ÉMILE ÉDOUARD CHARLES ANTOINE ZOLA was born in Paris in 1840. His childhood was spent in Aix and it was there that he received his early education. When he was eighteen he went to Paris, supported himself by becoming a clerk, and began to write. An early novel was followed by critical articles on art and literature which were published in *L'Événement*. After *Thérèse Raquin* (1867), the first of his typically naturalistic novels, Zola conceived the idea for his great work, the Rougon-Macquart series, which eventually encompassed twenty novels. To portray French life in its entirety through a detailed hereditary study of one family was the concept which motivated the series. *L'Assommoir* (1877), which examines taverns and their effects, was an immediate success and went through many editions. *Nana* (1880), the story of a courtesan who brings ruin to her clients and eventually to herself, increased Zola's reputation. The last novel in the series, *Doctor Pascal* (1893), brings all the previous novels into focus by means of the central character, himself a member of the Rougon family, who is scientifically investigating his own family. In 1898 Zola was forced to leave France and to live in England for a time because of his famous letter *J'accuse,* published in the *Aurore,* which agitated in favor of Alfred Dreyfus. He returned to Paris in 1899 and died there, having completed *Truth,* a novel based on the Dreyfus trial, in 1902. His graveside oration was delivered by Anatole France.

Germinal

by Emile Zola

Translated by
Stanley and Eleanor Hochman
With an Afterword by Irving Howe

(With a Revised and Updated Bibliography)

A SIGNET CLASSIC
NEW AMERICAN LIBRARY
NEW YORK AND SCARBOROUGH, ONTARIO

To David—
Because . . .
—S.H.
E.H.

 SIGNET CLASSIC TRADEMARK REG. U.S. PAT. OFF. AND FOREIGN COUNTRIES
REGISTERED TRADEMARK—MARCA REGISTRADA
HECHO EN CHICAGO, U.S.A.

SIGNET, SIGNET CLASSIC, MENTOR, ONYX, PLUME, MERIDIAN AND
NAL BOOKS are published *in the United States* by
NAL PENGUIN INC.,
1633 Broadway, New York, New York 10019,
in Canada by The New American Library of Canada Limited,
81 Mack Avenue, Scarborough, Ontario M1L 1M8

FIRST PRINTING, JUNE, 1970

9   10   11   12   13   14   15   16   17

PRINTED IN THE UNITED STATES OF AMERICA

Part ONE

1

On the flat plain, under a starless sky as thick and black as ink, a lone man was following the route from Marchiennes to Montsou—six miles of paved road cutting straight across the beet fields. He was unable to see the dark ground in front of him, and it was only the March wind, coming in mid-sea bursts and chilled by its sweep over miles of marshes and bare land, that made him aware of the immense, flat horizon. Not one tree was silhouetted against the sky, and the road spread before him as straight as a jetty through the blinding darkness of the shadows.

The man had left Marchiennes at about two o'clock. He was walking with long strides, shivering in his thin cotton jacket and corduroy trousers. A small bundle knotted in a checkered handkerchief kept getting in his way. He pressed it against his sides, first with one elbow and then with the other, so that he could keep both hands in his pockets; they were numb and bleeding from the lash of the east wind. Unemployed and homeless, he could think of only one thing—that perhaps the cold would be less sharp after sunrise. He had been striding along like this for about an hour when, on his left, about a mile from Montsou, he saw red flames—three braziers that seemed to be suspended in the sky. Frightened at first, he hesitated, but then he could no longer resist the painful need to warm his hands for a moment.

The road dipped into a hollow. Everything disappeared. On his right was a wooden fence, a wide-planked wall closing off a railroad track. On his left, at the top of a grassy slope, was a jumble of gables, suggesting a village of low-roofed houses, all alike. He walked another hundred yards. Suddenly, at a turning in the road, the fires reappeared; they were closer, but he still could not understand how they could burn so high in the lifeless sky, like smoky moons. Just then something at

5

ground level caught his attention. It was a thick mass, a tangle
of low buildings from which rose the outline of a factory
chimney. Here and there a light was shining out from a
grimy window; outside, five or six dim lanterns were hanging
from scaffolding, the blackened wood of which vaguely suggested the form of gigantic trestles. From this fantastic apparition drowned in night and smoke came only one sound: the
heavy, labored breathing of an unseen exhaust pump.

Then the man saw it was a coal mine. He was overcome by
shame: why bother?—there wouldn't be any work. Instead of
going toward the buildings, he decided to climb up the slag
heap to where three coal fires were burning in metal baskets
to heat and light the work area. The repairing shift must
have worked late—waste material was still being carried out.
He could hear the workers pushing the trains along the
trestles, he could see the moving shadows tipping over the
carts near each fire.

"Morning," he said, drawing near one of the braziers.

The cartman, an old man in a purple wool sweater and a
rabbit-skin cap, was standing with his back to the fire while
his horse, a big, yellow nag, waited in stonelike immobility
for the six carts it had drawn up from the mine to be
emptied. The tilterman doing this work was a red-haired,
rawboned fellow who seemed to be in no particular hurry; he
looked half asleep as he pressed down on the lever. Up above,
the wind was growing stronger—an icy north wind whose
great regular gusts were passing over them like the sweeps of
a scythe.

"Morning," replied the old man.

There was a silence. Feeling that they were looking at him
suspiciously, the young man immediately gave his name.

"I'm Etienne Lantier. I'm an engineman. There wouldn't
be any work here, would there?"

The light from the fire showed him to be about twenty-
one, dark, handsome, and strong in spite of his thin build.

Reassured, the cartman shook his head.

"Work for an engineman? I'm afraid not. Two others
came around asking yesterday. No, there isn't a thing."

A gust of wind interrupted them. Then, pointing to the
dark jumble of buildings at the foot of the slag heap, Etienne
asked:

"It's a mine, isn't it?"

This time the old man could not answer at once. He was
choked by a violent fit of coughing. Finally he spat up, and
his saliva left a dark spot on the flame-crimsoned ground.

"Yes, it's a mine, Le Voreux. . . . Look, the village is over there."

Raising his arm in turn, he pointed into the night at the village, the roofs of which the young man had spotted earlier. But by now the six carts were empty and the old man went after them, his legs stiffened by rheumatism; the big yellow horse started off on its own, not needing the whip, and pulled heavily between the rails, its coat ruffled by a fresh blast of wind.

Le Voreux was beginning to emerge from the night. Brooding in front of the fire and warming his bleeding hands, Etienne looked about and identified each part of the mine: the tarred screening shed, the headframe over the shaft, the enormous hoisting-engine room, and the square tower of the drainage pump. With its dumpy brick buildings huddled at the bottom of the hollow and its chimney thrusting upward like a menacing horn, the mine seemed evil-looking, a hungry beast crouched and ready to devour the world. As he examined it, Etienne thought about himself, about the vagabond existence he had led during the past week while looking for work. He saw himself back at the railroad shop, lashing out at his boss and being chased from Lille, being chased from everywhere. By Saturday he had reached Marchiennes, where he had been told there was work at Les Forges. Nothing. Neither at Les Forges nor at Sonneville. He had had to spend Sunday hidden among the piles of wood in a wheelwright's yard, and the watchman had just chased him out—at two o'clock in the morning. Nothing. Not a sou, not a crust. What was going to happen to him, wandering aimlessly along the roads like this, not even knowing where to shelter from the wind? Yes, it was a mine, all right. The few lanterns lit up the yard, and through a suddenly opened door he had caught a glimpse of the furnaces in a dazzling blaze of light. Now he could understand even the long, heavy respiration of the pump, which went on without stop and which was like the congested breathing of a monster.

The man emptying the carts, his back muscles bulging, had not even looked at Etienne, who was about to pick up his little bundle from the ground when a fit of coughing announced the cartman's return. He was slowly emerging from the shadows, followed by the yellow horse pulling six more loaded carts.

"Are there any factories at Montsou?" asked the young man.

The old man spat black, then answered into the wind:

"Oh, there are plenty of factories. You should have seen

this place three or four years ago. Everything was booming—
there weren't enough workers, wages had never been so
high—and now we're all tightening our belts again. There's
real misery everywhere—men are being fired and factories
are closing down one after the other. . . . Maybe it's not the
Emperor's fault, but why is he going off to fight in America?
And on top of everything else, the animals are dying of
cholera, just like the people."

In short phrases, stopping as the wind took their breath
away, they continued to recite their troubles. Etienne told
about his fruitless wanderings during the past week: would he
just die of hunger?—soon the roads would be full of beggars.
Yes, said the old man, it will all lead to trouble; damn it, you
can't just toss so many decent people out into the streets.

"People don't even have meat every day."

"At least if we had bread!"

"That's right! If we at least had bread . . ."

Their voices were lost in the gusts of wind that carried the
words away in a dismal howl.

"Look!" the cartman began again, loudly. He turned
toward the south. "That's Montsou over there."

Raising his arm again, he pointed to some invisible
spots, naming them one after the other. Down below, in
Montsou, the Fauvelle Sugar Refinery was still working, but
the one at Houton had let men go; only the Dutilleul Flour
Mill and the Bleuze Cable Works were still holding on. Then,
with a sweeping gesture to the north, he indicated half the
horizon: the Sonneville Construction Company had only received one third of its usual orders; only two of the three
blast furnaces of the Marchiennes Forges were lit; and finally, at the Gagebois Glassworks there was threat of a strike
because there was talk of a wage cut.

"I know, I know," the young man repeated after each
name was mentioned. "I've just come from there."

"As for us, it's been all right up to now," added the
cartman. "But the mines aren't turning out as much. And
look at La Victoire, on the other side—there are only two
coke furnaces burning over there too."

He spat, and after harnessing his sleepy horse to the empty
carts, he left again.

Now Etienne could see over the whole area. The darkness
was still thick, but the old man's pointing hand had filled it
with great suffering, which the young man could sense everywhere around him in that limitless space. Wasn't that a cry of
hunger that the March wind was rolling across the naked
plain? The raging gusts seemed to be announcing the death of

work, and a famine that would kill many men. Looking
around, he tried to pierce the darkness, tormented by both
the desire to see and the fear of seeing.

Everything was hidden in the impenetrable depths of the
gloomy night. All he could see, a long way off, were some
blast furnaces and coke ovens. The latter, with their batteries
of a hundred oblique chimneys, were outlined in red flames,
while farther to the left the two towers blazed blue, like giant
torches, against the empty sky. It was a melancholy sight, for
these nocturnal fires were the only stars rising on the threatening horizon of this land of coal and iron.

"Are you from Belgium?" asked the cartman, coming up
behind Etienne once more.

This time he had only brought three carts. There had been
an accident—a broken screw nut on the cage—and work
would be stopped for a good quarter of an hour, but these
three might as well be emptied. At the bottom of the slag
heap there was now silence; the trammers were no longer
making the trestles shake with the vibrations from the constant rumbling. The only noise from the mine was the distant
sound of a hammer beating on sheet metal.

"No, I'm from the Midi," answered the young man.

The tilterman, who had been emptying the carts, sat down,
glad of the accident; he maintained his savage silence, merely
lifting his large lusterless eyes to the cartman as though
annoyed by so much talk. And actually, the old man did not
usually talk so much. He must have liked the stranger's face
and been overcome by one of those sudden urges to speak
that sometimes makes old people begin to talk even if only to
themselves.

"I'm from Montsou," he said; "my name is Bonnemort."

"That's a nickname, isn't it?" asked Etienne, surprised.

The old man grinned happily and pointed to Le Voreux.

"Oh yes, three times they've pulled me out of there more
dead than alive—once with my hair scorched, another time
with my insides full of dirt, and a third time with my belly
swollen with water, like a frog. . . . When they saw that nothing could kill me, they called me Bonnemort for a joke."

His laugh grew louder; it sounded like the screech of a
badly oiled pulley and ended in a terrible fit of coughing. His
large head with its scanty white hair and his pale face with its
bluish blotches were now completely illuminated by the brazier. He was short, with a powerful neck, legs that turned out
and toes that turned in, and long arms from which massive
hands dangled to his knees. For the rest, like his horse that
stood so motionless, he seemed made of stone, troubled by

neither the cold nor the gusts of wind whistling about his ears. When he coughed, his throat was torn by a harsh rasping; he spat at the foot of the basket and the earth blackened.

Etienne looked at him, then at the stain on the ground.

"Have you been working at the mine a long time?"

Bonnemort flung out his arms.

"A long time? I guess you could say that. I wasn't eight years old when I went down—right here in Le Voreux—and I'm fifty-eight now. Figure that out! I've done everything— first a mine boy, then a hauler when I was strong enough to wheel the stuff, and then, for eighteen years, a cutter. Then, because of my damn legs, they put me to repairing, banking, patching—right up to the time when the doctor said that if they didn't bring me up I'd stay down there for good. And now for the last five years I've been a cartman.... That's something, isn't it? Fifty years with the mine, forty-five of them down below!"

As he was talking, fragments of burning coal occasionally fell from the brazier, lighting his pale face with their bloody reflection.

"They tell me to rest," he continued. "Not me! I'm not that crazy! I'll stick it out for another two years—until I'm sixty—and then I'll have my hundred and eighty franc pension. If I quit now, they'd only give me a hundred and fifty. They're pretty clever, those bastards! Besides, I'm fine except for my legs. You see, it's all that water from when I'd get soaked down in the stalls. There are days when I can't move without screaming."

Another fit of coughing interrupted him.

"And that's what makes you cough, too?" asked Etienne.

He shook his head violently. Then, when he could talk again:

"No, no. I caught a cold last month. I never used to cough, but now I can't get rid of it.... And the funny thing is that I spit ... I spit ..."

The rasping noise came from his throat again, and he spat another black blob.

"Is it blood?" Etienne finally had the courage to ask.

Bonnemort slowly wiped his mouth with the back of his hand.

"It's coal. I've got enough in my guts to heat me till the day I die. And I haven't set foot down there for the last five years! I guess I stored it up without even knowing about it. Well, it keeps your insides from spoiling."

In the silence that followed, the regular beats of the

far-away hammer rose from the mine, and the wind wailed in the dark night like a cry of hunger and weariness. Standing in front of the wildly dancing flames, the old man, speaking more softly now, continued to mull over his memories. Oh yes, it had been quite a while since he and his family had started working the vein. His family had been with the Company's Montsou mine from the beginning—and that was a long time ago, a hundred and six years. . . . His grandfather, Guillaume Maheu, a fifteen-year-old boy at the time, had been the one to find the soft coal deposit at Réquillart, down near the sugar refinery. It was abandoned now, but it had been the Company's first shaft, and everybody here knew his grandfather had discovered it. The proof was that they even called it the Guillaume vein, after him. . . . He had never known him, but people said he'd been big and strong, and he'd died of old age at sixty. Then his father, Nicholas Maheu—they used to call him Red—had died in Le Voreux when he was barely forty: they had been excavating it and the roof fell in, squashed him. The rocks had drunk his blood and swallowed his bones. Later on, two of his uncles and his three brothers had also died down there. He, Vincent Maheu, had come out pretty much in one piece, except for his twisted legs, and everyone thought he was pretty clever. . . . Well, what could you do? You had to work, and this work is passed on from father to son just like any other kind of work. Now his son, Toussaint Maheu, was killing himself in the mine, and his grandsons, and all the rest of the family. They all lived in the village over there. A hundred and six years of hacking away, the young ones after the old ones, all for the same company. What do you think of that?—there are lots of rich people who couldn't give as good an account of themselves!

"At least if you have something to eat," Etienne murmured again.

"Just what I say. As long as there's bread, you can manage."

Bonnemort stopped talking. His eyes turned toward the village, where lights were going on one after another. The clock in the Montsou tower was striking four, the cold becoming more bitter.

"Is your company rich?" asked Etienne.

The old man raised his shoulders, then let them fall again, as if bowed down by an avalanche of gold coins.

"Is it! Maybe not as rich as the Anzin Company nearby, but millions and millions all the same. They can't even count it anymore. Nineteen mines, thirteen in operation—Le

Voreux, La Victoire, Crèvecoeur, Mirou, Saint-Thomas, Madeleine, Feutry-Cantel, lots of others—and then six for drainage or ventilation, like Réquillart. Ten thousand workers, concessions in sixty-seven communities, five thousand tons a day taken out, a railroad connecting all the mines, and workshops, and factories . . . Oh yes, there's plenty of money there!"

The sound of carts rolling on the trestles suddenly made the big yellow horse prick up its ears. The cage down below must have been fixed and the workers gone back to their jobs. As he was harnessing the animal for another trip down, the cartman spoke to it gently:

"Mustn't get used to talking so much, you lazy good-for-nothing. If Monsieur Hennebeau knew how you were wasting your time . . ."

Etienne looked thoughtfully into the night and asked:

"Does the mine belong to Monsieur Hennebeau?"

The old man answered:

"No, he's just the general manager. He's on the payroll, just like us."

The young man gestured toward the massive darkness.

"Who does it all belong to, then?"

But at that moment Bonnemort had another attack, so violent this time that he couldn't catch his breath. Finally, after he had spat and wiped the black froth from his lips, he answered into the still-rising wind:

"What? Who does it belong to? . . . Who knows? To somebody."

He pointed vaguely into the shadows at some far-off and unknown place, peopled with these "somebodies" for whom the Maheus had been working the vein for more than a hundred years. His voice had taken on a quality of almost religious fear and awe, as if he had been talking about some inaccessible tabernacle in which was hidden a glutted and crouching god to whom they had all given their flesh but whom they had never seen.

"At least if you have enough bread to eat," Etienne repeated for the third time, without any apparent transition.

"Sure, but if we always had enough bread, that would be too good!"

The horse had already gone; the cartman, limping along unsteadily, disappeared too. The man who emptied the carts had not stirred; he was still there, all curled up in a ball, his chin between his knees, his large lusterless eyes fixed on nothingness.

Etienne picked up his bundle but made no move to leave.

While his chest was being roasted in front of the big fire the icy gusts were freezing his back. Maybe it would be a good idea to inquire at the mine office after all—maybe the old man didn't really know. And besides, he didn't care, he would take any kind of work. Where else could he go, what else could he do, in this country that was starving for lack of work?—leave his dead body behind a wall, like a stray dog? But still he hesitated; something was bothering him—a fear of Le Voreux, planted here in the middle of this flat plain, submerged in the thick night. Each gust of wind seemed stronger than the last, as if it were blowing from an ever more distant horizon. No hint of dawn paled the dead sky, and only the furnaces and the coke ovens flamed out, reddening the darkness but shedding no light on its mystery. And at the bottom of its hole, like an evil crouching beast, Le Voreux curled still more tightly and breathed still more heavily, as if troubled by its painful digestion of human flesh.

2

In the middle of fields of wheat and beets Village Number 240 was sleeping under the black skies. Four large blocks of small houses, set back-to-back and laid out as regularly as barracks or hospital buildings—geometric, parallel, and separated by three wide lanes divided into uniform garden plots—could vaguely be distinguished. The only sound on this deserted plain was that of the gusts of wind rattling the loose trellises against the garden walls.

At the Maheus', Number 16 of Block 2, nothing was stirring. Thick shadows pressed in on the only room on the first floor, as if to crush the sleep of those who—their presence felt rather than seen—were lying there, heaped together, open-mouthed, overcome by fatigue. Despite the bitter cold outside, the heavy air had an oppressive warmth—that stuffy heat, the smell of the human herd, found in even the best-kept barracks.

The cuckoo clock downstairs struck four; there was no sign of life other than the whistle of sharp breathing and a duet of heavy snores. Suddenly Catherine got up. As usual, she had counted the four strokes coming through the floor, but in her exhaustion she had not found the strength to come completely awake. Then, thrusting her legs from beneath the covers, she felt around, finally striking a match and lighting the candle. But she remained seated, her head so heavy that it sank back between her shoulders, giving way to the irresistible need to collapse onto the bolster.

The candle lit up the square, two-windowed room into which three beds had been crowded. There was also a closet, a table, and two old walnut chairs whose dark color stood out against the light walls. And nothing else, except some tattered clothing hung on nails and a pitcher resting on the tile floor near a red earthenware bowl that was used as a washbasin. In the bed on the left, Zacharie, the eldest, aged twenty-one, was asleep alongside his brother Jeanlin, who was almost eleven; in the bed on the right two young children, Lénore and Henri, the first six years old, the other four, were asleep in each other's arms. Catherine shared the third bed with her sister Alzire, a nine-year-old who was so frail that the older girl would never have known she was lying beside her if the little invalid's hump had not dug into her ribs. The glass door was open, and in the alcove on the landing, a kind of narrow passageway, the mother and father could be seen sleeping in a fourth bed, next to which they had had to place the cradle of their youngest child, Estelle, who was not quite three months old.

Catherine made a desperate effort. She stretched, and clenched her hands in the reddish hair tangling over her forehead and neck. Thin for her fifteen years, she was wearing a tight-fitting chemise that exposed only her bluish feet— which seemed to be tattooed by coal—and her delicate arms, whose milk-white color contrasted sharply with her sallow complexion, already spoiled by constant washing with harsh soap. Her somewhat large mouth, with its superb teeth in their greenish gums, opened in a final yawn; her gray eyes teared with suppressed sleep, a sad anguish that seemed to inflate her whole naked body with fatigue.

At that moment there was a groan from the alcove, and then the sound of Maheu's thick, stumbling voice:

"Damn it, it's time! ... Is that you lighting the candle, Catherine?"

"Yes, it's me. ... I just heard the clock downstairs."

"Well, hurry up, you good-for-nothing! If you had done a little less dancing Sunday, you'd have gotten us up earlier. ... How lazy can you get?"

And he continued to grumble at her until he himself fell back to sleep, his complaints jumbling together and melting into a new snore.

Barefooted and in her chemise, the young girl moved

about the room. As she passed the bed in which Henri and Lénore slept, she re-covered them with the blanket, which had slipped off. They were sunk in the deep sleep of childhood and did not awaken. Alzire, her eyes wide open, had silently moved into the warm spot vacated by her big sister.

"Come on, Zacharie! And you too, Jeanlin! Come on!" Catherine repeated as she stood beside her two brothers, who remained sprawled on the bed, their faces buried in the bolster.

She had to grab the elder by the shoulder and shake him; then, while he cursed at her, she decided to pull the cover off. The sight of the boys' bare legs flailing about struck her as funny, and she started to laugh.

"Idiot, let me alone!" Zacharie growled nastily as he sat up. "I don't like this fooling around. . . . Oh Christ, is it really time?"

He was thin and gawky, his long face was spotted with the suggestion of a beard, and he had the blond hair and the anemic pallor of the rest of the family. His nightshirt had crept up and he pulled it down, not out of modesty but because he was cold.

"The clock downstairs has struck," repeated Catherine. "Let's go. Father's getting angry!"

Jeanlin, who had curled himself up, shut his eyes and said: "Get the hell out of here! I'm asleep."

She broke into another good-natured laugh. He was so small, the joints of his thin legs and arms so terribly swollen, that she just picked him up in her arms. His wrinkled, monkeylike face, pierced by two green eyes and extended by two big ears, paled with helpless rage. He said nothing, but he bit into her right breast.

"You louse!" she murmured, repressing a cry and putting him down on the ground.

Alzire, lying silently with the covers up to her chin, had not gone back to sleep. With the intelligent eyes of an invalid, she watched her sister and brothers as they dressed. Another quarrel broke out at the washbasin: the boys shoved their sister aside because she was taking too much time getting washed. They threw off their nightshirts, and still puffy with sleep, they casually relieved themselves with all the nonchalance of a litter of puppies that has been brought up together. Catherine was ready first. She put on her miner's trousers, slipped on her coarse cloth jacket, fastened her blue cap over her piled-up hair—and in these Monday-morning work clothes she looked like a little man. Nothing was left of her own sex except the slight sway of her hips.

"When the old man comes in," Zacharie said spitefully, "he'll sure be glad to find the bed messed up. . . . And I'll tell him it was all your fault."

The "old man" was Grandfather Bonnemort, who worked at night and slept during the day, so the bed never got a chance to cool off; there was always somebody snoring away in it.

Without answering, Catherine started to straighten the cover and tuck it in. But for some time now noises from the neighboring house had been coming through the wall. These Company-built brick buildings were so cheaply made that the slightest sound penetrated them. From one end of the row to the other, everybody lived elbow to elbow, and no aspect of personal life could be hidden—not even from the children. A heavy step had shaken the staircase, and then there was a soft *plop*, followed by a sigh of relief.

"There!" said Catherine. "Levaque's gone down and Bouteloup's gotten into La Levaque's bed."

Jeanlin snickered, and even Alzire's eyes shone. Every morning they were amused by the activities of the trio next door: a cutter had taken in a repairman as a boarder, which meant that his wife had two men—one at night and one during the day.

"Philomène's coughing," said Catherine, after having listened for a moment.

She was talking about the Levaques' eldest, a tall nineteen-year-old girl who was Zacharie's mistress and who had already borne him two children. Her lungs were so delicate that she was a screener at the mine; she had never been well enough to work down below.

"Ah, don't kid yourself about Philomène!" Zacharie answered. "She doesn't give a damn, she just sleeps! The lazy pig sleeps till six o'clock!"

As he was putting on his trousers, he suddenly thought of something and opened the window. Outside in the darkness the village was getting up—one by one lights were appearing between the slats of the shutters. And that started another argument: he was leaning out to see if he could spot the Voreux foreman, who was said to be sleeping with La Pierronne, leave her house, but his sister was shouting to him that the husband had gone on the day shift at the loading station yesterday, so Dansaert couldn't possibly have slept there last night. While the cold blasts of air were sweeping through the room, both of them lost their tempers, each insisting on the accuracy of his own information. Suddenly, cries and tears were heard—it was Estelle in her cradle, protesting against the cold.

Maheu sat up. What was wrong with him? He'd gone back to sleep just like some loafer. . . . He swore so loudly that the children in the next room hardly dared breathe. Zacharie and Jeanlin lethargically finished washing. Alzire, wide-eyed, was still watching. The two little ones, Lénore and Henri, their arms wrapped around each other, had not moved; they went on breathing softly despite all the noise.

"Catherine, give me the candle!" shouted Maheu.

She finished buttoning her jacket and brought the candle to her father, leaving her brothers to search for their clothes by the faint light coming through the door. Her father jumped out of bed, but she didn't wait; feeling her way, she went downstairs in her heavy woolen stockings, lit another candle, and started to make the coffee. The whole family's sabots were under the cupboard.

"Will you keep quiet, you pest!" Maheu roared, exasperated by Estelle's continuing cries.

He was short, like Old Bonnemort, and had the same heavy build, big head, flat, livid face, and very short fair hair. The baby screamed louder than ever, terrified by the large gnarled arms waving above her.

"Let her alone. You know she won't shut up," said La Maheude, stretching out in the middle of the bed.

She too had just awakened and was irritated—it was idiotic not to be able to sleep the night through. Couldn't they just leave quietly? She was buried under the cover, and nothing of her showed but her large-featured long face, the heavy beauty of which was already deformed, at thirty-nine, by a life of misery and the seven children she had borne. Staring up at the ceiling, she spoke slowly while her husband dressed. Neither of them paid any attention to the baby, who was choking with tears.

"I don't have any money left, you know, and it's only Monday—six more days till you get paid. Things can't go on like this. All of you together only bring in nine francs. How do you expect me to manage?—there are ten of us in the house."

"What do you mean, nine francs?" protested Maheu. "Zacharie and me each get three, that makes six . . . Catherine and my father get two, that makes four . . . four and six make ten . . . and Jeanlin gets one—that makes eleven."

"Sure, eleven, but there are Sundays and days when there's no work. . . . Never more than nine, I tell you."

He was busy fumbling around on the floor for his leather belt and didn't answer. Then, straightening up, he said:

"Don't complain. At least I'm still in good shape. There are plenty who've been put to repairing at forty-two."

"Maybe, but that doesn't get us any bread. . . . What am I supposed to do? I don't suppose you have anything?"

"I've got two sous."

"Oh, keep that for a beer. . . . My God, what am I going to do? Six days is a long time. We owe sixty francs to Maigrat and he kicked me out the day before yesterday. That won't keep me from going back, but if he's going to be stubborn . . ."

And she went on in a mournful voice, her head rigid, her eyes sometimes closing against the cheerless light of the candle. She said that the cupboard was empty, that the children were asking for bread and butter, that there wasn't any coffee, that the water gave them cramps, and that the days were spent trying to fill up on boiled cabbage leaves. She had to keep raising her voice to be heard over Estelle's wailing. The cries were becoming unbearable, and Maheu suddenly seemed to become aware of them; beside himself with rage, he grabbed the baby from her cradle and threw her onto her mother's bed, stammering furiously:

"Here, take her before I knock her brains out! Christ, what a kid! It's got everything it wants, it's got the tit, and still it complains louder than everybody else."

And Estelle had in fact taken the breast. Snuggled under the cover and calmed by the warmth of the bed, she was now making only small, greedy sounds with her lips.

"Didn't those people at La Piolaine tell you to come see them?" continued Maheu after a moment of silence.

His wife pursed her lips dubiously.

"Yes, they met me. They were carrying clothes to poor children. . . . All right, I'll take Lénore and Henri there this morning. If only they'll let me have five francs!"

It was quiet again. Maheu was ready. He stood motionless for a moment, then said in his expressionless voice:

"Well, what can you do about it? That's the way things are. Figure something out for dinner. . . . There's no point in talking about it. I'd better get down to work."

"I suppose so," she answered. "Blow out the candle. I don't have to see the color of my thoughts."

He blew out the candle. Zacharie and Jeanlin were already on their way down and he followed them, the stairs groaning under their heavy, stockinged feet. The room and the passageway on the landing had fallen back into darkness. The children were asleep, and even Alzire's eyes were shut, but the mother remained staring into the shadows while Estelle tugged at her tired, pendulous breasts and purred like a kitten.

Downstairs Catherine had first taken care of the fire—a cast-iron unit, with a center grate and two side ovens, in which a coal fire burned at all times. Every month the Company gave each family about twenty-two bushels of hard coal picked up along the galleries. It was difficult to make it catch, so the girl banked the fire every evening and then shook it down in the morning, adding small, carefully selected pieces of soft coal. After that, she put on the kettle and crouched down in front of the cupboard.

The fairly large room took up the whole ground floor. It was painted apple-green and kept as spotless as a Dutch interior, its flagstones washed down with pails of water and then sprinkled with white sand. In addition to the varnished pine cupboard, the furniture consisted of a table and chairs of the same wood. Pasted on the walls were garishly colored prints—Company-presented portraits of the Emperor and Empress, soldiers and saints splattered with gold. They were in sharp contrast with the stark bareness of the room. The only other decorations were a pink cardboard box on the cupboard and a gaudily painted cuckoo clock, the loud ticking of which seemed to fill the room. Near the staircase door was another door, this one leading down to the cellar.

Despite the cleanliness, the stale warm air, always acrid with the smell of coal, was now also heavy with the sealed-in odor of onions cooked the evening before.

In front of the open cupboard doors, Catherine thought for a moment. There was only a little piece of bread, and just about enough white cheese, but scarcely more than a dab of butter—and she had to make sandwiches for the four of them. At last she made up her mind. She cut a few slices of bread, smeared cheese on some and brushed butter on others, then slapped them together. This was the *briquet*, the sandwich taken into the mines every morning. Soon the four sandwiches were lined up on the table and portioned out with strict justice, from the big one for the father to the little one for Jeanlin.

Though Catherine seemed to be absorbed in her work, she must nevertheless have been mulling over the gossip Zacharie had reported about the chief foreman and La Pierronne, because she opened the front door slightly and glanced out. The wind was still blowing, and more and more lights were flickering in the squat houses of the village, from which rose

the vague stirs of morning. Doors were already closing and
black lines of workers were disappearing into the night. It
was silly to stand there getting chilled—the loader was sure
to be asleep till it was time to start his six o'clock shift. Still,
she stood there and kept looking at the house on the other
side of the garden. The door opened and her curiosity was
inflamed. But no, it was only Lydie, the little Pierron girl,
leaving for the mine.

The sound of hissing steam made her turn around. She
closed the door and started to run—the water was boiling
over and putting out the fire. There was no more coffee, and
the best she could do was pour water over yesterday's
grounds. Then she put some brown sugar into the coffeepot,
and by that time her father and two brothers were coming
down.

"Damn!" Zacharie said when he had put his nose into the
bowl. "Do you call this coffee?"

Maheu shrugged in resignation.

"Well, it's not too bad—at least it's hot."

Jeanlin had gathered together the crumbs from the sandwiches and added them to his bowl. When Catherine had
finished drinking, she emptied the rest of the pot into their tin
flasks. The four of them were standing in the light of the
smoking candle, quickly gulping down their coffee.

"Aren't we ready yet?" asked the father. "You'd think we
were bankers!"

A voice came from the stairway, the door of which had
been left open. It was La Maheude, shouting:

"Take all the bread. I've got some vermicelli for the
children."

"All right," Catherine answered.

She had banked the fire and propped up the remainder of
last night's soup on a corner of the grate so that her grandfather would find it hot when he came home at six o'clock.
Each of them took his sabots from under the cupboard, slung
his flask over his shoulders, and stuffed his sandwich between
the back of his shirt and his jacket. And they left, first the
men and then the girl, who blew out the candle and locked
the door. The house was dark again.

"Well, it looks like we're leaving together," said a man
who was closing the door of the neighboring house.

It was Levaque, with his twelve-year-old son Bébert, Jeanlin's best friend. Astonished, Catherine choked back a laugh
and whispered to Zacharie: "This is something new! Bouteloup doesn't even wait until the husband is gone."

Now the lights in the village were going out. A last door

slammed and everything was asleep again, women and babies dozing off once more in the now roomier beds. And from the darkened village to the panting mine there was a slow stream of shadows moving under the gusty wind—the miners on their way to work, their shoulders hunched, their awkward arms crossed over their chests, their backs humped by their sandwiches. Despite the fact that they were shivering in their thin clothes, they did not hurry, but straggled along the road with a herdlike shuffling.

3

Etienne came down from the slag heap and went into Le Voreux. He spoke to some men and asked if there was any work, but they all shook their heads and told him to wait for the chief foreman. He was left free to wander about the badly lit buildings with their many dark corners and confusing complex of rooms and levels. After climbing a half-destroyed, gloomy stairway, he had found himself on a shaky footbridge; then he walked through the screening shed, where it was so midnight-black that he had to hold his hands outstretched to keep from bumping into anything. Suddenly, two enormous yellow eyes pierced the darkness ahead of him. He was under the headframe in the landing room, at the mouth of the shaft.

A foreman, old Richomme, a big fellow with a good-natured face and a gray handlebar moustache, was just at that moment going toward the checker's office.

"You wouldn't need anybody for any kind of job at all, would you?" asked Etienne again.

Richomme was going to say no, but he changed his mind and, walking off, answered as the others had:

"Wait for Monsieur Dansaert, the chief foreman."

Four lanterns were fixed there, and the reflectors, which threw all their light on the shaft, brightly illuminated the iron railings, the levers for the signals and catches, and the timber guides between which the two cages rode. The rest of the enormous navelike room was lost in a host of moving shadows. Only the lamproom was blazing in the background, while in the office of the checker a weak lamp was burning dimly, like a star about to go out. The cages were back in operation; there was a continuous rumble of a never-ending line of coal carts being rolled over the cast-iron flooring, and an incessant coming and going of workers, whose long bent backs could just be made out in this noisy, black, heaving tangle.

Deafened and blinded, Etienne stood motionless for a moment. Drafts were blowing in from all corners, and he was chilled. Then he took a few steps forward, drawn by the engine, whose steel and copper he could now see shining. It was on a higher level, about twenty-five yards back from the shaft, and so solidly set on its brick base that though it was going at full steam, with all the force of its four-hundred horsepower, the rise and fall of its enormous piston, moving with well-oiled ease, didn't even cause the walls to vibrate. Standing at the operating lever, the engineman was listening to the various signals and keeping his eyes fixed upon the indicator, on which the shaft and its different levels were shown by a vertical slot in which moved suspended lead weights representing the cages. Each time the engine started again, the drums—two immense thirty-foot wheels around the hubs of which two steel cables wound and unwound in opposite directions—turned so quickly that they were nothing but a gray blur.

"Watch out there!" shouted three workmen who were dragging a gigantic ladder.

Etienne had almost been crushed. But now his eyes were beginning to adjust, and he looked up at the speeding cables— more than a hundred feet of steel coil that rushed up into the headframe, passed over the pulleys, then plunged down into the shaft to the extraction cages. The pulleys were set in an iron scaffold similar to that of a high clock-tower. This rapid flight, the ceaseless to and fro of this incredibly heavy cable that could lift up to twenty-five tons at a speed of thirty feet a second, was all smooth and noiseless—a birdlike rush and glide.

"For God's sake, watch out!" shouted the workmen again as they pushed the ladder around to the other side in order to inspect the left-hand pulley.

Etienne slowly went back to the landing room. Shivering in the drafts, dazed by this monstrous whirling above his head, he watched the movements of the cages, his ears deafened by the thundering of the carts. Next to the shaft was the signal, a hammer-headed lever which a cord pulled from below would cause to strike against a block. One stroke to stop, two to descend, three to rise: an unending series of crashes, followed by the piercing ring of a bell, dominated the tumult, while the worker directing the operation added to the din by using a megaphone to shout orders to the engine-man. Amid all this pandemonium the cages kept appearing and disappearing, were emptied and filled, without Etienne's being able to understand a thing about any of the compli-cated maneuvers.

He understood only one thing: the shaft was swallowing men in mouthfuls of twenty and thirty, and in such easy gulps that it didn't seem to feel them going down. The workers had begun the descent at the stroke of four. They came from the dressing shed barefoot, their lanterns in their hands, and stood around in small groups until enough of them collected to make a load. Noiselessly, with the soft spring of a nocturnal beast, the cage, with its four levels each containing two carts loaded with coal, leaped out of the darkness and gripped the catches. On each landing trammers removed the carts and replaced them with others, either empty ones or those that had previously been loaded with timber; and it was into the empty carts that the workers piled, five in each one, so that there would be as many as forty when all the compartments were free. From the megaphone came an indistinct and toneless bellow, and the cord of the bell down below was pulled four times—the "meat signal"—as a sign that this load was one of human flesh. After a slight upward jerk the cage plunged silently, falling like a stone and leaving behind only the vibrant play of the cable.

"Is it deep?" Etienne asked a miner who was standing next to him, half asleep.

"Eighteen hundred and twenty-eight feet," answered the man, "but there are four landings before the bottom—the first at ten hundred and fifty-six feet."

They both fell silent, their eyes on the climbing cable. Etienne continued:

"And when it breaks?"

"Oh, when it breaks . . ."

The miner concluded with a gesture. His turn had come, the cage having reappeared with its effortless, tireless move-ment. He crouched down with his comrades and it plunged again, then leaped up again after less than four minutes to swallow down another load of men. For the next half hour the shaft kept devouring men in the same way—with a more or less gluttonous gulp depending on the level of the landing to which they were descending, but always without a stop, always ravenous, its giant bowels capable of digesting an entire nation. It kept stuffing itself and stuffing itself, but the darkness below remained lifeless, and the cage kept rising from the emptiness with the same silent voracity.

Eventually Etienne was overtaken by the same uneasiness he had already experienced on the slag heap. Why insist? This chief foreman would only send him away as the others had. A vague fear made him come to a sudden decision; he left, and once outside, didn't stop until he was in front of the boiler house. Through the wide-open door he could see seven two-furnaced boilers. In a cloud of white steam, and to the accompaniment of the hissing valves, a fireman was busy stoking one of the furnaces; the intense heat could be felt even at the doorway. The young man, glad to be warm, was drawing nearer when he ran into another group of workers arriving at the mine. It was the Maheus and the Levaques. At their head was Catherine, and at the sight of her gentle, boyish air, something told him to make one more attempt.

"Say there, friend, they wouldn't need anyone for any kind of work, would they?"

She looked at him, surprised and a little frightened by this unexpected voice coming from the shadows. But Maheu, behind her, had overheard, and he answered, stopping to talk for a moment. No, they didn't need anyone. This poor devil who seemed to have lost his way interested him, and after leaving Etienne, he caught up with the others and said:

"That could be any of us. . . . I guess we shouldn't complain—there are some who don't get the chance to die of overwork!"

They continued on and went straight to the dressing shed, a huge, roughly plastered room lined with padlocked cabinets. In the middle was an iron, doorless stove, glowing now, and so stuffed with incandescent coal that pieces kept bursting out and rolling across the firmly packed earthen floor. The only light in the room came from this fire, and its bloody reflections danced along the grimy walls and up the blackened ceiling.

As the Maheus entered, laughter was ringing out in the stifling heat. About thirty workers were standing with their backs to the fire and happily toasting themselves. Before going down into the mine everybody came here to soak up some heat and carry off a good slug of it in their skins in order to be able to face the dampness of the mine. But this morning they were more cheerful than usual; they were teasing Mouquette, a buxom, eighteen-year-old hauler whose enormous breasts and rear end seemed ready to split her jacket and trousers. She lived in Réquillart with her father, Old Mouque, a stableman, and her brother Mouquet, a trammer. However, since their working hours weren't the same, she came to the mine alone, and in the summer in the middle of the wheat fields and in the winter against a wall, she would take her pleasure with her current lover. Every man in the mine had had his turn in this fraternal, open-hearted fun-for-all. Once, when someone had accused her of having taken a Marchiennes nailmaker for a lover, she almost exploded with rage, shouting that she thought too much of herself for that and that she'd cut her arm off if anyone could claim he'd seen her with anybody but a miner!

"Isn't it Big Chaval anymore?" asked a miner, snickering. "Is it that little runt now? Why, he'll need a ladder! I saw you both behind Réquillart—he had to stand on top of a mile-stone!"

"So?" answered Mouquette cheerfully. "What difference does it make to you? We didn't ask you to come over and push, did we?"

And this good-natured vulgarity increased the men's hilarity; their shoulders, half roasted by the fire, heaved with laughter, while she herself, shaking with amusement, paraded before them in her obscene get-up, her grotesquely exaggerated bulges of flesh both comic and disturbing.

But the laughter soon stopped. Mouquette was telling Maheu that Fleurance, Big Fleurance, wouldn't be coming anymore. They had found her the day before, stretched out stiff on her bed; some said from a heart attack, others said from a bottle of gin drunk too quickly. Maheu was in despair: another rotten break! He'd lost one of his haulers and there was no immediate chance of replacing her. Four of them—he, Zacharie, Levaque, and Chaval—worked a section as a team and were paid by the load; if there was only Catherine to do the hauling, they wouldn't be able to send out as much. . . . Suddenly he exclaimed:

"Hey! What about that fellow who was looking for work?"

Dansaert happened to be passing the dressing shed, so Maheu told him the whole story and asked permission to hire the man. He pointed out that the Company wanted to re-place the haulage girls with boys, as had been done at Anzin. The chief foreman smiled at first, because the idea of replac-ing the women at the bottom usually upset the miners, who were more worried about jobs for their daughters than con-cerned about questions of morality or health. Finally, after some hesitation, he gave his permission, but he added that the decision would have to be approved by Monsieur Négrel, the engineer.

"He must be pretty far away by now, at the rate he was going," said Zacharie.

"No," said Catherine, "I saw him stop at the boiler house."

"Well, go after him, lazy!" shouted Maheu.

The girl rushed off just as a group of miners left for the shaft, making room at the fire for others. Without waiting for his father, Jeanlin, accompanied by Bébert, a fat, simple-minded boy, and Lydie, a sickly little girl of ten, went to get his lamp. Mouquette, who had preceded them, started to scream on the dark staircase, calling them dirty brats and threatening to slap them if they pinched her.

In the boiler house Etienne was still talking to the fireman, who was feeding coal into the furnaces. The very thought of having to go back into the night made him feel bitterly cold, but he was just making up his mind to leave when he felt a hand placed on his shoulder.

"Come with me," said Catherine. "There's a job for you."

At first he didn't understand. Then, in a burst of joy, he pumped the girl's hands energetically.

"Thanks, friend . . . you're a real pal, honest!"

She started to laugh, looking at him in the red glow from the furnace. Her figure was still undeveloped and her long hair was piled up under the miner's cap—it amused her that he had taken her for a boy. He was also laughing happily, and for a moment the two of them stood there, their cheeks aflame, laughing at each other.

In the dressing shed Maheu was squatting in front of his locker, taking off his sabots and his heavy woolen stockings. When Etienne got there everything was arranged in a few words: thirty sous a day and a backbreaking job, but one he would quickly learn. The cutter suggested that he keep his shoes on, and he lent him an old leather cap to protect his skull—a precaution scorned by both the father and the children. The tools taken out of the locker included Fleurance's shovel. Then, after Maheu had locked up their sabots and stockings, as well as Etienne's bundle, he cried out in sudden impatience:

"Where the hell is Chaval? Probably tumbling some slut on a pile of stones. . . . We're a half hour late today!"

Zacharie and Levaque were calmly toasting their shoulders, but the former asked:

"Are you waiting for Chaval? He got here ahead of us and went right down."

"You mean to say you knew that and you didn't tell me? Come on, come on! Let's hurry!"

Catherine had been warming her hands but had to follow

the rest now. Etienne let her go first and followed behind her. Once again he was moving through a labyrinth of stairways and dark corridors, their bare feet making a soft, slippered sound. But light blazed from the lamproom, a windowed room filled with tiers of racks on which were lined hundreds of Davy lamps that had been inspected and cleaned the day before and now were burning like tapers in a funeral chapel. At the checkout window each worker took the lamp stamped with his number, then examined it and closed it himself, while from behind a table the checker entered on his register the time the miner went down.

Maheu had to intercede to get his new hauler a lamp, and then there was another check: the workers had to pass in front of an inspector who made sure that all the lamps were tightly closed.

"Damn it, it's not too warm down here," muttered Catherine, shivering.

Etienne merely nodded. He found himself again standing in front of the shaft, in the vast draft-swept room. Though he considered himself reasonably brave, he was gripped by an uncomfortable sensation caused by the rumbling of the carts, the thumping of the signals, the muffled bellowing from the megaphone, and the continuous flight of the cables swiftly rolling and unrolling on the drums. The cages were rising and falling with the slither of nocturnal beasts, endlessly swallowing the men that the gaping hole seemed to drink down. It was his turn now. He was cold, and his nervous silence made Zacharie and Levaque snicker; they had both been against hiring this stranger—especially Levaque, who was hurt because he had not been consulted. Catherine was therefore pleased to hear her father explaining things to the young man.

"Look at the top of the cage. It has a safety device with cramp irons that grip the guides in case of a cable break. It works . . . usually. . . . Yes, the shaft's divided into three parts sectioned off by boards from top to bottom. The cages are in the middle, there's a ladder-well on the left . . ."

But he stopped to complain, though he was afraid to raise his voice:

"For God's sake, what's going on? They have no right to keep us freezing here like this!"

Richomme, the foreman, who was also waiting to go down, his open lamp fastened to a nail in his leather cap, heard him complain.

"Careful, somebody might overhear," he murmured paternally, in the spirit of a former miner whose loyalties were still to the workers. "Things take time. . . . Here we go! You and your team get in."

And in fact the cage, resting flat on its catches, banded with sheet iron and covered with a close-meshed screen, was waiting for them. Maheu, Zacharie, Levaque, and Catherine slid into a cart at the back, and since there had to be five, Etienne also got in. But all the good places were taken and he had to squeeze in next to the girl, whose elbow jammed into his stomach. He didn't know what to do with his lamp. Someone suggested that he hook it into a buttonhole on his jacket, but he didn't hear this and kept holding it awkwardly in his hand. The loading was still going on above and below: a confused animal cargo. Couldn't they get started? What was happening? It seemed as though he had been waiting for a long time. At last there was a jolt and things fell away; everything around him seemed to fly up, and a dizzying sensation of falling made his stomach churn. The feeling lasted as long as he was in the light, passing the two landing levels and the whizzing flight of the timberwork. Then, falling into the utter darkness of the mine, he became confused and no longer knew exactly what he felt.

"Here we go," said Maheu tranquilly.

The others all seemed relaxed. As for him, there were times when he wondered if he was going up or down. At moments the cage seemed to rush down without touching the guides; then there were sudden quiverings, a kind of rattling between the planks, which made him fear that a terrible accident was at hand. In addition, he couldn't see the walls of the shaft from behind the wire mesh against which he was pressing his face. The lamps barely lit up the bodies huddled around him. Only the open lamp of the foreman in the next cart shone out like a beacon.

"This one has a fifteen-foot diameter," said Maheu, continuing his explanations. "It really needs a new casing—the water is leaking in from all sides. . . . Listen, we're getting down to the water level. . . . Do you hear it?"

Etienne had already begun to wonder about the noise. It sounded like a downpour. At first a few large drops had beat on the roof of the cage, like the beginning of a shower; now the rain was getting heavier, streaming down and becoming a real deluge. The roof must have had holes in it, because a trickle of water falling on his shoulder soaked him to the skin. The cold was becoming icy. They were sinking into a damp darkness when, in a sudden flash of light, he had a vision of men moving around in a cave. Then they were falling into nothingness again.

Maheu was saying: "That was the first loading station. We're ten hundred and fifty-six feet down. . . . Look at the speed we're traveling at."

Lifting his lamp, he shone it on the timbers of the guides, which were speeding past like a rail under a train going full steam ahead. Nothing else could be seen. Three other loading platforms passed in sudden flashes of light. The deafening rain beat down into the darkness.

"How deep it is," murmured Etienne.

The fall seemed to have been going on for hours. The awkward position he had taken was uncomfortable, but he didn't dare move, and Catherine's elbow was particularly painful. She didn't say a word; he was only conscious of the warmth against him. When the cage finally stopped at the bottom, 1,828 feet down, he was surprised to find that the descent had only lasted a minute. But the sound of the catches taking hold and the sensation of something solid beneath him suddenly cheered him, and he laughingly said to Catherine:

"What have you got under your skin that keeps you so warm? I suppose you know that your elbow's digging into my stomach? . . ."

At this, she too started to laugh. What an idiot he must be to still think she was a boy! Was he blind?

"My elbow must be in your eyes," she answered, amid a burst of laughter that the surprised young man could not understand.

The cage was emptying and the workers crossed the loading platform, a kind of room carved out of the rock, reinforced with masonry, and lit by three large open-flame lamps. The loaders were charging along the cast-iron flooring with full carts. Dampness oozed from the walls, and warm gusts from the nearby stable mixed with the chilly smell of saltpeter. Four gaping galleries opened into the area.

"This way," Maheu said to Etienne. "You're not there yet. We've still got more than a mile to go."

The miners were separating into groups and disappearing into the black holes. About fifteen of them had entered the one on the left, and Etienne brought up the rear, behind Maheu, who was preceded by Catherine, Zacharie, and Levaque. It was a good haulage tunnel, cutting through rock so solid that only partial timbering had been necessary. By the tiny flame of their lamps, they kept walking forward in single file, never saying a word. The young man stumbled at every step, catching his feet in the rails. For some time now he had been worried by a muffled sound: the far-off noise of a storm that seemed to be growing in violence and coming from the very bowels of the earth. Was it the rumble of a cave-in that would bring crashing down on them the enormous mass that cut them off from the light of day? A light pierced the darkness and he could feel the rock vibrate; when he had flattened himself up against the wall just like the others, he saw, passing close to him, a big white horse harnessed to a string of carts. Bébert was sitting on the first cart and holding the reins, while Jeanlin, his hands straining against the edge of the last cart, was running along barefoot.

They started walking again. Farther on there was a junction; two more galleries opened up and once more the group divided, the miners gradually dropping off at all the workings. Now the haulage tunnel was timbered; oak props supported the roof and held the sagging rock behind a framework of wood through which could be seen bands of slate, shining with mica, and the heavy masses of dull, rough sandstone.

Strings of empty or full carts kept passing and crossing one another, their rumblings carried off into the darkness by shadowy animals with ghostly steps. On a double rail of a siding a long black serpent was sleeping—a parked string of carts whose snorting horse was so wrapped in darkness that its vaguely distinguishable rump seemed like a mass fallen from the vault above. Ventilation doors banged, closing slowly. And the farther they went, the narrower the tunnel, the lower and more uneven the roof, so that they were constantly forced to bend over.

Etienne struck his head sharply. If he hadn't been wearing the leather cap, his skull would have been fractured. Yet he had been carefully following the least gesture of Maheu, whose dark outline ahead of him could be seen by the light of the lamps. Not one of the other workers bumped into anything—they seemed to know every little hump of the ground, every protruding knot of the timbers, every swelling of the rocks. Etienne was also bothered by the slippery ground, which was becoming wetter and wetter. At times he passed through actual pools, discovered only as his feet sloshed through the muddy slop. But what astonished him most were the sudden changes in temperature. At the bottom of the shaft it had been very cold, and in the first haulage tunnel, through which the air for the mine passed, the narrow walls raised the strong icy blasts to storm level. But afterward, as they got into the other passageways, which had to compete for the available ventilation, the wind died and the heat increased—a suffocating, leaden heat.

Maheu had not spoken another word. He now went into a gallery on the right and, without turning, merely said:

"The Guillaume vein."

This was the vein in which their stall was located. After the first few steps Etienne bruised his head and elbows. The sloping roof came down so low that for as much as twenty or thirty yards at a time he had to walk doubled over. The water reached his ankles. They went on like this for about two hundred yards; then suddenly he saw Levaque, Zacharie, and Catherine vanish—as if they had been swallowed up into a narrow crack that opened ahead of him.

"You'll have to climb," said Maheu. "Hook your lamp into one of your buttonholes and hold on to the timbers."

He too disappeared and Etienne had to follow. This narrow chimney left in the vein was used by the miners to reach the secondary passageway. It was just the width of the coal seam, scarcely two feet. Luckily Etienne was thin. With the same awkwardness he had shown throughout, he hoisted himself with a wasteful expenditure of energy, pulling in his shoulders and buttocks and advancing hand over hand, clinging to the timbers. Fifty feet up they came to the first secondary passageway, but they had to go farther: the stall in which Maheu's group was working was in the sixth passageway—in hell, as they called it. The passageways were superimposed on one another, and fifty feet after fifty feet they climbed through this narrow endless cranny that scraped against back and chest. Etienne was gasping, as if the weight of the rocks had crushed his limbs; his hands were skinned, his legs were bruised, and worst of all, he was suffocating. He thought the blood was going to burst through his skin. In one of the passageways he could dimly see two crouching animals, a little one and a big one, pushing carts: Lydie and Mouquette, already at work. And he still had the height of two more stalls to climb! Sweat blinded him, and he despaired of being able to catch up with the others, whose agile limbs he could hear gliding along the rock.

"That's it—here we are!" said Catherine's voice.

But as he got there, another voice cried out from the rear of the stall:

"What's going on? Are you trying to make a fool out of me? I've got more than a mile to walk from Montsou, and I get here first!"

It was Chaval, a tall, thin, bony fellow, about twenty-five, with strong features. He'd been waiting and he was angry. When he saw Etienne he asked with surprised contempt:

"What's this?"

After he had heard the story from Maheu, he added,
between his teeth:

"So the men are taking the bread away from the girls
now!"

The two men exchanged a look infused with one of those
instinctive hatreds that flame up suddenly. Etienne had felt
the insult without quite understanding it. Silence fell and
everybody started to work. Gradually the veins had filled
with workers; the faces were being cut at every level, to the
end of every passageway. The ravenous mine had swallowed
its daily ration of men, and nearly seven hundred workers
were now laboring in this giant anthill, tunneling the earth
from all sides, riddling it until it was like an old piece of
worm-eaten wood. In the midst of this heavy silence, under
the crushing weight of the many levels above, by putting your
ear to the rock you could have heard these human insects at
work, from the whizzing of the cable that raised and lowered
the cage to the bite of the tools digging into the coal at the
bottom of the mine.

Etienne turned and once more found himself pressed up
against Catherine; but this time he became aware of the
curve of her budding breasts and suddenly understood the
warmth that had penetrated him.

"So you're a girl . . ." he mumbled in amazement.

She replied in her cheerful manner, without blushing:

"Of course I am. . . . It certainly took you long enough to
find out!"

4

The four cutters had stretched themselves out, head to toe,
over the whole surface of the sloping face. Separated by
hooked planks that caught the loosened coal, each of them
occupied about fifteen feet of the vein, which was so narrow—
scarcely twenty inches at this point—that they were squashed
in between the roof and the wall. They had to drag themselves along on their knees and elbows, and were unable to
turn without bruising their shoulders. To get at the coal, they
had to lie sideways, their necks twisted and their raised arms
wielding the short-handled picks at an angle.

Zacharie was at the bottom, Levaque and Chaval above
him, and Maheu at the very top. Each one was hacking away

at the bed of shale with his pick, cutting two vertical grooves in the vein, then driving an iron wedge into the top of the block and freeing it. The coal was soft, and the block crumbled into pieces and rolled down their stomachs and thighs. When these pieces, caught by the planks, had heaped up beneath them, the cutters disappeared, walled up in the narrow crevice.

Maheu was the one who suffered most. The temperature at the top climbed as high as ninety-five degrees; the air did not circulate, and the suffocating heat eventually became unbearable. In order to see clearly, he had had to hang his lamp on a nail right next to his head, and this additional heat beating down on his skull made his blood sing in his ears. But the worst was the dampness. Water was continually dripping down from the rock only a few inches above his face, and there was a never-ending stream of drops falling, with a maddening rhythm, always on the same spot. It was no use twisting his neck or turning his head: the drops kept beating against his face, splattering and spreading without stop. At the end of a quarter of an hour he was soaked through, coated with his own sweat, and steaming like a tub of laundry. That morning a drop ceaselessly trickling into his eye made him swear, but he wouldn't stop cutting, and his mighty blows jolted him so violently between the two layers of rock that he was like a plant-louse caught between two pages of a book—in constant danger of being completely crushed.

Not a word was said. They were all hammering away, and nothing could be heard except these irregular blows, muffled and seemingly far away. The sounds were harsh in the echoless, dead air, and it seemed as though the shadows had a strange blackness, thickened by the flying coal dust and made heavier by the gases that weighed down on their eyes. Behind metal screens, the wicks of their lamps gave off only reddish points of light, and it was hard to see anything. The stall opened out like a large, flat, oblique chimney in which the soot of ten winters had built up an unrelieved darkness. Phantom forms moved about, dull beams of light giving glimpses of a rounded haunch, a brawny arm, a distorted face blackened as if in preparation for a crime. Occasionally, as blocks of coal came loose, they would catch the light and shoot off crystal-like glitters from their suddenly illuminated facets. Then it would be dark again, the picks would beat out heavy dull blows, and there was nothing but the sound of panting breaths, grunts of discomfort and fatigue in the stifling air, and the dripping water from the underground streams.

Zacharie, his arms heavy from too much celebrating the night before, soon stopped work on the pretext of having to timber, an operation that allowed him to daydream and whistle softly, his eyes gazing vacantly into space. Behind the cutters, about ten feet of the vein had already been excavated, but indifferent to the danger and avaricious of their time, they had not yet taken the precaution of propping up the rock.

"Hey there, your highness," Zacharie called to Etienne, "get me some timber!"

Etienne, who was learning from Catherine how to use his shovel, had to stop and bring some timbers up to the stall. There were still a few left from last time. Usually they would bring some down every morning, already cut to the size of the seam.

"Get a move on, will you!" complained Zacharie, watching the new hauler awkwardly hoist himself up through the coal, his arms loaded with four pieces of oak.

With his pick, Zacharie cut one notch in the roof and another in the wall, then wedged in the two ends of the timber so that it would support the rock. In the afternoon the men on the repairing shift would take the rubble the cutters left at the ends of the galleries and fill in the excavated parts of the vein, burying the timbers and leaving only the upper and lower haulage paths intact.

Maheu stopped grunting. At last he had detached his block. Wiping his dripping face on his sleeve, he complained about what Zacharie was busy doing behind him.

"Let that alone," he said. "We'll take care of it after lunch. . . . We'd better keep cutting if we want to fill our quota of carts."

"But it's coming down," answered Zacharie. "Look, there's a crack. I'm afraid the whole thing will cave in."

His father merely shrugged his shoulders. Cave in? Not likely! And if it did, it wouldn't be the first time; they'd manage somehow. Finally he lost his temper and ordered his son back to the face.

As a matter of fact, all of them were slacking off. Levaque, still on his back, was swearing as he examined his left thumb, the flesh of which had been torn by some falling sandstone. Chaval, in a fit of fury, was stripping to the waist so that he wouldn't be so hot. They were already black with coal and covered with a fine dust which mixed with their sweat and ran down them in streams and pools. Maheu was the first to go back to hacking, this time at a lower point, with his head right up against the rock. And now the drops of water kept falling on his forehead so insistently that he thought he could feel them drilling a hole in his skull.

"Don't mind them," Catherine explained to Etienne. "They're always yelling about something."

In a friendly manner she went on with her explanations.

Each loaded cart was tagged before it left the stall, so that when it reached the top the checker could credit it to the team. It was therefore important that the cart be full and the coal clean; otherwise it would be rejected.

The young man, whose eyes were becoming adjusted to the dark, studied her. Her skin was still a sickly white; he couldn't really be sure of her age, but she was so frail that he guessed her to be about twelve. Yet she had a boyish freedom and a naïve impudence that he found somewhat disturbing, and he sensed that she must be older. He did not find her attractive: her pale Pierrot face with its forehead outlined by the cap seemed too clownish. But what surprised him most was the strength of this child—a nervous strength in which there was also a great deal of skill. With rapid and regular shovelfuls, she could fill her cart faster than he filled his, then push it to the incline with one slow, smooth motion, passing easily under the low rocks. He, on the other hand, bruised himself terribly, ran his cart off the rails, and became hopelessly stuck.

In truth, it was not a very easy road. It was about two hundred feet from the face to the incline, and the path, not yet enlarged by the men on the repairing shift, was as narrow as a tube, with an uneven roof bulging with bumps. At some points there was just room enough for the loaded cart to get through, and the hauler had to flatten himself out and push on his knees so as not to smash his skull. In addition, the timbers were already bending and breaking; long, pale cracks showed where they had given in the middle, just like crutches too weak to bear any weight. You had to be careful not to skin yourself against these splinters, and you crawled along on your stomach, under the dead weight that shattered thigh-thick oak logs, with the oppressive fear of suddenly hearing your back crack.

"Not again!" said Catherine, laughing.

Etienne had just derailed his cart on the most difficult stretch. He didn't seem to be able to push straight ahead on these rails that sank into the damp earth, and he swore, lost his temper, and tore wildly at the wheels—which he could not set back on the track despite his most strenuous efforts.

"Wait a minute," continued the girl; "you'll never manage if you get excited."

She quickly slipped down and backed beneath the cart, then, with a heave of her hip, lifted it and put it back in place. It weighed about fifteen hundred pounds. Amazed and ashamed, he mumbled his apologies.

She had to show him how to spread his legs and buttress his feet against the timbers on both sides of the tunnel to give himself solid support. The body had to be bent and the arms straight, so as to be able to push with all the muscles of the shoulders and hips. For one trip he followed her and watched her hurry along, her back stretched out, her hands so low that she seemed to be trotting on all fours, like one of those dwarfed animals in a circus. She sweated, she panted, she cracked her joints, but with the indifference born of habit she never complained—as if the common plight of all mankind was to live bent over this way. But he could not do the same; his shoes bothered him and his body ached from walking doubled over. After a few minutes this position became a torture, an intolerable agony so painful that he had to get on his knees for a moment to straighten his back and catch his breath.

Then at the incline there was another problem. She showed him how to shove his cart off quickly. At the top and the bottom of this incline, which served as the stalls between one landing and another, were mine boys—a brake operator above and a receiver below. These rascals, twelve to fifteen years old, kept shrieking obscenities at each other, and to catch their attention you had to shout even louder and more obscenely than they did. As soon as there was an empty cart to bring up, the receiver would give the signal and the hauler shoved off her full cart, the weight of which would draw up the other one when the boy released the brake. In the gallery at the bottom, trains of carts were made up and then pulled to the shaft by horses.

"Hey there, you good-for-nothings!" Catherine shouted into the incline, which was timbered all along its hundred-yard length and reverberated like a megaphone.

The mine boys must have been taking a break, for neither of them answered. The hauling was at a standstill at every level. Finally the shrill voice of a young girl called out:

"One of them is probably on top of Mouquette."

There was an explosion of laughter, and the girls in every part of the vein roared as if they would burst.

"Who was that?" Etienne asked Catherine.

She answered that it was little Lydie, an urchin who knew

more than she should and who pushed her cart as well as a full-grown woman, in spite of her doll-like arms. As for Mouquette, she was quite capable of keeping both mine boys busy at the same time.

Just then the receiver's voice called up, telling them to shove off a cart. A foreman was probably passing by down below. The hauling started again on all nine levels, and nothing could be heard but the periodic calls of the mine boys and the snorting of the haulage girls as they reached the incline, steaming like overloaded mares. A breath of bestiality swept through the mine: the sudden desire of the male when a miner came across one of these girls on all fours, her haunches in the air and her buttocks straining against her trousers.

And on every trip back to the stall Etienne rediscovered the same suffocating heat, the dull, interlocking cadence of the picks, the painful gasps of the cutters hard at work. All four of them had stripped to the bone, and covered with black mud up to their very caps, they seemed to be swallowed up by the coal. Once Maheu had nearly suffocated and they had had to work him loose—release the hooked boards so the coal would slide down to the ground. Zacharie and Levaque were cursing the vein; they said it was becoming hard—a factor that would make the terms of their contract disastrous. Chaval turned on his back for a moment and swore at Etienne, whose presence evidently exasperated him.

"You little worm, you! My God, it hasn't got the strength of a girl! ... Fill up that cart, will you! What're you doing, trying to save your energy? ... Christ, I'll see that you're docked if one of them is turned down because of you!"

Etienne did not answer; he was happy to have found this enslaving work, and he accepted the brutal distinction made between the skilled and the unskilled worker. But he couldn't walk; his feet were bleeding, his limbs twisted by terrible cramps, and his waist ringed with iron. Luckily it was ten o'clock and everybody decided to stop for lunch.

Maheu had a watch, but he did not bother to look at it. Even at the bottom of this starless night, he was never five minutes off. They all put on their shirts and jackets, and then, coming down from the face, they crouched down with their elbows against their sides and their buttocks resting on their heels—a posture so natural to miners that they use it even outside the mine, and never feel the need for a cobblestone or a beam to sit on. Each of them took out his sandwich and chomped away solemnly on the thick slices, occasionally mumbling something about the morning's work. Catherine, who had remained standing, finally joined Etienne, who, some distance apart from the others, had stretched out across the rails with his back against the timbers. It was reasonably dry there.

"Aren't you eating?" she asked him, her mouth full, her sandwich in her hand.

Then she remembered that he had been wandering around in the night, without a sou and probably without so much as a piece of bread.

"Would you like part of mine?"

And when he refused, swearing that he wasn't hungry, his voice trembling with the rumbling of his stomach, she continued gaily:

"Oh, if the idea disgusts you . . . but look, I've only bitten out of this half—I'll give you the other one."

She'd already broken the sandwich in two. Etienne took his half and kept himself from wolfing it down; he rested his arms on his thighs so she wouldn't see how they were shaking. In her calm, friendly way, she had stretched out alongside him on her stomach, resting her chin in one hand and slowly eating with the other. They could see each other by the light of the two lamps between them.

Catherine looked at him in silence for a moment. She must have found his fine features and black moustache handsome, for she smiled with an undefined pleasure.

"So you're an engineman and you've lost your job on the railroad. . . . Why?"

"Because I hit my boss."

She was speechless, all her inherited ideas of subordination and passive obedience upset.

"I ought to tell you that I'd had a few drinks," he went on, "and when I drink it makes me sort of crazy. I could kill myself and everybody near me. . . . I can't take a few drinks without wanting to tear into somebody. . . . And then I'm sick for the next two days."

"You shouldn't drink," she said seriously.

"Oh, don't worry, I know I shouldn't."

He nodded his head; he hated liquor with the hatred of the last-born of a race of drunkards, the hatred of one who suffered so from a wild, alcohol-steeped inheritance that the least little drop was poison to him.

"It's because of my mother that I'm upset about losing my job," he said, after swallowing a mouthful. "She's got a hard life, and I used to send her a few francs from time to time."

"Where is your mother?"

"In Paris. . . . She's a laundress on the rue de la Goutte-d'Or."

There was a silence. When he thought about these things a sudden fear shone in his dark eyes, a pang caused by the corruption incubating in the very core of his youthful vigor. For a moment he stared absently into the darkness of the mine, and here, down below, under the crushing weight of the earth above, he relived his childhood: his pretty and courageous mother, deserted by his father and then reclaimed again after she had married another, living between the two men who both exploited her and drunkenly rolling with them in the filthy gutters. He could remember the very street, and all the details came back to him: the dirty linen heaped in the middle of the shop, the drinking bouts that smelled up the house, the jaw-breaking blows.

"Well, I won't be able to send her anything from the thirty sous I make here," he resumed dreamily. "That much is sure, anyhow. . . . She's in for some rotten times."

He shrugged his shoulders hopelessly and bit into his sandwich.

"Do you want something to drink?" asked Catherine, opening her flask. "Don't worry, it's only coffee, it won't hurt you. . . . The bread will stick in your throat unless you drink something."

But he refused; it was enough that he had taken half her sandwich. However, she generously insisted, saying:

"Look, I'll drink first since you're so polite. . . . Only now you can't refuse, it wouldn't be nice."

And she held out her flask. She had gotten up on her knees and he could see her, close to him, in the light from the two lamps. What had made him think she was ugly? Now that she was all black, her skin coated with coal dust, she had a peculiar charm. In this face obscured by shadows, the teeth in her large mouth were of a dazzling whiteness, the eyes seemed to have become larger and were shining with a greenish light, like the eyes of a cat. A lock of reddish hair had escaped from her cap and was tickling her ear, making her laugh. She no longer seemed so young; she was probably at least fourteen.

"Well, since you want me to," he said, drinking and returning the flask.

She took another swallow and made him take one too, saying she wanted to share, and they amused themselves by passing the narrow-necked flask from one mouth to the other. It suddenly occurred to him that maybe he ought to grab her, to kiss her large, pale lips which were emphasized

by the coal and which were tormenting him with a growing
desire. But he was intimidated by her and didn't dare. In
Lille he had only had the lowest kind of whore, and he didn't
know how to behave with a working girl who still lived at
home.

"You must be about fourteen, aren't you?" he asked, biting
into his sandwich again.

She was amazed, almost angry.

"What? Fourteen? Why, I'm fifteen! ... It's true that I'm
not very big. Girls around here don't grow very fast."

He went on questioning her and she told him everything,
without being either brazen or embarrassed. As a matter of
fact, she knew everything about what went on between men
and women, even though he felt sure she was still a virgin—a
childish virgin whose development had been checked by the
bad air and the constant exhaustion in which she lived. When
he tried to disconcert her by mentioning Mouquette, she told
him terrible stories, her voice untroubled and amused. Oh,
that one! She really carried on! And when he asked her if she
herself didn't have a lover, she laughingly replied that she
didn't want to upset her mother, but it was sure to happen
some day. Her shoulders were hunched over, and she was
shivering a little in her sweat-dampened clothes, her face
resigned and gentle, ready to submit to the force of things
and of men.

"I guess it's easy to find a lover when everybody lives
together this way, isn't it?"

"Of course it is."

"And it doesn't hurt anybody.... There's no need to tell
the priest."

"Oh, the priest! I don't give a damn about him.... But
there's the Black Man."

"What do you mean, the Black Man?"

"The ghost of the old miner who comes back here and
strangles bad girls."

He stared at her, afraid she might be making fun of him.

"Do you mean to say you believe in that kind of nonsense?
Don't you know anything?"

"Of course I do. I know how to read and write.... It's a
good thing to know, and when my mother and father were
young they didn't get a chance to learn."

She was really very sweet. He made up his mind that when
she finished her sandwich he'd kiss her large pink lips. It was
a decision born of shyness, a notion of violence that choked
his voice. Those boy's clothes, the jacket and trousers, on this
girl's body excited and disturbed him. He had already swal-

lowed his last piece of bread, and after drinking from the flask, he gave it back to her to finish. Now the time for action had come, and he was glancing nervously toward the others when suddenly a shadow blocked the gallery.

Chaval had been standing there for some time, watching them from a distance. After making sure that Maheu couldn't see him, he came forward; since Catherine was still sitting on the ground, he grabbed her by the shoulders, pushed back her head, and calmly crushed her lips beneath a brutal kiss—quite deliberately, and pretending not to pay any attention to Etienne. The kiss seemed a claim to possession, a kind of jealous decision.

But the girl became angry.

"Let me alone, will you!"

He held her head and stared into her eyes. His reddish moustache and small beard flamed out of his black face with its large aquiline nose. Then he let her go and went off without a word.

Etienne felt chilled. It was idiotic to have waited. No, he wouldn't kiss her now because she would think he was only trying to imitate Chaval. In his wounded vanity, he felt a real anguish.

"Why did you lie?" he asked in a low voice. "He's your lover, isn't he?"

"No, I swear he isn't!" she protested. "There's nothing like that between us. Sometimes he likes to fool around. . . . Why, he doesn't even come from here—he came from the Pas-de-Calais six months ago."

They both got up. It was time to go back to work. His sudden coldness seemed to upset her. She certainly found him more handsome than the other and would probably have preferred him, so she searched for some friendly and conciliating gesture. Seeing that he was looking at his lamp, which was burning blue in a large, pale ring, she tried at least to distract him.

"Come here, I want to show you something," she murmured in a frank and open manner.

She led him to the bottom of the stall and showed him a crack in the vein. A slight hiss escaped from it—a tiny noise like the whistling of a bird.

"Put your hand there, you can feel the draft. . . . It's firedamp."

He was surprised. Was that all it was, that terrible stuff that blew everything up? She laughed and said it must be pretty strong today to make the lamps burn so blue.

"Any time you're ready, you two good-for-nothings!" called Maheu's rough voice.

Catherine and Etienne hurriedly filled their carts and pushed them to the incline, their backs rigid as they scurried under the uneven roof of the tunnel. After the second trip they were soaked with sweat and their bones were aching again.

At the face the cutters had gone back to work. They often shortened their lunch time so they wouldn't stiffen, and their sandwiches, eaten in ravenous silence so far from the sun, seemed like lead in their stomachs. Stretched out on their sides, they hacked harder than ever, obsessed by the idea of filling as many carts as possible. Nothing seemed to matter but this desperate battle to make a little more money. They no longer felt the water that was trickling over them and swelling their limbs, or the cramps caused by their awkward positions, or the suffocation of the darkness in which they faded like plants that have been put into a cellar. Yet as the day went on, the air became more and more unbreathable, heated by the lamps, by their own foul breaths, by the poisonous firedamp fumes. It seemed to cling to their eyes like cobwebs, and it would only be swept away by the night's ventilation. Meanwhile, at the bottom of their molehill, under the weight of the earth, with no breath left in their overheated lungs, they kept hacking away.

5

Without looking at his watch, which he had left in his jacket, Maheu stopped and said:

"It's almost one o'clock. . . . Are you finished, Zacharie?"

Zacharie had been timbering for some time, but he had stopped in the middle of the job and was now stretched on his back, his eyes blank, dreaming of the games of *crosse* he had played the day before. He shook himself and answered:

"Yes, it'll do. We can check it tomorrow."

And he went back to his place at the face. Levaque and Chaval had also put down their picks and everybody was taking a break. They all wiped their faces on their bare arms and looked up at the cracks and splits in the shaley roof. They hardly ever spoke about anything except their work.

"Another lousy break," muttered Chaval; "—getting a sec-

tion that's buckling. They didn't allow for that in the contract."

"The swindlers!" grumbled Levaque. "They're always looking for ways to do us in."

Zacharie started to laugh. He didn't give a damn about the
work or anything else, but he liked to hear the Company
abused. In his quiet way Maheu pointed out that the nature
of the ground changed every sixty or seventy feet. They had
to be fair: nobody could predict everything in advance. But
when the other two continued railing against the bosses, he
became nervous and glanced around.

"Sh! That's enough now!"

"You're right," said Levaque, also lowering his voice. "It's
not healthy."

Even all the way down here they were obsessed by the fear
of company spies—as if the stockholders' coal, still in the
vein, had ears.

"Anyhow," Chaval added loudly, with an air of defiance,
"if that bastard Dansaert talks to me the way he did the
other day, I'll shove a brick into him. . . . *I'm* not the one
who stops him from treating himself to those soft-skinned
blondes!"

At this Zacharie burst out laughing. The affair between the
chief foreman and La Pierronne was a constant source of
humor in the mine. Even Catherine, leaning on her shovel at
the foot of the face, held her sides and with a few words
explained the situation to Etienne. But Maheu, gripped by a
fear that he no longer tried to hide, lost his temper.

"Shut up, damn it! . . . Wait till you're alone if you're
looking for trouble."

While he was still talking there was a sound of footsteps in
the upper gallery, and almost immediately afterward, the
engineer of the mine—Little Négrel as the workers called
him among themselves—appeared at the head of the stall
accompanied by Dansaert, the chief foreman.

"What did I tell you?" muttered Maheu. "There's always
one of them ready to spring from the ground."

Paul Négrel, Monsieur Hennebeau's nephew, was twenty-six
years old, slender and handsome, with curly hair and a dark
moustache. His sharp nose and lively eyes made him look like
a friendly ferret, but his usual manner of detached and
skeptical intelligence would change to one of brusque author-
itarianism when he dealt with the workers. He was dressed
the way they were, and smeared with coal the way they
were; and to compel their respect he showed a reckless
courage, going into the most dangerous places and always

being the first to arrive at a cave-in or a firedamp explosion.

"This is it, isn't it, Dansaert?" he asked.

The chief foreman, a heavy-faced Belgian with a large, sensual nose, answered with exaggerated politeness:

"Yes, Monsieur Négrel. . . . And there's the man that was hired this morning."

They both slid down to the middle of the stall. Etienne was summoned, and the engineer, lifting his lamp, stared at him without saying a word.

"All right," he said at last. "But I don't like this business of taking strangers off the road. . . . Don't do it again."

He did not listen to the explanations offered about the demands of the work and the desirability of replacing girls with men for hauling. He had begun to inspect the roof, and the cutters were taking up their picks again. Suddenly he shouted:

"What the hell do you think you're doing, Maheu? My God, you'll all be buried alive down here!"

"Oh, it's solid enough," the worker answered quietly.

"Solid? . . . Why the rock's already beginning to settle and your timbers are more than six feet apart—as if you couldn't spare them! You're all the same—you'd rather have your skulls squashed than stop cutting long enough to do a decent job of timbering. I want all that shored up immediately. Twice as many timbers, do you hear?"

And when the miners began to argue, saying that they were the best judges of their own safety, he became furious.

"And I suppose that when you have your heads broken you'll take the consequences? Oh no, not you! It'll be the Company that will have to pay out the pensions to you or your wives. . . . I tell you we *know* you people—you'd give your very lives to have two extra carts of coal at quitting time!"

In spite of his steadily rising anger Maheu still spoke calmly.

"If they paid us enough, we'd timber better."

The engineer shrugged, but did not answer. He had gone down the length of the face, and from there he called out his final words:

"You've still got an hour, so get to work, all of you! And I might as well tell you that I'm fining this team three francs."

The cutters greeted this news with low growls, and only the force of the hierarchy kept them in line—the military hierarchy that kept each of them, from the mine boys to the chief foreman, bent one under the other. Even so, Chaval and Levaque made angry gestures, while Maheu shot them a warning look and Zacharie mockingly shrugged his shoulders. But it was Etienne who he had entered this pit of hell, rebellion had smoldered in him. He looked at Catherine, whose back was bent in resignation. Was it possible?—could people really slave away in this deadly darkness and not even make the few sous needed for food?

Meanwhile Négrel had gone off with Dansaert, whose role had been to nod his head in complete approval of everything said. Suddenly their voices could be heard once more; they had stopped again and were examining the timbering of the gallery, which the cutters had to maintain for a distance of thirty feet back from the face.

"Didn't I tell you they don't give a damn about anything!" shouted the engineer. "And you, damn it—don't you keep an eye on things?"

"Of course I do, of course I do," stammered the chief foreman. "We get tired of repeating the same thing to them over and over."

"Maheu! Maheu!" Négrel called furiously.

They all came down, and he went on:

"Take a look at this, do you expect it to hold? . . . It's not worth a damn! Why, it was put up in such a hurry that the cap-piece isn't even resting on the uprights! My God, now I know why maintenance costs us so much! You only want it to hold for as long as you're responsible, don't you? Then the whole thing comes crashing down and the Company has to send out an army of repairmen. . . . Look over there, will you—it's a real mess!"

Chaval wanted to say something, but Négrel shut him up.

"No, I know what you're going to say. You want to be paid better, right? Well, I warn you that you're forcing the management to a decision—we'll pay you separately for the timbering, but the price per cart will be cut proportionally. We'll see if you come out ahead that way. . . . In the meantime, I want all of that retimbered immediately. I'll check on it tomorrow."

And before the shock caused by this threat had a chance to wear off, he left. Dansaert, who had been so mild-mannered while Négrel was there, stayed behind for a few moments to tell the men harshly:

"You're getting me into trouble. . . . Watch out or it won't be only a three-franc fine that you get from me!"

When he too was gone, Maheu finally exploded:

"Damn it! What isn't fair isn't fair! I like to keep calm because it's the only way to come to any sort of understanding, but they always drive you too far. Did you hear that? They're going to give us less per cart and pay for the timbering separately! Just another way of paying us even less. . . . God damn it!"

He was looking for someone to vent his rage on when he caught sight of Catherine and Etienne standing around empty-handed.

"How about getting some timbers? Is this any of your business? How'd you like a kick somewhere?"

Without taking offense at his tone Etienne went off for some timbers; he himself was so angry at the bosses that he thought the miners were being much too good-natured.

Levaque and Chaval had eased themselves with a stream of obscenities, and now everybody, even Zacharie, was timbering furiously. For the next half hour all that could be heard was the sound of the maul wedging the timbers into place. Not another word was said: breathing heavily, they fought against the rock, which they would have shoved back with a heave of their shoulders if they had been able to.

"That's enough," said Maheu at last, worn out by anger and fatigue. "Half past one. . . . What a day this has been! We probably haven't made fifty sous! . . . I'm going. The whole business makes me sick."

Though there was still half an hour to go, he got dressed and the others followed suit. The very sight of the face enraged them. Catherine had gone back to her hauling; irritated by her zeal, they called to her to let the coal walk out on its own two feet! And all six of them, their tools under their arms, set off to face the long walk back to the shaft by the same road they had taken that morning.

In the chimney, Catherine and Etienne stopped for a moment, while the cutters slid down to the bottom. They had run into little Lydie, who was waiting in the middle of a passageway to let them go by, and she told them that Mouquette had disappeared. About an hour ago she had had such a heavy nosebleed that she'd gone off somewhere to wash her face, and nobody knew where. When Catherine and Etienne left her, the child went back to pushing her cart—exhausted, muddy, stretching her insectlike arms and legs, like a thin black ant struggling with a load too heavy for it. They, meanwhile, slid down on their backs, flattening their shoulders so they wouldn't skin their faces, and they skimmed so quickly along the rock polished by the rear ends of all the miners that from time to time they had to catch hold of the timbers—to keep their buttocks from catching fire, they said jokingly.

At the bottom they found themselves alone. Red stars were disappearing in the distance around a bend in the gallery. Their good humor vanished, and they started off at a pace heavy with fatigue, she first, he behind. Their lamps had become smudged, and he could hardly see her; she seemed drowned in a smoky fog. The knowledge that she was a girl made him uncomfortable; he thought it was stupid not to kiss her, to let the memory of Chaval stop him. Of course she had lied: Chaval was her lover and they probably made love on top of every pile of slack; he could see that she already had the swaying walk of a tramp. For no particular reason he was angry with her, as though she had cheated on him. She, on the other hand, kept turning around to warn him of some obstacle, and seemed to be inviting friendliness. They were so alone, they could have had such good laughs together! At last they came out into the haulage gallery and he was relieved of the indecision that had been torturing him; she, however, threw him a final sad look, as if mourning a lost happiness that they would never find again.

And now the underground life was rumbling all around them, with an incessant passing of foremen and a constant coming and going of strings of carts being moved briskly along by horses. Everywhere there were lamps, studding the night with stars. They had to keep flattening themselves against the rock to make way for shadows of men and animals, whose breaths they could feel on their faces. Jean-lin, running barefoot behind his string of carts, called out some obscenity, which they could not hear above the thunder of the wheels. They walked on, she now silent, he not recognizing the intersections and passageways they had taken that morning and thinking she was getting him more and more lost under the ground. He suffered most from the cold, an increasing chill that had gripped him as soon as he had left the face and which was making him shiver more and more as he got closer to the shaft. Once again the blasts of air were storming through the narrow passageway walls. He was beginning to think that they would never get there when, suddenly, they turned into the loading station.

Chaval glanced at them, his lips twisted with suspicion. The others were also there, sweating in the icy drafts and, like him, mutely swallowing angry complaints. They had come too soon, and the cage operators wouldn't take them up for half an hour, especially since they were busy with some complicated maneuvers necessary for the bringing

down of a horse. Carts were still being loaded with a deafening noise of rattling metal, and the cages flew up and disappeared into the pelting rain that fell from the dark hole
above. Below, a sump—a thirty-foot sinkhole filled by this
stream—was also exhaling its muddy dampness. Men kept
moving around the shaft, pulling signal cords, pressing down
levers, in the middle of this spray of water that soaked their
clothes. The reddish light of the three open lamps threw large
moving shadows and gave this underground room the look of
a secret cave, a bandit's forge beside a torrent.

Maheu made one more attempt and went up to Pierron,
who had gone on duty at six o'clock.

"Come on now, I'm sure you can let us up."

But the loader, a handsome fellow with a muscular body
and a gentle face, refused with a frightened gesture.

"I can't. Ask the foreman. . . . They'd fine me."

Another burst of complaints was stifled, and Catherine,
leaning over, whispered into Etienne's ear:

"Come see the stable. It's really nice there."

They had to slip off without being seen because it was
against the rules to go there. The stable was on the left, at
the end of a short gallery. About eighty feet long and fifteen
feet high, cut into the rock and vaulted with bricks, it could
hold about twenty horses. And it *was* nice there, with the
good warmth of living animals and the clean smell of well-
kept stalls. The one lamp gave off the peaceful glow of a
night light. Resting horses turned their heads and gazed at
them with big, childlike eyes, then slowly went back to their
oats, as was fitting for fat, healthy workers loved by everybody.

But as Catherine was reading aloud the names on the zinc
plates over the mangers, a body suddenly reared up in front
of her, and she let out a slight cry. It was Mouquette,
terrified, jumping up from a pile of straw in which she had
been sleeping. On Mondays, when she was tired from all the
Sunday good times, she would give herself a violent punch on
the nose, leave the face with the excuse that she had to look
for water, and slip in among the animals in the warm stalls.
Her father, who had a great weakness for her, would overlook it even at the risk of getting into trouble himself.

As it happened, Old Mouque came in just at that moment.
Short, bald, and worn-out, he was nevertheless quite heavy,
which was unusual in a fifty-year-old miner. From the time
he had been made a stableman, he had chewed tobacco so
constantly that the gums bled in his black mouth. He lost his
temper when he saw these other two with his daughter.

"What are you all doing here? Come on! Out! What do you tramps mean by bringing a man in here! ... Imagine using my clean straw for your dirty tricks!"

Mouquette thought that was very funny and broke into guffaws, but Etienne was embarrassed and walked away as Catherine smiled at him. The three of them reached the loading station just as Bébert and Jeanlin were arriving with a string of carts. There was a pause while they waited for the cages to be ready, and the girl went up to their horse and patted him in as she told Etienne his history. He was Bataille, an old favorite in the mine—a white horse that had been down there for ten years. During all that time he had lived in this hole, always occupying the same corner of the stable, always doing the same work in the long dark galleries, without ever again having seen daylight. He was fat and content, and his hide glistened; he seemed to lead a calm life, sheltered from all the troubles of the world above. In addition, down in this darkness he had developed great cleverness. The passageway along which he worked had eventually become so familiar to him that he learned to use his head to push open the ventilation doors and to dip so as not to bump it in places where the ceiling was too low. He probably also counted his trips, because when he had completed the required number he refused to begin another and had to be taken back to his manger. But now he was growing old, and at times his cat eyes seemed to be veiled in sadness. Perhaps in his dim dreamings he could vaguely remember the place where he had been born—the mill near Marchiennes, a mill set on the banks of the Scarpe and surrounded by large green fields through which the wind always blew. Something used to burn high in the air—an enormous lamp, the exact nature of which escaped his animal memory. And he stood there with his head down, trembling on his old legs and vainly trying to remember the sun.

In the meantime operations in the shaft were still going on. The signal hammer had beat out four blows; they were bringing down the horse. This was always exciting, because sometimes the horse would become so terrified that it would be dead when it was unloaded. At the top of the shaft, bound in a net, it would paw about wildly; then, as soon as it felt the solid ground give way, it would become petrified and sink from sight without so much as a tremble of its hide, its eyes wide and staring. The one being brought down now was too big to pass between the guides and had had to be suspended from the bottom of the cage, its head pulled down and tied to its flank. The descent lasted about three minutes, the engine having been slowed down as a precaution, and as a result, the excitement was growing. What the hell were they going to do, just leave it dangling in the dark? At last it appeared, as motionless as stone, its staring eyes dilated with terror. It was a bay, scarcely three years old, called Trompette.

"Careful, careful!" cried Old Mouque, who was responsible for receiving him. "Bring him here. Don't untie him yet."

Soon Trompette was set down in a heap on the iron flooring. He still had not moved; he seemed to be caught in the nightmare of this bottomless dark hole, this huge room ringing with noise. They were beginning to untie him when Bataille, just unharnessed, came up and stretched out his neck to sniff at this new arrival fallen from the earth above. The workers laughingly made room for him in the circle. Well—did he like the smell? Deaf to the mocking comments, Bataille grew animated. Perhaps he recognized the smell of fresh air, the almost forgotten scent of the sun on the grass. And suddenly he broke into a loud whinny, a song of happiness in which there was also a wistful sob. It was his welcome—joy at this whiff of things long past, and grief over this new prisoner who would never return to the surface alive.

"Oh, that Bataille!" called out the workers, amused by the carryings-on of their favorite. "Look at him talking to his friend!"

Trompette, now untied, still did not move. He remained on his side, choked with fear, as if he still felt gripped by the net. At last they got him up with a lash of the whip and he stood there, confused, his limbs shaking violently. Then Old Mouque led away the two horses, who were getting to know each other.

"Well, can we go up now?" asked Maheu.

But they had to unload the cages, and besides, there were still ten minutes to go. Little by little all the working areas were emptying out, and the miners were gathering from every gallery. About fifty men were already there, soaked and shivering in the pneumonia-heavy drafts blowing in from all sides. Pierron, for all his gentle looks, slapped his daughter Lydie because she had left the face too early. Zacharie was sneakily pinching Mouquette in an attempt to warm himself up. But the discontent was growing; Chaval and Levaque told about the engineer's threat—the price per cart lowered and timbering paid for separately—and the news was greeted with outcries; rebellion was taking root in this cramped space more than eighteen hundred feet underground. Soon the voices were rising without restraint, and these men, filthy with coal and frozen by the delay, were accusing the Company of killing half its workers down in the mine and letting the other half starve to death. Etienne listened, trembling with excitement.

"Hurry up! Hurry up!" the foreman Richomme kept saying to the loaders.

He was trying to speed up preparations for the ascent, not wanting to have to call the men to order and pretending not to hear. However, the protests became so violent that he was forced to pay attention. Behind him they were shouting that things couldn't go on this way, and that one fine day the whole business would blow up.

"You know how things are," he said to Maheu. "Make them shut up. When you're not the strongest you have to be the most sensible."

But Maheu, who was calming down and beginning to get worried himself, did not have to intervene. Suddenly the voices stopped. Négrel and Dansaert, back from their inspection, were emerging from one of the galleries, both of them soaked in sweat like all the others. The habit of discipline brought the men into line while the engineer walked past the group without a word. He got into one cart and the chief foreman into another; the signal cord was pulled five times— the indication for "big meat," as the bosses were called—and the cage shot up into the air amid a dismal silence.

6

In the rising cage, piled into a cart with four others, Etienne decided he would return to his hungry wanderings along the roads. He might just as well die right away as go back down into that pit of hell and not even make enough money for food. Catherine, who was in a compartment above him, was no longer pressing her lulling warmth against his side, and anyway, he didn't want to think of such foolishness; he only wanted to leave. Better educated than the rest of them, he knew he could not accept their herdlike resignation and would probably end by strangling one of the bosses.

Suddenly he was blinded. The ascent had been so rapid that he was dazzled by the daylight, and his eyes were blinking in the brightness to which he had already become unaccustomed. Still, it was a relief to feel the cage settle on

its catches. A trammer opened the door and a flood of
workers poured out of the carts.

"Say, Mouquet," Zacharie whispered to the trammer. "Are
we going to the Volcan tonight?"

The Volcan was a cabaret in Montsou. Mouquet winked
his left eye and his mouth opened in a silent laugh. Small and
heavy like his father, he had the devil-may-care look of a
rascal who would spend his last cent without worrying about
the next day. As his sister was also getting out just then, he
gave her a mighty whack on her behind in brotherly affection.

Etienne could hardly recognize the high nave of the landing station, which had previously seemed so disturbing in the
mysterious, shifting light of the lanterns. Now it only looked
bare and dirty. A grayish daylight was coming in through the
grimy windows; the only bright thing was the engine, its
copper fittings shining. The grease-covered steel cables were
speeding along like inky ribbons; and the pulleys above, the
enormous scaffolding that supported them, the cages, the
carts, the whole fantastic mass of metal, darkened the room
with the dull grayness of old iron. Rumbling wheels were
ceaselessly shaking the iron flooring, and the coal being
pushed about was giving off a fine dust that blackened the
ground, the walls, and even the beams of the headframe.

Chaval had gone to look at the tag board in the receiver's
small glassed-in office, and he returned in a rage. He had
found out that two of their carts had been refused, one
because it didn't have the full amount of coal and the other
because the coal was dirty.

"That does it!" he shouted. "Another twenty sous gone! . . .
That's what comes of taking on loafers whose arms are as
useful as a pig's tail!"

And his sidelong glance at Etienne completed his unspoken
thought. The latter was tempted to answer with his fists, but
then he asked himself, why bother?—he was going to leave
anyway. This settled it.

"You can't expect anything else the first day," said Maheu
to keep the peace. "He'll do better tomorrow."

They were all still tense, however, and looking for a fight.
When they went to the lamproom to return their lamps,
Levaque started a quarrel with the man in charge, whom he
accused of not having cleaned his lamp properly. They only
began to really unwind when they got to the dressing shed,
where the fire was still burning. In fact, the stove must have
been overloaded, because it was blazing, and the light cast on
the walls by the blood-red brazier made the large windowless

room seem on fire. With grunts of pleasure, they all stood a little way off and toasted themselves, steaming like kettles of soup; when their backsides were burned, they baked their bellies. Mouquette had calmly lowered her trousers to dry her shirt. Some of the boys teased her, then everybody burst out laughing because she suddenly shoved her rear end at them, which was her way of expressing complete contempt.

"I'm going," said Chaval, after having put his tools into his locker.

Nobody moved except Mouquette, who hurried after him, saying they were both going back to Montsou. Everybody continued to laugh, because they knew he wanted nothing more to do with her.

Meanwhile Catherine, who had been looking somewhat disturbed, whispered something to her father. Surprised at first, he had then nodded his approval and called Etienne over to give him his bundle.

"See here," he said in a low voice, "if you don't have any money, you'll never make it till payday. . . . Would you like me to see if I can arrange some credit for you?"

The young man was embarrassed for a moment; he had really been planning to ask for his thirty sous and leave. But he was ashamed in front of the girl. She was watching him closely, and perhaps she would think he was just trying to get out of working.

"I can't promise you anything," Maheu continued, "but they can only say no."

Etienne decided not to refuse. They would say no. Besides, he wouldn't be obligated in any way, he could still leave after having eaten something. Then he saw Catherine's pleasure—her lovely smile, her friendly looks, her joy in having been able to help him—and he was irritated with himself for not having refused. What was the use of all that?

When they had once more put on their sabots and closed their lockers, the Maheus left the dressing shed behind some of the others who were also going off one by one as soon as they had warmed up. Etienne followed them, and Levaque and his son joined the group. But as they were passing the screening shed a violent scene caught their attention.

The shed was enormous, with beams coated black with dust and with large louvers through which blew a continuous blast of air. Carts of coal, which came directly from the landing station, were dumped by the tiltermen into hoppers, long, sheet-iron chutes; to the left and right of these, screening girls stood on steps and with shovels and rakes sorted out the stones and pushed along the clean coal, which then fell through funnels into railroad cars on tracks laid below the shed.

Philomène Levaque was there, pale and thin, her face the sheeplike white of a blood-spitting consumptive. Her head protected by a scrap of blue woolen cloth, her hands and arms black to the elbows, she was sorting on a level below that of an old hag, the mother of La Pierronne—La Brûlé, as she was called—a terrifying apparition with the eyes of a wood owl and a mouth as tight as a miser's purse. The two women were grappling with one another, the young woman accusing the older one of raking away so many of her stones that she had only been able to fill one basket in ten minutes. They were paid by the basket, so these quarrels were constantly breaking out. Hair flew and fingers made black marks on red faces.

"Go on! Let her have it!" Zacharie shouted down to his mistress. All the screening girls roared with laughter. But La Brûlé turned on the young man fiercely.

"You piece of filth, you! Why don't you give a name to the two brats you filled her belly with!... Imagine that! An eighteen-year-old beanpole that can't even stand up!"

Maheu had to keep his son from going down to investigate, as he put it, the color of the old witch's complexion. But then a supervisor came running up and the rakes went back to rummaging in the coal. From the top to the bottom of the chutes, all that could be seen were the bent backs of women frantically competing for stones.

Outside, the wind had suddenly dropped, and a cold damp was falling from the gray sky. The miners hunched up their shoulders, crossed their arms, and left, straggling along with a lurching step that made their big bones stand out under their thin clothes. In the light of day they seemed like a band of Negroes who had tripped in the mud. Some of them hadn't finished their sandwiches, and the remaining bread, carried home again between shirt and jacket, made them look like hunchbacks.

"Look! Here comes Bouteloup," snickered Zacharie.

Without stopping, Levaque exchanged a few words with his boarder, a big, dark fellow of about thirty-five, with a placid, respectable face.

"Dinner ready, Louis?"

"I think so."

"Then the wife's in a good mood today?"

"Pretty good, I think."

The men on the repair crews were arriving now, new groups that were engulfed by the mine one after the other. It was the three o'clock shift: more men for the hungry mine, fresh crews to replace the teams of cutters in the depths of the tunnels. The mine was never at rest; night and day there were human insects digging away at the rock some eighteen hundred feet beneath the beet fields. Meanwhile, the young people were walking on ahead. Jeanlin was explaining to Bébert a complicated scheme he had for getting four sous' worth of tobacco on credit, while Lydie followed a respectful distance behind. Catherine came next, with Zacharie and Etienne. Nobody spoke, and it was not until they got to L'Avantage, an inn, that Maheu and Levaque caught up with them.

"Here we are," Maheu said to Etienne; "do you want to come in?"

The group separated. Catherine stood still for a moment, taking a last look at the young man; her large eyes, which had the greenish limpidity of spring water, seemed the more clear for being set off by her blackened face. She smiled, and disappeared with the others up the hilly road that led to the village.

The tavern was located between the village and the mine, at the intersection of two roads. It was a two-story brick building, whitewashed from top to bottom, its windows decorated with a wide sky-blue border. On a square sign nailed over the door was printed in yellow letters: "L'Avantage. Proprietor, Rasseneur." Behind the house was a ninepin alley screened off by a row of hedges. The Company had done everything it could to buy up this small plot in the midst of its vast holdings, and it was greatly annoyed by the little tavern that had sprung up in the middle of the fields, at the very entrance to Le Voreux.

"Come on in," Maheu repeated to Etienne.

The little room was small, bare, and bright, with its white walls, its three tables, its dozen chairs, and its pine bar no bigger than a kitchen cupboard. There were no more than ten mugs on it, three bottles of liqueur, a water pitcher, and a little zinc beer keg with a pewter spigot: nothing else—not a picture, not a shelf, not a game. A small coal fire was burning in a polished and shining iron fireplace. The floors were covered with a thin layer of white sand to soak up the perpetual humidity of this sodden countryside.

"A beer," Maheu ordered of a big, blond girl, a neighbor's daughter who sometimes took care of the place. "Is Rasseneur here?"

As she turned the spigot the girl replied that the proprietor would be back soon. Without putting his glass down, the

miner slowly drank half his beer to flush away the dust that
was clogging his throat. He did not offer his companion a
drink. The one other customer, another damp and coal-
smeared miner, was sitting at a table and drinking his beer in
silence, with an air of profound meditation. Another came
in, signaled for a beer, was served, paid, and left without a
word.

Then a heavy-set man of thirty-eight appeared, a carefree
smile on his round, clean-shaven face. It was Rasseneur, a
former cutter who had been fired by the Company three
years earlier at the end of a strike. An excellent worker, he
was also a good speaker and had presented all the workers'
grievances, so that he had ended by being the leader of all
those who were dissatisfied. His wife, like so many other
miners' wives, already kept a bar, and when he was thrown
out of work he took it over himself, raised some money, and
set up his place right in front of Le Voreux, like a challenge
to the Company. His tavern was doing very well and was
becoming a gathering place; he was growing prosperous on
the anger he had little by little inflamed in the hearts of his
former comrades.

"This is the fellow I hired this morning," Maheu explained
immediately. "Is one of your two rooms free, and could you
let him have it on credit till payday?"

Rasseneur's broad face immediately became suspicious. He
barely glanced at Etienne and answered, without bothering to
express his regrets:

"Both my rooms are taken. It's impossible."

Etienne was expecting this refusal, yet he was hurt by it,
and surprised at the sudden disappointment he felt at having
to leave. It didn't matter, though; he would go as soon as he
got his thirty sous. The miner who had been drinking at a
table had left. Others kept coming in, one by one, to rinse
their throats, then walked out again with the same awkward
gait. It was simply a swabbing-down operation—a joyless,
passionless, silent satisfaction of a need.

"Is anything going on?" Rasseneur significantly asked Maheu, who was sipping the rest of his beer.

The latter glanced around and saw that only Etienne was
there.

"What's going on is that we've had another tangle. . . . This
time about timbering."

He told the whole story. The innkeeper's face reddened
and swelled; a violent emotion was surging through him, and
his skin glowed and his eyes flamed. Finally he exploded:

"Well, if they decide to lower the prices, they're done for."

Etienne's presence bothered him, but he went on, occasionally glancing at him out of the corner of his eyes. With caution and innuendo, he made allusions to the director, Monsieur Hennebeau, his wife, and his nephew, little Négrel, but he never named them; he kept repeating that things couldn't go on this way and that one of these fine days everything would blow up. The misery was too great, he said, citing the factories that were closing and the workers who were leaving the area. For a month now, he'd been doling out more than six pounds of bread a day; yesterday he'd been told that Monsieur Deneulin, the owner of a neighboring mine, didn't know how he'd manage, and in addition he had just gotten a letter from Lille, filled with disturbing news.

"It came from that person you saw here one evening," he murmured.

But he was interrupted by the entrance of his wife, a tall, thin, intense woman with a long nose and flushed cheeks. She was much more politically radical than her husband.

"Pluchart's letter?" she said. "Ah, if he was in charge here, things would soon get better!"

Etienne, who had been listening for some time, was beginning to understand and be roused by this talk of wretchedness and retribution. The sudden mention of Pluchart's name made him start, and he said out loud, as though in spite of himself:

"I know Pluchart."

They looked at him and he had to add:

"Yes. I'm an engineman and he was my foreman in Lille. . . . He's a good man. I've often discussed things with him."

Rasseneur looked Etienne over again and his face showed a swift change, a sudden sympathy. He said to his wife:

"Maheu brought this young man here, one of his haulers, to see if there's a room free upstairs and if we can let him have credit till payday."

The matter was arranged in a few words. There was a room—the occupant had just left that morning. The innkeeper, now very excited, became expansive, insisting that he only asked what was possible from the bosses and never expected, as so many others did, things that were too hard to get. But his wife shrugged her shoulders, claiming that what was right was right.

"Well, good-bye," interrupted Maheu. "None of this will keep us from having to go down into the mine, and as long as we go down there'll be plenty of us who'll croak there. . . . You seem a happy enough fellow now that you've been out of it for three years. . . ."

"Yes, I've gotten back on my feet," said Rasseneur complacently.

Etienne accompanied the parting miner to the door and thanked him, but Maheu only nodded, without saying a word; the young man watched him wearily trudge up the road to the village. Madame Rasseneur, who was busy serving customers, had just asked him to wait a minute so that she could take him to his room, where he would be able to clean up. Should he stay? He was gripped by uncertainty again, an uneasiness that made him nostalgic for the freedom of the open road, for hunger under the sun, gladly suffered in the joy of knowing he was his own master. Since his arrival on the wind-swept slag heap, he seemed to have spent long years underground, flat on his belly in the dark tunnels. He was repelled by the notion of going down again—it was too unjust, too hard, and his masculine pride rebelled at the thought of being a beast that could be blinded and crushed.

And while Etienne was struggling to come to a decision, his eyes wandered over the immense plain, taking it in little by little. He was amazed; he had not imagined the horizon this way when old Bonnemort had pointed it out to him, still buried in darkness. True, in front of him he was able to recognize, in a dip in the terrain, Le Voreux with its buildings of wood and brick, the tarred screening shed, the tiled headframe, the engine house, and the tall, pale-red smoke stack, all menacingly heaped together. But around these buildings spread the yard, and he had not thought it so large; it was transformed into a lake of ink by the billowing waves of stockpiles of coal, porcupined with high trestles that carried the rails of the elevated tracks, and cluttered in one corner with supplies of timber, looking like the crop of a harvested forest. To the right the slag heap cut off his view. It seemed a colossal barricade built by giants, its older part already covered with moss, the other end consumed by an interior fire that had been burning for a year, giving off a thick smoke and leaving long trails of bloody rust on the surface of the pale gray of the shale and sandstone. Beyond this were the spreading fields—the endless fields of wheat and beets, bare at this time of year; marshes of hardy vegetation broken by a few stunted willows; and the far-off prairies divided by thin rows of poplars. In the distance, small white spots indicated the towns—Marchiennes to the north and Montsou to the south—while to the east the forest of Vandame bordered the horizon with a purplish line of leafless

trees. And under the livid sky, on this colorless winter afternoon, it seemed as if all the black of Le Voreux, all the flying
coal dust, had settled on the plain, powdering the trees,
sanding the roads, sowing the earth.

Etienne kept looking, and what surprised him most of all
was a canal, the canalized Scarpe, which he had not seen in
the darkness of the night. This canal flowed in a straight line
from Le Voreux to Marchiennes, a five-mile ribbon of dull
silver, an avenue bordered with large trees, rising above the
flat land, disappearing into infinity with its green banks and
its pale water over which skimmed the red-painted sterns of
barges. Near the mine there was a landing dock with moored
barges, which were filled directly from carts on an overhead
track. Then the canal turned sharply, cutting across the
marshes, and the whole soul of the flat plain seemed to be
concentrated there, in that geometrical line of water cutting
across it like a giant highway, carrying coal and iron.

Etienne's eyes turned from the canal to the village, which
was built on a plain, and of which he could see only the red
roof tiles. Then they turned back to Le Voreux and paused
at the bottom of the clayey slope, where there were two
enormous piles of bricks, made and fired right on the spot. A
branch of the Company's railroad ran alongside a wooden
fence and serviced the mine. The last of the repair shift must
have been going down. The only sound was the shrill screech
of a car being pushed along by some men. Gone were the
mysterious shadows, the inexplicable thunderings, the flam-
ing-out of unknown stars. In the distance the tall blast furnaces and the coke ovens had paled with the dawn. All that
remained unchanged was the steady sound of the exhaust
from the pump, still wheezing with the same heavy, labored
breathing—the respiration of an ogre whose appetite nothing
could satiate and whose steaming breath he could now see.

Etienne came to a sudden decision. Perhaps he imagined
he could see Catherine's eyes up there, at the entrance to the
village; more likely it was the wind of rebellion sweeping
from Le Voreux. He wasn't sure, but he wanted to go back
into the mine to suffer and to fight. He thought wrathfully
about those "somebodies" Bonnemort had spoken of, and
about this unknown, glutted, and crouching god to whom ten
thousand starving people fed their flesh.

Part TWO

1

La Piolaine, the property of the Grégoires, was about a mile east of Montsou, on the road to Joiselle. A large, square house of no particular style, it had been constructed at the beginning of the eighteenth century, and of the vast estate it had originally been a part of, only about seventy-five walled-in and easily maintained acres remained. Its orchard and kitchen garden were said to produce the finest fruits and vegetables in the region, but there were no grounds to stroll on—only a small wooded area. The avenue of old linden trees, which formed a leafy arcade along the three hundred yards from the gate to the steps of the house, was one of the curiosities of this flat plain on which, from Marchiennes to Beaugnies, large trees were a rarity.

The Grégoires had gotten up at eight o'clock that morning. Generally, they never stirred until an hour later, for they slept long and deeply, but the storm during the night had set them on edge. While her husband had immediately gone out to see if the wind had done any damage, Madame Grégoire had just come down to the kitchen in her slippers and flannel robe. She was short and fat, and though she was fifty-eight years old, her chubby face was still rosy and wide-eyed under her dazzling white hair.

"Mélanie," she said to the cook, "as long as the dough is ready you might as well make a brioche this morning. Mademoiselle won't be up for at least another half hour, and she could have some with her chocolate. . . . It would be a nice surprise for her."

The cook, a scrawny old woman who had been with them for thirty years, started to laugh.

"You're right, it would be a wonderful surprise. . . . My stove's going and the oven should be hot by now. And Honorine can help me."

Honorine, a girl of about twenty who had been taken in as a child and raised in the house, was now the chambermaid. Aside from these two women, the only other domestic was the coachman, Francis, who also did the heavy work. A gardener and his wife took care of the fruits, the vegetables, the flowers, and the poultry. Since the entire household was run along patriarchal lines in a calm and friendly family atmosphere, the little group got along very well together.

Madame Grégoire, who had dreamed up the surprise of the brioche while she was still in bed, stayed to see the dough put into the oven. The kitchen was enormous, and its spotlessness, together with the battery of casseroles, utensils, and pots that filled it, showed it to be the most important room in the house. It had the good smell of good cooking, and food supplies were bulging from the shelves and the cupboards.

"And make sure it's a nice golden brown," urged Madame Grégoire as she went into the dining room.

Although the house had central heating, this room was brightened by a coal fire. There was no sign of luxury: the big table, the chairs, and the buffet were all of simple mahogany, and only the two deep armchairs betrayed a love of comfort and the habit of long, postprandial digestive sessions. No one ever went into the drawing room; the family gathered here.

Just then Monsieur Grégoire, dressed in a thick fustian jacket, came back; he too was rosy-cheeked for his sixty years, and his large, friendly, and honest features were snow-capped with curly white hair. He had seen the coachman and the gardener and could report that there hadn't been much damage—just a chimney pot blown down. He enjoyed making a daily inspection of La Piolaine; it wasn't big enough to cause any worry, yet it gave him the pleasant feeling of proprietorship.

"Where's Cécile?" he asked. "Isn't she getting up today?"

"I don't know," answered his wife. "I thought I heard her stirring."

The table had been set—three bowls on a white cloth. Honorine was sent to see what Mademoiselle was doing, but she came right down, choking back a laugh and whispering as though she were still in the girl's bedroom:

"Oh, if Monsieur and Madame could only see Mademoiselle! . . . She's asleep . . . sleeping like an angel. . . . You can't imagine how pretty it is to see. . . ."

The mother and father exchanged tender looks, and he said, smiling:

"Will you come and see?"

"The little darling," she murmured. "Yes, I'm coming."

And they went up together. The room was the only luxurious one in the house. It was hung with blue silk, and its lacquered furniture was white, highlighted with fillets of blue —the whim of a spoiled child indulged by her parents. In the shadowy whiteness of the bed, under the half-light that filtered through the drawn curtains, a young girl was sleeping with her cheek against her bare arm. She was not really very pretty—she was much too healthy, much too buxom, fully developed at eighteen—but her glorious skin had a milky freshness set off by her chestnut hair, and the willful little nose in her round face was submerged in two plump cheeks. The blanket had slipped off, and she was breathing so gently that her already full bosom scarcely moved.

"That awful wind must have kept her from falling asleep," said her mother gently.

The father hushed her with a gesture. The two of them bent over and adoringly gazed at—in her virgin nudity—this long-desired daughter, whom they had had late in life after they had given up all hope. To them she was perfect: not too fat, indeed, never well-enough fed. She slept on, without sensing their presence or their faces so close to hers. But a slight quiver passed over her immobile face, and they trembled lest she awaken; they tiptoed away.

"Sh!" said Monsieur Grégoire at the door. "If she didn't sleep during the night, we must let her sleep now."

"As long as she wants, the darling," Madame Grégoire agreed. "We'll wait."

They went downstairs and settled themselves in the dining-room armchairs while the two servants, laughing over Mademoiselle's deep sleep, uncomplainingly kept the chocolate hot on the stove. Monsieur Grégoire had taken up his newspaper and Madame Grégoire was working on the large coverlet she was knitting. It was very warm inside, and not a sound came from the silent house.

The Grégoires' money, an income of about forty thousand francs a year, came entirely from stock in the Montsou mines. They loved to tell people the story of its origin, which went back to the very formation of the Company.

At about the beginning of the eighteenth century a mad passion for coal-prospecting had swept from Lille to Valenciennes. The successes of the concession holders who were later to form the Anzin Company had given everybody wild ideas. In every commune soil borings were made; corporations were organized and concessions sprang up overnight. Among the most determined men of that time was the Baron

Desrumaux, who had left behind a legend of the most titanic intelligence. For forty years he had fought against endless obstacles without weakening: unsuccessful initial research, new mines abandoned after long months of work, landslides that filled in the diggings, sudden inundations that drowned workers, and hundreds of thousands of francs poured into the earth; then there were administrative problems, stockholders' panics, and battles fought against the noble landowners who were resolved not to recognize the royal concessions unless arrangements were first made with them. At last he set up Desrumaux, Fauquenoix and Company to exploit the concession at Montsou, and the mines were just beginning to show some slight profit when two neighboring concessions—the one at Cougny, which belonged to the Count de Cougny, and the one at Joiselle, which belonged to the Cornille and Jenard Corporation—almost crushed him under the terrible weight of their competition. Luckily, on August 25, 1760, an agreement was arrived at which consolidated the three concessions into one. In this way the company exploiting the Montsou mines was created in its present form. In allotting shares, the entire property was divided up, according to the monetary system of the time, into twenty-four sous, each of which was subdivided into twelve deniers, which made 288 deniers in all; since each denier was worth ten thousand francs, the entire capital came to almost three million. Though Desrumaux was on his deathbed, he was victorious; his share had come to six sous and three deniers.

In those days the baron owned La Piolaine with its seven hundred acres, and he employed as his steward a young fellow from Picardy, Honoré Grégoire—the great-grandfather of Léon Grégoire, Cécile's father. At the time of the Montsou agreement, Honoré, who had hidden fifty thousand francs of savings in a stocking, tremblingly supported his master's unshakable faith. He parted with ten thousand francs in hard cash and took a denier, horrified at robbing his descendants of such a sum. The dividends received by his son Eugène were, in fact, very meager, and since the young man had decided to become a gentleman and had stupidly lost the other forty thousand francs of his paternal heritage in a disastrous adventure, he could barely make ends meet. But little by little the interest on the denier began to rise, and the family fortune began with Félicien, who was able to realize the dream on which he had been raised by his grandfather, the former steward: he was able to buy La Piolaine when it was broken up and sold as a state property for a ridiculously

low sum. The following years, however, were bad, and the
family had to wait out first the climax of the revolutionary
catastrophes and then the blood-drenched fall of Napoleon.
It was actually Léon Grégoire who benefited, in an overwhelming progression, from the timid and worried investment
of his great-grandfather. Those pitiful ten thousand francs
kept growing and swelling with the prosperity of the Company, and by 1820 they were returning one hundred percent
—ten thousand francs. In 1844 they were producing twenty
thousand, and in 1850, forty thousand. Two years previously
the dividend had risen to the fantastic figure of fifty thousand
francs: the value of the denier was quoted on the Lille stock
market at one million—a hundredfold increase in the course
of a century.

Monsieur Grégoire, who had been advised to sell when the
price went to a million, had refused with smiling condescension. Six months later an industrial crisis erupted and the
denier fell to six hundred thousand francs; but he kept right
on smiling and didn't regret a thing, because by this time the
Grégoires had a stubborn faith in their mine. It would go up
again—God himself was not more solid! Mixed with this
religious belief was also a profound gratitude toward a holding that for more than a century had nourished the family in
idleness. It was like a private god, one who, in their egoism,
they worshiped as the benefactor of their hearth, one who
rocked them in their large bed of ease and fattened them at
their groaning board. It had gone on from father to son: why
take the chance of irritating fate by doubting it? And behind
their faith was a supersititious terror: the fear that the
million represented by the denier would suddenly melt away
if it were cashed in and put away in a drawer. They felt it
was safer in the earth, that earth from which a people of
miners, famished generations, kept extracting it for them, a
little each day, according to their needs.

Fortune showered their house with other blessings, too.
Monsieur Grégoire, while still very young, had married the
daughter of a Marchiennes pharmacist, an ugly young lady
who had no money but whom he adored and who had
brought him all possible joy. Her life was centered around
the house and she adored her husband, having no other will
but his. They were never divided by differences in taste; a
single ideal of well-being united their desires, and for forty
years they had been living thus in tenderness and mutual
consideration. It was a well-ordered existence; the forty thousand francs were spent unobtrusively, and their savings used
for Cécile, whose late birth had for a moment upset their

budget. They were still satisfying all her whims—a second horse, two other carriages, dresses from Paris—but this was an additional pleasure for them; nothing was too good for their daughter, though they themselves had such a horror of personal display that they had even kept to the styles of their youth. Any outlay that did not return a profit seemed stupid to them.

Suddenly the door opened and a hearty voice called out:

"What! Don't tell me you're eating breakfast without me?"

It was Cécile, who had just gotten up and whose eyes were still swollen with sleep. She had merely put up her hair and slipped on a white wool dressing gown.

"Of course not," said her mother. "You can see that we're waiting for you. . . . Poor darling, that wind must have kept you awake. . . ."

The girl stared at her in surprise.

"Was there a wind? . . . I don't know anything about it. I didn't stir all night."

It struck them as funny and all three began to laugh; and the servants, who were bringing breakfast in, also broke into guffaws—so amusing did it seem to the entire household that Mademoiselle had slept for an unbroken twelve hours. The sight of the brioche added the final happy touch to their already joyful faces.

"What, it's already baked?" Cécile kept repeating. "What a trick to play on me. . . . Mmmm, how good that'll be, all hot in the chocolate!"

They sat down at last; the chocolate steamed in the bowls, and for some time nobody spoke of anything but the brioche. Mélanie and Honorine remained in the room, going into great detail about kitchen activities, watching them stuff themselves and get their lips all greasy, saying it was a pleasure to bake a cake when you saw with what good appetite your employers ate it.

Then the dogs began to bark and they thought it must be the piano teacher, who came from Marchiennes every Monday and Friday. A professor of literature also came every week. The girl's entire education had been received at La Piolaine, in happy ignorance and with a childish capriciousness; as soon as a question bored her she would toss the book aside.

"It's Monsieur Deneulin," said Honorine, coming back into the room.

Behind her, Deneulin, a cousin of Monsieur Grégoire, entered without ceremony. Loud-voiced and quick-gestured, he carried himself like a retired cavalry officer, and though he was over fifty, his close-cropped hair and large moustache were inky black.

"Yes, it's me.... Good morning. Please don't let me disturb you."

He had seated himself while the family was expressing its surprise, and now everyone went back to his chocolate.

"Was there anything you wanted to tell me?" asked Monsieur Grégoire.

"No, nothing at all," Deneulin answered quickly. "I was out riding for a little exercise, and since I was passing your house I thought I'd drop in to say hello."

Cécile asked him about Jeanne and Lucie, his daughters. They were both fine, the first all wrapped up in her painting, the other, the elder, practicing her singing at the piano from morning to night. There was a slight tremble in his voice, an uneasiness that he was hiding beneath bursts of gaiety.

"Is everything all right at the mine?" Monsieur Grégoire continued.

"Well, I've taken some hard knocks from this crisis, just like everyone else.... Ah, we're paying for the good years now! Too many factories were built, too much railroad track laid down, too much capital tied up in the hope of tremendous production—and now money is tight and there isn't enough available to keep the whole thing going.... Luckily, things aren't hopeless, and I'll manage in spite of everything."

Like his cousin, he had inherited a denier in the Montsou mines; but he, an enterprising engineer, tormented by the desire for a royal fortune, had sold as soon as the denier had reached the million mark. For months he had been hatching a scheme. His wife had inherited from an uncle the small Vandame concession, in which only two mines—Jean-Bart and Gaston-Marie—were open; they were both so run-down, their equipment in such a state of disrepair, that the output barely covered the operating expenses. He had gotten the idea of repairing Jean-Bart, renovating the apparatus and enlarging the shaft so as to be able to sink it further down, and of using Gaston-Marie only for drainage. He said there would be gold by the shovelful down there. The idea was a good one, but he had poured his million francs into it and then the damned industrial crisis broke out just when the big profits were about to prove that he had been right. In addition, he was a bad manager, brusquely generous with his workers, and since his wife's death he had allowed himself to be taken advantage of; he also gave free rein to his daughters: the elder was talking of going on the stage and the younger had already had three landscapes refused by the Salon. But both of them laughed at the financial disaster, and, in fact, the menacing prospect of poverty was showing them to be excellent housekeepers.

"You know, Léon," he went on in a hesitant voice, "you were wrong not to sell when I did. Everything's collapsing now and you may ... If you had let me take care of your money, you'd have seen what we would have done at Vandame, in our own mine!"

Monsieur Grégoire finished his chocolate unhurriedly and replied quietly:

"Never! ... You know I don't care to speculate. I lead a peaceful life and it would be too stupid to have to wrack my brains about business affairs. And as for Montsou, even if it continues to go down, we'll still have enough for our needs. There's no need to be so greedy, you know! And besides, you're the one who'll be biting your fingernails someday, because Montsou will climb again and it will still be buying white bread for Cécile's children's children."

Deneulin listened to him with an uncomfortable smile.

"So," he mumbled, "if I were to ask you to put a hundred thousand francs into my business, you would refuse?"

But the alarm on the Grégoires' faces made him sorry that he had gone so fast, and he put off his idea of a loan until later, reserving it for a more desperate time.

"Oh, I'm not at that point yet! ... It was just a little joke. My God, perhaps you're right—the money that others earn for you is the money that fattens you up with the least risk."

They began to talk of other things. Cécile returned to the topic of her cousins, whose tastes intrigued her even though she found them shocking. Madame Grégoire promised that she would take her daughter to see the dear girls on the first sunny day. Meanwhile Monsieur Grégoire seemed lost in thought; he was not following the conversation. Suddenly he said out loud:

"Myself, if I were in your place I wouldn't hold out any longer. I'd try to come to an agreement with Montsou. . . . They're very eager to, and you'd be able to get your money back."

He was alluding to the old dispute between the Montsou concession and the one at Vandame. Despite the latter's slight importance, its powerful neighbor was furious at the existence of these two square miles that didn't belong to it, set right in the middle of its sixty-seven communes; having vainly tried to drive it out of business, Montsou was now plotting to buy Vandame at a low price as soon as the latter

entered its final agony. The war went on without a let-up,
each concession extending its galleries to within approximate-
ly six hundred feet of the other. It was a duel to the death,
even though the directors and engineers maintained polite
relations among themselves.

Deneulin's eyes had blazed.

"Never!" he cried in his turn. "As long as I'm alive
Montsou will never get Vandame. . . . I had dinner at Hennebeau's on Thursday, and I noticed how he kept circling
around me. Why, even last autumn—when the big shots
came to see the manager—they tried to butter me up. . . .
Yes, yes, I know them, those marquises and dukes, those
generals and ministers—thieves who'd catch you in a neck
of the woods and steal the shirt off your back!"

He went on and on, and in any case Monsieur Grégoire
was not defending the management of Montsou—the six managers set up by the 1760 agreement, who governed the Company despotically. Whenever one of them died, the five sur-
vivors chose a new member from among the richest and most
powerful stockholders. In the opinion of the owner of La
Piolaine, whose own demands were so reasonable, these
gentlemen sometimes went too far in their exaggerated love
of money.

Mélanie had come in to clear the table. Outside, the dogs
began to bark again, and Honorine was starting for the door
when Cécile, uncomfortable with the heat and the food, got
up from the table.

"I'll go. That must be my teacher."

Deneulin also got up. He watched the young girl leave,
then asked, smiling:

"And what about this marriage with Little Négrel?"

"Nothing's been settled," said Madame Grégoire. "It's just
an idea. . . . We still have to think about it."

"No doubt," he continued with a sly smile. "I think the
nephew and the aunt . . . What really bowls me over is that
Madame Hennebeau should take to Cécile as she does."

But Monsieur Grégoire became indignant. Such a distinguished woman, and fourteen years older than the young
man! The idea was monstrous, and he didn't like people to
joke about such things. Still laughing, Deneulin shook hands
and left.

"That wasn't the teacher either," said Cécile, coming back.
"It's that woman with the two children—you know, Mama,
the miner's wife we met. . . . Shall I have them come in
here?"

There was a moment's hesitation. Were they very dirty?

No, not very, and they could leave their sabots on the steps outside. The father and mother were already ensconced in their deep armchairs, digesting; the fear of a change in air finally decided them.

"Have them come in, Honorine."

So La Maheude and her little ones came in—frozen, famished, gripped by a fearful bewilderment at suddenly finding themselves in this warm room that smelled so wonderfully of brioche.

2

Up in the still-shuttered room, gray bars of light had begun to fan out across the ceiling, and the closed-in air became heavier as they all continued their deep sleep: Lénore and Henri in each other's arms; Alzire, her head thrown back, lying on her hump; and Old Bonnemort, sleeping alone in Zacharie and Jeanlin's bed, snoring away with his mouth open. Not a sound came from the alcove, where La Maheude, her breasts sagging to the side, had fallen asleep again while nursing Estelle, who, equally exhausted, gorged with milk, was lying across her mother's belly, her face sunk in the soft flesh.

Downstairs the cuckoo struck six. From the village streets could be heard the sound of slamming doors, followed by the clatter of sabots on the cobblestone walks: the screening girls were going off to the mine. Then silence fell again until seven o'clock, when shutters were thrown back and the sounds of yawns and coughs could be heard through the walls. For a long time a coffee mill screeched without waking anyone in the room.

But suddenly a storm of slaps and shrieks in the distance made Alzire start up. She became aware of the time and ran barefooted to shake her mother awake.

"Mama, Mama, it's late! You have to go somewhere.... Be careful!—you'll crush Estelle."

And she rescued the infant, who was half-suffocating under the weight of the enormous breasts.

"God, what a life!" grumbled La Maheude, rubbing her eyes. "You get so worn-out that all you want to do is sleep all day.... Get Lénore and Henri dressed, I'm taking them

with me. You can stay with Estelle. I don't want to drag her
along, she might get sick in this rotten weather."

She washed quickly and put on an old blue skirt, her
cleanest, and a gray woolen jacket on which she had sewn
two patches the night before.

"And the soup! God, what a life," she mumbled again.

While her mother went downstairs, bumping into things on
her way, Alzire carried Estelle, who had begun to cry, back
into the bedroom with her. She was used to the infant's
rages; at eight, she could already use a woman's tender tricks
to calm and distract her. She gently laid her in the still-warm
bed and lulled her to sleep by giving her a finger to suck. And
not a minute too soon, either, for there was another outburst
of noise and she had to separate Lénore and Henri, who had
finally awakened. Those two did not get along at all, only
hugging each other lovingly when they were asleep. As soon
as she was awake, the six-year-old girl fell upon the boy, who
was two years younger and did not even try to return her
slaps. They both had heads that were too big, as though
swollen, and tangles of blond hair. Alzire had to pull her
sister off by the legs and threaten to skin her alive. Then she
had to put up with their stamps of rage at being washed, and
again at each piece of clothing that she put on them. The
shutters were kept closed so as not to disturb Old Bonnemort's sleep, and he continued to snore through all the
horrible racket made by the children.

"Everything's ready! What are you doing up there?" called
La Maheude.

She had thrown back the shutters, shaken up the fire, and
added some coal. She had hoped against hope that the old
man hadn't gobbled up all the soup, but she found the
saucepan wiped clean, so she cooked a handful of vermicelli
she had been keeping in reserve for the past three days. They
would have to swallow it plain, without butter—there
couldn't be any of last night's little dab left; she was surprised
to find that Catherine, in preparing the sandwiches, had
managed by some miracle to leave a bit about the size of a
nut. But now the cupboard was really empty: nothing, not a
crust, not a scrap, not so much as a bone to gnaw on. What
was to become of them if Maigrat kept refusing them credit
and if the people at La Piolaine didn't give her a few francs?
When Catherine and the men came back from the mine they
would have to have something to eat—unfortunately, nobody
had yet figured out how to live without eating!

"Aren't you ever coming down?" she called up angrily. "I
should be gone by now."

When Alzire and the children appeared, she divided the vermicelli among the three small plates. She herself wasn't hungry, she said. Although Catherine had already poured water over last night's coffee grounds, she did it a second time and swallowed two large mugs of a coffee so diluted that it looked like rusty water. Still, it would keep her going.

"Listen," she repeated to Alzire. "Let your grandfather sleep, and see to it that Estelle doesn't hurt herself. If she wakes up and begins to yammer too much, here's a piece of sugar—you can dissolve it and give her a few spoonfuls. . . . I know you're a good girl and won't eat it yourself."

"And what about school, Mama?"

"School? Well, some other day . . . I need you today."

"And the soup? Do you want me to make it if you come back late?"

"The soup, the soup . . . No, wait for me."

Alzire, who had the precocious intelligence of the sickly child, knew very well how to make the soup, but she obviously understood, and said no more about it. By now the whole village was awake and groups of children were going off to school, noisily scraping their clogs. It stuck eight; a growing murmur of chatter came from the left, from the Levaques'. The women's day was beginning: they stood around the coffeepots, their hands on their hips and their tongues turning as endlessly as grindstones. A faded face, with thick lips and a squashed nose, pressed against a pane of the window, calling:

"Listen to what I've heard!"

"No, no, later!" answered La Maheude. "I have to go somewhere."

And frightened that she might succumb to the offer of some hot coffee, she prodded Lénore and Henri and quickly left with them. Upstairs, Old Bonnemort was still snoring, with a rhythmic snore that rocked the house.

Once outside, La Maheude was surprised to find that the wind had stopped and that there had been a sudden thaw. The sky was the color of earth, the walls slimy with a greenish dampness, the roads sticky with mud—a mud peculiar to mining regions, as black as liquid soot and so thick and gluey that your sabots stuck in it. As soon as they were on the way she had to slap Lénore because the child was amusing herself by using the tips of her clogs to shovel along the mud. On leaving the village, she had walked past the slag heap and followed the canal road, taking shortcuts along furrowed paths that led through empty lots enclosed by mossy fences. Shed followed shed: long factory buildings with tall chimneys spitting soot and blackening the ravaged countryside of the industrial suburb. Behind a clump of poplars could be seen the crumbling headframe of the Réquillart mine; only the large structural pieces were still standing. Here La Maheude turned to the right, onto the main road.

"Just wait! Just wait, you little pig!" she screamed. "I'll teach you to make mudballs!"

This time it was Henri—he had picked up a handful of mud and was molding it into a ball. The two children, slapped indiscriminately, came back to order and contented themselves with squinting down at their footprints in the mounds of mud. They were floundering, already exhausted by their efforts to free their clogs at every step.

In the direction of Marchiennes the road unrolled its five miles of cobblestone, running straight between the reddish fields like a greasy ribbon. In the other direction it wound down across Montsou, which was built on the slope of a broad rise in the plain. Here in the Nord roads that go straight from one manufacturing town to another are gradually being laid out, and they seem to turn an entire Department into one industrial complex. The small brick houses that lined both sides of the road winding down to the bottom of the slope were gaily painted to brighten the atmosphere—some yellow, some blue, others—no doubt with their final fate already in mind—black. A few large two-story houses, the homes of factory executives, broke the line of narrow facades. A church, also of brick, looked like a new model for a blast furnace, with its square bell-tower already begrimed by the flying coal dust. But what stood out most from among all the sugar refineries, rope factories, and flour mills were the dance halls, the taverns, and the bars—so numerous that they accounted for five hundred out of every thousand houses.

Arriving at the Company's yards—a vast series of warehouses and workshops—La Maheude decided to take Lénore and Henri by the hand, one on the right and the other on the left. Just beyond was the residence of the manager, Monsieur Hennebeau—a sort of enormous chalet separated from the road by an iron fence and a garden in which some scrawny trees were struggling for existence. A carriage was drawn up at the door, and a gentleman with a rosette in his lapel and a lady in a fur coat were descending from it—probably some visitors who had gotten off the Paris train at the Marchiennes station, for Madame Hennebeau, who could be seen in the half-light of the vestibule, let out an exclamation of surprise and pleasure.

"Walk, you little loafers!" scolded La Maheude, pulling at the two children lagging behind in the mud.

She had reached Maigrat's place and was in a turmoil. Maigrat lived right alongside the manager, only a wall separating the mansion from his small house, and there he had a general store—a long building whose windowless front opened onto the road. He stocked a little bit of everything: groceries, all kinds of pork, and fruit; and he sold bread, beer, and pots and pans. Formerly an inspector at Le Voreux, he had begun with a modest canteen; then, thanks to the protection of the Company, his business had expanded, gradually killing off Montsou's small shops one after the other. He brought all kinds of merchandise together, and his large number of customers from the Company villages enabled him to sell more cheaply and to extend more credit. He was still under the control of the Company, which had built both his house and his store.

"It's me again, Monsieur Maigrat," said La Maheude humbly, finding him standing at his door.

He looked at her without answering. He was fat, cold, and polite, and he prided himself on never changing his mind.

"Come now, you're not going to send me away like yesterday. We've got to eat between now and Saturday. . . . Of course I know we've owed you sixty francs for two years now . . ."

In awkward, broken phrases, she tried to explain. It was an old debt, contracted during the last strike. They had often promised to pay it off, but they couldn't—they just couldn't manage the two francs every payday. Then too, she'd had trouble the day before yesterday—she'd had to pay twenty francs to a shoemaker who was threatening to have their belongings seized. That's why they didn't have a sou now. Otherwise they'd have managed till Saturday, just like everybody else.

Stomach out, arms crossed, Maigrat shook his head at each supplication.

"Only two loaves of bread, Monsieur Maigrat—I'm reasonable, I'm not asking for coffee. . . . Only two three-pound loaves a day."

"No!" he finally shouted as loud as he could.

His wife had appeared—a sickly creature who spent her days bent over an account book, never daring to raise her head. Terrified at seeing La Maheude turn imploring eyes to her, she slipped away. People said that she gave over the conjugal bed to the haulage girls who were customers; it was a known fact that when a miner wanted an extension of credit he had only to send his daughter or his wife—it didn't matter if she was beautiful or ugly, so long as she was compliant.

La Maheude, who was still looking at Maigrat pleadingly, was embarrassed by the gleam in the pale little eyes that seemed to be undressing her. It made her angry; she might have understood it if she'd still been young, before she'd had seven children. She turned away, violently pulling at Lénore and Henri, who were busily gathering and inspecting nutshells from the gutter.

"This will bring you bad luck, Monsieur Maigrat. Remember I said so!"

Now her only hope was the people at La Piolaine. If they wouldn't part with at least five francs, she and her family might just as well lie down and die. She had turned left and taken the road to Joiselle. The Company offices were there at a corner of the road, a real brick palace to which the bigwigs from Paris—the princes, the generals, the government officials—came every autumn for lavish dinners. As she walked along she was already spending her five francs: first bread and coffee; then a quarter of butter and a bushel of potatoes for the morning soup and the evening stew; and finally, maybe a little headcheese for Old Bonnemort, who needed some meat.

The curé of Montsou, the Abbé Joire, came by, hiking up his cassock with the delicacy of a well-nourished cat; he was fearful of soiling his habit. He was a gentle little man who tried not to get involved in anything, so as to irritate neither the workers nor the bosses.

"Good morning, Father."

Without stopping, he smiled at the children and left her standing there in the middle of the road. She was not at all religious, but she had suddenly gotten the idea that this priest was going to give her something.

And the struggle through the black and clinging mud began again. There was still more than a mile to go, and the children, unhappy, no longer having fun, had to be dragged more forcefully. On both sides of the road stretched the same empty lots enclosed by mossy palings, the same factory buildings begrimed by smoke and bristling with tall chimneys. Then, out in the open country, the flat fields unfolded—immense, like an ocean of brown clods, without one tree for a mast, all the way to the purplish line of the Vandame Forest.

"Carry me, Mama."

She carried each of them in turn. The road was pocked

with puddles and she kept her skirt held up, afraid she would be too dirty when she got there. Three times she almost fell, so slippery was the road. And when they finally arrived at the steps of the house, two enormous dogs rushed at them, barking so loudly that the children screamed in terror. The coachman had to use his whip.

"Leave your sabots outside and come in," Honorine said.

In the dining room the mother and the two children stood immobile, dazed by the sudden warmth and embarrassed by the looks from the old gentleman and lady stretched out in their armchairs.

"Cécile," said the latter, "distribute your little presents."

The Grégoires let Cécile handle all their charity; it was part of their notion of bringing her up well. One had to be charitable, and they said of themselves that it was the good Lord's house. They also flattered themselves that they dispensed their charity intelligently—they lived in constant fear of being hoodwinked into encouraging vice—and they never gave money. Never! Not ten sous, not two sous, because it was a known fact that as soon as the poor got their hands on two sous they drank them away. So their charity was always given in kind—especially in warm clothes that were distributed during the winter to needy children.

"Oh, the poor darlings!" exclaimed Cécile. "They're blue with cold.... Honorine, go get the package in my closet."

The servants were also looking at the poor wretches, with both the pity and the tremor of uneasiness common to the well-fed. While the maid went upstairs, the cook just stared; she had put the rest of the brioche on the table, and her hands were hanging free.

"Luckily," Cécile continued, "I have two more woolen dresses and a few small shawls.... You'll see how warm the poor darlings will be!"

At this point La Maheude found her tongue and stammered:

"Thank you very much, Mademoiselle.... You are all very kind."

Tears filled her eyes; she felt sure of getting her five francs and was only worried about how she might best ask for them if they weren't offered. The maid still hadn't come back, and there was a moment of awkward silence. From behind the folds of their mother's skirt the children were staring, wide-eyed, at the brioche.

"Are these two your only children?" asked Madame Grégoire, to break the silence.

"Oh no, Madame, I have seven."

Monsieur Grégoire, who had gone back to reading his paper, started indignantly.

"Seven children! But good heavens, why?"

"It's unwise," murmured the old lady.

La Maheude made a vague gesture of apology. What could you do? You didn't think about it, they just came naturally. And besides, when they grew up, they earned a little something and helped keep the house going. They'd have been able to make out if not for the grandfather, who was getting too old, and if, out of all the children, more than just the two boys and the eldest girl could go down into the mine. The young ones had to be fed even though they didn't do anything.

"So," Madame Grégoire continued, "you've been working in the mines for a long time?"

A silent laugh lit up La Maheude's pale face.

"Oh yes, oh yes . . . I went down until I was twenty. When I had my second baby the doctor told me I'd die down there because it seemed it was doing something to my bones. Anyway, I got married just then and I had enough to do in the house. . . . But in my husband's family, you know, they've been going down for years and years. It must have begun with Grandfather's grandfather. Nobody really knows, but it was right at the very beginning, when they first began to swing the picks down in Réquillart."

Monsieur Grégoire looked thoughtfully at the woman and her two pitiful children, with their waxy flesh, their colorless hair, their bodies shrunken by degeneracy, riddled with anemia, looking like woefully ugly starvelings. Silence fell again, and nothing could be heard but the spurts of gas from the burning coal-fire. The warmly humid room had that heavy feeling of well-being in which happy middle-class nests lull themselves to sleep.

"What can be keeping her?" exclaimed Cécile impatiently. "Mélanie, run up and tell her the package is at the bottom of the closet, on the left."

Meanwhile Monsieur Grégoire had begun to voice out loud the reflections inspired in him by the sight of these starving creatures.

"It's true that life is very difficult, but, my good woman, it must be said that the workers are hardly very sensible. . . . For example, instead of putting aside a few sous the way our peasants do, the miners drink, get into debt, and end up by not having enough to feed their families with."

"Oh, Monsieur is so right," answered La Maheude seriously. "They don't always follow the straight and narrow path.

That's what I always tell the good-for-nothings when they complain.... As for me, I've been lucky, my husband doesn't drink. True, he sometimes takes a little too much on Sundays, but it never goes any further than that. And it's especially nice of him because before we were married he drank like a pig—no offense meant.... And yet, his being so good doesn't help very much. There are days like today when you could turn every drawer in the house upside down without making even a centime fall to the ground."

She wanted to bring up the matter of the five francs, and she went on in a soft voice, explaining about the fatal debt that had begun modestly enough but which had soon gotten out of control and become all-consuming. You could pay regularly for months, but then one day you fell behind and it was all over; you could never catch up again. The gap would keep getting bigger and bigger, and the men would get disgusted with working because they didn't bring in enough to meet the payments. And that was it! You were in the soup for the rest of your life! And besides, you had to understand— a miner needed a mug of beer to flush away the coaldust. That's the way it began, and then when trouble came, he just stayed in the cabarets. Maybe—not that she wanted to blame anyone—but maybe the workers really weren't paid enough.

"I thought," said Madame Grégoire, "that the Company lets you live rent-free and gives you your coal?"

Out of the corner of her eye, La Maheude glanced at the flaming coal in the fireplace.

"Yes, yes, they give us coal. Not very good coal, but it burns.... As for the rent, it's only six francs a month—that doesn't seem like much, but sometimes it's very hard to pay.... Why, today, if you were to cut me into little pieces you couldn't get two sous from me. You can't get blood from a stone."

The lady and gentleman, reclining cozily, fell silent, slowly becoming bored and uneasy before the display of such misery. La Maheude was afraid she had insulted them, so she added in the frank and calm manner of a practical woman:

"Oh, I'm not complaining. That's the way things are and that's the way you have to take them—especially since it wouldn't do any good to struggle. It probably wouldn't change a thing. The best thing is to try to manage honestly in the corner where the good Lord has put you, isn't that so?"

Monsieur Grégoire approved heartily.

"With such sentiments, my good woman, misfortune can't touch you."

At last Honorine and Mélanie brought in the package.

Cécile opened it and took out two dresses, then added some
shawls and even some stockings and mittens. It would all do
wonderfully, and she hurriedly had the two servants wrap up
the garments. Her piano teacher had just come in, and so she
began to edge the mother and children toward the door.

"We're really very short just now," stammered La Maheude, "and if we only had five francs . . ."

She choked on the sentence; the Maheus were proud, they
did not beg. Cécile looked at her father uneasily, but with a
righteous air he bluntly refused.

"No, I'm afraid we don't do that. We can't."

Moved by the mother's stunned face, Cécile wanted to do
something special for the children. They were still staring at
the brioche; she cut off two pieces, which she gave to them.

"Here, this is for you."

Then she took the pieces back and asked for an old
newspaper.

"Wait a minute, you'll share it with your brothers and
sisters."

And with her parents watching tenderly, she finally managed to get them to the door. The poor children, who had no
bread, went off respectfully clutching the brioche in their
cold-swollen hands.

Again La Maheude was dragging her children along the
road, but no longer seeing either the deserted fields or the
black mud or the colorless swirling sky. On her way back
through Montsou she strode into Maigrat's store and im-
plored him so passionately that she ended by carrying away
two loaves of bread, some coffee, some butter, and even her
five francs, since the man also lent money at usurious rates.
He was not interested in her, but in Catherine—she understood as much when he suggested she send her daughter the
next time she needed anything. Well, they'd see about that.
Catherine would slap him if he tried to get funny with her.

3

Eleven o'clock was striking at the little church of Village
240, a brick chapel where the Abbé Joire came to say mass
on Sundays. Alongside the church was the school, also of
brick, and the braying voices of children could be heard even
through the closed windows, shut against the cold. The small

back-to-back gardens, created by dividing the long lanes separating the four groups of uniform houses, lay deserted; ravaged by winter, they mournfully displayed their clayey earth,
broken and untidy with the last vegetables. The soup was
being made, and the chimneys were smoking. From time to
time a woman would appear down one of the streets, open a
door, and vanish inside. Even though it was no longer raining, the gray sky was so heavy with humidity that the
rainspouts were steadily dripping into the barrels standing
alongside the cobblestoned walks. The village, hastily thrown
up in the middle of this vast plain and bordered with black
roads like mourning bands, displayed only one sign of cheerfulness—the regular rows of red tiles, constantly washed
clean by the downpours.

Before returning home, La Maheude had to make a detour
to buy some potatoes from the wife of an inspector, a
woman who still had some left from her crop. Behind a
curtain of puny poplars, the only trees that grew on this flat
plain, was a group of isolated buildings—houses in groups of
four, surrounded by their gardens. Since the Company reserved this new area for foremen, the miners had nicknamed
this corner of the hamlet Silk Stocking Village, just as they
called their own area Pay-Your-Debts, in a good-natured but
ironic jibe at their own misery.

"Ouf! Here we are," said La Maheude, laden with packages
and pushing Lénore and Henri, muddy and exhausted, inside.

In front of the fire, Estelle, cradled in Alzire's arms, was
howling. Having no more sugar and not knowing what to do
to keep the infant quiet, Alzire had decided to pretend to
give her the breast. The trick often succeeded, but this time
it had done no good to open her dress and press the infant
mouth against her scrawny, sickly, eight-year-old chest; the
baby was screaming with rage at not being able to draw
anything from the skin on which she was biting.

"Let me have her," said the mother as soon as she had put
down the bundles, "or she won't let us have a moment's
quiet."

When she had produced from her dress a breast swollen as
a wineskin, and when the squalling infant clutching at the
nipple fell suddenly quiet, they could at last talk. But everything was going well: the little housekeeper had kept up the
fire, swept, put the room in order. And in the silence they
could hear the grandfather snoring upstairs, with the same
rhythmic snores that had not stopped for a moment.

"What a lot of things," murmured Alzire, smiling at the

sight of the groceries. "If you want, Mama, I'll make the
soup."

The table was loaded: a package of clothes, two loaves of
bread, potatoes, butter, coffee, chicory, and half a pound of
headcheese.

"Oh, the soup," said La Maheude, wearily. "We'd have to
pull up some sorrel and some leeks.... No, I'll make some
later for the men.... Boil some potatoes, we'll eat them with
a little butter.... And some coffee, right? Don't forget the
coffee!"

Suddenly she remembered the brioche. She looked at the
empty hands of Lénore and Henri, who had already recovered from their fatigue and were now fighting on the floor.
Had those little pigs sneakily eaten the brioche on the road?
She slapped them, while Alzire, who was putting the pot on
the fire, tried to calm her.

"Let them alone, Mama. If it's me you're worried about,
you know I don't care about the brioche. They were hungry
after having walked so far."

It struck noon, and they could hear the clogs of the
children coming out of school. The potatoes were cooked and
the coffee, heavily thickened with chicory, was passing
through the filter with a musical drip-drop. A corner of the
table was cleared, but only the mother ate there; the three
children sat with plates on their knees, and the little boy,
with mute voracity, stared at the headcheese, the greasy
wrappings of which excited him beyond words.

La Maheude was drinking her coffee in small sips, her
hands wrapped around the glass to warm them, when Old
Bonnemort came down. Usually he got up later and his
dinner would be waiting for him on the fire, so he began to
complain because the soup wasn't ready. When his daughter-
in-law told him that things didn't always work out the way
we wanted them to, he ate his potatoes in silence. From time
to time he would get up and spit into the fireplace, a
concession to cleanliness; then, huddled on his chair again, he
would roll the food around the back of his mouth, his head
bowed and his eyes unseeing.

"Oh, I forgot, Mama," said Alzire. "Our neighbor was
here...."

Her mother interrupted her:

"She's a nuisance!"

She was bitter against La Levaque, who had pleaded
poverty the night before so as not to have to lend her
anything—and yet La Maheude knew she was pretty well off
just now because the boarder, Bouteloup, had paid his rent in

advance. Actually, there was very little lending from house to house in the village.

"Oh, you've just reminded me," La Maheude continued; "—wrap up a millful of coffee and I'll take it back to La Pierronne. . . . I owe it to her from the day before yesterday."

When her daughter had prepared the packet, La Maheude added that she would be back soon to put the soup up for the men. Then she went out, carrying Estelle in her arms and leaving Old Bonnemort slowly chomping on his potatoes while Lénore and Henri fought over who would eat the skins that fell from the table.

La Maheude, afraid that La Levaque would see her, cut through the gardens instead of going all the way around. It so happened that her garden was back to back with the Pierrons' garden, and the dilapidated latticework fence that separated them had a gap through which the families were able to pass to visit each other. The well used by the four houses was also located there. To one side, behind a group of straggly lilac bushes, was the hutch, a low shed full of old tools, in which the rabbits they ate on holidays were raised one by one. One o'clock struck—coffee time; not a soul was to be seen at any door or window: only one man, someone on the repair shift, was spading his vegetable garden while waiting for it to be time to go down. He never raised his head. But as La Maheude reached the other group of buildings, she was surprised to see a gentleman and two ladies appear in front of the church. She stopped for a moment, then recognized them: it was Madame Hennebeau showing the village to her guests, the gentleman with the decoration and the lady with the fur coat.

"Oh, you didn't have to make a special trip!" exclaimed La Pierronne when La Maheude had returned the coffee. "There was no hurry."

La Pierronne was twenty-eight, and with her dark hair, low forehead, large eyes, and small mouth, she was considered the prettiest woman in the village. She was also vain, as fastidious as a cat, and—since she had never had any children—her breasts were still fine. Her mother, La Brûlé, was the widow of a cutter who had been killed in the mine. She had sent her daughter to work in a factory, swearing she would never let her marry a miner, and had never forgiven her for having, rather late in life, married Pierron—who in addition to everything else was a widower with an eight-year-old daughter. Yet the couple lived happily, despite the gossip and the stories about the wife's lovers and the husband's complaisance: not a single debt, meat twice a week, and a

house so spotlessly kept that you could see yourself in the
pots and pans. As an extra bit of luck, thanks to certain
connections the Company had authorized her to sell candies
and cookies, which she displayed in large jars on two shelves
in her window. This meant six or seven sous' profit every
day, sometimes twelve on Sundays. Only La Brûlé and little
Lydie did not share in the general contentment: the former
roared against the bosses with the rage of an old revolutionary and demanded that her husband's death be avenged, and
the latter received all-too-frequent slaps attesting to the
family's vivacity.

"How big she is already!" La Pierronne cooed at Estelle.

"Oh, what trouble she is! Don't get me started on that!"
said La Maheude. "You're lucky not to have any. At least
you can keep things clean."

Though her own place was in order and she scrubbed it
every Saturday, she cast a housewife's envious glance over
this bright room that even had some purely decorative
touches: gilt vases on the cupboard, a mirror, three framed
prints.

La Pierronne was having her coffee alone, since everyone
else in the household was down in the mine.

"You must have some with me," she said.

"No, thanks, I've just had mine."

"What difference does that make?"

And indeed it made no difference. They drank slowly.
From between the jars of cookies and candies they looked
out at the houses across the way, with their windows from
which hung curtains whose whiteness or lack of it proclaimed
the degree of each woman's housewifely virtues. Those of the
Levaques were very dirty—hardly better than rags that
seemed to have been used to scrub the bottoms of pots.

"How can they live in such filth?" murmured La Pierronne.

La Maheude's tongue was loosened by this, and now there
was no stopping her. Oh, if she had only had a boarder like
that Bouteloup, she would have managed differently! When
you knew how to go about it a boarder was an excellent
proposition. You just had to make sure you didn't sleep with
him. And besides, everybody knew that Levaque drank, beat
his wife, and ran after the girls who sang in the Montsou
cabarets.

La Pierronne assumed an expression of great disgust.
Those singers spread all kinds of diseases. There was one at
Joiselle who had infected an entire mine.

"What surprises me is that you let your son have anything to do with their daughter."

"I'd like to know how you can stop it! Their garden is right alongside ours. In the summertime Zacharie and Philomène were always behind the lilac bushes, and they didn't give a damn what they did on that hutch! Why, you couldn't even get water from the well without catching them at it!"

It was the usual story of village promiscuity, with the girls and the boys going to hell together, playing the beast with two backs on tops of the low slanting roofs of the hutches as soon as night fell. All the haulage girls made their first babies there, unless they took the trouble to go to Réquillart or into the wheat fields to do it. It didn't make any difference, they got married eventually; the only ones to object were the mothers of sons who began too soon, because the boy who got married didn't bring anything into the house anymore.

"If I were you, I'd just as soon get it all over with," continued La Pierronne sensibly. "Your Zacharie has already given her two, and they'll only go off somewhere to live together. . . . The money's lost in any case."

Furious, La Maheude raised her arms heavenward.

"I tell you, if they set up house together it will be with my curse! . . . Doesn't Zacharie owe us some consideration? He cost us enough, didn't he? Well then, he's got to pay us back before he saddles himself with a wife. . . . What would happen to us if our children started to work for others right away? We might just as well drop dead!"

Then she calmed down.

"I'm just talking in general. We'll see later. . . . Your coffee is very strong—it's the real thing."

And after another fifteen minutes of talk she hurried away, exclaiming that the men's soup was not yet made. Outside, the children were going back to school, and some of the women were at their doors, watching Madame Hennebeau walking down one of the streets and pointing out some features of the village to her guests. Their visit was beginning to stir the village up. The man on the repair shift stopped spading for a minute, and two frightened hens fluttered through the gardens.

As La Maheude neared her door she ran into La Levaque, who had come out to catch Dr. Vanderhagen, a Company doctor—a hurried little man who was crushed by overwork and who gave his consultations on the run.

"Doctor," she said, "I can't sleep anymore and I hurt all over. . . . I've got to talk to you about it."

Without stopping, he answered unceremoniously:

"Don't bother me! You drink too damn much coffee!"

"And what about my husband, Doctor?" asked La Maheude in her turn. "You ought to see him.... He still has those pains in his legs."

"That's because you're wearing him out. Stop bothering me!"

Both women stood there, watching his receding back.

"Come on in," said La Levaque after she and her neighbor had exchanged despairing shrugs. "I want to tell you something.... You'll have a cup of coffee, won't you? I've just made some."

La Maheude didn't want to, but she gave in. Well, just a drop so as not to hurt her feelings. And she went in.

The room was black with filth—the floor and the wall spotted with grease, the cupboard and table sticky with dirt. There was a stomach-turning smell of bad housekeeping. Near the fire, his elbows on the table and his nose sunk in his plate, Bouteloup was finishing up some boiled beef. Heavy-set and placid, he was still young-looking at thirty-five. Standing beside him, little Achille, who was almost three and Philomène's elder, was watching with the mute appeal and the imploring expression of a hungry beast. Every once in a while the boarder, whose great brown beard hid a tender heart, would shove a piece of meat into the child's mouth.

"Wait, let me sugar it," said La Levaque, putting the brown sugar right into the coffeepot.

Six years older than Bouteloup, she was worn out and hideous, with her beasts sagging onto her belly and her belly sagging onto her thighs; there were sprouts of grayish bristle on her flat face, and her hair was always uncombed. He had taken her naturally, without any more thought than he gave to his soup, in which he found floating hairs, or to his bed, on which the sheets remained for three months running. She was part of the room and board, and her husband was fond of repeating that honest accounts make for good friends.

"I just wanted to tell you," she continued, "that somebody saw La Pierronne hanging around Silk Stocking Village yesterday. Mr. You-Know-Who was waiting for her behind Rasseneur's, and they went off together along the canal. What do you think of *that* for a married woman!"

"Well," said La Maheude, "before he married her, Pierron used to give the foreman rabbits—now he saves money by lending him his wife."

Bouteloup burst into a hearty laugh and threw a piece of gravy-soaked bread into Achille's mouth. The two women continued their tirade against La Pierronne, who was a coquette—no prettier than anyone else, but always busy inspecting every pore in her body, washing herself, and rubbing in skin lotions. Well, it was her husband's business if that's the way his tastes ran. Some men were so eager to get ahead that they'd wipe the bosses' rear ends just to hear them say thanks. And on they went, until they were interrupted by the arrival of a neighbor bringing back a nine-month-old baby, Desirée, Philomène's youngest child. The latter had her lunch at the screening shed, and she had made arrangements for the baby to be brought there so she could give her the breast while she sat down for a minute in the middle of the coal.

"I can't leave mine for a minute, she starts screaming right away," said La Maheude, looking at Estelle, who had fallen asleep in her arms.

But she couldn't escape the challenge she had been reading for some time in La Levaque's eyes.

"Listen, we've got to settle this business."

At first, the two mothers, without any need to discuss it, had been in complete agreement about not arranging a marriage. If Zacharie's mother wanted to keep collecting her son's pay as long as possible, Philomène's mother grew wild at the idea of giving up her daughter's. There was no particular hurry, and La Levaque had even wanted to keep the baby, as long as there was only one. But now Achille was growing up and eating bread, and another had come; she found she was losing by the deal and relentlessly pushed for the marriage, determined not to give up another sou.

"Zacharie's lot's been drawn and he won't be called up. There's nothing else in the way. . . . Come on, now, when is it to be?"

"Let's put it off till the weather gets nice," answered La Maheude, embarrassed. "What a nuisance this all is! As if they couldn't have waited to be married before going together! I swear I'd strangle Catherine if I found out *she'd* played the fool."

La Levaque shrugged her shoulders.

"Don't be silly—her turn will come too."

With the ease of a man completely at home, Bouteloup ransacked the cupboard, looking for some bread. Vegetables for Levaque's soup, potatoes and leeks, lay on a corner of the table, half-peeled and taken up and put down a dozen times in the course of incessant gossiping. La Levaque had just gone back to them again when she suddenly dropped them once more to plant herself in front of the window.

"What's going on out there? . . . Why, it's Madame Henne-

beau with some people. Take a look. They're going into La
Pierronne's." In a flash they were back at the topic of La
Pierronne. It never failed: whenever the Company wanted to
show off the village they brought the visitors straight to her
place because it was so clean. But they probably never
mentioned the stories about the chief foreman! Oh, it's easy
enough to be clean when you have lovers who earn three
thousand francs plus rent and heat, and without counting
presents. If everything was clean on the surface, it certainly
wasn't underneath! And for all the time the visitors remained
across the way they rattled on.

"They're leaving now," said La Levaque at last. "They're
going to make the rounds. . . . Look! They're going into your
place!"

La Maheude was horrified. Had Alzire sponged off the
table? And *her* soup wasn't ready either! She mumbled a
good-bye and took off, going straight home without so much
as a glance to either the left or the right.

But everything was shining. Seeing that her mother had
not come home, Alzire, very serious, a towel tied around her
waist, had begun to make the soup. She had pulled up
the last leeks from the garden, gathered some sorrel, and was
just then cleaning the vegetables, while the water for the bath
the men would take when they got home was heating in a
large cauldron on the fire. By luck, Henri and Lénore were
quiet, busily tearing up an old calendar. Old Bonnemort was
silently smoking his pipe.

La Maheude was still panting when Madame Hennebeau
knocked.

"You don't mind, do you, my good woman?"

Tall, blond, somewhat heavy in the superb ripeness of her
forties, she was smiling in an attempt at affability and managing not to make too obvious her fear of staining her
bronze-colored silk dress and the black wrap she wore over
it.

"Come in, come in," she repeated to her guests. "Nobody
will mind. . . . See, isn't this one clean too? And this good
woman has seven children! All our homes are like this. . . . As
I was saying, the Company rents them the house for six
francs a month. A large room on the ground floor, two
rooms upstairs, a cellar, and a garden."

The gentleman with the decoration and the lady in the fur
coat, who had gotten off the morning train from Paris, looked
about vaguely, their faces showing their confusion at all these
strange, disorienting sights.

"And a garden," the lady repeated. "Why, I could live here myself—it's charming."

"We give them more coal than they can burn," Madame Hennebeau went on. "A doctor visits them twice a week, and when they're old they get pensions, even though nothing is taken off their wages."

"It's the Garden of Eden," murmured the gentleman ecstatically.

La Maheude had rushed to offer them seats, but the ladies refused. Madame Hennebeau was already weary of it all; in the boredom of her exile, she had been happy to distract herself for a moment with this role of zoo attendant, but she had soon been repelled by the stale odor of poverty, which was stronger than the cleanliness of even the carefully selected houses into which she ventured. Besides, all she did was parrot bits of sentences she had overheard, without ever troubling herself further about this world of workers living alongside her in suffering and need.

"Oh, what beautiful children," said the lady, who was really repelled by their overly large heads matted with straw-colored hair.

And La Maheude had to tell them how old the children were, and answer the polite questions they asked about Estelle. Old Bonnemort had respectfully taken his pipe out of his mouth, but he was so ravaged by his forty years down below—his legs stiff, his body broken, his face ashen—that he nevertheless remained a disturbing presence; when he was seized by a violent fit of coughing, he was afraid that his black sputum would probably upset the visitors, so he decided to leave the room and spit outside.

Alzire was the star attraction. What a lovely little housekeeper, with her dishtowel tied around her! Her mother was complimented for having a little girl who was so mature for her age. Nobody mentioned her hump, but uneasy, compassionate looks were directed at the poor little invalid.

"And now," Madame Hennebeau concluded, "if you're asked about our villages in Paris, you'll know what to say. . . . Never noisier than this, strong family ties, everybody healthy and happy, as you can see—in fact, a place you should come to for a bit of a rest, with pure air and peaceful surroundings."

"It's marvelous, marvelous!" exclaimed the gentleman in a final burst of enthusiasm.

They left as delighted as though they had come from a sideshow, and La Maheude, who had accompanied them to the door, remained at the threshold while they slowly walked off, speaking very loudly. The streets had become crowded, and they had to pass through groups of women drawn by the rapidly spread news of their visit.

In fact, La Levaque, standing in front of her door, had stopped La Pierronne, who had come running up to take a look. They both pretended to be shocked and surprised. Were those people going to sleep at the Maheus'? It wasn't all that enjoyable!

"Never any money, in spite of all they earn! . . . Well, that's what you can expect if people carry on like that!"

"I just heard that she went to beg from those people at La Piolaine this morning, and that Maigrat, who'd refused her credit, let her have some groceries. . . . And we all know how *he* gets paid!"

"What, her? Oh no, that would take real courage! . . . He gets his from Catherine."

"Huh! And not half an hour ago she had the nerve to tell me she'd strangle Catherine if she ever caught her fooling around! . . . As if that Chaval hadn't tumbled her bottom on the hutch a long time ago!"

"Sh! Here they come."

After which La Levaque and La Pierronne, standing about quietly, without any unseemly curiosity, had contented themselves with sidelong glances at the departing visitors. Then they had urgently signaled to La Maheude, who was still carrying Estelle in her arms, and all three stood motionless, watching the well-clothed backs of Madame Hennebeau and her guests withdraw down the street. When they were some little distance away, the gossip started again, with redoubled violence.

"Those women certainly spend enough on their backs! Their clothes are probably worth more than they are!"

"You can say that again! . . . I don't know the other one, but the one from here—I wouldn't give *that* for her, big as she is. The things I've heard . . ."

"Really? What things?"

"Well, men, of course. . . . To begin with, the engineer—"

"That skinny little thing? He's too small—she'd lose him in the sheets!"

"What difference does that make as long as she enjoys it? . . . Myself, I always think something's wrong when I see a lady who turns her nose up at everything and never seems to be happy with anything. . . . Just look at her wiggle her rear end—as if she thinks she's better than the rest of us! You call that decent?"

The strollers were walking at the same slow pace, still

talking, when a barouche drew up in front of the church and a man in his late forties got out. He was dressed in a tight-fitting black frock coat, his skin was tanned, and his expression was one of authority and formality.

"Her husband," whispered La Levaque, seized by the hierarchical fear the manager inspired in his ten thousand workers and automatically lowering her voice as if he could hear her. "You can almost see the horns sprouting from his head."

Now the whole village was outside. The women's curiosity was growing; little groups of them were merging together, forming a crowd, and on the sidewalks bands of snotty-nosed brats were standing around, gaping. There was even a momentary glimpse of the pale face of the schoolteacher, watching from over the schoolhouse ledge. The man who was digging in the middle of the gardens stopped, his foot on the spade, his eyes open wide. And the murmur of the gossiping gradually swelled like the rattling noise of the wind blowing through dry leaves.

The crowd in front of La Levaque's door was especially large. First there were two women, then ten, then twenty. Now that there were so many ears about, La Pierronne cautiously fell silent. La Maheude, one of the more sensible women, also contented herself with merely watching; to quiet Estelle, who was awake and screaming, she had calmly taken out her udderlike breast, which hung down as though stretched by the continual flow of milk. When Monsieur Hennebeau had seated the ladies in the carriage and started off toward Marchiennes, there was a last explosion of jabbering voices, with all the women gesticulating and shouting into each other's faces—the tumult of an anthill in rebellion.

Just then three o'clock struck. The workers on the repair shift—Bouteloup and the others—had left. Suddenly, around the corner of the church, came the first of those returning from the mine, their faces black, their clothing soaked, their arms crossed, their backs bent. The women dispersed quickly, running home with the flurry of housekeepers who had been guilty of too much coffee and too much talk. All that could be heard was the nervous exclamation, pregnant with family quarrels:

"Oh my God, the soup! My soup isn't ready yet!"

4

When Maheu got home, after having left Etienne at Rasseneur's, he found Catherine, Zacharie, and Jeanlin sitting at the table, finishing their soup. They were all so hungry on their return from the mine that they ate in their damp clothes, without even washing up. Nobody waited for anybody else—the table remained set from morning till night and there was always somebody seated at it, gulping down his portion at whatever hour his work schedule permitted.

Maheu spotted the groceries from the door. He didn't say anything, but his worried expression brightened. All that morning the thought of the empty cupboard, of the house without coffee or butter, had gnawed at him, had caused him torments of anguish as he hacked away at the vein in the suffocating depths of the stall. How would his wife manage? And what would become of them if she came home empty-handed? And now there was enough of everything! She would tell him all about it later. He laughed with relief.

Catherine and Jeanlin had already gotten up and were drinking their coffee standing, while Zacharie, who had hardly been filled by his soup, had cut off a thick slice of bread and was spreading butter on it. He was very conscious of the headcheese on a plate, but he didn't touch it; meat was for the father when there was only enough for one. They had all just washed down their soup with a big bumper of water, the refreshing drink of the last days of the pay period.

"I don't have any beer," said La Maheude when the father had sat down at the table in his turn. "I wanted to keep back a little of the money. . . . But if you want some, Alzire can run over and get a pint."

He looked at her, beaming. What?—she had money too?

"No, no," he said. "It's all right, I've had some."

And he slowly began to spoon down the mash of bread, potatoes, leeks, and sorrel that had been heaped into the bowl he used as a plate. La Maheude, without putting Estelle down, helped Alzire to make sure he had everything he wanted, pushed the butter and the headcheese close to him, and put his coffee back on the fire so it would be hot.

Meanwhile, alongside the fire, the bathing was beginning in the cut-down barrel that had been turned into a tub. Cather-

90

ine, who went first, had filled the tub with lukewarm water and was calmly undressing, removing her cap, her jacket, her trousers, and even her shift. She had done so ever since she was eight years old, growing up without ever seeing anything wrong in it. She merely turned her back so her stomach was facing the fire, then vigorously scrubbed herself with the harsh soap. Nobody paid any attention to her; even Lénore and Henri were no longer interested in seeing how she was made. When she was clean she went up the stairs, completely nude, leaving her drenched shift and her other clothes in a pile on the floor. Then a quarrel broke out between the two brothers. Jeanlin had hurriedly leaped into the tub, using as an excuse the fact that Zacharie was still eating, and now the latter was pulling at him, demanding his turn and shouting that even though he was nice enough to let Catherine soak herself first, that didn't mean he wanted to bathe in the slop of brats—especially since after this particular one had been in the water it could be used to fill the inkwells at school! They ended by bathing together, both turned toward the fire, and even helping each other by scrubbing one another's backs. Then they too disappeared up the stairs, like their sister completely nude.

"What a mess they make!" grumbled La Maheude, picking the clothes off the floor and putting them to dry. "Alzire, mop up a little, will you?"

Before she could continue, she was interrupted by an outburst from the other side of the wall—a man swearing, a woman weeping, and all the thrashing noises of a battle, with dull blows sounding like thuds on an empty gourd.

"La Levaque's getting hers," Maheu commented tranquilly as he continued to scrape the bottom of his bowl with his spoon. "That's funny—Bouteloup said the soup was ready."

"Ready my foot!" said La Maheude. "I saw the vegetables on her table and they weren't even peeled!"

The shouts grew louder, there was a terrible crash that shook the wall, and then everything fell silent. The miner swallowed his last spoonful of soup and summed everything up in a tone of judicious impartiality:

"I don't blame him, if the soup isn't ready."

Then, after drinking a full glass of water, he started on the headcheese, cutting it into small squares, spearing them with the end of his knife, and eating them on his bread, without a fork. Nobody spoke while the father ate, and he too was silent. He didn't recognize the headcheese as having come from Maigrat, so it must have come from somewhere else, but he asked no questions. He only wanted to know if the old man was still upstairs sleeping. No, the grandfather had already gone out for his usual stroll. And then there was silence again.

But the odor of the meat had drawn the attention of Lénore and Henri, who were amusing themselves on the floor by tracing streams in the slopped-over bath water. They came over to their father, the little boy in front, and planted themselves in front of him. Their eyes followed each morsel, hopefully watching it leave the plate and disappointedly seeing it vanish into his mouth. Finally their father noticed the hungry desire that was making them pale and moistening their lips.

"Did the children have any?" he asked.

And, as his wife hesitated:

"You know I don't like this kind of unfairness. It takes my appetite away to see them standing around me, begging for a bite."

"But they did have some!" she exclaimed angrily. "If you paid any attention to them, you'd have to give them your share and everybody else's too. They'd stuff themselves till they burst. . . . Didn't we all have some of the headcheese, Alzire?"

"Of course, Mama," answered the little hunchback, who in such situations lied with all the aplomb of an adult.

Lénore and Henri, who were whipped if they didn't tell the truth, were paralyzed with shock, revolted by such lying. Their little hearts swelled, and they wanted to protest, to say that they hadn't been there when the others had eaten their share.

"Come on, get away from here," repeated the mother, chasing them to the other end of the room. "You should be ashamed of yourselves, always sticking your noses into your father's plate. And even if he is the only one to have any, isn't he the one who works? You, you good-for-nothings, you're only an expense—and an expense that's bigger than you are!"

But Maheu called them back and put Lénore on his left knee and Henri on his right. Then he finished the headcheese, making a game out of sharing it by dividing it up and cutting their share into small pieces. The children wolfed it down ecstatically.

When he had finished, he said to his wife:

"No, don't give me my coffee yet. I'm going to wash first. . . . Here, help me empty this dirty water."

They each grasped a handle of the tub and were emptying it into the gutter in front of the door when Jeanlin came down dressed in dry clothes—a pair of trousers and a woolen overblouse, both threadbare hand-me-downs from his brother, both too big for him. Seeing him sneak out through the open door, his mother stopped him.

"Where are you going?"

"Over there."

"Where over there?. . . Listen, what you're going to do is pick a dandelion salad for tonight, understand? If you don't come back with a salad, you'll hear from me about it."

"All right, all right."

Jeanlin left, his hands in his pockets, shuffling his sabots and rolling his pathetically meager ten-year-old hips like an old miner. Zacharie came down next. He was more carefully put together, his chest molded in a black jersey with blue stripes. His father called out to him not to come home too late, but he went out without answering, shaking his head and clenching his pipe between his teeth.

The tub was once again full of lukewarm water, and Maheu was already slowly taking off his jacket. Responding to a warning glance, Alzire took Lénore and Henri outside to play. The father didn't like to bathe with the whole family around, although it was done in many other houses of the village. Not that he criticized anybody; he merely said that washing up together was fine for children.

"What are you doing up there?" La Maheude called upstairs.

"I'm fixing my dress—I tore it yesterday," Catherine answered.

"All right. . . . Don't come down now, your father's bathing."

Maheu and La Maheude were alone. She had decided to put Estelle on a chair, and by some miracle, the child, finding herself comfortable near the fire, wasn't crying; her staring eyes, blank with an infant's unawareness, followed her parents. Maheu, naked, crouched in front of the tub, had begun by plunging in his head, which had first been lathered with the harsh soap whose time-honored usage had discolored and bleached the hair of the whole race. Then he got into the water and soaped his chest, belly, arms, and thighs, scrubbing himself energetically with both fists. His wife stood watching him.

"I saw that look of yours when you got home," she began. "You were worried, and the sight of the groceries was a relief, wasn't it?. . . Would you believe that those people at La Piolaine didn't let me have a sou? Oh, they're nice enough—they gave me some clothes for the children—but I

was ashamed to beg. It makes me sick to have to ask for
anything."

She stopped for a moment to fix Estelle more firmly on the
chair so that she wouldn't fall. The father continued to scrub
himself, asking no questions to speed along this interesting
tale, but merely waiting patiently to understand.

"Maigrat refused me—absolutely—and put me out like a
dog.... You can see what a fix I was in! Woolen clothes
keep you warm, but they don't put anything into your stomach, do they?"

He raised his head but still didn't say anything. Nothing at
La Piolaine, nothing at Maigrat's: then how? But La Maheude had just rolled up her sleeves, as she usually did, to
wash his back and the other areas that were difficult for him
to reach. He liked to have her soap him, to scrub him all
over with wrist-breaking energy. She took some soap and
worked on his shoulders while he braced himself against the
tub.

"So I went back to Maigrat's and told him a few things—
oh, did I tell him a few things! I said it wasn't right to be so
heartless, that it would bring him bad luck if there was any
justice in the world.... He didn't like that at all—he kept
shifting his eyes every which way, and you could see he
wanted to get away...."

Her hands had worked down from his back to his buttocks, and while she was at it she ventured further, digging
into every fold of flesh, not skipping one spot on his body,
making him shine like her three pots on Saturdays, when she
did a special clean-up. But all this back-and-forth motion of
her arms was making her sweat, and she was so shaken up
and out of breath that her words came in gasps.

"Then he called me an old leech.... But we'll have bread
till Saturday, and what's more, he let me have five francs. I
got butter, coffee, and chicory from him, and I was even
going to take some headcheese and potatoes, when I saw he
was beginning to grumble.... Seven sous for headcheese,
eighteen sous for potatoes—and I've still got three francs
seventy-five for a stew and some boiled beef.... Well, I
didn't waste my morning, did I?"

Now she was drying him, patting the spots that were still
wet. He, happy and without a thought for the day the debt
would come due, broke into a loud laugh and grabbed her in
his arms.

"Stop it, idiot! You're still wet, you're making me
damp.... There's one thing, though—I'm afraid Maigrat has
some idea ..."

She was going to mention Catherine, but stopped. Why bother him? It would only start trouble.

"What idea?" he asked.

"Well, the idea that he can cheat us. Catherine will have to go over his bill with a fine-tooth comb."

He grabbed her again and this time did not let go. The bath always ended this way. She would get him excited by rubbing so hard, then by drying him with the towel, which tickled the hair on his arms and chest. In fact, in every house in the village this was the hour of foolishness, the time when more children than were wanted were planted. At night the whole family was around. He pushed her toward the table, joking, enjoying the one good moment of the day, saying he was having his dessert—and a dessert for which there was no charge! Her hips and breasts twisting, she fought him off for a moment just for the fun of it.

"Stop it, idiot, stop it! Look, Estelle's watching us! Wait till I turn her around."

"Oh, at three months, what can she understand?"

When he got up, Maheu put on only a pair of dry trousers. His special pleasure, when he was clean and had had some fun with his wife, was to remain for a while with his chest bare. His white skin, as white as that of an anemic girl, was tattooed by the scratches and gashes of the coal—"grafts," the miners called them. He was proud of them, and he spread his large arms and broad chest, which shone like blue-veined marble. In the summer, all the miners stood at their doors like that, and even now, in spite of the damp weather, he went there for a moment and called out some racy comment across the gardens to a friend who was also standing bare-chested at *his* door. Others appeared, and the children standing around on the pavement looked up and laughed at the joy of all this weary workers' flesh exposed to the open air.

While drinking his coffee, and without having yet put on a shirt, Maheu told his wife how angry the engineer had been about the timbering. He was calm and relaxed, and he listened, nodding approvingly, to the good advice of La Maheude, who showed excellent sense in these matters. She always said that there was nothing to be gained by fighting the Company. Then she told him about Madame Hennebeau's visit; though they didn't say so, they were both proud of it.

"Can I come down?" called Catherine from the top of the stairs.

"Yes, yes, your father's drying himself."

The young girl had put on her Sunday dress, an old

dark-blue poplin, faded and worn-out at the pleats. She was wearing a plain black tulle bonnet.

"You're all dressed up. . . . Where are you going?"

"To Montsou, to buy a ribbon for my bonnet. . . . I took the old one off, it was too dirty."

"You mean you have some money?"

"No, Mouquette promised to lend me ten sous."

Her mother let her go, but called her back when she reached the door.

"Listen, don't buy your ribbon at Maigrat's—he'd only cheat you, and he'd think we're rolling in money."

Her father, who had squatted in front of the fire to dry his neck and armpits more quickly, added:

"And try not to spend the whole night hanging around outside."

Maheu spent the afternoon working in his garden. He had already planted potatoes, beans, and peas, and yesterday he had heeled in some cabbage and lettuce plants and was now going to replant them. This bit of garden furnished all their vegetables except for potatoes, of which they never had enough. He had a green thumb and even managed to raise artichokes, which his neighbors considered an affectation. As he was getting his row ready, Levaque came out to smoke a pipe in his own garden and have a look at the romaine lettuce Bouteloup had planted that morning—if the boarder had not had the energy to do the spading, nothing would have grown there but nettles. A conversation sprang up over the fence. Levaque, refreshed and stimulated by having beaten his wife, tried in vain to get Maheu to go to Rasseneur's with him. What! did the idea of a beer frighten him? They'd have a game of ninepins, stroll around with some friends, and then come back for dinner. . . . That was the way to live after a day down in the mine. Maheu admitted there was probably no harm in it, but he wouldn't give in: if he didn't replant his lettuces, they'd all be wilted by the next day. Actually, he refused out of a sense of what was right; he did not want to ask his wife for any of the change from the five francs.

It was striking five when La Pierronne came by to find out if her Lydie had gone off with Jeanlin. Levaque answered that she must have, since Bébert had also disappeared, and the three of them were always sniffing around at each other. When Maheu had quieted them by telling them about the dandelion salad, he and his friend started joking with La Pierronne, crudely but good-naturedly. She got angry, but because she was actually tickled by the indecencies that made her hold her sides and shriek, she did not leave. A skinny woman, whose stuttering anger sounded like the clucking of a hen, came to her aid, and other women took up the cudgels from the safety of their doorways. Now that school was over, swarms of children were hanging about, squealing, rolling, fighting, while those fathers who were not off drinking were gathered in groups of three and four, squatting on their heels the way they did down in the mine, smoking their pipes and exchanging an occasional word in the shelter of some wall. When Levaque wanted to feel La Pierronne's thigh to see if it was firm, she left in a rage, and Levaque decided to go to Rasseneur's by himself, leaving Maheu to his planting.

It suddenly grew dark, and La Maheude lit the lamp, irritated because her daughter and the boys had not yet come home. She should have known: they never managed to all sit around the table for the one meal they could have eaten together. And she was still waiting for the dandelions, too. What could that damn kid gather at this hour, in this pitch dark? A salad would go so well with the vegetable stew she had simmering on the fire—potatoes, leeks, sorrel, all fricas-seed with fried onions! The whole house smelled of fried onions—that wonderful smell which turns rancid so quickly and penetrates the bricks of the mining villages with such a stench that you can smell them from far off in the country by that strong odor of the poor man's cooking.

When night fell Maheu came in from the garden and immediately sank into a chair, his head against the wall. As soon as he sat down in the evening he fell asleep. The cuckoo struck seven, and Henri and Lénore had just broken a plate by insisting on helping Alzire, who was setting the table, when Old Bonnemort came in first, in a hurry to eat and get back to the mine. La Maheude woke Maheu:

"Let's eat. Too bad for them. . . . They're big enough to find their way home. But it's a shame about that salad. . . ."

5

At Rasseneur's, after having eaten some soup, Etienne went up to his tiny top-floor room facing Le Voreux and fell onto his bed, fully clothed and overwhelmed by weariness. He had had less than four hours' sleep in the past two days. When he awoke, it was dusk; for a moment he was confused

and did not know where he was. He felt so uncomfortable,
and his head was so heavy, that he painfully got to his feet
with the idea of getting some fresh air before having dinner
and going to bed for the night.

Outside, the weather was milder; the sooty sky was turning
the color of copper, and the warm, damp air was heavy with
the approach of one of those long rains of the Nord. Night
was falling like a cloud of smoke, engulfing the far horizons
of the plain. Over the immense sea of reddish fields, the
lowering sky seemed to be melting into a black dust, with not
a breath of wind stirring the darkness. It was all dim, dismal,
funereal.

Etienne walked aimlessly, interested only in shaking off his
feverishness. When he passed in front of Le Voreux—already
dark at the bottom of its hole, but with not one lamp yet
shining—he stopped to watch the day laborers leaving: it
must be six o'clock; trammers, loaders, and stablemen were
going off in groups, together with the screening girls—laughing shadows in the dusk.

First came La Brûlé and her son-in-law Pierron. She was
bickering with him because he hadn't backed her up in an
argument with an inspector about how many stones she had
raked out.

"You spineless thing, you! How can you call yourself a
man and still crawl like that in front of these bastards who're
eating us alive?"

Pierron was following her calmly, without answering. Finally he said:

"I suppose you would've liked me to start up with the
boss? No thanks, I don't need any more trouble!"

"Why don't you bend over so they can beat you more
easily?" she shrieked. "My God, if only my daughter had
listened to me! . . . It's not enough that they killed my husband—I suppose you'd like me to thank them for it! No, I
tell you, I'll have their hides some day!"

Their voices faded away. Etienne watched her disappear,
with her eagle's beak, her wild white hair, and her long,
skinny, furiously gesticulating arms. But then, from behind
him, a conversation between two young men caught his
attention. He recognized Zacharie, who had been waiting
there and whose friend Mouquet had just come up to him.

"Are you ready?" asked the latter. "We'll have something
to eat, and then off to the Volcan."

"Later. There's something I have to do first."

"What?"

Then Mouquet turned around and saw Philomène coming out of the screening shed. He thought he understood.

"Oh, I see. . . . I'll go on ahead."

"Right—I'll catch up with you."

As Mouquet walked away, he ran into his father, Old Mouque, who was also leaving Le Voreux; the two men merely said good evening to each other, and the son took the main road while his father went off along the canal.

Zacharie was already shoving Philomène down the same secluded path, in spite of her objections. She was in a hurry, some other time—they were arguing like an old married couple. It wasn't funny, this being able to see each other only outdoors, especially in the winter when the ground was damp and there wasn't even the wheat to stretch out on.

"No, it's not that," he muttered impatiently. "I've got something to say to you."

He was holding her by the waist and gently leading her along. Then, when they were in the shadow of the slag heap, he asked her if she had any money.

"What for?"

He began a confused tale about a two-franc debt that was going to drive the whole family into complete misery.

"Stop lying! . . . I saw Mouquet, and you're both going to the Volcan, where all those dirty singers are."

He denied it, beat against his chest, gave his word of honor. Then, since she simply shrugged her shoulders at this, he suddenly said:

"Come along with us if you want to. . . . You'll see that your being there won't bother me at all. What the hell would I want with those singers? . . . Will you come?"

"And what about the baby?" she answered. "Do you think you can go anywhere with a kid that cries all the time? . . . You'd better let me go home—I bet they can't hear themselves think anymore."

But he held on to her and kept begging. Didn't she understand? It was just so he wouldn't look silly in front of Mouquet, whom he had promised to meet there. A man couldn't go to bed with the chickens every night. Giving in, she lifted the flap of her jacket and, slitting the stitching with her fingernails, took a few ten-sou coins out of the hem. Fearful of being robbed by her mother, she hid there whatever she made from working extra hours at the mine.

"Look, I've got five," she said. "I'm willing to give you three . . . but you've got to swear to me that you'll talk your mother into letting us marry. I've had enough of this kind of

life! And on top of everything, Mama counts every mouthful
I eat. . . . Swear, you've got to swear first."

She spoke with the passionless resignation of an overgrown, sickly girl who was, quite simply, tired of her existence. He swore, and protested that it was a promise sworn
before God; then, when he had the three coins, he kissed her,
tickled her, made her laugh, and he would have pushed things
further, there in this corner of the slag heap which was the
winter quarters of this long-established couple, if she had not
kept saying no, it wouldn't be any fun. She returned to the
village alone, while he cut across the fields to catch up with
his friend.

Etienne had watched them from a distance, automatically,
without understanding what was really going on, thinking it
was only a simple rendezvous. The girls in the mine were
precocious, he thought, and he remembered the girls at Lille
whom he used to wait for behind the factories—those
bunches of girls corrupted by a complete surrender to misery
by the time they were fourteen. But another encounter surprised him even more, and he stopped.

At the bottom of the slag heap, in a kind of ditch formed
by some big stones that had slid down, little Jeanlin was
violently bawling out Lydie and Bébert, who were seated on
either side of him.

"What did you say? . . . What I'll give you is a smack, if
you want. . . . Whose idea was it, anyway?"

And it had been Jeanlin's idea. After having wandered for
an hour through the fields along the canal with the two
others, gathering dandelions, he had looked at the pile of
salad greens and decided that they'd never eat that much at
home; so instead of going back to the village, they had gone
on to Montsou, where he set Bébert to act as lookout while
he made Lydie knock at the doors of the bourgeois families
and offer the dandelions for sale. Already wise in the ways of
the world, he said girls could sell anything they wanted to. In
the excitement of the enterprise, the whole heap had been
sold, but at least Lydie had made eleven sous. Now, empty-
handed, they were dividing the profits.

"It's not fair!" shouted Bébert. "You've got to divide it
into three equal shares. . . . If you take seven sous, we'll only
have two apiece."

"What do you mean, not fair?" Jeanlin answered furiously.
"To begin with, I picked more than you did!"

Usually Bébert gave in out of a fearful admiration and a
credulity that made of him a perpetual victim. Though he

was older and stronger, he even let himself be hit. But this time the idea of all that money spurred him to resistance.

"He's robbing us, isn't he, Lydie? . . . If he doesn't share, we'll tell his mother."

In a flash Jeanlin had his fist under Bébert's nose.

"Just say that again! It's me who'll go to *your* house and tell them you've sold Mama's salad. . . . Anyhow, jackass, how can you divide eleven sous into three equal shares? Try it if you're so smart. . . . Here's two sous for each of you, and you'd better take them fast or I'll put them back in my pocket."

Vanquished, Bébert took the two sous. Lydie, trembling, had said nothing, for Jeanlin inspired in her the fear and tenderness of an abused little wife. When he offered the two sous she put out her hand with a submissive smile, but suddenly he changed his mind.

"Hell, what are you going to do with all that? Your mother'll swipe it for sure if you don't know where to hide it. . . . I'd better keep it for you. When you need money, you can ask me for it."

And the nine sous disappeared. To seal her mouth he had laughingly grabbed her and was rolling around with her on the slag heap. She was his little wife, and in dark corners they attempted together the lovemaking they saw and heard at home behind the partitions and through the cracks in the doors. They knew everything, but were still too young to do much of anything, so they groped and played for hours, like vicious puppies. He called it "playing mama and papa," and she came running whenever he called, letting herself be taken with an instinctive, delicious trembling, often angry but always yielding in the hope of something that never happened.

As Bébert was never allowed to participate in these games, and punches rained down on him as soon as he even tried to touch Lydie, he was always embarrassed, choked with anger and uneasiness, whenever the other two amused themselves—which they did without being in any way inhibited by his presence. Because of this, his one idea was always to frighten them, to break it up by yelling out that somebody could see them.

"Watch it, there's a man looking!"

This time he wasn't lying; it was Etienne, who had decided to continue his walk. The children jumped up and ran off, and he went on, around the slag heap and along the canal, amused at having thrown such a scare into those scamps. No doubt they were beginning too young, but what could you do?—they saw so much, they heard so much, that you'd have

had to tie them down to restrain them. Nevertheless, at heart
Etienne was saddened by it.

A little further on he came across some more couples. He
was nearing Réquillart, and there, among the old ruins, all
the girls from Montsou would slink about with their lovers. It
was the common meeting place, the remote and deserted
corner where all the haulage girls came to make their first
baby when they didn't dare risk it on top of a hutch. The
broken palings opened to all of them the old yard, now a
wasteland cluttered with the debris from the two collapsed
sheds and studded with the skeletons of still-standing uprights.
Heaps of broken carts and stacks of half-rotted timber were
everywhere, and some kind of hardy vegetation was reclaim-
ing this piece of land, spreading out in a thick growth and
springing up as young, but already sturdy trees. Every girl
felt herself at home here; there were forgotten little corners
for all of them, and their sweethearts would toss them down
on the beams, behind the piles of timber, or in the carts.
They would settle down, elbow to elbow, without paying any
attention to their neighbors, and it was as though all around
this lifeless machine, next to this shaft weary of spewing
forth coal, the powers of creation were taking their revenge—
unbridled love, under the lash of instinct, planting babies in
the bellies of girls scarcely more than children themselves.

Yet there was a watchman living there—Old Mouque, to
whom the Company had given two rooms almost directly
under the ruined headframe and continually threatened with
destruction by the expected fall of the last of the scaffolding.
He had had to prop up part of the ceiling, but all in all he
lived there very comfortably with his family—he and Mouquet in one room and Mouquette in the other. Since the
windows no longer had a single pane of glass, he had decided
to nail them up with boards; you couldn't see very well
inside, but it was warm. In any case, this watchman didn't
watch over anything; he went off to take care of his horses at
Le Voreux and never bothered about the ruins of Réquillart,
the shaft of which was the only part kept in order, and that
only so it could serve as a chimney for a furnace that
ventilated the neighboring mine.

And so it was that Old Mouque was spending his declining
years surrounded by lovemaking. La Mouquette, from the
time she was ten, had been tossed in every corner of the
ruins, not as a green and frightened child like Lydie, but as a
fully developed girl, fit for bearded youths. Her father never
complained, because she was always respectful and never
brought her lovers home. Besides, he was used to such things.

Every time he came from or went to Le Voreux, every time he left his corner, he couldn't take so much as a step without stumbling over a couple in the grass, and at the other end of the enclosure, where he gathered wood to cook his soup or looked for burdock for his rabbit, it was even worse: then he would see the greedy noses of all the girls of Montsou pop up, and he had to be careful not to trip over the legs stretched across the paths. But gradually these encounters had come to embarrass nobody, neither Old Mouque, who simply took care not to fall, nor the girls, whom he let go about their business while he discreetly turned away like a good fellow undisturbed by the workings of nature. And just as the girls now knew him, so he had ended by knowing them, in the same way you know the thieving magpies that carry on in the pear trees of your garden. Ah, these young people, how they enjoyed themselves, how they went at it! Occasionally he would shake his head with silent regret as he turned away from the noisy wenches breathing too heavily in the shadows. Only one thing annoyed him: there was one couple that had gotten into the bad habit of embracing against the wall of his room. It wasn't that it kept him from sleeping, but they pushed so hard that they were damaging the wall.

Every evening Old Mouque was visited by Bonnemort, who always took the same walk before dinner. The two old men scarcely spoke to each other, exchanging no more than a dozen words during the half hour they spent together. But being together and thinking of old times without having to talk about them seemed to cheer them; they would sit alongside one another on a beam, there at Réquillart, speak a few words, then drift off, each into his private daydream. During these times they probably felt themselves young again, for all around them lovers were hiking their mistresses' skirts, there was a murmur of kisses and laughter, and the warm smell of young girls mingled with the cool smell of crushed grass. It was behind this same mine, forty-three years ago, that Old Bonnemort had first possessed his wife, a haulage girl who was so sickly that he used to set her up on a cart so he could kiss her more comfortably. Ah, those were the days! And the two old men, shaking their heads, would finally take leave of each other, often without even saying good night.

This evening, just as Etienne came up, Old Bonnemort was rising from the beam to go back to the village, and he said to Mouque:

"Well, good night friend. . . . Tell me, did you know La Roussie?"

Shrugging his shoulders, Mouque was silent for a moment, then, as he went into the house he said:

"Good night, friend, good night!"

Etienne sat down on the same beam. Without knowing why, he was becoming more and more melancholy. The old man whose retreating back he now watched reminded him of his arrival that morning and of the flood of words the nerve-racking wind had torn from this now-silent figure. What misery! And all these bone-weary girls who were still silly enough to come here in the evening and make more babies whose flesh was doomed to toil and suffering! It would never end, so long as they kept filling themselves with ever more paupers. . . . Shouldn't they rather plug their bellies and clench their thighs, as if at the approach of disaster? But perhaps he was only brooding about these morose notions because he was depressed at being alone while all the others were going off in pairs to take their pleasure. He felt stifled by the mugginess of the air; raindrops, still infrequent, were falling on his feverish hands. Yes, sooner or later all the girls took their turn at it—it was stronger than reason.

While Etienne was sitting motionless in the shadows, a couple coming from Montsou brushed past without seeing him and continued on their way into the waste space of Réquillart. The girl—probably still a virgin—was fighting, resisting, pleading in low whispers, but the young man kept silently pushing her into the darkness of a still-standing shed in which there were piles of moldy ropes. It was Catherine and Big Chaval, but Etienne hadn't recognized them as they passed, and now he followed them with his eyes, waiting to see the end of this little incident and caught in the grip of a passion that changed the course of his thoughts. Why should he interfere? When girls said no, it was because they liked to be pushed around a little first.

On leaving Village 240, Catherine had taken the main road into Montsou. Ever since the age of ten, when she had begun to earn her keep in the mine, she had run about the countryside alone, enjoying the complete freedom customary in mining families, and if now, by fifteen, no man had yet had her, it was thanks to her delayed development; the decisive change into womanhood was still to come. When she reached the Company yards she crossed the street and went into the laundress', where she was sure she would find Mouquette, for the latter spent her time there with a group of women who kept treating each other to coffee from morning to night. But she was doomed to disappointment—Mouquette had stood a treat in her turn and could no longer let her have the promised ten sous. To make it up to her they tried to give her a steaming hot glass of coffee, but she refused, and did not even want her friend to borrow for her from one of the other women. She was seized by a sudden fit of economy, a sort of superstitious fear—the certainty that if she were to buy that ribbon now it would bring her bad luck.

She hurried off along the road back to the village and had already reached the houses on the outskirts of Montsou when a man called to her from the doorway of Piquette's place.

"Hey, Catherine, where are you running to?"

It was Big Chaval. She was annoyed, not because she didn't like him but because she was in no mood to fool around.

"Come on in and have something to drink.... A little glass of something sweet, all right?"

She refused politely: it was almost dark and they were waiting for her at home. He had come forward, and standing in the middle of the road, was pleading with her in a low voice. For some time he had been wanting to get her to come up to his room on the first floor of Piquette's, a nice room with a big bed, big enough for a couple. Why did she always refuse—was she afraid of him? She laughed good-humoredly and said she would go up there the week that no babies sprouted. Then one thing led to another, and somehow she was telling him about the ribbon she hadn't been able to buy.

"Why, I'll buy it for you!" he exclaimed.

She blushed, feeling she would be wiser to refuse, but very much wanting her ribbon. She thought again of a loan, and ended by accepting on the condition that she would pay him back whatever he laid out for her. That made them start joking again: it was agreed that if she didn't sleep with him, she would pay him back his money. But then another difficulty arose when he talked of going to Maigrat's.

"No, not to Maigrat's. Mama said not to go there."

"Don't be silly—you don't have to say where you got it! ... He has the prettiest ribbons in Montsou."

When Maigrat saw Big Chaval and Catherine come into his store, like two lovers buying their wedding presents, he became red as a beet, and he showed his blue ribbons with all the fury of a man who is being made fun of. After the young people had been served, he stood in his doorway and watched them disappear into the dusk, and when his wife came out and timidly asked him about something, he fell on her with curses, shouting that some day he'd make all these ungrateful bastards sorry—they ought to be down on the ground, licking his boots!

Big Chaval walked along the road beside Catherine, his arms swinging clear, but nudging her with his hip and guiding her without seeming to. Suddenly she noticed that he had made her leave the main road and that they were on the narrow path leading to Réquillart. But she had no time to get angry; his arm was already around her waist and he was confusing her with a flood of tender words. How silly she was to be afraid!—would he hurt a little darling like her, as soft as silk and good enough to eat? He kept blowing behind her ear and down her neck, making a shiver run up and down her body. She was confused, and could think of nothing to say. It was true that he seemed to be in love with her. Last Saturday night, after blowing out her candle, she had asked herself what she would do if he behaved this way, and as she was falling asleep she had dreamed, all soft with pleasure, that she was no longer saying no. Why then did the same idea today fill her with repugnance, with something like regret? While he was tickling the back of her neck with his moustache, so gently that it made her shut her eyes, the shadow of another man, the young fellow she had caught a glimpse of that morning, passed on the screen of her closed eyelids.

Suddenly Catherine looked around her. Chaval had led her into the rubble of Réquillart, and she drew back, shuddering, before the shadows of the broken-down shed.

"Oh no, oh no," she murmured. "Please let me go!"

The fear of the male—the fear that upon the approach of the conquering man stiffens the muscles in instinctive self-defense even when the girls are willing—made her frantic. Her virginity, though it had nothing new to learn, grew terrified, as if at the menace of a blow, of a wound whose unknown pain she dreaded.

"No, no, I don't want to! I'm too young, I tell you. . . . Honest! Later, when I'm ready."

He growled harshly:

"Idiot! Then there's not even anything to be afraid of. . . . What difference does it make to you?"

He said no more. He had gotten a good grip on her and thrown her into the shed. She fell back on some old ropes and stopped resisting—submitting to the male, before her time, with that hereditary submission which made the girls of her race tumble in the open air while still in their childhood. Her frightened stuttering stopped, and nothing could be heard but the passionate breathing of the man.

Meanwhile, Etienne had listened without moving. Another one taking the plunge! And now that he had seen the little comedy, he got up, disturbed by a feeling of uneasiness, a sort of jealous excitation mingled with anger. He no longer tried to be quiet—those two were much too busy to pay any attention to him—and he strode over the beams. He was therefore surprised to see, after he had gone some distance down the road and had turned around, that they were already up and seemed, like himself, to be returning to the village. The man had his arm around the girl's waist again, hugging her gratefully and still whispering into her ear; she was the one who appeared to be in a hurry, who wanted to get home and was irritated by the delay.

Then Etienne felt a strong desire to see their faces. It was idiotic, and he walked a little faster so as not to give in to it. But his feet slowed down of themselves, and he ended by hiding himself in the darkness at the first lamp post. He was absolutely stunned when he recognized Catherine and Big Chaval as they went by. At first he wasn't sure: was it really she, this young girl in the dark-blue dress and the bonnet? Was that really the same little urchin he had seen in trousers, a cloth cap on her head? That was why she had been able to brush right past him without his recognizing her! But now he no longer doubted it; he had just recognized her eyes, the limpid green of spring water, so clear and so deep. What a slut! And he felt a burning need to revenge himself—for no particular reason—by despising and scorning her. And she didn't even look nice, dressed as a girl; she was hideous.

Catherine and Chaval had slowly passed him. They didn't know they were being watched, and he kept stopping her, kissing her behind the ear; his caresses made her laugh and she began to slow down. Etienne was now behind and had to follow them, annoyed because they were blocking his way and he was forced to witness things that only exasperated him. So it was true, what she had sworn that morning: she had not been anybody's mistress yet, and he hadn't believed her, had deprived himself of her so that he wouldn't seem to be behaving like the other one, had just let her be taken from under his very nose, had pushed his stupidity to the point of actually amusing himself by watching them! It drove him mad; he clenched his fists and felt he could have eaten that man alive in one of those wild needs to kill someone that sometimes overcame him.

The walk lasted half an hour. When Chaval and Catherine drew near Le Voreux, they slowed down even more, stopping twice alongside the canal, three times near the slag heap;

they were both very gay now and were amusing themselves
with tender little games. Etienne had to stop whenever they
did, lest he be seen. He forced himself to feel nothing more
than a brutal regret: this would teach him to try to spare a
girl's feelings out of respect! Then, after they passed Le
Voreux and he was free to go and have his dinner at
Rasseneur's, he continued to follow them as far as the village, where he stood in the shadows for a quarter of an hour,
waiting for Chaval to let Catherine go inside the house. And
when he was sure they were no longer together, he started
walking again and went some distance on the road to Marchiennes, just tramping along, not thinking of anything in
particular, too choked up and unhappy to shut himself in his
room.

It was not until an hour later, about nine o'clock, that
Etienne came back through the village, telling himself that he
had to eat and go to bed if he wanted to get up at four
o'clock in the morning. The village was already asleep, sunk
in the darkness of night. Not so much as a glimmer of light
slipped through the closed shutters, and the long rows of
houses were sleeping heavily, like snoring barracks. The only
sign of life was a cat running across the empty gardens. It
was the end of the day; the workers, exhausted, had fallen
into bed straight from the table, heavy with fatigue and food.

There was still a light on at Rasseneur's; an engineman and
two workers on the day shift were drinking their beers.
Before going inside, Etienne stopped and looked once more
into the shadows. It was the same immense blackness he
remembered from the morning, when he had arrived in the
midst of the hurling wind. In front of him Le Voreux was
crouching like a terrible beast—shadowy, and pocked with
some few lantern lights. The three braziers on the slag heap
were blazing like bloody moons, at times silhouetting the
enormous shadows of Old Bonnemort and his yellow horse.
Beyond, on the flat plain, the night had covered everything—
Montsou, Marchiennes, the forest of Vandame, the vast sea
of beets and wheat; only the blue flames of the blast furnaces
and the red flames of the coke ovens shone like distant
lighthouses. Little by little the darkness was thickening; the
rain was now falling slowly, continuously, covering the nothingness below with its monotonous streaming; only one voice
could still be heard—the heavy, labored breathing of the
drainage pump, ceaselessly panting, night and day.

Part THREE

1

The next day and the following days Etienne went back to his work in the mine. He became accustomed to it, and his life began to revolve around the new job and the new habits that had seemed so hard at the beginning. Only one incident broke the monotony of the first two weeks—a passing fever kept him in bed for forty-eight hours, his limbs aching, his head burning, dreaming in a semi-delirium that he was pushing his cart through a tunnel so narrow his body could not squeeze through it. But that was only the stiffness of apprenticeship, an excessive exhaustion from which he soon recovered.

Day followed day; weeks, months, went by. Now, like all the others, he got up at three o'clock, drank his coffee, and took the sandwich Madame Rasseneur had prepared for him the night before. Each morning on the way to the mine he would meet Old Bonnemort going home to sleep, and each afternoon, leaving the mine, he would run into Bouteloup coming to work. He had his cap, trousers, and cloth jacket; he shivered and he toasted his back at the big fire in the dressing shed. Then there was the barefooted wait at the landing station, always swept by furious drafts—but he was no longer fascinated by the engine with its steel components and copper surface shining in the shadows above, nor by the cables speeding by like the black and silent wings of a nocturnal bird, nor by the cages ceaselessly springing up and plunging down amid the bedlam of signals, shouted orders, and the rattle of carts on the iron flooring. His lamp wasn't working well—that damn lampman probably hadn't cleaned it—and he would come to life only when Mouquet was packing them all in, clowning around and giving the girls resounding slaps on their behinds. The cage would start and fall like a stone to the bottom of a well, but he never lifted

his head to see the daylight disappear. He never gave a
thought to a possible fall, and the deeper he sank into the
darkness, under the pelting water, the more he felt at
home. Down at the loading station, after the meek and
sanctimonious Pierron had let them out, there was always the
same herdlike trampling as the teams shuffled off to their
stalls. By now he knew the galleries of the mine better than
the streets of Montsou; he knew he had to turn here, bend
down a bit farther on, avoid a puddle somewhere else. He
had become so used to the more than a mile walk underground that he could have done it without a lamp, his hands
in his pockets. And each time there would be the same
encounters—a foreman shining his lamp in their faces as he
passed them, Old Mouque bringing along a horse, Bébert
leading the snorting Bataille, Jeanlin running behind the train
to close the ventilation doors, and fat Mouquette and scrawny
Lydie pushing their carts.

In time, Etienne also found that he was suffering considerably less from the dampness and airlessness of the stall. The
chimney seemed easy to climb, as if he had shrunk and could
now pass through cracks where formerly he would not have
dared put even a hand, and he could breathe the coal dust
without discomfort, see in the dark, and sweat unconcernedly, quite used to the sensation of damp clothes on his body
from morning to night. In addition, he no longer wasted his
strength in awkward movements; the whole team was
amazed at his quickness and skill. At the end of three weeks
he was considered one of the best haulers in the mine:
nobody rolled his cart to the incline more swiftly or shoved it
off more efficiently. His small build made it possible for him
to slip in everywhere, and though his arms were as thin and
white as a woman's, he worked so energetically that it
seemed as if his soft skin must be covering iron. Even when
he was broken with fatigue, he never complained—out of
pride, no doubt. The only thing to be said against him was
that he couldn't take a joke; he got angry as soon as anyone
tried to tease him. In the end, as each day's backbreaking
routine further reduced him to little more than a machine, he
was accepted and looked upon as a real miner.

Maheu, who had great respect for work well done, was
particularly taken with Etienne. Also, like the others, he
realized that the young man's education was better than his
own: he saw him read, write, make little diagrams, and he
heard him talk of things he, Maheu, did not even know
existed. This was not surprising—miners are rough men, not
as quick-witted as enginemen—but he *was* surprised by the

boy's courage, by the boldness with which he had gotten into the swing of mining so as not to die of hunger. He was the first casual laborer ever to have caught on to things so quickly. As a result, whenever there was a lot of work at the face and Maheu did not want to stop one of the cutters, he would have Etienne take care of the timbering, sure that the work would be done properly and solidly. The bosses kept nagging at him about this damn timbering business—he was always afraid that the engineer Négrel would appear, followed by Dansaert, and shout and argue and demand that everything be done over again, and he had noticed that his hauler's timbering seemed to satisfy these gentlemen better, despite their way of never looking pleased and their repeated threats that one day or another the Company would have to take strong measures. Things dragged on, and a dull anger was fermenting in the mine. Even Maheu, generally so placid, got to the point of clenching his fists.

At first there had been some rivalry between Zacharie and Etienne. One evening each had threatened to punch the other. But Zacharie, who was really a good fellow and interested only in his pleasure, had immediately been appeased by the friendly offer of a beer, and he soon had to acknowledge the newcomer's superiority. Levaque was also friendly now, and talked politics with the hauler, who had, he said, some good ideas. In fact, of all the men on the team it was only on the part of Big Chaval that Etienne sensed a feeling of deep hostility. Not that they actually quarreled—on the contrary, they had become good friends—but as they joked around together their eyes would betray their mutual dislike. Catherine, between the two of them, went on in her tired and resigned way, bending her back, pushing her cart, always kind to her fellow hauler—who now in his turn always helped her—but also always obeying her lover, to whose caresses she publicly submitted. It was an accepted situation, a recognized relationship to which even the family closed its eyes—so much so that Chaval would take the girl behind the slag heap every evening and then bring her back to her parents' door, where he would give her a last kiss in full view of the whole village. Etienne, who thought he had come to terms with the situation, often teased her about these walks, jokingly using such obscenities as were common among the young girls and boys at the bottom of the mine, and she would reply in the same manner, boastfully relating all her lover had done to her. But she became pale and uneasy whenever her eyes met Etienne's, and they would both turn their heads away and not speak to each other for as much as an hour—as if they hated each other because of things buried deep within them, things they never discussed.

Spring had come. One day as Etienne came out of the mine he suddenly got a strong whiff of April's warmth—the good odor of sweet earth, tender green shoots, and pure fresh air; and now, every time he came up, spring smelled better and better and warmed him more and more after his ten hours of work in the eternal winter at the bottom of the shaft, among the damp shadows that no summer ever dissipated. The days grew longer, and by May he was going down at sunrise, with the red sky bathing Le Voreux in the misty haze of dawn and the white steam rising, all pink, from the exhaust pipes. There was no more shivering; a warm breath blew from far across the plains, and the larks sang in the sky, high above. Then, at three o'clock, he would be dazzled by a burning sun which was setting fire to the horizon and reddening the bricks beneath their grimy coats of coal. In June the wheat was already tall, its bluish green clashing with the dark green of the beets. It was an endless sea, undulating at the least breeze; he saw it spreading and growing from day to day, and he was sometimes surprised in the evening to find it more swollen with green than it had been in the morning. The poplars along the canal were plumed with leaves. Grass was invading the slag heap, flowers were covering the fields, and a whole world was germinating, springing from the earth, while he, down below, was groaning with wretchedness and exhaustion.

Now when Etienne went walking in the evening it was no longer behind the slag heap that he would startle pairs of lovers. He could follow their wake in the wheat, spot their lecherous nests by the shaking of the yellowing kernels and the big red poppies. Zacharie and Philomène went back there out of long habit; La Brûlé, always on Lydie's trail, was constantly flushing her out with Jeanlin, the two of them burrowed down so deeply that you had to step on them to make them start up; and as for Mouquette, she camped everywhere—you couldn't cross a field without seeing her head plunge down and her feet fly up as she took her pratfalls. But they were all free to do as they wished; Etienne found it shameful only on those evenings when he would meet Catherine and Chaval. Twice as he drew near he saw them suddenly drop down in the middle of a patch of wheat, the stalks suddenly going completely still. Another time, as he was walking along a narrow path, Catherine's limpid eyes showed above the wheat, then disappeared. Then it would

seem as though the vast plain was too small, and he preferred
to spend the evening at Rasseneur's place, L'Avantage.

"Madame Rasseneur, let me have a beer. . . . No, I'm not
going out tonight, I can barely stand on my feet."

And he would turn to a friend, a man who usually chose to
sit at a back table, his head against the wall.

"Souvarine, won't you have one?"

"No, thanks."

Etienne had gotten to know Souvarine because they both
lived at Rasseneur's. Souvarine was an engineman at Le
Voreux and he occupied the furnished room upstairs, alongside Etienne's. About thirty, slim and blond, his fine features
were framed by a thick head of hair and a thin beard. His
white, pointed teeth, his thin nose and mouth, his rosy complexion, all gave him the look of a girl—a look of gentleness,
which could, however, be transformed into one of sudden
savagery by steely flashes from his gray eyes. There was
nothing in his poor workingman's room except a box of
papers and books. He was Russian, never spoke of himself,
and paid no attention to the rumors going around about him.
The miners, always suspicious of strangers and spotting him
as someone from another class by his small, gentleman's
hands, had at first imagined some kind of adventure—
perhaps he was a murderer fleeing from justice. But then he
had shown himself so friendly, so lacking in arrogance, so
quick to give the children in the village every sou in his
pocket, that they now accepted him, reassured by the phrase
"political refugee"—a vague phrase seeming to provide an
excuse even for crime, and suggesting a kind of camaraderie
of suffering.

During the first few weeks Etienne had found his reserve
impenetrable, and as a result he did not learn his history until
later. Souvarine was the youngest son of a noble family in
the province of Tula. In St. Petersburg, where he was studying medicine, the wave of Socialist enthusiasm that was then
breaking over all the youth of Russia had made him decide
to learn a manual trade, that of engineman, so that he could
mingle with the people, get to know them, and be able to
help them like a brother. And now, having fled his country
following an unsuccessful attempt against the Emperor's life
—for a month he had lived in a fruit-seller's basement, digging a tunnel beneath the street and preparing his bombs
under the constant threat of blowing up both himself and the
house—he made his living with this trade. Disowned by his
family, without money, blacklisted by French workshops as a
foreigner who could only be a spy, he was dying of hunger

when the Montsou Company had finally hired him during a
labor shortage. He had been working there for a year now,
and was an excellent employee—sober, silent, taking the day
shift one week and the night shift the next, so dependable
that the bosses held him up as a good example.

"Aren't you ever thirsty?" Etienne asked him, laughing.

He answered in his soft, almost accentless voice:

"I'm thirsty when I eat."

Etienne then teased him about women, swearing he had
seen him in the wheat fields near Silk Stocking Village with
one of the haulage girls. He merely shrugged his shoulders
with calm indifference. A haulage girl?—what for? For him a
woman was sexless—a comrade if she had a man's courage
and sense of fraternity, and if she hadn't, why make yourself
vulnerable by forming an attachment? He wanted neither
mistress nor friend—he wanted no ties; he was responsible to
no one for his own blood or that of others.

Every night at about nine o'clock, when the bar would
empty out, Etienne stayed on to talk to Souvarine. He would
drink his beer in small sips, while the engineman would
smoke one cigarette after another, his thin fingers discolored
by the tobacco. His veiled, mystic's eyes would dreamily
follow the smoke; his unoccupied left hand would nervously
move in the air. He usually ended up by putting a tame
rabbit—a large female one, always swollen with pregnancy
and allowed the freedom of the house—on his lap. The
rabbit, whom he had named "Poland," had grown to love
him, and she would come to sniff at his trousers, sit up, and
scratch with her paws until he would pick her up, like a child.
Then, huddled against him, her ears flat back, she would
close her eyes while he endlessly stroked the gray silk of her
fur with an unconscious, caressing gesture, finding tranquillity in the soft and living warmth.

"You know, I've gotten a letter from Pluchart," Etienne
said one evening.

There was no one else in the place but Rasseneur. The last
customer had left, returning to the sleeping village.

"Well!" exclaimed the landlord, standing in front of his
two roomers. "Pluchart! What's he up to?"

For two months Etienne had been carrying on a steady
correspondence with the Lille mechanic, whom he had decided to tell about his job at Montsou and who was now
indoctrinating him, jumping at this chance to use Etienne to
propagandize among the miners.

"What he's up to is that association, which is going very
well ... It seems people from all over are joining up."

"And what do *you* think of their association?" Rasseneur asked Souvarine.

The latter, gently scratching Poland's head, blew out a jet of smoke and murmured quietly:

"More foolishness."

But Etienne became excited. The initial illusions of his ignorance and his natural predisposition to rebelliousness both acted to throw him into the fight of labor against capital. The association they were talking about was the Workers' International, the famous International that had just been set up in London. Wasn't that a wonderful effort, a campaign in which justice would finally be victorious? No more frontiers, but workers from all over the world rising up and joining together to guarantee the workingman the bread he earns. And what a magnificently simple organization: at the bottom, the section, representing the commune; then the federation, grouping all the sections from the same province; then the nation; and finally, above all of these, humanity itself, incarnated in a general council in which each nation was represented by a corresponding secretary. Within six months they would conquer the earth and lay down the law to the bosses if they fail to fall into line!

"Just foolishness!" repeated Souvarine. "Your Karl Marx is still at the stage of wanting to let natural laws operate. No politics and no conspiracies, isn't that right? Everything done in the open, and higher salaries the only aim. . . . Well, don't talk to me about your evolution! Burn the cities, mow down the nations, wipe everything out—and when there's nothing left of this rotten world, maybe a better one will grow in its place."

Etienne began to laugh. He did not always understand what his friend was talking about, and this theory of destruction seemed only a pose to him. Rasseneur, more practical-minded, and with the common sense of the well-established man, did not even bother getting angry. He was interested only in precise information.

"Then you're going to try to set up a section in Montsou?"

That was what Pluchart, who was secretary of the Federation of the Nord, wanted, and he kept emphasizing the help the International would be able to give the miners if they ever went on strike. Actually, Etienne did think a strike was imminent: the business of the timbering would end badly; it would take only one more unreasonable demand on the part of the Company to bring all the mines into a state of rebellion.

"The trouble is the dues," said Rasseneur judiciously. "Fif-

ty centimes a year for the general fund and two francs for
the section doesn't seem like much, but I'll bet lots of men
will refuse to give it."

"Especially," Etienne added, "since we would first have to
set up an emergency fund, which could be turned into a strike
fund if necessary. . . . Still, now's the time to think of these
things. I'm ready, if the others are."

There was a silence. The oil lamp smoked on the bar.
Through the open door they could hear the sound of a
shovel—a fireman feeding one of the furnaces at Le Voreux.

"Everything is so expensive!" broke in Madame Rasseneur,
who had come in and was listening with a somber air, her
height exaggerated by her eternal black dress. "Would you
believe it if I told you I paid twenty-two sous for eggs today?
Something's got to give!"

This time the three men were of the same opinion. First
one, then another spoke in desolate voices, and the grievances poured forth. The workers couldn't manage any
longer, the Revolution had only aggravated their misery; it
was the middle classes that had been growing fat since '89, so
greedy they didn't even leave the workers the plates to lick
clean. Could anybody claim that the workers had had their
reasonable share in the extraordinary growth of wealth and
comfort during the last hundred years? They were told they
were free and that was the end of it: yes, free to starve to
death, and that was just what they were doing! Voting for
those rascals who only went on to stuff themselves without
thinking any more of the poor than of their old boots didn't
put any bread in their cupboards! No, one way or another, it
all had to come to an end—either nicely, by legislation, by
friendly understanding, or brutally, by setting fire to everything and by going at one another's throats. The children
would certainly see it even if their parents didn't, because the
century could hardly end without another revolution—a
workers' revolution this time, a blow-up that would clean
society from top to bottom and rebuild it with more decency
and justice.

"Something's got to give!" Madame Rasseneur repeated
vigorously.

"Yes, yes," they all cried, "something must give!"

Souvarine was brushing back Poland's ears, and her nose
was quivering with pleasure. With a faraway look in his eyes,
he said in a hushed voice, as if to himself:

"Raise wages—can it really be done? They are fixed by the
iron law that sets them at the lowest sum possible, just
enough so the workers can eat dry bread and make ba-

bies. . . . If they fall too low, the workers starve to death and the shortage of labor makes wages go up again. If they go too high, the increased labor supply makes them fall. . . . Empty stomachs keep the balance steady, and the result is a perpetual condemnation to starvation."

When he forgot himself in this way and started talking about Socialist theory, Etienne and Rasseneur became uneasy, disturbed by the pessimistic assertions to which they had no answers.

"Listen," he continued in his usual quiet manner, looking at them now. "Everything must be destroyed or hunger will spring up again. Yes, anarchy!—nothing left, the earth washed in blood and purified by fire! . . . After that, we'll see."

"The gentleman is absolutely right," declared Madame Rasseneur, who in spite of her revolutionary enthusiasm was very polite.

Etienne, depressed by his own ignorance, did not want to continue the discussion. He got up, saying:

"Let's go to bed. None of this will keep me from having to get up at three o'clock."

After snuffing out the cigarette butt stuck to his lips, Souvarine gently put his hand under the rabbit's big belly and set her on the floor. Rasseneur locked up. They separated in silence, their ears ringing and their heads bursting with the serious questions they were turning over in their minds.

And every evening, over the single mug of beer that Etienne took an hour to empty, there were similar conversations in the bare room. A world of shadowy ideas that had lain dormant in him was beginning to stir and grow. Devoured by a rage to learn, he had nevertheless hesitated to borrow any of his neighbor's books, most of which were unfortunately either in German or Russian; but he had finally borrowed a French book on cooperatives—more foolishness, said Souvarine—and he was also regularly reading a newspaper Souvarine subscribed to, *Combat*, an anarchist sheet published in Geneva. As for the rest, in spite of their daily meetings he found Souvarine as reserved as ever, always seeming to be just passing through life, without interests, affections, or possessions of any kind.

About the beginning of July, things suddenly improved for Etienne. An accident intruded on the monotonously repetitious life of the mine: the teams working in the Guillaume vein had come across a disturbance in the stratum and said that surely meant there was a fault ahead—and indeed they soon reached the fault, which the engineers, despite their detailed knowledge of the terrain, had known nothing about.

The whole mine was in an uproar: no one talked of anything
but the lost vein, which had probably slid down on the other
side of the fault. The older miners were sniffing around like
good hunting dogs unleashed on the scent of the coal, but
meanwhile the teams could hardly sit around with their arms
folded; notices were put up, announcing that the Company
would auction off new contracts.

One day at quitting time Maheu walked along with Etienne and offered him a job on his team as a cutter, to replace
Levaque, who had gone to work on another team. The
arrangement had already been cleared with the chief foreman and the two engineers, who both seemed well pleased
with the young man. Etienne had only to accept this rapid
advancement, and he did, gratified by Maheu's increasing
esteem.

That evening they went back to the mine to look over the
notices. The stalls up for bids were in the Filonnière vein in
the north gallery of Le Voreux. They didn't seem terribly
advantageous ones; Maheu shook his head as Etienne read
him the terms. And when they went down the next day to see
the vein, Maheu pointed out the distance from the loading
station, the crumbly nature of the terrain, the narrowness of
the seam, and the hardness of the coal. However, if they
wanted to eat they would have to work, so the following
Sunday they went to the auction, which took place in the
dressing shed and which was presided over, in the absence of
the division engineer, by the engineer of the mine, assisted by
the chief foreman. Five or six hundred miners were there,
standing in front of a little platform set up in a corner, and
the bidding was so fast that nothing could be heard but a dull
rumble of voices—the shouts of numbers being drowned out
by other numbers.

For a moment Maheu was afraid he would not get one of
the forty contracts being offered by the Company. Upset by
rumors of a crisis and panicked by the fear of unemploy-
ment, the competitors kept lowering their prices. Seeing their
frenzy, the engineer Négrel took his time and let the bids fall
as low as possible, while Dansaert, who wanted to speed
things up, lied about the quality of the lots. To get his
150-foot heading, Maheu had to bid against a comrade who
also seemed determined to have it; they took turns cutting
each other's bids by a centime a cartful, and though Maheu
finally won, he had had to lower his price so much that the
foreman Richomme, standing behind him, muttered between
his teeth and nudged him, angrily grumbling that he would
never be able to manage at that price.

Etienne was swearing as they came out. He exploded in front of Chaval, who was just returning from a stroll in the wheat fields with Catherine, while his father-in-law had been taking care of more serious matters.

"My God, how they bleed us!" he shouted. "They make worker fight against worker these days!"

Chaval got angry—*he* would never have lowered his price! And Zacharie, who had merely come out of curiosity, said it was disgusting. But Etienne shut them up with a violent gesture.

"It won't always be like this! Some day we'll be the masters!"

Maheu, who hadn't said a word since the auction, suddenly seemed to wake up. He repeated:

"The masters. . . . God damn it, it can't be too soon!"

2

It was the last Sunday in July, the feast day of the patron saint of Montsou. On Saturday evening the good housekeepers of the village had washed down their living rooms with floods of water—whole bucketfuls sloshed over the flagstones and against the walls—and though the floors had been spread with white sand, which was a costly luxury for the purses of the poor, they were still not dry. The day promised to be very hot, with one of those summer skies, heavy with storm clouds, that seem to weigh down on the endlessly stretching, flat, bare plains of the Nord.

On Sundays, everybody at the Maheus' got up at a different time. By five o'clock Maheu could no longer bear to be in bed and would get up and dress, but the children would sleep away the morning until nine. On this particular Sunday Maheu went out to smoke a pipe in his garden, then went back inside to have some bread and butter, alone, while waiting for the others. He spent the morning doing odd jobs: he repaired the tub, which had a leak in it, and he pasted up a picture of the imperial prince, which had been given to the children, under the cuckoo clock. Meanwhile, the others came down one by one. Old Bonnemort had taken a chair outside to sit in the sun. La Maheude and Alzire had immediately started cooking dinner. Then Catherine appeared, pushing along Lénore and Henri, whom she had just dressed. By the time Zacharie and Jeanlin finally came down, still yawning, their eyes swollen with sleep, eleven o'clock was striking and the house was already filled with the odor of rabbit stewing with potatoes.

For that matter the whole village was stirred up by the holiday and feverish with excitement, rushing through dinner so everyone could go off to Montsou with his friends. Troops of children were running about, and men in shirtsleeves and slippers were walking around with a lazy holiday shuffle. Through the doors and windows, open wide to the fine weather, could be seen the rows of rooms, each one overflowing with gestures and cries and the rumble of family life; and from one end of the rows of houses to the other, on this day the odor of rabbit, the smell of rich cooking, was competing with the habitual one of fried onions.

The Maheus ate at the stroke of noon. They were quiet compared with the other groups, with their gossiping from door to door and the continual hubbub of the women, exchanging shouts and answers, borrowing and returning, slapping at brats to drive them away or get them inside. Actually, for the past three weeks there had been a coolness between them and their neighbors, the Levaques, because of the marriage between Zacharie and Philomène. The men still got together, but the women pretended not to know each other. This quarrel had brought about a closer relationship with La Pierronne, but she had gone off, early in the morning, to spend the day with a "cousin" in Marchiennes, leaving Pierron and Lydie with her mother. Everybody laughed at this, for they all knew the cousin: she had a moustache and was the chief foreman at Le Voreux. La Maheude felt that it really wasn't decent to leave your family on such a holiday.

Besides the rabbit and potatoes—a rabbit they had been fattening up in the hutch for a month—the Maheus also had a thick soup and beef. The day before had been payday, and they couldn't remember ever having had such a feast. Even last St. Barbara's Day, that holiday during which the miners do nothing for three days, the rabbit had not been so fat or so tender, and the ten pairs of jaws, from little Estelle's, whose teeth were beginning to come in, to Old Bonnemort's, whose teeth were beginning to fall out, set to work with such good will that the very bones disappeared. It was good to have meat, but because they had it so rarely they digested it badly. They ate everything; only a bit of boiled beef was left for the evening. They'd have it with bread and butter if they were hungry.

Jeanlin was the first to disappear. Bébert was waiting for

him behind the school, but they had to hang around for a long time before they were able to lure Lydie away, for La Brûlé, having made up her mind not to go out herself, wanted to keep the child at home too. When she noticed that Lydie had slipped away, she screamed and waved her scrawny arms about, while Pierron, irritated by the racket, went off for a quiet stroll with the air of a husband who is able to enjoy himself without guilt because he knows that his wife is having a good time too.

Old Bonnemort was the next to leave, and then Maheu decided to get some fresh air and asked La Maheude to join him later. No, she didn't really think she could, it was just too much trouble with the children; well, maybe she would, she'd think about it, they'd find each other. Outside, he paused for a moment, then went next door to see if Levaque was ready. Instead, he found Zacharie waiting for Philomène; La Levaque had just started in again on the eternal subject of the marriage and was shouting that they were trying to make a fool of her, that she'd have it out with La Maheude once and for all. What kind of life was it, having to take care of her daughter's fatherless children while the girl was gallivanting around with her lover? Philomène having calmly finished putting her bonnet on, Zacharie led her off, saying it was all right with him if it was all right with his mother. Since Levaque had already slipped away, Maheu also referred his neighbor to his wife and hurriedly left. Bouteloup, elbows on the table, was finishing a piece of cheese and stubbornly refused the friendly offer of a beer. He was staying home, like a good husband.

Little by little the village was emptying out, the men going off one after another and the girls, after waiting at their doors, setting out in the other direction on the arms of their lovers. Just as her father was turning the corner at the church, Catherine saw Chaval and rushed to join him so they could go to Montsou together. La Maheude, left alone with the squabbling children, didn't even have the strength to get up from her chair, but poured herself a second cup of boiling coffee and drank it in small sips. Only the wives were left in the village, and they invited each other in to drain the coffeepots around tables still warm and greasy from dinner.

Maheu suspected that Levaque was at L'Avantage, so he slowly walked down to Rasseneur's. And yes, there he was in the small hedged garden behind the tavern, having a game of ninepins with some friends. Old Bonnemort and Old Mouque were standing there, following the game with such absorption that they even forgot to nudge each other. A hot sun was beating directly down, and there was only a sliver of shadow alongside the building; Etienne was there, sitting at a table and drinking beer, annoyed because Souvarine had just left him to go up to his room. Almost every Sunday the engine-man shut himself in to read or write.

"Do you want to play?" Levaque asked Maheu.

The latter refused. He was too hot, and he was already dying of thirst.

"Rasseneur!" called Etienne. "Let's have a beer here."

And turning to Maheu, he said:

"This one's on me."

They were all on easy, familiar terms now. Rasseneur didn't hurry himself; he had to be called three times and in the end it was Madame Rasseneur who finally brought the warm beer. The young man had lowered his voice to com-plain about how the place was run: they were good people, of course, people whose ideas were all right, but the beer wasn't worth a damn and the soup was terrible! He'd have looked for another place to live long before this, but he hated the idea of the long walk to Montsou. Still, one of these days he'd end up looking for a room with some family in the village.

"Yes, of course," said Maheu in his slow way; "of course. You'd be much better off in a family."

There was a sudden outcry—Levaque had knocked down all the pins with one ball. In the midst of the uproar, Mouque and Bonnemort, never lifting their eyes from the ground, stood in deep, silent approval. The general excitement pro-voked by such a feat boiled over into jokes, especially when the players saw Mouquette's laughing face appear over the hedge. She had been circling around for an hour, and now, emboldened by the laughter, she came nearer.

"What!—you're alone?" Levaque shouted. "Where are your lovers?"

"My lovers?—I've given them all the gate!" she answered with gay impudence. "I'm looking for a new one now."

Everybody offered himself and tried to excite her with obscenities. She shook her head and laughed the louder, playing coy. Her father heard it all but just stood there, never taking his eyes off the fallen ninepins.

"Go on!" continued Levaque, shooting a glance toward Etienne. "We all know the one you'd like! ... You'll have to take him by force."

Etienne began to laugh. It was true—he *was* the one the haulage girl had been circling around. He turned her down, amused, but feeling no desire at all for her. She remained behind the hedge a few minutes longer, staring at him with wide eyes, then slowly walked away; her face was saddened now, as though the burning sun had suddenly become too much for her.

Etienne had already resumed his whispered explanations to Maheu about why the Montsou miners should set up an emergency fund.

"Since the Company insists we're free to do as we want, what are we afraid of? All we've got is their pensions, and since nothing is taken out of our pay for them, they give those out any way they please.... Instead of depending on them, it would be a good idea to set up a mutual aid association that we could at least count on in case of urgent need."

And he went into the details, discussed the actual organization, and promised to take on all the work himself.

"All right, I'm willing," said Maheu, finally convinced. "But what about the others? . . . Try to sign them up."

Levaque had won, and everybody left the game to have some beer. Maheu refused a second one: maybe later, the day wasn't over yet. He had just thought of Pierron—where could he be? Probably at Lenfant's place. He persuaded Etienne and Levaque to join him, and all three left for Montsou just as a new group took over the ninepins at L'Avantage.

On the way they had to stop in at Casimir's bar and then at Le Progrès. Friends called to them from the open doors: there was no way to refuse. Each time it meant a beer—two, if they stood a round in their turn. They remained about ten minutes, talked a bit, then repeated the process farther on; it was quite safe—they knew the beer and could fill up on it without giving themselves any more trouble than having to piss it out right away, as clear as spring water. At Lenfant's they ran into Pierron, who was finishing his second beer and who couldn't refuse to down another in a toast. They joined him, of course. There were four of them now, and they left to look for Zacharie at Tison's. The place was empty, but they ordered a beer and waited a while. Next they thought of the Saint-Eloi, where they accepted a round from the foreman Richomme, then continued their wandering from bar to bar with no other excuse now but the fun of it.

"Let's go to the Volcan!" said Levaque suddenly; he was getting a little high.

The others laughed, hesitated, then accompanied their friend through the growing holiday throng. In the long and narrow Volcan, on a wooden platform set up at the rear, five singers, the rejects of the streets of Lille, were parading around in low-cut dresses and flaunting themselves with outrageous gestures; if a customer wanted one of them, he paid ten sous to have her behind the platform. The place was crowded with haulers, trammers, and even some fourteen-year-old mine boys—all the youth of the mines, drinking more gin than beer.

Some of the older miners were there too—the lickerish family men from the villages, those whose homes were going to pieces.

As soon as their group was seated around a small table, Etienne latched on to Levaque so he could explain his idea about an emergency fund. Like most new converts who think they have a mission in the world, he was a persistent propagandist.

"Every member can easily pay in twenty sous a month," he repeated. "With these twenty sous piling up, we'll have a real hoard in four or five years—and when you have money you're strong, no matter what happens. . . . Well, what do you say?"

"It's all right with me," Levaque answered absentmindedly. "We'll talk about it some time."

He was all worked up about a big blonde, and he insisted on staying behind when Maheu and Pierron, having finished their beers, decided to leave without waiting for another song.

Etienne, who had left with them, ran into Mouquette outside; she seemed to be following them, for there she was again, still staring at him with her big eyes and laughing her good-natured laugh, as if to say, "How about it?" The young man made some joke and vanished into the crowd.

"I wonder where Chaval is?" asked Pierron.

"He must be at Piquette's," said Maheu. "Let's go there."

But as the three of them neared Piquette's the sounds of a brawl at the door stopped them. Zacharie was shaking his fist at a Walloon nailmaker, a stolid, sturdy type, while Chaval stood by, his hands in his pockets, and watched.

"Well, there's Chaval," Maheu said calmly. "He's with Catherine."

For five long hours the haulage girl and her lover had been wandering through the fair. All along the Montsou road—that wide route with low, gaily painted houses winding down the hill—a stream of people was flowing along under the hot sun like an army of ants, lost in the utter emptiness of the flat plain. The eternal black mud had dried, and the black dust was rising like a storm cloud. The cabarets, their tables set out to the edge of both sides of the road, were thronged, as were the peddlers' stalls—a double line of open-air bazaars, with shawls and mirrors for the girls, knives and caps for the boys, and candies, sugar-coated almonds, and cookies for everybody. There was an archery stand in front of the church, and games of *boules* opposite the Company yards. At the corner of the Joiselle road, in a fenced-in area near the Company's offices, people had swarmed to see a cockfight between two large, red, metal-spurred cocks, their slashed throats bleeding. Farther on, at Maigrat's, aprons and trousers were being given out as prizes at billiards. And there were long silences as the crowd dumbly drank and stuffed itself; a mute indigestion of beer and fried potatoes spread in the heavy heat—a heat made hotter still by the kettles of oil boiling in the open air.

Chaval bought Catherine a mirror for nineteen sous and a shawl for three francs. At every corner they kept running into Mouque and Bonnemort, who had come to the fair and were slowly walking through it, side by side, lost in thought. But another meeting made them angry—they saw Jeanlin energetically urging Bébert and Lydie to steal bottles of gin from a makeshift bar that had been set up at the edge of an empty lot. Catherine managed to slap her brother, but Lydie was already rushing off with a bottle. Those damn kids would end up in jail!

When they got to La Tête Coupée Chaval decided to take his mistress inside to watch a finch contest that had been advertised on the door for a week. Fifteen nailmakers from Marchiennes had accepted the challenge, each one with a dozen cages; the dark little cages with the blinded finches motionless inside them were hooked onto a fence in the courtyard, and the point was to see which one would sing out his tune the most often in the course of an hour. Each nailmaker had a slate and stood behind the cages, keeping track, checking on his neighbors and being checked on himself. The finches were divided into *chichouïeux*, which had a full-throated song, and *batisecouics*, which had a higher pitch, and they all started timidly—first risking only an occasional phrase, then exciting each other to more and more frequent repetitions, and finally being carried away by such a rage of emulation that a few of them even collapsed and died. The nailmakers frenziedly urged them on, screaming at them in Walloon to sing again, again, again, just once more, while about a hundred spectators stood in absorbed silence amid the infernal music made by 180 finches all repeating the same tune at different tempos. A *batisecouic* won the first prize, a metal coffeepot.

Catherine and Chaval were still there when Zacharie and
Philomène came in. They shook hands and stayed together,
but suddenly Zacharie became angry; he surprised a nailmaker, one of those who had come with some friends to watch,
pinching his sister's thighs. She turned red but made him keep
quiet, terrified at the thought of the slaughter that would
ensue should all these nailmakers throw themselves at Chaval
if he too objected to her being pinched. Of course she had
felt the man, but she had prudently not said anything. Her
lover, however, just laughed, and all four of them left; the
matter seemed closed. And then, as soon as they had entered
Piquette's, there was the nailmaker again, provoking them,
daring them, defiantly brushing up against them. Zacharie,
whose family feelings were outraged, rushed at the fellow.

"That's my sister, you bastard! . . . Just you wait, damn it!
I'll teach you to show some respect!"

The two men were kept apart, while Chaval, quite calm,
continued to repeat:

"Forget it—it's my business, and I tell you I don't give a
damn about him."

Just then Maheu arrived with his friends, and he was able
to quiet Catherine and Philomène, who were already in
tears. The nailmaker had disappeared and the crowd was
laughing now. To put an end to the incident, Chaval, who
was very much at home at Piquette's, stood a round of beers.
Etienne had to clink glasses with Catherine, and they all—the
father, the daughter and her lover, the son and his mistress—
drank together, with a polite "good health to everybody."
Then Pierron insisted on paying for a round and everything
was going smoothly when Zacharie saw his friend Mouquet
and flew into a rage again. He called him over and they both
left—to settle things with the nailmaker, he said.

"I'll slaughter him! . . . Chaval, you and Catherine keep an
eye on Philomène. I'll be back."

Now Maheu offered a round of beers. After all, if the boy
wanted to avenge his sister, it would set a good example. But
from the time she had caught sight of Mouquet, Philomène
had calmed down and merely shaken her head. She was sure
the two rascals had only slipped away to the Volcan.

Feast-day celebrations always ended with a dance at the
Bon Joyeux. The proprietor of this cabaret was the widow
Désir, a hearty, fifty-year-old matron, round as a barrel but
so full of juice that she still had six lovers—one for each day
of the week, she said, and all six on Sunday. She called all
the miners her children and was quite sentimental about the
flood of beer she had poured out for them over the past

thirty years, and she also boasted that not one single haulage girl became pregnant without having first limbered up her legs a little at the Bon Joyeux. The place consisted of two rooms: the cabaret proper, in which were the bar and tables, and, communicating with this room through a large opening, the dance hall, an enormous room that had wooden planking in the middle and flagstone paving around the edges. The decoration consisted of two garlands of paper flowers that crossed from one corner of the ceiling to the other and were joined in the center by a wreath of similar flowers, and the walls were covered with gilt shields bearing the names of saints: Saint Eloi, patron of the ironworkers, Saint Crépin, patron of the shoemakers, Sainte Barbe, patroness of the miners—in fact, a calendar of all the trades. The ceiling was so low that the three musicians on their stand, which was no bigger than a pulpit, kept scraping their heads. To light the place at night, an oil lamp was hung at each of the four corners of the hall.

On this Sunday the dancing had begun at five o'clock, when light still streamed in through the windows, but it wasn't till about seven that the place really began to fill up. Outside, a stormy wind had risen and was blowing great clouds of black dust that blinded everybody and crackled in the kettles of frying oil. Maheu, Etienne, and Pierron, who had come into the Bon Joyeux to sit down, found Chaval dancing with Catherine, while Philomène, all alone, looked on. Neither Levaque nor Zacharie had reappeared. Since there were no benches around the dance floor, Catherine came to rest at her father's table after each dance. They called to Philomène, but she preferred to stand. It was growing dark; the three musicians were playing wildly, and nothing could be seen in the room but the movement of hips and breasts and a mad confusion of arms. The appearance of the four lamps was greeted enthusiastically, and suddenly everything was illuminated—red faces, tumbled hair pasted against skin, flying skirts sweeping along the strong smell of sweating couples. Maheu drew Etienne's attention to Mouquette, who, round and fat as a bladder of lard, was swinging violently in the arms of a tall, thin trammer: she had had to console herself and find another man.

It wasn't until eight o'clock that La Maheude appeared, Estelle at her breast and followed by her brood, Alzire, Henri, and Lénore. She had unerringly headed straight for the Bon Joyeux to join her husband. They would eat later. Everybody's stomach was drowned in coffee and swollen with beer; nobody was hungry now. Other wives were arriving, and

there was some whispering when La Levaque came in behind
La Maheude and accompanied by Bouteloup, who was leading Achille and Désirée, Philomène's children, by the hand.
The two women seemed to be getting on quite well, one
turning around and talking to the other. They had had it all
out on the way, and La Maheude had resigned herself to
Zacharie's marriage; she was desperate at the idea of losing
her eldest's wages, but she had to admit that she could no
longer keep them without injustice. Though she tried to put a
good face on it, her heart was anxious, and as a housekeeper,
she was wondering how she would make both ends meet now
that the major part of her income was about to disappear.

"Sit there," she said to her neighbor, pointing at a table
near the one at which Maheu sat drinking with Etienne and
Pierron.

"Isn't my husband with you?" asked La Levaque.

The men told her he would be back soon. All of them,
including Bouteloup and the children, were so bunched together, so squeezed in by the crush of drinkers, that the two
tables seemed to be one. They ordered beers. Catching sight
of her mother and her children, Philomène decided to join
them. She accepted a chair and seemed pleased to learn that
she was finally to be married, and when Zacharie was asked
for, she said in her soft voice:

"I'm waiting for him. He's around somewhere."

Maheu had exchanged glances with his wife. Had she
really consented? He grew quiet and smoked in silence. He
too was caught up in the fear of tomorrow, and he brooded
about the ingratitude of these children who got married, one
after the other, and left their parents in wretched poverty.

People were still dancing. The end of a quadrille clouded
the dance hall in red dust; the walls were bulging, a cornet
was screeching like a locomotive in distress, and when the
dancers stopped they were steaming like horses.

"Do you remember," said La Levaque, leaning over to
speak into La Maheude's ear, "how you talked about strangling Catherine if she played the fool?"

Chaval had brought Catherine back to the family table and
the two of them, standing behind Maheu, were finishing their
beers.

"Bah," La Maheude mumbled, seemingly resigned. "It's
just one of those things people say. . . . The one thing that
keeps me from worrying is that she can't have a baby—of
that I'm sure! . . . Why, if she were to have a child and I had
to marry her off—how would we ever eat?"

Now the cornet was screeching out a polka, and as the

tumult started up again, Maheu quietly told his wife about an idea he had. Why not take a boarder? Etienne, for example. He was looking for a place, and now that Zacharie was going to leave they'd have the room. The money they'd lose on the one hand they'd partly make up on the other. La Maheude's face brightened: why not? It was a good idea, they'd have to arrange it. Once again she seemed to have been saved from starvation, and her spirits were so sharply revived that she ordered another round of beers.

Meanwhile, Etienne was trying to indoctrinate Pierron, to whom he was explaining his idea about an emergency fund. He had just got him to promise to join when he imprudently let slip his true purpose.

"And you can see how useful the fund will be if we go on strike. We can tell the Company to go to hell—for the first time we'll have a fund that will allow us to fight back. . . . Well, what do you say? Are you with us?"

Pierron lowered his eyes and paled. He stuttered:

"I'll think about it. . . . But behaving is the best insurance of all."

Then Maheu got hold of Etienne and without beating about the bush frankly proposed that he come and board with them. The young man accepted immediately, since he very much wanted to live in the village and be closer to his fellow-workers. It was all settled in a few words, La Maheude adding that they would wait until after the children had married.

Just then Zacharie finally returned with Mouquet and Levaque. All three brought with them the odors of the Volcan—gin on their breaths and the bitter smell of cheap whores. They were very drunk and very pleased with themselves, poking each other in the ribs and snickering. When he found out that he was at last to be married, Zacharie laughed so hard he began to choke, at which Philomène philosophically declared she'd rather see him laugh than cry. There were no more chairs, so Bouteloup made room for Levaque on his, and the latter was so touched at seeing the whole family together that he ordered still another round of beers.

"Hell, we don't have fun like this very often!" he thundered.

They stayed until ten o'clock. Wives kept coming in to find their husbands and take them home, troops of children followed along behind them, mothers unconcernedly exposed breasts as long and pale as sacks of oats and daubed their chubby little babies with milk, and children old enough to walk, bulging with beer and crawling on all fours under the

tables, relieved themselves without shame. It was a rising tide
of beer; the widow Désir's barrels were broached, beer
swelled bellies and flowed from everywhere—noses and eyes
and elsewhere too. Everybody had so blown up that each one
had an elbow or a knee shoved into a neighbor, and the
contact seemed only to amuse and excite them. Every mouth
was open in a continuous ear-to-ear laugh. Since it was as
hot as an oven, everybody made himself comfortable by
stripping down to the flesh, a flesh browned by the thick
smoke of pipes; and the only problem was when you had to go
outside for a minute. Every once in a while one of the girls
would get up and go to the rear, near the pump, hike up her
skirts for a minute, then go back. Under the garlands of
colored paper the dancers were sweating so much that they
could no longer see each other, and this encouraged the mine
boys to knock over the haulage girls with a sudden thrust of
their hips. But when one of the wenches fell with a man on
top of her, the cornet would cover their fall with its mad
tooting, and the thumping feet would roll them around until
they felt as though the whole dance hall had fallen on top of
them.

Somebody stopped by and told Pierron that his daughter
Lydie was sleeping outside, sprawled across the pavement.
Her share of the stolen bottle had made her drunk, and he
had to carry her home in his arms while Jeanlin and Bébert,
steadier on their legs, followed in the distance, finding it all
very funny. This broke the party up; families began to leave
the Bon Joyeux, and the Maheus and the Levaques decided
to return to the village. Bonnemort and Old Mouque left at
the same time, both with the same sleepwalker's step and
both still sunk in the silence of their memories. They all went
back together, going through the fair for a last time, past the
kettles of congealing oil, past the bars from which the last
mugs of beer were running down in streams to the middle of the road. The storm was still threatening, and the
sound of laughter rose as soon as they had left behind the
lighted houses and disappeared into the dark countryside. A
breath of passion swept from the ripening wheat; many
children must have been planted that night. At last they
straggled into the village. Neither the Levaques nor the
Maheus ate with much appetite, and the latter fell asleep
over their morning's boiled beef.

Etienne had taken Chaval to Rasseneur's for another
drink.

"Count me in!" said Chaval, when Etienne had explained
the emergency fund to him. "Shake! You're all right!"

The first signs of drunkenness were blazing from Etienne's eyes, and he shouted:

"That's right, let's not argue. . . . I tell you, drink and women mean nothing to me alongside the idea of justice. There's only one thing that warms my heart—the thought that we're going to crush the bosses!"

3

In the middle of August, Zacharie, now a married man, was able to obtain from the Company a vacant house in the village for Philomène and their two children, and Etienne moved in with the Maheus. At first he found Catherine's presence somewhat embarrassing.

They lived in constant intimacy; he replaced the elder brother everywhere, even to the extent of sharing Jeanlin's bed, which stood in front of his big sister's. Going to bed, getting up, he had to undress and then re-dress right next to her, had to see her as she herself took off or put on her clothes. When the last petticoat would fall, she would stand revealed in her pale whiteness—the transparent, snowy whiteness of anemic blondes—and he was always troubled by it; though her hands and face were spoiled, the rest of her looked as if she had been dipped in milk from her heels right up to her neck, where a line of roughened skin cut across like an amber necklace. He would pretend to look away, but little by little he began to know her: first her feet, which his lowered eyes could see, then a flash of knee as she used to slide under the cover, then her small, firm breasts when she would bend over the washbasin in the morning. As for her, without looking at him, she would hurry as fast as she could, and in ten seconds was undressed and stretched out beside Alzire—a movement so supple and snakelike that he had hardly taken his shoes off before she had disappeared, turning her back and showing nothing more than her heavy knot of hair.

Actually, she never had any reason to be angry with him. If, in spite of himself, a kind of obsession made him watch for the moment when she got into bed, he nevertheless avoided any pleasantries and prudently kept his hands to himself. Her parents were there, and besides, his feeling for her was one of both friendship and bitterness; he could not

treat her as a man treats the girl he desires despite the fact
that the life they shared was such a promiscuous one: they
washed together, ate together, worked together, and nothing
about either of them remained a secret to the other, not even
their most intimate needs. The family's entire sense of modesty was now confined to the daily bath, which the girl took
alone in the upstairs room while the men, one after the
other, bathed below. And by the end of the first month they
no longer seemed to see each other when they moved about
the room, undressed, before blowing out the candle. She no
longer hurried, and had gone back to her old habit of doing
up her hair as she sat on the edge of the bed—her arms in
the air, her chemise raised to her thighs; he, with his trousers
already off, would sometimes help her search for the pins she
had dropped. Habit killed all shame at being naked, and they
found it natural, for they weren't doing anything wrong—and
anyway, it wasn't their fault if there was only one room for
everybody. And yet, at moments when they were thinking of
nothing shameful, they would suddenly become troubled.
After not having paid any attention to the paleness of her
body for many evenings, he would once again notice her
whiteness, a whiteness that would send a shiver through him
and make him turn around lest he give way to the desire to
have her. On other evenings, for no apparent reason, it was
she who would be overcome by modesty and slip between the
sheets as if she had felt his hands seize her. Then, once the
candle was out, they would both realize that they wouldn't
sleep, that in spite of their fatigue they were thinking of each
other. The experience would leave them disturbed and sullen
all the next day; they preferred the quiet evenings when they
could be comfortable with each other, like friends.

Etienne had nothing to complain about except Jeanlin,
who slept all curled up like a hunting dog. Alzire breathed
softly, and Lénore and Henri were found in the morning
just as they had been put to bed, in each other's arms. In the
darkened house there was no noise but the snores of Maheu
and his wife, rolling out at regular intervals like a black-
smith's bellows. All in all, Etienne was better off than he had
been at Rasseneur's—the bed wasn't bad and the sheets were
changed once a month. The soup was better too, though he
suffered from a lack of meat. But they were all in the same
boat, and he could hardly expect to have rabbit at every
meal for his forty-five francs. Those forty-five francs helped
the family, and by leaving some small debts unpaid they were
finally able to make both ends meet. As a result, the Maheus
showed themselves grateful to their boarder—his clothes

were washed and mended, his buttons resewn, and all his
things kept in order; in short, he felt himself enveloped by a
woman's care and attention.

It was during this period that Etienne began to understand
more clearly some of the ideas that had been vaguely buzzing
about in his brain. Until then, surrounded by the confused
ferment among his fellow-workers, he had merely felt an
instinct to rebel, but now he became aware of muddled
questions working in him: why poverty for some? why
wealth for others? why the former under the heel of the
latter without the hope of ever being able to exchange
places? His first step had been to realize his own ignorance.
Since then, a secret shame, a hidden grief, gnawed at him: he
knew nothing, so he didn't dare talk about the things that
moved him most—the equality of all men and the justice that
called for a sharing among them of the goods of the earth.
As a result, he was gripped by the uneducated man's methodless passion for study. He was now corresponding regularly
with Pluchart, who was better educated than he and deeply
involved with the Socialist movement. He was sending for
books, the badly digested reading of which added to his
fervor—especially *The Health of the Miner,* a work on
medicine in which a Belgian doctor listed all the diseases the
mining population was dying of. But there were also works
on political economy, so technically arid as to be incompre-
hensible; anarchist pamphlets that overwhelmed him, and old
issues of newspapers that he kept as irrefutable proofs for
possible future discussions. In addition, Souvarine was lending
him some books, and one volume, on cooperative societies,
had set him dreaming for a whole month about a universal
system of exchange in which money would be abolished and
the functioning of society based on the value of work itself.
As he felt himself beginning to think, the shame of his
ignorance left him, and in its place came a sense of pride.

During these first months Etienne remained at the level of
the fervent neophyte; his heart overflowed with noble indignation against the oppressors and strained toward the hope of
the coming triumph of the oppressed. All his random reading
had not yet led him to construct his own system; within him
Rasseneur's practical demands were warring with Souvarine's
demands for destructive violence, and when he left L'Avantage, where everyone met almost every day to rail against the
Company, he would walk about as though in a dream, seeing
visions of the radical regeneration of nations brought about
without so much as a broken window or a drop of blood. For
that matter, the means of achieving all this remained ob-

scure; his head began to ache as soon as he tried to formu-
late a program, and he preferred to believe that things would
work out well on their own. He even showed himself to be
illogically moderate, sometimes saying that politics should be
banished from the social problem—a phrase he had read
somewhere and which seemed a good thing to say to the
phlegmatic miners among whom he lived.

Every evening now the Maheus would spend a half hour
talking before going up to bed, and Etienne always took up
the same theme. Now that his sensitivities were becoming
more defined, he was increasingly offended by the promiscui-
ties of the village. Were they animals to be penned up this
way, one against the other in the middle of the fields, so
heaped together that they couldn't change their clothes without showing their bottoms to their neighbors? It wasn't
healthy, and how corrupt it made the boys and girls who had
to grow up like that!

"Of course," Maheu would reply, "if we had more money
we'd be more comfortable. . . . But all the same, it's true that
it's not good for anybody to live one on top of the other. It
always ends with drunken men and pregnant girls."

And this would set the family off, each one having to have
his say while the oil lamp further fouled the air of the room,
which already reeked of fried onions. No, life wasn't very
amusing. You worked like a dumb beast at a job that used to
be punishment for galley slaves in the old days, more often
than not you kicked off before your time, and for all that you
didn't even have meat for your evening meal. True, you did
get some slop, you did eat—but very little, just enough so
you could suffer without actually dying, crushed by debts and
hounded as if you had stolen your bread. When Sunday came
around you slept from exhaustion. The only pleasures left
were to get drunk or to make your wife pregnant—and even
then the beer gave you a pot belly, and the child grew up and
didn't give a damn about you. No, no, there was nothing very
amusing about it.

Then La Maheude would put in:

"The worst thing is when you have to admit that things
will never change. When you're young and keep imagining
that you'll be happy, you keep hoping for things, but then the
misery always begins all over again and you stay caught in it.
. . . I don't wish anybody any harm, but there are times when
this injustice is too much for me."

A silence would fall and for a moment they would all
breathe heavily, vaguely uneasy at the thought of this sealed
horizon. Only Old Bonnemort, if he was there, would open

his eyes in surprise, because in his day you didn't worry yourself like this: you were born in the coal and you tore away at the vein without asking for anything else—but now there was something in the air that made the miners more ambitious.

"There's no point in spitting on things you're stuck with," he would murmur. "A good beer is a good beer. . . . The bosses are often bastards, but there'll always be bosses, won't there? It's a waste of time to knock yourself out thinking about it."

Then Etienne would become excited. What, weren't the workers to be allowed to think? Why, things were going to change just *because* the workers were finally thinking. In the old man's day a miner lived in the mine like an animal, like a coal-extracting machine—always underground, his ears and his eyes shut to what was going on outside. And that was why the rich people who ran things could agree among themselves so easily, could buy him and sell him and gobble him up alive: he never even suspected anything. But now the miner was waking up down there; he was germinating in the earth just like a real seed, and one day you'd see what would spring up in these fields: men would spring up—yes, an army of men who would reestablish justice. Weren't all citizens equal since the Revolution? Well, if all men could vote, why should the workers remain the slaves of the bosses who paid them? The big companies and their machines were crushing everything, and you didn't even have the security you had in the old days, when people in the same trade united in guilds and knew how to defend themselves. By God, that was why—and for other reasons, too—everything would blow up some day, thanks to education. You had only to look around the village: the grandfathers hadn't been able to sign their names, the fathers were already able to, and as for the sons, they could read and write like professors. Oh yes, it was growing—little by little a hardy crop of men was growing and ripening in the sun! Now that they didn't have to be stuck in one place for their whole lives, now that they could hope to take their neighbor's place, why shouldn't they use their fists and try to be the strongest?

Maheu, though deeply stirred, remained suspicious.

"As soon as you try anything they give you back your work book," he said. "The old man's right. The miner will always suffer, and without even the hope of some meat now and then as a reward."

La Maheude, who had been quiet for some time, seemed to shake off a dream.

"At least if what the priests said was true—if the poor of this world will be the rich of the next."

She was interrupted by a burst of laughter, and even the children shrugged their shoulders. Up here, in the open air, they were all unbelievers; though they were secretly afraid of ghosts when they were down in the mine, they mocked at the empty heavens.

"Oh, the priests!" exclaimed Maheu. "If they really believed all that, they'd eat less and work more, to reserve a good place for themselves up there. . . . No, when you're dead you're dead."

La Maheude sighed heavily.

"Oh my God, oh my God!"

Then, with her hands on her knees and an air of utter despair:

"So it's true, there's no hope for us."

They would all look at each other. Old Bonnemort would spit into his handkerchief, Maheu would let his extinguished pipe hang forgotten from his mouth. Alzire, sitting between Lénore and Henri, asleep at the edge of the table, would listen. But it was Catherine, her chin resting on her hands, who never took her bright eyes off Etienne while he protested, proclaimed his faith, and held up to them a vision of the enchanted future of his dream society. Around them the village would be going to bed, and the only sound would be the faint weeping of a child or the loud arguments of a drunk getting home late. Inside the room the cuckoo would tick slowly, and a cool dampness would rise from the sanded flagstones into the stuffy heat.

"And that's another silly idea," said the young man. "Why do you have to have God and his paradise to be happy? Can't you make your own happiness here on earth?"

His passionate voice went on endlessly, and suddenly the sealed horizons would open up and light would stream into the somber lives of these poor people. The eternally recurrent misery, the animal-like work, the destiny of a beast that gives its wool and then is slaughtered—all this misfortune disappeared, as if swept away by a burst of sunlight, and justice descended from the sky in a fairylike dazzle. Since God was dead, justice would ensure men's happiness by setting up the rule of equality and fraternity. One day a new society would spring up, as in their dreams—a tremendous city, as splendid as a mirage, in which every citizen lived by his labor and had his share in the common joys. The old, rotten world would have fallen into dust; humanity, reborn and purged of its crimes, would make up a single nation of workers, having for its motto: To each according to his worth, and his worth according to his work. And the dream kept expanding, growing more and more beautiful and more and more seductive as it soared higher and higher into the impossible.

At first La Maheude, gripped by an undefinable fear, had refused to listen. No, no, it was too beautiful; you shouldn't give yourself up to these ideas—they made life too unbearable, and then you'd do anything for a chance at such happiness. When she saw Maheu disturbed, then won over, a light shining in his eyes, she would become upset and interrupt Etienne, exclaiming:

"Don't listen, husband! You can see he's only telling fairy tales. Do you think the bosses will ever agree to work the way we do?"

But little by little the charm of it would begin to affect her too. She would end by smiling, her imagination awakened, on the threshold of a marvelous world of hope. It was so wonderful to forget the sad reality for a little while! When you live like an animal, your head bent to the earth, you've got to have a little corner of dreams, where you can relax by treating yourself to things you know you will never have. And what really excited her, what finally put her in agreement with the young man, was the idea of justice.

"Ah, there you're right!" she cried. "If something's just, I'll let myself be hacked to bits for it. ... And it would certainly be just for us to have our turn at enjoying life."

At this Maheu dared to let himself go.

"Damn it, I'm not rich, but I'd gladly give a hundred sous to see this happen before I die! ... What a blow-up! Will it be soon? How do we go about it?"

Etienne would begin to talk again. The old society was cracking; it couldn't last more than a few more months, he would affirm categorically. He was a bit more vague about the ways and means, jumbling up all his reading and not hesitating, since he was dealing with uneducated people, to launch into explanations in which he himself lost the thread. All the various theories were thrown in, softened by his certainty of an easy victory and the universal embrace that would end this misunderstanding between the classes—though of course there would probably be some stubborn ones among the bosses and the bourgeois who might have to be forced to see reason. And the Maheus would seem to understand, approve, and accept these miraculous solutions with the blind faith of converts, like those Christians, in the first days of the Church, who expected the perfect society to be

born on the dump heap of the ancient world. Little Alzire
would catch an occasional word, and happiness appeared to
her in the form of a warm house in which children played
and ate as much as they wanted. Catherine, without moving,
chin still in hand, would keep her eyes fixed on Etienne, and
when he fell silent she would tremble and go all pale, as if
suddenly chilled.

But La Maheude would look at the cuckoo clock.

"It's after nine! We'll never be able to get up tomorrow
morning."

And the Maheus would leave the table, their hearts heavy
and sunk in despair. It seemed to them that they had just
been rich, and now they had once again dropped into their
dung. Old Bonnemort would leave for the mine, grumbling
that none of this talk made the soup any better, while the
others went upstairs one behind the other, terribly aware of
the damp walls and the stifling, poisonous air. Upstairs, with
the rest of the village already deep in heavy sleep, Catherine,
the last one to get into bed, would blow out the candle, and
Etienne would hear her tossing about feverishly before falling
asleep.

Neighbors would often join these sessions: Levaque, who
was enthusiastic at the idea of sharing; Pierron, who prudently left for bed as soon as the Company came under attack;
sometimes Zacharie, who was bored by politics and who
preferred to go to L'Avantage for a beer; and Chaval, who
went further than the others and even called for blood. He
would spend an hour at the Maheus' almost every evening,
his constancy owing much to an unacknowledged jealousy, a
fear that Catherine might be taken from him. This girl, of
whom he was already beginning to tire, had become more
dear to him now that a man slept near her and could take
her during the night.

Etienne's influence kept growing, and he was gradually
revolutionizing the village. His was an undercover propaganda that gained in effectiveness as he grew in everybody's
esteem. As a prudent housewife, La Maheude distrusted his
ideas, but she gave him the special consideration due a young
man who always paid her on time, who neither drank nor
gambled, and who always had his nose buried in a book. She
built up his reputation with the neighbors as an educated
man, and they took advantage of this by asking him to write
their letters for them. He became a sort of advisor on all
business matters, taking care of correspondence and consulted by the various households on delicate matters. As a
result, by September he had been able to set up his much

talked-about emergency fund. It was still somewhat shaky, for it included only the people of the village, but he hoped to get the men from all the other mines to join—especially if the Company remained passive and didn't interfere any more than it had. He had been named secretary of the association and was even paid a small sum for keeping the books; as a result, he was almost rich. A married miner could not make both ends meet, but a serious-minded bachelor with no one dependent on him could even manage to save a bit.

From that time on, a slow change took place in Etienne. His innate vanity and love of comfort, lulled during his period of poverty, were aroused, and spurred him to buy some good clothes. He treated himself to a pair of fine boots, and this immediately qualified him for a position of leadership; the whole village looked up to him. His ego delighted in it, and these first experiences with popularity intoxicated him: to be a leader of others, to command—he who was so young and who only yesterday had been a laborer—filled him with pride and bolstered his dream of a coming revolution in which he would play an important part. His very face changed, and he became serious, impressed with the sound of his own voice; his newborn ambition fired his theories and led him to more militant ideas of battle.

But meanwhile autumn was upon them and the October frosts had blasted the village's kitchen gardens. The mine boys were no longer tumbling the haulage girls on top of the rabbit hutches behind the scraggly lilac bushes, and there were only a few winter vegetables left: cabbages pearled with white frost, leeks, and pickling vegetables. Once again the rains were beating down on the red tiles, streaming into the barrels under the rainpipes with a torrential roar. Inside the houses the stoves never had a chance to cool, but were constantly fed with coal, poisoning the closed rooms. Another season of poverty and misery was beginning.

On one of these first frosty October nights Etienne, over-excited by what he had spoken of downstairs, couldn't fall asleep. He had watched Catherine slide under the cover, then blow out the candle. She too seemed restless, tormented by one of those occasional surges of modesty that made her hurry so awkwardly that she only exposed even more of herself. In the darkness she lay as though dead, but he could sense that she was not asleep either and that she was thinking of him just as he was thinking of her: this mute exchange between them had never before so troubled them. Minutes slipped by; neither of them moved, and despite their efforts at control, their breathing became more awkward. Twice he

was on the point of getting up and taking her. It was stupid
for them to want each other so much and never satisfy their
desire. Why should they fight against it so stubbornly? The
children were asleep, and she was quite willing; he was sure
that she was waiting, all choked up, and that she would
silently enclose him in her arms, her teeth clenched. Almost
an hour went by. He did not go to her and she did not turn
around, fearful lest she seem to be calling to him. The longer
they lived together, the higher grew the barrier of shame, of
repugnance, of scruples of friendship that they would not
have been able to explain even to themselves.

4

"Listen," said La Maheude to her husband, "since you're
going to Montsou for your pay, bring me back a pound of
coffee and two pounds of sugar."

He was restitching one of his shoes in order to save the
cost of having it repaired.

"All right," he mumbled, without looking up from his
work.

"And I'd also like you to stop at the butcher's. . . . How
about a bit of veal? We haven't had any for a long time."

This time he raised his head.

"Do you think I'm going to get hundreds of thousands?
There won't be much money this pay period, what with their
damn idea of stopping work all the time."

It was after lunch on a Saturday at the end of October.
Using as an excuse the fact that payday upset work routines,
the Company had once more suspended extraction operations
in all its mines for the day. Panic-stricken by the growing
industrial crisis, not wanting to augment its already heavy
stockpiles, it took advantage of the slightest pretext to force
its ten thousand workers into idleness.

"Etienne's waiting for you at Rasseneur's, you know," La
Maheude went on. "Take him along with you. He'll be
cleverer than you about arguing with them if they don't give
you credit for the right number of hours."

Maheu nodded in agreement.

"And talk to them about this business with your father.
The doctor does whatever the Company wants him to. . . .

The doctor's wrong, though, isn't he, old man? You can still work, can't you?"

For the past ten days Old Bonnemort, his "paws," as he put it, swollen, had been more or less nailed to his chair. She had to repeat her question before he grumbled:

"Of course I can still work. A man isn't finished just because he has a little trouble with his legs. It's just an excuse they've made up so they won't have to give me my hundred and eighty franc pension."

La Maheude thought about the forty sous the old man might never bring in again, and she uttered an anguished cry:

"My God, we'll all soon be dead if this keeps up!"

"At least when you're dead you're not hungry anymore," said Maheu.

He hammered a few more nails into his shoes and decided to leave. Village 240 would not be paid until about four o'clock, so the men were in no hurry; dawdling, they set off one by one, their wives calling out to them to come right back. Many women gave their husbands errands to keep them from spending too much time in the bars.

Etienne had gone to Rasseneur's for news. There were some disturbing rumors—the Company was said to be more and more dissatisfied with the timbering. The workers were being loaded with fines, and a conflict seemed inevitable. But this was only the acknowledged cause, a screen for the underlying network of other, more secret and serious issues.

As a matter of fact, when Etienne had come in, one of the men who had just returned from Montsou was drinking a beer and talking about an announcement that had been posted at the paymaster's—but he was not quite sure what the announcement really said. Another man came in, then a third, and each one told a different story. It seemed clear, however, that the Company had come to some decision.

"What do you think about all this?" asked Etienne, sitting down next to Souvarine at a table on which, instead of a glass, there was only a package of tobacco.

Without haste the engineman finished rolling a cigarette.

"I think it could easily have been foreseen. They're going to push you to the wall."

He was the only one with enough understanding to analyze the situation, and he explained it in his usual quiet way. The Company was in the grip of a crisis and had to reduce expenses if it didn't want to go under, and naturally, it would be the workers who would have to pull in their belts; the Company would invent any sort of excuse to chip away at their wages. For two months the coal had been piling up in

the yards because the factories were shut down. Since the
Company didn't dare shut down too—an idle plant could be
ruinous—it was trying to think of some middle course,
maybe a strike, by means of which the miners would emerge
tamed, and less well paid. It was also worried by the new
emergency fund, which was becoming a threat to the future;
a strike would eliminate that threat by using up the fund
while it was still small.

Rasseneur had sat down beside Etienne, and they were
both listening with a worried air. They could speak freely
because nobody was there but Madame Rasseneur, who was
sitting behind the counter.

"What an idea!" muttered the innkeeper. "Why should they
bother with that? The Company has nothing to gain from a
strike and neither have the workers. The best thing would be
to come to some agreement."

It was a sensible idea. He was always in favor of reasonable demands. In fact, ever since his former boarder's rapid
rise to popularity, he had carried his theory of progress
within what was possible to the point of declaring that you
didn't get anything at all if you wanted everything at once.
His fat man's beer-nourished good nature was being eaten
away by a secret jealousy, aggravated by the fact that the
men from Le Voreux seemed to have deserted his bar,
coming less frequently to drink and to listen to him hold
forth; and sometimes, forgetting his old bitterness at having
been fired, he even defended the Company.

"So you're against a strike?" cried Madame Rasseneur
from her seat.

And when he emphatically answered yes, she shut him up.

"You're spineless! Let these gentlemen talk."

Etienne was thinking, his eyes fixed on the beer she had
brought him. Finally he raised his head.

"Everything our friend says is very possible, and we'll have
to make up our minds about this strike if it comes to that.
. . . As a matter of fact, Pluchart has written me about this in
his letters. He's also against a strike, because the worker
suffers from it as much as the boss, and he doesn't accomplish anything decisive by it. The only thing is that he sees it
as a good opportunity of convincing our men to join up with
him. . . . Look, here's his letter."

Pluchart, discouraged by the suspicion the International
was meeting with from the Montsou miners, did indeed hope
they would join en masse if a conflict obliged them to line up
against the Company. Despite his efforts, Etienne had not
been able to sign up a single member—though it was true

that he used the greater part of his influence for his emergency fund, which had found more favor. But as Souvarine pointed out, the fund was still so meager that it would quickly be exhausted, and then the strikers would have no choice but to join the Association of workers so that their brothers in every country could come to their aid.

"How much is in the fund?" Rasseneur asked.

"Just about three thousand francs," answered Etienne. "And I suppose you know that the management called me in the day before yesterday. Oh, they're very polite—they kept telling me they didn't want to keep their employees from setting up a reserve fund—but I soon saw that they wanted control of it. . . . There's no doubt but what we're in for trouble about that."

Rasseneur had begun to walk up and down, whistling scornfully. Three thousand francs!—what the hell could you do with that? It wouldn't pay for a week's bread, and if you were counting on foreigners, people who lived in England, you might just as well lie down and die right away. No, it was too stupid, this idea of a strike!

Then, for the first time, angry words were exchanged between these two men whose common hatred of capital had always previously led them to end in agreement.

"And you, what do you think?" repeated Etienne, turning toward Souvarine.

The latter answered with his usual word of contempt.

"Strikes? Foolishness!"

Breaking into the angry silence that followed, he added softly:

"Oh, I don't really have anything against it, if your hearts are set on it—one side is ruined, the other is killed off, and there's at least that much cleared away. . . . But at that rate it would take a thousand years to rebuild the world. Why not begin by blowing up this prison in which you're all rotting?"

With his delicate hand he pointed to Le Voreux, whose buildings could be seen through the open door. Then he was interrupted by an unexpected incident: Poland, the fat, tame rabbit, had ventured outside and now came bounding back, fleeing from the stones of a group of mine boys; terrified, her ears flat back and her tail up, she sought refuge between his legs, scratching at him and begging to be picked up. When he had placed her on his lap he cupped his hands around her, and as always, the feel of this soft, warm fur plunged him into a deep reverie.

Almost immediately afterward, Maheu came in. In spite of Madame Rasseneur's polite insistence—she sold her beer as though she were giving it away—he refused a drink. Etienne had jumped to his feet and the two of them left for Montsou.

On Company paydays Montsou had a holiday air—like on a lovely Sunday fair-day. Miners poured in from all the villages, and since the paymaster's office was small, they preferred to wait outside, standing about on the road in groups and blocking the way with a constantly renewed line. Peddlers took advantage of the opportunity and set up their carts, displaying everything from china to pork products, but it was the taverns and inns that did especially well, for the miners went there before being paid, to while away the time, and returned to celebrate as soon as they had pocketed their money. Those who did not go on to the Volcan seemed reasonable comparatively.

That day as Maheu and Etienne passed among the groups of men they sensed a rising anger. There was none of the usual lighthearted atmosphere compounded of money received—and then squandered—in the bars; instead, fists were clenched and angry words were flying from mouth to mouth.

"Then it's true?" Maheu asked Chaval, whom he ran into in front of Piquette's. "They've really done this shitty thing?"

But Chaval merely answered with a furious growl and a sidewise glance at Etienne. Having become more and more jealous of Etienne—this newcomer who had set himself up as a leader and whose boots, he said, were being licked by the whole village—Chaval had joined up with another team when the new contracts were made. The situation was complicated by a lovers' quarrel; he never took Catherine to Réquillart, or behind the slag heap, without accusing her in obscene language of sleeping with her mother's boarder—after which he would exhaust her with the violence of his rekindled savage passion.

Maheu asked him another question.

"Have they started paying the men from Le Voreux yet?"

And since he turned his back on them after having nodded yes, the two men decided to go inside.

The paymaster's office was a small rectangular room cut in two by a grilled partition. Five or six miners were waiting on benches along the walls, while the paymaster, assisted by a clerk, was paying off another, who stood at the window, cap in hand. A yellow bulletin had been pasted up above the bench on the left, its freshness contrasting with the smoky gray of the wall, and since early morning the men had been filing past it. They came in by twos and threes, stood there motionless for a while, then went out without a word, shoulders bowed as if their spines had been broken.

Two miners were standing there now, a young man with a blunt, brutal face, and a very thin old man whose face was besotted by age. Neither knew how to read; the younger one was spelling out the letters while the older one merely looked on stupidly. Many men came in like this, to look even if they couldn't understand.

"Read it to us," Maheu said to Etienne. Reading was not one of *his* strong points either.

Etienne began to read the bulletin aloud. It was a notice from the Company to the men in all its mines, and it announced that in the face of the men's carelessness about timbering, and weary of setting useless fines, it had decided to introduce a new method of payment for the extraction of coal. From now on it would pay for timbering separately—by the cubic yard of wood brought down and used, and taking as a measure the amount necessary for good work. Naturally the price for a cartload of coal would have to be lowered from fifty centimes to forty centimes, but allowance would be made for the nature and the distance of the face. And this was followed by a complicated set of figures intended to establish that the ten-centime cut would be exactly compensated for by the price paid for timbering. The Company also added that in order to allow everybody time to convince himself of the advantages offered by this new method, it would not go into effect until Monday, December 1st.

"How about reading a little lower over there!" shouted the paymaster. "You can't hear yourself think."

Etienne paid no attention to the remark and continued to read. His voice was quivering, and when he had finished, the others continued to stare at the bulletin. The old miner and the young one seemed to be waiting for something more, but then they left, their shoulders drooping.

"Christ!" muttered Maheu.

He and Etienne had sat down. Engrossed, their heads bent, they did some calculations while the parade of men continued to file past the yellow paper. Did the Company think they were fools? The timbering would never make up for the ten centimes lost on each cartful. The most they could make would be eight centimes, and that meant the Company was stealing two centimes from them—without even taking into account the time that careful work would require. So this was what the Company really had in mind—a disguised cut in wages! It was going to save money by taking it out of the miners' pockets.

"Christ!" repeated Maheu, raising his head. "If we let them get away with this we deserve what we'll get!"

But the window was now free, and he went up to be paid. In order to save time, the team leaders were the only ones to present themselves at the paymaster's; they received the money for the whole team and divided it among their men afterward.

"Maheu and team," said the clerk. "Filonnière vein, face number seven."

He checked his lists, which were made up from books in which the foremen entered the number of carts extracted each day by every team, and then repeated:

"Maheu and team, Filonnière vein, face number seven. ... One hundred and thirty-five francs."

The paymaster handed over the money.

"Excuse me, sir," stammered the cutter, dumbfounded. "Are you sure you're not making a mistake?"

An icy shudder pierced his heart; he stared at the small sum of money without picking it up. He had, to be sure, expected a bad pay-period, but it couldn't have come to so little unless he had completely miscalculated. After giving their shares to Zacharie, Etienne, and the man who had replaced Chaval, only fifty francs at most would be left for himself, his father, Catherine, and Jeanlin.

"No, there's no mistake," said the clerk. "You have to deduct for two Sundays and four lay-off days—that leaves only nine working days."

Maheu followed this explanation, doing the arithmetic under his breath: nine days meant about thirty francs for him, eighteen for Catherine, and nine for Jeanlin. As for Old Bonnemort, he had only put in three days. But still, if you added the ninety francs for Zacharie and the two other men, it surely came to more.

"And don't forget the fines," concluded the clerk. "Twenty francs in fines for defective timbering."

The cutter made a despairing gesture. Twenty francs in fines, four lay-off days—well, that was it! And to think that when Old Bonnemort was still working and Zacharie hadn't gotten married, there were some paydays when he had taken home as much as a hundred and fifty francs!

"Well, are you going to take it?" shouted the paymaster impatiently. "You can see there's somebody else waiting. . . . If you don't want it, say so."

As Maheu was about to pick up the money with his large, trembling hand the clerk stopped him.

"Just a minute, I've got your name down here. Toussaint Maheu, right? ... The Company secretary wants to talk to you. Go in, there's nobody with him."

The stunned worker found himself in an office furnished with old mahogany and faded green rep. For the next five minutes he listened to the secretary, a tall, pale man who talked to him across some papers on his desk, without even getting up. But a buzzing noise in his ears kept him from hearing. He vaguely understood that it had to do with his father, whose retirement with a pension of a hundred and fifty francs was being taken under consideration: fifty years old and forty years of service.* Then it seemed to him that the man's voice was becoming colder, harder. It was a reprimand. He was being accused of meddling with politics, and something was said about his boarder and the emergency fund; finally it was suggested that he would be better off not getting mixed up with such nonsense—he who was one of the best workers in the mine. He wanted to protest, but he could only mumble a few disconnected words, twist his cap in his feverish hands, and withdraw, stammering:

"Of course, sir . . . I can assure you, sir . . ."

Outside, when he had found Etienne, who was waiting for him, he exploded:

"What a coward I am! I should have told him off. . . . Not enough money to buy bread, and insults to the bargain! And he's got it in for *you*—he told me the whole village was being corrupted. . . . And what the hell can we do about it?—just take it and say thank you. He's right, it's the best thing to do."

Maheu fell silent, gripped simultaneously by anger and fear. Etienne, in a somber mood, was thinking. Once again they passed through the groups of men blocking the road. The anger was growing, the contained anger of a generally placid people, the grumble of a storm hanging threateningly over this sullen mass. A few who were good at figures had made their calculations, and news of the two centimes won by the Company on the timbering was circulating through the crowd, exciting even the dullest. But more than anything else it was a rage against this disastrous pay-period, the revolt of hunger against lay-offs and fines. They didn't have enough to eat now—what would happen to them if wages were lowered still more? Their anger found voice in the taverns, so parching their gullets that the little money they had received remained on the counters.

---

*Zola's error. On p. 10 Bonnemort says he is fifty-eight, has worked fifty years in the mine, and has two years to go before getting a hundred-and-eighty-franc pension.

Not a word was exchanged between Etienne and Maheu as
they walked from Montsou to the village. When her husband
came in, La Maheude, who was alone with the children, saw
immediately that he was empty-handed.

"Well, you're a nice one!" she said. "What about my coffee
and my sugar and my meat? A little piece of veal wouldn't
have ruined you!"

Strangled by suppressed emotion, he made no answer.
Then, in the heavy face of this man hardened to labor in the
mines, there was a welling up of despair, and large tears fell
like warm rain from his eyes. He had dropped into a chair
and was weeping like a child as he tossed the fifty francs on
the table.

"Take it," he faltered. "Here's what I've got for you. . . .
It's for the work of all of us."

La Maheude looked at Etienne; seeing him silent and
crushed, she too began to cry. How could nine people live on
fifty francs till the next payday? Her eldest had left them and
the old man could no longer move his legs: death stared
them in the face. Alzire threw her arms around her mother,
terrified at seeing her cry. Estelle shrieked, Lénore and
Henri sobbed.

And soon the same cry of misery rose from the entire
village. The men had come home, and each household was
weeping over the calamity of this disastrous payday. Doors
flew open and women rushed out, shouting into the street the
complaints that could not be contained under the roofs of
their sealed houses. A fine rain was falling, but they didn't
feel it; they called to each other from the walks and displayed in the palms of their hands the money they had
received.

"Look! This is what they gave him! They don't give a
damn about anybody, do they?"

"Look at what I've got!—why, I haven't even got enough
to pay for bread till next payday!"

"And what about me? Figure it out—I'll have to sell my
underwear!"

Like the others, La Maheude had also gone outside. A
group had formed around La Levaque, who was shouting the
loudest because her drunkard of a husband hadn't come back
at all, and she knew that much or little, his wages would melt
away at the Volcan. Philomène was watching for Maheu, so
as to keep Zacharie from siphoning off any of his money.
Only La Pierronne seemed calm; that hypocrite Pierron
somehow always managed—nobody knew how—to have
more hours credited in his foreman's book than the other

men. But La Brûlé thought that was shameful of her
son-in-law, and she sided with those who were angriest; gaunt
and straight, she stood in the middle of the group and shook
her fists at Montsou.

"And to think," she shouted, without naming the Hennebeaus, "that this morning I saw their maid go by in a
carriage! . . . Yes, the *cook* in a carriage pulled by two
horses! Going to Marchiennes for some fish, no doubt!"

A clamor rose, the fury broke out again. That white-
aproned maid on her way to the market of a neighboring
village in her master's carriage excited their indignation. Did
they have to have fish even when the workers were dying of
hunger! Well, maybe they wouldn't always have fish; the turn
of the poor would come. And the ideas sown by Etienne took
root and grew in this cry of rebellion. There was an impatience for the promised age of gold, a haste to have their
share of the happiness just beyond the horizon of wretchedness that closed them in like a tomb.

The injustice was becoming intolerable; since the very
bread was being taken from their mouths, they would end by
insisting on their rights. The women especially would have
liked to storm this ideal city of progress immediately—that
city in which there would be no more poor. It was almost
dark, the rain was falling more heavily, but, surrounded by a
band of screaming children, they continued to fill the village
with their tears.

That evening at L'Avantage a strike was decided upon.
Rasseneur no longer fought it, and Souvarine accepted it as a
first step. Etienne summed up the situation in a few words: if
the Company really wanted a strike, a strike is what it would
get.

5

A week passed, and work went on in an atmosphere of
gloom and suspicion brought on by the anticipation of the
approaching conflict.

For the Maheus, the next payday promised to be even
more meager than the last, and La Maheude, in spite of her
moderation and good sense, was becoming more and more
bitter. In addition to everything else, her daughter Catherine
had taken it into her head to sleep away from home one

night! The next morning she had come back from this escapade so worn-out and sick that she hadn't been able to go
to work; she wept and kept saying that it wasn't her fault—
Chaval had made her stay, threatening to beat her if she ran
away. He was madly jealous and wanted to keep her from
going back to Etienne's bed—where, he said, he knew the
family made her sleep. La Maheude was furious; she forbade
her daughter to see such a brute again and talked of going to
Montsou and settling things herself with a slap. But meanwhile it was a day's work lost, and the girl, now that she had
this lover, preferred not to change.

Two days later there was more trouble. On Monday and
Tuesday Jeanlin, supposedly sensibly at work down in Le
Voreux, had gone off on a spree to the marshes and the
forest of Vandame with Bébert and Lydie. He had enticed
them into going with him, and nobody ever knew what
dishonest tricks or precocious games they had been up to. La
Maheude disciplined him firmly—she turned him over her
knee in the very street, right in front of all the horrified brats
of the village. Can you imagine?—her very own children,
who had been costing them a fortune since the day they had
been born and who should now finally be bringing some
money in! And in this outcry there was the memory of her
own harsh childhood—the hereditary poverty that made of
every child in the brood no more than a future breadwinner.

That morning, when the men and the girl had left for the
mine, La Maheude sat up in her bed and said to Jeanlin:

"If you do anything like that again, you little devil, I'll skin
you alive!"

The work at Maheu's new stall was difficult. This part of
the Filonnière vein was so narrow that the cutters, squeezed
in between the wall and the roof, skinned their elbows as
they worked. It was also getting very wet, and they were
afraid there might be a flash flood, one of those sudden
torrents that can break through the rocks and sweep the men
away with its force. The day before, Etienne, withdrawing
his pick after a forceful blow, had received a jet of spring
water in his face; but it was just a warning, and the only
result was that the stall became even wetter and more
unhealthy. Besides, he hardly ever thought about the possibility of accidents; he was as indifferent to danger as the others
were. They all lived in an atmosphere of firedamp, unaware
either of its weight on their eyelids or of the spiderweb veil it
left hanging on their lashes. Only sometimes, when the flames
in their lamps would become paler and bluer, would they
think about it for a moment, and a miner would put his ear

against the vein to listen to the faint hiss of gas—the sound of air bubbling through every crack. But the real danger was in the possibility of landslides, for not only was the timbering defective—it was still slapped together too quickly—but the ground itself was water-soaked and would not hold it.

That day Maheu had had to have the timbering reinforced three times. It was two-thirty and the men were almost ready to go up. Stretched out on his side, Etienne was finishing the loosening of a block when a far-off rumble of thunder shook the whole mine.

"What's that?" he cried, dropping his pick to listen.

He had thought the whole gallery was caving in behind him.

Maheu was already skidding down the sloping face, saying:

"It's a slide. . . . Quick, quick!"

They all scrambled down as fast as they could, swept by a feeling of anxiety for their comrades. The lamps were dancing in their hands as they scurried along the tunnels in a deathly silence, one behind the other, their backs bent as though they were galloping on all fours; without slowing down, they threw back short answers to each other's questions: where was it?—in the stalls? No, it was coming from below!—more likely in the haulage tunnel! When they came to the chimney they dropped inside, falling over each other without worrying about bruises.

Jeanlin, his bottom still red from the beating the day before, had not run away from the mine that day. He was trotting barefoot behind his string of carts, shutting the ventilation doors one after the other; occasionally, when he didn't think he would run into a foreman, he would climb onto the last cart, which was forbidden lest he fall asleep there. But his biggest joy came when the carts were pulled over to let another string go by; without using his lamp, he would sneak up front, where Bébert was holding the reins, give his friend a vicious pinch, then play as many tricks as a mischievous monkey—his yellow hair, big ears, and thin face somehow lit up by his small green eyes that shone in the darkness. Unhealthily precocious, he seemed to have the peculiar intelligence and the swift movements of the incompletely human being, a throwback to animal origins.

In the afternoon Mouque gave the mine boys Bataille, whose tour of duty it was, and at one point, as the horse was panting on a siding, Jeanlin slipped up to Bébert and asked:

"What's the matter with this old nag, stopping short like that? . . . He'll make me break my legs."

Bébert was not able to answer; he had to restrain
Bataille, who was becoming excited at the approach of another train of carts. Even from a distance the horse had
sensed his friend Trompette, for whom he had felt a great
tenderness since the day he had first seen him being unloaded
in the mine. It was a little like the affectionate pity that
might be felt by an old philosopher trying to comfort a
young friend by instilling in him some of his own resignation
and patience, for Trompette was not acclimating himself; he
pulled his carts spiritlessly, his head hanging, blinded by the
darkness and forever mourning the sun. Each time Bataille
met him he would stretch out his neck, snort, and encourage
him with a damp nuzzle.

"Christ!" swore Bébert. "There they go, licking each
other's hides again!"

Then, when Trompette had passed, he answered Jeanlin's
question about Bataille.

"The sly old devil is pretty sharp. . . . When he stops like
that it's because he knows there's trouble ahead—a stone or
a hole—and he takes good care of himself, he doesn't want
to break anything. . . . I don't know what's bothering him
today—when we get to the door he pushes it and then stands
stock still. . . . Did you notice anything?"

"No," said Jeanlin. "But there's a lot of water—I'm up to
my knees in it."

The string of carts started up again. On the next trip, after
having opened the ventilation door with a nudge of his head,
Bataille once again refused to move, standing there whinnying and trembling. At last he made up his mind and shot
ahead.

Jeanlin had closed the door and remained behind. He bent
down to inspect the pool he was wading in, then lifted his
lamp and noticed that the timbers had bent under the constant seepage from a spring. At that moment a cutter named
Berloque, who was known as Chicot, came hurrying up from
his stall on his way to see his wife, who was in labor. He too
stopped and examined the timbering. Then suddenly, just as
the boy was about to run after his cart-train, there was a
deafening crash, and the cave-in had swallowed up both man
and child.

There was a great silence. A thick dust, raised by the
turbulence of the slide, was spreading through the tunnels.
Blinded and choked by it, the miners came down from every
direction, from the farthest stalls, their jiggling lamps barely
lighting the stampede of black men through the deep mole-
tunnels. When the first of them reached the cave-in they

shouted and called out to their comrades. Another group of men had come from the stalls in the opposite direction and were now on the other side of the mound of earth that was obstructing the gallery. It was soon clear that not more than a dozen yards of the roof had collapsed. The damage was not serious. But then a dying groan rose from the rubble and every heart sank.

Bébert, leaving his string of carts, came running up, repeating:

"Jeanlin is under there! Jeanlin is under there!"

Just then Maheu, along with Zacharie and Etienne, came tumbling out of the chimney. In his wild despair, he could only curse.

"Christ! Christ! Christ!"

Catherine, Lydie, and Mouquette, who had also come running up, began to sob, to wail with horror, in the terrifying chaos intensified by the darkness. The men tried to quiet them, but they were hysterical and only shrieked the louder at every groan.

The foreman Richomme had also raced to the scene, miserable because neither the engineer Négrel nor Dansaert was in the mine. He pressed his ear against the rocks and listened, finally announcing that the groans were not those of a child—there was a man there, for sure. Maheu had already called out Jeanlin's name many times, but there was not even a whisper of sound. The boy must have been squashed flat.

And still the monotonous groaning continued. They spoke to the dying man and asked his name, but the only reply was another groan.

"Hurry," Richomme, who had already organized the rescue operation, kept repeating. "We'll talk about it later."

With pick and shovel the miners attacked the cave-in from both sides. Chaval was shoveling in silence alongside Maheu and Etienne, while Zacharie saw to the removal of the excavated earth. It was past quitting time and none of them had eaten, but there was no going off to eat while comrades were in danger. However, it did occur to some of them that the village would be worried if nobody came back, and it was suggested that the women be sent home. But neither Catherine nor Mouquette nor even Lydie wanted to leave; riveted in place by the need to know, they stayed and helped clear the rubble. Finally Levaque agreed to go up and explain the cave-in as being just some small damage that had to be repaired. It was almost four o'clock; in less than an hour the men had done the equivalent of a day's work: half the rubble would already have been removed if more rocks had not

fallen from the roof. Maheu was working with such a stubborn fury that he had only a terrible gesture of refusal for
the person who offered to relieve him for a while.

"Careful," said Richomme at last. "We're almost there. . . .
We don't want to finish them off."

And in truth the groaning was becoming more and more
distinct. It was this unceasing sound that was guiding the
diggers, and now it seemed to be right under their picks.
Suddenly it stopped.

They looked at one another in silence, shivering with the
sensation of having felt the chill of death in the shadows.
They dug on, soaked in sweat, their muscles tensed to the
breaking point. A foot was uncovered, and from then on they
cleared the rubble away by hand, freeing the limbs one by
one. The head was undamaged. The lamps lit it, and the
name of Chicot passed from mouth to mouth. He was still
warm; his spine had been broken by a rock.

"Wrap him up and put him in a cart," ordered the foreman. "Let's get the boy now—hurry!"

Maheu struck a final blow and an opening appeared; they
were in communication with the men who were digging on
the other side. They shouted that they had just come upon
Jeanlin—unconscious, both legs broken, but still breathing. It
was the father who carried the boy in his arms; his jaws were
clenched and he still said nothing but "Christ"—a word into
which he poured all his grief. Catherine and the other women
began to shriek again.

The procession was quickly formed. Bébert had brought
back Bataille, who was harnessed to the two carts: in the
first lay the body of Chicot, supported by Etienne; in the
second sat Maheu, holding on his lap the unconscious Jeanlin, covered by a piece of cloth torn from a ventilation door.
They started walking. On each cart a lamp was shining like a
red star. Behind the carts followed the line of miners, some
fifty shadowy figures in Indian file. Overwhelmed with exhaustion, they were dragging their feet, slipping in the mud,
as balefully mournful as a herd of cattle stricken by an
epidemic. It took almost half an hour to reach the loading
platform—an underground funeral procession endlessly winding through the thick darkness of galleries that forked,
turned, circled, advancing without end.

Richomme had gone on ahead to the loading platform and
given orders for an empty cage to be held ready. Pierron
quickly loaded the two carts. Maheu remained in one with
his injured son on his knees, while in the other Etienne had to
hold Chicot's corpse steady in his arms. When everyone else

had piled into the other compartments the cage mounted. It took two minutes. The water streaming from the casing was very cold, and the men looked up, impatient to see daylight again.

Luckily, the mine boy sent to Dr. Vanderhagen had found him at home and brought him back. Jeanlin and the dead man were carried into the foremen's room, where a large fire was kept burning all year round. The buckets of hot water put out for footwashing were set aside, two mats were spread on the floor, and the man and the boy were laid upon them. Only Etienne and Maheu went in. Outside, the haulage girls, the miners, and the boys who had come running were all standing in a group and speaking in whispers.

As soon as the doctor had taken one look at Chicot, he murmured:

"He's had it. . . . You can wash him."

Two inspectors undressed and then sponged down the coal-blackened corpse, still damp with the sweat of work.

"His head's all right," continued the doctor, kneeling on Jeanlin's mattress. "So's his chest. . . . Ah—he got it in the legs."

He himself undressed the child, unfastening the cap, removing the jacket, pulling off the trousers and shirt with the skill of a nurse. And the poor little body appeared, insect-thin, coated with black dust and yellow earth, marbled with bloodstains. The doctor could make nothing out, so Jeanlin too had to be washed. He seemed to get thinner under the sponge, and his flesh was so pale, so transparent, that the bones showed through. It was pitiful to see—this final degenerate offshoot of a wretched race, this little bit of suffering flesh, half-crushed by the weight of the rocks. When he was clean they saw the bruises on his thighs, two red blotches on the white skin.

Coming out of his faint, Jeanlin whimpered. Maheu was standing at the foot of the mat, his arms hanging at his sides, and looking at him; large tears rolled down his cheeks.

"Oh, so you're the father?" asked the doctor, raising his head. "Don't cry, you can see he isn't dead. . . . You'd do better to help me."

He found two simple fractures, but he was worried about the right leg: it would undoubtedly have to be amputated.

Just then the engineer Négrel and Dansaert, who had finally been informed, came in with Richomme. Négrel listened to the foreman's account with a resentful air, then he exploded. Always that damn timbering! Hadn't he told them a hundred times that it would cost lives! And yet the idiots

were talking of going on strike if they were forced to timber
more solidly! And the worst of it was that now the Company
would have to pay for the damage. Monsieur Hennebeau
would certainly be overjoyed!

"Who is it?" he asked Dansaert, who was standing mutely
by while the corpse was being wrapped in a sheet.

"Chicot, one of our best workers," answered the chief
foreman. "He's got three children. . . . Poor bastard!"

Dr. Vanderhagen wanted Jeanlin taken home immediately.
It was six o'clock and already growing dark; they might just
as well take the corpse along too. The engineer gave orders
for a wagon to be made ready and a stretcher to be brought.
The injured child was put on the stretcher, and the corpse
and the mat were loaded into the wagon.

The haulage girls were still standing outside, talking to
some miners who had lingered to get a look. When the door
of the foremen's room opened, the group fell silent. Another
procession was formed—the wagon in front, the stretcher
next, and all the others bringing up the rear. They left the
mine yard and slowly climbed the steep road to the village.
The first frosts of November had denuded the immense plain,
and night was slowly enveloping it like a shroud falling from
the leaden sky.

Etienne softly suggested to Maheu that he send Catherine
on ahead to warn La Maheude and soften the blow. The
father, walking behind the stretcher as if stunned, nodded his
agreement, and since they were almost there, the girl ran
ahead as fast as she could. But the wagon, that well-known
black box, had already been spotted. Women were frantically
rushing out from their houses, and three or four of them,
bareheaded, began to race down the street in anguish. Soon
there were thirty, then fifty, all choked by the same terror.
Had somebody been killed? Who was it? The story told by
Levaque, which had at first reassured them, now threw them
into a nightmare of exaggerated fear: it was no longer one
man who had been killed, but ten, and the wagon would be
bringing them back one by one.

Catherine had found her mother in a state of agitated
foreboding, and at the girl's first stumbling words La Maheude had cried out:

"Your father is dead!"

The young girl protested in vain and tried to tell her about
Jeanlin, but La Maheude had darted out without listening.
Seeing the wagon turn the corner of the church, she had
grown pale and faint. Some of the women, speechless with
shock, stayed at their doors and craned their necks; others

followed the procession, fearfully watching to see at whose house it would stop.

The wagon passed and La Maheude saw Maheu walking behind the stretcher. Then, when the stretcher had been set down at her door, when she saw Jeanlin alive, with his legs broken, she reacted so sharply that she almost choked with rage. Dry-eyed, she stammered:

"So that's it! Now they're crippling our children! . . . Both legs!—my God, what do they expect me to do with him?"

"Quiet!" said Dr. Vanderhagen, who had come along to bandage Jeanlin. "Would you rather he'd been killed down there?"

But La Maheude only stormed the more, while Alzire, Lénore, and Henri wept. Even as she helped carry the injured boy upstairs and gave the doctor what he needed, she was cursing her fate, asking how they expected her to get the money to feed invalids. Wasn't the old man enough? Now the boy was losing his feet too! And she went on and on, while from a nearby house came other cries, lacerating lamentations: Chicot's wife and children were weeping over his body. It was completely dark now, and the exhausted miners were finally eating their soup; a mournful silence, broken only by the loud wailing, had fallen over the village.

Three weeks went by. It had not been necessary to amputate, and Jeanlin would keep both legs—but he would always be lame. After an investigation the Company had resigned itself to a fifty-franc contribution. It had also promised to find the little cripple a job on the surface as soon as he was better. Meanwhile, the family's misery increased, for Maheu had been so shaken by the experience that he fell sick with a high fever.

Today was Sunday, and Maheu had been back at the mine since Thursday. In the evening Etienne talked about the coming December 1st, and was preoccupied with the question of whether or not the Company would carry out its threat. They stayed up till ten o'clock waiting for Catherine, who must have been lingering with Chaval, but she didn't come home. Without saying a word, La Maheude furiously bolted the door. It took Etienne a long time to fall asleep—the empty bed, in which Alzire took up so little space, made him nervous.

The next morning there was still no sign of her, and it was only later in the day, after work, that the Maheus learned that Chaval was keeping Catherine with him. He had made such terrible scenes that she had decided to move in with him. To avoid their complaints he had abruptly left Le

Voreux and taken a job at Jean-Bart, Monsieur Deneulin's
mine, and Catherine followed him there as a haulage girl.
The new couple would continue to live in Montsou, at Piquette's.

At first Maheu talked of punching Chaval and bringing his
daughter back with a few kicks in the rear. Then he
shrugged: why bother? It always ended this way—you
couldn't keep girls from moving in with a man when they
wanted to. The best thing was to wait quietly for the wedding. But La Maheude didn't take it so well.

"Did I ever beat her when she went with Chaval?" she
shouted at Etienne, who was listening to her in silence, very
pale. "Tell me, you're a sensible man. . . . We let her have
her freedom, didn't we?—my God, they all go the same way,
anyway! Take me, for example. I was pregnant when I got
married, but I didn't leave my parents—I would never have
been so indecent as to turn my pay over to a man who didn't
need it while I was still so young. . . . Why, it's disgusting!
People will stop having children!"

And as Etienne merely kept nodding, she went on:

"A girl who went out every night, wherever she wanted to!
What's the matter with her? Couldn't she wait for me to
marry her off after she'd helped us get on our feet? Wouldn't
that have been the right thing to do? After all, you have a
daughter so that she can work. . . . But we were too good to
her. We should never have let her fool around with a man.
Give them an inch and they take a mile."

Alzire was nodding her agreement. Lénore and Henri,
frightened by this storm, were weeping quietly while their
mother proceeded to enumerate the family's misfortunes: first
there was Zacharie, whom they'd had to let get married; then
Old Bonnemort, who sat in his chair with his crippled feet;
then Jeanlin, who wouldn't be able to leave his room for
another two weeks, his bones not properly knit; and now, the
final blow—that tramp Catherine, run off with a man! The
family was coming apart at the seams. Only the father was
left to work at the mine. How were they to live—seven
people not counting Estelle!—on his three francs? They all
might as well throw themselves into the canal.

"There's no point eating your heart out," said Maheu
heavily. "Maybe things will work themselves out."

Etienne, who had been staring at the floor, raised his head;
his eyes were fixed on a vision of the future, and he murmured:

"It's time, by God, it's time!"

Part FOUR

1

That Monday the Hennebeaus were supposed to have the Grégoires and their daughter Cécile to lunch. Plans had also been made for the afternoon: after the meal, Paul Négrel was to take the ladies on a visit to Saint-Thomas, a mine that was being expensively refitted. However, all of this was only an amiable pretext, for Madame Hennebeau had designed the entire project as part of a scheme to hasten the marriage of Cécile and Paul.

Then suddenly, that very Monday, at four o'clock in the morning, the strike had broken out. When the Company had put its new wage system into effect on the 1st of December, the miners had remained calm. Two weeks later, on payday, not one of them had made the least complaint. Everybody, from the manager down to the least important inspectors, thought the new rate had been accepted, and there was thus great surprise at this declaration of war, which was carried out with a strategy and a unanimity that seemed to indicate a strong leadership.

At five o'clock Dansaert woke Monsieur Hennebeau to tell him that not one man had gone down at Le Voreux. Village Number 240, which he had just passed through, was fast asleep, its windows and doors closed. And from the moment the manager had jumped out of bed, his eyes still heavy with sleep, he was deluged with communications: messengers came running in every fifteen minutes, and a hailstorm of dispatches fell onto his desk. At first he hoped that the rebellion was confined to Le Voreux, but with every passing minute the news became worse: Mirou and Crèvecoeur were affected, and so was Madeleine, where only the stablemen had appeared; at La Victoire and Feutry-Cantel, the two best-disciplined mines, only a third of the men had gone down. Only Saint-Thomas seemed to have its full comple-

ment of men and to have remained untouched by the general
movement. Until nine o'clock he dictated dispatches tele-
graphing everywhere—to the prefect of Lille, to the Company
directors, informing the authorities, asking for orders. He
sent Négrel on a tour of the neighboring mines in order to
get precise information.

Suddenly Monsieur Hennebeau remembered the luncheon,
and he was about to send his coachman to tell the Grégoires
that the plans for the afternoon would have to be postponed,
when a hesitation, an inability to come to a decision, stopped
him—he who with a few decisive words had just prepared his
field of battle in the best military fashion. He went up to
Madame Hennebeau and found her in her dressing room,
where a maid was doing her hair.

"Ah, they're on strike," she said calmly, when he had
explained the situation. "Well, what difference does that
make? . . . I assume we're not going to stop eating, are we?"

And she persisted, despite his telling her that the luncheon
would be awkward and the visit to Saint-Thomas impossible.
She had an answer for everything. Why waste a lunch that
was already on the fire? And as for visiting the mine, they
could cancel that later if it really turned out to be unwise.

"Besides," she went on after her maid had left, "you know
why I want to have these good people. This marriage ought
to concern you more than the foolishness of your workers.
. . . In any case, I insist, so please don't argue with me."

A tremor ran through him as he looked at her, and the
stern, cold face of this man of discipline betrayed the secret
pain of a wounded heart. She sat there bare-shouldered,
already overripe, but still dazzling and desirable—a Ceres
gilded by autumn. For a moment he felt a brutal desire to
take her, to roll his head between her exposed breasts, here
in this warm room with its lingering odor of musk, its
emanation of the intimate luxury of a sensual woman, but he
restrained himself; for the past ten years the couple had slept
in separate bedrooms.

"If you insist," he said as he left her. "We'll go ahead as
planned."

Monsieur Hennebeau had been born in the Ardennes, and
he had had the difficult beginnings of the poor young man
thrown as an orphan on the streets of Paris. At twenty-four,
after having just managed to complete his studies at the
School of Mines, he had gone to La Grand-Combe as an
engineer at the Sainte-Barbe mine. Three years later he
became division engineer at the Marles mines in the Pas-de-
Calais, and it was there that he married, by one of those

strokes of fortune that seem so usual among mining engineers, the daughter of a rich spinning-mill owner in Arras. For the next fifteen years the couple lived in the same small provincial town, and nothing happened to break the monotony of their existence, not even the birth of a child. A growing discontent gradually alienated Madame Hennebeau from her husband; brought up to have a respect for money, she was scornful of this husband who worked hard for a mediocre income that provided her with none of the satisfactions to her vanity that she had dreamed of as a schoolgirl. Uncompromisingly honest, he never speculated, and stayed at his post like a soldier. Their disharmony continued to increase, aggravated by one of those peculiar sensual misunderstandings that can cool even the most ardent; he adored his wife, who had the voluptuous appetites of a sensual blonde, yet they were already sleeping apart, awkward with one another and easily wounded. From that time on, though he didn't know it, she had a lover. Finally he left the Pas-de-Calais and went to Paris to take an office job, thinking she would be grateful. But Paris—the Paris she had been longing for from the time she had gotten her first doll—was to complete their separation, for in this Paris she washed off all traces of the provinces within a week and became an elegant woman, caught up in the turmoil of all the luxurious follies of the period. The ten years she spent there were filled by a great passion, a public liaison with a man whose desertion of her nearly killed her. This time her husband had not been able to remain ignorant, and after some terrible scenes he resigned himself to the situation, helpless before the untroubled amorality of this woman who took her pleasure where she found it. It was after the end of this romance, when he saw her sickened with grief, that he had taken the job of managing the Montsou mines, hoping that in this bleak desert of black land he could still reform her.

Since they had been living in Montsou the Hennebeaus had relapsed into the irritated boredom of the early days of their marriage. At first she had seemed soothed by the great quiet; she enjoyed the peace of the unbroken monotony of the immense plain and buried herself like a woman whose life is over, behaving as though her heart were dead and she so uninterested in the world that not even putting on weight bothered her. Then, beneath this indifference, a last fever flamed up, a need to come alive again, which she pacified for six months by redoing and refurnishing to her own taste the small residence assigned to the manager. She said it was dreadful, and filled it with tapestries, bibelots, and a display of artistic luxuries that was talked about as far away as Lille. But now the countryside began to exasperate her; its idiotic fields spreading out to infinity, its everlasting black, treeless roads along which swarmed hideous creatures, both disgusted and frightened her. Lamentations of exile began; she accused her husband of having sacrificed her to a forty-thousand-franc salary, a pittance that was barely enough to keep the house running. Why hadn't he done as the others did—demanded a share, obtained some stock, succeeded in something? And she carried on with all the cruelty of an heiress who has brought a fortune as her dowry. He, always perfectly polite, dissimulated behind his mask of the cold and correct administrator a ravaging desire for this creature, one of those violent, late-developing desires that increase with age. He had never possessed her as a lover, and he was haunted by an inescapable vision—to have her, if only once, as she had given herself to another. Every morning he dreamed of conquering her that evening; then, when she looked at him with her cold eyes, when he felt that everything in her rejected him, he avoided letting even so much as his hand brush against her. It was a pain without possible relief, hidden beneath the stiffness of his behavior—the pain of a tender nature secretly dying because it hadn't found happiness at home. At the end of six months, when Madame Hennebeau had completely furnished the house and had nothing to occupy her, she sank into a languorous boredom, behaving like a victim whom exile would kill—and who, she said, would be just as happy to die of it.

It was then that Paul Négrel came to Montsou. His mother, who was the widow of a Provençal captain and lived in Avignon on a small income, had had to make do with little more than bread and water in order to send him to the Polytechnical Institute. He had graduated low in the class, and his uncle, Monsieur Hennebeau, had got him to resign his commission by offering to take him on as an engineer at Le Voreux. From then on he was treated as if he had been their own son; he had his own room, and took his meals and lived there, all of which enabled him to send his mother half of his three-thousand-franc salary. To disguise his kindness, Monsieur Hennebeau explained how difficult it was for a young man to keep house for himself in one of the little cottages reserved for the mine engineers. Madame Hennebeau had immediately taken on the role of the good aunt, addressing him familiarly and watching over his well-being. In the first months, especially, she displayed a maternal interest in him, rich in advice on the smallest matters. Nevertheless she remained a woman, and she soon slipped into personal confidences. This very young and practical fellow, whose intelligence was unfettered by scruples and who professed philosophical theories about love, amused her by his vivacious pessimism, which was leaving its mark on his already pointed nose and thin face. Naturally, he found himself in her arms one evening; she seemed to be giving herself out of pure goodness, insisting all the while that her heart was dead and that she only wanted to be his friend. And certainly she was not jealous; she teased him about the haulage girls, who were horrible, he said, and almost sulked because he had none of the usual young man's extravagant tales to tell her. Then the idea of arranging a marriage for him took hold of her. She dreamed of sacrificing herself, of personally turning him over to some rich young girl. Their relationship continued—an amusing recreation into which she poured all the autumn tenderness of an idle woman whose life was over.

Two years went by. One night Monsieur Hennebeau heard bare feet brush past his door, and he became suspicious. This new adventure repelled him—in his own house, between this mother and this son! But the very next morning his wife told him that she had chosen Cécile Grégoire for their nephew, and she went about arranging this marriage with so much enthusiasm that he blushed at his own monstrous imaginings. He was left with only a feeling of gratitude to the young man for having made the house less mournful since his arrival.

Coming down from his wife's dressing room, Monsieur Hennebeau met Paul returning from his errand. The strike situation seemed to amuse him.

"Well?" asked his uncle.

"Well, I've just completed a tour of the villages and they all seem to be very quiet. . . . But I think they're going to send you some delegates."

Just then Madame Hennebeau's voice called from upstairs. "Is that you, Paul? . . . Come up and tell me the news. How silly of these people to be naughty when they're so well off!"

And since his wife was summoning his messenger, the manager had to give up all hope of learning any more. He returned to his desk, on which another bundle of dispatches had piled up.

When the Grégoires arrived at eleven o'clock, they were somewhat startled to see Hippolyte, the manservant, standing guard at the door; after he had looked nervously up and down the road, he hustled them inside without ceremony. The drawing-room curtains were closed, and the Grégoires

were shown directly into Monsieur Hennebeau's office, where
he apologized for receiving them in such a way, but explained that the drawing room looked out on the street and it
was pointless to seem deliberately provocative.

"What! You don't know?" he said, seeing their surprise.

When Monsieur Grégoire learned that the strike had
finally broken out, he calmly shrugged his shoulders. Bah! It
wouldn't amount to much, the people here were basically
decent. Madame Grégoire was nodding her head, approving
his confidence in the time-honored resignation of the miners,
while Cécile—very gay that day and looking radiant with
health in a deep-orange dress—was smiling at the mention of
the word "strike," which made her think of charitable visits
to the villages.

Just then Madame Hennebeau came in, dressed in black
silk and followed by Négrel.

"Isn't it a bore!" she exclaimed as she crossed the threshold. "As if those men couldn't have waited! . . . Do you
know that Paul refuses to take us to Saint-Thomas?"

"We'll stay here then," said Monsieur Grégoire obligingly.
"It will be a great pleasure."

Paul had merely bowed to Cécile and her mother. Irritated by this lack of enthusiasm, his aunt shot him a look
that sent him scurrying over to the young girl, and when she
heard them laughing together, she enveloped them in a
glance of maternal affection.

Meanwhile Monsieur Hennebeau finished reading the
dispatches and prepared some replies. The conversation continued around him, his wife explaining that she hadn't done a
thing to this office, which had, indeed, kept its old, faded red
wallpaper, its heavy mahogany furniture, its much-worn
cardboard file cases. After three quarters of an hour they
were about to go in to lunch when the servant announced
Monsieur Deneulin, who entered excitedly and bowed to
Madame Hennebeau.

"What!—you here?" he said, noticing the Grégoires.

Then he briskly turned to the manager.

"So it's happened, eh? I've just heard about it from my
engineer. . . . At my place all the men went down this
morning—but it may spread. I'm not easy about it. . . . How
are things with you?"

He had raced over on horseback, and his nervousness
betrayed itself in his loud voice and abrupt gestures, which
made him seem like a retired cavalry officer.

Monsieur Hennebeau was beginning to explain to him

exactly how things stood when Hippolyte opened the dining-room door. He broke off and said:

"Have lunch with us. I'll tell you the rest over the dessert."

"Just as you like," answered Deneulin, so preoccupied that he accepted without further ceremony.

But he became aware of his rudeness and turned to Madame Hennebeau with apologies. Her response was gracious. She had a seventh place set and seated her guests: Madame Grégoire and Cécile on either side of her husband; then Monsieur Grégoire and Deneulin on her own right and left; and finally Paul, whom she placed between the young girl and her father. As they lit into the hors d'oeuvres she said with a smile:

"I must apologize—I wanted to give you oysters. . . . A shipment comes into Marchiennes from Ostende on Mondays, and I had planned to send my cook in the carriage. . . . But she was afraid of being stoned. . . ."

They interrupted her with a roar of laughter. Everyone found this a really amusing story.

"Sh!" Monsieur Hennebeau was annoyed; he looked toward the window, through which the road could be seen. "There's no need for everyone to know that we're entertaining today."

"Well, in any case, here's one slice of sausage they won't get," declared Monsieur Grégoire.

The laughter broke out again, but more discreetly this time. The room, hung with Flemish tapestries and furnished with old oak cabinets, gave them a feeling of ease as they made themselves comfortable. Pieces of silver plate shone behind the glass of the credenzas, and there was a large, burnished-copper hanging lamp in whose rounded surfaces were reflected a palm and an aspidistra growing in majolica pots. Outside, the December day was chilled by a sharp cold wind from the northeast, but not so much as a breath of it came inside to disturb the hothouse warmth, made fragrant by the subtle odor of sliced pineapple in a cut-glass bowl.

"Shouldn't we draw the curtains?" suggested Négrel, amused at the idea of terrifying the Grégoires.

The maid, who was helping the butler, thought it was an order and went to draw one of the curtains. This started an interminable round of pleasantries: no glass or fork was set down without elaborate precautions; each dish was greeted like something salvaged from looting in a conquered city—and behind the forced gaiety there was a suppressed fear, betrayed by involuntary glances in the direction of the road, as if a band of beggars were out there, spying on the table.

After the scrambled eggs with truffles came the river trout. The conversation had turned to the industrial crisis, which had been worsening for the past eighteen months.

"It was inevitable," said Deneulin. "The last few years were much too prosperous and could only lead to this. . . . Think of the enormous amount of immobilized capital—the railroads, the ports, the canals—think of all the money sunk in the maddest kinds of speculation! Just in this neighborhood alone they set sugar refineries up as if the Department would have *three* beet harvests. . . . Of course money has become scarce, and there's nothing to do but wait for the interest to come back on the millions that have been spent. Meanwhile, the result is a deadly congestion, and the complete stagnation of business."

Monsieur Hennebeau argued against this theory but agreed that the good years had spoiled the workers.

"When I think," he exclaimed, "that these fellows in our mines were once able to make as much as six francs a day—twice what they make now! They lived well and developed expensive tastes. . . . Today of course they find it difficult to go back to their former frugality."

"Monsieur Grégoire," interrupted Madame Hennebeau, "do have a little more trout. . . . They're delicious, aren't they?"

The manager continued:

"But is it really our fault? We've been hit hard too. . . . With the factories closing down one after another we've had the devil's own time unloading our stock, and given the decreasing demand, we're forced to lower our production costs. . . . That's what the workers don't want to understand."

A silence fell. The butler offered roast partridges while the maid began filling the glasses with Chambertin.

"There's been a famine in India," Deneulin went on in an undertone, as though speaking to himself. "America has delivered a hard blow to our blast furnaces by stopping its orders for iron and cast-iron. Everything's connected. A far-off shock is enough to shake the whole world. . . . And the Empire was so proud of the fever pitch of industry!"

He attacked his partridge wing. Then, raising his voice:

"The worst thing about it is that if you want to lower production costs you've got to produce more—otherwise the cut comes from wages, and the worker is right in saying that he's the one to bear the brunt of it."

This admission, forced on him by his own honesty, gave rise to a discussion. The ladies were bored, but everybody was in the first flush of appetite and was busy with his plate. When the butler came back, he seemed to want to say something, but he hesitated.

"What is it?" asked Monsieur Hennebeau. "If there are any dispatches, let me have them. . . . I'm waiting for some replies."

"No, sir, it's Monsieur Dansaert. He's waiting in the hall, but he's afraid he may be disturbing you."

The manager made his excuses and had the chief foreman brought in. The latter remained standing, a few feet from the table; everybody turned to look at him, huge and breathless with the news he was bringing: the villages were quiet, but they had decided to send a delegation. It would probably be there in a few minutes.

"Very well, thank you," said Monsieur Hennebeau. "I want a report morning and evening, understand?"

And as soon as Dansaert had left, the guests returned to their pleasantries and fell on the Russian salad with zeal, saying there was not a moment to lose if they wanted to finish it. Their gaiety knew no bounds when Négrel asked the maid for some bread and she replied with a "yes, sir" that was so low and terrified that it seemed as though a band of murderers and rapists must be at her back.

"You can speak up," said Madame Hennebeau serenely. "They aren't here yet."

The manager, to whom a packet of letters and dispatches had been brought, decided to read one of the letters out loud. It was from Pierron, respectfully informing them that he was obliged to go on strike with the others to keep them from turning on him, and adding that he hadn't even been able to avoid making one of the delegation, although he disapproved of this step.

"So much for freedom to work!" exclaimed Monsieur Hennebeau.

The talk then returned to the strike and he was asked his opinion.

"Oh," he replied, "we've been through it before. . . . There'll be a week of idleness, or two weeks at most, like the last time. They'll make the rounds of the cabarets, then when they're really hungry, they'll go back to the mines."

Deneulin shook his head.

"I'm not so sure. . . . This time they seem better organized. Don't they have an emergency fund?"

"Yes, but it's barely three thousand francs. What do you think they can do with that? . . . I suspect that a certain Etienne Lantier is their leader. He's a good worker and I'd

hate to have to send him packing the way I did Rasseneur,
who is still infecting Le Voreux with his ideas and his beer.
. . . But no matter, half the men will go down again in a
week, and in two weeks all ten thousand of them will be
down there."

He was convinced of this. His only worry was about the
possibility of disgrace if the Company directors were to hold
him responsible for the strike. For some time now he had felt
himself less in favor with them. He therefore abandoned the
spoonful of Russian salad that he had taken and reread the
replies from Paris, trying to penetrate the meaning behind
each word. Allowance was made for him, and the meal
turned into a military luncheon eaten on the battlefield before the first shots were fired.

Now the ladies joined in the conversation. Madame Grégoire expressed pity for those poor people who were going to
be hungry, and Cécile could already see herself distributing
coupons for bread and meat. But Madame Hennebeau was
amazed at this talk of the poverty of the Montsou miners.
Weren't they very well off? People who were given houses,
heat, and medical care at the Company's expense! Her indifference toward this herd was such that all she knew about it
was the little lecture she had learned by heart, that lecture
with which she dazzled visiting Parisians and which she had
ended by believing herself; she was quite indignant at the
workers' ingratitude.

Meanwhile Négrel was continuing to frighten Monsieur
Grégoire. He didn't dislike Cécile, and he was quite willing
to marry her if his aunt insisted; but he wasn't feverishly in
love, and he behaved like an experienced young man who, as
he said, could no longer be carried away by it all. He thought
of himself as a republican, which, however, didn't prevent
him from keeping extremely tight control over his workers,
or from subtly making fun of them in the company of ladies.

"I don't share my uncle's optimism either," he went on.
"I'm afraid there will be serious trouble. . . . As a matter of
fact, Monsieur Grégoire, I advise you to lock up La Piolaine. It may be pillaged."

At that very moment, his kindly face lit, as usual, with a
smile, Monsieur Grégoire was outdoing his wife in the
expression of paternal feelings toward the miners.

"Pillaged?" he cried, stupefied. "Why would they pillage
my place?"

"Aren't you a Montsou stockholder? You don't *do* anything—you live off the work of others. Why, you're the
infamous capitalist himself, and that's enough. . . . You can

be sure that if the revolution triumphs it will force you to restore your fortune as stolen money."

Monsieur Grégoire suddenly lost the childlike tranquillity, the serene unawareness, in which he lived. He stammered:

"My fortune stolen! Didn't my great-grandfather earn—and through hard labor—the money he invested? Haven't we run all the risks of the enterprise? And do I make bad use of my income now?"

Madame Hennebeau, alarmed at seeing both mother and daughter pale with fear, hastily intervened, saying:

"My dear Monsieur Grégoire, Paul is only teasing you."

But Monsieur Grégoire was beside himself. The butler passed around a dish of crayfish, and he took three of them without knowing what he was doing; he began breaking their claws with his teeth.

"Oh, I don't deny that there are stockholders who take advantage. For example, I've been told about ministers who receive Montsou stock as hush money for services rendered the Company. And there's that nobleman whose name I won't mention—a duke, the biggest of our stockholders—whose life is a scandal of wastefulness! Millions squandered on women, orgies, and foolish luxuries. . . . But we, we live quietly, like the honest folk we are—we don't speculate, we content ourselves with living sensibly on what we have, and we give the poor their proper share. . . . Come now, the workers would have to be real thieves to steal from us!"

Négrel himself, though he was amused by Monsieur Grégoire's anger, had to calm him. The crayfish were still going around, and the crackling of shells could be heard as the conversation turned to politics. Monsieur Grégoire, still trembling, proclaimed himself a liberal in spite of everything; he pined for the days of Louis-Philippe. As for Deneulin, he was for a strong government and declared that the Emperor was sliding down the slippery path of dangerous concessions.

"Remember '89," he said. "It was the nobility that made the Revolution possible by its complicity, its taste for philosophic novelties. . . . Well, today the middle class is playing the same stupid game, with its passion for liberalism, its rage for destruction, its flattery of the workers. . . . Yes, yes, you're sharpening the teeth of the monster so it can devour us. And it *will* devour us, you can be sure of that!"

The ladies made him stop, changing the subject by asking for news of his daughters. Lucie was at Marchiennes, where she was singing with a friend, and Jeanne was painting the head of an old beggar. But he told them this with a distracted air and kept his eyes on the manager, who was absorbed

in the reading of his dispatches and oblivious of his guests.
Behind the thin sheets of paper he could feel the presence of
Paris and the directors, whose orders would decide about the
strike, and he couldn't keep himself from once more giving
way to his preoccupation.

"Well, what are you going to do?" he asked suddenly.

Monsieur Hennebeau started, then avoided the issue with a
vague reply.

"We'll see."

"Yes, of course—you people are well established and can
afford to wait," Deneulin said, thinking out loud. "But as for
me, if the strike spreads to Vandame, I've had it. Even
though I've completely modernized Jean-Bart, the only way I
can make ends meet with just one mine is by constant
production. . . . Things don't look too bright for me, I assure
you!"

This involuntary confession caught Monsieur Hennebeau's
attention. As he listened, a plan began to form in his mind:
should the strike go badly, why not use it to let things
deteriorate to the point of ruining his neighbor, whose concession could then be bought at a low price? It would be the
surest way of putting himself back in the good graces of the
directors, who had been longing to take over Vandame for
years.

"If Jean-Bart is so much of a worry," he said, smiling,
"why not let us have it?"

But Deneulin already regretted his complaints. He shouted:
"Never!"

They were amused by his violence, and by the time dessert
appeared, they had finally managed to forget the strike. The
apple-charlotte meringue was praised to the skies. Then the
ladies discussed the recipe for the pineapple dish, which was
also declared to be delicious. Fruit—some grapes and pears—
provided the final mellowing touch attendant on such a
copious lunch. Completely relaxed, everyone was talking at
once while the butler poured out a Rhine wine, champagne
being considered too vulgar.

And the marriage between Paul and Cécile certainly took
an important step forward during the conviviality accompanying the dessert. Under the pressure of significant glances
from his aunt, the young man made a special effort to please,
and his honeyed manner quite reconquered the Grégoires,
who had been terrified by his talk of pillage. Seeing the close
understanding between his wife and his nephew, Monsieur
Hennebeau again felt the terrible suspicion stir in him—as if
he had surprised a physical caress behind the looks they

exchanged. But he was once again reassured by the idea of this marriage being arranged before his very eyes.

Hippolyte was serving the coffee when the maid rushed in, terrified.

"Sir, sir, they're here!"

It was the delegation. Doors slammed, and a breath of terror could be felt sweeping through the nearby rooms.

"Show them in to the drawing room," said Monsieur Hennebeau.

Around the table the diners looked at each other, anxious and uncertain. Silence reigned. Then they attempted to return to their little jokes: they pretended to put the rest of the sugar in their pockets and talked of hiding the silver. But the manager remained serious and the laughter died away; the voices fell to whispers as the heavy steps of the delegates could be heard crushing the carpet in the adjoining drawing room.

Lowering her voice, Madame Hennebeau said to her husband:

"I hope you'll have your coffee first."

"Of course," he answered. "Let them wait."

Though he seemed to be thinking of nothing but his cup of coffee, he was nervous, aware of every sound.

Paul and Cécile had risen from the table and he had induced her to peep through the keyhole. They stifled their laughter and spoke in hushed tones.

"Do you see them?"

"Yes. . . . There's a big one, and two smaller ones behind him."

"Well, don't they look fierce?"

"Not at all, they're very nice."

Monsieur Hennebeau suddenly rose from his chair, saying that the coffee was too hot and he would drink it later. As he left the room he put a finger to his lips to recommend prudence. They were all sitting again, and they stayed at the table, silent, no longer daring to move, straining their ears and listening intently, uneasy at the sound of those loud, male voices.

2

At a meeting held the day before at Rasseneur's, Etienne and several of his comrades had chosen the delegates who were to see the manager on the following day. That evening, when La Maheude learned that her husband was to be one of the group, she was in despair, and asked him if he wanted them all to be thrown into the street. Maheu himself hadn't accepted without reluctance. Despite feeling the injustice of their poverty, when the moment came to act, both of them sank again into the traditional resignation of their race; they feared the consequences of action and preferred to submit to their fate passively. In matters relating to the practical problems of their lives, Maheu usually relied on his wife's judgment, for she always offered good advice. This time, however, he ended by getting angry, especially since he secretly shared her fears.

"Let me alone, will you!" he said, getting into bed and turning his back on her. "*That* would be a nice thing, letting the others down! . . . I'm doing what I have to do."

She got into bed too. Neither of them spoke. Then, after a long silence, she replied:

"You're right, go ahead. But you realize it's the end for us."

They sat down to lunch as it was striking twelve. The rendezvous was set for one o'clock at L'Avantage, and from there they would go to Monsieur Hennebeau's. There were some potatoes, but since there was only a little butter left nobody took any of it. They would have bread and butter in the evening.

"You know we're counting on you to be our spokesman," Etienne suddenly said to Maheu.

The latter was stunned—struck dumb with emotion.

"Oh no—that's going too far!" exclaimed La Maheude. "I'm willing enough for him to go, but I forbid him to be the leader. . . . And why him rather than anybody else?"

Etienne explained with his usual passionate eloquence. Maheu was the best worker in the mine, the best liked and the most respected, the one who was always cited for his good sense. As a result, coming from him the miners' complaints would take on added weight. At first he, Etienne, was sup-

172

posed to have spoken, but he hadn't been in Montsou long
enough. They would listen more readily to an old-timer. And
finally, the men were entrusting their interests to the one
most worthy; he couldn't refuse—it would be cowardly.

La Maheude gestured hopelessly.

"Go ahead, husband, go ahead. Sacrifice yourself for the
others. I guess I agree after all."

"But I'll never be able to," Maheu stammered. "I'll only
say a lot of foolishness."

Happy to have convinced him, Etienne slapped him on the
back.

"You'll say what you feel and it will be fine."

His mouth full, Old Bonnemort, whose legs were getting
better, shook his head and listened. A silence fell. When they
ate potatoes, the children choked them down and remained
very quiet. After having swallowed, the old man slowly
mumbled:

"Say whatever you want—it'll be the same as if you hadn't
said anything. . . . I've seen this kind of thing before, I have!
Forty years ago the manager drove us out with swords.
Today he may let you in, but you won't get any more of an
answer than you would from that wall. . . . Hell, they've got
the money and they couldn't care less!"

There was another silence. Maheu and Etienne got up and
left the dispirited family sitting in front of their empty plates.
They picked up Pierron and Levaque on the way, then all
four went to Rasseneur's, where the delegates from the
neighboring villages were arriving in small groups. When the
twenty members of the delegation had assembled, they drew
up the conditions they would oppose to those of the Company and set off for Montsou. A sharp northeast wind was
sweeping across the road. They arrived at the stroke of two.

At first the butler told them to wait and closed the door on
them; then he came back and showed them into the drawing
room and pulled aside the curtains. Daylight filtered dimly
through the lace. Left alone, the miners were afraid to sit
down; they were embarrassed, starchily clean, dressed in
their Sunday best, fresh-shaven, their blond hair and
moustaches gleaming. Twisting their caps in their hands, they
glanced out of the corners of their eyes at the furniture—a
jumble of all styles, made fashionable by the taste for dubious antiques: Henri II armchairs, Louis XV chairs, a seven-
teenth-century Italian cabinet, a fifteenth-century Spanish
contador, an altar frontal draping the mantelpiece, and embroidery from old chasubles sewn on to the portières. These
old golds, these fawn-colored silks, all this churchly richness,

inspired them with an uneasy respect. Their feet seemed to be sinking into the deep pile of the Oriental carpets. But what most overwhelmed them was the heat; their cheeks still frozen from the wind along the road, the unvarying furnace heat enveloped and surprised them. Five minutes went by. Their uneasiness was increasing in the comfort of this opulently furnished room, so luxuriously snug.

At last Monsieur Hennebeau appeared, militarily buttoned, and wearing in his lapel the neat little rosette of his decoration. He was the first to speak.

"Ah, here you are! . . . It seems you're up in arms. . . ."

Then he stopped, to say with stiff politeness:

"Sit down, I'm quite willing to talk to you."

The miners turned around and looked for seats. A few of them risked the chairs, but the others, worried by the embroidered silks, preferred to remain standing.

There was a silence. Monsieur Hennebeau, who had pushed his armchair to the fireplace, was looking them over quickly and trying to recognize their faces. He had just seen Pierron, hidden in the back, and now his eyes stopped at Etienne, who was seated in front of him.

"Well, what do you have to say to me?" he asked.

He was expecting Etienne to do the talking, and he was so surprised to see Maheu step forward that he could not help adding:

"What, you? A good worker who's always been so sensible, an old-timer in Montsou, a man whose family has worked at the bottom since the first blow of the pick! . . . Ah, that's too bad, I'm really hurt to see you at the head of these malcontents!"

Maheu listened, his eyes lowered. Then he began to speak, his voice low and hesitant at first.

"Sir, it's just because I'm a quiet fellow nobody can complain about that my comrades chose me. It should prove to you that this isn't a revolt of troublemakers or malcontents who are just trying to upset things. All we want is justice. We're tired of starving, and we think the time has come to arrange things so that we at least have enough bread for every day."

His voice grew firmer. He raised his eyes, and looking straight at the manager now, he went on:

"You know very well that we can't accept your new system. . . . They say we don't timber well and it's truc—we don't spend the time that we should on this work. But if we did, the time we'd have left for cutting would be shorter yet, and since we can't make enough to feed ourselves even with things as they are, that would be the end of everything, the last straw that would finish off your men for good. Pay us more and we'll timber better—we'll put in the necessary time on it instead of concentrating on the cutting, which is the only job that brings anything in. There's no other arrangement possible—if you want the job done it's got to be paid for. . . . And what have you thought up instead?—something we can't even consider! You lower the price per cart and say you're compensating for it by paying for the timbering separately. Even if this were true we'd still be getting cheated, because timbering always takes more time. But what really gets us is that it isn't even true! The Company isn't compensating us at all—it's only putting two centimes per cart into its own pocket, that's all!"

"Yes, yes, that's the truth," murmured the other delegates, seeing Monsieur Hennebeau make a sudden move as if to interrupt.

But it was Maheu who stopped the manager short. Now that he had started, the words were coming of themselves, and at moments he listened to himself in surprise, as though some stranger within him were speaking. Everything that had built up in the depths of his being, things he didn't even know were there, came pouring out from his overflowing heart. He described the poverty common to all of them, the backbreaking work, the brutalizing life, the women and children starving at home. He cited the last disastrous paydays—the ridiculous sums eaten away by fines and lay-offs and brought home to weeping families. Had the Company determined to kill them all off?

"And so, sir," he concluded, "we've come to tell you that if we've got to starve we might as well starve without working. At least we won't be so tired. . . . We've left the mines and we won't go down again unless the Company accepts our conditions. The Company wants to lower the price per cart and pay us for the timbering separately. We want things to stay as they were, and in addition, we want five centimes more per cart. . . . And now it's up to you to decide if you're for justice and for work."

Some of the miners called out:

"That's right. . . . He's said what we all feel. . . . We only want what's fair."

Others, without speaking, merely nodded their agreement. The luxurious room with its gold and embroidery, its jumble of mysterious, would-be antiques, had disappeared; the men were no longer even aware of the carpet, crushed under their heavy boots.

"Give me a chance to answer, will you?" finally shouted
Monsieur Hennebeau, who was getting angry. "First of all,
it's not true that the Company is gaining two centimes per
cart. . . . Let's look at the figures."

A confused discussion followed. In an attempt to create a
division among them, the manager called on Pierron, who
stutteringly squirmed out of answering. On the other hand,
Levaque had set himself up as the leader of the most aggres-
sive, jumbling everything and affirming facts he knew nothing
about. The loud murmur of voices was muffled by the tapestries, stifled by the hothouse heat.

"If you all talk at once," continued Monsieur Hennebeau,
"we'll never get anywhere."

He had regained his calm, once again showing the cold
unruffled politeness of a manager who has received his orders
and is determined to carry them out. From the very first
words he had kept his eyes fixed on Etienne, working to draw
the young man from the silence in which he had shut himself. He therefore abandoned the argument about the two
centimes and suddenly adopted a larger view of the problem.

"No, admit the truth—you're all reacting to hateful propaganda. It's a veritable plague that's sweeping through the
workers and infecting even the best of them. . . . Oh, I don't
need anybody's confession. I can see for myself that all of
you, who used to be so level-headed, have changed. You've
been promised more butter than bread, haven't you? You've
been told that it's your turn to be the bosses. . . . In fact,
you've all been signed up in the International, that army of
bandits whose dream is to destroy society. . . ."

At this Etienne interrupted him.

"You're mistaken, sir. Not one of the men from Montsou
has signed up yet. But if you push them to it, the men in all
the mines will join. It depends on the Company."

From that moment on, the battle was between Monsieur
Hennebeau and Etienne; it was as if the other miners were
no longer there.

"The Company is a real godsend for these men and you're
wrong to threaten it. This year it spent three hundred thousand francs to build mining villages that don't return two
percent, and I'm not even considering the pensions it pays
out or the medication it provides. You who seem so intelligent, who in only a few months have become one of our best
workers—wouldn't you do better to spread these truths than
to ruin yourself by associating with people of bad reputation?
Yes, I'm talking about Rasseneur, whom we had to get rid of
in order to save our mines from Socialist rot. . . . You're

always seen at his place, and he is surely the one who got you to set up this emergency fund—which we'd be very willing to tolerate if it were only a savings fund, but which we can see is a weapon against us, a reserve fund to pay the expenses of war. And I should mention at this point that the Company means to have control over this fund."

Etienne had let him go on, his eyes fixed on those of the manager, his lips twitching nervously. He smiled at the last sentence and replied simply:

"Then that's a new demand, sir, since up to this point you've overlooked asking for such control. . . . Unfortunately, what we want is for the Company to be less concerned with us—not to play God, but just to show that it's fair by giving us our due—the profit we make that it keeps all for itself. Is it right, every time there's a crisis, to let the workers die of hunger just to save the stockholders' dividends? . . . No matter what you say, sir, the new system is a cover-up for a cut in wages, and that's what we're against, because if the Company has to save money, it's unfair to do it only at the workers' expense."

"Ah, we're finally there!" exclaimed Monsieur Hennebeau. "I was waiting for this accusation of starving the workers and living on their sweat! How can you say such idiotic things, you who should know about the enormous risks that capital runs in industry—in the mines, for example. These days a completely equipped mine costs from one and a half to two million francs—and what trouble before you can get a piddling return from the enormous sums swallowed up! Almost half the mining companies in France are going bankrupt. . . . Besides, it's ridiculous to accuse the successful ones of being cruel. When their workers suffer, they themselves suffer. Don't you think the Company has as much to lose in the present crisis as you have? It can't set wages the way it wants—it has to meet competition or be ruined. Blame the facts of the situation, not the Company. . . . But you don't want to listen, you don't want to understand!"

"On the contrary," said the young man; "we understand very well that there can be no possible improvement for us as long as things go on as they are—and that's why, one day or another, the workers will end by seeing to it that things go differently."

These words, on the surface so moderate, were said in a low voice, but with such conviction and implied menace that a long silence followed. A constraint, a breath of fear, passed through the quiet drawing room. The other delegates, who only half-understood what had been said, nevertheless felt that their comrade, here in the midst of all this well-being, had just demanded their share, and once again they began to look out of the corners of their eyes at the thick hangings, the comfortable chairs, and all the luxury of the room, the least bauble of which would have paid for a month's soup.

At last Monsieur Hennebeau, who had remained sunk in thought, rose to dismiss them. Everybody else got up too. Etienne had lightly nudged Maheu's elbow, and the latter, already tongue-tied and awkward, resumed:

"Well then, sir, if that's all you have to say . . . We'll tell the others that you've rejected our conditions."

"*Me*, my good man?" the manager exclaimed, "*I'm* not rejecting anything! I'm just an employee like you, and I have no more say in this matter than the least of your mine boys. I get my orders, and my job is to see that they are properly carried out. I've told you what I thought is my duty to tell you, but I wouldn't dream of making a decision. . . . You have let me know your demands, I shall bring them to the attention of the directors, and then I shall give you their answer."

He was speaking in the formal manner of an administrator—with the cold correctness of a mere instrument of authority who avoids any involvement in a problem. And now the miners were looking at him suspiciously, wondering what he was up to, what interest he might have in lying, what he could be getting for putting himself between them and the real bosses this way. He must be some sort of schemer, this man who got paid just like a worker and yet who lived so well!

Etienne again ventured to intervene.

"Then you see, sir, how unfortunate it is that we can't present our case in person. We would be able to explain many things, use arguments that you couldn't possibly be expected to think of . . . if we only knew where to go!"

Monsieur Hennebeau did not lose his temper. He even smiled.

"Well, things begin to get complicated if you don't have confidence in me. . . . You'd have to go over there."

The delegates followed his vague gesture, his hand pointed toward one of the windows. Where was "over there"? Paris, probably. But they weren't really sure—it all seemed so terrifyingly far away, in some inaccessible, sacred land ruled over by the unknown god crouching in the recesses of his tabernacle. They would never see him, but they felt him as a far-off force, bearing down on the ten thousand miners of

Montsou. And when the manager spoke, it was this hidden force, uttering oracles, that he had behind him.

A feeling of profound discouragement overcame them, and even Etienne shrugged his shoulders to signify that they might as well leave. Meanwhile, Monsieur Hennebeau was amicably clapping Maheu on the back and asking for news of Jeanlin.

"It's a terrible lesson for you, and yet you're the one who defends sloppy timbering! . . . Think it over, my friends, and you will see that a strike would be a disaster for everybody. Before the end of a week you will be dying of hunger. How will you be able to manage? . . . However, I'm counting on your good sense and I'm convinced that you will go back down by Monday at the latest."

They all walked out, leaving the drawing room like a shuffling herd of cattle, their backs bent, not replying by so much as a word to this expectation of their submission. The manager accompanied them to the door and was obliged to sum up the results of the meeting: on one side, the Company and its new rates; on the other, the workers with their demand for an increase of five centimes per cart. So as not to inspire any false hopes, he thought it his duty to warn them that the directors would certainly reject their demands.

"Think it over before doing anything foolish," he repeated, disturbed by their silence.

In the hall Pierron bowed obsequiously while Levaque was pointedly putting on his cap. Maheu was still searching for some final word when Etienne again nudged his elbow, and they all left in an ominous silence. The only sound was the slamming of the door.

When Monsieur Hennebeau went back to the dining room he found his guests sitting immobile and mute over their liqueurs. In a few words he brought Deneulin, whose face clouded over even more, up to date. While he was drinking his cold coffee, an attempt was made to talk of other things, but the Grégoires themselves kept returning to the strike, astonished that there were no laws to stop workers from leaving their jobs. Paul was reassuring Cécile, telling her that they were expecting the police.

Finally Madame Hennebeau summoned the butler.

"Hippolyte, before we go into the drawing room, open the windows and air the place out."

3

Two weeks had gone by, and on the Monday of the third week the time sheets sent in to the manager showed a further decrease in the number of workers who had gone down. Management was expecting work to be resumed that morning, but the directors' determination not to give in had exasperated the miners. Le Voreux, Crèvecoeur, Mirou, and Madeleine were no longer the only idle mines—scarcely a quarter of the men were going down at La Victoire and at Feutry-Cantel, and even Saint-Thomas was affected. Little by little the strike was becoming general.

At Le Voreux a heavy silence was hanging over the yard. It was a dead factory, empty and deserted—an industrial complex from which the breath of work has departed. Up above, against the gray December sky, three or four abandoned carts on the overhead tracks had the mute sadness of lifeless things. Below, between the thin legs of the trestles, the stockpiles of coal were giving out, leaving the ground black and bare, and the piles of timber were rotting in the heavy rain. At the landing dock of the canal a half-loaded barge seemed to be sleeping in the muddy water; on the deserted slag pile, where decomposing sulphides were smoking in spite of the rain, the shafts of a wagon dismally seemed to implore the sky. But above all the buildings themselves seemed benumbed—the screening shed with its closed shutters, the headframe into which the rumbling from the landing station was no longer rising, the now-cold boiler shed, the enormous smokestack that was too large for the occasional wisps of smoke. The hoisting engine was only fired up in the mornings, when the stablemen brought down the horses' fodder; only the foremen—laborers once more—went down with them, in an attempt to protect the galleries against the destruction that begins as soon as maintenance ceases. After nine o'clock all other arrivals and departures were by means of ladders. And from these corpselike buildings in their winding sheets of black dust came only the sound of the exhaust of the pump, with its long, labored breathing—all that remained of the life of the mine, which the water would destroy if that breathing were ever to stop.

On the hill opposite the mine, Village 240 also seemed to

be dead. The prefect of Lille had come running, and gendarmes had patrolled the roads; but given the orderly behavior of the strikers, the prefect and the gendarmes had decided to go home again. The village had never before set such a good example to the others on this immense plain. The men, to avoid going to the cabarets and bars, slept through the day; the women, by cutting down on their coffee drinking, became more reasonable, less stirred up by gossip and quarrels; and even the bands of children seemed to understand, and were so well-behaved that they would run around barefoot and fight with one another noiselessly. The watchword was repeated from mouth to mouth: let's be on our best behavior.

Nevertheless, the Maheus' house was busy with a constant coming and going of people. It was there that Etienne, as secretary, had divided among the needy families the three thousand francs in the emergency fund. A few hundred francs more had been obtained by subscriptions and collections from various sources, but now all resources were exhausted, the miners had no more money with which to support the strike, and the threat of hunger was upon them. After having promised everybody two weeks' credit, Maigrat had suddenly changed his mind at the end of a week and cut off all supplies. He usually took his orders from the Company; perhaps the latter wanted to finish things quickly by starving out the villages. In addition, he was behaving like a capricious tyrant, either giving or refusing bread according to the looks of the girl the parents had sent for the groceries. He especially closed his door to La Maheude; bitter and resentful, he was determined to punish her because he had not had Catherine. And to top their misery, it was freezing cold; the women watched their dwindling coal supplies with the gnawing realization that there would be no more coal from the mines so long as the men refused to go down. As though it weren't enough to die of hunger, they were also going to die of cold!

The Maheus had already run out of everything. The Levaques were still eating, thanks to a twenty-franc piece lent by Bouteloup. As for the Pierrons, they still had money, but to seem as famished as the others lest they be besieged by requests for loans, they bought on credit from Maigrat, who would have tossed his whole shop at La Pierronne if she had only held out her skirt. Beginning on Saturday, many families had gone to bed without supper, yet even in the face of the terrible days that were setting in, not one complaint was heard; everybody obeyed the watchword with quiet courage. Despite everything, there was absolute confidence—a re-

ligious faith, the blind dedication of a race of believers. Since they had been promised an age of justice,
they were ready to suffer for the conquest of universal
happiness. Hunger went to their heads, and the sealed-in
horizon had never before opened onto as promising a future
for these poor people as in their starving state of exaltation.
When their eyes began to swim they looked beyond—to the
ideal city of their dreams, now close and almost real, with its
people of brothers, its golden age of labor, its food shared at
a common board. Nothing could shake their conviction that
they were at last about to enter it. The fund was exhausted,
the Company would not yield, each passing day could only
aggravate the situation, and still they kept their faith,
showing a smiling contempt for mere facts. If the earth was
about to open beneath them, a miracle would save them.
This faith served in lieu of bread, and warmed their stomachs. When the Maheus and the others had gulped down
their watery soup too quickly, they went into a half-swoon—
the same ecstatic vision of a better life that had made the
martyrs give themselves up to the beasts.

Etienne was now the uncontested leader. In their evening
conversations he delivered himself of oracles that reflected
the new awareness resulting from his studies, which were
leading him into every area of thought. He spent his nights
reading and received an increasing number of letters; he had
even subscribed to *Vengeur*, a Socialist sheet from Belgium,
and this paper, the first to come into the village, had won
him extraordinary respect from his comrades. His growing
popularity excited him more with each passing day. To
maintain a widespread correspondence, to discuss the fate of
the workers in every part of the province, to give advice to
the miners, and, above all, to become a focal point, to feel
the world revolve around him—all this constantly inflated the
vanity of the former engineman, the cutter with black and
sweaty hands. He was climbing a rung of the social ladder,
he was entering that accursed middle class, with an intellectual pleasure and a sense of well-being that he did not dare
admit even to himself. Only one thing was still bothering
him—his awareness of his lack of education, which made him
awkward and timid whenever he found himself faced with a
gentleman in a frock coat. Though he continued his efforts to
educate himself, devouring everything, his lack of method
made assimilation of the material very slow; the resulting
confusion was such that he ended by "knowing" things he
had not really understood. Because of this, at moments when
his good sense had the upper hand, he felt certain doubts

about his mission and feared that he might not be exactly the right man for the job. Perhaps what was needed was a lawyer, a learned man who knew how to talk and what to do without compromising his comrades? But then a reaction would set in and restore his self-confidence. No, no—no lawyers! They were all swindlers, men who made use of their skill to fatten themselves at the expense of the people. No matter what happened the workers had to handle their own affairs. And once again his uneasiness would be lulled by his dream of being a leader of the people: Montsou at his feet, Paris in the misty future, and—who could tell?—a deputy one day; he saw himself on the platform of a magnificent hall, blasting the bourgeoisie with the first speech ever to be delivered in a parliament by a worker.

For the past few days Etienne had been disturbed. Pluchart was writing letter after letter, offering to come to Montsou and stir up the strikers' enthusiasm. On the surface it was only a question of organizing a closed meeting, over which the engineman would preside, but actually it was a plan to exploit the strike and win the miners over to the International, of which they had so far remained suspicious. Etienne was afraid of possible trouble, but he would have let Pluchart come if Rasseneur had not been so passionately opposed to this intervention. In spite of his power, Etienne had to take the innkeeper into consideration, for his services were of an earlier date and he had many followers among his customers. As a result, Etienne was still hesitating about his reply to Pluchart.

As it happened, that Monday at about four o'clock another letter came from Lille while Etienne was alone with La Maheude in the room downstairs. Maheu, restless at his enforced leisure, had gone fishing: if he were lucky enough to catch a good-sized fish below the canal lock, he would be able to sell it and buy bread. Old Bonnemort and little Jeanlin had gone off to test the use of their newly recovered legs, and the children were out with Alzire, who spent hours on the slag heap, gathering cinders. La Maheude, unbuttoned, her breast out of her blouse and hanging down to her belly, was sitting beside the small fire, which they no longer dared build up, and nursing Estelle.

When Etienne folded up the letter she asked:

"Good news? Are they going to send us some money?"

He shook his head and she went on:

"I don't know how we're going to manage this week. . . . Never mind, we'll manage somehow. When you've got justice on your side it gives you courage, and you always end up being the strongest, right?"

By this time, having thought the matter through, she was for the strike. It would have been better to make the Company behave fairly without having to stop work, but since they had stopped, they ought not to go back before seeing justice done. On this point she was uncompromising. Better to die than seem to have been wrong when you were right!

"Oh," exclaimed Etienne, "if only a good plague would break out and rid us of all these Company people who exploit us so!"

"No, no," she answered. "You mustn't wish for anybody's death. It wouldn't even help us, because others would spring up to take their place. ... All I want is for them to behave more reasonably, and I'm sure they will, there are good people in every group. ... You know I don't agree with your political ideas at all."

And in truth she was always finding fault with his violent way of expressing himself; she thought him too belligerent. It was reasonable to want to be paid fairly for your work, but why get mixed up with all kinds of other things like the bourgeois and the government? Why get involved in other people's business? You would only get hurt that way. But she thought well of Etienne nevertheless—he didn't get drunk and he paid her his forty-five francs board money regularly. When a man knew how to behave decently, you could overlook a lot of other things.

Etienne then began to talk about the republic, which would guarantee bread for everybody. But La Maheude shook her head; she remembered 1848, a black year that had left her and her husband stripped to the bone during their early life together. Oblivious of everything around her, her eyes staring into space, her breast still bared, she droned on about the troubles of that earlier time while her daughter Estelle, without letting go of the nipple, fell asleep on her lap. And Etienne, also lost in thought, kept staring at her enormous breast, the soft whiteness of which so contrasted with the ruined and yellow complexion of her face.

"Not a centime," she murmured, "not so much as a crumb to eat, and all the mines shut down. Just like now, for that matter—the slow starvation of the poor!"

But at that moment the door opened, and they stared in silent surprise at Catherine, who had not returned to the village since her flight with Chaval. She was so upset that she didn't even close the door, but stood there trembling and speechless. She had counted on finding her mother alone, and the sight of the young man drove from her mind the speech she had prepared on the way.

"What the hell are you doing here?" shouted La Maheude, without even getting up. "I don't want anything more to do with you. Get out!"

Catherine groped for words.

"Mama, I brought some coffee and sugar . . . for the children. . . . I put in some extra hours—I thought I could help them. . . ."

She pulled from her pockets a pound of coffee and a pound of sugar, and screwing up her courage, she put them on the table. She was tortured by the thought that Le Voreux was on strike while she was still working at Jean-Bart, and the only way she could think of to help her parents a little was to use the excuse about doing it for the children. But her generosity had no softening effect on her mother, who replied:

"Instead of bringing us luxuries you'd have done better to stay here and help us earn enough for bread."

She raged at Catherine, relieving her pent-up emotions by saying to her face everything she had been repeating about her for a month. To go off with a man, to live with him when you're only sixteen and you have a family in desperate straits! You have to be the most unnatural kind of daughter to do such a thing! She could easily enough overlook a mistake, but no mother could ever forgive a trick like that! And it wasn't as if they'd kept her on a short leash! Not at all—she'd been as free as air, and all they asked was that she come home to sleep.

"Tell me, what kind of fire do you have in your blood at your age?"

Standing motionless by the table, her head hanging down, Catherine listened to her mother. A shiver ran through her thin, underdeveloped body and she struggled to reply.

"Oh, if it was just *me* . . . for all the pleasure *I* get out of it! It's him. When he wants to, I pretty much have to, don't I? Because he's stronger than I am, you know. . . . Who can ever tell how things are going to turn out? Never mind, it's done and it can't be undone—it might as well be him as another, now. He'll have to marry me."

She defended herself without indignation, with the passive resignation of the girl who submits to the male early in life. Wasn't it always this way? She had never dreamed of anything else—an assault behind the slag heap, a baby at sixteen, shared poverty if her young man married her. She wasn't blushing and trembling out of shame, but only because she was being treated like a tramp in front of this young man, whose presence somehow oppressed her and filled her with despair.

Meanwhile Etienne had gotten up and was pretending to shake down what was left of the fire so as not to get in their way. But their eyes met, and he saw that she was pale and exhausted—though still pretty, with those bright eyes shining out of her yellowing face; he became aware of a strange feeling—his bitterness was gone, and all he wanted was for her to be happy with the man she had preferred to him. He felt a need to look after her, a desire to go to Montsou and make this other fellow behave decently. But Catherine saw nothing but pity in this continued tenderness—he must really despise her to look at her that way! And she felt so heartsick that she choked up, unable to mumble another word of excuse.

"That's right, you might as well keep quiet," continued La Maheude, implacable. "If you've come back to stay, come in. If not, get out right away and consider yourself lucky that I can't get up—or you'd have already felt my foot somewhere!"

Suddenly, as if this threat were immediately being translated into action, Catherine received a swift kick in the rear, a kick so violent that it stunned her with surprise and pain. It was Chaval, who had bounded in through the open door and let fly his foot like an unruly horse. He had been watching her for a few minutes from outside.

"You bitch!" he roared. "I followed you. I knew damn well you'd come back here to get yourself screwed to the eyeballs! And you even pay him for it! You soak him in coffee at my expense!"

La Maheude and Etienne were too stupefied to move. With a furious gesture Chaval drove Catherine toward the door.

"Get the hell out of here!"

As she sought refuge in a corner, he turned on her mother.

"A fine thing—playing watchdog while your whore of a daughter is upstairs with her legs in the air!"

He caught Catherine by the wrist and, shaking her, dragged her outside. At the door he turned again to La Maheude, who remained nailed to her chair. She had even forgotten to tuck her breast back into her blouse. Estelle had fallen asleep with her nose pressed into her mother's woolen skirt, and the enormous breast was hanging free and bare, like the udder of a huge cow.

"When the daughter isn't here the mother gets *her* innings

in," Chaval shouted. "Go ahead, parade your tits in front of him! He won't turn his nose up, your son of a bitch of a boarder!"

Etienne was overcome by a desire to hit him. Fear of stirring up the village by a fight had kept him from tearing Catherine from Chaval's hands, but now he too was swept by rage, and the two men stood face to face with murder in their eyes. It was their old hatred, a long-unavowed jealousy, exploding into the open, and one of them would have to destroy the other.

"Watch out!" Etienne muttered through closed teeth. "I'll get you for this!"

"Try!" answered Chaval.

They stared at one another for a few seconds, so close that the hot breaths of each scorched the other's face. It was finally Catherine who imploringly took her lover's hand and led him away. She dragged him from the village, fleeing without a backward glance.

"What a brute!" Etienne murmured as he slammed the door shut. He was so shaken by anger that he had to sit down.

La Maheude sat opposite him, still motionless. She made a sweeping gesture, and the silence that followed was awkward and heavy with things unspoken. In spite of himself, his eyes went back to her breast, that flow of white flesh whose dazzle now embarrassed him. True enough, she was forty and she was shapeless, like a good brood mare who had put down too often, but many still found her desirable—large, solid, her face now drawn and faded, but with remnants of former good looks. Slowly and calmly she had taken her breast in both hands and put it back inside her blouse. A rosy corner was still peeking out and she pushed it in with a finger, then buttoned herself up so that she was now all black and dumpy again in her old jacket.

"What a pig he is," she said finally. "Only a dirty pig like that would have such disgusting ideas. . . . Not that I give a damn! He didn't even deserve an answer."

Then, without taking her eyes off the young man, she added in a frank voice:

"I have my faults, of course, but that's not one of them. . . . Only two men have ever laid a hand on me—a haulage boy once, when I was fifteen, and then Maheu. If he had left me the way the other did, I don't really know what would have happened. And I'm not boasting about having been faithful to him since our marriage, because often when you behave well it's because there's been no opportunity to do otherwise. . . . But I'm telling you the way things are, and I know a few neighbors who wouldn't be able to say as much, could they?"

"That's true enough," answered Etienne, getting up.

And he left while she, having put the sleeping Estelle down on two chairs, began to relight the fire. If Maheu had caught and sold a fish, they'd still be able to make a soup.

Outside, night was already falling, a glacial night, and Etienne walked along with his head down, gripped by a black despair. It was no longer just anger against the man or pity for the poor, mistreated girl—the brutal scene was fading, dimming, and he was brought back to the sufferings of all of them, to the abominations of poverty. Once again he saw the breadless village, the women and children who would have nothing to eat that night, all of them fighting on empty stomachs. And in the terrible melancholy of dusk the doubts that sometimes stirred within him sprang up again, torturing him with a force he had never felt before. What a frightful responsibility he had taken upon himself! Was he to urge them further, make them stubbornly resist now that there was neither money nor credit? And what would happen if no help came, if hunger quenched their courage? Suddenly he had a vision of disaster: children dying, mothers sobbing, while thin, emaciated men were going down into the mines once again. He walked on, his feet kicking against the stones, and the thought that the Company would prove the stronger and that he would be responsible for the suffering of his comrades filled him with unbearable anguish.

When he raised his head he found himself in front of Le Voreux. The black mass of the buildings grew heavier in the increasing darkness. The deserted mine yard cluttered with enormous motionless shadows was like a corner of an abandoned fortress. As soon as the hoisting engine had stopped, the very soul of the place seemed to have left. At this time of night nothing was alive—not a lantern, not a voice—and the exhaust of the pump itself was no more than a far-off groan coming from some unknown place, here in this annihilation of what had once been a mine.

As Etienne watched, his courage revived. If the workers were suffering from hunger, at least the Company was having to dig into its millions. Why should it turn out to be the stronger in this war of labor against capital? In any case it would find victory expensive. They would count their dead afterward. Once again he was gripped by the fury of battle, the savage desire to banish poverty even at the price of death. The village might just as well die all at once as

continue to die piecemeal of starvation and injustice. His
badly digested reading came back to him, bringing to mind
examples of people who had set fire to their cities to stop the
enemy, vaguely remembered stories of mothers who saved
their children from slavery by dashing their brains out
against the cobblestones and of men who let themselves die of
starvation rather than eat the bread of tyrants. It all went to
his head, and a flaming joy sprang from his black despair,
chasing doubt and making him ashamed of his momentary
cowardice. And in this rebirth of his faith, gusts of pride
exalted him further—the joy of being a leader, of seeing
himself obeyed to the point of sacrifice, the expanded dream
of his power and of the day of his triumph. He could already
imagine the scene of simple grandeur in which he would refuse power for himself and restore authority to the hands of
the people once he had triumphed.

But he was startled out of his reverie by the sound of
Maheu's voice telling him about his good luck—the magnificent trout he had caught and sold for three francs. There
would be soup tonight. Etienne let his friend go back to the
village alone, saying he would follow, then went into L'-
Avantage and sat down at a table; he waited for a customer to
leave before bluntly informing Rasseneur that he was going
to write to Pluchart and ask him to come immediately. He
had made up his mind; he wanted to organize a closed
meeting because he was convinced that victory was assured if
the mass of Montsou miners were to join the International.

4

The closed meeting was set for two o'clock Thursday at
the widow Désir's Bon Joyeux. Outraged by the suffering
inflicted upon her "children," the widow was firm in her
support, especially since her cabaret was nearly empty. Never
had there been a less thirsty strike; the drunkards locked
themselves up at home lest they disobey the command to be
on their best behavior. Montsou, which swarmed with people
on fair-days, desolately displayed its silent and funereal main
street. No beer flowed from bar or belly; the gutters were
dry. At Casimir's and at Le Progrès, nothing could be seen
but the pale faces of the bar girls, searching up and down the
road, and in Montsou itself the entire string of bars from

Lenfant's to Tison's, by way of Piquette's and La Tête-
Coupée, was deserted; only the Saint-Eloi, which was fre-
quented by the foremen, was still serving an occasional beer.
The emptiness even reached the Volcan, where the ladies
were unemployed due to the lack of admirers—despite the
fact that they had lowered their price from ten to five sous
because of the hard times. It was as if the whole countryside
were in deep mourning.

"My God!" the widow Désir had exclaimed, slapping her
thighs with both hands. "It's all the fault of the gendarmes!
Let them throw me in jail if they want, but I've got to get
back at them!"

For her, all the authorities, all the bosses, were "gendarmes"—a term of general contempt in which she enveloped
all the enemies of the people. She had received Etienne's
request with enthusiasm; her whole place belonged to the
miners, she would let them have the dance hall free, and she
herself would send out the invitations, since that was what
the law required. And if the law didn't like it, so much the
better—she'd give them an earful! The very next day Etienne
brought her some fifty letters to sign—he had had them
copied out by those neighbors in the village who knew how
to write—and then the letters were sent off to the mines: to
the delegates and to the men they were most sure of. The
ostensible business of the day was to discuss the continuation
of the strike, but actually they were expecting Pluchart and
counting on him to make a speech that would result in mass
adherence to the International.

On Thursday morning Etienne became worried; his old
foreman, who had promised in a telegram to come on
Wednesday evening, had not yet arrived. What could be
wrong? He was upset at not being able to talk things over
with him before the meeting. By nine o'clock Etienne was in
Montsou, thinking that Pluchart might have gone straight
there without stopping at Le Voreux.

"No, I haven't seen your friend," answered the widow
Désir. "But everything is ready—come and see."

She led him into the dance hall. The decorations were still
the same—garlands from the ceiling holding up a wreath of
colored paper flowers, and shields of gilded cardboard displaying the names of the saints along the walls—but the
musicians' platform had been replaced by a table and three
chairs in one corner of the room, and there were diagonal
lines of benches to complete the decor.

"That's perfect," said Etienne.

"And remember," the widow said, "you're at home here.

Shout and argue as much as you want. . . . If the gendarmes come, they'll only get in over my dead body."

Despite his uneasiness, Etienne couldn't help smiling as he looked at her. She seemed enormous; her breasts were so large that each one would have required a man for itself—which made people say that these days she had to use two of her six weekday lovers each night because of the heavy workload!

But Etienne was surprised to see Rasseneur and Souvarine come in, and when the widow left the three of them alone in the large empty room he exclaimed:

"What!—you here already?"

Since the enginemen were not on strike, Souvarine had worked that night at Le Voreux and had merely come along out of curiosity. As for Rasseneur, he had seemed upset for the past couple of days, and his fat round face had lost its good-natured smile.

"Pluchart hasn't come and I'm very worried," Etienne added.

The innkeeper avoided his eyes and muttered:

"That doesn't surprise me. I'm not expecting him."

"What?"

Rasseneur took courage, and looking Etienne straight in the eyes, he said boldly:

"Well, if you want to know the truth, I sent him a letter too, and in that letter I begged him not to come. . . . I think we should handle things ourselves, without asking help from strangers."

Etienne, trembling and beside himself with anger, his eyes locked with those of his comrade, stammeringly repeated:

"You did that? You did that?"

"Yes, I did that—and yet you know how much confidence I have in Pluchart! He's clever and he's dependable and you can work with him. . . . But you see, as for your ideas, I don't give a damn about them! All this stuff about politics and government is crap! What I want is for the miner to be treated better. I worked down there for twenty years, and I sweated out so much misery and exhaustion that I swore I'd try to make it easier for the poor bastards who are still down there—and the one thing I know is that you won't get anywhere with all your rigmarole, you'll only make things worse for the miner. . . . When hunger forces him to go down again he'll be cheated even more—the Company will pay him off in blows, like an escaped dog driven back to his kennel. . . . And that's what I want to prevent, understand?"

Planted solidly on his thick legs, his belly thrust out, he

raised his voice, and the whole nature of this sensible and patient man manifested itself in the lucid sentences that flowed forth so effortlessly. Wasn't it idiotic to think that you could suddenly change the world overnight, put the workers in the place of the bosses, share out all the money the way you share an apple? It might take thousands and thousands of years for that to happen. Well, you could take those miracles and shove 'em! The best thing to do if you didn't want to mess everything up was to go straight ahead and insist on reforms that were possible, to improve the worker's life at every opportunity. That's why, if he were in charge, he'd get the Company to agree to better working conditions; if they did anything else, if they were pigheaded, they'd all end up starving to death.

Speechless with indignation, Etienne had let him talk. Now he shouted:

"My God, don't you have any blood in your veins?"

In another minute he would have struck Rasseneur, and to resist the temptation he strode through the room, taking out his anger by kicking a path through the benches.

"At least close the door," said Souvarine. "There's no need for everybody to hear."

He closed it himself, then calmly sat down on one of the chairs at the table. He had rolled a cigarette and was watching the others with his gentle, intelligent eyes, his lips drawn in a slight smile.

"Getting angry won't help," Rasseneur continued judiciously. "At first I thought you were level-headed. It was a good idea to urge the men to remain calm, to force them to stay home, to use your power to maintain order. But now you're heading them straight into trouble!"

After each lunge through the benches Etienne would come back to the innkeeper, grab him by the shoulders, and shake him as he shouted his answers into his face.

"But, God damn it, I *am* for keeping calm! Yes, I've imposed discipline on them! Yes, I'm still advising them not to start trouble! But in the end we can't let ourselves be made fools of! . . . You're lucky you can remain cool, but as for me, there are times when I feel my head's going to explode!"

This was a confession on his part. He was mocking at his own neophyte illusions, his religious dream of a world in which justice would soon reign over men who had become brothers. A fine idea just to cross your arms and wait—if you wanted to see men devour one another like wolves until the end of the world! No! Action had to be taken or injustice would be eternal, and the rich would always be sucking blood from the poor! That was why he could not forgive himself the stupidity of having once said that politics should be excluded from the social problem. At that time he had known nothing, but since then he had read, he had studied, and now his ideas had matured; he could boast of having a system. Unfortunately he explained it badly, in confused phrases that still had little bits and pieces of all the theories he had successively come across and then abandoned. Crowning everything were the ideas of Karl Marx: capital was the result of theft, and labor had the duty and the right to reconquer this stolen wealth. To put the theory into practice, he had at first let himself be won over by Proudhon's foolish dream of mutual credit, of a vast bank of exchange which would eliminate middlemen; then he had become wildly enthusiastic about Lasalle's cooperative societies, set up by the state and gradually transforming the world into a single industrial city—but he had become discouraged by the difficulty of controlling the scheme; more recently, he had taken up the notion of collectivism and was demanding that all instruments of work be collectively owned, but it was all still very vague; he did not know how to realize this newest dream, for he was still inhibited by scruples arising from sensitivity and reason, and he couldn't bring himself to the absolute affirmations of the dogmatists. He had only reached the stage of saying that the first thing was to seize the government. After that, they would see.

"But what's got into you? Why are you lining up with the bourgeois now?" he went on violently, coming back and planting himself in front of the innkeeper again. "You yourself used to say: 'things will have to blow up!' "

Rasseneur blushed slightly.

"Yes, I said that, and if things blow up you'll see I'm no more of a coward than the next man. . . . Only I refuse to be with those who make trouble just to get something out of it."

It was Etienne's turn to blush. The two men were no longer shouting, but their bitter rivalry had made them sharp and nasty. Indeed, it was this very rivalry that made them push their systems to the extreme, forcing the one into an exaggerated revolutionary stance, pushing the other to adopt an affectation of prudence, carrying both of them, in spite of themselves, beyond their real ideas by the ineluctable pressure of roles forced upon them and not freely chosen. And Souvarine, who was listening to them, let a silent contempt play over his fair, girlish face—the crushing contempt of a man ready to give his own life without fanfare, without even the glory of martyrdom.

"I suppose you mean me by that?" asked Etienne. "Are you jealous?"

"Jealous of what?" answered Rasseneur. "*I* didn't set myself up as a great man. *I'm* not trying to organize a section at Montsou so I can become secretary of it!"

Etienne started to interrupt him, but he continued:

"Be honest! You don't give a damn about the International—all you want is to be our leader and to play the gentleman by corresponding with your wonderful Federal Council of the Nord."

A silence fell. Then, trembling, Etienne replied:

"All right, then. . . . I thought I'd been fair about it all. I always consulted you because I knew you had been carrying on the struggle long before I came. But since you can't stand sharing the leadership, from now on I'll do things on my own. . . . And to begin with, you might as well know that the meeting will take place even if Pluchart doesn't come, and that the men will join up in spite of you."

"Oh, join up," muttered the innkeeper. "That's not all there is to it. . . . You'll have to get them to pay their dues."

"Not at all! The International allows workers on strike to postpone their payment. We'll pay later, but the International will come to our aid right away."

Rasseneur suddenly flew into a rage.

"All right, we'll see! . . . I'll be at your meeting and I'll speak out. I won't let you turn my friends' heads. I'll show them where their real interest lies. We'll see which one of us they'll follow—me, whom they've known for thirty years, or you, who've upset everything here in less than a year. . . . No, no—get off my back! We'll see which of us will crush the other!"

And he left, slamming the door behind him. The paper garlands trembled under the ceiling and the gilded shields rattled against the walls. Then the large room returned to its heavy silence.

Seated in front of the table, Souvarine went on smoking in his calm way. After having walked up and down for a while in silence, Etienne was giving vent to his feelings at great length. Was it his fault if everybody was abandoning that big good-for-nothing and rallying to him? And he denied having sought popularity, he didn't even know how it had all happened—the good will of the village, the confidence of the miners, the power he now had over them. He was indignant at being accused of wanting to make trouble just because of personal ambition, and he beat his chest, protesting his feelings of fraternity.

Suddenly he stopped in front of Souvarine and shouted:

"Listen, if I thought I was responsible for wasting one drop of a friend's blood, I'd take off for America immediately!"

The engineman shrugged his shoulders and again his lips thinned into a smile.

"Oh, blood," he murmured. "What does that matter? The earth has need of it."

Etienne calmed down, took a chair, and sat down opposite him, his elbows leaning on the table. That fair face, whose dreamy eyes would occasionally be illuminated by red glints that made them look savage, upset him and had a peculiar effect on his will. Without his friend having spoken, vanquished by just this heavy silence, he felt as if he were being gradually absorbed.

"Look here," he asked, "what would you do in my place? Isn't it right for me to try to do something? . . . The best thing for us is to join the Association, isn't it?"

Souvarine slowly exhaled a jet of smoke and replied with his favorite word:

"Foolishness! But meanwhile it's something. . . . Besides, their International will soon get going. He's working on it."

"Who is?"

"He!"

Souvarine had pronounced this word in a hushed voice, in a tone of religious fervor, while glancing toward the east. He was speaking of the master, of Bakunin the Exterminator.

"Only he can give the final blow," he continued. "All your learned gentlemen with their talk of evolution are cowards. . . . Under his orders, within three years the International will have crushed the old world."

Etienne was listening with complete attention. He was burning with a desire to learn, to understand this cult of destruction about which the engineman would only rarely and mysteriously speak, as if he were keeping the secret for himself.

"But tell me—what is your goal?"

"To destroy everything. . . . No more nations, no more governments, no more property, no more God or religion."

"I understand that, but where will it get you?"

"To the primitive and formless community, to a new world, to a fresh start."

"By what means? How do you expect to go about it?"

"By fire, by poison, by the dagger. The outlaw is the true hero, the avenger of the people, the revolutionary in action— someone who has no need of fancy phrases from books. A

terrifying series of assassinations is needed to frighten those
in power and arouse the people."

As he spoke, Souvarine became terrible. Ecstasy lifted him
from his chair, a mystic flame darted from his pale eyes, and
his delicate hands murderously grasped the edge of the table.
Gripped by fear, Etienne watched him, remembering the
half-confided stories about mines laid under the Czar's palace; police chiefs knifed like wild boars; his mistress, the only
woman he had ever loved, hanged in Moscow one rainy
morning while he, there in the crowd, was kissing her with
his eyes for the last time.

"No, no," murmured Etienne, with a gesture meant to
sweep aside these abominable visions. "We haven't sunk to
that yet, here. Assassination, arson—never! It's monstrous,
it's unjust—all the comrades would rise up to strangle the
guilty one."

He still did not understand, his race rejected this dark
dream of the extermination of the world, of a world razed to
the earth like a field of wheat. What would happen afterward? How would the people spring up again? He demanded
an answer.

"Explain your program to me. We want to know where
we're going, the rest of us."

His eyes staring into space, Souvarine coolly summed up:

"All discussions about the future are criminal because they
prevent pure destruction and impede the march of the revolution."

This made Etienne laugh, despite the chill the answer sent
through him. He willingly admitted there was much to be
said for these ideas, the terrifying simplicity of which attracted him, but it would make things too easy for Rasseneur if
they were to be spread among the comrades. They had to be
practical.

The widow Désir suggested they have lunch. They accepted and went into the bar, which on weekdays was separated from the dance hall by a movable partition. When they
had finished their omelet and cheese the engineman wanted
to leave. His friend tried to detain him, but he said:

"What for?—just to hear you talk a lot of foolishness? . . .
I've had my fill of it! Good-bye."

And he walked out in his gentle but determined way, a
cigarette dangling from his lips.

Etienne's anxiety was increasing. It was one o'clock and
Pluchart was obviously not going to keep his word. At about
one-thirty the delegates began to show up, and he had to
receive them because he wanted to check on those coming

in, lest the Company had sent its usual spies. He examined
every letter of invitation and looked everybody over; many
people, of course, were admitted without letters of invitation—
the door was open to anybody he knew. As two o'clock was
striking he saw Rasseneur arrive, go to the bar, and stand
there slowly finishing his pipe and talking. This mocking calm
was the last blow to Etienne's self-possession, especially since
the clowns—Zacharie, Mouquet, and some others—had also
come, just to see the fun. They couldn't have cared less about
the strike and were happy not to have to work; taking a
table, they spent their last sous on beer and were teasing and
sneering at the others, the dedicated ones who were about to
be bored to death.

Another quarter of an hour went by. The men were
beginning to get impatient, and Etienne, desperate, had just
decided they should go in when the widow Désir, who was
peering down the street, called out:

"Here comes your gentleman now!"

And it was in fact Pluchart, coming in a carriage drawn by
a winded horse. He immediately leaped to the road; thin and
dandified, with a squarish head much too big for his body,
under his black frock coat he was dressed in the Sunday best
of a prosperous workingman. For the past five years he had
not lifted so much as a file, and made vain by his platform
success, he took great pains with his appearance, paying
special attention to his hair; but he was still stiff-jointed, and
the nails on his big hands, eaten away by the iron, had never
grown in again. Very active, he advanced his ambition by
traveling endlessly up and down the countryside to spread his
ideas.

"Don't be angry with me," he said, forestalling all questions and reproaches. "Yesterday a lecture at Preuilly in the
morning and a meeting at Valençay in the evening. Today
lunch at Marchiennes with Sauvagnat.... Finally I was able
to get a carriage. I'm exhausted, you can tell from my voice.
But it doesn't matter, I'll speak anyway."

He was crossing the threshold of the Bon Joyeux when he
suddenly stopped short.

"Damn—I'm forgetting the cards! We'd be in a fine mess."

He went back to the carriage, which the coachman was
drawing up, took from the trunk a small black wooden box,
and carried it off under his arm.

Beaming, Etienne followed in his shadow, while Rasseneur,
embarrassed, hadn't the courage to offer his hand. But
Pluchart had already grabbed it, saying only a quick word
about his letter: what a funny idea! why not have this

meeting? you should always have a meeting whenever you could. The widow Désir offered him a drink but he refused. Pointless!—he didn't need a drink to speak. The only thing was that he was in a hurry—he planned to go on to Joiselle that evening because he wanted to talk things over with Legoujeux. They entered the dance hall as a group, with Maheu and Levaque, who had come late, following them. The door was then locked so they would be undisturbed, and this made the clowns snicker even louder, Zacharie calling out to Mouquet that the result of all this hocus-pocus would probably be a baby.

About a hundred miners sat waiting on the benches in the stuffy room, in which the warm odors of the last dance seemed to be rising from the floor. Whispers flew and heads turned as the new arrivals took their seats. Everyone looked at the gentleman from Lille, whose black frock coat occasioned a certain surprise and uneasiness.

But on a motion from Etienne they immediately set up a committee. He called out names and the others approved by raising their hands. Pluchart was elected chairman, and then Maheu and Etienne himself were named members. There was a shuffling of chairs and the committee took its seats. For a moment everybody was looking for the chairman; he had disappeared behind the table and was putting away the box, which had till then not left his hands. Reappearing, he rapped his fist on the table to get attention, then began in a husky voice:

"Citizens . . ."

A little door opened and he had to stop. It was the widow Désir, coming in through the kitchen and carrying six beers on a tray.

"Don't let me disturb you," she whispered; "people get thirsty when they talk."

Maheu took the tray from her and Pluchart was able to continue. He said that he was touched by the wonderful reception given him by the workers of Montsou, and he apologized for being late, mentioning his fatigue and his sore throat. Then he gave the floor to citizen Rasseneur, who was asking for it.

Rasseneur had already planted himself beside the table, next to the beers. A turned chair served him as a speaker's platform. He seemed deeply stirred and he cleared his throat before shouting out:

"Comrades . . ."

His influence over the miners lay essentially in his facility with words—the ease with which he was capable of talking to them for hours without getting tired. He would make no gesture, remaining stolid and smiling, and would overwhelm them, dazzle them, until they would call out: "Yes, yes, it's true, you're right!" That day, however, from his very first words, he had sensed a stubborn opposition. He therefore proceeded very carefully and began by arguing only against the continuation of the strike, waiting to be applauded before attacking the International. Of course, honor militated against giving way to the demands of the Company, but what suffering, what a terrible future lay before them if they had to hold out much longer! And without actually coming out for surrender, he sapped their courage; he described the villages dying of hunger and asked what resources those who were for holding out could count on. Three or four of his friends called out their approval, but this only accentuated the cold silence of the majority, their increasingly irritated disapproval of his talk. Then, despairing of winning them over, he lost control and predicted trouble if they let their heads be turned by provocations from outsiders.

Two-thirds of the men had risen to their feet; they were angry, they wanted to prevent him from saying more—he was insulting them by treating them like children who were incapable of taking care of themselves! Taking swallow after swallow of beer, he nevertheless went on talking through the tumult, shouting angrily that the man who could keep him from doing his duty was not yet born!

Pluchart was on his feet. As he did not have a bell, he was banging his fist on the table, repeating in his hoarse voice:

"Citizens ... citizens ..."

He was finally able to obtain a little order, and the meeting having been consulted, he withdrew the floor from Rasseneur. The delegates who had represented the miners in the interview with the manager led the others, all of them maddened by hunger and stirred up by new ideas. The outcome of the vote was a foregone conclusion.

"*You* don't give a damn—*you've* got enough to eat!" cried Levaque, shaking his fist at Rasseneur.

Etienne had leaned over behind the chairman's back to calm Maheu, who was red with rage at this hypocritical speech.

"Citizens," said Pluchart, "let me say a few words."

A deep silence fell. He spoke. His voice sounded painful and hoarse, but he was used to it—everywhere he went he paraded both his laryngitis and his program. Little by little he let his voice swell out, making it play on the sympathy of his audience. His arms were outstretched, and he punctuated his

phrases by the sway of his shoulders; his eloquence had
something of the pulpit about it, and the religious way of
letting the ends of his sentences drop made for a monotonous
droning that ended by winning his listeners over.

He took as his theme the power and the benefits of the
International—the theme he always began with in places
where he was unknown. First he explained its goal: the
emancipation of the workers; then he outlined its imposing
structure: at the bottom the commune, higher up, the province, then the nation, and at the summit, humanity itself. His
arms rose slowly, piling up the levels and building the immense cathedral of the world of the future. Then he explained its internal organization: he read the statutes, talked
of the congresses, pointed out the growing importance of the
work and the enlargement of the program—which having
started with the question of wages was now working toward
the destruction of the system itself, so that the entire question
of wages would be finished with once and for all. No more
nationalities—the workers of the whole world united in a
common need for justice, sweeping out bourgeois rot, finally
setting up a free society in which those who did not work
would not reap! He was roaring, and his breath shook the
colored paper flowers under the low grimy ceiling that sent
his voice echoing back down.

The men's heads bobbed as if on a tidal wave. Some of
them cried out:

"That's right! . . . We're with you!"

He went on. In three years the world would be theirs. He
listed those who had been won over. Memberships were
pouring in from all sides; no new religion had ever made so
many converts! Then, when they were the masters, they
would dictate the laws to the bosses and have them by the
throats in their turn!

"That's right! . . . They'll be the ones to go down into the
mines!"

He gestured for silence. Now he took up the question of
strikes. In principle he was against them—they were too slow
a method and they tended to increase the suffering of the
workers. But for lack of anything better, when strikes became inevitable you had to go through with them because
they had the advantage of disorganizing capital. And he cited
some examples to show how the International was a godsend
for the strikes: in Paris, during a strike of bronze-workers,
the bosses had suddenly agreed to everything, terrified at the
news that the International was sending help; in London, the
International had saved some coal miners by repatriating, at

its own expense, a group of Belgians called in by the owner. Just signing up was enough to make the companies quake— the workers were joining the great army of laborers who were ready to die for one another rather than remain the slaves of capitalist society.

He was interrupted by applause. Wiping his forehead with his handkerchief, he refused a beer offered by Maheu. When he tried to continue, another burst of applause interrupted him.

"They're ripe!" he said quickly to Etienne. "They've had enough. . . . Quick, the cards!"

He dived under the table and reappeared with the little black wooden box.

"Citizens," he shouted, dominating the tumult, "here are the membership cards. Let your delegates come up and I'll give them some to pass around. . . . We'll straighten everything out afterward."

Rasseneur rushed up and again protested. Etienne was also getting excited, for he too had a speech to make. Complete confusion followed. Levaque was cocking his fists as though ready to fight. Maheu was on his feet, talking, but not a word could be heard. In the mounting excitement the dust was rising from the floor—the flying dust of former dances, poisoning the air with the strong smell of haulage girls and mine boys.

Suddenly the little door opened and the widow Désir filled it with her belly and breasts, saying in a thundering voice:

"For God's sake, be quiet! . . . The gendarmes are here!"

The local chief of police had come, a little late, to draw up a report and disband the meeting. He was accompanied by four gendarmes. For five minutes the widow had stalled them at the door, saying she was in her own house and certainly had the right to have some friends in. But they had shoved her aside and she had run ahead to warn her "children."

"You'll have to get out this way," she continued. "One of them's guarding the courtyard. It doesn't matter, my little woodshed opens onto the alley. . . . But hurry up!"

The police chief was already beating his fist against the door, and since nobody was opening it, he was threatening to break it down. Some spy must have given them away, for he was shouting that the meeting was illegal because many of the miners were there without letters of invitation.

Inside the room the confusion was becoming even greater. They couldn't just slip away like this—they hadn't voted either for joining up or for continuing the strike. Everybody

insisted on talking at the same time. Finally the chairman
had the idea of taking a vote by acclamation. Hands were
raised, delegates hastily declared they were joining up in the
name of absent comrades. And it was in this way that ten
thousand Montsou miners became members of the International.

Meanwhile the stampede had begun. To protect the retreat
the widow Désir had gone over to lean against the door,
which was shaking under the thumps of the gendarmes' rifle
butts. Striding over the benches, the miners were slipping
out, one after another, through the kitchen and the woodshed. Rasseneur was one of the first to disappear, and Levaque followed him, forgetting his insults and hoping for the
offer of a beer to revive his spirits. Etienne, after having
grabbed up the little box, was waiting with Pluchart and
Maheu, who felt honor-bound to be the last to go. Just as
they were leaving, the lock gave, and the police chief found
himself in front of the widow, whose belly and breasts were
still blocking his way.

"I hope you're satisfied now that you've torn my place
apart," she said. "You can see there's no one here."

The chief, a slow-moving man who didn't care much for
excitement, merely threatened to lock her up, and taking his
four men with him, he went off to make his report—followed
by the snickers of Zacharie and Mouquet, who were struck
with admiration at the good trick their friends had pulled and
quite indifferent to armed authority.

Out in the alley Etienne, awkwardly holding the box, raced
ahead, followed by the others. Suddenly he thought of Pierron and asked why nobody had seen him; Maheu, as he ran,
answered that Pierron was sick: a convenient illness—the
fear of compromising himself. They wanted Pluchart to stay,
but without stopping he said he was leaving immediately for
Joiselle, where Legoujeux was waiting for orders. At this they
shouted good-bye to him, and without slowing down, their
heels in the air, they raced through Montsou. Between gasps
they exchanged a few words. Etienne and Maheu were laughing confidently, sure of victory now: once the International
had sent help the Company would beg them to go back to
work. And in this surge of hope, in this gallop of heavy boots
resounding on the cobblestones of the road, there was also
something else, something wild and menacing—a violence
that was to sweep through and inflame the villages in the
four corners of the countryside.

5

Another two weeks went by. It was the beginning of January, and cold fogs numbed the immense plain. The misery had increased; the villages were dying hour by hour under the growing famine. The four thousand francs sent from London by the International had not bought even three days' bread. Since then, nothing more had come. With this great hope dead, the miners' courage was broken. Whom were they to count on, now that even their own brothers were abandoning them? They felt lost in the midst of the endless winter, cut off from the world.

By Tuesday, Village 240 was at the end of its resources. Etienne and the delegates had tried everything: they started new drives for support in the neighboring cities, and even as far away as Paris; they asked for contributions; they organized meetings. But all these efforts led nowhere, for the public, which had been stirred at the beginning, was losing interest now that the strike was dragging on peacefully, without any exciting incidents. The meager contributions barely sufficed to sustain the poorest families; the others lived by pawning their clothes and selling their household goods piece by piece. Everything found its way to the secondhand dealers—the wool stuffing from mattresses, kitchen utensils, even furniture. At one point they thought they were saved; the small storekeepers of Montsou, whose business had been killed off by Maigrat, had offered credit in the hope of winning back their customers, and for a week Verdonck, the grocer, and Carouble and Smelten, the two bakers, kept open shop: then their supplies gave out and all three called a halt. The marshals were overjoyed; the end result of all this was that the miners were building up a crushing load of debts that would grind them down for a long time. No more credit anywhere, not so much as an old pot to sell—all they could do was crawl into a corner and die like starving curs!

Etienne would have sold his very flesh. He had given up his salary as secretary, and he had gone to Marchiennes to pawn his good frock coat and trousers, happy to keep the pot boiling a little longer at the Maheus'. All he had left were his boots, and he was only holding on to them to keep his feet in good shape, he said. His greatest regret was that the strike had broken out too soon, before the emergency fund had had a chance to build up. He saw this as the sole cause of the disaster, because obviously the workers would surely triumph over the bosses on the day the fund was large enough to enable them to resist. And he remembered how Souvarine had accused the Company of forcing the strike in order to wipe out the fund before it could build up.

The sight of the village, of these poor people without food or heat, wrenched his heart. He preferred to go out, to exhaust himself in long walks. One evening, as he was passing Réquillart on his way home, he saw an old woman lying unconscious at the side of the road; she was obviously dying of starvation, and after having gotten her up, he called to a girl he could see on the other side of the fence.

"Oh, it's you," he said, recognizing Mouquette. "Help me. We've got to make her drink something."

Moved to tears, Mouquette quickly ran back to her house, the tottering hovel her father had put together in the midst of the rubble, and returned almost immediately with some gin and some bread. The gin soon revived the old woman, who then silently and gluttonously gnawed at the bread. She was the mother of a miner and lived in a village near Cougny; she had fallen on her way back home from Joiselle, where she had gone in a vain attempt to borrow ten sous from a sister. As soon as she had eaten, she went off, still dazed.

Etienne had remained in the deserted grounds of Réquillart, the rotting sheds of which were disappearing under the brambles.

"Well, won't you come in and drink something?" Mouquette asked him laughingly.

And as he hesitated, she continued:

"Don't tell me you're still afraid of me?"

He followed her inside, won over by her laugh and touched by the fact that she had given her bread so willingly. She did not want them to stay in her father's room and led him into her own, where she immediately poured out two small glasses of gin. The room was very clean and he complimented her on it. Actually, the family did not seem short of anything: the father was still working as a stableman at Le Voreux, and she, just so as not to sit around with her hands in her lap, had gone to work as a laundress, which brought in thirty sous a day. Just because a girl fools around with men doesn't mean she's lazy!

"Tell me," she murmured suddenly, coming over and putting her arms tenderly around his waist, "why won't you love me?"

She had said it so sweetly that he began to laugh.

"But I do," he answered.

"No, no—not the way I want. . . . You know I'm dying for it. . . . Well?—it would give me so much pleasure!"

It was true, she had been asking him for the last six months. He looked at her as she clung to him, hugging him with her trembling arms, her face lifted in such a plea for love that he was very moved. There was nothing beautiful about her big round face with its yellowed complexion ruined by the coal, but her eyes were burning with such fire, such charm emanated from her, she quivered so with desire, that suddenly she seemed fresh and young. Faced with this gift so humbly and ardently offered, he could no longer refuse.

"Oh, you will, you will," she stammered, transported. "You will!"

And she gave herself to him as awkwardly and ecstatically as a virgin, as if it were the first time she had ever been with a man before. Then, when he left her, it was she who was overcome with gratitude: she thanked him and kissed his hands.

Etienne was a little ashamed of his good fortune. There was nothing to boast of in having had Mouquette, and as he left, he swore to himself that it wouldn't happen again. Still, he was fond of her; she was really a good-hearted creature.

When he got back to the village he learned of serious developments that made him forget the incident. There was a rumor abroad that the Company might consent to some concessions if the delegates were to make another appeal to the manager. At least that was what the foremen had been saying. The truth of the matter was that in this struggle the mine was suffering even more than the miners. On both sides obstinacy was causing ruin: labor was dying of hunger, but capital too was destroying itself. Each day of idleness was draining off hundreds of thousands of francs. Every idle machine was a dead machine. The plant and the equipment were both deteriorating, and the immobilized money was dribbling away like water soaking into sand. The small stock of coal in the Company yards was giving out, and customers were talking of turning to Belgian sources; this carried a threat for the future. But what especially frightened the Company, though it carefully hid the fact, was the increasing damage in the galleries and the faces. The foremen

could not handle the maintenance work; timbers were collapsing everywhere, and not an hour passed without some cave-
in. The damage had soon become so great that months of
repairs would be required before the cutters could begin
work again. Stories were already going around: at Crèvecoeur, nine hundred feet of tunneling had collapsed in one
single piece, blocking all access to the Cinq-Paumes vein, and
at Madeleine the Maugrétout vein was crumbling away and
filling up with water. At first the management refused to
acknowledge these facts, but two accidents, one following on
the heels of the other, had forced them to an admission. One
morning, near La Piolaine, a fissure appeared above the
north gallery of Mirou because of a cave-in the night before;
and the next day there was an internal subsidence in Le
Voreux which so shook a corner of the suburb that two
houses were almost destroyed.

Etienne and the delegates were reluctant to make another
move without knowing where the Board of Directors stood.
Dansaert, whom they questioned, avoided any definite answer: of course the misunderstanding was regretted and
everything possible would be done to bring about an agreement, but he said nothing specific. They finally decided to see
Monsieur Hennebeau again just so that they could not later
be accused of having refused the Company an opportunity to
acknowledge its errors. However, they swore not to give an
inch and to maintain their demands no matter what, since
justice was on their side alone.

The interview took place on Tuesday morning, the day on
which the village had sunk to its lowest ebb, and was less
cordial than the first one. Again it was Maheu who spoke,
explaining that his comrades had sent them to find out if the
directors had anything new to say to them. At first Monsieur
Hennebeau pretended to be surprised: he had received no
orders, and nothing could change so long as the miners
persisted in their odious rebellion. And his rigid authoritari-
anism had the most unfortunate effect; even if the delegates
had come with conciliatory notions, the manner in which
they were received would have been enough to confirm them
in their resistance. Then, after this beginning, the manager
seemed disposed to look for some grounds for mutual concessions: for example, the workers might agree to be paid
separately for timbering and the Company might raise payment for it by the two centimes the men said it was trying to
gain. However, he added that he was taking it upon himself
to make this offer; nothing had been agreed on, but he

flattered himself that he could obtain this concession from Paris. The delegates refused and repeated their demands: the retention of the old system, with an increase of five centimes per cart. At this point Monsieur Hennebeau admitted that he was empowered to negotiate with them directly, and he urged them to accept his offer in the name of their starving wives and children. But with their eyes fixed on the floor, their minds made up, they continued to say no with a fierce insistence. The meeting ended badly. Monsieur Hennebeau slammed the door behind them, and Etienne, Maheu, and the others, their heavy boots stamping on the cobblestones, set off in the mute fury of beaten men pushed to the wall.

At about two o'clock the women of the village made a move of their own and went to see Maigrat. The only hope left was to soften this man, to wrest another week of credit from him. The idea had come from La Maheude, who often counted too much on people's good nature. She got La Brûlé and La Levaque to go with her, but La Pierronne begged off by saying she could not leave Pierron, whose illness was still dragging on. Some other women joined the group, making about twenty in all. When the people of Montsou saw them coming—a somber and wretched line of women stretched across the road—they shook their heads nervously. Doors were shut, and one lady hid her silver. It was the first time the women had turned out, and nothing augured worse for the future: things must be pretty bad for the women to take to the roads like that. At Maigrat's there was a violent scene. He began by showing them in, snickering and pretending to think they had come to pay their debts— now that was nice of them, to get together so they could bring the money at one time. Then, as soon as La Maheude had spoken, he put on a show of anger. They must think he was crazy! More credit?—did they want to put him out of business? No, not so much as a potato, not so much as a crust of bread! And he suggested they go back to the grocer Verdonck and the bakers Carouble and Smelten, since that was where they took their custom these days. The women listened to him in frightened humility, apologized, searched his face for some sign of softening. He went back to his crude jokes, saying he would let La Brûlé have the whole shop if she would take him as a lover. They were all so eager to please that they began to laugh, and La Levaque even went so far as to say that *she* would be willing enough. But suddenly he became rough and shoved them toward the door. As they continued to persist in their pleas, he even struck one of them. Outside on the street, while the others

called him a traitor, La Maheude, shaking her clenched fists
in a gesture of vengeful fury, shrieked that she hoped he
would die, that a man like that didn't deserve to eat.

Their return to the village was a lugubrious affair. When
the women returned empty-handed the men stared at them,
then bowed their heads. It was all over now; the day would
end without so much as a spoonful of soup, and all the days
to follow stretched ahead into a cold darkness from which
not even a ray of hope glimmered. But it had been their own
choice, and nobody spoke of giving up. The very excess of
their misery made them even more stubborn, and they silently resolved to die like hunted beasts who remain at the
bottom of their holes rather than come out. Who would have
dared be the first to talk of giving up? They had all sworn to
stick together, and stick together they would, just as they did
in the mine when one of them was buried under a cave-in.
That's what they would have to do, and the mines had given
them plenty of experience in how to endure; when you had
been bred on fire and water from the time you were twelve,
you could certainly tighten your belt for a week. And their
determination was strengthened by a soldierly spirit of sacrifice—a spirit that came of pride in one's profession and
glory in the daily struggle against death.

That evening was a terrible one at the Maheus'. They all
sat in silence around the dying fire in which the last cake of
slack was smoking. The day before yesterday, after having
emptied the mattress handful by handful, they had finally
decided to sell the cuckoo clock for three francs, and the
room seemed bare and dead now that it was no longer filled
with the sound of the familiar tick-tock. The only little
luxury left was the pink cardboard box in the center of the
cupboard, an old gift from Maheu to which La Maheude
clung as though it were a jewel. The two good chairs were
gone, and Bonnemort and the children were squeezed together on an old mossy bench that had been brought in from the
garden. The deepening gray twilight seemed to intensify the
cold.

"What shall we do now?" La Maheude kept repeating,
crouched in front of the stove.

Etienne was standing there, staring at the portraits of the
Emperor and Empress pasted on the wall. He would have
torn them down a long time ago if the family, which found
them decorative, had not prevented him from doing so, and
he now muttered from between clenched teeth:

"And to think we won't get so much as two sous from
those popinjays who are watching us starve!"

"Suppose I pawn the box?" said La Maheude, pale and hesitant.

Maheu, who was seated on the edge of the table, his legs dangling and his chin sunk on his chest, straightened up:

"No! I don't want you to do that!"

La Maheude got up painfully and walked around the room. My God, could they really have come to such misery?—the cupboard without a crust in it, nothing left to sell, not even an idea about how to get a loaf of bread—and now the fire was going out! She turned angrily to Alzire, whom she had sent out that morning to search for cinders on the slag heap and who had returned empty-handed, saying that the Company would no longer allow that. Who cared about the Company? As if it was stealing to gather bits of waste coal! Despairingly, the child explained that a man had threatened to hit her, but she promised to go back the next day and let herself be beaten if necessary.

"And what about that good-for-nothing Jeanlin?" cried the mother. "Where is he now, I ask you? ... He was supposed to bring back some salad—at least we could have chewed a little grass, like the animals. Wait, you'll see—he won't come home tonight. He didn't come home last night. I don't know what he's up to, but the wretch always looks well-fed!"

"Maybe he picks up a few sous along the road," said Etienne.

At that she shook her fists, beside herself with rage.

"If I thought that! ... What, my children beg? I'd rather kill them and then kill myself afterward!"

Maheu had again sunk down on the edge of the table. Lénore and Henri, surprised that there was no supper, began to whine, while Old Bonnemort was silently and philosophically rolling his tongue around his mouth to make himself think he was eating. Nobody said anything. They were all exhausted by the aggravation of their various illnesses—the grandfather coughing and spitting up his black blobs, once more troubled by the rheumatism that was threatening to become dropsy; the father asthmatic, with water on his knees; the mother and children wracked by hereditary scrofula and anemia. Of course all of this went with the work: they only complained when a lack of food began to finish them off, and people in the village were already dropping like flies. They *had* to find something to eat. My God, what were they to do?—where were they to go?

Then, in the dusk whose gloom was darkening the room more and more, Etienne, heartbroken, after some hesitation finally made up his mind.

"I'll be back in a while," he said. "I just want to take a look around."

And he went out. He had thought of Mouquette. She must surely have a loaf of bread and would willingly let him have it. He was annoyed at having to go back to Réquillart: the girl would kiss his hands like a love-sick servant; but a man couldn't let his friends down when they were in trouble, and he'd be nice to her again if he had to.

"I'll take a look around too," said La Maheude. "Sitting here won't help."

She opened the door again and slammed it shut violently, leaving the others motionless and mute in the scant light of a candle that Alzire had just lit. Outside, she stopped to think for a moment. Then she went into the Levaques' house.

"Listen, the other day I loaned you a loaf of bread. How about letting me have one back?"

But she stopped, for the sight that met her eyes was scarcely encouraging; the house seemed more miserable than her own.

La Levaque was staring into her dead fire while Levaque, who had been made drunk on an empty stomach by some nailmakers, was sleeping on the table. Bouteloup was leaning against the wall and mechanically scratching his shoulders, with the confused air of a good fellow whose savings have been spent by others and who is now somewhat surprised to have to tighten his belt.

"A loaf of bread!" answered La Levaque. "Why, I was hoping to borrow another one from you!"

Just then her husband groaned in his sleep with pain, and she pushed his face against the table.

"Shut up, you pig! I hope your insides rot! . . . Instead of getting them to stand you to drinks, couldn't you have asked one of your friends for twenty sous?"

She continued in this vein, swearing and giving vent to her feelings, there in the filthy house which had been neglected for so long that an unbearable odor was rising from the floor. It could all blow up, she didn't care! To top it off, her son, that tramp Bébert, had been gone since morning, and she kept shrieking that it would be so much the better if he didn't come back! Then she said she was going to bed. At least she'd be warm. She elbowed Bouteloup.

"Come on, let's go! . . . The fire's dead and there's no point in lighting a candle just to see the empty plates. . . . Are you coming, Louis? We're going to bed, I said. A little bit of loving will make us feel better. . . . And I hope this drunken bastard freezes to death down here!"

Once outside again, La Maheude cut resolutely through the gardens to the Pierrons' house. There was a sound of laughter from inside. She knocked, and there was sudden silence. It took some time for the door to be opened.

"Oh, it's you!" said La Pierronne, pretending complete surprise. "I thought it was the doctor."

Without letting La Maheude get a word in, she pointed to Pierron, who was seated in front of a roaring coal fire.

"He's not well, he's still not well. He looks all right, but the trouble's in his stomach. He needs to be kept warm, so we're burning everything we have."

And in truth Pierron seemed quite hearty, his complexion rosy, his body well-fed; it was in vain that he tried to play the invalid and gasp for breath. Besides, La Maheude had caught a strong whiff of rabbit as she had come in—though of course they had cleared the table. A few crumbs remained, however, and in the center of the table she noticed a forgotten bottle of wine.

"Mama has gone to Montsou to see if she could get a loaf of bread," La Pierronne continued. "We're just waiting for her to get back."

But her voice died in her throat; she had followed her neighbor's glance and she too now saw the bottle. She caught herself immediately and began to explain: yes, it was wine; the people from La Piolaine had brought the bottle for her husband because the doctor had prescribed Bordeaux for him. And she went on babbling her gratitude to those good people—especially the young girl; not a bit proud, that one, coming into the workers' homes and distributing her charities herself!

"Yes," said La Maheude. "I know them."

She was miserable at the idea that things always went to those who needed them least. It never failed; those people from La Piolaine would have brought water to a river. How could she not have seen them in the village? She might have been able to get something out of them after all.

"I came," she finally admitted, "to see if things were any better here than at our place. . . . Do you at least have some vermicelli you could lend me?"

La Pierronne broke into exclamations of regret.

"Nothing at all, my dear. Not so much as a grain of semolina. . . . If Mama doesn't come back it means she's had no luck, and we'll have to go to bed without supper."

Just then the sound of weeping rose from the cellar, and she angrily banged her fist against the door. It was that little slut Lydie—she'd locked her up, she said, to punish her for not having come back till five o'clock after a whole day of gadding about. They couldn't control her anymore; she was always disappearing.

La Maheude was just standing there, unable to make up her mind to leave. The roaring fire penetrated her with a painful sense of comfort, and the knowledge that there was food here made her feel more famished than ever. They had obviously sent the old woman away and locked the little girl up so they could feast on their rabbit. Ah, no matter what you said, if a woman carried on, her family benefited!

"Good night," she said suddenly.

Outside, night had fallen, and the moon behind the clouds was shedding a sickly light on the ground. Miserable, lacking the courage to return home directly, La Maheude went around the long way instead of cutting across the gardens; every door along the row of lifeless house fronts gave off an air of famine and misery. Why bother knocking?—it was Poverty & Company everywhere. In the weeks since they had stopped eating, even the odor of onions had disappeared— that pungent odor which proclaimed far into the countryside that a village was near; now there was only the odor of old cellars, the dampness of holes in which nothing lives. Vague sounds were dying away in the air—stifled weeping and trailing curses—and in the slowly deepening silence one could hear the approach of the sleep of hunger—the exhaustion of bodies thrown across beds and in the grip of empty-stomached nightmares.

As she was passing in front of the church she saw a swiftly gliding shadow. Hope made her hasten her step, for she had recognized the Abbé Joire, who said mass on Sundays in the village chapel: he must be coming from the sacristy, where he'd been called on some errand. Bent forward, he was scurrying along—a plump and mild man who wanted to live at peace with everybody. If he had been doing his errand at night, it must have been to avoid compromising himself with the miners. People said that he had just gotten a preferment, and he had already been seen walking with his successor, a thin abbé with eyes like burning coals.

"Father Joire, Father Joire," stammered La Maheude.

But he did not stop.

"Good evening, good evening, my good woman."

She found herself in front of her own house. Her legs could carry her no further, and she went inside.

No one had moved. Maheu was still sitting on the edge of the table, and Old Bonnemort and the children were still huddled together on the bench to lessen the cold. And no one had spoken; only the candle had burned down—so short now that there would soon be no more light. At the sound of the opening door the children turned their heads, but on seeing their mother come in empty-handed, they went back to staring at the floor, restraining a strong urge to cry lest they be scolded. La Maheude fell back into her place near the dying fire. Nobody questioned her, the silence remained unbroken. They had all understood, and it was pointless to wear themselves out with further talk. Spiritless now, their courage gone, they waited for whatever help Etienne might have been able to unearth somewhere. The minutes went by and they no longer counted even on that.

When Etienne did return he had a dozen cold boiled potatoes wrapped in a cloth.

"This is all I was able to find," he said.

There had been no bread at Mouquette's either: it was her own dinner that she had wrapped up and forced him to take, kissing him with all her heart.

"No thanks," he said when La Maheude offered him his share. "I had something while I was out."

He was lying, and he watched gloomily as the children threw themselves on the food. The father and mother were also holding back in order to leave a little more for them, but the old man was greedily gulping everything down. They had to take a potato away from him for Alzire.

Then Etienne told them he had heard some news. The Company, angry at the obstinacy of the strikers, was talking of giving their workbooks back to those miners involved in the strike. There was no doubt about it, the Company wanted war. And there was an even more serious rumor going around—the Company was boasting of having been able to convince a large number of workers to go down again: the next day La Victoire and Feutry-Cantel were supposed to have their full complement of miners, and even at Madeleine and Mirou a third of the men were expected to report. The Maheus were furious.

"Damn it," shouted Maheu, "if there are traitors, we'll have to take care of them!"

And springing up he gave way to his rage and his suffering:

"Tomorrow evening in the forest! ... Since they won't let us meet at the Bon Joyeux, we'll make the forest our meeting place!"

This cry aroused Old Bonnemort, whose gluttony had made him drowsy. It was an old rallying cry—the meeting

place to which in former days the miners used to go to plot
their resistance to the king's soldiers.

"Yes, yes, on to Vandame! I'll join you if that's where
you're going!"

La Maheude made a forceful gesture.

"We'll all go. There must be an end to these injustices and
treacheries!"

Etienne decided to send word to all the villages that a
meeting would be held the next evening. But the fire was
dead, just as at the Levaques', and the candle suddenly went
out. There was no more coal, no more oil; they had to grope
their way to bed in the bitter cold that penetrated to the
bone. The children were weeping.

6

Jeanlin had recovered and was on his feet again, but his
bones had knit so badly that he limped on both legs; he was
a sight to see as he waddled along like a duck, but he moved
as quickly as ever, with all the skill of some evil, thieving
animal.

That evening at dusk he and his inseparable companions,
Bébert and Lydie, were keeping watch on the road to
Réquillart. Jeanlin was hidden in an empty lot behind a
fence, just opposite a ramshackle grocery that had been set
up at the corner where a path joined the road. The old,
nearly blind woman who ran the store had put out three or
four sacks of lentils and beans, all black with dust, but it was
an ancient dried codfish, hanging in the doorway and discolored by flyspecks, that Jeanlin's narrowed eyes were longingly
fixed upon. Twice already he had started Bébert on his way
to pull it down, but each time somebody had come around
the bend in the road. Some nosybody was always getting in
the way—you couldn't get a thing done!

A gentleman on horseback appeared, and the children,
recognizing him as Monsieur Hennebeau, flattened themselves
out along the bottom of the fence. Since the beginning of the
strike, he was often seen riding the roads like this, traveling
alone through the rebellious villages and showing quiet courage in personally checking on the state of the countryside.
No stone had ever whistled past his ears; he met only with
silent men who were slow to greet him, and, more often,

lovers who could not have cared less about politics and were busy enjoying themselves in every hidden corner. Trotting along on his mare, his eyes straight ahead so as not to disturb anybody, he would pass through these feasts of unrestrained love and his heart would swell with unsatisfied longings. He was perfectly aware of the children, the little boys in a heap on top of the little girl—why, even the youngsters had already learned to amuse themselves by rubbing their wretchedness together! His eyes grew moist, and straight in the saddle, buttoned up in his coat with military correctness, he disappeared from view.

"What rotten luck!" said Jeanlin. "This will never end. . . . Run, Bébert, pull it by the tail!"

But now two other men were coming, and the boy stifled a curse as he heard the voice of his brother Zacharie telling Mouquet how he had discovered forty sous sewn into his wife's skirt. They were both laughing heartily and pounding each other on the back. Mouquet suggested a big game of *crosse* for the next day: they'd leave at two o'clock from L'Avantage and go on to Montoire, near Marchiennes. Zacharie agreed. Why the hell were people bothering them about the strike?—as long as they weren't doing anything, they might as well have a good time. They were turning the corner of the road when Etienne, who was coming from the canal, stopped them and began talking.

"Are they going to sleep here?" said Jeanlin angrily. "It's nearly dark, and the old woman's taking in her sacks."

Another miner came along, on his way to Réquillart. Etienne went off with him, and as they were passing the fence the boy heard them talking about the forest: the meeting had been put off till the following day lest there not be enough time to alert all the villages in the one day.

"Listen!" Jeanlin whispered to his companions. "The big meeting's on for tomorrow. We've got to be there! We'll take off in the afternoon, right?"

Then, since the coast was finally clear, he sent Bébert off again.

"Go to it! Grab it by the tail! . . . And watch out for the old lady's broom."

Luckily it was dark now. Bébert had made one leap, clutched at the cod, and broken the string. He started to run, waving the cod behind him like a kite, and the other two followed him at top speed. Astonished, the old woman came out of her shop, but she was unable to understand what had happened, or to make out the group vanishing into the shadows.

The scamps had become the terror of the countryside,
which they had invaded, little by little, like a savage horde.
At first they had been satisfied with the yard at Le Voreux,
where they rolled around in the piles of coal, becoming black
as Negroes, and played hide-and-seek through the stacks of
timber among which they wandered as though in a virgin
forest. Then they had taken over the slag heap, where they
would slide on their behinds down the bare parts, still hot
with interior fires, and dart among the brambles of the older
parts—hidden all day and as busy as mischievous mice with
their quiet little games. Enlarging their territory still further,
they fought among the piles of bricks until blood flowed;
raced through the fields, eating all sorts of juicy herbs without bothering about bread; searched the banks of the canal
for mudfish, which they swallowed raw; and roamed ever
further afield, traveling as far as the forest of Vandame,
where they would stuff themselves with strawberries in the
spring and hazelnuts and huckleberries in the summer. Soon
the whole immense plain belonged to them.

But what sent them ceaselessly prowling along the roads
from Montsou to Marchiennes, their eyes blazing like those
of young wolves, was their growing passion for plunder.
Jeanlin was always the captain of these expeditions, launching
the little band against all kinds of quarry, ravaging the onion
fields, pillaging the orchards, and attacking the grocers' vegetable stands; the people of the region accused the striking
miners and talked of a large, organized gang. One day
Jeanlin had even forced Lydie to steal from her mother; he
had made her bring him two dozen sticks of barley sugar that
La Pierronne kept in a glass jar on a shelf in her window,
and though the child had been mercilessly pummeled, she so
feared his authority that she had not betrayed him. The
worst of it was that he always took the lion's share for
himself. Bébert also had to turn every bit of booty over to
him, and he considered himself lucky if the captain didn't hit
him and keep it all.

For some time, though, Jeanlin had been going too far. He
beat Lydie as though she were his wedded wife, and he took
advantage of Bébert's credulity to get him involved in all
kinds of nasty scrapes, finding it amusing to make a donkey
of this strapping boy who was so much stronger than he was
and who could have crushed him with one blow. He despised
both of them and treated them like slaves, telling them he
had as a mistress a princess to whom they were unworthy of
even being introduced. And, indeed, for the past week he had
taken to disappearing suddenly—at the end of a street, at a

turn in a path, in fact anywhere he happened to be—after having ordered them, in a terrible way, back to the village. But only after he pocketed the booty.

And that is what happened on this evening.

"Hand it over," he said, tearing the cod from his friend's hands when the three of them stopped at a turn in the road near Réquillart.

Bébert protested.

"I want some too, you know! I'm the one who took it!"

"So what!" shouted Jeanlin. "You'll get some if I feel like giving you any—but not tonight, that's for sure. Maybe tomorrow, if there's any left."

He gave Lydie a shove and lined the two of them up like soldiers at shoulder arms. Then, slipping behind them, he said:

"Now stay there for five minutes and don't turn around. . . . By God, if you turn around you'll be eaten by wild animals! . . . Afterward, go straight home—and if you touch Lydie on the way, Bébert, I'll know about it and you'll both get it!"

Then he vanished into the shadows with such a light step that his bare feet made no sound. For the next five minutes the two children stood there motionless, never looking back lest they receive a blow from some invisible force. Their common terror had slowly given birth to a great affection between them. Bébert was always thinking of squeezing her in his arms, the way he'd seen grown-up couples do, and Lydie would have been willing enough for it to happen—it would have been nice to be gently caressed for a change— but neither he nor she would have dared disobey Jeanlin; and so though it was pitch-black when they set off, they did not even put their arms around each other, but walked side by side, yearning and despairing, sure that if they so much as touched each other their captain would clout them from behind.

At this same time Etienne had reached Réquillart. The night before, Mouquette had begged him to come back, and back he had gone—ashamed to discover, though he refused to admit it, that he was becoming fond of this girl who adored him as if he were the Christ. He told himself that he was going there with the intention of breaking off. He would see her and explain that she mustn't keep after him. This was no time to be enjoying oneself—it was dishonest to treat yourself to such pleasure when everybody was dying of hunger! Not having found her at home, he had decided to

wait, and he was now peering into the darkness, watching for
a moving shadow.

The old, half-blocked shaft gaped beneath the ruined
headframe. Above the black hole a vertical beam, to which a
scrap of roofing still clung, looked like a gallows, and two
trees, a service tree and a plane, thrust forth from the broken
coping of the masonry as though they were growing from the
very bowels of the earth. It was a wild, abandoned spot, the
grass-choked entrance to an abyss, clogged with old timbers
and dotted with blackthorn and hawthorn bushes among
which the warblers built their nests in the springtime. For the
past ten years the Company, which wished to avoid heavy
maintenance costs, had been thinking of filling in this dead
shaft; but it was waiting until a ventilator could be installed
at Le Voreux, because the ventilation furnace of the two
shafts, which were connected, was at the bottom of Réquillart and the former extraction shaft was now serving as a
chimney. Meanwhile nothing had been done except to hold
the casing in place with horizontal props, which made any
extraction impossible; the top galleries had been abandoned,
and only the bottom one was kept in repair. There an
enormous coal furnace blazed like an inferno, causing such a
powerful draft that the air rushed at hurricane force from
one end of the neighboring mine to the other. As a safety
precaution, orders had been given to maintain the ladder well
so that people could still go up and down; however, nobody
was in charge of this, so the ladders were rotting in the
humidity and some of the platforms had already fallen apart.
A large bramble bush blocked the entrance to the shaft, and
since the first ladder had lost some rungs, it was necessary to
hang from a root of the service tree and then let yourself
drop blindly into the darkness.

Etienne was waiting, hidden behind a bush, when he heard
a rustling sound among the branches. At first he thought he
had frightened off a snake. But he was stupefied with amazement as a struck match suddenly illuminated Jeanlin, who
was lighting a candle and seemingly sinking into the earth.
His curiosity was so aroused that he went up to the edge of
the hole: the boy had disappeared, but a faint light was
shining from the second platform. For a moment he hesitated; then, holding on to the roots, he let himself drop. At
first he thought he was going to fall the whole seventeen
hundred feet that measured the depth of the shaft, but he
finally felt a rung under his feet and quietly continued down.
Jeanlin must not have heard anything, for Etienne could still
see the light going down ahead of him. The boy's huge and

frightening shadow danced along as he made his way with his waddling gait. He was clambering down with the skill of a monkey, catching on with his hands, his feet, and even his chin wherever there were missing rungs. The ladders succeeded one another every twenty feet or so, some still solid, others shaky and cracking, ready to break; narrow platform followed narrow platform, so moldy and rotten that stepping on them was like stepping on moss; and the farther down Etienne went the more suffocating the heat became because of the furnace below—which fortunately had not been going full blast since the beginning of the strike, for under ordinary circumstances, when the furnace consumed its daily ration of five tons of coal, nobody could have ventured there without being roasted alive.

"What a little devil!" swore Etienne, gasping. "Where the hell can he be going?"

Twice he had almost fallen head over heels. His feet slipped on the slimy wood. At least if he had had a candle, like the boy—but since his only guide was the faint, ever-receding glimmer beneath him, he kept bumping into things. It was already the twentieth ladder, and they were still going down. He began to count: twenty-one, twenty-two, twenty-three, and down, down, he went. His head was ready to burst with the heat, and he felt as though he were falling into a furnace. At last he came to a loading station and saw the candle vanishing down a gallery. Thirty ladders—that was more than six hundred feet.

"How long is he going to keep this up?" he thought. "He must hole up in the stable."

But the passageway on the left that led to the stable was blocked by a cave-in, and the trek began again, more difficult and more dangerous than before. Startled bats fluttered about or clung to the roof of the loading station. He had to hurry in order not to lose sight of the light, and he quickly turned into the same gallery; the only trouble was that where the boy seemed to pass through easily, with all the suppleness of a serpent, he could not squeeze through without bruising every limb. Like all the old passageways, this gallery had shrunk, and was continuing to shrink every day under the ceaseless pressure of the earth; in some places it was little more than a tube, which would itself disappear some day. As a result of this strangulating pressure, the split and shattered timbers were a menace, threatening to cut him, to skewer him on splinters as sharp as swords. He made his way carefully, on knees or belly, probing the darkness ahead of him with his hands. Suddenly a swarm of rats rushed over

him, running over his whole body from his head to his feet in
a panic flight.

"For God's sake! Aren't we there yet?" he grumbled,
broken-backed and out of breath.

They were. After more than half a mile the tubelike tunnel
abruptly became wider, and they were in a wonderfully
preserved part of the gallery. It was the end of an old
haulage tunnel which cut across the seam and made a natural
cave. He had to stop; in the distance he could see the boy set
down his candle between two stones and move about, calm
and relaxed, like a man happy to be home again. He had
turned this part of the gallery into a comfortable habitation.
A heap of straw in one corner provided a soft bed, and on
some old timbers set up to form a table a little feast was
spread out—some bread, some apples, a few half-started
bottles of gin: a real bandit's cave, with loot that had been
piling up for weeks, even useless loot like soap and polish,
stolen for the sheer pleasure of stealing. And there was the
boy, alone with all this booty, taking a bandit's pride in it.

"Don't you give a damn about anybody else?" exclaimed
Etienne when he had caught his breath. "You come down
here and stuff yourself while up above the rest of us are
dying of hunger?"

Panic-stricken, Jeanlin began to tremble. But when he
recognized Etienne he quickly recovered his composure.

"Would you like to join me for dinner?" he asked. "How
about a little grilled cod? . . . Just wait, you'll see."

He had never let go of his cod, and he now carefully
began to scrape off the flyspecks with a handsome new knife,
one of those little daggers with mottoes inscribed on their
bone handles. This one bore the single word "Love."

"That's a nice knife you've got there," Etienne commented.

"It's a present from Lydie," answered Jeanlin, neglecting
to add that Lydie had stolen it, on his orders, from a
peddler's stand in front of La Tête-Coupée.

Then, still scraping, he added proudly:

"I've made things pretty comfortable here, haven't I? . . .
It's warmer than it is up there, and it smells a hell of a lot
better!"

Etienne had sat down, curious to hear what the boy had to
say. His anger had passed, and he found himself interested in
this little devil who was so hardy and industrious in his vices.
And to tell the truth, he *was* comfortable at the bottom of
this hole: it was no longer too hot, and even though a
blistery December was wracking the bodies of the wretches

up above, down here there was an even, constant warmth, like that of a tepid bath. As the galleries aged, they cleansed themselves of noxious gases; the firedamp was gone, and the only odor was that of rotting timbers—a subtle smell of ether, faintly sharpened by the scent of something like clove. Even the timbers themselves looked interesting: some had a yellowish, marblelike pallor and were fringed with lacy-white, flaky vegetable growths that seemed to drape them with an embroidery of silk and pearls; others bristled with mushrooms. And there were swarms of white moths, snowy flies and spiders flying about—a colorless world that had never known the sun.

"Aren't you afraid?" asked Etienne.

Jeanlin looked at him in astonishment.

"Afraid of what? There's nobody here but me."

He had finally finished scraping the cod. He lit a small wood fire, spread out the glowing embers, and grilled the fish. Then he cut a loaf of bread in half. It was a terribly salty feast, but delicious to strong stomachs.

Etienne had accepted his share.

"I'm not surprised that you keep getting fatter while the rest of us all get thinner. But you know, it's piggish of you to stuff yourself this way! ... Don't you ever think about the others?"

"Why are they so stupid?"

"Anyway, you're right to hide yourself like this. If your father found out you were stealing, he'd tan your hide!"

"As if the rich didn't steal from us! You're the one who's always saying so. This bread I swiped from Maigrat was probably one he owed us!"

The young man fell silent, his mouth full. Troubled, he studied this boy who—with his greedy muzzle, his green eyes, his large ears, his abortive intelligence and savage cunning—was slowly reverting to an ancient animality. The mine, which had formed him, had applied the finishing touches by breaking his legs.

"And what about Lydie?" Etienne asked. "Do you ever bring her down here?"

Jeanlin broke into a scornful laugh.

"Here? Not on your life! ... Women talk too much."

And he went on laughing, full of disdain for Lydie and Bébert. Had anyone ever seen such idiots? It tickled him to think that they had swallowed all his lies and gone off empty-handed while he, warm and comfortable, was now eating the cod. He summed up with the gravity of a little philosopher:

"It's best to be alone—then there are no arguments."

Etienne had finished his bread. He drank a swallow of gin.
For a moment he had wondered whether to repay the boy's
hospitality by taking hold of his ear and dragging him out of
the mine by force, warning him that if he did any more
stealing he would tell his father everything. But as he examined this buried retreat he had an idea: wasn't it possible that
he or his comrades might have need of it some day if things
should go badly up there? He made Jeanlin swear not to
sleep away from home, as he had sometimes done when he
found himself too comfortably settled in his straw bed, and
taking a candle he went off without waiting, leaving the boy
tranquilly setting his house in order.

Despite the intense cold, Mouquette was sitting outside on a
timber beam, waiting for Etienne in anxious desperation.
When she saw him she threw her arms around his neck, and
when he told her of his determination not to see her anymore
it was as though he had plunged a knife into her heart. But
my God, why?—didn't she love him enough? Fearing he
might succumb to his desire to go inside with her, Etienne led
Mouquette toward the road, explaining as gently as possible
that she was compromising him in the eyes of his comrades,
compromising their political cause. She was amazed—what
connection could this have with politics? Then it occurred to
her that perhaps he was ashamed to be seen with her—she
wasn't offended, it was quite understandable—and she offered
to let him slap her in public to make it look as if he were
breaking off with her. But he would come to see her,
wouldn't he, just for a little while, every now and then? She
begged him wildly, swore that she would keep out of sight,
that she wouldn't detain him for more than five minutes. He
was extremely moved, but he continued to refuse. This was
the way it had to be. When he was about to leave her he felt
he at least wanted to kiss her good-bye. Step by step they had
reached the first houses of Montsou, and as they were standing with their arms around each other under the big full
moon, a woman passed near them and suddenly started, as if
she had tripped over a stone.

"Who's that?" Etienne asked uneasily.

"It's Catherine," answered La Mouquette. "She's on her
way back from Jean-Bart."

The woman continued on her way, her head bowed, her
steps faltering, her entire being expressing extreme weariness.
And Etienne watched her go, in anguish at having been seen
by her, his heart breaking with senseless remorse. Wasn't she
living with a man? Hadn't she made him suffer the very same

pain, here on this same road to Réquillart, when she had given herself to that man? But despite all that, he was unhappy to have done the same to her.

"You want to know something?" Mouquette murmured tearfully as she left. "If you don't want me, it's because there's somebody else you want."

The next day the weather was superb, one of those beautiful winter days when there is a clear frosty sky above and the earth rings underfoot like crystal. Jeanlin had slipped away just after one o'clock, but he had to wait for Bébert behind the church and they almost left without Lydie, whose mother had locked her in the cellar again. She had just been let out, given a basket, and told to bring it back full of dandelion greens or risk being locked up with the rats overnight. Terrified, she wanted to go after the salad immediately, but Jeanlin talked her out of it: they'd take care of the salad later. For some time now Poland, Rasseneur's big rabbit, had been on his mind, and as it happened, just as they were passing in front of L'Avantage the rabbit hopped out onto the road. With one swooping movement he seized her by the ears and shoved her into Lydie's basket; then the three of them raced off. It would be lots of fun to make the rabbit run like a dog all the way to the forest.

But they stopped to watch Zacharie and Mouquet, who, after having had a beer with a couple of friends, were about to begin their game of *crosse*. The stakes, which had been left with Rasseneur, were a new cap and a red scarf. Split into teams of two, the four players began to bid for the first lap, from Le Voreux to the Paillot farm—about two miles; Zacharie won by bidding to do it in seven strokes against Mouquet's eight. They had set the *cholette*, a little boxwood egg, on the road, its pointed end up. Each player had a *crosse*, a mallet with an oblique iron head and a long handle around which string had been tightly wound. Two o'clock was striking as they began. For his first turn, which consisted of three strokes, Zacharie mightily shot the *cholette* more than four hundred yards across the beet fields—it was forbidden to play in the villages or on the roads because people had been killed by being struck by the *cholette*. Mouquet, also a fine player, drove it back with such a powerful blow that his one stroke sent the *cholette* flying a hundred and fifty yards. And so the game continued, one team driving ahead, the other team driving back, always racing over the frozen furrows that hurt their feet.

At first Jeanlin, Bébert, and Lydie had run behind the players, excited by the staggering strokes. Then they remem-

bered Poland, who was being shaken up in Lydie's basket,
and deserting the game in the open fields, they brought out
the rabbit to see how fast she could run. She immediately
raced away, and they launched themselves after her in a
chase that lasted a full hour. It was a wild scramble, with
zigzagging back and forth, shouts meant to frighten her, and
outstretched arms closing on nothing. If she had not been
pregnant, they would never have caught her.

As they were catching their breath, the sound of curses
made them turn around. They had gotten in the way of the
crosse game, and Zacharie had almost split his brother's
head. The players were on their fourth lap: from the Paillot
farm they had gone toward Quatre-Chemins; then from Quatre-Chemins to Montoire; and now, in six strokes, from
Montoire to Pré-des-Vaches. That made more than six miles
in an hour, and they had even stopped for some beers at
Vincent's and at Les Trois Sages on the way. This time
Mouquet was ahead. He had two strokes to go and victory
was sure—but then Zacharie, taking his turn with a malicious
laugh, drove the *cholette* back so skillfully that it landed in a
deep ditch. Mouquet's partner could not drive it out and the
result was disastrous. All four were shouting and getting
more and more excited; they were neck and neck and would
have to begin all over again. From Pré-des-Vaches it was
about a mile and a half to Herbes-Rousses: five strokes. Once
there, they would freshen up with a few beers at Lerenard's.

But Jeanlin had an idea. Letting the players start off, he
took a piece of string out of his pocket and tied it to Poland's
left hind leg. How funny it was—the rabbit running along in
front of the three rascals, dragging her foot, limping in such
a comical fashion that they had a better laugh than ever
before in their lives! Next they tied the string around her
neck so she could really go; and when she got tired, they
dragged her along, on her belly or her back, just like a
pull-toy. This went on for more than an hour and the rabbit
was close to death, when they suddenly stuffed her back into
the basket—they had heard, near the woods at Cruchot's, the
crosse teams into whose field of play they had once more
wandered.

Zacharie, Mouquet, and the two others were now lapping
up the miles, stopping only long enough to swallow a few
beers in each of the bars they set up as their goals. From
Herbes-Rousses they had raced to Buchy, then to Croix-de-
Pierre, then to Chamblay. The ground reverberated under
their stampeding feet as they ran without let-up after the
cholette bounding over the frozen earth: it was a good time

to play because there was no danger of sinking into soft mud—only the risk of breaking a leg. In the clear cold air the mighty strokes of the *crosse* rang out like rifle shots. Muscular hands gripped the corded handles, the whole body followed through on each swing, as if to fell an ox, and on it went for hours, from one end of the plain to the other, over ditches, hedges, road embankments, and low walls. You had to be strong-winded and have iron-jointed knees to play, and the cutters were wild about this game which drove from their muscles the cramps and kinks put in by their work in the mine. At twenty-five, there were a few fanatics who could do more than twenty miles; at forty, nobody played anymore—they were all too heavy.

Five o'clock struck and dusk was already falling. Just one more lap, this time all the way to the forest of Vandame, to decide who would win the scarf and cap. Zacharie, with his clownish indifference to politics, joked about what fun it would be to turn up there, right in the middle of their friends. As for Jeanlin, the forest had been his goal ever since they had left the village, even though he might have seemed to be wandering at random. With an angry gesture he threatened Lydie, who, tormented by remorse and fear, was talking of returning to Le Voreux to gather her dandelions. What—miss the meeting?—no, he wanted to hear what the men had to say. He shoved Bébert along and suggested they amuse themselves on the way to the forest by freeing Poland and chasing her with rocks. His notion was to kill her; he wanted to carry her off to his cave at the bottom of Réquillart and eat her. The rabbit began running again, her nose wrinkled up and her ears flat back; one stone skinned her back and another cut her tail, and despite the growing darkness it would have been the end of her if the rascals hadn't spotted Etienne and Maheu standing in the middle of a clearing. They threw themselves wildly on the animal and once more stuffed her into the basket. At almost the same moment Zacharie, Mouquet, and the two others let fly the final strokes that sent the *cholette* rolling to within a few yards of the clearing. They had all ended up at the very center of the meeting place.

Ever since dusk had begun to fall, the whole countryside had been covered with a stream of dark shadows slipping, singly or in groups, along the roads and paths or across the flat plain, toward the tall, purplish treetops of the forest. Every village had emptied, the women and even the children leaving as though for a stroll under the great clear sky. Now the roads were nearly dark, and though it was impossible to

see the marching crowd that was heading toward the same
goal, its presence could be felt—shuffling, hesitant, moved by
a single spirit. From between the hedges and among the
bushes there was nothing but a gentle rustling, the faint
murmur of voices in the night.

Monsieur Hennebeau, mounted on his mare, was on his
way home just then, and he listened to these indistinct
sounds. He had met a number of couples, a long, slow parade
of strollers out to enjoy the beautiful winter evening. More
lovers, mouth pressed against mouth, off to take their pleasure behind the walls! Wasn't that what he usually met
with—girls being tumbled at the bottom of every ditch,
beggars gorging themselves on the only pleasure that cost
nothing? And the idiots complained of their lives when they
could have their fill of that only true happiness—love! How
gladly he would have accepted their starvation if he could
have begun life all over again with a woman who would give
herself to him on top of these stones with all her being and
all her heart! *His* unhappiness was inconsolable; he envied
these poor wretches. Head bowed, he rode slowly toward
home, tormented by the long-drawn-out sounds coming from
the depths of the black countryside—sounds which, to his
ears, could only be the sound of kisses.

7

The meeting was at the Plan-des-Dames, a vast clearing
created by recent tree-felling. It spread out in a gentle slope
and was surrounded by tall trees—superb beeches whose
straight and regular trunks encircled it with a white colon-
nade stained by green lichens. Some of the gigantic felled
trees still lay on the grass; to the left, a stack of sawn timber
rose in a geometric cube. As dusk fell the cold grew sharper,
and the fallen mosses crackled underfoot. It was darkest
night at ground level, but the high branches above were
silhouetted against a pale sky, in which the rising moon
would soon quench the light of the stars.

About three thousand miners—a seething crowd of men,
women, and children that was gradually filling the clearing
and spilling out under the trees—had come to gather here,
and latecomers were still arriving; a sea of heads, drowned in
darkness, stretched as far as the bordering underbrush. There

was a dull muttering sound, like a storm wind sweeping through the still and glacial forest.

Etienne was standing at the top of the slope with Rasseneur and Maheu. A quarrel had broken out, and their voices could be heard in sudden spurts. The men nearest them were listening: Levaque, with his fists clenched; Pierron, with his back turned to them, uneasy because he had no longer been able to plead sickness; and Bonnemort and Old Mouque, seated side by side on a stump and seemingly sunk in profound reflection. Behind them were the clowns—Zacharie, Mouquet, and some others—who had just come for a good laugh. The women, in contrast, formed a solemn group, as serious as though they were in church. La Maheude was silently shaking her head at La Levaque's muffled curses. Philomène was coughing, her bronchitis bothering her again now that winter was here. Only Mouquette was laughing; she was amused at the way La Brûlé was accusing her daughter of being an unnatural child who had sent her mother away so *she* could stuff herself on rabbit, a turncoat who grew fat on the cowardice of her husband! Jeanlin had climbed to the top of the timber pile, hoisted Lydie after him, and forced Bébert to follow; the three of them stood outlined against the sky, higher than anyone else.

The quarrel had been started by Rasseneur, who wanted to follow parliamentary procedures and elect a committee. His defeat at the Bon Joyeux had enraged him, and he had sworn to have his revenge; he flattered himself that he would be able to reestablish his former authority as soon as he could confront the mass of miners themselves, instead of merely the delegates. Etienne thought the idea of a committee here in the middle of the forest idiotic—they were being tracked down like wild beasts, so they would have to act like savages; revolutionary methods were called for.

Seeing that the argument could drag on forever, he suddenly seized command of the crowd by mounting a tree trunk and calling out:

"Comrades! Comrades!"

Maheu smothered Rasseneur's protests, and the crowd's confused murmuring slowly died out in a long sigh. Etienne went on in a thundering voice:

"Comrades, since they forbid us to speak, since they set the police on us as if we were criminals, we have had to come here to meet! Here we are free, here we are at home, here nobody can silence us any more than they can silence the birds or the animals!"

There was a thunderous reply of shouts and exclamations.

"Yes, yes, the forest is ours, we have the right to speak here! ... Speak!"

For a moment Etienne stood motionless on the tree trunk. The moon was still too low on the horizon to light anything but the highest branches, and the crowd, gradually becoming calm and silent, remained shrouded in darkness. Etienne was also black, a bar of darkness standing at the top of the slope.

He slowly raised an arm and began, but his voice was no longer thundering—he had adopted the level tone of a simple representative of the people making a report on the situation. He was finally able to use the speech that the police chief had forestalled at the Bon Joyeux, and he began with a rapid history of the strike, expressing himself with the borrowed authority of scientific language: the facts, nothing but the facts. First he related his dislike of the strike: the miners hadn't wanted it, but management had provoked them to it with its new system of paying separately for the timbering. Then he recalled the delegates' first visit to the manager's house, the bad faith of management, and later, after the delegates' second visit, its tardy concession of the two centimes it had tried to steal. And that's how things stood now. He went on to account for the expenditures that had exhausted the emergency fund, told how the money sent from outside had been used, and devoted a few sentences to excusing the International—Pluchart and the others—for not being able to do more for them, given their own troubles in the battle to conquer the world. The situation was therefore daily growing worse—the Company was returning workbooks and threatening to bring in miners from Belgium, and in addition, it was intimidating the weaklings and had persuaded some of the miners to go back to work. He kept to his monotonous tone, as if to emphasize all this bad news, and he described how hunger was winning out, hope dying, and the struggle down to the last flickers of courage. Then suddenly, without raising his voice, he summed up:

"And it is under these circumstances, comrades, that you must come to a decision this evening. Do you want to go on with the strike? And if so, what measures are you ready to take to win out over the Company?"

A great silence fell from the starry sky. The night-shrouded crowd was silent, speechless under the lash of these heartbreaking words, and the only sound was its hopeless sigh sifting through the trees.

But Etienne was already speaking again, this time in a different voice. He was no longer the secretary of an association but a commander of troops, an apostle bringing the truth. Were any of them so cowardly as to go back on their oaths? What!—were they to have suffered uselessly for a month? Were they to go back to the mines with their tails between their legs and let their eternal misery begin all over again? Wasn't it better to die immediately, in an attempt to destroy this tyranny of capital that was starving the workers? Wasn't it time to call a halt to this stupid submission to hunger, this submission that would only last until hunger would once again drive even the mildest of them to revolt? And he painted a picture of the exploited miners, bearing the whole brunt of the disastrous crises and reduced to starvation every time the demands of competition forced prices down. No! The new system of paying for timbering was not acceptable—it was only a disguised economy for the Company, an attempt to steal from each man one hour of his work each day. But this time they had gone too far, and the day was coming when the wretched of the earth, pushed beyond endurance, would see to it that justice was done.

He paused, his arms outstretched. At the word "justice" the crowd shuddered with excitement and broke out into a burst of applause that swept along like a storm of dry leaves. Voices called out:

"Justice! . . . The time has come! . . . Justice!"

Little by little Etienne was warming up. He did not have Rasseneur's free and easy eloquence; he was often at a loss for words and got entangled in his sentences, finishing them only through an effort of will that made his whole body strain forward. But this very stumbling effort gave birth to forceful images drawn from their common, familiar toil, images that seized the imagination of his audience; and his workingman's gestures—his elbows drawn back, then thrust forward with clenched fists, his jaws suddenly jutting out as though to bite—also had an extraordinary effect on the men. They all said the same thing—he wasn't very big, but he knew how to make himself listened to.

"Wages are a new form of slavery," he resumed in a more vibrant voice. "The mine must belong to the miner just as the sea belongs to the fisherman, just as the earth belongs to the farmer. . . . Listen to me! The mine belongs to *you*, to all of you who have paid for it for more than a century with so much blood and misery!"

And he resolutely plunged into obscure legal questions, becoming hopelessly embroiled in the endless series of special mining laws. That which was under the earth belonged to the people just as did the earth itself; only a hateful privilege guaranteed a monopoly to the companies, and this was espe-

cially true of Montsou, where the alleged legality of the
concessions was complicated by agreements made long ago
with the owners of the former fiefs, pursuant to the old
custom of Hainault. The miners therefore had only to reconquer that which belonged to them—and his outstretched
arms embraced the whole countryside beyond the forest. Just
at that moment the rising moon slid over the high branches,
and he was bathed in light. When the crowd, still in darkness,
saw him, white with that light, open-handedly distributing
fortune, they again broke into prolonged applause.

"Yes, yes, he's right!"

From that point on, Etienne was astride his favorite topic—
the attribution of the instruments of production to the collec-
tivity, as he put it in a phrase whose barbarous jargon gave
him immense pleasure. He had undergone a complete evolution. Beginning with the sentimental notions of the recent
convert—the need to reform the wage system—he had arrived at the political theory of doing away with wages completely. His collectivism, which at the time of the meeting at
the Bon Joyeux was still formless and humanitarian, had
since stiffened into a complicated program, every article of
which he scientifically reasoned out. First he postulated that
liberty could only be obtained by destroying the State. Then,
when the people had seized control of the government, the
reforms could begin: a return to the primitive commune, the
substitution of an egalitarian and free family for the narrow-
minded and oppressive family, absolute equality in civil,
political, and economic matters, the guarantee of individual
independence thanks to the possession of the instruments of
labor and the fruits thereof, and, finally, free technical training paid for by the community. All this would demand a
total recasting of the old corrupt society; he attacked marriage and the rights of inheritance, he set limits to personal
fortunes, and he toppled the iniquitous monuments of dead
centuries—all with a repeated sweeping gesture of his arm,
the gesture of a reaper mowing down the ripe harvest; then,
with his other hand, he built up the humanity of the future,
constructing the edifice of truth and justice that would grow
in the dawn of the twentieth century. At this pitch of intellectual strain, reason crumbled and only the single-
mindedness of the fanatic remained. The scruples of his
sensibility and common sense were swept away, and nothing
seemed easier than the realization of this new world: he had
it all planned, and he spoke of it as though it were a
mechanism he could set up in a couple of hours, heedless of
the cost in fire and blood.

"Our turn has come!" he shouted in a final outcry. "It's our turn to have the power and the wealth!"

From the depths of the forest the acclamations rolled toward him. By now the moon was bathing the whole clearing in white light, throwing into sharp relief the swelling sea of heads that stretched all the way out to the vague outlines of the underbrush between the great gray tree trunks. And under the glacial sky there was a seething mass of faces—burning eyes, open mouths, a whole people in heat, starving men, women, and children unleashed to justly pillage the ancient inheritance of which they had been dispossessed. They no longer felt the cold; Etienne's burning words had warmed them to the marrow. A religious exaltation lifted them from the earth—like the feverish hope of the first Christians awaiting the coming reign of justice. Many of the obscure sentences had escaped them; they understood little of the technical and abstract reasoning, but the very obscurity and abstraction seemed to widen the scope of the promises and sweep them into a dazzling future. What a dream!—to be the masters, to suffer no longer, to finally come into possession!

"That's right, by God! It's our turn! . . . Death to the exploiters!"

The women were delirious—La Maheude driven from her usual calm by the giddiness of hunger; La Levaque shrieking; old La Brûlé beside herself, waving her witchlike arms; Philomène seized by a fit of coughing; and Mouquette so excited that she was calling out endearments to the speaker. Among the men, Maheu, completely won over, had shouted angrily as he stood between Pierron, who was trembling, and Levaque, who was talking too much; Zacharie and Mouquet, the clowns, tried to joke about it, but they were ill at ease, and astonished that a man could talk so long without stopping for a drink. Jeanlin, on the timber pile, was making more noise than anybody, egging on Bébert and Lydie and waving the basket containing Poland.

The clamor started up again and Etienne enjoyed the intoxication of popularity. The three thousand breasts whose hearts beat higher at a word from him seemed the materialization of his power. If Souvarine had deigned to come, he would have applauded his ideas, insofar as he recognized them, been content with his pupil's progress in anarchist theory, and satisfied with the entire program except for the matter of training—a vestige of sentimental foolishness, for healthy ignorance was to be the bath in which the metal of

men would be retempered. As for Rasseneur, he shrugged his
shoulders in contempt and anger.

"Let me speak!" he shouted to Etienne.

The latter jumped down from the tree trunk.

"Speak if you want to—we'll see if they listen to you!"

Rasseneur had already taken his place and was gesturing
for silence, but the noise continued. His name passed through
the crowd, from those in the nearest ranks who had recognized him to those in the furthest ones lost under the
beeches, and they refused to listen to him; he was a fallen
idol, the very sight of whom irritated his former followers.
His facility with words, the easy, relaxed manner in which he
spoke, everything that had for so long charmed them was
now considered to be so much tepid tea, fit only to soothe
cowards. He tried in vain to talk over the noise; he wanted
once more to take up his usual pacification speech about how
it was impossible to change the world with laws and how you
had to give social evolution enough time to work itself out.
They laughed at him, shouted at him to shut up; the defeat
begun at the Bon Joyeux worsened and became irremediable.
They ended by throwing handfuls of frozen moss at him, and
one woman cried out shrilly:

"Down with the traitor!"

He tried to explain why the mine could not belong to the
miner the way the loom belonged to the weaver, and he
called for a system of profit-sharing under which the worker
would have a vested interest in the organization, as if he
were a member of the family.

"Down with the traitor!" repeated a thousand voices, and
stones began to fly through the air.

At this he paled, and despair filled his eyes with tears. It
was the collapse of his whole life, twenty years of ambitious
camaraderie shattered by the ingratitude of the crowd.
Heartsick, unable to continue, he stepped down from the tree
trunk.

"You think it's funny," he spluttered, turning to the triumphant Etienne. "All right, I hope the same thing happens
to you. . . . It *will* happen, believe me!"

And with a sweeping gesture, as though to disclaim all
responsibility for the troubles he could foresee, he turned
away and walked off alone through the white and silent
countryside.

A chorus of jeers arose, and then suddenly everybody was
surprised to see Old Bonnemort standing on the tree trunk
and trying to make himself heard through all the tumult.
Until then he and Mouque had been lost in thought, seeming

in their usual way to be mulling over the old, long-gone days. No doubt he was giving way to one of those sudden urges toward babbling that would sometimes stir up the past so violently that old memories would rise from his depths and flow from his lips for hours. It had become very quiet, and everybody listened to the old man, so ghostly pale in the moonlight; as he was talking about things that had no obvious connection with the discussion, long stories that nobody could understand, their astonishment increased. He spoke of his youth, told of his two uncles who had been crushed to death at Le Voreux, then went on to the pneumonia that had carried off his wife. Through it all, however, he never lost hold of his one idea: things had never been right and they never would be right. For example, five hundred of them had gathered here in the forest because the king hadn't wanted to shorten the work day—but he never finished that story and began to tell of another strike instead: he had seen so many of them! They all ended up under these trees, here at the Plan-des-Dames, there at La Charbonnerie, or even further away, toward Saut-du-Loup. Sometimes it was freezing, sometimes it was hot. One evening it had rained so hard that they'd had to disband before they'd been able to say a word. And the king's soldiers would come and it would all end in bursts of rifle fire.

"We'd raise our hands like this and we'd swear we'd never go down. . . . Oh, I've sworn, yes, I've sworn!"

The crowd was listening, open-mouthed and uneasy, when Etienne, who had been watching the scene, leaped up on the fallen tree, keeping the old man beside him. He had just recognized Chaval standing among his friends up front. The idea that Catherine might be there had stirred a new fire within him, a need to have her see him acclaimed.

"Comrades, you've heard what one of our old-timers has had to say—what he has suffered and what our children will suffer if we don't put an end to these thieves and murderers once and for all!"

He was terrifying. Never before had he spoken so violently. He was holding on to Old Bonnemort with one arm, displaying him like a flag of misery and mourning, crying for vengeance. In a few swift sentences he went back to the first Maheu, and he showed how this whole family had been worn out by the mine, devoured by the Company—and how it was now, after a hundred years of work, more starved than ever; then, as a contrast, he drew a picture of the big-bellied board members stinking of money, and of the whole bunch of stockholders who for a century had been kept like whores, doing nothing, living off the sweat of the miners. Wasn't it disgusting?—a whole people dying down below, from father to son, just so ministers could be bribed and generations of aristocrats and bourgeois could give parties or grow fat by their firesides! He had studied the diseases of the miners and he listed them all, going into frightening detail: anemia, scrofula, black bronchitis, choking asthma, paralyzing rheumatism. They were miserable wretches, thrown like fodder to the machines, herded like cattle into villages, swallowed bit by bit by the large companies that were codifying slavery and threatening to regiment all the workers in the country, millions of men, just for the benefit of a thousand good-for-nothings! But the miner was no longer ignorant, no longer a brute buried in the bowels of the earth. An army was springing up from the depths of the mines, a harvest of citizens whose seed was germinating and would burst through the earth one sunny day. And then they'd see if after forty years of service they would dare offer a hundred and fifty franc pension to a sixty-year-old man who spat coal and whose legs were swollen from the water in the stalls! Oh yes, labor would demand an accounting from capital, from that impersonal god, unknown to the worker, who crouched somewhere in his mysterious tabernacle and sucked the life from the starving wretches who fed him! They would go there, they would make him show his face in the light of the destructive fires, they would drown him in blood, the filthy pig, the monstrous idol gorged with human flesh!

He fell silent, but his arms were still outstretched, still pointing to the enemy "over there"—he didn't know where, but somewhere. This time the clamor of the crowd was so loud that the bourgeois in Montsou heard it and looked toward Vandame, worried lest it be some terrible landslide. Night birds flew out from the woods into the great clear sky.

And now Etienne wanted to bring matters to a head:

"Comrades, what is your decision? . . . Do you vote to continue the strike?"

"Yes, yes!" thundered the voices.

"And what steps will you take? . . . If any cowards go down tomorrow, we're sure to be defeated."

Again the voices thundered:

"Death to the cowards!"

"Then you are determined to remind them of their duty, of the oath they swore. . . . Here's what we can do—we'll show up at the mines, and the traitors will understand that they can't get away with it and the Company will see that we're all in agreement—that we'll die sooner than give in."

"That's right, let's go to the mines! To the mines!"

All the time he had been speaking, Etienne had been searching for Catherine among the pale, roaring faces in front of him. No, she definitely wasn't there. But he did keep seeing Chaval, who shrugged his shoulders and pretended to be amused by it all, but who was devoured by jealousy and ready to sell his soul for even a little of Etienne's popularity.

"And if there are spies among us, comrades," Etienne went on, "they'd better be careful, we know who they are. . . . Yes, I see some miners from Vandame who are still on the job. . . ."

"Do you mean me?" blustered Chaval.

"You or anybody else. . . . But since you're the one who's spoken, you might as well understand that those who eat have nothing in common with those who are hungry. You're working at Jean-Bart. . . ."

A mocking voice broke in:

"Him, work? . . . He's got a woman working for him."

Chaval swore, his face in flames.

"Damn it, doesn't a man have the right to work?"

"No!" shouted Etienne. "When your friends are suffering for the good of all, you don't have the right to be selfish and line up with the bosses to save your own neck! If the strike had been general, we'd have won a long time ago. . . . Should even one man at Vandame have gone down when the men of Montsou were out? The thing to do would be to stop work everywhere, at Monsieur Deneulin's as well as here. Do you understand? All the men in the stalls at Jean-Bart are traitors —you're all traitors!"

The crowd around Chaval was becoming threatening. Fists were raised, and there was a rumble of "kill him! kill him!" He paled. But his rage to triumph over Etienne gave him an idea.

"Listen to me, will you! Come to Jean-Bart tomorrow and you'll see if I'm working! . . . They sent me to tell you that we're all with you. The fires should be put out and the enginemen should go out on strike too. If the pumps stop, so much the better—the water will ruin the mines and that'll be the end of everything!"

He in turn was now wildly applauded, and from then on Etienne himself was swept aside. Orator succeeded orator on the tree trunk, gesticulating into the clamor and urging terrifying proposals. It was a mad outburst of faith, the impatience of a religious sect that was tired of waiting for the hoped-for miracle and had decided to make it happen. Heads emptied by famine saw red, and dreamed of fire and blood—

an apotheosis of glory from the midst of which universal
happiness was ascending. And the calm moon bathed this
surging mass, and the profound silence of the deep forest
embraced this cry of massacre. Only the frozen moss
crackled underfoot, and the beeches rose powerfully, the
delicate tracery of their branches black against the white sky,
neither seeing nor hearing the miserable creatures swarming
at their feet.

The crowd began to push and shove, and La Maheude
found herself next to Maheu; the two of them, driven out of
their minds by the mounting exasperation that had gnawed at
them for months, shouted approval of Levaque, who was
demanding the heads of the engineers. Pierron had disappeared. Bonnemort and Old Mouque were both talking at the
same time, saying vague and violent things that nobody could
understand. As a joke, Zacharie called for the destruction of
the churches, while Mouquet beat the earth with his *crosse*
just to add to the noise. The women were wild: La Levaque,
her hands on her hips, started fighting with Philomène,
whom she accused of having laughed; Mouquette talked of
putting the police out of commission with a few strategically
placed kicks; La Brûlé, who had just slapped Lydie for not
having either the basket or the salad, continued to strike into
the air blows intended for all the bosses she would have liked
to have in her hands. For a moment Jeanlin was terrified, for
Bébert had learned from one of the mine boys that Madame Rasseneur had seen them steal Poland; but as soon as he
had decided to go back and secretly let the animal loose at
the door of L'Avantage, he began to shout louder than ever,
and he opened his new knife and waved the blade about,
insanely proud of how it flashed in the dark.

"Comrades, comrades!" Etienne kept repeating, exhausted,
his voice hoarse from the effort to get a moment's silence so
that they could come to a final decision.

At last they listened to him.

"Comrades! Tomorrow morning at Jean-Bart, agreed?"

"Yes, yes, at Jean-Bart. Death to the traitors!"

The hurricane of the three thousand voices filled the sky
and faded away in the pure light of the moon.

Part *FIVE*

1

The moon had set, and at four o'clock the night was pitch-black. Everybody was asleep at the Deneulins', and the old brick house, its door and windows sealed, stood silent and somber at the end of the sprawling, badly kept garden that separated it from the Jean-Bart mine. The other side of the house looked out on the deserted road to Vandame, an overgrown village hidden behind the forest, about two miles away.

Deneulin, worn-out by having spent part of the previous day down in the mine, was snoring away with his nose against the wall when he dreamed that someone was calling him. He finally awoke, heard an actual voice, and ran to open the window. One of his foremen was standing in the garden.

"What's the matter?" asked Deneulin.

"Sir, it's a rebellion. Half the men want to stop work, and they're keeping the others from going down."

Deneulin didn't understand; his head was heavy and buzzing with sleep, and the bitter cold lashed at him like an icy shower.

"Damn it, force them to go down," he mumbled.

"It's been going on for an hour," the foreman continued. "We thought we'd better come and get you. You're the only one who might be able to make them listen to reason."

"All right, I'll come."

He dressed quickly, fully awake now and very worried. The whole house could have been pillaged—neither the cook nor the servant had budged. But now, from the other side of the landing, he could hear the sound of alarmed whispering, and when he went out, he saw the door of his daughters' room open and both girls appear in the white dressing gowns they had hastily thrown on.

237

"Father, what's happening?"

The elder girl, Lucie, was already twenty-two, tall, dark, and dignified; Jeanne, the younger one, was scarcely nineteen, small, blond, and enchanting.

"Nothing serious," he answered reassuringly. "It seems that some loudmouths are making a fuss down there, and I'm going over to look into it."

They protested that they wouldn't let him leave until he had had something hot—otherwise he'd come home sick, his stomach all upset as usual. He objected, insisting he was really in too much of a hurry.

"Listen," said Jeanne finally, hanging her arms around his neck, "either you drink a small glass of rum and eat a couple of biscuits, or else I won't let you go and you'll have to carry me along with you."

He swore that the biscuits would stick in his throat, but he had to give in, and the girls preceded him downstairs, each with her candlestick. Below, in the dining room, they hurried to serve him, one pouring rum and the other running to the pantry for a package of biscuits. Having lost their mother while still very young, they had grown up all alone, undisciplined and spoiled by their father. The elder was haunted by the dream of singing on the stage, and the younger was mad about painting and showed an unusually bold taste. But when serious business losses had made it necessary for them to trim their style of life, both of these somewhat impetuous girls suddenly turned into careful and shrewd housekeepers whose eyes could spot an error of centimes in a bill; and now, with their boyish, bohemian air, they controlled the purse strings, pinched pennies, argued with tradesmen, constantly made over their dresses, and, in short, managed to put a decent face on things in spite of their increasing financial embarrassment.

"Eat, Papa," Lucie kept repeating.

Then, noticing his silent and grave preoccupation, her fear returned.

"It must be serious to make you look like that, isn't it? . . . Suppose we stay here with you? They can get along without us at this luncheon."

She was referring to an excursion that had been planned for that morning. Madame Hennebeau was first to go to the Grégoires' in her carriage and pick up Cécile; then she would come for them and they would all go on to Marchiennes to lunch at Les Forges at the invitation of the manager's wife. It was an opportunity to visit the workshops, the blast furnaces, and the coke ovens.

"Of course we'll stay," declared Jeanne in turn.

But he became angry.

"What an idea! I tell you it's nothing. . . . You will please go back to your beds and be ready at nine o'clock as was arranged."

He kissed them and rushed off. They could hear the fading sound of his boots on the frozen garden earth.

Jeanne carefully replaced the cork in the bottle of rum while Lucie locked up the biscuits.

The room had the cold cleanliness common to those in which the meals served are frugal ones. The girls took advantage of this early morning descent to make sure that everything had been set to rights the night before. A napkin had been left lying around—the servant would hear about it. Finally they went back upstairs.

As Deneulin took the short cut through the narrow paths of his kitchen garden, he thought of his threatened fortune—of the Montsou *denier*, of the million he had realized on it and which he had dreamed of increasing tenfold, but which was now in such danger. There had been an uninterrupted run of bad luck—enormous and unforeseen repair bills, ruinously high operating expenses, and then this disastrous industrial crisis just when the profits were beginning to come in. If the strike spread to his mine he was done for. He pushed open a little door; against the dark sky the mine buildings were of a denser darkness, starred by an occasional lantern.

Jean-Bart was not as important as Le Voreux, but its renovation had made it into a "nice little mine," as the engineers put it. Not only had the shaft been widened by a yard and a half and sunk to a depth of more than twenty-three hundred feet, but it had been completely reequipped—the hoisting engine was new, the cages were new, and in fact all the equipment was new and represented the last word in scientific achievement. There were even some touches of elegance in the buildings—the screening shed had a scalloped lambrequin, the headframe boasted a clock, both the landing room and the engine house were rounded like Renaissance chapels, and over everything towered the smokestack, a mosaic spiral of red and black bricks. The pump had been set up in the other shaft of the concession, in the old Gaston-Marie pit, now used exclusively for drainage. At Jean-Bart there were only two subsidiary shafts to the right and left of the main extraction shaft, one a ladder well and one for the steam-driven ventilator.

That morning Chaval had been the first to arrive; at three

o'clock he was arguing with the men and trying to convince them that they had to do what the Montsou miners were doing and demand an increase of five centimes per cart. Soon the four hundred men who worked at the bottom had overflowed from the dressing shed into the landing room amid a tumult of cries and gestures. Those who wanted to work were barefoot, their lamps in their hands and their shovels or picks under their arms; the others, still wearing their sabots, their coats around their shoulders because of the bitter cold, were barring the entrance to the shaft. The foremen had shouted themselves hoarse trying to restore order, begging the men to be reasonable and not keep those who wanted to go down from doing so.

When Chaval saw Catherine in her trousers and jacket, her blue cap on her head, he was furious, for on getting up he had ordered her in no uncertain terms to stay in bed. In despair at not working, she had nevertheless followed him; he never gave her any money and she often had to pay for him as well as for herself. What would happen to her if she stopped earning anything? . . . She was obsessed by a fear— the fear of a Marchiennes brothel, which was where the haulage girls ended up when they had nothing to eat and no place to go.

"God damn it, what the hell are you doing here?" Chaval shouted.

She stammered that she didn't have an income and she wanted to work.

"So you're setting yourself up against me, are you? You slut! . . . Go back home or I'll send you on your way with a few kicks in the ass!"

She timidly retreated, but didn't leave; she was determined to see how things would work out.

Deneulin arrived by way of the stairway from the screening shed. Despite the dim light given off by the lanterns, he quickly took in the whole scene—the shadowy mob of cutters, loaders, trammers, haulage girls, and even mine boys, every one of whose faces was familiar to him. In the still-new and clean landing room, all work had come to a halt, and everything seemed to be waiting: the engine, steam up, was hissing gently; the cages hung from the motionless cables; the abandoned carts cluttered the iron flooring. Only some eighty lamps had been taken out; the rest were blazing in the lamproom. But surely it would take only a word from him for everything to start up again.

"Well, boys, what's going on here?" he asked in a hearty

voice. "What's bothering you? Tell me about it and we'll straighten it all out."

Though he demanded a great deal of work from the men, his attitude toward them was generally paternal. Authoritarian, brusque in manner, he would first try to win them over with a loud and breezy good humor, and he often succeeded in earning their admiration. They respected him, above all, as a man of courage, always down in the stalls with them, always the first on the spot when an accident spread terror through the mine. Twice, after firedamp explosions, he had been let down by means of a rope under his arms when even the boldest had hung back.

"Come now," he continued, "you're not going to make me regret having vouched for you. You know that I refused to have police stationed here. . . . Just be calm, I'm listening to you."

Embarrassed, they all fell silent and moved away from him, and it was Chaval who finally said:

"It's like this, Monsieur Deneulin. We can't go on working—we want five centimes more per cart."

Deneulin looked surprised.

"What!—five centimes! What's this demand based on? *I'm* not complaining about your timbering, *I'm* not trying to impose a new pay scale, like the management at Montsou."

"That may be true, but just the same our comrades at Montsou are right. They're rejecting the pay scale and demanding an increase of five centimes because a man can't do a decent job under the present contract. . . . We want five centimes more, don't we, men?"

There were shouts of approval, and the hubbub started up again, accompanied by violent gestures. Little by little they were all gathering around him in a tight circle.

Deneulin's eyes blazed, and he clenched his fists—those fists of a man who liked strong governments—to keep from giving way to the temptation of seizing one of them by the scruff of the neck. He preferred to discuss the matter, talk it over sensibly.

"You want five centimes more, and I agree the work is worth it. The trouble is, I can't give it to you. If I do, I'll be ruined. . . . You've got to understand that for you to be able to survive, *I* have to survive first. And I'm at the end of my rope—the least increase in my costs would finish me off. . . . You may remember that two years ago, at the time of the last strike, I gave in—I could still manage it then. But that pay increase was ruinous, and for two years now I've been struggling. . . . As things stand now, I'd rather put a padlock

on the door right away than not know where to get the
money to pay you with next month."

Chaval snickered nastily at this employer who was so
candidly explaining his affairs. The others lowered their
heads, stubborn, unbelieving, unwilling to get it through their
skulls that a boss might not be making millions off his
workers.

But Deneulin persisted. He described his fight against
Montsou, which was always on the alert, always ready to
gobble him up any time he made a slip. It was the savage
competition that was forcing him to economize, especially
since the great depth of Jean-Bart made the cost of extraction higher for him—a factor which was barely compensated
for by the great width of his coal seams. He would never
have raised wages after the last strike if he hadn't had to
match those at Montsou lest his men leave him. And then he
conjured up a menacing future for them—what would they
have gained if they forced him to sell and they themselves
passed under the terrible yoke of the Montsou Company! *He*
wasn't lording it over them from some faraway, unknown
tabernacle; *he* wasn't one of those stockholders whom the
men never saw and who fleeced the workers through paid
managers! He was a real boss, and he risked considerably
more than his money—he risked his intelligence, his health,
his life. A work stoppage would quite simply be the end of
him, for he had no stock and yet he had to fill his orders. In
addition, the capital invested in his installation could not
remain dormant. How would he meet his commitments? Who
would pay the interest on the money his friends had entrusted
to him? It would mean bankruptcy.

"And that's it, men," he concluded. "I wanted to show
you. . . . You can't ask a man to cut his own throat, can you?
And if I let you have your five centimes or if I let you go on
strike, it's the same as cutting my throat."

He fell silent. A murmur went through the crowd. Some of
the miners seemed to be hesitating, and some moved toward
the shaft.

"At least," said the foreman, "let everybody be free to
choose. . . . Who wants to work?"

Catherine was one of the first to step forward, but Chaval
pushed her back angrily, shouting:

"We're all in agreement. Only a son of a bitch would
doublecross his friends!"

From that point on, conciliation seemed impossible. The
shouting began again, and men were pushed away from the
shaft and almost crushed against the walls. For a moment the

manager, in desperation, tried to fight on alone, to force the mob to his will; but it was a foolish attempt and he had to leave. Winded and exhausted, so bewildered by his impotence that he hadn't so much as an idea of what to do next, he sat in the checker's office for a few minutes. Then he calmed down and told one of the supervisors to bring Chaval to him. When the latter had agreed to talk to him, he waved everybody else outside.

"Leave us alone."

Deneulin's notion was to see what this fellow was made of. From Chaval's very first words he spotted him as being vain and devoured by jealousy, so he began to flatter him, pretending to be surprised that such a good worker would compromise his future in this way. To listen to him, he had for some time had an eye on Chaval with a view toward rapid advancement, and he ended by frankly offering to make him a foreman later. Chaval listened to him in silence, his fists clenched at first, then gradually relaxing. His mind was in a turmoil: if he insisted on going ahead with the strike, he'd never be anything more than Etienne's lieutenant, whereas now another ambition was presenting itself—the possibility of becoming one of the mine bosses. A hot flush of pride rose to his face and intoxicated him. Besides, the strikers he had been waiting for since early morning would never show up now; something must have stopped them, maybe the police: the time had come to give in. But still he kept shaking his head, playing the incorruptible man and indignantly beating his chest. Finally, without telling his employer about the rendezvous he had planned with the Montsou miners, he promised to calm the men and get them to go down.

Deneulin remained out of sight, and even the foremen kept away. For an hour they heard Chaval, standing on one of the landing room carts, lecture and argue. Some of the workers booed him, and a hundred and twenty of them left in exasperation, stubbornly abiding by the decision he had persuaded them to make. It was already after seven o'clock; day was breaking, a bright, sparkling, frosty day. And suddenly the noise of the mine started up again, and the halted work resumed. First it was the engine, its connecting rods plunging, rolling and unrolling the cables on the drums. Then, amid a din of signals, the descent began; the cages were filled, swallowed down, and brought up again as the shaft devoured its ration of mine boys, haulage girls, and cutters, and the trammers pushed their carts along the iron sheeting in a rumble of thunder.

"For God's sake, what the hell are you doing there?"

Chaval shouted to Catherine, who was waiting her turn.
"Will you stop loafing around and go down!"

At nine o'clock, when Madame Hennebeau arrived in her
carriage with Cécile, she found Lucie and Jeanne all ready
and very elegant, despite the fact that their clothes had been
made over twenty times. But Deneulin was surprised to see
Négrel accompanying the carriage on horseback. What?—
were the men to be included? Madame Hennebeau explained
in her maternal manner that she'd been made nervous—it
was said that the roads were filled with unsavory people, and
she preferred to bring along a protector. Négrel laughed and
reassured them: nothing to worry about—the usual
loudmouthed threats, but no one would dare throw a stone
through a window. Still elated by his success, Deneulin told
about the suppressed revolt at Jean-Bart; now, he said, he
felt pretty sure everything would be all right. And there on
the road to Vandame, while the young ladies were getting
into the carriage, they all enjoyed the exhilaration of this
superb day, unaware of the long, swelling shudder in the
distant countryside—the sound of a people whose marching
steps they would have heard had they put their ears to the
ground.

"So it's settled," repeated Madame Hennebeau. "You'll
come for these young ladies in the evening, and you will dine
with us. . . . Madame Grégoire has also promised to come
fetch Cécile."

"You can count on me," Deneulin answered.

The carriage started off toward Vandame. Jeanne and
Lucie leaned out to smile at their father, who stood at the
side of the road, while Négrel trotted gallantly behind the
spinning carriage wheels.

They crossed the forest and took the road from Vandame
to Marchiennes. As they were approaching Tartaret, Jeanne
asked Madame Hennebeau if she had ever seen the Green
Hill; the latter, though she had been living in the area for five
years, admitted that she had never passed that way, so they
made a detour. Tartaret, at the edge of the forest, was an
uncultivated wasteland of volcanic sterility, under which a
coal mine had been burning for centuries. Its beginning was
lost in legend, and the local miners told the following story:
a fire from heaven had once fallen on this Sodom in the
bowels of the earth—where the haulage girls used to indulge
in obscene abominations—and it had happened so quickly
that the girls had not had time to get out and were still
flaming away at the bottom of that hell to this very day. The
dark-red calcined rocks were covered with an efflorescence

of alum, like a leprosy. Yellow flowers of sulfur spread
from the edges of the fissures, and the daredevils who were
bold enough to look down these cracks at night swore they
could see flames—the condemned souls roasting in the fire
below. Flickering lights moved along the ground; hot vapors
stinking of filth and of the devil's foul kitchen smoked day
and night; and in the middle of this accursed wasteland of
Tartaret, like a miracle of eternal spring, rose the Green
Hill, with its perpetually green grass, its beech trees with
their endlessly renewed leaves, and its fields in which as many
as three crops a year would ripen. It was a natural hothouse,
heated by the fire in the buried depths. Snow never lay there.
The great clumps of green alongside the leafless trees of the
forest were spread out under this December day, and the
frost had not even browned its edges.

Soon the carriage was speeding across the plain. Négrel
joked about the legend and explained how fires generally
broke out at the bottom of a mine due to spontaneous
combustion of the coal dust; when it couldn't be controlled, it
burned on endlessly, and he described how a Belgian mine
had been flooded by changing the course of a river and
directing it into the shaft. But then he fell silent, for bands of
miners had been passing the carriage for the last few minutes. They went by silently, glancing sidewise at this luxurious
turnout that was forcing them to the side of the road. Their
number kept increasing, and the horses had to be slowed to
a walk on the little bridge over the Scarpe. What was
happening to make all these people come out onto the roads
like this? The ladies were becoming frightened, and Négrel
began to suspect trouble somewhere in the seething countryside; it was a relief when they finally arrived at Marchiennes.
Under a sun that seemed to blot out their fires, the batteries
of the coke ovens and the chimneys of the blast furnaces were
belching clouds of smoke, sending down a never-ending rain
of soot.

2

At Jean-Bart Catherine had been pushing her carts to the
relay point for an hour, and she was so soaked in sweat that
she had to stop for a moment to mop her face.

Chaval, hacking away at the vein with the rest of his team

at the bottom of the stall, was surprised at no longer hearing the rumble of the wheels. The lamps were burning badly, and the coal dust was too thick for him to be able to see.

"What's the matter?" he shouted.

When she replied that she was about to melt and that her heart was ready to give out, he replied furiously:

"Idiot, do what we've done! Take off your shirt."

They were 2,336 feet down, toward the north, in the first gallery of the Désirée vein—almost two miles from the loading platform. The local miners would pale and lower their voices when they talked of this area of the mine, as if they were talking of hell; most often, in fact, they merely shook their heads, preferring not to talk about these burning depths at all. The farther north the galleries ran, the closer they came to Tartaret, beginning to penetrate into that interior fire which had calcined the rocks above. At the point the team had now reached, the stalls had an average temperature of 113 degrees. They were actually in the infernal city, surrounded by the flames that spewed forth the sulfur and the foul vapors visible to passersby on the plain above through the cracks in the ground.

Catherine, who had already taken off her jacket, hesitated, then took off her trousers too; with her arms and thighs now bare, her shift tied around her waist like a blouse with a piece of cord, she went back to her hauling.

"Well, it should be more comfortable like this," she said aloud.

Her sense of suffocation was mixed with a vague fear. During the five days they had been working there, she had found herself ceaselessly thinking about those tales she had heard from the cradle on—stories about the haulage girls of olden days who were still burning under Tartaret as punishment for things that could not even be spoken of. Oh, of course she was too old now to believe in such foolishness, but still—what would she do if she were to see a girl, as red as a stove and with eyes like flaming coals, suddenly come out of the wall? The very thought made her sweat twice as much.

At the relay point, 264 feet from the stall, another haulage girl took the cart and pushed it 264 feet farther—right to the foot of the inclined plane—so the receiver could send it off with the others coming from the galleries above.

"Well, you really make yourself at home!" said the other woman, a scrawny widow of thirty, when she saw Catherine in her shift. "I can't do that—the boys on the incline are always after me with their dirty tricks."

"Oh," the young girl replied, "I can't worry about the men, I'm too uncomfortable!"

She set off again, pushing an empty cart. The worst of it was that there was another reason, besides the fact that this bottom gallery was so close to Tartaret, for the heat to be so unbearable. The tunnel ran alongside some old workings—a very deep abandoned gallery of Gaston-Marie—where ten years ago a firedamp explosion had set fire to the vein, and this fire was still burning behind the *corroi*—a clay wall that was built here and kept in constant repair in order to contain the disaster. Without air, the fire should have died out, but it was probably being fed by some concealed drafts and had been burning all this time, heating the clay of the *corroi* just the way bricks of a furnace are heated, so that anyone passing by was roasted. And for more than 300 feet the haulage was done alongside this wall in a temperature of 140 degrees.

After two more trips Catherine was gasping again. Luckily the tunnel was wide and easy in this désirée vein, which was one of the thickest in the region. The seam was about six feet high and the men could work standing up, but they would have preferred a less comfortable position and some cooler air.

"Hey, are you asleep there?" Chaval called out roughly, as soon as he could no longer hear Catherine moving about. "How the hell did I ever get stuck with a slut like that! Fill your cart and start moving!"

She was at the foot of the face, leaning on her shovel; she felt so sick that she could only gape at them stupidly, making no move to obey. In the reddish light of the lamps they were hardly visible—naked as animals, and so black, so coated with sweat and coal, that their nudity did not even embarrass her. Theirs was a shadowy labor, a labor of apelike spines stretching and straining, a hellish vision of scorched limbs exhausting themselves amid dull thuds and groans. But evidently they could see her better, for the picks stopped beating and they teased her for having taken off her trousers.

"Hey, be careful, you'll catch cold!"

"That's a pretty good pair of legs! Hey, Chaval, there's enough for two!"

"Let's see! Pull it up a little! Higher than that, higher!"

Without troubling himself about the laughter, Chaval started in on her again.

"That's enough, damn it! ... Oh, she's willing enough when it comes to dirty jokes—she'd stand there listening till tomorrow!"

Painfully, Catherine had managed to fill her cart; now she pushed it off. The gallery was too wide for her to be able to brace herself against the timbers on both sides, and her bare feet were twisting between the rails, searching for a point of purchase: she was moving ahead slowly, her arms held out stiffly in front of her, her body bent double. And as soon as she came alongside the *corroi* the fire torture began again, and the sweat ran from every pore, like a rainstorm.

Before she had gone a third of the way to the relay point she was drenched, blinded, as caked with black mud as the men were. Her tight shift seemed soaked in ink, and it stuck to her skin and worked its way up her back with every movement of her legs, restricting her so painfully that she had to stop again.

What was the matter with her today? She'd never felt her bones turned to water like this before. The air must be bad. There was no ventilation here in this far-off gallery. You breathed in all kinds of vapors that came bubbling out of the coal—sometimes they were so heavy that the lamps wouldn't burn—to say nothing of the firedamp, which nobody paid any attention to anymore because they sniffed up so much of it from one end of the week to the other. She knew it well, this bad air—"dead air," the miners called it—with the heavy asphyxiating gases down at the bottom, and up above, the light gases that catch fire and can destroy all the workings of a mine, hundreds of men, in a single clap of thunder. She had swallowed down so much of it from childhood on that she was surprised to find it bothering her so, making her ears buzz and her throat burn.

She couldn't stand it anymore—she would have to take off her shift too. It was torture, this cloth whose every wrinkle cut into her, burned her. She tried to resist, tried to go on with the hauling, but she had to stop and straighten up. Then suddenly, telling herself she would put it on again at the relay point, she took it all off, the cord, the shift, everything; she was so feverish that she would have torn her skin off if she had been able to. And now, naked, pitiful, reduced to the level of an animal hunting for food in the filth of the roads, she struggled on, her haunches smeared with soot, her belly caked with mud, like a mare pulling a carriage. Down on all fours, she kept pushing.

Despair swept over her as she realized that being naked brought no relief. What else could she take off? The buzzing in her ears was deafening her, and her temples felt as though they were clamped in a vise. She fell to her knees. The lamp propped against the coal in the cart seemed to go out. Her mind swimming in confusion, she clung to one idea—she had to raise the wick. Twice she brought the lamp down to the ground in front of her to examine it, and twice she saw it grow pale, as if it too were out of breath. Suddenly the lamp went out. Everything whirled around in the darkness; a millstone was turning in her head, and her heart grew faint and stopped beating, benumbed by the same terrible fatigue that had overcome her limbs. She had fallen over on her back and was gasping in the asphyxiating air along the ground.

"By God, I think she's loafing again!" growled Chaval.

He listened from the top of the stall but couldn't hear the sound of the wheels.

"Hey, Catherine, you damn slug!"

His voice faded away down the dark gallery, and not so much as a whisper replied.

"Do you need some help from my foot to get you going?"

Nothing stirred; the deathly silence remained unbroken. Furious, he went down, and holding his lamp, ran along in such a wild rage that he almost stumbled over the girl's body, which was stretched across the path. He stared at her, open-mouthed. What was the matter? Was she only pretending, just to catch a little snooze? But the lamp, which he had lowered to light up her face, threatened to go out. He raised it, lowered it again, and then he understood: she must have swallowed some bad air. His anger disappeared, and the miner's devotion to a comrade in danger stirred within him. He shouted for them to bring his shirt; he had lifted the naked, unconscious girl in his arms and was holding her as high as possible. When their clothes had been thrown over his shoulders, he set off at a trot, supporting his burden with one hand and carrying the two lamps in the other. The deep galleries unfolded before him; he ran, turning to the right, turning to the left, trying to find the frosty life-giving air that was swept down the ventilator from the plain above. Finally, the bubbling sound of a spring flowing from a rock stopped him. He was at a junction with a large haulage gallery that had formerly served Gaston-Marie. The air here was blowing through the ventilator like a tempest, and it was so cold that he started to shiver as he settled his still-unconscious mistress on the ground, her back against the timbers.

"For God's sake, Catherine, stop kidding around! . . . Try to sit up while I dip this in the water."

It frightened him to see her so lifeless, but he managed to dip his shirt in the spring and bathe her face with it. She was like a corpse—it was as if her thin underdeveloped body, in

which the forms of puberty were still hesitating, was already
buried in the earth. Then a shudder ran through the childish
breasts, belly, and thighs of this pitiful little girl deflowered
before her time, and she opened her eyes and stammered:

"I'm cold."

"Ah, that's better!" exclaimed Chaval in relief.

He re-dressed her, slipping on her shift quickly, but swearing as he struggled to put on her trousers, for she could do
little to help. She was stunned, unable to understand where
she was or why she was naked. When she remembered, she
was overcome with shame. How could she have dared take
everything off! And she questioned him: had they seen her
like this, without even a handkerchief to cover her? He
teased her and made up all kinds of stories; he said he had
carried her there through a crowd of miners lining the way.
What a mad idea to have taken him seriously and exposed
her ass to the air! But then he swore that he had run so
quickly that the men couldn't have seen whether it was round
or square.

"Damn it, I'm freezing!" he said, putting his own clothes
on.

She had never known him so nice. Generally, every kind
word she got from him was immediately followed by two
insults. Yet it would have been so good to live together
peacefully! A feeling of tenderness mingled in her with the
languor of exhaustion. She smiled at him and murmured:

"Kiss me."

He kissed her and lay down beside her, waiting till she
would be able to walk.

"You see," she went on, "you were wrong to yell at me
before—I really couldn't stand it anymore! It's not that hot
for you in the stall, but if you only knew how I was roasting
in that tunnel!"

"Well sure," he replied, "it would be more comfortable
under the trees. . . . You poor kid, I know it's rough down
here."

She was so touched to hear him admit this that she tried to
make light of the difficulties.

"Oh, it's just that I don't feel well. And the air is so rotten
today. . . . But in a few minutes you'll see if I'm a slug! If
you've got to work, you work, right? Me, I'd rather die than
give in."

There was a silence. He had his arm around her waist,
hugging her against his chest to keep her from catching a
chill, and she, though she felt strong enough to go back to
work, was lingering in delight.

"The only thing is," she continued in a low voice, "I'd like it so much if you were a little kinder. ... It's so nice when we try to love each other."

She began to cry softly.

"But I do love you!" he exclaimed. "Haven't I taken you to live with me?"

She only shook her head. Men often took women just to have them, without caring at all if they were happy or not. Her tears flowed more freely—she was brokenhearted at the thought of how good her life would be if she had only fallen in with another man, one whose arms would always have been around her waist like this. Another?—and through her anguish floated the vague image of that other. But that was over, and all she wanted now was to live out her days with this one, if only he wouldn't be so rough with her.

"Then promise me," she said, "that you'll try to be like this every once in a while."

She choked on another outburst of sobs and he kissed her again.

"What a goose you are! ... Look, I promise to be nice. Come on now, I'm no worse than anybody else."

She looked at him and began to smile again through her tears. Maybe he was right; after all, you didn't see many happy women around. And though she had no particular confidence in his promise, she gave herself up to the pleasure of seeing him so kind. Oh, if only it could last! They had put their arms around each other again and were locked in a long embrace when the sound of footsteps made them get to their feet. Three of the men who had seen them pass had come to find out how things were.

They all went back together. It was almost ten o'clock and they had their lunch in a cool corner before going back to sweat at the bottom of the stall. They were just finishing their *briquets* and about to take a swallow of coffee from their flasks when a noise from some distant stalls made them uneasy. What now?—another accident? They stood up and began to run, meeting cutters, haulage girls, and mine boys at every step, but nobody knew anything and they were all shouting; it must be something terrible. Little by little the alarm spread throughout the entire mine; terrified shadows were pouring out from the galleries, lanterns dancing and bobbing in the darkness. Where was it? Why didn't somebody tell them?

Suddenly a foreman ran by, shouting:

"They're cutting the cables! They're cutting the cables!"

Panic broke out, and there was a wild stampede through

the dark tunnels. They couldn't understand. Why were they cutting the cables?—and who was cutting them, while the men were still down at the bottom? It seemed a monstrous thing to do.

Another foreman's voice boomed out, and then died on the air:

"The men from Montsou are cutting the cables! Everybody out!"

When Chaval understood what was happening, he stopped Catherine short. His legs grew heavy at the thought of having to face the miners from Montsou. So they had come, those men he had thought were in the hands of the gendarmes! For a moment he considered retracing his steps and going up by way of Gaston-Marie, but it was too late for that. He swore, hesitated, tried to hide his fear, repeated that it was stupid to run like this. They wouldn't just be left down there on the bottom, would they?

The foreman's voice sounded again, closer this time.

"Everybody out! Use the ladders! Use the ladders!"

And Chaval was swept along with the others. He shoved Catherine and complained she wasn't running fast enough. Did she want them to be left at the bottom of the shaft, to die of hunger?—because those bastards from Montsou were quite capable of destroying the ladders without waiting for everybody to get out! This horrifying possibility unhinged them all, and through every gallery there was a mad stampede, a frantic race to be the first to get to the ladders and to climb out ahead of the others. Some of the men were shouting that the ladders were broken and that *nobody* would get out. And as the terrified groups poured into the loading station it was like a tidal wave, with men hurling themselves at the shaft and crushing one another in the narrow entrance to the ladder well. An old stableman, who had prudently just finished putting the horses back in the stable, watched them with contemptuous indifference; he was used to spending a night in the mine and was sure they'd manage to get him out somehow.

"For God's sake, climb up ahead of me!" Chaval shouted at Catherine. "At least that way I can catch you if you fall."

Confused, breathless, soaked in sweat again from running nearly two miles, Catherine mindlessly gave herself up to the pushing of the crowd. Chaval pulled her by the arm so hard that he almost broke it; she cried out in pain, and tears sprang to her eyes: he was already forgetting his promise, she would never be happy.

"Go on up!" he roared.

But she was too afraid of him. If she went first, he would keep shoving and pushing at her. So she hung back, and the flood of maddened miners swept them aside. The water seeping into the shaft was falling in large drops, and the loading platform, trembling under the trampling footsteps, was shaking above the muddy sump, thirty feet deep. Two years ago, right here at Jean-Bart, there had been a terrible accident—a cable had broken and the cage had dropped to the bottom of the sump; two men had been drowned. Everybody was thinking about this, sure that the same thing would happen to the lot of them if they all kept crowding together on the boards.

"You damn blockhead!" shouted Chaval. "Die and good riddance!"

He began to climb and she followed him.

From the bottom of the mine up to the surface there were a hundred and two ladders, each about twenty-three feet long and set on a narrow platform extending the width of the well, with a square opening barely big enough for a man's shoulders to pass through. It was like a flat twenty-three-hundred-foot-high chimney, between the wall of the shaft and the partition of the cage shaft—a damp, endless, black tube in which almost perpendicular ladders succeeded one another at regular intervals. It took a brawny man twenty-five minutes to crawl up this gigantic column, though in fact the well was no longer used except in emergencies.

At first Catherine climbed energetically enough. Her bare feet, used to the sharp edges of the coal that lined the tunnels, were not bothered by the square rungs, which were covered with iron rods to keep them from wearing out, and her hands, callused from hauling the carts, were able to grip the uprights effortlessly, even though they were too large for her grasp. As a matter of fact, this unexpected climb gave her something to think about; this long human serpent, slithering and hoisting itself three to a ladder so that its head would reach daylight while its tail was still lingering above the sump, made her forget her unhappiness. But there was still a long way to go—the first of the men must still be only a third of the way up. Nobody was speaking now, and the only sound was of the dull tread of climbing feet; at the same time, the lamps, like moving stars, were spaced out from the bottom to the top in an ever-lengthening line.

Behind her, Catherine heard a mine boy counting the ladders, and that gave her the idea of counting too. They had already climbed fifteen of them and were coming to a loading level. Just then she bumped into Chaval's legs. He swore,

and shouted at her to be more careful. Gradually, one man
after another, the whole column stopped moving. What
now?—what was happening? And each of them found his
voice again to question in terror. Their anxiety had increased
as they climbed, and the closer they got to daylight the more
they felt their fear of that unknown thing waiting for them
up above. Somebody announced they would have to go back
down, that the ladders were broken. It was what had been
worrying all of them—the dread of finding themselves suspended in emptiness. Then another explanation traveled
down from mouth to mouth—a cutter had slipped from a
rung. Nobody was sure of anything; the shouts kept them
from hearing. Were they going to have to sleep there? Finally, knowing no more than before, they began to climb again
with the same slow and painful movements, amid the same
tread of feet and dancing of lamps. They would probably get
to the broken ladders higher up.

At the thirty-second ladder, as they were passing a third
loading level, Catherine felt her arms and legs go stiff. At
first she had felt a slight tingling all over her body, but now
she was losing the sensation of wood and iron under her feet
and in her hands. A dull burning pain, which slowly became
more intense, was searing her muscles. And as she grew
fainter she remembered Old Bonnemort's stories of the days
when there had been no ladder well, of the time when girls
of about ten used to carry the coal out on their shoulders by
climbing up completely exposed ladders, and if one of them
slipped, or if so much as one piece of coal rolled from a
basket, three or four of the children would tumble headfirst
from the ladders. The cramps in her limbs were becoming
unbearable—she would never make it to the top.

Whenever the movement up the ladders stopped, she was
able to catch her breath, but each time she was left more
dazed by the terror that swept down from above. The
breathing of the people above and below her was becoming
labored, and the interminable climb was making them all
giddy and nauseous. She was suffocating, wild with the
darkness and maddened by the crush of the walls against her
flesh. She was also trembling from the humidity, her body
sweating under the great drops that fell on her. They were
approaching the water level, and the rain was pouring down
so heavily that it threatened to put out the lamps.

Twice Chaval called to Catherine without getting any
reply. What the hell was she doing down there? Had her
tongue fallen out? She could at least tell him if she was all
right. They had been climbing for half an hour, but so

painfully that they were only up to the fifty-ninth ladder. Forty-three more to go. Catherine finally mumbled that she was doing all right; if she had admitted how tired she was, he would have called her a slug. The iron on the rungs was cutting into her feet, as if it were sawing at the bone. Each time she reached up, she expected to see her hands slip from the uprights, for they were so skinned and stiff that she couldn't close her fingers; she felt as though she were falling backward, shoulders and thighs strained and wrenched by the unremitting effort. What bothered her most was the fact that the ladders were almost perpendicular, so she had to pull herself up by the wrists, with her stomach pressed against the wood. By now the heavy panting was muffling the sound of treading feet; a tremendous groan, echoed and intensified by the walls of the well, was rising from below and dying away in the air above. There was a moan, and word was passed along that a mine boy had just cracked open his skull against the edge of a ladder platform.

And Catherine kept climbing. They had passed the water level; the downpour had stopped and the cellarlike air was heavy with vapor, stinking of old iron and rotting wood. Mechanically she went on counting under her breath: eighty-one, eighty-two, eighty-three; nineteen to go. Only the rhythmic repetition of these numbers sustained her. She was no longer aware of her movements. When she raised her eyes the lamps above her were spinning in a spiral. She was bleeding, she felt she was dying, a mere breath would tumble her. Worst of all, those below her were pushing now, and the whole column was thrusting itself forward, giving way to a growing fury born of fatigue, of a terrible need to see the sun again. The first of the men were already out, so the ladders were still all right; but the idea that they could still be broken, that the last of the men might be kept from getting out while others were already breathing in the fresh air up above, drove them completely mad. When there was another halt there was another outburst of cursing, and they all kept moving, shoving, climbing over each other's bodies in their determination to make it out no matter what.

And then Catherine fell. She had cried out Chaval's name in a desperate appeal, but he hadn't heard; he was fighting, kicking a man in the ribs so he could get ahead of him. She was rolled over and trampled on, and as she lay unconscious she had a dream: she thought she was one of the little haulage girls of olden days, and that a piece of coal, fallen from a basket above her, had caused her to drop to the bottom of the shaft like a sparrow hit by a stone. Only five

more ladders to climb; they had been at it for almost an
hour. She never knew how she got to the top—carried on
shoulders, kept from falling by being wedged against the
walls of the well—but suddenly she found herself in the
dazzling sunlight, surrounded by a screaming, hooting crowd.

3

Ever since before dawn the villages had been seething with
excitement, and this same excitement was now spreading
along the roads and through the entire countryside. The
miners had not been able to start out at the hour agreed
upon, for word had gone out that soldiers and gendarmes
were patrolling the plain. It was said that they had come
from Douai during the night, and people accused Rasseneur
of having sold out his comrades by warning Monsieur Hennebeau; a haulage girl even swore that she had seen his servant
taking the message to the telegraph office. In the pale light of
early morning the miners clenched their fists and watched for
the soldiers from behind their shutters.

At about seven-thirty, just as the sun was rising, the
impatient men were able to take heart from another rumor:
it was only a false alarm, one of the military exercises that
the general, acting on the request of the prefect of Lille, had
ordered from time to time since the outbreak of the strike.
The strikers hated this official, whom they accused of having
fooled them with the promise of conciliatory intervention—
an intervention that turned out to be nothing more than a
parade of troops through Montsou once a week in order to
keep the miners in line. As a result, as soon as the soldiers
and the gendarmes finally set off for Marchiennes, after
having done no more than deafen the villages with the
hoofbeats of their horses on the hard earth, the miners
laughed at this naïve prefect and his troops who turned heel
just as things were about to get interesting. Until nine o'clock
they stood calmly outside their houses, peacefully watching
the jaunty backs of the last of the gendarmes disappear down
the road. Snug in their large beds, the bourgeois of Montsou
were still asleep, their heads buried in their pillows. At the
manager's house, Madame Hennebeau had just been seen
driving off in her carriage, presumably leaving Monsieur
Hennebeau at work, for the shuttered and silent residence

seemed dead. Not one of the mines was guarded by soldiers—
a perfect example of fatal carelessness at the hour of danger,
of the stupidity that inevitably accompanies catastrophe, and,
in short, of every error a government can make when it is
ignorant of the facts. Nine o'clock was striking when the
miners finally started for Vandame to keep the rendezvous
they had agreed upon in the forest the night before.

Etienne realized immediately that the three thousand miners he had counted on would not be at Jean-Bart. Many of
them believed the demonstration had been postponed, and
what was even worse, the two or three groups already on the
way would only compromise the cause if he didn't somehow
place himself at their head. About a hundred of them, who
had left before dawn, must have taken refuge under the
beeches in the forest while waiting for the others. Souvarine,
whom Etienne went up to consult, shrugged his shoulders:
ten determined men could accomplish more than a mob. And
he turned back to the book he had been reading and refused
to have anything to do with the affair; it would probably
turn into something emotional, when all that was necessary
was to burn down Montsou—a simple enough thing to do. As
Etienne left the house he caught a glimpse of Rasseneur, very
pale, sitting by his stove, while his wife, larger than life in her
eternal black dress, was lecturing him in cutting but perfectly
polite language.

Maheu felt they had to keep their word—a rendezvous
such as this was sacred. All of them had calmed down during
the night, and he was now afraid of a disaster; but he
explained that it was their duty to be there and to support
the just demands of their comrades. La Maheude nodded her
approval. Etienne kept repeating complacently that they had
to act in a revolutionary manner, but without endangering
anyone's life. Before leaving, he refused his share of a loaf of
bread, which had been given him the previous night, along
with a bottle of gin; but he downed three shots of the gin in
quick succession, just to keep warm—and he even took a full
flask of it along with him. Alzire would look after the
children. Old Bonnemort, his legs swollen from all the activi-
ty of the night before, had stayed in bed.

They prudently decided not to leave together. Jeanlin had
disappeared long ago. Maheu and La Maheude slipped off in
one direction, taking a shortcut to Montsou, while Etienne
started for the forest, where he hoped to rejoin his comrades.
On the way he caught up with a group of women, among
whom he recognized La Brûlé and La Levaque: as they
walked, they were eating chestnuts brought by Mouquette,

swallowing them shells and all to help fill their stomachs. But he found nobody in the forest—the men were already at Jean-Bart. He raced on and arrived at the mine just as Levaque and about a hundred others were entering the yard. Miners were swarming in from all sides—the Maheus from the main road, the women from across the fields, all helter-skelter, without leaders, without arms, simply flowing there as naturally as water that overflows its banks and courses down-hill. Etienne caught sight of Jeanlin, perched on a footbridge and looking for all the world as if he were at a theater. He ran faster and caught up with the men in front. There were scarcely three hundred of them.

They came to a halt when Deneulin appeared at the top of the stairway that led to the landing room.

"What do you want?" he asked in a loud voice.

After having watched the departure of the carriage, from inside which his daughters were still smiling at him, he had returned to the mine, feeling once more vaguely uneasy. However, everything seemed to be all right—the men had gone down, the coal was coming up, and he was reassured: he was talking to the chief foreman when somebody told him of the approaching strikers. He quickly posted himself at a window of the screening shed, and at the sight of this mounting flood that was pouring into the yard, he immediate-ly realized his own impotence. How could he defend these buildings which were open on all sides? He would hardly be able to muster twenty of his workers around him. He was lost.

"What do you want?" he repeated, white with suppressed anger, making an effort to accept his ruin courageously.

There was some shoving and muttering in the crowd. Finally Etienne stepped forward and said:

"Monsieur, we haven't come to do you harm, but all work everywhere has got to stop."

Deneulin openly treated him as a fool.

"And do you suppose you'll be doing me *good* by shutting down my mine? You might just as well step up behind me and shoot me right in the back. ... Yes, my men are down below—and they won't come up unless you kill me first."

These uncompromising words provoked an uproar. Maheu had to restrain Levaque, who rushed forward threateningly while Etienne was still negotiating and trying to convince Deneulin of the legitimacy of their revolutionary action. But the latter kept insisting on the individual's right to work, and in any case he refused to dignify such foolishness by discuss-ing it—he insisted on being the master in his own place. He only regretted not having a few gendarmes around to sweep this scum out.

"This is all my fault, I deserve what's happening. There's only one thing people like you understand—force. And the government thinks it can win you over with concessions! Why, as soon as it's furnished you with arms, you'll just overthrow it!"

Etienne, though he was trembling with rage, managed to control himself. He lowered his voice.

"Monsieur, I beg you to order your men up. I can't answer for my control over my comrades. Only you can prevent a catastrophe."

"No! Get out of here! Who the hell are you, anyway? You're not employed here, and you and I have nothing to say to each other. . . . Only pillaging thieves would race around the countryside this way!"

His voice was drowned by shouts and curses, and it was the women who were hurling their insults loudest of all. He continued to stand his ground, his candor even bringing a measure of relief to his authoritarian nature. Since he was faced with ruin in any case, he felt useless platitudes to be cowardly. But the strikers' number kept increasing; already more than five hundred of them were pushing toward the door, and he would have been torn to pieces if his chief foreman had not pulled him back abruptly.

"For God's sake, sir! . . . It'll be a massacre. Why should men be killed for nothing?"

He struggled, protested, and in a last cry shouted his defiance at the crowd:

"You pack of thieves! We'll see about this when we've got the upper hand again!"

He was pulled away just as a sudden rush pushed the front of the crowd against the stairway, buckling the ramp. The women were shoving, yelping, inciting the men. The door was boltless, merely closed on a latch, and it gave way immediately. But the stairway was narrow, and it would have taken the mob, crushed together as it was, a long time to get in if the tail end of the besiegers had not decided to go through the other openings. They burst in from all sides—from the dressing shed, the screening shed, the boiler house—and in less than five minutes they had taken over the entire mine, thronging through the three floors in a fury of shouts and gestures, carried away by the élan of their victory over this boss who had dared resist them.

Maheu, afraid of what might happen, had rushed ahead, saying to Etienne:

"They mustn't kill him!"

Etienne was already running, but when he realized that Deneulin had barricaded himself in the foremen's room, he replied:

"And what if they do?—would it be our fault? A madman like that!"

Nevertheless, he was worried; he himself was still too controlled to give way to this surge of anger, and besides, his pride as a leader had been wounded by the sight of the strikers escaping from his authority and acting with wild excitement, instead of coldly executing the will of the people, as he had planned. In vain he kept calling for calm, shouting that they mustn't provide their enemies with ammunition by committing acts of pointless destruction.

"To the boilers!" screamed La Brûlé. "Put out the fires!"

Levaque had found a file and was waving it around like a dagger, dominating the tumult with a terrible cry:

"Cut the cables! Cut the cables!"

Soon they were all repeating it. Only Etienne and Maheu protested, but deafened by the noise, shouting into the clamor, they were unable to obtain silence. Finally Etienne was able to make himself heard:

"But there are men at the bottom, comrades!"

The uproar increased, and voices rose from all sides.

"Too bad for them!—they shouldn't have gone down! . . . serves the traitors right! . . . That's right, let them rot down there! . . . And anyway, they've got the ladders!"

And once they had thought of the ladders they became still more insistent, and Etienne realized he would have to give in. In an effort to limit the disaster he rushed toward the engine, hoping to at least be able to have the cages brought up; that way, when the cables were sawn through above the shaft, the cages would not be crushed by the enormous force of their fall. The engineman had already disappeared, as had the few men who worked on the surface, so he grabbed the starting lever and pulled it, while Levaque and two other men clambered up the iron scaffolding that supported the pulleys. The cages had barely been fixed on their catches when the rasping sound of a file biting into steel was heard. Everything became very quiet, and this sound seemed to fill the entire mine; all of them were looking up, watching, listening, seized by a strong emotion. Standing in the front ranks, Maheu experienced a terrible joy, as if the teeth of the file were delivering them from wretchedness by eating the cable of one of those pits of misery into which no one would ever again go down.

But La Brûlé had disappeared along a stairway leading to the dressing shed, still shrieking:

"We've got to dump the fires! To the boilers! To the boilers!"

Some of the women were following her. La Maheude hurried after to keep them from wrecking everything, just as her husband had tried to restrain the men. She was the calmest of them—after all, they could demand their rights without tearing down other people's property! By the time she got to the boiler shed the women were already driving out the two firemen, and La Brûlé, armed with a large shovel, was crouched in front of one of the furnaces and energetically emptying it, tossing the glowing coals onto the brick floor, where they continued to burn with a black smoke. There were ten furnaces for the five boilers. Soon the women were hard at work—La Levaque plying her shovel with both hands, Mouquette pulling her skirt up over her thighs so as not to catch fire, all of them bloody in the reflection of the flames, sweating and disheveled in this devil's kitchen. The piles of coal were growing higher—the burning heat was beginning to crack the ceiling of the enormous room.

"Enough!" shouted La Maheude. "The place is on fire!"

"So much the better," replied La Brûlé. "That makes less for us to do. . . . By God, I always said I'd make them pay for my husband's death!"

Just then they heard Jeanlin's shrill voice.

"Watch it! I'll put it out! I'm going to open the valves!"

One of the first to enter, he had run through the crowd, enchanted by all the uproar and looking about to see what mischief he could do; he had just decided to open the valves and release the steam. The jets exploded with the violence of gunshots, and the five boilers emptied out in a stormy rush, hissing and rumbling so thunderously that they threatened to burst everyone's eardrums. Everything was veiled with steam—the red coal paled, the women were only awkwardly moving shadows. Behind the whirlwind of white mist only the boy could be seen; high up in the gallery, in a state of rapture, his mouth gaped with joy at having released this hurricane.

It lasted nearly a quarter of an hour. A few pails of water had been thrown on the heaps of coal to make sure they were out, and there was no longer any danger of fire. But the anger of the crowd was not appeased, but rather whipped up. Some of the men came down with hammers, the women armed themselves with iron bars, and there was talk of smashing the boilers, destroying the engines, demolishing the entire mine.

When Etienne was warned of this he came rushing up with Maheu. He himself was becoming intoxicated, beginning to be carried away by this burning fever of revenge, but he fought against it and urged them to be calm, now that the cut cables, the doused fires, and the empty boilers had made all work impossible. They wouldn't listen to him, and he was about to be swept aside again when the sound of shouts and hoots was heard from outside, next to a small, low door that was the exit from the ladder well.

"Down with the traitors! . . . Down with the dirty cowards! . . . Down with them! Down with them!"

The miners who had been at the bottom were beginning to come out. The first of them, blinded by the daylight, were standing there blinking their eyes. Then they started to move along, trying to get to the road and escape.

"Down with the cowards! Down with the traitors!"

All the strikers had come running. In less than three minutes nobody was left in the buildings, and those from Vandame who had been treacherous enough to go down now had to run a gauntlet formed by the five hundred men and women who had come from Montsou. And as each new miner appeared at the door of the ladder well, his clothes in tatters and covered with the black mud of his labors, the hooting redoubled and he was greeted by ferocious jibes: look at *him*—so short his ass scrapes along the ground! and get a load of that one—his nose half rotted away thanks to the whores at the Volcan! and this other one—there's enough wax leaking out of his eyes to keep ten cathedrals supplied with candles! and there's a thin, no-assed wonder, as tall as Lent is long! Then an enormous haulage girl tumbled out, her breasts disappearing into her belly and her belly looking like a second behind, and she was met by a storm of laughter. Everybody wanted to touch her, the jokes grew wilder, turning cruel, and soon fists would begin to fly—and meanwhile the poor creatures kept coming out, shivering, silent under the storm of insults, on the watch for blows, happy when they finally managed to get away from the Company area.

"Look at that! How many are down there?" asked Etienne.

He was surprised to see them still coming, and angry because it was obviously not only a matter of a few workers driven by hunger and terrorized by the foremen. Had he been lied to in the forest?—almost all of Jean-Bart had gone down. Then he saw Chaval standing at the threshold and he let out a cry and ran forward.

"My God! Is this the rendezvous you made with us?"

There was an explosion of curses and the crowd surged forward to get the traitor. He had sworn with them the night before, and now they find he has been at the bottom with the others? Was he trying to make fools of them?

"Get him! Throw him down the shaft! Throw him down the shaft!"

Pale with fear, Chaval was trying to stammer out an explanation, but Etienne, beside himself with anger and possessed by the same fury as the others, cut him short.

"You wanted to be one of us—well, you will be! . . . Move, you son of a bitch!"

Another shout drowned out his voice. Catherine had just appeared and was standing there, dazzled by the bright sunlight and bewildered at finding herself surrounded by this savage crowd. Her legs about to collapse after the hundred and two ladders, her palms bleeding, she was gasping for breath when La Maheude saw her and rushed forward, her hand raised as if to strike.

"Ah, you too, you slut! . . . While your mother starves to death, you betray her for your pimp!"

Maheu caught at her hand and prevented the blow. But he shook his daughter and reproached her for her conduct as furiously as his wife had, both of them losing their heads and shouting louder than anyone else.

The sight of Catherine had been the last straw for Etienne. He kept repeating:

"Let's go! Let's go to the other mines! And you, you filthy pig, you're coming with us!"

Chaval had barely enough time to get his sabots from the dressing shed and to slip his woolen sweater over his shivering shoulders. They kept pulling at him, forcing him to race along in their midst. In a daze, Catherine also put on her sabots, buttoned to the neck the worn man's jacket which she had been wearing since the weather had turned cold, then ran along behind her lover, not wanting to abandon him because they were surely going to kill him.

Jean-Bart emptied in about two minutes. Jeanlin, who had found a watchman's horn somewhere, was blowing it and making raucous sounds, as if he were calling in the cattle. The women—La Brûlé, La Levaque, and Mouquette—were holding their skirts so they could run, while Levaque was twirling an ax in his hand as if it were a drum major's baton. More miners kept joining the crowd, and now they were nearly a thousand—a disorderly band once more flowing onto the road like a river overrunning its banks. The gate of

the compound was too narrow, so they ripped out some
fence palings.

"To the mines! Down with the traitors! No more work!"

And suddenly Jean-Bart was deathly silent. Not a man
could be seen, not a breath stirred. Deneulin came out of the
foreman's room, and with a gesture that forbade anyone to
follow him, set out all alone to inspect the mine. He was pale
and very calm. First he stopped in front of the shaft, raised
his eyes, and stared at the cut cables: the sawn ends of steel
were hanging uselessly—the bite of the file had left a gaping
wound, an open sore shining out from the black grease. Next
he climbed up to the engine and contemplated the motionless
piston, like the joint of some colossal limb stricken by paraly-
sis; he touched the already cooled metal and the cold made
him shiver, as though he had touched a corpse. Then he went
down to the boiler house and walked slowly past the extinguished furnaces, gaping and flooded; when he kicked them
they gave forth an empty, hollow sound. Well, it was all
over—his ruin was complete. Even if he could fix the cables,
even if he could start the furnaces again, where would he find
the men? Another two weeks of the strike and he would be
bankrupt. And now that his disaster was certain he no longer
hated the Montsou bandits; he felt that everybody was to
blame—the fault was general, centuries old. Oh, they were
brutes, no doubt, but brutes who could not read and who
were dying of hunger.

4

And the crowd, flowing off the road and trampling through
the beet fields, swarmed across the bare plain, white with
frost under the anemic winter sun.

Etienne was in charge by the time they reached Fourche-
aux-Boeufs. Without calling a halt, he shouted orders and
organized the march. Up front, Jeanlin was sounding wild
music on his horn. Behind him, in the front ranks, came the
women, some of them armed with sticks: La Maheude,
wild-eyed, seeming to search the horizon for the promised
city of justice, and La Brûlé, La Levaque, and Mouquette
striding along in their rags like soldiers setting off for war. If
there was any trouble, they'd see if the gendarmes would
dare attack women! After them came the men, a straggling,

spreading herd, bristling with iron bars over which loomed Levaque's ax, its blade glittering in the sunlight. Etienne was in the center, keeping an eye on Chaval by forcing him to march in front of him, while behind them Maheu kept darting murderous glances at Catherine, the only woman among all these men; she insisted on trotting along beside her lover in order to keep the others from hurting him. They were all bareheaded and disheveled, and the only sound was the thumping of their sabots—a clatter like that of a herd of cattle turned loose and stampeded by the savage urging of Jeanlin's horn.

But suddenly a new cry went up.

"Bread! Bread! We want bread!"

It was noon, and the hunger built up by six weeks on strike and sharpened by this race through the fields was stirring in their bellies. The few breakfast crusts of the lucky ones, the handful of chestnuts brought by Mouquette, were long forgotten; their stomachs were crying for food, and the pain added to their rage against the traitors.

"To the mines! No more work! We want bread!"

Etienne, who had refused his share of the food back at the village, now felt his insides twisting unbearably. He did not complain, but from time to time he mechanically reached for his flask and gulped down a swallow of gin, feeling so shaky that he thought he would never be able to continue without it. His cheeks were burning, his eyes blazing, but he kept his head; he was still hoping to avoid useless destruction.

As they reached the Joiselle road a Vandame cutter, who had joined them to take vengeance on his employer, urged the men toward the right, shouting:

"To Gaston-Marie! Stop the pump! Flood Jean-Bart and wreck it!"

Despite Etienne's protests and his pleas to let the pumps continue their work, the crowd was already beginning to turn around. But what good would it do to destroy the galleries?— despite his fury, Etienne's whole workingman's soul was revolted by the idea. Maheu also thought it was unfair to take it out on a machine. But the cutter kept shouting his cry of vengeance, and Etienne had to outshout him:

"On to Mirou! There are traitors down there! . . . On to Mirou! To Mirou!"

He waved the crowd back onto the road to the left, while Jeanlin, running to take the lead again, blew his horn all the louder. The men swirled around. Gaston-Marie was safe, at least for now.

Racing across the endless plain, they covered the two and

a half miles to Mirou in half an hour. On this side, the canal cut across the plain like a long ribbon of ice. Only the leafless trees, transformed by the frost into giant candelabra, broke the monotonous flatness that stretched ahead endlessly, like a sea, until it merged with the sky. Montsou and Marchiennes were hidden by a slight groundswell, and there was only a bare, empty immensity.

When they arrived at the mine they saw a foreman waiting for them on a footbridge to the screening shed. They all recognized Quandieu, the senior of the Montsou foremen—an old man of almost seventy, whose skin and hair were both white and who was, for a miner, a miracle of good health.

"What do you tramps want here?" he shouted.

The crowd stopped. This was no boss, but a comrade, and they were restrained by a feeling of respect for the old worker.

"There are men at the bottom," said Etienne. "Make them come up."

"Yes, there are men down there," said Old Quandieu, "about six dozen of them. The others were afraid of you, you good-for-nothings! . . . But I warn you that before one of them comes up, you'll have to deal with me!"

There was a roar of exclamation, the men surged forward, the women began to advance. The foreman had quickly come down from the footbridge and was barring the door.

At this point Maheu decided to intervene.

"Listen, old man, we've got a right to do this. How can we make the strike general if we don't force all the men to join us?"

The old man was silent for a moment. Evidently when it came to questions of solidarity he was as ignorant as the cutter. Finally he answered:

"I don't say you haven't got the right—but as for me, I only know my orders. . . . There's nobody here but me. The men are supposed to be down at the bottom till three o'clock, and there they'll stay till three o'clock."

His last words were drowned in jeers. Fists were shaken, and the women were already deafening him, blowing their hot breaths into his face. But with his short beard and his hair white as snow, he held his head high, he stood his ground, and courage so swelled his voice that it could be heard distinctly above all the tumult.

"By God, you're not going any further! . . . Just as sure as there's a sun in the sky, I'd rather let myself be killed than let you lay a hand on the cables. . . . So don't take another step or I'll throw myself down the shaft right before your eyes."

A shudder passed through the crowd and it drew back, overawed. He went on:

"Is there any man here who's so rotten he can't understand that? . . . I'm only a workingman, just like the rest of you. I've been told to guard the place, and guard it I will."

Old Quandieu had reached the limit of his intelligence, and there he stood, pigheaded, inflexible in his soldierly conception of duty, his eyes dimmed by the black gloom of half a century underground. The men looked at him, for what he was saying stirred them, raised in them some echo of military obedience, of fraternity, of resignation in the face of danger. Thinking they were still about to push forward, he repeated:

"I warn you, I'll throw myself down the shaft right before your eyes!"

The crowd recoiled, turned, and again took up its stampede along the straight, endless road that ran between the open fields. Again the cries arose:

"To Madeleine! To Crèvecoeur! No more work! We want bread! We want bread!"

But there was a sudden tussle in the center of the hurrying crowd. Word went out that it was Chaval, who had tried to take advantage of the confusion to escape. Etienne had grabbed his arm and was threatening to break his back if he tried anything. Chaval was struggling, protesting furiously:

"What's this all about? Isn't a man free anymore? . . . I've been freezing for an hour now, and I've got to clean up. Take your hands off me!"

It was true that the coal plastered to his skin by the sweat was painful, and that his sweater was not of much use against the cold.

"Move—or *we'll* see to cleaning you up!" answered Etienne. "You shouldn't have tried to go us one better by screaming for blood."

They were still running; finally Etienne turned to Catherine, who was still managing to keep up with them. It wrung his heart to know that she was so close to him, so wretched, shivering in her man's jacket and her mud-caked trousers. She must be nearly dead with fatigue, but she kept running all the same.

"*You,* you can go home," he said.

She seemed not to hear. Her eyes met Etienne's for a moment, and her only response was a flicker of reproach. She did not stop. Why did he want her to abandon her man? True, Chaval wasn't very nice, and sometimes he even beat her—but he was her man, the one who had had her first, and it made her furious that they were more than a thousand to

one against him. She would have defended him out of pride,
if not out of tenderness.

"Go away!" Maheu repeated.

This order from her father made her hesitate for a moment. She trembled, and tears welled up in her eyes. Then, in
spite of her fear, she reclaimed her place and kept running.
After that they let her be.

The crowd followed the road to Joiselle, then went for a
short distance along the road to Cron before turning toward
Cougny. Here the flat countryside was dotted with factory
chimneys, and the road was lined with wooden sheds—
brickmaking factories—with large, dusty windows. They
passed the low houses of two neighboring mining villages,
180 and 76, and from each one, in response to the trumpet-
ing of the horn and the clamor that went up from the crowd,
whole families piled out, men, women, and children, and ran
to join the march of their comrades. By the time they got to
Madeleine there were fifteen hundred of them. The road
sloped down gently, and the rumbling flood of strikers had to
go around the slag heap before spreading through the yard of
the mine.

It was just a little after two o'clock, but the foreman had
been warned and had pushed up quitting time, so when the
crowd arrived, the last of the miners—about twenty of them—
were getting out of the cage. They fled under a hail of
stones. Two of them were beaten, and another left behind the
sleeve of his jacket. This action against the men saved the
equipment, and neither the cables nor the boilers were
touched. The human flood was already on its way, surging
toward the neighboring mine.

This one, Crèvecoeur, was only about five hundred yards
from Madeleine, and here too the crowd arrived just as the
miners were coming up. The women caught and whipped a
haulage girl, splitting her trousers and exposing her buttocks
as the men stood by and laughed. The mine boys were
slapped, and the cutters' bodies were black and blue, their
noses bleeding, before they made their escape. And through
this growing ferocity, this ancient need for revenge that was
driving them mad, rose the ceaseless cries, torn from their
throats; they screamed death to the traitors, shouted hatred
of badly paid work, and roared of bellies hungry for bread.
They began to cut the cables, but the file wouldn't bite—and
anyway, it would take too long now that they were in such a
fever to keep moving, to keep pushing on and on and on. A
steam cock was broken at the boiler shed, and the iron grates

cracked when pailfuls of water were thrown into the furnaces.

Outside again, there was talk of marching on Saint-Thomas. This was the best-disciplined of all the mines and the strike had not touched it; some seven hundred men must have gone down, and the thought of it was infuriating. They would wait for the miners with sticks and bats, and they would see who would come off best in a pitched battle! But a rumor went around that the gendarmes were at Saint-Thomas, the same gendarmes they had mocked that very morning. How did they know this? Nobody could say, but they were afraid; they decided on Feutry-Cantel instead. And again they were seized by the intoxication, again they were back on the road, clattering along in their sabots, again they were rushing onward: to Feutry-Cantel! to Feutry-Cantel! There were still probably about four hundred sons of bitches there—they'd have some fun! The mine was about two miles away, hidden in a dip in the earth next to the Scarpe. They were already climbing the slope of Les Plâtrières, past the Beaugnies road, when a voice—nobody ever knew whose—shouted out that maybe the soldiers were at Feutry-Cantel. And from one end of the column to the other word was passed along that the soldiers *were* there. The march slowed down, and little by little the breath of panic was growing, spreading through this countryside rendered lifeless by the strike, this countryside over which they had been trampling for hours. Why hadn't they run into the soldiers? This very impunity troubled them, foreshadowed the repression they felt must lie ahead.

Though nobody knew where it came from, a new order suddenly launched them toward another mine.

"To La Victoire! To La Victoire!"

Were there then no soldiers or gendarmes at La Victoire? Nobody knew, but they all seemed reassured. And turning on their heels they went down the slope toward Beaumont and cut across the fields to rejoin the Joiselle road. The railroad line barred their way, but they tore down the fence palings and crossed it. They were approaching Montsou, and the gently rolling countryside flattened; the sea of beet fields stretched into the distance, all the way to the dark houses of Marchiennes.

This time they had to cover more than three miles, but they were so carried away that they felt neither their terrible fatigue nor their bruised and aching feet. The column of men kept growing, added to by comrades picked up along the road and in the villages. When they had crossed the Magache bridge over the canal and were in front of La Victoire, there were two thousand of them. But it was after three o'clock, and the men had all come up—not a one was left at the bottom. They vented their frustration in pointless threats; all they could do was welcome the oncoming repair shift with a hail of broken bricks. It was an easy victory for them—the deserted mine was theirs. And in their fury at not having any traitors to pummel, they attacked the things. A pocket of bitterness was bursting in them, a poison pocket of slow but ever-swelling growth. Years and years of hunger were torturing them, whetting their appetite for death and destruction.

Behind one of the sheds Etienne saw some loaders filling a coal cart.

"Get the hell out of here!" he shouted. "Not one piece of coal leaves this yard!"

About a hundred strikers came running up in response to his call, and the loaders had barely enough time to get away. Some of the men unharnessed the horses, prodding them in the rump and frightening them off, while others overturned the cart and broke its shafts.

Levaque, wielding his ax with a vengeance, had attacked the trestles in order to knock down the footbridges, but he made no headway and, instead, got the idea of tearing up the rails and thus destroying the track that ran from one end of the yard to the other. Soon the whole crowd was working at it. Maheu, using a crowbar as a lever, was tearing up iron rail-chairs; meanwhile La Brûlé, leading the women, invaded the lamproom, where their vigorously swinging sticks soon had the ground covered with the debris of broken lamps. La Maheude, now beside herself with rage, was lashing out as frenziedly as La Levaque. All of them were soaked in oil, and Mouquette was wiping her hands on her skirt, laughing at having gotten so dirty. Jeanlin had emptied a lamp down her back just for the fun of it.

But none of these vengeful acts brought them anything to eat. Their stomachs were rumbling louder and louder, and the great cry rose once again:

"Bread! Bread! We want bread!"

It so happened that a retired foreman ran a canteen at La Victoire. He had probably been frightened off, and his shack was deserted. When the women came back from the lamproom and the men had finished tearing up the tracks, they all attacked the canteen, whose shutters gave way immediately. They found no bread—only two pieces of raw meat and a sack of potatoes—but as they looted the place they did come across some fifty bottles of gin, which disappeared like a drop of water soaked up in sand.

Etienne had emptied his flask and was able to refill it. Little by little a nasty drunkenness, the drunkenness of the starving, was making his eyes bloodshot and exposing the protruding, wolflike teeth between his drawn, pale lips. And then he suddenly noticed that Chaval had managed to slip away in the confusion. He swore, some men were sent looking, and they found the fugitive hiding with Catherine behind the woodpile.

"Ah, you son of a bitch—so you're afraid to get mixed up in this!" roared Etienne. "You were the one in the forest to call for an engineman's strike to stop the pumps, and now you're trying to crap out on us! . . . Well, by God, we're going back to Gaston-Marie and I'm going to see to it that *you* smash the pump. Yes, damn it, *you're* going to smash it!"

He was drunk; he himself was launching his men against the very pump he had saved a few hours earlier.

"To Gaston-Marie! To Gaston-Marie!"

Cheering him, they all rushed forward, while Chaval, still asking to be allowed to wash, was seized by the shoulders and roughly pushed and dragged along.

"Get out of here!" Maheu shouted at Catherine, who had also started to run again.

This time she did not hesitate; she merely looked at her father with her burning eyes and went on running.

Once again the crowd plowed across the bare plain, retracing its steps over the straight road through the spreading fields. It was four o'clock, and the setting sun was casting the lengthened shadows of the wildly gesticulating mob over the frozen ground.

They bypassed Montsou and joined the Joiselle road above it, and to avoid the detour at Fourche-aux-Boeufs they passed alongside the walls of La Piolaine. The Grégoires had just left, having an appointment to see their lawyer before going to dine at the Hennebeaus', where they were to pick up Cécile. The estate, with its avenue of bare lindens, its vegetable garden and orchards denuded by winter, seemed asleep. Nothing stirred inside the house, the sealed windows of which were befogged by the warm air within, and the deep silence gave off an impression of cheerfulness and comfort—a patriarchal feeling made up of warm beds and well-laden tables and the tranquil joys amid which the owners spent their lives. Without stopping, the crowd glared darkly through the railings and along the length of protecting wall, which bristled with broken bottle ends. Again the cry went up:

"Bread! Bread! We want bread!"

The only answer was the angry barking of a pair of tawny-coated Great Danes, who reared up with open mouths. Standing behind a closed shutter were the two servants, Mélanie the cook and Honorine the chambermaid; sweating and pale with fear, drawn there by the sound of this cry, they watched the parade of savages. When they heard a single stone fly through a nearby window, they fell to their knees and thought they were dead. It was one of Jeanlin's tricks: he had made a sling with a piece of string and was saying hello to the Grégoires as he passed. He was already back at his horn-blowing, and the crowd was disappearing into the distance with the fading cry of:

"Bread! Bread! We want bread!"

By the time they arrived at Gaston-Marie their number was swollen still more—over twenty-five hundred madmen, breaking and sweeping everything before them with the pent-up force of an unleashed torrent. The gendarmes had been there an hour earlier, but had been misled by some peasants and had gone off toward Saint-Thomas in such a hurry that they had not even taken the precaution of leaving a few men behind to guard the mine. In less than fifteen minutes the fires were put out, the boilers emptied, and all the buildings broken into and wrecked. But it was the pump they were really after. It was not enough for them that it had stopped as the last breath of steam died—they threw themselves on it as though it were a living person whose life they were determined to have.

"The first blow belongs to you," repeated Etienne, putting a hammer in Chaval's hand. "Come on, now, you swore with the rest of us."

Chaval was trembling, and he drew back; in the frenzied shoving he dropped the hammer, but the other men, without waiting, struck at the pump with crowbars, bricks, anything they happened to have in their hands. A few of them even broke their sticks on it. The nuts flew off, and pieces of steel and copper fell away like amputated limbs. A massive blow from a pick smashed the iron body, and the water flowed out with a tremendous gurgle, like a death rattle.

It was all over. The maddened crowd found itself outside and pressing behind Etienne, who was still holding onto Chaval.

"Kill the traitor! Down the shaft with him! Down the shaft."

Livid with terror, the poor wretch kept returning to his idiotic obsession, his need to clean up.

"Oh, if that's what's bothering you," said La Levaque, "here's a tub you can use!"

They were near a pool made by seepage from the pump. It was covered with a thick white layer of ice, and they dragged him over to it, broke the ice, forced him to put his head in the freezing water.

"In you go, you bastard," repeated La Brûlé. "By God, if you don't do it yourself, we'll do it for you! . . . And now, how about a little drink? That's right, like an animal, with your snout in the trough!"

He was made to get down and drink on all fours. Everybody was laughing cruelly. One woman pulled his ears, another threw a handful of fresh manure from the road right into his face. His old sweater was in shreds, and he stumbled along, haggard, kicking out with his feet in an effort to escape.

Maheu had shoved him about, and La Maheude was among the wildest of the women—both of them evening up old scores; and even Mouquette, who usually remained good friends with her lovers, was raging at this one, calling him a son of a bitch and saying they ought to take his pants off to see if he was still a man.

Etienne made her stop.

"That's enough! There's no need for everybody to get in on this. . . . You, if you want to, we can settle this between the two of us."

His fists were clenched, his eyes blazing with murderous fury; his drunkenness was becoming a need to kill.

"Are you ready? One of us isn't going to leave this spot. . . . Somebody give him a knife. I've got mine."

Catherine, exhausted and horrified, stared at him. She was remembering what he had told her—that thanks to the filth his drunken parents had poured into his blood, after three drinks he felt as though he could eat a man alive. Suddenly she rushed forward and beat at him with her two small hands, shouting into his face, choking with indignation.

"Coward! Coward! Coward! . . . Isn't all this terrible enough? Do you want to kill him now that he can hardly stand?"

She turned on her mother and father and on all the others.

"Cowards! You're all cowards! . . . Kill me, too! If you touch him again, I'll scratch your eyes out! Oh, you cowards!"

And she planted herself in front of her man and defended

him, forgetting the blows, forgetting their miserable life together, thinking only of the fact that she belonged to him
because he had taken her, and that when he was treated this
way the shame was also hers.

Etienne had grown pale under the girl's blows. He had
been on the point of striking her, but then, after passing a
hand over his face like a man sobering up after a drunk, he
said to Chaval, amid a great silence:

"She's right, that's enough. . . . Get out of here."

Chaval took off immediately, Catherine following behind
him. Stunned, the crowd watched them disappear around the
bend in the road. Only La Maheude murmured:

"You made a mistake. You should have held onto him.
He'll betray us somehow, I'm sure."

But the crowd had set off again. It was almost five o'clock,
and the red-hot sun, squatting on the horizon, was setting the
whole immense plain on fire. A passing peddler told them the
soldiers were near Crèvecoeur, so they turned around once
more and a new order went out:

"To Montsou! To the manager's house! . . . Bread! Bread!
We want bread!"

5

Monsieur Hennebeau had gone to the window of his study
to watch the departure of the carriage that was taking his
wife to lunch at Marchiennes. For a moment his eyes had
followed Négrel trotting along beside the carriage door, then
he had calmly turned back to his desk. The house seemed
empty, with neither his wife nor his nephew to animate it
with their comings and goings. In addition, on that particular
day the coachman was driving Madame; Rose, the new maid,
was off until five o'clock; and the only ones left behind were
Hippolyte, the manservant, shuffling through the rooms in his
slippers, and the cook, busy since dawn with her pots and
pans and completely given over to preparations for the dinner her employers were giving that evening. Monsieur Hennebeau was therefore looking forward to getting a lot of work
done in the quiet, deserted house.

At about nine o'clock, though he had been ordered to
admit no one, Hippolyte took it upon himself to announce
Dansaert, who was bringing news. It was only then that the

manager heard about the meeting held the night before in the forest, and the details were so complete that as he listened he found himself thinking about the man's love affair with La Pierronne, an affair so notorious that every week he received two or three anonymous letters denouncing the debaucheries of the chief foreman. It was obvious that the husband had babbled—the whole report had the odor of pillow talk about it. Monsieur Hennebeau took advantage of the occasion to make it plain that he knew all about the affair, but he contented himself with merely recommending prudence, lest a scandal break out. Dansaert, confused by these reproaches in the middle of his report, denied everything, stuttering excuses even while the sudden redness of his big nose was confessing to everything. But he was glad to get off so easily, and he did not insist, for generally, whenever an employee treated himself to a good-looking girl in the mine, the manager would demonstrate the implacable severity of the highly moral man. The conversation returned to the strike—the meeting in the forest was only loudmouthed boasting, nothing serious. In any case, thanks to the respect and fear inspired by the military maneuvers that morning, the villages would surely not make any move for at least a few days.

Nevertheless, when Monsieur Hennebeau was alone again he was on the point of sending a message to the prefect. Only the fear of betraying his anxiety, perhaps pointlessly, held him back. As it was, he could not forgive himself for having been so lacking in perspicacity as to have told everyone—and even to have written to the Board of Directors—that the strike would not last more than two weeks. To his great surprise, it had now been dragging on for almost two months, and he was in despair; he felt his prestige diminish with each passing day, he felt more and more compromised—and he kept trying to imagine some bold stroke by which he would be able to get back into the good graces of the directors. He had just asked them for orders in case of a riot, but their reply had not yet come; he was expecting it in the afternoon mail. He kept telling himself that there would always be time to send off telegrams and put the mines under military guard—if that was what these gentlemen thought should be done. He himself felt such a move would certainly mean a battle, with blood and corpses, and despite his usual decisiveness, he was reluctant to assume such responsibility.

He worked on, undisturbed, until about eleven o'clock, with no sound in the deserted house other than the distant noise of Hippolyte polishing the floor of an upstairs room. Then he received two dispatches, one on the heels of the

other—the first reporting how Jean-Bart had been invaded by
the band from Montsou, and the second describing the cut
cables, the extinguished fires, and all the other damage. He
did not understand. Why had the strikers gone to Deneulin's
instead of attacking one of the Company's mines? Well, so
far as he was concerned, they could wreck Vandame—it
would only further his plan to take it over. And at noon,
served by Hippolyte moving about soundlessly in his slippers,
he ate alone in the vast dining room. The solitude added to
the gloom of his thoughts, and a cold shiver went through
him when a foreman, who had come on the double, was
shown in and described the crowd's march on Mirou. Almost
immediately afterward, just as he was finishing his coffee, a
telegram informed him that Madeleine and Crèvecoeur were
now also being threatened. His perplexity became extreme. He
was waiting for the two o'clock mail: should he ask for
troops immediately, or would it be better to wait and not
take any action before knowing what the directors' orders
were? He returned to his study, deciding to look over a note
to the prefect that he had asked Négrel to prepare the night
before. But he couldn't find it, and it occurred to him that
perhaps the young man had left it in his room, where he
often did his writing at night. And without making any
decision, preoccupied as he was by the idea of this note, he
ran upstairs to look for it in his nephew's bedroom.

Upon entering, Monsieur Hennebeau was surprised: due,
no doubt, to either Hippolyte's forgetfulness or his laziness,
the room had not been done. It gave off a damp warmth—
the stuffy warmth of a long night, made all the heavier by a
hot-air register that had been left open—and his nostrils were
assailed by a penetrating perfume, which he assumed must be
the odor coming from the unemptied washbasin. The room
was in complete disorder, with clothes scattered everywhere,
damp towels tossed over the backs of chairs, the bed unmade,
a sheet pulled loose and trailing on the carpet. At first,
however, he barely noticed any of this; he had headed for a
table covered with papers and was searching for the missing
note. Twice he went through the papers one by one, but it
obviously was not there. Where the devil could that scatter-
brained Paul have put it?

And as Monsieur Hennebeau came back to the middle of
the room, he glanced around at each piece of furniture and
noticed something shining on the unmade bed, something that
flashed like a spark. Mechanically he went over and put out
his hand for it. It was a little golden flacon, lying in a fold of
the sheet. He had immediately recognized it as one of Ma-

dame Hennebeau's—a flacon of ether that she always kept
with her. But he couldn't understand what it was doing
there: how could it be in Paul's bed? And suddenly he turned
deathly pale. His wife had slept there!

"Excuse me, sir," Hippolyte murmured from the doorway,
"I saw you come up . . ."

The servant had come in, and the disorder of the room
upset him.

"My God, that's right! The room hasn't been done! Rose
went out and left everything for me to do!"

Monsieur Hennebeau had hidden the flacon in his hand,
gripping it almost hard enough to break it.

"What do you want?"

"Sir, there's another man here. . . . He's come from
Crèvecoeur and he has a letter."

"All right, you may go. Tell him to wait."

His wife had slept there! When he had locked the door he
opened his hand and stared at the flacon, which had left a
red mark on his flesh. Suddenly he saw it all, he understood
everything—this filthy affair had been going on in his very
own house for months! He remembered his old suspicion, the
brushing against the doors, the bare feet padding through the
silent house at night. Yes, of course, it was his wife going up
there to sleep!

He fell into a chair opposite the bed, which he stared at
fixedly, and sat there for a long time, as if stunned. A noise
roused him—somebody was knocking at the door and trying
to open it. He recognized the servant's voice.

"Sir . . . Ah, the door's locked. . . ."

"What is it now?"

"It seems to be very urgent—the workers are destroying
everything. Two more men are downstairs, and there are
some dispatches, too."

"Let me alone, damn it! I'll be down in a minute!"

He had just thought of something that made his blood run
cold—if Hippolyte had done the room that morning, he
would have been the one to find the flacon! But he supposed
the servant must know—there must have been scores of
times when he had found the bed still warm with adultery,
Madame's hairs trailing on the pillow, disgusting stains soiling
the sheets. And it was pure nastiness that made him keep
bothering him now. Perhaps he had even listened at the door
and been excited by the debauchery of his masters.

Monsieur Hennebeau did not stir. He kept staring at the
bed, and the long years of his suffering unrolled before his
eyes—his marriage to this woman, their immediate disagree-

ment of both the heart and the flesh, the lovers she had had
without his knowing about them, and the one he had tolerated for ten years' in the same way one might tolerate the
depraved tastes of an invalid. Then their arrival at Montsou,
his wild hope of curing her, the months of languishing, of
drowsy exile and the approach of old age, which would give
her to him at last. And then the arrival of their nephew, this
Paul to whom she became a mother, to whom she would
speak of her dead heart, buried forever under ashes. And he,
like the fool of a husband he was, had foreseen nothing! He
adored this woman who belonged to him, whom other men
had had and whom he alone could never have! He adored
her with such a shameful passion that he would have fallen to
his knees if she had only deigned to give him the leftovers of
others! But these leftovers she was giving to this child!

Just then the sound of a distant bell made Monsieur
Hennebeau start. He recognized it as the bell rung on his
orders whenever the mailman arrived. He got up, and in a
loud voice he gave vent to a flood of obscenity that tore from
his throat in spite of himself.

"I don't give a damn! I don't give a good goddamn about
their dispatches and their letters!"

Now he was overcome by rage, by a need for some kind
of sewer into which he could kick all this filth. The woman
was a slut, and he searched for obscene terms with which to
besplatter her image. The sudden memory of the marriage
she was so calmly arranging between Cécile and Paul served
only to inflame him further. Was there no longer even any
passion, any jealousy, at the core of this burning sensuality?
Was this having of men now only a perverse pastime?—a
habit?—a recreation enjoyed the way one enjoys a familiar
dessert? And it was she whom he blamed for everything,
absolving of almost all responsibility this child whom she had
bitten into with this reawakening of appetite just as one
might bite into some green fruit stolen from the roadside.
Whom would she devour, to what depths would she sink,
when there would no longer be any obliging nephews sensible
enough to join the family and accept within it board, bed,
and wife?

There was a timid scratching at the door, and Hippolyte's
voice whispered through the keyhole:

"Sir, the mail is here . . . and Monsieur Dansaert is back—
he says there's been bloodshed."

"I'm coming, for God's sake!"

What should he do to them? When they returned from
Marchiennes he would drive them into the streets, like stink-

ing beasts he would no longer keep in the house. He would take a stick to them, tell them to do their poisonous coupling elsewhere. It was their sighs, their intermingled breaths, that made the warm air of the room so unbearably heavy; the penetrating odor that had suffocated him was the scent of musk given off by his wife's flesh—another one of her perverse tastes, this physical need for violent perfumes. All about him—in the jars scattered about, in the unemptied basins, in the disordered bedclothes and furniture, in the whole room reeking of vice—he could sense the heat and the smell of their fornication, the living presence of adultery. In a fury of impotence he flung himself at the bed, beating it with his fists, pummeling the places that still held the imprint of their two bodies, maddened by the tossed-back covers and the rumpled sheets that lay soft and lifeless under his blows, as if they too were exhausted by the long night of love.

But suddenly he thought he heard Hippolyte returning. A feeling of shame brought him back to himself. He paused for a moment, and panting, he wiped the sweat from his brow and tried to still the wild beating of his heart. He stood in front of the mirror and studied his face, so ravaged that he could hardly recognize himself. Then, after he had watched it slowly grow more calm, he made a supreme effort and went downstairs.

Five messengers and Dansaert were waiting for him. All of them brought news of the increasing seriousness of the strikers' march from one mine to another, and the chief foreman gave him a detailed report of what had happened at Mirou and how it had been saved by the exemplary behavior of Old Quandieu. He listened and nodded his head, but he heard nothing; his whole being had remained upstairs, in the bedroom. Finally he dismissed them, saying he would take whatever measures were necessary, and when he was once more alone he sat down at his desk, put his head in his hands, closed his eyes, and seemed to doze off. His mail was there, and at last he brought himself to go through it for the expected letter from the directors, every line of which seemed at first to dance up and down before his eyes. Eventually, however, he managed to understand that the gentlemen were hoping for some kind of trouble: oh, of course they did not suggest that he make things worse, but they let it be understood that such outbreaks would hasten the end of the strike by provoking strong repressive measures. He no longer hesitated; he sent off messages in all directions—to the prefect of Lille, to the army headquarters at Douai, to the gendarmerie at Marchiennes. It was a relief;

now he could shut himself in, and he even announced that he
was suffering from an attack of gout. He remained hidden in
his study all afternoon, receiving no one and merely reading
the dispatches and letters that continued to rain down on
him. In this way, from a distance, he followed the progress of
the mob from Madeleine to Crèvecoeur, from Crèvecoeur to
La Victoire, and from La Victoire to Gaston-Marie. From
other sources he also learned of the gendarmes and soldiers—
completely at sea, blundering about, continually marching
away from the mines being attacked. For all he cared, they
could slaughter one another and destroy everything. He had
put his head down into his hands again, his fingers crossed
over his eyes, and he sank into the deep silence of the empty
house, a silence broken only by the occasional rattle of the
pots and pans of the cook, who was completely immersed in
her preparations for that evening's dinner.

It was five o'clock and dusk was already darkening the
room when a sudden disturbance made Monsieur Hennebeau
start up, confused, listless, his elbows still buried in his
papers. He thought it was the two wretches coming home,
but the tumult increased and a terrible cry rang out just as he
drew near the window.

"Bread! Bread! We want bread!"

It was the strikers, who were invading Montsou just as the
gendarmes, thinking Le Voreux was about to be sacked, were
galloping away in the other direction to occupy that mine.

At just about the same time, a little more than a mile
away from the houses on the outskirts of town and just below
the junction where the main road met the road to Vandame,
Madame Hennebeau and the young ladies had just seen the
crowd march by. The day at Marchiennes had been a de-
lightful one—a charming lunch at the home of the manager
of Les Forges, then an interesting tour of the workshops and
a trip to a nearby glass factory to fill the afternoon. Later, as
they were returning home in the dying light of the beautiful
clear winter day, Cécile had noticed a small farmhouse
bordering the road and had expressed a sudden desire to stop
for a cup of milk. They had all got out of the carriage,
Négrel had gallantly leaped off his horse, and the farmer's
wife, flustered by all these splendid people, was soon bustling
about and talking of laying a tablecloth before serving them.
But Lucie and Jeanne wanted to see the cow milked, so they
had all gone down to the stable with their cups and made a
picnic of it, laughing as their feet sank into the straw.

Madame Hennebeau, all maternal indulgence, was daintily

sipping her milk when she was startled by a strange, rumbling noise outside.

"What's that?"

The stable, which was built right at the edge of the road, also served as a barn and thus had a door wide enough for carts to pass through. The young ladies, peering outside, were astonished to see a black flood on their left, a howling mob pouring out of the road to Vandame.

"The devil!" murmured Négrel, who had also come out. "Are our loudmouths finally going to turn nasty on us?"

"It must be the miners again," said the farmer's wife. "That's the second time they've come past. Things don't seem to be going too well—I hear they've taken over the whole countryside."

Her words were spoken with caution, and she watched their effect on the faces about her; when she noticed how frightened they all were, the profound anxiety the encounter was producing in them, she hastened to add:

"Oh, the good-for-nothings, the good-for-nothings!"

Négrel, realizing that it was too late to get back into the carriage and return to Montsou, ordered the coachman to drive it quickly into the farmyard, where it was hidden behind a shed. He himself tied his horse, the reins of which a small boy had been holding, in the same shed. When he came back, he found his aunt and the young ladies in a state of panic and about to follow the farmer's wife, who was offering them refuge inside the house. But he felt they were safer where they were—nobody would come looking for them in all this hay. The barn door, however, did not quite close, and there were so many cracks in it that they could see the road from between the worm-eaten boards.

"Come—a little courage," he said. "We'll sell our lives dearly!"

This pleasantry only increased their fears. The noise was growing louder, nothing could yet be seen, and a wind seemed to be whistling down the deserted road, like one of those sudden gusts that precede a great storm.

"No, no, I don't want to watch," said Cécile, huddling in a corner of the hay.

Madame Hennebeau, very pale, furious with these people who were spoiling her outing, was standing a little back, with a look of disgust; but Lucie and Jeanne, though they were quaking, did not want to miss any of the spectacle and had their eyes glued to a crack.

The thunderous rumble was coming nearer, the earth shook, and Jeanlin, blowing his horn, was the first to race by.

"I suggest you take out your scent bottles, the sweaty masses are about to pass," murmured Négrel, who, despite his republican convictions, liked to mock the riffraff when he was with the ladies.

But his witty sally was lost in the hurricane of shouts and gestures. The women had appeared—nearly a thousand of them, their hair disheveled from racing across the country-side, their bare flesh showing through tattered clothes and exposing the nudity of female animals weary of giving birth to starvelings. Some of them had babies in their arms and were lifting them over their heads, waving them about like banners of mourning and vengeance. Others, younger, like full-bosomed Amazons, were brandishing sticks, while the old women, a terrifying sight, were shrieking so loudly that the cords of their emaciated throats seemed about to burst. Next came the men—two thousand madmen, a single, compact, swarming mass of mine boys, cutters, and repairers, so squeezed together that their faded trousers and their tattered woolen sweaters had merged into one uniform earth color. Their eyes were blazing, and all that could be seen were their gaping black mouths singing the *Marseillaise*, the stanzas of which were lost in a confused bellow accompanied by the clatter of sabots on the hard ground. Above their heads, among the bristling iron bars, reared a vertical ax, and that single ax, the crowd's banner, was silhouetted against the clear sky like the blade of a guillotine.

"What dreadful faces," faltered Madame Hennebeau.

Négrel muttered between clenched teeth:

"The devil take me if I can recognize a single one of them! Where can all these ruffians come from?"

And it was true—anger, hunger, two months of suffering, and this wild stampede from mine to mine had turned the placid faces of the Montsou miners into those of long-jawed, howling beasts. The sun was setting, and its last, crimson rays were turning the plain blood-red; the road seemed awash with blood as the men and the women, besplattered as butchers in a slaughterhouse, kept coming on.

"How superb!" murmured Lucie and Jeanne, their artistic sense stirred by the magnificent horror of it all.

Nevertheless they were frightened, and they moved back to join Madame Hennebeau, who was leaning against a manger. The idea that a single glance between the gaping planks of the door would be enough to bring about their massacre froze her to the marrow; and even Négrel, usually so courageous, felt himself pale as he was invaded by a terror stronger than himself, one of those terrors that spring from the unknown. Cécile, huddled in a corner of the hay, did not stir. The others, despite themselves, could not keep from staring out.

It was an apocalyptic vision of the revolution that would inevitably sweep them all away on some bloody evening of this dying century. Yes, one day the people would slip its harness and, unleashed, race along the roads just like this; it would make the blood of the bourgeois flow, it would parade their severed heads on pikes, it would scatter the gold of disemboweled cashboxes. The women would shriek and the men would have those wolflike jaws open to bite. Yes, there would be the same rags, the same thunder of heavy sabots, the same terrifying mob, with its dirty flesh and stinking breath, sweeping aside the old world in a wild, barbaric onslaught. Fires would blaze, not so much as a stone would be left standing in the cities, and after the enormous rut, the enormous orgy during which the poor, in a single night, would ravage the women and empty the cellars of the rich, there would be a return to the savage life of the forest. Nothing would be left, not a sou of the great fortunes, not a deed of possession, until the day when a new world would perhaps spring up. Yes, all this was what was passing along the road like a force of nature, and the terrible blast of it was striking them full in the face.

A great cry went up, dominating the *Marseillaise:*

"Bread! Bread! We want bread!"

Lucie and Jeanne clung to Madame Hennebeau, who was herself in a near faint, while Négrel stationed himself in front of them, as though to protect them with his body. Was it to be this evening, then, that the old society would crack? And what they saw next completed their stupefaction. The crowd had flowed on, and only a few stragglers were still passing, when suddenly Mouquette appeared. She was lingering at the rear of the column, searching out any of the bourgeois who might be at the doors of their gardens or the windows of their homes, and when she found any, since she couldn't spit in their faces, she showed them what was for her the supreme expression of her contempt. She must have just caught sight of one, because she suddenly raised her skirt, stuck out her buttocks, and showed her enormous rear end, naked in a last blaze of sunlight. There was nothing obscene about this rear end, and nothing laughable; it was of a savage ferocity.

Everything disappeared; the flood was rolling on toward Montsou along the winding road between the low, gaudily painted houses. The carriage was brought out from the farmyard, but the coachman would not dare take it upon himself to deliver Madame and the young ladies safely if the strikers were in control of the road. The worst of it was that there was no other way back.

"But we *must* get home, dinner is waiting for us!" said Madame Hennebeau angrily, exasperated by fear. "These filthy workers had to choose a day when I have company! That's what comes of trying to be nice to such rabble."

Lucie and Jeanne were trying to coax Cécile from the hay, but she resisted, thinking that the savages were still parading past, and insisting that she did not want to see them. Finally they all took their places in the carriage. Then Négrel, back on his horse, had the idea of returning through the back lanes of Réquillart.

"Go slowly," he told the coachman, "it's a terrible road. If they try to keep you from rejoining the main road further on, stop behind the old mine and we'll continue on foot and get in through the garden gate. You can leave the carriage and horses anywhere—in the shed of some inn."

They started off. In the distance the crowd was streaming through Montsou, where the townspeople had been scurrying around in a wild panic ever since they had seen the gendarmes and the soldiers pass through a second time. Terrible rumors were circulating, and there was talk of handwritten posters threatening to disembowel the bourgeois; nobody had read them, but this didn't keep people from citing actual phrases of the text. At the notary's, especially, the terror was at its height, for somebody had just slipped under his door an anonymous letter in which he was warned that a barrel of gunpowder had been buried in his cellar and was ready to go off if he did not declare himself on the side of the people.

It so happened that the Grégoires, whose visit had been extended by the arrival of this letter and who were discussing it, were just deciding that it was the work of a prankster when the mob invaded the street and utterly panicked the household. The Grégoires merely smiled. Lifting a corner of a curtain, they looked out and refused to admit that there was any danger whatever—it would all end peacefully, they said. It was only five o'clock, and they had plenty of time to wait till the street was clear before crossing over to dine at the Hennebeaus', where Cécile, surely back by now, must be waiting for them. But nobody else in Montsou seemed to share their confidence: people were running about frantically, doors and windows were being slammed shut. Across the road they saw Maigrat barricading his store with a profusion of iron bars, and he was so pale and trembling that it was his weak little wife who had to tighten the nuts.

The crowd had come to a halt in front of the manager's house, and from all sides came the cry:

"Bread! Bread! We want bread!"

Monsieur Hennebeau was standing at the window when Hippolyte came in to close the shutters lest the glass panes be smashed by a hail of stones. He closed all the ones on the ground floor, then went upstairs; soon one could hear the squeaking of the hasps and the banging of shutter after shutter. Unfortunately, the window of the kitchen, which was in the basement, could not be sealed off in the same way, and that was dangerous, for through it could be seen the fires under the pots and the spit.

Monsieur Hennebeau, who wanted to get a better view, mechanically went up to the third floor and into Paul's room, which was the best situated, for it was on the left side of the house and commanded a view of the road right up to the Company yards. He stood behind the shutters and looked down on the crowd. But the room—its washstand sponged and cleaned, the sheets neatly and tightly drawn over the cold bed—upset him once again. All his rage of that afternoon, his furious battle in the depths of his immense, silent solitude, had turned now to a tremendous weariness. His whole being was, like the room, cooled—the morning's filth swept out, everything set to rights again. What good would a scandal do? Had anything really changed? His wife had simply taken another lover, and the fact that she had chosen him from among the family scarcely made things worse; it might even offer some advantages, since at least appearances would be saved. His mad fit of jealousy now seemed pitiful. How ridiculous to have pounded the bed with his fists! Since he had tolerated that other man, he could very well tolerate this one; it would only mean a little more contempt and disgust. A bitter, poisonous taste invaded his mouth—the pointlessness of everything, the eternal pain of existence, the shame he felt for himself at still adoring and desiring this woman even in the filth to which he was abandoning her.

Beneath the window the shouts broke out in redoubled violence.

"Bread! Bread! We want bread!"

"Idiots!" said Monsieur Hennebeau through clenched teeth.

He heard them curse him because of his large salary, calling him a fat-bellied good-for-nothing and a dirty pig who stuffed himself with delicacies until he was sick while workingmen were dying of hunger.

The women had spotted the kitchen, and a storm of

obscenities was unleashed against the roasting pheasant, against the sauces whose rich odors tormented their empty stomachs. Oh, these bourgeois bastards—someday they'd stuff enough champagne and truffles down their throats to make their guts burst!

"Bread! Bread! We want bread!"

"Idiots!" Monsieur Hennebeau repeated. "Do you think *I'm* happy?"

Anger rose in him against these people who could not understand. He would gladly have made them a present of his high salary in exchange for their tough hides and their easy, casual lovemaking. If he could only seat them at his table and stuff them with his pheasant while he went off to fornicate behind the hedges, tumbling the girls and not giving a damn if anybody else had tumbled them first! He would have given everything—his education, his comfort, his luxury, his power as a manager—if for only one day he could have been the least of the wretches under his command, free in his flesh, boorish enough to beat his wife and take his pleasure with the wives of his neighbors. And he felt that he too wanted to be starving, to have an empty, churning stomach that would make him faint and dizzy with pain; maybe that would have deadened his everlasting grief. Oh, to live like an animal, to have nothing of one's own, to be able to roll in the wheat with the ugliest and filthiest of the haulage girls and find contentment!

"Bread! Bread! We want bread!"

Hearing this, he lost his self-control and shouted furiously into the uproar:

"Bread! Do you think that's enough, you idiots!"

He had enough to eat, and still he groaned in pain. His ravaged home, his whole torture-racked life, rose in his throat like a death rattle. Bread was not enough to make everything all right. Who was fool enough to think that sharing the wealth would make for happiness in this world? Those empty-headed revolutionaries could tear down this society and build up another, but giving everyone his slice of bread and butter would not add a single joy to humanity, nor spare it a single pain. In fact, they would only increase the misery of the world: they would someday make the very dogs howl with despair by raising them from the simple satisfaction of their instincts to the unassuageable torment of their passions. No, the only good was not to be at all, or if be one must, to be a tree, a stone, or even less—a grain of sand that cannot bleed under the heels of passersby.

And in the pain of his torment, tears filled Monsieur

Hennebeau's eyes and coursed down his cheeks in burning drops. Dusk was covering the road in darkness when the stones began to batter the front of the house. No longer angry at these hunger-maddened wretches, enraged only by the searing pain in his heart, he continued to stammer through his tears:

"The idiots! The idiots!"

But the cry of the belly dominated everything, and a roar like a tempest swept everything before it.

"Bread! Bread! We want bread!"

6

Though sobered by Catherine's slaps, Etienne had remained at the head of his comrades. But even as he was hoarsely urging them on to Montsou, he could hear another voice within him, the astonished voice of reason, asking why all this was happening. None of it had been part of his plan. He had set out for Jean-Bart with the idea of acting unemotionally and thereby preventing a disaster—how then had it happened that he was ending the day, which had gone from violence to violence, by besieging the manager's house?

It was certainly he who had just shouted "Halt!" but he had only done it to protect the Company yards, which there was talk of sacking. And now that stones were flying at the walls of the manager's house, he was vainly racking his brain for some legitimate prey against which he could launch the crowd in order to avoid even worse trouble. As he stood there, isolated and powerless in the middle of the road, someone called to him—a man standing in the doorway of Tison's place, which had hastily been shuttered up by the owner so that only the door was free.

"Yes, it's me. . . . Listen to me."

It was Rasseneur. Some thirty men and women, almost all from Village 240, having remained at home in the morning and come for news in the evening, had crowded into the bar at the approach of the strikers. Zacharie and his wife, Philomène, were at one table. Farther inside, Pierron and La Pierronne had their backs turned and were hiding their faces. No one was drinking; they had simply taken shelter there.

Etienne recognized Rasseneur and started to move on, but the latter said:

"The sight of me bothers you, doesn't it? . . . I warned you, you're in for trouble. Now you can ask for bread all you want, but lead is what you'll get."

At this Etienne turned back and replied:

"The only thing that bothers me are the cowards standing around with their arms folded, watching the rest of us risk our necks."

"You mean you intend to sack that house then?" asked Rasseneur.

"I intend to stay with my friends to the very end, so that at least we will all die together."

And in despair Etienne rejoined the crowd, prepared to die. Three children in the road were throwing stones, and he kicked out at them lustily, shouting for the benefit of the men that nothing would be solved by breaking windows.

Bébert and Lydie had just rejoined Jeanlin, who was showing them how to use his sling. Each of them shot off a stone to see who could do the most damage. Lydie's awkwardness resulted in a cracked skull for one of the women in the crowd, and the two boys were holding their sides with laughter. Bonnemort and Mouque sat behind them on a bench, watching. Bonnemort's swollen legs were so unsteady that he had dragged himself this far only with great difficulty, and since he had the ashen face typical of him on the days when not a word was to be gotten out of him, no one could figure out just what curiosity had driven him forward.

Nobody was obeying Etienne any longer. Despite his orders, the stones continued to fly, and he was amazed and frightened by these brutes he had unleashed—men slow to anger, but then terrible in the ferocious tenacity of that anger. All the old Flemish blood was there—dull and placid, taking months to boil over, but then throwing itself into acts of abominable savagery and refusing to listen to reason until the beast within was sated with atrocities. In the Midi, where he came from, crowds flared up more quickly, but they did less damage. He had to fight with Levaque to get his ax away from him, and he did not know how to restrain the Maheus, who were throwing stones with both hands. It was the women who frightened him most; La Levaque, Mouquette, and the others, whipped up to a murderous fury, their teeth and nails bared, were howling like bitches under the urgings of La Brûlé, whose gaunt figure towered above them.

But suddenly everything stopped, and a momentary surprise brought about a little of the calm that Etienne's pleas had not been able to obtain. It was simply that the Grégoires had decided to leave the notary's and cross the street to the

manager's house; and they looked so untroubled, they seemed
so sure that this was just a joke on the part of their good
miners, whose resignation had been nourishing them for a
century, that the latter, in their astonishment, had actually
stopped throwing stones lest they hit this old lady and gentleman who had fallen from the sky. They let them enter the
garden, walk up the front steps, ring at the barricaded door
that nobody was in any hurry to open. Just then, Rose, the
chambermaid, returned from her afternoon off; she laughed
at the raging miners, all of whom she knew because she was
a native of Montsou, and it was she who beat her fists against
the door until Hippolyte finally opened it a crack. It was
none too soon; the hail of stones began again just as the
Grégoires disappeared within. Recovered from its astonishment, the crowd was shouting louder than ever.

"Death to the bourgeois! Long live socialism!"

In the hall, as though amused by the whole adventure,
Rose continued to laugh, repeating to the terrified manservant:

"Oh, they're not really bad, I know them."

Monsieur Grégoire methodically hung up his hat. Then,
after he had helped Madame Grégoire take off her heavy
coat, he added in his turn:

"I'm sure there's no real malice in them. When they've had
their fill of shouting, they'll go home and eat with a heartier
appetite."

Just then Monsieur Hennebeau came down the stairs. He
had watched the scene and was now coming to receive his
guests in his usual polite and formal manner. Only his pallor
betrayed the tears that had shaken him. The man in him had
been conquered; all that was left was the careful administrator, resolved to do his duty.

"You know," he said, "that the ladies haven't come back
yet."

For the first time the Grégoires felt uneasy. Cécile not
back!—how would she get in if the miners went on with this
joke?

"I thought of clearing the way to the front of the house,"
added Monsieur Hennebeau. "Unfortunately, not only am I
alone here, but I don't know where to send my servant for
four men and a corporal to come and sweep this rabble
away."

Rose, who was still there, was so bold as to again murmur:

"Oh, sir, they're not really bad."

The manager shook his head, while outside the tumult

increased, and they could hear the dull thud of stones striking against the front of the house.

"I don't blame them, and I can even find it in my heart to excuse them. Only people as ignorant as they are could think that we make a deliberate effort to keep them in misery. However, I'm responsible for maintaining the peace. . . . To think that there are gendarmes out on the roads, or so I'm told, and that I haven't been able to find even one of them all day!"

He broke off, and moving to one side, said to Madame Grégoire:

"I beg you, Madame, please don't stand out here. Come into the drawing room."

But the cook, climbing up the stairs from the basement in a state of exasperation, detained them in the hall for several minutes longer. She declared that she could no longer accept the responsibility for the dinner—she had ordered *vol-au-vent* shells from the pastry shop in Marchiennes and expected them to be delivered at four o'clock, but obviously the baker must have gotten lost on the way, frightened by these bandits. Perhaps they had even pillaged his delivery baskets. She imagined her *vol-au-vent* shells barricaded behind a bush, besieged, then swelling the bellies of the three thousand wretches who were demanding bread. In any case, Monsieur couldn't say she hadn't warned him—she would rather throw her dinner into the fire than have it be spoiled because of the revolution.

"Just be patient," said Monsieur Hennebeau. "Nothing is lost yet—the baker may still come."

And as he was turning back to Madame Grégoire and opening the door of the drawing room for her, he was surprised to see a man sitting on the hall bench, a man whom the growing darkness had prevented him from noticing earlier.

"It's you, is it, Maigrat? What's the matter?"

Maigrat had risen, and his face could be made out, fat and pale, distorted by terror. He had lost his heavy, stolid assurance, and he humbly explained that he had slipped into the manager's house to ask for aid and protection if the bandits attacked his store.

"As you can see, I myself am in danger, and I have no one here," replied Monsieur Hennebeau. "You would have done better to stay at home and stand guard over your merchandise."

"Oh, I've barred the door, and anyhow, my wife is there."

The manager lost his patience and made no effort to hide

his contempt. A fine guard she was, that sickly creature wasted by blows!

"There's really nothing I can do. Try to defend yourself. And I suggest you get back immediately, because they're beginning to shout for bread again. . . . Listen."

It was true. The tumult was starting up again and Maigrat thought he heard his name among the cries. On the one hand, he thought it was too late to go back, they would tear him to pieces; and on the other, he was racked by the thought of his impending ruin. He pressed his face against the glass panel of the door and stood there, sweating, trembling, expecting disaster. Meanwhile the Grégoires finally decided to enter the drawing room.

Monsieur Hennebeau calmly tried to do the honors of the house, but it was in vain that he begged his guests to be seated; the sealed and barricaded room, lit by two lamps while it was still daylight, was filled with terror at each new uproar from outside. Muffled by the drawn curtains, the rumble of the crowd's anger was even more menacing, like a vague yet terrible threat. Still they talked, constantly returning to the topic of this inconceivable revolt. As for Monsieur Hennebeau, he was surprised not to have foreseen it, and the information he had received was so faulty that his anger was primarily directed at Rasseneur, whose detestable influence he claimed to recognize. No matter, the gendarmes would soon come; it was inconceivable that they should just abandon him! As for the Grégoires, their only thought was for their daughter: the poor dear was so easily frightened! But perhaps, given the danger, the carriage had turned back to Marchiennes. They waited in this way for another quarter of an hour, made more tense by the noise from the road and the sound of stones striking against the closed shutters, making them resound like drums. The situation had become intolerable; Monsieur Hennebeau was talking of going outside, driving the loudmouths away singlehanded, and then going to meet the carriage, when suddenly Hippolyte appeared, shouting:

"Sir, sir! Madame is here—they're killing Madame!"

The carriage had not been able to go beyond the Réquillart lane because of the threatening groups, so Négrel had carried out his plan of walking the remaining hundred yards to the house and knocking on the garden door near the sheds: the gardener would hear them, or someone else would be there to open it for them. And at first everything had gone perfectly; Madame Hennebeau and the young ladies were already knocking at the door when some of the women, alerted to their arrival, rushed down the lane. From then on things went from bad to worse. Nobody came to open the door, so Négrel had made a vain attempt to break it down with his shoulder. The flood of women was increasing, and because he was afraid his aunt and the girls would be overrun, he made the desperate decision to push them before him, right through the besiegers and up to the front steps. But this maneuver led to a scuffle: the shrieking band of women followed them, determined not to let them get away, while the rest of the crowd flowed in from all sides, not knowing what was happening, but amazed to find these smartly dressed ladies wandering about in the midst of the battle. At this point the confusion became so great that it resulted in one of those strange and inexplicable incidents that occur in times of panic. Lucie and Jeanne had reached the steps and slipped through the door, which was being held half-open by the maid; Madame Hennebeau had managed to follow them; and then Négrel came in behind the ladies and shot the bolts, convinced that he had seen Cécile go in first of all. But she was not there; somewhere along the way she had disappeared, so maddened by terror that she had turned her back on the house and run right into the heart of the danger.

A cry immediately went up:

"Long live socialism! Death to the bourgeois! Kill them!"

From a distance, and because she was wearing a veil that hid her face, some of the women took her for Madame Hennebeau. Others thought she was a friend of Madame Hennebeau's—the young wife of a neighboring manufacturer hated by his workers. But it did not matter who she was—it was her silk dress, her fur coat, and even the white feather in her hat that infuriated them. She smelled of perfume, she wore a watch, she had the soft skin of a do-nothing who never even touched a piece of coal.

"Just wait!" shrieked La Brûlé. "We'll shove that lace up your ass!"

"Those bitches steal all that from us," La Levaque picked up. "They cover themselves with fur while we freeze to death.... Let's strip her naked to teach her a lesson!"

Mouquette immediately rushed forward.

"Yes, yes, let's whip her!"

And in this savage rivalry the women, reaching out tatter-clad arms, pressed forward, each one wanting a piece of this rich man's daughter. Her behind was surely no better than anybody else's. Why, more than one of these bitches was completely rotten under her frills! This injustice had gone on too long—now they would be forced to dress like working-women, all these whores who dared spend fifty sous to have a skirt laundered!

Surrounded by these furies, her legs paralyzed, Cécile was shaking with fear, stammering out the same phrase over and over again:

"Ladies, please, ladies, don't hurt me."

Then she let out a hoarse cry: cold hands had just grabbed at her neck. It was Old Bonnemort—the crowd had pushed her near him and he had seized her. Intoxicated by starvation, dazed by his long years of misery, he seemed suddenly to have shaken off the resignation of half a century under the prodding of some mysterious urge for vengeance. During the course of his life he had saved dozens of his comrades from death and risked his neck in firedamp explosions and cave-ins, but now he was giving in to something he could not explain, to an overwhelming need to do what he was doing, to a fascination with the white neck of this young girl. And since this was one of his silent days, when he seemed to have lost the use of his tongue, he merely tightened his fingers, looking all the while like some old, sick animal ruminating over his memories.

"No, no!" shrieked the women. "Strip her ass, strip her ass!"

As soon as those in the house had realized what was happening, Négrel and Monsieur Hennebeau had boldly opened the door to rush to Cécile's aid. But the mob was now pushing against the garden gate and it was hard to get out. There was a struggle, during which the horrified Grégoires appeared on the front steps.

"Let her alone, old man, it's the young lady from La Piolaine!" La Maheude shouted at Bonnemort when she recognized Cécile, whose veil had been torn by one of the women.

Etienne, appalled by these reprisals against a mere child, was trying to make the crowd let her go. He had a sudden inspiration and brandished the ax he had torn from Levaque's hands.

"Let's get Maigrat's place, damn it! . . . There's bread inside. Let's tear the place down!"

And swinging wildly he brought the ax down on the door of the store. Some of the men had followed him—Levaque, Maheu, and a few others—but the women were determined not to be put off. Cécile had passed from the hands of Bonnemort into those of La Brûlé. Down on all fours, Lydie and Bébert, led by Jeanlin, were crawling under her skirts to see the lady's behind. The women were pulling at her, and

her clothes were already splitting when a man on horseback
appeared, urging his mount forward and using his whip on
those who were slow to get out of his way.

"Ah, you scum, now you want to beat our daughters, do
you!"

It was Deneulin, coming to keep his dinner engagement.
He swiftly jumped down, took Cécile by the waist with one
hand, and used his other to maneuver the horse with extraordinary skill and force, making of it a living shield; then he
cut through the crowd, which fell back from the horse's
hoofs. At the gate the battle was still going on, but he got
through, bruising and battering limbs as he went. This unexpected help saved Négrel and Monsieur Hennebeau, both of
whom were in serious danger as curses and blows rained
down on them. And while Négrel carried Cécile, who had
fainted, inside, Deneulin, who was protecting the manager
with his large body, was hit by a stone as he got to the top of
the steps, and the blow almost dislocated his shoulder.

"That's right!" he shouted. "Break my bones now that
you've broken my machines!"

He quickly closed the door. A broadside of stones struck
the wood.

"What madmen!" he continued. "Another two seconds and
they would have cracked my skull like an empty gourd. . . .
But what can you expect? There's no talking to them—
they're beyond understanding, and all you can do is cut them
down."

In the drawing room the Grégoires wept as they watched
Cécile return to consciousness. She had not been hurt, had
not suffered so much as a scratch: only her veil was lost. But
they were more alarmed than ever when they saw their cook,
Mélanie, standing there and describing how the mob had
demolished La Piolaine. Mad with fear, she had run to warn
her masters. Without anybody noticing, she too had entered
through the half-open door during the struggle; and in her
interminable account, Jeanlin's one stone, which had broken
a single window, became a veritable cannonade that had
battered down the walls. Hearing this, Monsieur Grégoire
was in a turmoil: his daughter attacked, his house razed to
the ground—was it then true that the miners could really
dislike him for living quietly and decently on the fruits of
their labor?

The chambermaid, who had brought in a towel and some
cologne, repeated:

"I still think it's strange—they're not really bad."

Madame Hennebeau sat there, very pale and unable to

recover from the emotional shock; it was only when somebody congratulated Négrel that she began to smile again.

Cécile's parents were especially grateful to the young
man—the marriage was now a foregone conclusion. Monsieur
Hennebeau watched in silence, his eyes going from his wife,
to the lover whom that morning he had sworn to kill, to the
young girl who would probably soon rid him of the fellow.
He was in no hurry; his one fear now was that he might see
his wife sink even lower, perhaps to some footman.

"And you, my darlings?" Deneulin asked his daughters.
"Nothing broken, I hope?"

Lucie and Jeanne had been terribly frightened, but they
were glad to have seen it all. They were laughing now.

"Good lord," continued their father, "this has been quite a
day! . . . If you want a dowry, you'll have to earn it
yourselves—and you may even have to take care of me as
well."

He was making light of it, but his voice trembled. His eyes
filled with tears as his two daughters threw themselves into
his arms.

Monsieur Hennebeau had heard this confession of ruin.
His face lit up. True—Vandame would fall to Montsou; this
was the hoped-for compensation, the lucky chance that
would put him back in the good graces of the board of
directors. At every crisis in his life he took refuge in the
strict execution of orders, and he created his small share of
happiness out of the military discipline under which he lived.

But everyone was quieting down, and a weary peace descended on the drawing room, with the calm light of its two
lamps and the muffling warmth of its hangings. What could
be happening outside? The ruffians were quiet, stones were
no longer striking the house, and the only sound was a dull,
heavy thudding, like the sound of ax blows in the distant
forest. To find out what was going on, they went back into
the hall to venture a peek through the glass panel in the
door. Even the ladies went upstairs to peer out from behind
the shutters.

"Do you see that scoundrel Rasseneur standing there in the
doorway of that bar?" Monsieur Hennebeau asked Deneulin.
"I suspected as much—I knew he'd have to be mixed up in
this."

However, it was not Rasseneur—it was Etienne, who was
breaking down Maigrat's store with the ax. He kept shouting
to his comrades: didn't all the merchandise inside belong to
the miners? Didn't they have the right to take back their own
from this thief who had been exploiting them for so long,

who let them starve at a word from the Company? Little by little they gave up the attack on the manager's house and ran over to pillage the neighboring store. The cry of "Bread! Bread! We want bread!" thundered out again. Well, behind that door they would find bread. A rage of hunger swept over them, as if they could not wait any longer without dying right there on the road. There was such a rush toward the door that every time Etienne raised the ax he was afraid he would hurt somebody.

Meanwhile Maigrat had left the hall of the house and had at first taken refuge in the kitchen; but he had no idea of what was going on from there, and he kept imagining all kinds of abominable attacks against his store. He had just gone outside, and he was hiding behind the pump when he distinctly heard his door breaking down and the shouts of looting, among which he could distinguish his own name. So it wasn't a nightmare: if he still could not see, he could at least hear, and his ears buzzing, he followed the attack. Each blow of the ax went right to his heart. One of the hinges must have given way; another five minutes and the store would be theirs. With his mind's eye he saw the terrifyingly realistic images—the bandits rushing in, the drawers forced, the sacks ripped open, everything eaten, everything drunk, the very furnishings carried off, nothing left—not so much as a stick with which to go begging through the villages. No, he would not let them bring about his ruin, he would rather die. All the while he had been standing there, he had seen, through a window at the side of his house, the scrawny silhouette of his wife, pale and blurred through the glass: she was probably watching the attack like the poor, silent, beaten creature she was. Beneath the window there was a shed, so situated that one could get to the top of it from the garden of the manager's house by climbing up the trellis on the dividing wall; from there it was easy to reach the window by crawling along the roof tiles. And because he felt such remorse at having left his store, he was now obsessed by the possibility of returning there in this way. There might still be time to barricade the store with the furniture, and he even invented other heroic defenses—like pouring boiling oil or flaming kerosene down from above. But the love for his merchandise had to fight against his fear, and he was gasping with the effort to vanquish his cowardice. Suddenly another blow of the ax, louder this time, made him come to a decision. Avarice won out. He and his wife would cover the sacks with their bodies rather than give up a single loaf of bread.

A few seconds later there was an outburst of catcalls.

"Look! Look! . . . The tomcat is up there! Let's get the cat! Let's get the cat!"

The crowd had just noticed Maigrat on the roof of the shed. His excitement had enabled him, despite his heaviness, to climb the trellis with great agility, careless of the splintering wood; and now he was stretched out along the tiles, trying to reach the window. But the slope of the roof was very steep, his belly was in the way, his nails were breaking off. Nevertheless, he would have been able to drag himself to the top if he had not started to tremble with the fear of being stoned, for the mob below, which he could no longer see, kept shouting:

"Let's get the cat! Let's get the cat! . . . Let's beat the hell out of him!"

And suddenly, both hands losing their grip simultaneously, he rolled down like a ball, bounced over the rain gutter, and fell across the dividing wall so awkwardly that he bounded off it and onto the road, where he split his skull on the corner of a milestone. His brains had spilled out. He was dead. Up above, his wife, pale and blurred behind the window, was still watching.

At first they were all stupefied. Etienne had stopped, the ax falling from his hands. Maheu, Levaque, and all the others, their eyes fixed on the wall—down which a thin red stream was slowly flowing—forgot about the store. The shouting had stopped, and a deep silence spread through the growing darkness.

Then the hooting began again. It was the women, drunk with blood-lust, who were rushing forward.

"So there's a God after all! Ah, you dirty pig, it's all over with you now!"

They swarmed around the still-warm body, laughing at it insultingly, calling his cracked head an ugly mug, shrieking into the dead man's face the long bitterness of their starved lives.

"I owed you sixty francs, and now you've been paid, you thief!" said La Maheude, as enraged as the others. "You won't ever refuse me credit again. . . . Wait! Just wait—I have to fatten you up a little more!"

And scratching at the earth with all ten fingers, she brought up two handfuls of dirt and crammed it into his mouth.

"Here, eat that! . . . Go on, eat it the way you used to eat us!"

The insults redoubled, and all the while the dead man lay on his back, staring with wide-open eyes at the enormous sky from which night was falling. The earth in his mouth was the bread he had refused, and it was the only bread he would eat from now on. Starving the poor had not brought him much luck.

But the women had other things to avenge themselves for. They circled about, sniffing at him like she-wolves. They tried to think of some outrage, some act of savagery that would relieve their feelings.

La Brûlé's shrill voice was heard.

"Let's cut it off, like with a tomcat!"

"Yes, yes, get the cat, get the cat! . . . He's done it too often, the bastard!"

Mouquette was already at work, pulling his trousers off while La Levaque held up his legs. Then La Brûlé, with the dry hands of old age, spread his naked thighs and grabbed his dead virility. She clutched it all, tearing at it with a force that arched her thin back and cracked her long arms. The soft flesh resisted, and she had to try again; at last she was able to rip it loose—a lump of hairy bleeding flesh that she waved around with a triumphant laugh:

"I've got it, I've got it!"

Shrill voices saluted the horrible trophy with curses.

"Ah, you bastard, now you won't screw our daughters anymore!"

"That's right, no more paying you with our bodies! We won't all have to offer our bottoms just to get a loaf of bread!"

"Come to think of it, I owe you six francs. Would you like a little something on account? Me, I'm willing—if you still can!"

This sally shook them with terrible gaiety. They pointed the bloody little lump out to one another as though it were some evil beast that had made each of them suffer, a beast they had finally crushed and now saw before them, inert and in their power. They spat on it, they thrust out their jaws, they repeated in a furious outburst of contempt:

"He can't do it anymore! He can't do it anymore! . . . What's going to be shoved into the ground isn't even a man! . . . Go on and rot, that's about all you can do!"

Then La Brûlé stuck the lump on the end of her stick, and lifting it high in the air, waving it like a banner, she started down the road, followed by the shrieking mob of women. Drops of blood were raining down, and the pitiful flesh hung there like a scrap of waste in a butcher's stall. Up at the window Madame Maigrat had still not moved, but in the last light of the setting sun the imperfections of the glass distorted

her white face so that it seemed to be laughing. Beaten,
continually betrayed, bent over an account book from morning to night, perhaps she really was laughing as the mob of
women rushed past with the evil beast, the finally crushed
beast, at the end of the stick.

This horrible mutilation had taken place amid frozen
horror. Neither Etienne nor Maheu nor any of the others had
had the time to intervene: they remained motionless before
this stampede of furies. A few faces appeared at the door of
Tison's—Rasseneur, pale with disgust, Zacharie and Philomène, horrified by what they had seen. The two old men,
Bonnemort and Mouque, shook their heads gravely. Only
Jeanlin was enjoying himself; he kept nudging Bébert and
forcing Lydie to raise her eyes, from the ground. But the
women were already returning, circling back and passing
under the windows of the manager's house. Behind the shutters, the ladies and the young girls were craning their necks.
They had not been able to see the scene, which the wall cut
off from view, and now they could hardly see because it was
dark.

"What have they got on the end of that stick?" asked
Cécile, who had become bold enough to watch.

Lucie and Jeanne said it must be a rabbit skin.

"No, no," murmured Madame Hennebeau, "they must
have pillaged the butcher's—it looks like a scrap of pork."

Just then she shuddered and fell silent. Madame Grégoire
had nudged her with her knee. They both remained open-
mouthed. The girls, very pale, asked no further questions, but
they continued to stare as the red vision vanished into the
darkness.

Etienne brandished his ax again. But the uneasiness would
not be dispelled, and now the corpse was barring the road
and protecting the store. Many had drawn back—it was as
though their thirst had been slaked and they were no longer
interested. Maheu was standing there glumly when he heard
a voice at his ear, telling him to run. He turned around and
saw Catherine, still in her cast-off man's jacket, still dirty and
gasping for breath. He repulsed her with a wave of his hand.
He refused to listen, and even threatened to beat her. She
made a despairing gesture, hesitated, then ran toward Etienne.

"Run, run! The gendarmes are here!"

He too chased her away, cursing as he felt his cheeks flush
again at the memory of her slap. But she wouldn't give up;
she forced him to drop the ax and dragged him along, pulling
at him with both arms.

"But I tell you the gendarmes are here! . . . Listen to me.

It's Chaval who went for them and who's bringing them
here, if you must know. I was disgusted, so I came to warn
you. Run, I don't want them to get you."

And Catherine got him away just as the gallop of horses
could be heard in the distance. Suddenly a cry went up: "The
gendarmes! The gendarmes!" It was a rout—such a wild
scramble for safety that in two minutes the road was free,
absolutely empty, as if it had been swept clean by a hurricane.
Maigrat's corpse was the only stain on the white earth. In
front of Tison's Rasseneur stood alone; relieved and smiling,
he applauded the easy victory of armed authority. Meanwhile, in deserted and lifeless Montsou, behind the silent and
shuttered facades, the bourgeois—sweating with fear, their
teeth chattering—did not so much as dare risk a look. The
plain was drowned in the thick darkness, and only the blast
furnaces and the burning coke ovens could be seen against
the tragic sky. The heavy galloping of the gendarmes drew
closer—they swept in as an indistinguishable dark mass. And
behind them, confided to their protection, came the wagon of
the Marchiennes baker, from out of which jumped a delivery
boy who calmly began to unload the *vol-au-vent* shells.

Part SIX

1

The first two weeks of February crawled by, pitilessly prolonging the terrible winter of the destitute. The authorities had once again been in evidence: the prefect of Lille, a public prosecutor, a general. And the gendarmes had not been considered sufficient—troops had been sent to occupy Montsou, and an entire regiment was camped in the area from Beaugnies to Marchiennes. Armed guards were protecting the mines; soldiers were stationed at every engine. The manager's house, the Company yards, and even the homes of some of the bourgeois were bristling with bayonets. Nothing could be heard but the slow tramp of patrols up and down the cobbled highway. On top of the Voreux slag heap, where the icy winds never stopped blowing, there was a twenty-four-hour guard planted like a lookout tower above the flat plain, and every two hours, as if they were in occupied territory, the changing guards roared out:

"Who goes there? . . . Advance and give the password!"

Nowhere had the men gone back to work. On the contrary, the strike had spread: Crèvecoeur, Mirou, and Madeleine had followed the lead of Le Voreux and stopped operations; Feutry-Cantel and La Victoire were losing more workers every morning; there were not even enough men at Saint-Thomas, which had until then been untouched. The miners, faced with this deployment of force that outraged their pride, were responding with a silent obstinacy. The villages in the middle of the beet fields seemed deserted. Not a worker stirred, and if by chance one was seen, he would be alone, his head bent, glancing out of the corner of his eyes at the red trousers of the soldiers. But there was a misleading docility about this sense of great, somber peacefulness, this passive defiance pitting itself against rifles; it was like the forced, patient obedience of caged animals that keep their

eyes on the trainer and are ready to spring at his neck if he
so much as turns his back. The Company, which was being
ruined by this death of work, talked of hiring miners from
the Borinage, on the Belgian frontier; but it did not dare do
so, and the battle lines remained drawn in a stalemate between the miners shut up in their houses and the lifeless
mines guarded by the troops.

This peace had suddenly established itself the morning
after the terrible day, screening a panic so great that there
was the most complete silence about the damage and the
atrocities. An inquest was held, and it established that
Maigrat had died from his fall; the story of the horrible
mutilation of the corpse, already the subject of legends, remained vague and shadowy. The Company did not admit
how much damage it had sustained, nor did the Grégoires
wish to compromise their daughter by the scandal of a trial
at which she would have to give evidence. Nevertheless,
several arrests had been made—as usual, of foolish and
terrified bystanders who knew nothing. The men were still
laughing at the fact that Pierron had, by mistake, been taken
to Marchiennes in handcuffs. Rasseneur too had almost been
led off between two gendarmes. Management contented itself
with drawing up lists of men to be discharged, and returning
stacks of workbooks: Maheu had received his, and so had
Levaque and thirty-four of their comrades from Village 240
alone. The brunt of official wrath was directed at Etienne,
who had disappeared the evening of the riot and was now
being searched for, though not a trace of him could be
found. Chaval, in his hatred, had denounced him; but begged
by Catherine, who wanted to save her parents, he refused to
name any of the others. The days dragged by, everybody was
sure it was not yet over, everybody was waiting for the end,
hearts heavy with uneasiness.

From that time on, the bourgeois in Montsou started up
every night in panic, their ears ringing with the sound of an
imaginary tocsin, their nostrils haunted by the stench of
gunpowder. But what finally succeeded in driving them out of
their minds was a sermon by their new curé, the Abbé
Ranvier, that thin, fiery-eyed priest who had taken the place
of the Abbé Joire and who was such a far cry from the
smiling discretion of the latter, whose single concern had
been to get along with everybody, like the plump and smiling
man he was! Had not the Abbé Ranvier dared defend the
terrible bandits who were dishonoring the region? He found
excuses for the wickedness of the strikers, and he violently
attacked the bourgeoisie, at whose door he put the entire

blame. It was the bourgeoisie, by robbing the church of its
ancient rights in order to itself abuse them, that had made of
this world an accursed place of injustice and suffering; and it
was the bourgeoisie, by its refusal to return to the faith and
the fraternal traditions of the first Christians and by its
atheism, that was prolonging these misunderstandings and
bringing on a terrible catastrophe. And he had even dared to
threaten the rich, warning them that if they insisted on
ignoring the voice of God, God would surely align Himself
with the poor: He would reclaim the wealth of the unbelievers, and He would distribute it to the humble of the earth for
the triumph of His glory. The devout listened and trembled;
the notary declared that this was the worst sort of socialism;
and all of them could see the curé at the head of a mob,
brandishing a cross and wildly tearing down the bourgeois
society of '89.

When Monsieur Hennebeau was informed, he merely
shrugged his shoulders and said:

"If he makes too much trouble the bishop will get rid of
him for us."

And while this panic was sweeping from one end of the
plain to the other, Etienne was living underground, in Jeanlin's burrow at the bottom of Réquillart. It was there that he
had hidden himself, and nobody believed he could be so
close; the quiet audacity of this refuge in the very mine itself,
in this abandoned gallery of the old shaft, had thrown his
pursuers off the scent. Up above, the blackthorns and hawthorns that sprouted between the fallen timbers of the
headframe choked the entrance; no one dared go down that
way anymore, because you had to know the trick of hanging
from the roots of the service tree and then letting yourself
drop fearlessly until you reached the first of the ladder rungs
that was still solid. There were other obstacles to protect him
too—the suffocating heat of the ladder well, the four hundred feet of dangerous descent, and then the painful half-mile
slide on your stomach through the narrow tunnel before
coming upon the robber's hideout piled with booty. He was
living there in the midst of abundance, for he had found
some gin, the remainder of the dried cod, and provisions of
all kinds. The big bed of hay was excellent, and there were
no drafts—the equable temperature was like that of a warm
bath. Only light was in short supply. Jeanlin—who had made
himself Etienne's supplier and who was as cautious and
discreet as a savage, delighted at being able to thumb his nose
at the gendarmes—was able to bring Etienne almost every-

thing, even some pomade, but he had not been able to lay his hands on a package of candles.

After the fifth day Etienne lit a candle only to eat by. Food would simply not go down when he tried to swallow it in the dark. That interminable, unvarying, complete blackness caused his greatest suffering. It mattered not that he slept in safety, was warm and had enough to eat—never had night weighed so heavily on his head. It seemed to press down on him like the very crush of his thoughts. So now it was he who was living off theft! Despite his communistic theories, the old scruples of his upbringing rose in revolt, and he contented himself with dry bread and even pared down his portion of that. But what was he to do?—he had to live, his work was not finished. He was also overwhelmed by another shame—remorse for the savage drunkenness that had resulted from drinking gin in the bitter cold on an empty stomach, and which had thrown him on Chaval, knife in hand. A previously unknown terror stirred within him, a terror of that hereditary evil, of his long inheritance of drunkenness, which would not allow him so much as a drop of alcohol without making him give way to homicidal fury. Would he end up as a murderer? When he had reached safety, here in this great calm of the bowels of the earth, he was so satiated with violence that he had sunk for two days into the exhausted sleep of a glutted animal, and his despair persisted; he was crushed, there was a bitter taste in his mouth, his head ached as though after some terrible orgy. A week passed; the Maheus, though they had been told of his difficulty, were unable to send a candle: he had to do without light, even to eat by.

For long hours now Etienne remained sprawled on his hay, troubled by vague feelings he had never known he had. For instance, there was a feeling of superiority that was setting him above his comrades, a self-pride that had developed as he had educated himself. Never had he done so much thinking. He asked himself why he had felt such disgust the day after that furious race from mine to mine, and he dared not answer; he was repelled by the memory of the base greed, the brutal instincts, the odor of all that misery shaken out in the wind. Despite the torment of the darkness, he was beginning to dread the time when he would have to return to the village. It was so horrible, all those poor wretches living piled together, swilling from a common trough! Not one of them with whom to discuss politics seriously, an animal existence, always the same choking stench of onions! He wanted to broaden their horizons, raise them to the comfort and the good manners of the bourgeoisie by making *them* the masters—but what a lengthy task it would be and he no longer felt he had the courage to wait for victory in this prison of hunger. Slowly his vanity at being their leader, his feeling that he constantly had to think for them, was setting him apart and creating within him the soul of one of those bourgeois whom he so despised.

One evening Jeanlin brought him a candle end stolen from a carter's lantern, and this was a great relief for Etienne. Whenever the darkness, pushing down on his skull with a force that almost drove him crazy, got to be too much for him, he would light the candle for an instant; then, as soon as he had shaken off the nightmare, he would put the candle out, avaricious of this light that was as necessary to his life as bread. The silence rumbled in his ears; he could hear nothing but the flight of a swarm of rats, the cracking of old timbers, the tiny noise of a spider spinning its web. And staring into this tepid nothingness, he would return to his obsession—the question of what his comrades were doing up above. To abandon them would have seemed the worst sort of cowardice to him. If he was hiding like this, it was only so that he could remain free, to advise and to act. His long sessions of brooding had established his ambition: until something better came along, he would like to be like Pluchart, to quit his job and work only in politics—but alone, in a clean room, with the excuse that intellectual labor absorbs one's whole life and demands complete quiet.

At the beginning of the second week—Jeanlin having told him that the gendarmes believed he had slipped over the border into Belgium—Etienne risked leaving his hole as soon as night had fallen. He wanted to take stock and see if it was worth fighting on. He himself thought it was a lost cause; even before the strike he had been dubious about the end result and had simply given way to events, and now, after his orgy of rebelliousness, he was returning to his original doubts and despaired of making the Company give in. But he would not yet admit it; he was tortured by the thought of the miseries of defeat, of all the heavy weight of responsibility for suffering that would weigh down on him. The end of the strike—was it not the same as the end of his role, the destruction of his ambition, the return to the brutalization of the mine and the humiliations of the life of the village? And in all honesty, without any low, calculated dishonesty, he tried to find his faith again, to prove that resistance was still possible and that capital would destroy itself when faced with the heroic suicide of labor.

And in actual fact the rumble of ruin could be heard throughout the district. At night, as he would roam over the dark countryside like a wolf that has left its forest lair, he seemed to hear the crash of bankruptcies from one end of the plain to the other. Along the roads he walked there were only closed, lifeless factories, their buildings rotting under the leaden sky. The sugar refineries had especially suffered; the Houton and Fauvelle refineries, after first having cut down the number of their workers, had just shut down, one after the other. At the Dutilleul flour mill the last millstone had stopped on the second Saturday of the month, and the Bleuze ropeworks, which made mine cables, had been completely killed by the work stoppage. Around Marchiennes the situation was growing worse every day: all the furnaces out at the Gagebois glassworks, constant layoffs at the Sonneville construction works, only one of the three blast furnaces at Les Forges going, and not one battery of coke furnaces blazing on the horizon. The strike of the Montsou miners, itself born of the industrial crisis that had steadily been worsening for two years, had added to the crisis and brought about a complete industrial collapse. To the original causes of trouble—the drying up of orders from America and the immobilization of enormous sums of capital in a production surplus—was now added the unforeseen shortage of coal for the few boilers still operating, and this was the final death knell: the mines were no longer furnishing food for the machines. Frightened by the general depression, the Company, by cutting down its output and starving its miners, had found itself at the end of December without a single lump of coal in its yards. Everything was connected with everything else; infection spread from afar, one failure drew another in its traces, and industries toppled and crashed into one another in a series of catastrophes so rapid that the reverberations were felt even in such neighboring cities as Lille, Douai, and Valenciennes, where absconding bankers left entire families without a sou.

Often at a turning in the road Etienne would stop in the glacial night to listen to the ruin rain down. He would breathe the darkness in deeply and exult in the idea of complete destruction, the hope that day would dawn on the extermination of the old society, when egalitarianism would pass along the ground like a scythe and leave not one fortune standing. But it was the Company's mines and how they had fared in this trouble that particularly interested him, and he would start to walk again, blinded by darkness, and visit them one after another, happy when he learned of some new damage. Cave-ins were continuous, and the longer the tunnels were left abandoned, the more serious they became. Above the north gallery of Mirou the subsidence of the soil was such that about a hundred yards of the Joiselle road had been swallowed up, as if by an earthquake; the Company, made uneasy by the talk these accidents had aroused, had paid the proprietors for their vanished fields without any argument. Crèvecoeur and Madeleine, where the rock crumbled easily, were becoming more and more blocked. There was talk of two foremen who had been buried alive at La Victoire; a flash flood had inundated Feutry-Cantel; more than half a mile of a gallery at Saint-Thomas, where the timbers were in bad repair and were collapsing on all sides, would have to be walled off. And so it was that from hour to hour there were enormous expenses that opened breaches in the dividends of the stockholders—a rapid destruction of the mines themselves, which in the long run would end by eating up those famous Montsou "deniers" that had multiplied a hundredfold in the course of a century.

Etienne's hopes revived in the face of this series of disasters, and he began to believe that a third month of resistance would finish off the monster, the weary, glutted beast crouching somewhere over there like an idol in the unknown recesses of its tabernacle. He knew that a wave of strong emotion had swept the Paris newspapers as a result of the trouble at Montsou; violent polemics had raged between the official papers and the opposition papers, and terrifying stories were printed—stories used especially against the International, which the Empire, having first encouraged, was now becoming fearful of. Management had no longer dared turn a deaf ear, and two of the directors had deigned to come and conduct an investigation—but with such reluctance, so unworried about the outcome, so unconcerned, that they had left after three days, saying things could not be better. He had learned from other sources, however, that during their stay these gentlemen had been in constant session, feverishly active, busy with matters about which nobody close to them had breathed a word. He decided they had merely been playing at being confident, and he interpreted their departure as a wild rout; he was certain of victory now that those terrible men had given up.

But the next night Etienne was again in despair. The Company's back was too strong to be so easily broken; it could afford to lose millions, for it would get them all back later at the expense of the workers, by paring down their wages. That night he had gone as far as Jean-Bart, and he

realized the truth when a guard told him that there was talk
of turning Vandame over to Montsou. Rumor had it that a
pitiful poverty reigned at Deneulin's house—the poverty of
the rich, with the father sick at his powerlessness, aged by
money worries, and the daughters struggling to save what
they could from the creditors. There was less suffering in the
starving villages than in this middle-class house where they
felt they had to hide the fact that there was only water to
drink. Work had not started again at Jean-Bart, and it had
been necessary to replace the pump at Gaston-Marie; in
addition, despite the prompt precautions that had been taken,
there had been some flooding, and this too had necessitated
vast expenditures. Deneulin had finally risked asking the
Grégoires for a loan of a hundred thousand francs, and their
refusal, though it had been expected, had finished him; they
said that if they refused, it was out of pure affection for him,
to keep him from engaging in a hopeless struggle, and they
advised him to sell. He was still refusing, vehemently. It
enraged him to thus have to bear the cost of the strike—he
would rather die, with the blood rushing to his head, or
choking in a fit of apoplexy. But what was he to do?—and he
had finally listened to their offers. They haggled, belittling
this magnificent prize, this renovated, newly equipped mine
whose operation was paralyzed only by his lack of ready
cash. He would be lucky if he got enough out of it to pay off
his creditors. For two days he had fought against the directors camped in Montsou, furious at the calm way in which
they took advantage of his troubles, shouting "Never!" in his
vibrating voice. And that was the way things stood. They had
returned to Paris, to await his death rattle patiently. Etienne
understood how this would compensate for the Company's
other disasters and was once again overcome by discouragement; the power of big capital was so invincible, so strong in
battle, that it could even grow fat on defeat, by eating the
corpses of the smaller businesses fallen at its side.

Fortunately, the next day Jeanlin brought him some good
news. At Le Voreux the casing of the shaft was threatening
to split; water was leaking from every joint, and they had
had to rush a team of carpenters there to start making
repairs.

Until then Etienne, worried by the eternal black silhouette
of the sentinel planted on the slag heap high above the plain,
had avoided Le Voreux. The silhouette was unavoidable; up
in the sky, like a regimental flag, it dominated everything. At
about three o'clock in the morning the sky became overcast
and Etienne made his way to the mine, where some of his

comrades described the dangerous condition of the casing: they even thought it should be completely replaced, which, if done, would stop extraction operations for three months. He circled around for a long time, listening to the carpenters' mallets tapping away in the shaft. His heart grew lighter at the thought of this wound that had to be dressed.

As he was going back in the early dawn he saw the sentinel still on the slag heap. This time the man would surely see him. He walked on, thinking of these soldiers who were taken from among the people and then armed against the people. How easy the triumph of the revolution would become if the army were to suddenly side with it! The workers and peasants in the barracks would only have to remember their origins. For the bourgeois, that was the supreme peril, the great fear—their teeth chattered when they thought of a possible defection of the troops. Within two hours they would be swept away, exterminated, along with all the privileges and abominations of their iniquitous way of life. Rumor had it that whole regiments were already infected by socialism. Was it true? Would justice come thanks to the very bullets distributed by the bourgeoisie? And grasping at another hope, the young man dreamed that the regiments whose units were guarding the mines would come out in favor of the strike, shoot the entire Company, and at last give the mine to the miners.

He suddenly became aware of the fact that while his head had been buzzing with these notions he had started to climb the slag heap. Why should he not talk to the soldier? He would find out the color of his ideas. Assuming an air of indifference, he kept going closer, as if he were simply gathering old pieces of wood left among the rubble. The sentinel did not move.

"What rotten weather, comrade!" said Etienne finally. "I think we're going to have some snow."

The soldier was small and very blond, with a gentle, pale face covered with red freckles. In his military overcoat he had all the awkwardness of a recruit.

"Yes, I think so too," he murmured.

And his blue eyes stared at the livid sky—at that smoky dawn in which the soot seemed to hang like lead over the distant plain.

"They're idiots to stick you up here to freeze your ass off!" Etienne went on. "You'd think they were expecting the Cossacks. . . . And it's always so windy up here!"

The little soldier shivered but did not complain. There was, to be sure, a drystone hut in which Old Bonnemort used to

take shelter on gusty nights, but the soldier's orders being not
to leave the summit of the slag heap, he stayed put, his hands
so stiff with cold that he could no longer feel his rifle. He
belonged to a detachment of sixty men who were guarding
Le Voreux, and since his turn at this cruel tour of duty came
up frequently, he had already come close to dying up there,
his feet frozen. But it was all part of the job—a passive
obedience had ended by stultifying his brain, and he replied
to Etienne's questions with a few stuttered words, like a
drowsy child.

For a quarter of an hour Etienne tried in vain to make
him talk about politics. He said yes, he said no, but he did
not seem to understand; some of the men said the captain
was a republican, but he had no ideas about it and it made no
difference to him. If they ordered him to shoot, he'd shoot, so
he wouldn't be punished. The worker listened to him and was
gripped by hate, the hate of the people against the army,
against these brothers whose hearts could be changed by
slipping a pair of red trousers over their rears.

"What's your name?"

"Jules."

"Where are you from?"

"From Plogoff, over there."

He had pointed vaguely. It was in Brittany, that was all he
knew. His small, pale face became animated, and cheering
up, he began to laugh.

"I've got a mother and sister back there. Of course they're
waiting for me, but there's still a long time to go. . . . When I
left, they went with me as far as Pont-l'Abbé. We'd borrowed the Lepalmecs' horse, and he almost broke his legs at
the bottom of the hill at Audierne. Cousin Charles was
waiting for us with sausages, but the women were crying too
much and everything stuck in our throats. . . . Oh my God,
my God, this is a long way from home!"

Though he still laughed, his eyes grew moist. He could
suddenly see that deserted Plogoff moor, that savage, storm-
lashed Raz peninsula, as it was during heather season, in a
blaze of sunlight.

"Tell me," he asked, "if I don't get into any trouble, do
you think they'll give me a month's furlough in two years?"

At this Etienne began to talk of Provence, which he had left
when he was very young. It was growing lighter, and
snowflakes were beginning to whirl in the leaden sky. He
became nervous when he noticed Jeanlin circling around in
the brambles, looking amazed to see him up there. The boy
was waving to him. What was the point of this pipe dream of

fraternizing with the soldiers? It would take years and years, and he was as discouraged by his futile attempt as if he had counted on its success. But suddenly he understood Jeanlin's signal: they were coming to relieve the sentinel. He left, running all the way back to his hideout at Réquillart, once more heartbroken by the certainty of defeat, while the boy, running along beside him, kept accusing that damn soldier of having called the men out to fire on them.

At the top of the slag heap, Jules had remained immobile, his eyes staring blankly out at the falling snow. The sergeant approached with his men and the regulation cries were exchanged.

"Who goes there? . . . Advance and give the password."

And the heavy steps marched away again, resounding as though in a conquered country. Despite the growing light, there was no movement in the villages; the miners were raging in silence under the military heel.

2

Snow had been falling for two days, but it had stopped that morning; a bitter cold had turned the immense plain into a sheet of ice, and the black countryside, with its inky roads, its walls and trees powdered with coal dust, was all white— an overwhelming, endless whiteness stretching as far as the eye could see. Village 240 lay under the snow as though buried. Not one wisp of smoke was rising from a chimney; the houses were as cold as the cobblestones on the road, and because there were no fires the thick blanket of snow on the roof tiles never melted. The village was nothing more than a quarry of white stones in a white plain—a vision of a dead village wrapped in its shroud. The muddy tracks churned up by the passing patrols were the only marks on the streets.

At the Maheus' the last shovelful of clinkers had been burned the night before, and it was useless to think of gleaning the slag heap in this terrible weather, when the very swallows could not find a blade of grass. Because she had insisted on fumbling under the snow with her poor little hands, Alzire was now dying. La Maheude had wrapped her up in a shred of blanket and was waiting for Dr. Vanderhagen; she had already been to his house twice without finding him, but his maid had promised that he would get to

the village before nightfall and the mother was standing in
front of the window, watching for him, while the sick little
patient, who had insisted on coming downstairs, was shivering
on a chair, under the illusion that it was better there, next to
the fireless stove. Old Bonnemort, his legs gone bad again, sat
opposite her and seemed to be asleep. Neither Lénore nor
Henri, who were trudging along the roads with Jeanlin to beg
a few sous, had come home yet. Only Maheu moved around,
walking heavily back and forth across the bare room, each
time coming up against the wall like a stupid animal no
longer aware of its cage. There was no more lamp oil either,
but the snow outside was so white that its reflection was able
to dimly light the room even though night had already fallen.

There was a clatter of sabots, and La Levaque, furious,
flung open the door and started yelling at La Maheude from
the threshold:

"So you've been telling people I make my boarder give me
twenty sous every time he sleeps with me!"

La Maheude shrugged her shoulders.

"Don't be an idiot, I haven't said a thing. . . . Anyway,
who told you I said that?"

"Never you mind who. Somebody told me you said it. . . .
And you even said you could hear us do our dirty business
through the wall, and that my house was getting filthier and
filthier because I was always on my back. . . . Just try to deny
that you said it!"

Every day quarrels broke out because of the women's
constant gossiping. Arguments and reconciliations had always
been a daily occurrence, especially between the families that
lived alongside one another, but never before had they gone
at each other with such bitter nastiness. Since the strike,
hunger had aggravated resentments, and everyone had a need
to strike out at someone else: a dispute between two women
would generally end with a savage fight between their husbands.

And in fact just then Levaque came in, dragging Bouteloup
along with him.

"Here's the man himself—let him say if he's ever given my
wife twenty sous to sleep with her!"

The mild-natured boarder, hiding his alarm behind his big
beard, protested, stammering:

"Oh, no, never so much as a sou. Never!"

In a flash Levaque turned threatening and shook his fist
under Maheu's nose.

"You know, I don't like this. When you have a wife like

yours you have to whack her around. . . . Or do you believe what she said?"

"But for God's sake!" exclaimed Maheu, furious at being jolted from his depression, "what's all the fuss about? Aren't we miserable enough as it is? Shut up, or I'll let you have it! . . . And besides, who said my wife said that?"

"Who said it? . . . Why, La Pierronne said it, that's who."

La Maheude burst into a shrill laugh and, turning to La Levaque, said:

"Oh, it was La Pierronne, was it? . . . Well, let me tell you what she told *me!* She told me you slept with both your men at the same time, one on top and the other on bottom!"

After that no peace was possible. Everybody got angry, and the Levaques answered the Maheus by saying that La Pierronne had said a few words about them too—that they had sold Catherine, and that all of them were rotting away, even the children, because of some filthy disease Etienne had picked up at the Volcan.

"She said that, did she? She said that?" roared Maheu. "All right, I'm going there right now, and if she admits that she said it, she'll feel my fist on her jaw!"

He had rushed out, and the Levaques followed behind to bear witness while Bouteloup, who hated disputes, furtively slipped home. Kindled by the argument, La Maheude was also about to leave, but she was stopped by a moan from Alzire. She wrapped the shreds of blanket over the child's shivering body and returned to station herself in front of the window, her eyes staring into the distance. Would that doctor never come?

Just outside the Pierrons' house, Maheu and the Levaques found Lydie walking up and down in the snow. The shutters were closed, but there was a glimmer of light shining through a crack. At first the child answered their questions, though with reluctance: no, her papa wasn't there, he had gone to the wash house to meet La Brûlé and carry back the bundle of laundry. Then she became confused and refused to say what her mother was doing. Finally she blurted it out, with a sly, bitter laugh: her mother had thrown her out because Monsieur Dansaert was there and she kept them from talking. Since early that morning, Dansaert had been making the rounds of the village with two gendarmes, trying to gather workers by frightening the more timid and announcing everywhere that the Company was determined to hire miners from the Borinage area if the men were not down at Le Voreux on Monday. At nightfall, finding La Pierronne alone, he had

sent off the gendarmes and remained behind to have a glass
of gin in front of a good fire.

"Sh, quiet down! Let's get a look at them," murmured
Levaque with a lickerish laugh. "We'll straighten this other
business out later. . . . And you get away from here, you little
slut!"

Lydie drew back a bit as he put his eye to the crack in the
shutter. He stifled a few small cries, and his spine arched and
quivered. Then La Levaque took a turn looking, but she
doubled over, as though with sudden cramps, and said it
disgusted her. Maheu, who also wanted to see, had shoved
her aside and now declared that he was getting his money's
worth. And they began again, taking turns, each one getting
a peek, just like at a play. A cheerful fire was blazing in the
immaculately clean room, there were cookies on the table,
and a bottle and some glasses; it was a real celebration—so
much so that what they could see going on inside ended by
infuriating the two men, though under other circumstances
the scene would have given them enough to joke about for
six months. To see her with her skirts in the air and Dansaert
in her up to her neck was funny, all right, but for God's
sake, wasn't it piggish to treat yourself to it in front of such a
big fire, and to build up your energy for it with cookies,
when your friends didn't have a crust of bread or a scrap of
coal?

"Here comes Papa," cried Lydie, running off.

Pierron was calmly coming back from the wash house with
the bundle of laundry on his shoulder. Maheu challenged him
immediately.

"I hear your wife has been saying that I sold Catherine
and that everyone in our house was diseased. . . . Well, how
about what goes on in your house? How much does this
gentleman who's busy wearing out your wife's hide pay you
for her?"

Pierron was confused and did not understand, but just then
his wife, frightened by the tumult of voices, lost her head and
inched open the door to see what was going on. There she
was—all red, her blouse open, her skirt still raised and
caught in her belt—while in the background Dansaert was
frantically trying to get into his trousers. The chief foreman
ran off and disappeared, terrified lest such a story reach the
ears of the manager. There was an uproarious burst of
laughter, hoots, and insults.

"You're always saying that other people are dirty," La
Levaque screamed at La Pierronne. "Well, it's not surprising

that you're so clean—you get yourself so well scrubbed by the bosses!"

"She's just the one to talk!" added Levaque. "This is the bitch who said that my wife sleeps with both the boarder and me, one on top and the other on bottom! . . . Yes, yes, somebody told me you said it."

But La Pierronne was calm now, and she stood up to this foul language with a lofty disdain, contemptuous of them all in her certainty that she was the richest and most beautiful woman in the village.

"I said what I said and that's all there is to it! . . . What I do is no concern of yours. You're jealous of us because we put money in the bank! Go ahead, say what you want—my husband knows very well why Monsieur Dansaert was here."

And in fact Pierron was angrily defending his wife. The quarrel took a new tack; he was called a traitor, a spy, a Company watchdog, and they accused him of hiding behind closed doors to stuff himself with the delicacies the bosses gave him in return for his treachery. He replied by claiming that Maheu had slipped a threatening note under his door—a piece of paper with a drawing of crossbones and a dagger above them. Naturally enough, like all the women's quarrels now that hunger was enraging even the gentlest of them, it ended with the men rushing murderously at one another. Fists flying, Maheu and Levaque had hurled themselves at Pierron, and they had to be separated. By the time La Brûlé came back from the wash house, her son-in-law's nose was bleeding copiously. Informed of what had happened, she merely said:

"That pig is a dishonor to me."

The street became empty again; not a shadow stained the bare whiteness of the snow, and the village once more sank into its deathlike immobility, starving under the intense cold.

"And the doctor?" asked Maheu, closing the door.

"Hasn't come," replied La Maheude, still standing in front of the window.

"Are the children back?"

"No, not yet."

Looking like a stunned ox, Maheu resumed his heavy striding from wall to wall. Old Bonnemort, sitting stiffly on his chair, had not even lifted his head. Alzire said nothing either; to spare them pain, she was trying not to shiver, but despite her courage in suffering, she sometimes shook so violently that the quaking of her thin, sick body could be heard against the blanket; at the same time, her big, wide

eyes stared at the ceiling, lit by the pale reflection of the
all-white garden as though with moonlight.

The house was in its last agony, empty, fallen into complete and final destitution. The mattress covers had followed
the woolen stuffings to the secondhand shop, then the sheets
had gone, and the linen, and everything else that could be
sold. One evening they had sold one of the grandfather's
handkerchiefs for two sous. Tears flowed for each object the
poor household was forced to give up, and the mother was
still lamenting the fact that one day she had carried off the
pink cardboard box—her husband's old gift—hidden in her
skirt, as if it were a baby she was going to leave at somebody's doorstep. They were naked; they had nothing more to
sell but their skin, and that was so worn out and destroyed
that nobody would have given a centime for it. They no
longer even bothered to look for anything else—they knew
that there was nothing, that it was the end of everything, that
they could not hope for a candle, or a lamp, or a potato; and
thus they waited for death, not even angry except for the
children's sake—they were revolted by the pointless cruelty
of burdening Alzire with illness before finally finishing her
off.

"Here he comes at last!" said La Maheude.

A black shape passed in front of the window. The door
opened. But it was not Dr. Vanderhagen; it was the new
curé, the Abbé Ranvier, who did not seem at all surprised to
find himself in this lifeless house, without light, without fire,
without bread. He had already been to three neighboring
houses, for he was going, like Dansaert and his gendarmes,
from family to family, trying to recruit men of good will;
and in his feverish, fanatical voice he immediately came to
the point.

"Why didn't you come to Sunday Mass, my children?
You're wrong not to, only the Church can save you. . . .
Come now, promise me you'll be there next Sunday."

Maheu had stared at him, then without a word resumed
his heavy pacing. It was La Maheude who answered.

"To Mass, monsieur le curé?—what for? Does the good
Lord give a damn about us? . . . Can you tell me what my
little girl, who's sitting there shivering with fever, has ever
done to Him? I suppose we didn't have enough trouble
before, was that it?—He had to make her sick when I can't
even give her a cup of something hot!"

The priest just stood there and spoke for a long time. With

the ardor of a missionary who preaches to savages for the
greater glory of his religion, he exploited the horrible misery
and the bitterness exasperated by hunger. He said that the
Church was with the poor and that one day she would make
justice triumph by calling down the wrath of God on the
iniquities of the rich. And that day would dawn soon, because
the rich had taken God's place and, following their impious
theft of power, had even gone so far as to rule without God.
But if the workers wanted a just division of the goods of the
world, they would have to put themselves into the hands of
the priests immediately, just as on the death of Jesus the poor
and the humble had rallied around the apostles. What
strength the Pope would have! What an army the clergy
would have at its disposal when it could command the count-
less mass of workers! In one week the world would be purged
of evildoers, the unworthy masters would be banished, and
the true reign of God—when each man would be compensated according to his merits and universal happiness would
be based on the law of labor—would begin.

Listening to him, La Maheude was reminded of Etienne on
those autumn evenings when he used to prophesy the coming
end of their miseries. But she had always been suspicious of
cassocks.

"What you say, monsieur le curé, is very true," she said,
"but all it means is that you're not getting along with the
bourgeois anymore. . . . All our other curés used to dine at
the manager's house, and they always threatened us with
hell-fire as soon as we asked for bread."

He went on, speaking of the deplorable misunderstanding
between the Church and the people. Now, in veiled phrases,
he struck out at the city priests, at the bishops, at the high
clergy—all of them sated with luxuries and gorged with
power, working hand in hand with the liberal bourgeoisie and
not seeing, in their imbecilic blindness, that it was this same
bourgeoisie that was depriving them of empire over the
world. Deliverance would come from the country priests,
who would all, with the aid of the poor, rise up to reestablish
the Kingdom of Christ; and he held himself straight—like the
leader of a band of fanatics, like a bible-inspired revolutionary—and his eyes shone with such ardor that they lit up the
dark room, and he seemed already to be at their head. But
his fiery sermon had swept him into mystical language, and
these poor people had long since stopped being able to understand him.

"There's no need for so many words," growled Maheu

suddenly. "You would have done better to begin by bringing us a loaf of bread."

"Come to Mass on Sunday!" exclaimed the priest. "God will provide everything."

And he left, going to catechize the Levaques in their turn—so carried away by his dream of the Church's final triumph, and having such disdain for mundane facts, that he was able to go through the villages without alms and pass through that army of starving people with empty hands, himself only a poor devil who saw suffering as a spur to salvation.

Maheu kept striding back and forth, and all that could be heard was this regular tread that made the flagstones vibrate. Suddenly there was a noise like a rusty pulley; it was Old Bonnemort spitting into the cold fireplace. Then the regular beat of the footsteps began again. Alzire, dazed by fever, was softly raving, laughing, thinking that it was warm out and that she was playing in the sunshine.

"Oh my God," murmured La Maheude after feeling her cheeks, "now she's burning up. . . . I don't even expect that pig anymore—those thieves must have told him not to come."

She was referring to the doctor and the Company. Nevertheless she let out a cry of joy on seeing the door open again—but then her arms fell and she stood there stiffly, her face woebegone.

"Good evening," said Etienne in a low voice, after he had carefully closed the door behind him.

He often visited them like this, when it was pitch-black outside. The Maheus had known about his hideout from the second day, but they kept the secret; nobody else in the village knew just exactly what had become of the young man. As a result, he became a legendary figure. The people continued to have faith in him, and mysterious rumors made the rounds: he was going to appear with an army, with chests full of gold—and it was still the same religious anticipation of a miracle, the realization of an ideal, the sudden entry into the city of justice, that he had promised them. Some said they had seen him on the Marchiennes road in a carriage with three gentlemen; others insisted that he would return from England in two more days. After a while, however, distrust set in, and some of the clowns were even accusing him of hiding in a cellar, with Mouquette to keep him warm—his liaison with her was known and had done him no good. Under the steady pressure of now-despairing

former believers—whose number was increasing every day—
his popularity was beginning a slow decline.

"What rotten weather," he added. "Nothing new with you?
Things still going from bad to worse? . . . I've heard that
Little Négrel has gone to Belgium to find some Borinage
miners. My God, if that's true, we're sunk!"

A shudder had gone through him on coming into this
glacial room, where his eyes had had to accustom themselves
to the darkness before he could actually see the poor
wretches whose presence he could at first only sense as
blacker patches of darkness. He felt the repugnance and
uneasiness of a worker uprooted from his class, polished by
education, and seething with ambition. What misery—and the
odor, and the piled bodies, and the terrible, choking pity of
it! The sight of this agony so unmanned him that he groped
for the words with which to counsel submission.

But Maheu had come up to him and was shouting:

"Borinage miners!—they wouldn't dare, the sons of
bitches! Let them send the Belgians down—if they want us to
wreck the mines!"

Embarrassed, Etienne explained that the miners would not
be able to do a thing, that the soldiers guarding the mines
would protect the descent of the Belgian workers. Maheu
clenched his fists, saying that those bayonets at their backs
was what really got him angry. Weren't the miners their own
masters anymore? Were they to be treated like galley slaves?
Forced to work at gunpoint? He loved his mine, and it
pained him not to have gone down for two months; that was
why he saw red at the very idea of this insult, this threat to
send down those strangers. Then he remembered that his
workbook had been returned to him, and he was heartbroken.

"I don't know why I'm getting angry," he murmured.
"After all, I've got nothing to do with that bunch. . . . Once
they've chased me out of here I might just as well curl up on
the road and die."

"Stop that talk!" said Etienne. "If you want, they'll take
your workbook back tomorrow. Good workmen like you
aren't fired."

He suddenly stopped, amazed to hear Alzire laughing softly in the delirium of her fever. Until then he had only been
able to make out the stiff shadow of Old Bonnemort, and the
gaiety of this sick child terrified him. This was it—it was too
much if it was beginning to kill off the children. He made up
his mind to speak, and his voice began to tremble.

"Look, things can't go on this way. We're beaten. . . .
We've got to give in."

La Maheude, silent and immobile until then, suddenly
exploded, screaming into his face and swearing like a man:

"What did you say? . . . My God, *you* say that?"

He wanted to explain his reasons, but she would not let
him speak.

"By God, don't say that again or I'll batter your face with
my fists even if I am only a woman. . . . So we're to have
starved for two months, I'm to have sold everything in my
house, my children are to have fallen sick, and it's all to be
for nothing—so that injustice can begin all over again! . . .
Oh, the very thought of it makes my blood boil! No! No! I'd
sooner burn everything and kill everybody than give in!"

With a dramatic, menacing gesture she pointed into the
darkness at Maheu.

"Listen to me!—if my husband ever goes back to the
mine, I'll stand on the road and spit in his face and call him
coward!"

Etienne could not see her, but he felt the heat of her rage,
like the breath of a howling beast; he recoiled, dumbfounded
by this fury that was of his own making. He found her so
changed that he could no longer recognize her; previously she
had been all prudence and had reproached him for his
violence, saying that one should not wish for anyone's death,
and now she refused to listen to reason and was talking of
killing everybody. It was no longer he but she who was
discussing politics, who wanted to sweep away the bourgeoisie, who was calling for the republic and the guillotine so
the world might be rid of those rich thieves who had grown
fat on the work of the starving.

"Yes, I'd skin them alive with my own hands. . . . Enough
is enough! Our turn has come, you said so yourself. . . . When
I think that Father, Grandfather, Grandfather's father, and
all the ones who came before them suffered what we're
suffering, and that our sons and the sons of our sons will still
be suffering it in the future, it drives me mad, it makes me
want to reach for a knife. . . . We didn't do enough the other
day. We should have razed Montsou to the ground, down to
the last brick. And do you know?—I've only one regret, and
that's not having let the old man strangle the girl from La
Piolaine. . . . After all, they're letting my children be strangled by hunger!"

Her words fell like ax blows in the night. The sealed
horizon had refused to open, and in the depths of this grief-
crazed mind the impossible ideal was turning to poison.

"You didn't understand me," Etienne managed to say, beating a retreat. "We should be able to make some arrangement with the Company—I know the mines are suffering a lot of damage, so they'll probably be willing to come to some kind of agreement."

"No, no agreements!" she shrieked.

Just then Lénore and Henri came in, empty-handed. A gentleman had given them two sous, but the girl had kept kicking her little brother and the two sous had fallen into the snow; Jeanlin had helped them look, but they had not been able to find the money.

"Where is Jeanlin?"

"He ran off, Mama. He said he had things to do."

Etienne listened, heartbroken. In the old days she used to say she'd kill them if they put out their hands to beg. Now it was she herself who sent them out along the roads, and she even spoke of them *all* going—ten thousand Montsou miners, each one with a stick and a beggar's bag, sweeping over the terrified countryside.

The anguish in the dark room increased. The children had come back hungry, they wanted to eat—why couldn't they eat? And they complained, stumbled about, and ended by stepping on the toes of their dying sister, who then moaned. Beside herself, the mother slapped them, striking out blindly into the darkness. Then, as they began to cry even louder, begging for bread, she burst into tears and sank to the floor, gathering all of them, even the little invalid, in one embrace. For a long time she sat there weeping, the flowing tears bringing her a measure of relief, leaving her limp, exhausted, stuttering the same sentence calling for death over and over again: "My God, why don't you take us? My God, for pity's sake, take us and let it all be over!" The grandfather still sat, as immobile as an old tree twisted by the wind and the rain; the father still walked between the fireplace and the cupboard, without turning his head.

But the door opened again, and this time it was Dr. Vanderhagen.

"Damn!" he said. "A candle wouldn't hurt your eyes any. ... All right, let's go, I'm in a hurry."

As usual, worn out by his work, he was grumbling. Luckily he had some matches; the father had to strike six of them, one after the other, and hold them up so the doctor could examine the patient. Her blanket had come undone, and she was shivering under the wavering light—thin as a bird dying in the snow, so frail that nothing but the hump on her back could be seen. But still she was smiling, that distant smile of the dying, and her eyes were wide open, her pathetic hands clasped on her hollow chest. And when the sobbing mother asked if it was fair that this child, the only one who helped her with the house, so intelligent, so gentle, should be taken before her, the doctor lost his temper.

"There, she's gone. . . . She's died of hunger, this child of yours. And she's not the only one. I just saw another one go nearby. . . . You all send for me, but I can't do a thing. It's meat that you need to cure you."

Maheu, his fingers burned, dropped the match, and darkness fell again on the still-warm little corpse. The doctor had hurried off. Etienne could hear nothing in the black room but the sobs of La Maheude, who kept repeating her call for death, that lugubrious, endless lamentation:

"My God, it's my turn, take me! . . . My God, take my husband, take everyone—for pity's sake, let it all be over."

3

By eight o'clock that Sunday Souvarine was alone in L'-Avantage, sitting in his usual place, with his head against the wall. Not one miner knew where to get the two sous for a beer, and the taverns had never had fewer customers. Madame Rasseneur was therefore sitting motionless behind the counter in a state of silent irritation, while Rasseneur was standing in front of the cast-iron stove, seeming to watch the brownish coal-smoke with an air of profound meditation.

Suddenly the heavy quiet of the overheated room was broken by three sharp taps on a windowpane. Souvarine turned his head and rose to his feet; he had recognized the signal Etienne had used several times before, when from outside the latter could see him sitting at an empty table and smoking his cigarette. But before Souvarine could get to the door Rasseneur had opened it, and recognizing by the light from the window the man who was standing there, he said to him:

"Are you afraid I'll turn you in? . . . You'll be more comfortable talking in here than you would be on the road."

Etienne came in. Madame Rasseneur politely offered him a beer, but he refused with a gesture. The innkeeper added:

"I've known where you were hiding for a long time. If I

were the spy your friends say I am, I'd have turned you over to the gendarmes a week ago."

"You don't have to defend yourself," Etienne answered. "I know you've never stooped to anything like that. . . . People can have different ideas and still respect each other."

And once again there was silence. Souvarine had returned to his chair and was once more sitting with his back against the wall, his eyes following the spiraling smoke of his cigarette; but his febrile fingers were moving nervously up and down his lap, searching for the warm fur of Poland, who was not there that evening. His uneasiness was unconscious—he knew something was missing, but he did not know exactly what.

Sitting opposite him, Etienne finally said:

"Work starts again tomorrow at Le Voreux. Little Négrel has come back with the Belgians."

"Yes, they were brought in after dark," murmured Rasseneur, who had remained standing. "Let's hope there'll be no more killing!"

Then he raised his voice:

"Now look, I don't want to start quarreling with you again, but there'll be hell to pay if you insist on being stubborn. . . . As a matter of fact, what's happening to you here is exactly what's happening to your International. I ran into Pluchart the other day at Lille, where I had some business, and it looks like his whole organization's jumped the track."

He went into details. The Association, after having conquered the workers of the entire world in a burst of propaganda that had the bourgeoisie still trembling, was now being devoured, destroyed a little more every day by the internal conflicts caused by vanities and ambitions. Since the anarchists had ousted the evolutionists and taken over, everything was splitting at the seams; the original goal of wage reform was being lost sight of in the midst of all the factional wrangling, and the intellectual leadership, because of its hatred of discipline, was falling apart. It was already easy to foresee that this mass uprising, which had for a moment threatened to sweep away the old rotten society, was doomed to failure.

"Pluchart is sick over it," continued Rasseneur. "And on top of everything else, he's just about lost his voice. But he keeps on talking anyway, he wants to go talk to them in Paris, too. . . . And he told me three times that our strike's a failure."

Etienne kept his eyes on the ground, let him have his say,

and did not interrupt. The night before, he had talked with some of the men, and he had felt pass over him the breath of bitterness and suspicion—that first breath of unpopularity which foretells defeat. He was sullen, reluctant to admit his dejection to the very man who had predicted that he too would be hooted by the mob as soon as it needed a scapegoat for some miscalculation.

"Yes, the strike's probably done for, and I know it as well as Pluchart," he said. "But that was to be expected. We went into the strike unwillingly, and we weren't counting on it to get rid of the Company for us. . . . But people get excited, they begin to hope for all kinds of things, and then when the trouble starts they forget they should have expected it and they begin to complain and quarrel as though the catastrophe had fallen out of the sky."

"Well, if you think the game's been lost," said Rasseneur, "why don't you get the men to listen to reason?"

The young man stared at him.

"Listen, let's stop this right now. . . . You've got your ideas and I've got mine. I came in here to show you that I respect you all the same. But I still think that even if we die in the effort, our starved bodies will be of more use to the people's cause than all your prudent politics. . . . Ah, if one of those goddamned soldiers would only send a bullet into my heart—that would be the way to go!"

His eyes glistened with tears as this cry was torn from him—this cry that revealed the secret desire of the defeated for a refuge in which he might shake off his torment forever.

"Well said!" declared Madame Rasseneur, glaring at her husband with all the contempt of her radical opinions.

Souvarine, his eyes still staring into space and his hands still nervously moving up and down his lap, seemed not to have heard anything. His blond, girlish face with its thin nose and small pointed teeth had grown savage in response to some mystic reverie filled with bloody visions, and replying to a word plucked out of the conversation, something Rasseneur had said about the International, he had begun to dream out loud.

"They're all cowards. There was only one man who could have made their organization into a terrible instrument of destruction—but they'd have to want that, and nobody wants it. That's why the revolution will once more end in failure."

And while the two other men listened uneasily to these somnambulistic confessions spilling into the darkness, he continued to complain, in a voice heavy with disgust, about the imbecility of mankind. In Russia, nothing was going well, and he was in despair at the news he had received. His old comrades were all turning into politicians; those notorious nihilists who had made Europe tremble—those sons of popes, of petit bourgeois, of storekeepers—were not able to raise themselves above the idea of national liberation and seemed to think that the deliverance of the whole world would follow once they had killed their own despot; and as soon as he tried to speak to them of cutting down the old order of things like an overripe harvest, as soon as he even pronounced the childish world "republic," he felt himself misunderstood, feared, henceforth out-of-place, relegated to the ranks of those ineffectual princes of revolutionary cosmopolitanism. His patriotic heart fought on, however, and it was with painful bitterness that he kept repeating his favorite word:

"Foolishness! . . . They'll never get anywhere with their foolishness!"

Then, lowering his voice even more, he spoke in bitter words of his old dream of fraternity. He had renounced his rank and his fortune, he had joined the workers, for only one reason—the hope of finally seeing the establishment of a new society based on work in common. Every sou in his pocket had long since been given to the village urchins, and he had shown a brotherly tenderness toward the miners, smiling at their suspiciousness and finally winning them over by proving himself a careful and close-mouthed worker—but no true bond had been formed; his contempt for any kind of tie, his determination to remain free, uncorrupted by the allurements of fame and profit, kept him as much of a stranger as ever to them. And all that day he had been especially exasperated by an item that had appeared in the newspapers that morning.

His voice changed and his eyes suddenly focused; he turned them on Etienne and spoke directly to him.

"Do *you* understand it?—this business of those hatmakers in Marseilles who won the hundred-thousand-franc first prize in the lottery and who raced right off to invest it, saying they weren't ever going to lift a finger again? . . . Yes, that's what you all want, you French workers—you want to find a buried treasure somewhere and then retire to some corner and live on it in selfish idleness. Though you all complain about the rich, you don't have the guts to share with the poor whatever good fortune comes your way. . . . You'll never be worthy of happiness as long as you have something that's just your own—and as long as your hatred of the bourgeoisie is due to nothing more than a furious desire to take their place."

Rasseneur burst out laughing; the notion that the two workers from Marseilles should have given up the prize

seemed ridiculous to him. But Souvarine paled, his distorted
face reflecting one of those terrifying outbursts of religious
fury that can result in the extermination of whole nations,
and he shouted:

"You'll all be cut down, overthrown, tossed on the garbage
heap! Someday a man will be born who will annihilate your
race of cowards and pleasure-lovers. And look, do you see
these hands? If they could, these hands would take hold of
the world and shake it—like this—until it fell to pieces and
you would all be buried under the rubble!"

"Well said!" repeated Madame Rasseneur with her air of
polite conviction.

Another silence fell. Then Etienne went back to the subject of the Borinage workers. He questioned Souvarine about
the measures that had been taken at Le Voreux, but the
engineman was again lost in his personal preoccupations and
scarcely replied; he only knew that they were going to
distribute bullets to the soldiers guarding the mine. And the
restless, nervous movements of his fingers on his knees became
so marked that he finally became aware of what they were
searching for—the soft, soothing fur of the tame rabbit.

"Where's Poland?" he asked.

The innkeeper laughed again and looked at his wife. After
an embarrassed pause, he took courage.

"Poland?—oh, she's warm enough."

The plump rabbit had probably been injured during her
adventure with Jeanlin, for ever since then she had only given
birth to dead litters, and in order not to have to feed an
unproductive animal they had that very day resigned themselves to serving her up with some potatoes.

"Yes, you ate one of her legs tonight. . . . Why, you even
licked your fingers afterward!"

At first Souvarine had not understood. Then he became
very pale and he gagged with nausea, while despite his will
to stoicism, two big tears welled up in his eyes.

But nobody had time to notice this emotion; the door had
suddenly flown open and Chaval had appeared, pushing
Catherine before him. After having gotten drunk on beer and
boasting in all the Montsou cabarets, he had then decided to
go to L'Avantage and show his former friends that he was
not afraid. As he came in, he was saying to his mistress:

"By God, I tell you you're going to have a beer here, and
I'll break the neck of the first man who looks at me sideways!"

Catherine, startled by the sight of Etienne, went white.
When Chaval also noticed him, he sniggered nastily.

"Two beers, Madame Rasseneur! We're celebrating the return to work."

She poured them out without a word—a woman who would never refuse to sell her beer to anyone. Silence had fallen. Neither the innkeeper nor the two others had stirred from their places.

"I know some people have been saying I'm a spy," Chaval continued arrogantly, "and I'm waiting for those who said so to say it to my face, so we can finally have it out."

No one answered; the men turned their heads and stared blankly at the wall.

"There are some who are loafers, and there are some who aren't," he went on, raising his voice. "As for me, I've got nothing to hide—I've left Deneulin's damn place, and tomorrow I'm going down at Le Voreux with twelve Belgians they've put under me because they think so much of me. And if that bothers anyone, just let him say so and we'll talk it over."

Then, since the same contemptuous silence continued to greet his provocations, he turned on Catherine.

"Drink up, damn it! . . . Let's drink to the death of all the sons of bitches who refuse to work!"

She raised her glass for the toast, but with such a trembling hand that they could hear the rattling of the two glasses. Meanwhile, he had taken out of his pocket a handful of silver, which he was showing off with drunken ostentation, saying that that was what you got if you were willing to sweat for it, and that he defied loafers to show as much as ten sous. The men's attitude was exasperating him, and he switched to direct insults.

"So the moles come out at night, do they? I guess the gendarmes have to be asleep before the thieves will show themselves."

Etienne had risen, very calm and resolute.

"Look, you're beginning to annoy me. . . . Yes, you're a spy—your money still stinks of betrayal, and the idea of touching your treacherous flesh disgusts me. But never mind, I'm your man, if you want! For a long time now one of us has been fated to finish off the other."

Chaval clenched his fists.

"Let's go, then! You really have to lay it on to bring you to a boil, you dirty coward! . . . Just you and me, I'm ready—and you're going to pay for all the crap you made me go through!"

Her arms raised supplicatingly, Catherine was about to get between them, but they did not even have to push her

away—she realized the inevitability of the battle and withdrew of her own accord, slowly. She stood silently against the
wall, so paralyzed by anguish that she was no longer even
trembling, her wide-open eyes fixed on the two men who
were going to kill each other because of her.

Madame Rasseneur merely cleared the mugs off the counter lest they be broken, then reseated herself without showing
any unseemly curiosity. But two former comrades just could
not be allowed to slaughter each other, and Rasseneur insisted on trying to intervene; Souvarine had to take him by
the arm and bring him back to the table, saying:

"It's none of your business. . . . There's one too many of
them—the stronger one will survive."

Without waiting to be attacked, Chaval was already swinging his clenched fists in the air. He was the bigger of the two,
and the more awkward—he used his arms as though they
were handling sabers, aiming furious, slashing blows at
Etienne's face. And through it all he kept talking, playing up
to his audience with a stream of insults that served to excite
him.

"Ah, you damn pimp, I'll tear your nose off, and when I
do I'll shove it you know where! . . . Just let me at that face
of yours—that face the whores seem to like so much—and
I'll pound it into pigs' mash, and then we'll see if the sluts
keep running after you!"

Silent, his teeth clenched, his slim body crouched in the
prescribed position, Etienne was protecting his chest and face
with his two fists and waiting his chance before releasing
them in terrible jabs, with the force of springs.

At first they did each other little harm. The windmill blows
of the one and the calculated waiting of the other only
prolonged the fight. A chair was overturned; their heavy
shoes crunched the white sand strewn over the tiles. But
finally they became winded—their breath came in heavy
gasps, while their red faces blazed with an inner fire, the
flames of which seemed to dart through their eyes.

"Got you!" roared Chaval. "A nice one right on your
carcass!"

And so he had—his fists, coming from the side like a flail,
had smashed into his enemy's shoulder. Etienne stifled a
groan of pain; the only sound was that of a dull thud against
his bruised flesh. He replied with a blow right to the chest, a
blow that would have finished Chaval if he had not saved
himself by one of his continual, goatlike jumps. As it was, the
blow landed on his left side with such force that it made him
stagger, the wind knocked out of him. Feeling his arms

weaken from the pain, he became enraged, and he rushed at Etienne like a wild animal, aiming for his stomach with his heel.

"There's one for your guts!" he stammered in a strangled voice. "I'm going to pull them out into the fresh air!"

Etienne sidestepped the blow, but was so indignant at this infraction of the rules of fair play that he broke his silence.

"Shut up, you hulk! And goddamn it, don't use your feet again or I'll take a chair and beat your brains out!"

From then on the fight grew worse. Rasseneur was horrified and would have tried to intervene again, but he was restrained by a sharp look from his wife: what, didn't two customers have the right to settle an argument in their place? He contented himself by taking up his stand in front of the chimney, for he was afraid that one or both of them might fall into the fire. Souvarine, with apparent calm, had rolled a cigarette, but he had forgotten to light it. Catherine was still standing motionless against the wall; only her hands were moving—they had unconsciously risen to her waist and were mechanically twisting and tearing at the material of her dress. All her energy was concentrated in an effort not to cry out, not to kill one of them by screaming out her preference for the other—though she was so bewildered that she was not even sure which one she did prefer.

Chaval was soon exhausted, drenched in sweat, hitting out at random. Etienne, despite his anger, was continuing to protect himself and parried almost every blow, though a few of them managed to graze him. One of his ears was split, and a fingernail had dug into his neck; there was such smarting pain that he in turn began to swear, and launched one of his terrible straight jabs. Once again Chaval saved his chest by leaping aside, but he had bent down in doing so and the blow landed on his face, smashing his nose and getting an eye. Blood immediately began to stream from his nostrils, his eye swelled and became blue and puffed. Blinded by the red flood, stunned by the ringing in his head, the poor wretch kept beating the air wildly until one of Etienne's blows finally struck his chest and finished him off. There was a loud crash, and he fell on his back like a heavy sack of plaster being unloaded.

Etienne waited.

"Get up. If you'd like some more, we can begin all over again."

After lying on the floor for a few dazed seconds without answering, Chaval began to stir about and move his arms and legs. He drew himself up with difficulty and remained

crouched on his knees for a moment, his hand in his pocket
and occupied with something they could not see. Then, when
he was on his feet, he again rushed at Etienne, his throat
swelling with a savage cry.

But Catherine had seen, and in spite of herself a loud cry
escaped from deep within her, astonishing her by its acknowl-
edgment of a preference she herself had been unaware of.

"Watch out!—he's got his knife!"

Etienne had hardly had enough time to parry the first blow
with his arm. His woolen sweater was cut by the thick blade,
which was one of those fastened to a boxwood handle by a
brass ferrule. But he had already seized Chaval's wrist, and a
terrible struggle began—Etienne knowing he was lost if he let
go, the other trying to break loose and strike. Little by little
the knife was lowered, their stiff arms grew tired, and twice
Etienne felt the icy touch of the steel against his skin:
making a supreme effort, he was able to crush Chaval's wrist
in such a grip that the knife dropped from his open hand.
They both flung themselves on the floor; it was Etienne who
picked the knife up and brandished it in his turn. He was
holding Chaval pinned under his knee and threatening to slit
his throat.

"You goddamn traitor, now you're going to get it!"

A hideous voice was deafening him, rising from his guts,
beating hammer blows in his head—a sudden murderous
madness, a need to taste blood. He had never before been so
shaken by the fit—and yet he was not even drunk. And he
fought against this hereditary evil with the same hopeless
shuddering a maddened lover feels, struggling on the brink of
rape. He was finally able to control himself, and he threw the
knife behind him, mumbling hoarsely:

"Get up and get out!"

This time Rasseneur had rushed forward, being careful
however not to get between them lest he intercept a blow.
He did not want anybody to be murdered in his place, and he
was so angry that his wife, bolt upright behind her counter,
pointed out that he was always yelling before there was any
need. Souvarine, who had almost been hit in the leg with the
knife, finally lit his cigarette. Was it all over, then? Catherine
continued to stare at the two men, stupefied at finding them
both still alive.

"Get out!" Etienne repeated. "Get out or I'll kill you!"

Chaval rose to his feet and used the back of his hand to
wipe away the blood that kept flowing from his nose; his jaw
smeared with red, his eye swollen, he dragged himself away,
raging at his defeat. Catherine automatically began to follow

him, but at this he drew himself up and his hatred exploded in a flood of filthy abuse.

"Oh no! oh no!—since he's the one you want, go sleep with him, you dirty slut! And if you want to stay alive, don't you dare come back to my place again!"

He slammed the door violently. A heavy silence settled on the warm room, where the low hiss of the coal was all that could be heard. The overturned chair was still on the floor, and drops of blood were soaking into the sand on the tiles.

4

When they left Rasseneur's Etienne and Catherine walked along in silence. The thaw was beginning, a slow, cold thaw that dirtied the snow without melting it. In the livid sky high above, there were hints of a full moon behind the large clouds—those dark tatters that were being angrily tossed about by a stormy wind—but on the ground not so much as a breath was stirring, and the only sound was the dripping from the roofs, from which white bundles were tumbling down with soft thuds.

Etienne was embarrassed by this woman who had been handed over to him, and in his awkwardness he could find nothing to say. It seemed absurd to think of taking her to Réquillart with him and hiding her there. He had wanted to take her back to the village, to her parents' home, but she had refused in terror: no, no, anything rather than become a burden to them after having so unfeelingly deserted them! And neither of them said another word. They trudged along aimlessly, on roads that were turning into rivers of mud. At first they had gone down toward Le Voreux; then they turned to the right and walked between the slag heap and the canal.

"But you've got to sleep somewhere," he finally said. "If I only had a room, I'd gladly take you there. . . ."

But a strange access of timidity checked him. He thought of their past, of their intense desire for each other, and of the delicacy and shame that had kept them from becoming lovers. Was it because he still wanted her that he felt so troubled, that his heart was slowly warming with new desire? Instead of bitterness at the memory of the slaps she had given him at Gaston-Marie, he now felt excitement. He was surprised, and suddenly the idea of taking her to Réquillart seemed a natural one—an easy thing to do.

"Come on now, make up your mind. Where do you want me to take you? . . . Do you really hate me so much that you don't want to come with me?"

She was following him slowly, hindered by her sabots that kept slipping in the ruts, and without raising her head she murmured:

"My God, I have enough trouble as it is—don't make any more for me! What good would it be to do what you want, now that I have a lover and you yourself have a woman?"

She was referring to Mouquette. She believed the rumors she had been hearing during the past two weeks and assumed he was living with her; when he swore it wasn't true she shook her head, remembering the evening she had seen them kissing each other passionately.

He stopped and said in a low voice:

"This is all such a shame, isn't it? We'd have gotten along so well together!"

A slight tremor ran through her and she replied:

"Oh, don't feel sorry about it, you're not losing much. If you only knew it, I'm nothing but skin and bones—hardly bigger than a pat of butter, and so messed up inside that I'll never get to be a real woman!"

She spoke freely, accusing herself of her long-delayed puberty as though it were her own fault. She was demeaned by it, felt herself classed with the children despite the fact that she had a lover. After all, there is some excuse for it when you can at least have a baby.

"You poor little thing," murmured Etienne, overwhelmed with pity.

They were at the foot of the slag heap, hidden in the shadow of its enormous mass. An inky cloud was just passing across the moon; they could no longer see each other's faces, their breaths mingled, their lips sought the kiss they had so long and so ardently desired. But suddenly the moon reappeared, and they saw high above them, on the rocks bathed in white light, the erect figure of the Voreux sentinel. And without ever having finally kissed, they were separated by a sense of modesty—their old modesty made up of anger, a vague repugnance, and much affection. They began to trudge on again, ankle-deep in slush.

"Then you've made up your mind? You won't come with me?" asked Etienne.

"No," she answered. "You after Chaval, and then after

you somebody else ... No, the whole thing disgusts me, and since I don't get any pleasure out of it, what's the use?"

They fell silent again and walked on a little way without exchanging a word.

"Do you at least know where you're going?" he finally said. "I can't leave you outside on such a night."

She replied simply:

"I'm going home. Chaval is my man, and it wouldn't be right for me to sleep anywhere else."

"But he'll beat you!"

There was another silence. She had shrugged her shoulders in resignation. He would beat her, and when he was tired of beating her he would stop: wasn't that better than roaming the roads like a whore? Besides, she was getting used to being beaten; for consolation she told herself that eight out of ten girls were no better off than she was. If her lover decided to marry her some day, it would even be very nice of him.

Etienne and Catherine had mechanically headed toward Montsou, and the closer they got the longer their silences became. It was as if they had already separated. It hurt him to see her go back to Chaval, but he could think of nothing to say to make her change her mind. He was heartsick over it, but he could offer her nothing but a life of misery and flight, and a hopeless future if a soldier's bullet smashed his head. Maybe it was true—maybe it was better to suffer from what one knew rather than take the risk of exposing oneself to new suffering. And so, head bowed, he led her back to her lover, not even protesting when she stopped him on the highway near Les Chantiers, about twenty yards from Piquette's place, and said:

"Don't come any further. If he sees you, there'll only be more trouble."

The church clock was striking eleven; the bar was closed, but light was shining through the shutters.

"Good-bye," she whispered.

She had given him her hand; he was holding it, and she had to free it slowly, painfully, in order to leave him. Without turning around, she unlatched the side door and went in. He made no move to leave; he stood there, his eyes fixed on the house, worried about what was happening inside. He listened intently, terrified lest he hear the shrieks of a woman being beaten. But the house remained black and silent, except for a light that appeared at a second-floor window, and when the window opened and he recognized the thin shadow leaning out toward the road, he stepped forward.

Then, in a voice that was barely a whisper, Catherine said:

"He hasn't come back. I'm going to bed. . . . Please go away, please!"

Etienne went. The thaw was spreading—water was streaming from the roofs and sweating from the walls, the fences, and all the formless masses of this industrial suburb buried in the night. Exhausted and sick at heart, desiring only to disappear into the earth and vanish there forever, he headed first for Réquillart. Then his mind turned to Le Voreux again; he thought about the Belgian workers who were supposed to go down the next day, and about his comrades in the village who were exasperated by the soldiers and determined not to permit foreigners in their mine. And again he walked along the canal and through the puddles of melted snow.

Just as he was nearing the slag heap once more, the moon shone out bright and clear. He raised his eyes and looked at the sky, where the clouds were stampeding along under the lash of the wind on high; but now the clouds were becoming whiter, breaking up, getting thinner, and, muddily transparent, they passed across the face of the moon so swiftly that it remained veiled only for moments before reappearing in all its brightness.

His eyes filled with this pure light, Etienne was lowering his head when something at the top of the slag heap caught his attention. The sentinel, stiff with cold, was walking twenty-five paces toward Marchiennes and then turning back again toward Montsou. His bayonet was a white gleam shining above the black silhouette that was so clearly outlined against the pale sky. But what intrigued Etienne was that behind the shack in which Old Bonnemort used to take shelter on stormy nights he could see a moving shadow, a tense and crouching beast that he immediately recognized as Jeanlin by his weasel-like spine, long and supple. The sentinel could not see Jeanlin, and Etienne was sure that the thieving little boy was about to pull some trick, for he was as angry at the soldiers as ever, always asking when they would finally be rid of those murderers who had been sent to kill people with their rifles.

For a moment Etienne was on the verge of calling out to him to keep him from doing anything foolish. The moon had clouded over, and he had seen Jeanlin tense up, ready to spring; but the moon reappeared and the boy was still crouched there. Each time the sentinel would walk as far as the shack, then turn his back and walk the other way. Suddenly, just as another cloud made everything dark again, Jeanlin sprang onto the soldier's back with the great leap of a wildcat, clung there by his claws, then plunged his open knife into the man's throat. The soldier's horsehair collar was hard to pierce, and Jeanlin had to bear down with both hands, using all the weight of his body. He had often slit the throats of hens he had come on behind some farmhouse. It all happened so quickly that there was only a stifled cry in the night and the sound of a rifle clattering to the ground. The moon was already shining brightly again.

Frozen to the spot with amazement, Etienne continued to stare, the cry he had been about to give strangled before it reached his lips. Above him the slag heap was now bare—no silhouette was outlined against the wildly fleeing clouds. He ran up to the top of the heap and found Jeanlin squatting on all fours alongside the corpse, which lay on its back, arms outspread. In the clear moonlight the gray overcoat and the red trousers stood out starkly against the white snow. The knife was buried to the hilt in the man's throat, and not a drop of blood had flowed.

In a mad fury Etienne struck the boy and knocked him down beside the dead man.

"Why did you do that?" he stammered wildly.

Jeanlin drew himself up and dragged along on his hands, his thin back in a feline arch; his large ears, green eyes, and jutting jaw were quivering and glowing in the aftermath of his evil deed.

"My God, what made you do it?"

"I don't know, I just wanted to."

And he stuck to this answer. He had "wanted to" for the past three days. The idea had tormented him—he had thought about it so much that his head ached, there, right behind the ears. Why should they care about these rotten soldiers who had only come here to make trouble for the miners right on their very doorsteps? From those wild speeches in the forest, those cries of havoc and death that had resounded from mine to mine, some five or six words had penetrated, and he kept repeating them—a child playing at revolution. And that was all he knew—nobody had urged him on, it was his own idea, it had come to him just the way the desire to steal onions from a field sometimes came to him.

Horrified by this deadly flowering of crime in the mind of such a child, Etienne kicked him aside as if he were an animal. Every time the moon shone out, he looked fearfully toward the mine, terrified lest the guards posted at Le Voreux had heard the sentinel's muffled cry. But nothing had stirred, and he bent down, he felt the hands that were slowly turning cold, he put his ear to the heart that was no longer beating under the coat. Nothing could be seen of the knife but its bone handle, on which was engraved in black letters the simple sentimental message: Love.

His eyes went from the throat to the face. Suddenly he recognized the little soldier: it was Jules, the recruit with whom he had spoken one morning. And the sight of this gentle, freckled, fair face filled him with a great pity. The blue eyes were looking at the sky with the same wide stare with which he had searched the horizon for his home town. Where was this Plogoff that had appeared to him in a blaze of sunlight? Far, far away, over there. On this blustery night the sea was roaring in the distance, and the wind passing above them now had perhaps passed over that distant moorland. Two women, the mother and the sister, were standing there, clutching their billowing kerchiefs, they too searching the horizon—as if they might be able to see what their boy was doing at this moment, beyond the miles that separated them. They would wait for him forever now. What a terrible thing it was for poor devils to kill each other for the sake of the rich!

But the corpse would have to be disposed of. At first Etienne thought of throwing it into the canal, but the certitude that it would be found there made him decide against this. His anxiety increased as the minutes raced by. What should he do? He had a sudden inspiration: if he could carry the body to Réquillart, he could make it disappear forever.

"Come over here," he said to Jeanlin.

The boy was suspicious.

"No, you want to beat me. And besides, I've got things to do. Good-bye."

And it was true—he had made an appointment to meet Bébert and Lydie at a hiding place, a hole they had fixed up under the timber piles at Le Voreux. It was all a big scheme to sleep away from home, so they could be on the spot if the Belgians were going to be stoned when they went down in the morning.

"Listen," Etienne repeated, "come over here or I'll call the soldiers and they'll cut off your head."

And while Jeanlin was making up his mind, Etienne rolled up his handkerchief and wound it tightly around the soldier's neck, not withdrawing the knife because it was keeping the blood from flowing. The snow was melting, and the ground showed neither the red stain of blood nor any sign of a struggle.

"Take his legs."

Jeanlin took his legs and Etienne grabbed his shoulders and

slung the rifle behind his back; then the two of them went slowly down the slag heap, trying not to set any rocks rolling. Fortunately the moon was veiled, but as they hurried along beside the canal it came out again brightly: it was a miracle that they were not seen by the guards. They went quickly, silently, hindered by the swaying of the body and obliged to set it down every hundred yards. At the corner of the lane leading to Réquillart they heard a noise and their blood froze; they barely had time to hide behind a wall to escape a patrol. Farther on, they ran into a man, but he was drunk and went off swearing at them. When they finally arrived at the old mine they were drenched in sweat and so unnerved that their teeth were chattering.

Etienne had foreseen that it would not be easy to get the soldier down the ladder well. It was a horrible job. First Jeanlin, who had remained on top, had to pass the corpse down to Etienne, who, hanging from the bushes, accompanied it down to help it past the first two platforms, where some of the ladder rungs were broken. Then at each succeeding ladder he had to follow the same procedure—go down first, then catch the body in his arms; and at each of the thirty ladders, for more than six hundred feet, he felt that body continually drop down on him, the rifle scraping against his back. He had not wanted the boy to run ahead and get his avariciously guarded candle end, for what was the point? —a candle would only be a nuisance in this narrow passageway. However, when they arrived at the loading station, panting, he did send him for it and sat down near the corpse to wait in the darkness with wildly pounding heart.

As soon as Jeanlin came back with the light Etienne questioned him, for the boy had explored every part of these old works, even the passageways too narrow for grown men to get through. They set off again, dragging the corpse for more than half a mile through a labyrinth of ruined galleries. Finally the roof became so low that they found themselves on their knees, under crumbling rock held up by half-rotten timbers. The area was like a long box, and they laid the little soldier into it as though into a coffin; they set the rifle alongside him, then kicked the rotted timbers to make them collapse, even at the risk of being trapped there themselves. The rock cracked immediately, and they had barely enough time to crawl away on all fours. When Etienne turned around again, gripped by a desire to see, the roof was still crumbling, slowly crushing the body under its enormous weight. And then there was nothing, nothing but the heavy mass of the earth.

Jeanlin, finding himself back home in his bandit's hideout, stretched out on the hay and mumbled, in complete exhaustion:

"To hell with it! The brats will have to wait for me—I'm going to take a snooze."

Etienne had blown out the remaining bit of candle. He too was exhausted, but not sleepy; painful, nightmarish thoughts were beating like hammers inside his head. One of them was more persistent than the others, more tormenting and draining—a question to which he had no answer: why had he not killed Chaval when he had had him under his knife, and why had this child just slit the throat of a soldier whose name he did not even know? The problem made him question his revolutionary beliefs about the courage to kill, the right to kill. Was it that he was a coward? There in the hay the boy had begun to snore like a drunken man, as if he were sleeping off the intoxication of his murder and Etienne was repelled and irritated, unable to bear the idea of knowing Jeanlin was there, of hearing him. Suddenly he shuddered— the breath of fear had passed over his face. There was a faint rustle, a sob that seemed to have risen from the bowels of the earth. The image of the little soldier lying there under the rocks with his rifle sent a shiver down his spine and made his hair stand on end. It was idiotic, but the whole mine was filled with voices; he had to relight the candle, and he did not calm down until its pale light proved the emptiness of the galleries.

For the next quarter of an hour he kept thinking, his mind still obsessed with the same problem, his eyes fixed on the burning wick. Then there was a splutter, the wick was extinguished, and everything returned to darkness. He began to tremble again, and he was on the verge of hitting Jeanlin to make him stop his loud snoring. The boy's presence was so unbearable, his own need for fresh air so pressing, that he ran off, hurrying through the galleries and up the ladder well as though he could hear a ghost panting at his heels.

Up above, among the ruins of Réquillart, Etienne could finally breathe freely. Since he did not have the courage to kill, it was he who should die; and this idea of death, which had stirred within him before, was reborn, his mind grasping at it like a last hope. To die boldly, to die for the revolution— that would end everything, would square all his accounts, both good and bad, and keep him from thinking anymore. If his comrades attacked the Belgians, he would be in the first rank, and there would be a good chance of being shot. It was with determined steps that he returned to circle around Le

Voreux. The clock was striking two, and there was a loud sound of voices from the foremen's room, which was being used by the soldiers guarding the mine. The disappearance of the sentinel had thrown the post into a turmoil; the men had awakened the captain, and after a careful examination of the area it was decided that the soldier must have deserted. Listening in the darkness, Etienne remembered the Republican captain of whom the little soldier had spoken. Was it not possible to get him to side with the people?—the troops would mutiny, and that could be the signal for the massacre of the bourgeois. He was carried away by a new dream, and he no longer thought of dying; he stood there for hours, his feet in the mud, his shoulders soaked by the drizzle from the thaw, feverish with the hope that victory might still be possible.

He waited for the Belgians until five o'clock, then realized that the Company had been clever enough to have them sleep at Le Voreux. The descent was beginning, and the few strikers from Village 240 who had been posted as lookouts were unsure as to whether or not to warn their comrades. It was Etienne who alerted them to the Company's trick, and they raced off, leaving him waiting behind the slag heap on the towpath. Six o'clock was striking and the ashen sky was growing paler, lightening into a reddish dawn, when the Abbé Ranvier appeared, his cassock raised over his thin legs. He went to say an early Mass in the chapel of a convent on the other side of the mine every Monday.

"Good morning, my friend," he said in a loud voice, after his burning eyes had taken the young man in.

But Etienne did not answer. In the distance he had just seen a woman pass between the trestles of Le Voreux, and thinking he recognized Catherine, he anxiously began to run toward her.

Catherine had been trudging along the thawing roads since midnight. Chaval, coming home and finding her in bed, had immediately set her on her feet with a slap. He had roared at her, shouting that she had better leave by the door if she didn't want to leave by the window; and weeping, only half-dressed, her legs bruised by kicks, she was forced downstairs and pushed outside with a final blow. Dazed by this brutal rupture, she had sat on a milestone and looked at the house, waiting for him to call her back; he couldn't mean it—surely he was watching and would tell her to come back upstairs when he saw her shivering like this, abandoned, with nobody to turn to.

After two hours, half-dead with cold from sitting still like

a dog that had been thrown into the street, she came to a
decision. She left Montsou, then came back again, but she
did not dare either to call out from below or to knock at the
door. Finally she went off along the cobblestones of the
main road with the idea of going to her parents' house in the
village. But when she got there she was overwhelmed by such
shame that she ran back through the gardens to avoid being
seen and recognized, though everybody behind the closed
shutters was sunk in heavy sleep. And from then on she
wandered about, terrified by the slightest sound, trembling
lest she be picked up, like some tramp, and taken to that
Marchiennes brothel, the threat of which had been haunting
her like a nightmare for months. Twice she drew near Le
Voreux, but she was frightened by the loud voices of the
guards and ran away breathlessly, looking back to see if she
was being followed. Though the path near Réquillart was
always filled with drunks, she nevertheless returned there in
the vague hope of finding the man she had rejected only a
few hours earlier.

Chaval was to go down that morning, and this was what
brought Catherine back to the mine even though she knew it
was pointless to talk to him: it was all over between them.
There was no longer any work at Jean-Bart, and he had
sworn to strangle her if she went back to Le Voreux, where
he feared her presence might compromise him. What was she
to do?—go somewhere else, die of hunger, yield under the
blows of every passing man? She kept dragging herself along,
stumbling in the ruts, her legs buckling, mud-splattered to her
waist. The thaw was now flowing down the roads in rivers of
mud, and she sank into it as she kept walking, walking, not
even daring to look for a stone to sit on.

Day broke. Catherine had just recognized Chaval's back
cautiously disappearing around the slag heap when she saw
Lydie and Bébert poking their noses out of their hiding
place under the timbers. They had spent the night there, on
the watch, not daring to go home because Jeanlin had ordered them to wait for him; and while the latter was sleeping
off his murderous drunk at Réquillart, the two children had
tried to keep warm in each other's arms. The wind whistled
between the poles of chestnut and oak, and they huddled
together as if they were in some abandoned woodcutter's
hut. Lydie no more dared voice her suffering at being beaten
like a little wife than Bébert had the courage to complain of
cheeks that swelled under the captain's blows; but Jeanlin
had taken too much advantage of them, risking their necks in
mad escapades and then refusing them their share of the

loot, and their hearts rose in revolt; they had ended by embracing each other despite his prohibition, ready to accept the blow from the invisible with which he had threatened them. The blow never came, and with no thought of doing anything else, they continued to kiss each other gently, putting into the caress all the passion they had so long fought against, all their pain and tenderness. And so they had kept each other warm all night long, happier in this forsaken spot than they could ever remember being—happier even than on Saint-Barbe's day, when they had fritters to eat and wine to drink.

A sudden bugle blast made Catherine start. Looking up, she saw the guards at Le Voreux grab their rifles. Etienne was running up, Bébert and Lydie had jumped out of their hiding place, and beyond, in the growing daylight, a band of men and women were coming down from the village, gesticulating in wild anger.

5

All entrances to Le Voreux had just been closed, and the sixty soldiers, their rifles at parade rest, were barring the only door left open—the one that led by a narrow staircase to the landing level onto which opened the foremen's room and the dressing shed. To protect his men from an attack from the rear, the captain had lined them up against the brick wall in a double rank.

At first the band of miners that had come down from the village kept their distance. There were no more than thirty of them, and they were discussing the situation in anger and confusion.

La Maheude, unkempt under a hastily knotted kerchief, and with Estelle sleeping in her arms, had been the first to arrive, and she kept repeating in an impassioned voice:

"Don't let anybody in or out! We've got to nab them all inside!"

While Maheu was agreeing with her, Old Mouque arrived from Réquillart. They tried to keep him from going in, but he put up a struggle, insisting that his horses had to have their hay no matter what, and that they didn't give a damn about the revolution. Besides, there was a dead horse down there, and they were waiting for him so they could bring him up. Etienne extricated the old stableman from the crowd, and the soldiers permitted him to proceed to the shaft. A quarter of an hour later, as the slowly swelling band of strikers was becoming menacing, a large door opened on ground level and some men appeared; they dragged out the dead animal—a pitiful bundle still caught up in the rope net—and abandoned it among the puddles of melting snow. Everybody was so paralyzed by the sight that no attempt was made to stop the men from returning inside and barricading the door again. They had all recognized the horse by his head, bent and stiffened against his flank. Whispers ran through the crowd.

"It's Trompette, isn't it? It's Trompette."

It was indeed Trompette. Never since the day he had gone down had he been able to adjust to life underground. He remained listless and unwilling to work, as if tortured by regret for the lost light of day. Bataille, the senior horse in the mine, had tried to bestow on him a little of the resignation he himself had acquired after ten years at the bottom by brushing affectionately against his sides and nipping at his neck, but it was in vain. The caresses only increased his melancholy, and his flesh trembled under the confidences of this comrade grown old in the darkness; and each time they would meet and snort at each other, they would both seem to be lamenting, the older because he could no longer remember and the younger because he could still not forget. In neighboring stalls in the stable they would stand with lowered heads, nuzzle each other's noses, and exchange their never-ending dream of daylight—their visions of green grass, white roads, and luminous yellows stretching into infinity. Then when Trompette, drenched in sweat, had lain dying on his bed of straw, Bataille had begun to sniff at him hopelessly, with short snorts like sobs. He felt him grow cold; the mine was claiming his last joy, this friend who had fallen from above, still redolent of good smells that reminded him of his own youth in the open air. And when he had seen that his friend was no longer moving he had whinnied in terror and broken his tether.

Mouque had been warning the chief foreman for the past week, but it was hardly the time for anybody to be worrying about a sick horse! These gentlemen did not at all like the idea of shifting the horses from place to place, but now they would have to let him be brought up. The night before, Mouque and two other men had spent an hour tying Trompette up. To get the body to the shaft they harnessed Bataille. Slowly the old horse pulled and dragged his dead comrade through a gallery so narrow he had to jerk his way forward at the risk of skinning Trompette, and he was troubled by this—he kept swinging his head and listening to the long brushing sound made by the mass of flesh on its way to the tanner's. At the loading level, after he had been unharnessed, he mournfully watched the preparations for the ascent—the body pushed onto the boards over the sump, the net attached to the bottom of a cage. Finally the loaders rang the "meat call"; he raised his head to watch his friend go, slowly at first, then suddenly swallowed by the shadows, flown off forever up that dark hole. And he stood there with his neck stretched upward, his uncertain animal memory perhaps recalling some of the things up above. But it was all over; his comrade would never see anything again, and when his time came to ascend the shaft he too would be tied up in the same kind of pitiful bundle. His legs began to tremble, and the fresh air blowing from far-off fields choked him; he seemed to be drunk as he plodded heavily back to the stable.

In the yard the miners were standing gloomily around Trompette's body. A woman said in a low voice:

"At least a man only goes down if he wants to."

But another wave of strikers was coming from the village. At their head, followed by La Levaque and Bouteloup, marched Levaque, who was shouting:

"Death to the Belgians! We don't want any foreigners here! Death! Death!"

They were all rushing forward, and Etienne had to stop them. He had approached the captain—a tall, slim young man of no more than twenty-eight, with an expression of desperate resoluteness on his face—and was trying to explain the situation to him and win him over, watching to see the effect of his words. Why risk a pointless massacre?—wasn't justice on the side of the miners? They were all brothers, they should be able to get along together. At the word "republic" the captain had made a nervous gesture. Maintaining his military stiffness, he said brusquely:

"Stand back! Don't force me to do my duty!"

Three times Etienne started all over again. Behind him the men were grumbling. There was a rumor that Monsieur Hennebeau was at the mine, and there was talk of sending him down by a rope tied around his neck to see if he would hack his coal out himself. But the rumor was false; only Négrel and Dansaert were there, and both of them appeared for a moment at a landing-room window: the chief foreman, somewhat abashed since his escapade with La Pierronne, was hanging back a bit, but the engineer let his bright little eyes roam boldly over the crowd and smiled with the

usual mocking contempt he felt for both men and things.
Hoots went up, and the two men disappeared from view. In
their place only the blond face of Souvarine, who happened
to be on duty then, could be seen; since the beginning of the
strike he had not left his engine for even a single day, and he
was always silent now, increasingly absorbed by a fixed idea,
the steely reflection of which seemed to shine from the
depths of his pale eyes.

"Stand back!" the captain repeated loudly. "I'm not interested in what you have to say. I have orders to guard the
mine and guard it I will. . . . And don't crowd in on my men
or I'll have to take steps to make you draw back."

Although his voice was firm, the sight of the rising flood of
miners was making him increasingly pale and anxious. He
was supposed to be relieved at noon; but fearing he would
not be able to hold out till then, he had just sent one of the
mine boys to Montsou to ask for reinforcements.

His statement had been greeted with angry shouts.

"Death to the foreigners! Death to the Belgians! . . . We're
the ones who live here, and we'll decide what happens here!"

Etienne stepped back in despair. It was the end—there was
nothing left to do but fight and die. He stopped trying to
restrain his comrades, and the crowd surged up to the little
band of soldiers. There were almost four hundred of them—
the neighboring villages were emptying out and everybody
was coming on the run. They were all shrieking out the same
cry, and Maheu and Levaque were shouting furiously to the
soldiers:

"Get out of here! We have nothing against you, get out of
here!"

"This is none of your business," took up La Maheude; "let
us handle it our own way."

And behind her La Levaque added, more violently:

"Do we have to tear you apart to get through? We're
telling you to get the hell out of here!"

Even the shrill voice of Lydie, who with Bébert had
wormed into the thick of it, could be heard saying nastily:

"Have you ever seen such a clumsy bunch of soldiers in
your life?"

Catherine was standing a few feet away, watching and
listening, completely bemused by this new violence into the
midst of which unrelenting fate had plunged her. Was she not
suffering enough already? What sin had she committed to be
given no respite from trouble? Why, even as late as last night
she hadn't been able to understand the anger stirred up by
the strike—she thought that when you had your fair share of

blows it was silly to go looking for more—and yet now her heart was filled with a need to hate; she remembered the things Etienne used to say during those long evenings, and she tried to hear what he was saying to the soldiers now. He was treating them like comrades, reminding them that they too came from the people, and that they should stand with the people against those who would exploit their misery.

Just then there was a commotion in the crowd and an old woman erupted out of it. It was La Brûlé, whose exposed neck and arms were terrifying in their scrawniness; she was running at such a pace that strands of her gray hair were blowing into her eyes and blinding her.

"Ah, by God, I'm here with you at last!" she muttered, gasping for breath. "That traitor Pierron had me locked in the cellar!"

And without further ado she turned on the soldiers, her black mouth vomiting abuse.

"You dirty scum! You slimy toads! You lick the boots of your superiors, but when it comes to standing up against the poor you've got courage enough!"

The others joined their voices to hers in a salvo of insults. A few of them were still shouting "Long live the soldiers! Throw the officer down the shaft!" but soon there was only one roar: "Down with the red pants!" And these soldiers who had listened in silence, with unmoved and impassive faces, to appeals to fraternity and to friendly attempts to win them over, remained equally impassive under this hail of obscenity. Behind them the captain had drawn his sword; and since the crowd was coming closer, threatening to crush them against the wall, he ordered his men to raise their bayonets. They obeyed, and a double row of sharp steel was suddenly pointed at the breasts of the strikers.

"Oh, the bastards!" shrieked La Brûlé, falling back.

But they were already moving forward again, wildly contemptuous of death. The women surged ahead, La Maheude and La Levaque clamoring:

"Kill us then, kill us! We want our rights."

At the risk of cutting himself, Levaque had bunched three bayonets in his bare hands and was shaking them and pulling them toward him in an attempt to tear them loose; his strength increased tenfold by anger, he stood there twisting them while Bouteloup, sorry to have followed his lead, stood a little way off and watched him calmly.

"Come on and try it," Maheu kept repeating. "Come on, if you've got the guts!"

And he opened his jacket, pulled aside his shirt, and

exposed his naked chest, the hairy flesh tattooed by coal. Terrible in his insolence and his challenge, he pushed up against the steel points and forced them to be drawn back. One of the bayonets had pricked his breast, and this so maddened him with rage that he tried to force it in more deeply, so he could hear his ribs crack.

"Cowards, you don't dare! . . . There are ten thousand more behind us. Yes, you can kill us, but then there'll be ten thousand more to kill."

The soldiers' situation was becoming critical, for they had received strict orders not to use their arms except as a last resort. But how were they to keep these madmen from spitting themselves on the steel? And in addition to everything else, there was no more room—they were right up against the wall and unable to move back another step. The little troop, the handful of men facing the mounting tide of miners, was nevertheless holding fast and coolly executing the captain's clipped orders. The latter, his eyes bright and his lips nervously drawn, was afraid of only one thing—that his men might lose their temper in the face of all the abuse. A young sergeant, a tall thin fellow with a scanty bristling moustache, was already blinking his eyes in a disturbing way. Next to him a service-striped veteran, his skin tanned by twenty campaigns, had paled on seeing his bayonet twisted like a straw. Another—a recruit no doubt—still smelling of the fields, grew red every time he heard himself called scum and toad. And there was no end to the violence of clenched fists and foul words, of accusations and threats whipping across their cheeks. It required all the force of their orders to keep them motionless, their faces frozen in the sad, lofty silence of military discipline.

A clash was beginning to seem inevitable when the white-haired foreman Richomme appeared from behind the soldiers, his friendly policeman's manner swept away by an overwhelming emotion. He shouted out:

"For God's sake, this is stupid! This kind of idiocy can't go on."

And he threw himself between the bayonets and the miners.

"Friends, listen to me. . . . You know that I was a worker for a long time and that I've never stopped being one of you. Well, by God I promise you that if the bosses don't give you what's fair, I'll tell them off myself! . . . But this is going too far—you're not doing yourselves any good by shouting filth at these good fellows and trying to get your guts torn out."

They were listening, they were hesitating. Unfortunately

the sharp profile of Little Négrel reappeared at the upper window. He was probably afraid of being accused of sending a foreman instead of risking his own neck, and he tried to speak; but his voice was lost in such a tumult that he could only shrug his shoulders and once more leave the window. From then on it was useless for Richomme to beg them in his own name, or to insist that the matter could be settled in a peaceful manner among comrades: they pushed him to one side, they were suspicious of him. But he stubbornly insisted on remaining among them.

"By God, they may break my skull as well as yours, but I won't leave you as long as you keep being so damn foolish!"

Etienne, whom he was begging to help make them listen to reason, shrugged helplessly. It was too late, there were now more than five hundred people there—and not merely the fanatics who had come running to drive out the Belgians, but the rubbernecks and the clowns, who were finding the battle quite amusing. In the middle of a group some way back, Zacharie and Philomène were watching as if it were a show, so unconcerned that they had even brought along their two children, Achille and Désirée. A new stream was pouring in from Réquillart, in the midst of which were Mouque and Mouquette: Mouquet immediately began to guffaw and went over to pound his friend Zacharie on the back, while Mouquette, feverish with excitement, ran up to the front ranks of the zealots.

The captain kept looking toward the road from Montsou. There was still no sign of the requested reinforcements; his sixty men would not be able to hold out much longer.

Finally, as a way of impressing the crowd, he ordered his men to load their rifles in full view of everybody. The soldiers executed his order, but the excitement only increased—as did the boasting and the mocking shouts.

"Look, the loafers are getting ready for target practice," sniggered La Brûlé, La Levaque, and the other women.

La Maheude, clutching to her breast the little body of Estelle, who had awakened and was crying, went so close that the sergeant asked her what she was doing there with that poor little brat.

"What the hell do you care?" she answered. "Shoot us if you dare!"

The men nodded contemptuously. Not one of them believed the soldiers would fire on them.

"There aren't any balls in their cartridges," said Levaque.

"What are we, Cossacks?" yelled Maheu. "They won't fire on Frenchmen, for God's sake!"

Some of the others were shouting that they hadn't been afraid of lead when they had fought in the Crimean campaign, and all of them kept flinging themselves at the rifles. If there had been a volley at that moment the whole crowd would have been cut down.

Up front now, Mouquette was choking with rage at the idea that the soldiers were ready to riddle women's hides. She had already spat out every obscenity she knew, she could find nothing else vile enough to say, when suddenly—having only this final, mortal insult to launch at the heads of the soldiers— she showed her ass. Using both hands, she pulled up her skirts and stuck out her behind, emphasizing its enormous rotundity.

"There, this is for you!—and at that it's too clean for such a bunch of dirty bastards!"

She bent, she twisted, she turned from side to side so each of them would get a fair share, and at each thrust she cried out:

"This one's for the officer! This one's for the sergeant! And this one's for the troops!"

A storm of laughter went up; Bébert and Lydie were doubled over, and even Etienne, despite his dark apprehensions, applauded this insulting nudity. Now all of them, the clowns as well as the diehards, were hooting the soldiers, as if they had seen them being splattered with filth—only Catherine, standing a little to one side on some old timbers, remained silent, choking on a raging hatred whose heat she felt rising within her.

The crowd began to shove. To calm his men's tension, the captain decided to take some prisoners. Mouquette leaped back and escaped in one bound between the legs of her friends, but three miners, Levaque and two others, were plucked from among the most violent and imprisoned in the foremen's roon.

Négrel and Dansaert, from up above, were calling to the captain to join them inside. He refused, for he was convinced that these buildings, with their lockless doors, would be taken by assault and that he would be subjected to the shame of being disarmed. His little detachment was already grumbling impatiently—they could not possibly run before these sabot-clad wretches. Once again the sixty men, their backs to the wall and their rifles loaded, faced the mob.

At first the strikers, amazed by this show of force, retreated in deep silence. Then a cry went up, demanding the prisoners and insisting they be freed immediately. There were rumors going around that they were being slaughtered inside, and without any plans for concerted action, swept by the same impulse and the same thirst for revenge, everybody ran to the nearby pile of bricks—those bricks made of the clay from the marly soil and then fired on the spot. The children carried them one by one, the women filled their skirts with them. Soon everyone had a pile of ammunition at his feet and the battle of the bricks began.

La Brûlé was the first to let fly, breaking the bricks over her bony knee and simultaneously launching the two pieces, one with her left hand and one with her right. La Levaque—so heavy and flabby that she had to get up close to hit anything—almost dislocated her shoulders, though Bouteloup kept pulling her back and begging her to leave now that her husband was out of it. All the women were urging each other on; Mouquette, tired of bloodying herself by trying to break the bricks over her fat thighs, was tossing them unbroken, and even the children were part of the firing line, with Bébert showing Lydie how to throw underhand. There was a storm of enormous hailstones landing with heavy thuds. And suddenly there was Catherine among all these furies, her fists in the air, she too brandishing pieces of brick and hurling them with all the force in her scrawny arms. She could not have said why, but she was suffocating, bursting with a need to hurt somebody. Would it never be finished, this terrible life of misery? She had had enough of it, of being beaten and chased by her man, of wading through the muddy roads like a lost dog, of not even being able to ask her father for something to eat because he had as little as she. Things would never get better—as a matter of fact, they had been getting worse for as far back as she could remember—and with no other idea but to sweep everything away, so blinded by rage that she did not even see whose jaws she was cracking, she kept breaking the bricks and throwing them straight ahead.

Etienne, who had remained in front of the soldiers, almost had his head split open. His ear swelling, he turned around, and a shudder ran through him when he realized the brick had come from Catherine's feverish hands; at the risk of being killed, he stayed where he was and watched her. Many others were also caught up in the excitement of the battle; seeming to forget where they were, they too just stood there with their arms dangling at their sides. Mouquet was keeping track of the hits as though he were at some kind of game: oh, that was a good one! oh, too bad! Joking all the time, he kept nudging Zacharie, who was quarreling with Philomène because he had slapped Achille and Désirée after refusing to put them on his shoulders so they could see better. There

were spectators grouped all along the road into the distance.
And at the top of the hill, at the entrance to the village, Old
Bonnemort had just appeared, dragging himself along on his
stick and now motionless and upright for a moment against
the rust-colored sky.

As soon as the first bricks had begun to fly, the foreman
Richomme had again rushed between the soldiers and the
miners. Careless of danger, so anguished that big tears kept
welling up in his eyes, he was pleading with some, arguing
with others. Because of the tumult no one could hear a thing
he said; they could only see the quivering of his big gray
moustache.

But the hailstorm of bricks was becoming heavier, for the
men were following the women's lead and joining in.

La Maheude noticed that Maheu was standing back, empty-handed and sullen.

"What's the matter with you?" she cried. "Are you deserting your comrades? Are you going to let them be taken to
prison? . . . Ah, if I didn't have this child with me you'd soon
see what I would do!"

She was prevented from joining La Brûlé and the others
by Estelle, who was clinging to her neck and screaming; and
as her husband seemed not to hear her, she kicked some
bricks in front of him.

"Pick them up, for God's sake! Or would you rather have
everybody see me spit in your face to give you courage?"

He turned scarlet, broke some bricks, threw them. La
Maheude, half-stifling her daughter in the iron grasp with
which she was clutching her to her breast, stood behind him,
urging him on with banshee shrieks and howls for blood, and
he kept moving forward until he found himself facing the
rifles.

The little troop was all but lost from sight under this hail
of stones. Luckily the stones were striking above their heads—
the wall was pockmarked with them. What was to be done?
The idea of retreating inside the building momentarily turned
the captain's pale face purple, but it was no longer even
possible—they would be torn to pieces if they so much as
moved. A brick had just struck against the visor of his cap
and drops of blood were running down his forehead. Several
of his men were wounded, and he sensed that they were
beside themselves with rage, in the grip of that unbridled
instinct for self-preservation that overrides all notions of
obedience to orders. The sergeant had just roared out an
oath—his left shoulder was half-dislocated, his skin bruised
by a heavy blow that had sounded like the *thump* of a

washerwoman pounding her laundry. The recruit had been grazed by two bricks—his thumb was smashed and he was maddened by a burning pain in his right knee: how long were they going to put up with this? The veteran had been hit in the groin by a ricocheting rock—his face was green and his rifle trembled in his thin, outthrust arms. Three times the captain was on the point of giving the order to fire. He was in agony, and for seconds that seemed like eternities he struggled with clashing concepts of duty, with his beliefs as a man and a soldier. The rain of bricks redoubled, and just as he was about to open his mouth and shout: Fire! the rifles went off of their own accord—first three shots, then five, then a volley from the whole platoon, then, long afterward, a single shot that rang out in the great silence.

The miners were stupefied. The soldiers had fired, and the open-mouthed mob stood motionless, not yet able to believe what had happened. But there were blood-curdling shrieks as the bugle called for a cease-fire, and complete panic as the crowd fled frantically through the mud like a machine-gunned herd.

At the first three shots Bébert and Lydie had fallen down one upon the other, the girl hit in the face and the boy with a hole under his left shoulder. She had been killed instantly and now lay motionless. But he was still moving, and writhing in agony, he took her into his arms—as if he wanted to hold her once more the way he had held her in the dark hiding place where they had spent their last night. And just then Jeanlin, his eyes still swollen from sleep, finally came running up from Réquillart; hopping through the smoke, he was just in time to see Bébert clasp his little wife and die.

The other five shots had brought down La Brûlé and the foreman Richomme. Hit in the back while he was pleading with his comrades, he had first fallen to his knees, then dropped to the ground, where he lay drawing his last painful breaths, his eyes still wet with the tears he had wept. The old woman, her breast torn open, had fallen straight forward, crackling like dry firewood and muttering a final curse that mingled in her throat with a last surge of blood.

Then the volley had swept the whole area, cutting down groups of laughing bystanders who had been eyeing the battle from some hundred feet away. Mouquet received a bullet in his mouth and fell, his head shattered at the feet of Zacharie and Philomène, splattering their children with blood. At the same moment two bullets hit Mouquette in the belly. She had seen the soldiers take aim, and with instinctive generosity she had thrown herself in front of Catherine, yelling for her to

watch out; then she had shrieked and, bowled over by the
force of the bullet, fallen flat on her back. Etienne ran to her,
wanting to pick her up and carry her away, but she motioned
to him that it was no use. She painfully breathed her last, all
the while smiling at the two of them as though she was happy
to see them together now that she was going.

Everything seemed to be over, and the roar of bullets was
fading away among the distant buildings of the villages when
the last, isolated shot rang out, long after the others.

Maheu, hit in the heart, whirled around and fell face-down
in a coal-blackened puddle.

Dazed, La Maheude bent down.

"Come on now, get up. You're not really hurt, are you?"

Her hands were taken up with Estelle and she had to put
the child under her arm in order to turn her husband's head.

"Say something! Where does it hurt?"

His eyes were blank, his mouth filled with a bloody foam.
She understood; he was dead. Her daughter still tucked under
her arm like a bundle, she remained squatting in the mud,
staring uncomprehendingly at her husband.

The mine area was clear. With a nervous gesture the
captain had first removed and then replaced his stone-slashed
cap, and now, faced with the disaster of his life, he
maintained his habitual pale rigidity while his men mutely
reloaded their rifles. The horrified faces of Négrel and
Dansaert could be seen at the landing-room window. Behind
them stood Souvarine, his forehead furrowed by a deep
wrinkle, as if his obsession were indelibly and menacingly
posted there. At the edge of the plateau on the other side of
the horizon Bonnemort still stood, one hand leaning heavily
on his stick, the other shading his eyes so that he could more
clearly see the slaughter of his flesh and blood. The wounded
were shrieking, and the dead were stiffening in broken pos-
tures, splattered by the muddy thaw or, here and there,
half-buried by the inky patches of coal poking through the
soiled scraps of snow. And amid these bodies of men—so
small, so shrunken by their poverty and misery—lay the
corpse of Trompette, a monstrous and pitiful heap of dead
flesh.

Etienne had not been killed. He was still standing alongside
Catherine, who had crumpled from weariness and anguish,
when a vibrant voice made him start. It was the Abbé
Ranvier on his way back from Mass; he stood there, his arms
raised to the sky, and with the fury of a prophet he called
down the wrath of God on the assassins, prophesying
the coming era of justice and predicting that heavenly thun-

derbolts would soon strike down the bourgeoisie, for it had crowned its many crimes by causing the massacre of the workers and the wretched ones of the earth.

Part SEVEN

1

The rifle shots fired at Montsou had caused powerful reverberations, even as far off as Paris. For four days the opposition newspapers had been indignant, carrying horrifying stories on their front pages: twenty-five wounded and fourteen dead, among whom were two children and three women, and there were also prisoners taken—Levaque had become a sort of hero, and was credited with having responded to the examining magistrate with a reply worthy of an ancient Roman. The Empire, at whose heart these rifle balls had struck, pretended to the calm of the all-powerful, unaware of the seriousness of its wounds. It was simply a regrettable clash, an unimportant incident that had taken place somewhere in the black countryside, far away from the pavements of Paris where public opinion was formed. People would soon forget; the Company had received semi-official orders to hush up the affair and end the strike, the irritating duration of which was making it a danger to society.

The result was that by Wednesday morning three of the directors were seen arriving in Montsou. The little town, which till then had been so unnerved that it had hardly dared rejoice over the massacre, now breathed freely and savored the pleasure of finally being rescued. Even the weather had turned fine, and there was a bright shining sun, one of those early February suns whose warmth tinges the lilac bushes with green. All the shutters of the Company offices had been thrown back, and the great building seemed to have come to life again. Encouraging rumors filtered out from it—it was said that these gentlemen, much moved by the catastrophe, had come running with open arms to welcome back the poor lost sheep of the villages. Now that the blow had been struck—no doubt more energetically than they would have liked—they outdid themselves in their role as saviors and

354

decreed some excellent, though rather belated, measures. To begin with, they discharged the Belgians, making a great to-do about this extreme concession to their workers. Then they called off the military occupation of the mines, which the completely crushed strikers were no longer threatening. In addition they managed to stifle the affair of the sentinel who had disappeared from Le Voreux: the whole countryside had been scoured without turning up either the rifle or the corpse, and it was decided to declare the soldier a deserter even though there was a suspicion of crime. In every way they tried to minimize what had happened, for they trembled with fear at the thought of the future and judged it dangerous to acknowledge the irresistible savagery of a mob let loose among the crumbling foundations of the old world. And meanwhile these attempts at conciliation in no way kept them from the successful conclusion of some purely administrative business—Deneulin had been seen going to the Company offices for meetings with Monsieur Hennebeau. Negotiations over the purchase of Vandame were in progress, and rumor had it that he was going to accept the gentlemen's offers.

But what was causing the greatest stir throughout the region were the large yellow posters that the directors had caused to be pasted up on every wall. They carried the following announcements in very large type: "Workers of Montsou: We do not wish the outbursts, the sad results of which you have been able to see in recent days, to deprive the level-headed and willing workers of their means of livelihood. We will therefore open all the mines Monday morning, and as soon as work is again underway we shall consider carefully and with open minds those aspects of the situation that may call for improvement. We shall do whatever is fair and possible to do." And in one morning the ten thousand miners filed past those posters. Not one of them said anything; many of them shook their heads, others walked away wearily without having moved a muscle of their set faces.

Until then Village Number 240 had obstinately persisted in its fierce resistance. It was as if their comrades' blood, which had reddened the mud of the mines, was now barring the way to the others. Scarcely ten of them—Pierron and a few turncoats like him—had gone down again, and their departures and arrivals were observed with gloom, but without so much as a gesture or a threat. The poster pasted on the side of the church was therefore met with profound suspicion. There was not a word in it of the workbooks that had been returned: was the Company refusing to take them back? And the fear of reprisals, together with the fraternal idea of protesting against the dismissal of those who had been most compromised, made them all continue in their obstinacy. There was something suspicious about this, they would have to see, they would go back to the mines when these gentlemen would be good enough to explain themselves more clearly. A heavy silence weighed down on the low houses, and not even hunger mattered anymore—now that violent death had passed over their roofs they might as well all die.

But one house more than the others, that of the Maheus, was especially dark and silent, overwhelmed by its mourning. From the time she had followed her husband's body to the cemetery La Maheude had not opened her mouth. After the battle she had permitted Etienne to bring Catherine, covered with mud and half-dead, back to the house; and while, as the young man stood there, she was undressing the girl to put her to bed, she had thought for a moment that her daughter too had been returned to her with a bullet in her belly, for her shift was spotted with large bloodstains. But she soon understood that it was the arrival of puberty, finally brought on by the shock of that terrible day. Ah, another piece of good luck!—a fine gift that was, to be able to make children so the gendarmes could slaughter them later on! And she said not a word to Catherine, any more than she did to Etienne. The latter was so repelled at the thought of returning to the darkness of Réquillart that he felt he would prefer prison, and he was now sleeping with Jeanlin at the risk of being arrested; he shuddered with horror at the thought of that eternal night after all those deaths, and at his unconfessed fear of the little soldier who was sleeping there under the rocks—and besides, he longed for prison as for a refuge from the torment of his defeat. But no one bothered him, and he dragged himself through the weary hours without knowing how to tire out his body. Sometimes, however, La Maheude would look resentfully at the two of them, him and her daughter, and seem about to ask them what they were doing in her house.

Once again they were all sleeping jumbled together, Old Bonnemort occupying the bed of the two children, who were themselves sleeping with Catherine now that poor Alzire was no longer there to dig her hump into her big sister's ribs. It was at night, when the mother would get into her cold bed—suddenly become too large—that she felt the emptiness of the house. She tried to fill the space with Estelle, but in vain; the child was no substitute for her husband, and she would weep soundlessly for hours. Then the days began to go by as before: there was still no bread, and they were still not lucky enough to die once and for all; the little they managed to pick up here and there only did the poor wretches the bad turn of keeping them alive. Nothing in their existence had changed, except that she no longer had a husband.

On the afternoon of the fifth day Etienne, driven to despair by the sight of this silent woman, left the house and began to walk slowly down the cobblestoned village street. His restlessness, caused by his enforced inactivity, drove him to take never-ending walks, his arms hanging, his head bowed, always tortured by the same thought. After wandering about like this for half an hour, he suddenly felt even more uneasy and realized it was because the men were standing at their doors to watch him go by. The little that had remained of his popularity had vanished in the wake of the fusillade, and he could not go outside without being aware of the burning eyes that were fixed on him. When he raised his head he saw the men standing there menacingly and the women drawing aside the little window curtains to stare at him; and in the face of this still-silent accusation, the repressed anger of those eyes made large by hunger and tears, he became self-conscious and could no longer continue his walk. Always behind him he could sense the mounting force of the mute reproaches, and he was so afraid of hearing the whole village rush out and scream its misery at him that he returned home, trembling.

But the scene that awaited him at the Maheus' put the finishing touches to his dejection. Old Bonnemort was near the cold fireplace, nailed to his chair as he had been since the day of the slaughter, when two neighbors had found him, his walking stick in pieces beside him, crumpled on the ground like an old tree shattered by lightning. And while Lénore and Henri were trying to allay their hunger by scraping away with an ear-splitting noise at an old pot in which cabbages had been boiled the night before, La Maheude, having set Estelle on the table, was standing erect and shaking her fist at Catherine.

"Just say that again, by God! Just say that again!"

Catherine had announced her intention of returning to Le Voreux. The idea of not earning her keep, of being tolerated at her mother's like some burdensome and useless animal, was becoming more unbearable every day, and if she had not been afraid of Chaval doing some dreadful thing to her, she would have gone back down last Tuesday. Stuttering, she began again:

"But what do you expect?—you can't live without working. At least we'd have something to eat——"

La Maheude cut her short.

"Listen to me! I'll strangle the first one of you that goes back to work. . . . Ah, no, that would be too much—first to kill the father and then to continue exploiting the children! No, enough!—I'd rather see you all carried off in a pine box, like your father."

And her long silence broke under a furious flood of words. A lot of good Catherine's money would do!—barely thirty sous, and maybe you could add another twenty sous if the bosses were willing to find some work for that thief Jeanlin! Fifty sous and seven mouths to feed! The brats were good for nothing but guzzling down their soup. As for the grandfather, something must have broken in his head when he fell, because he seemed to have lost his mind—unless it had been the sight of the soldiers firing on his friends that had driven him mad.

"Isn't that right, old man?—they really finished you off. Your hands are still pretty strong, but it's all over with you."

Bonnemort looked at her uncomprehendingly with his dull eyes. He would sit there, staring ahead like that, for hours at a time, and he had only just enough intelligence left to spit into the plate of ashes that was put alongside him for the sake of cleanliness.

"And they didn't settle his pension," she went on, "and now I'm sure they never will, because of our ideas about things. . . . No, I tell you that's enough! I won't have anything more to do with those damn people!"

"But still," ventured Catherine, "they promised on their posters . . ."

"Will you shut up about your posters! . . . It's just another trap to catch us and swallow us down whole. They can afford to be nice, now that they've shot us to pieces!"

"But Mama, where shall we go? You can be sure they won't let us stay in the village."

La Maheude made a vague and terrible gesture. Where would they go?—she didn't know. She tried not to think about it, it drove her mad. They would go somewhere, someplace. And as the sound of the pot-scraping was becoming unbearable, she swooped down on Lénore and Henri and slapped them. Estelle, who had crawled to the edge of the table on all fours, now fell, increasing the uproar. The mother quieted her with a whack: it would have been a good thing if she had killed herself right then and there! She talked of Alzire and said she hoped the others would have as much luck. Then suddenly she put her head against the wall and burst into heavy sobs.

Etienne had stood there, not daring to intervene. He no longer counted for much in the house, and even the children held back from him suspiciously. But the tears of this unhappy woman tore at his heart, and he murmured:

"Come now, come now, courage!—we'll try to manage somehow."

She seemed not to hear him; she was complaining now, a low, continuous complaint.

"Oh, how can all this be? Somehow we made do, before all these horrors. We only had dry bread to eat, but at least we were all together. . . . And then what happened? My God, what did we do to be so miserable—some of us under the ground, and the rest of us wanting only to be there too? . . . It's true that they used to harness us up like workhorses, and when it came to sharing the rewards it wasn't fair for us always to get the brickbats, to keep swelling the moneybags of the rich without any hope of ever enjoying the good things of life ourselves. . . . When hope goes, the joy of living goes with it. Yes, we couldn't keep on that way much longer, we had to be able to live a little . . . but if we had only known! Is it possible to have become so unhappy just from wanting justice?"

Sobs welled up in her throat and her voice was choked by an immense sadness.

"And then there are always those clever ones who promise you that everything can change for the better if you only make an effort. . . . You get all worked up, and you suffer so much from what is that you begin to ask for what can never be. Look at me—my head was all full of foolish nonsense, I was imagining a life in which everybody in the world would be on good terms, I was off woolgathering, way up in the clouds! And then you tumble down into the filth again and really break your back. . . . It wasn't true, nothing that we thought we had seen was actually there. What was there was misery—oh, as much of that as you wanted—and a hail of bullets on top of everything else!"

Etienne listened to this lamentation, and each tear was a jab of remorse. He could find no words with which to calm La Maheude, who was shattered by the terrible fall from the heights of the ideal. She had come back to the middle of the room and was staring at him; she burst into a final contemptuous cry of rage:

"And you—are you thinking of going back to the mine too, after having gotten us all into this mess? . . . I'm not

blaming you, but just the same, if I were in your place I'd
have already died of shame at the thought of all the harm I'd
done my friends."

He wanted to answer, but then just shrugged his shoulders
hopelessly: why bother with explanations that she was suffering too much even to begin to understand? And finding it too
painful to stay, he went out and resumed his desperate
wanderings.

Outside, the village seemed to be waiting for him, the men
in the doorways, the women at the windows. As soon as he
appeared there was the sound of muttering, and the crowd
increased. The undercurrent of nasty talk that had been
intensifying for four days finally exploded in a general male-
diction. Fists were shaken at him, mothers bitterly pointed
him out to their sons, old men looked at him and spat. It was
the aftermath of the days of defeat, the inevitable decline of
popularity, a hatred aggravated by all the pointlessly endured
suffering. He was paying for the hunger and the death.

As Etienne left the house, Zacharie, who was just arriving
with Philomène, jostled him and sneered nastily.

"Well, well, he's growing fatter!—it looks as if some people thrive on other people's deaths!"

La Levaque, accompanied by Bouteloup, had already come
to her door. Referring to Bébert, her son who had been
killed by a rifle bullet, she cried out:

"Oh yes, there are cowards who are willing enough to have
children massacred. If he wants to give my boy back to me,
let him go look for him under the ground!"

She kept forgetting that her husband was a prisoner—after
all, her bed wasn't empty, for Bouteloup was still there—but
now she suddenly remembered him and continued in a shrill
voice:

"Look at that, will you! The rascals are walking around
free while the good men are rotting in jail!"

Attempting to avoid her, Etienne ran into La Pierronne,
who had come racing through the gardens. The latter had
welcomed as a release the death of her mother, whose violent
outbreaks had threatened them all with a gallows end, nor
did she weep over the death of Pierron's little girl, that slut
Lydie—good riddance to her! But in an attempt to reconcile
herself with the neighbors she joined in with the others.

"And what about my mother and my little girl? We saw
you, you were hiding behind them when they swallowed the
lead that had been meant for you!"

What was he to do?—strangle La Pierronne and the others? fight the whole village? For a moment Etienne wanted to

do just that. The blood was boiling in his head—and he now thought of his comrades as brutes, and he was vexed at seeing them so unintelligent and uncivilized as to blame him for what had been logically inevitable. How stupid! He was disgusted by his inability to recover his domination over them, and as though deaf to the insults he merely hastened his steps. Soon it became a flight, each household booing as he passed, some of the people trailing after him, all of them cursing him, as with a single voice, in an outburst of hate. It was he who was the exploiter, the assassin, the sole cause of their tragedy. He left the village at a gallop, pale, frantic, the howling mob at his back. At the main road many of them finally turned back, but a few of them were still persisting when at the bottom of the hill, in front of L'Avantage, he ran into another group leaving Le Voreux.

Old Mouque and Chaval were among them. Since the death of his daughter, Mouquette, and his son, Mouquet, the old man had gone on with his job as stableman without a word of complaint or regret. But suddenly, at the sight of Etienne, he was shaken by fury, tears sprang to his eyes, and a flood of abuse streamed from that mouth blackened and bloodied by tobacco.

"Bastard! Dirty pig! Skunk! . . . Just you wait—you've got to pay for the death of my poor children, and pay you will!"

He picked up a brick, broke it, and flung both halves.

"That's the idea! Let's get him!" sniggered Chaval excitedly, delighted by this opportunity for vengeance. "Now it's your turn. . . . Backed against the wall, aren't you, you slimy toad?"

And he too started throwing bricks at Etienne. A savage clamor went up, and everybody picked up bricks, broke them, hurled them, in an attempt to slaughter him the way they had wanted to slaughter the soldiers. Dazed, he no longer tried to flee, but faced them and tried to calm them with words. His old speeches, once so warmly applauded, rose to his lips. He was repeating the very words with which he had intoxicated them in the days when he had held them, like a faithful flock, in the palm of his hand; but his power was dead, and the stones were his only reply. He had just been hit on the left arm and was retreating in peril of his life when he found himself backed up against the wall of L'-Avantage.

Rasseneur had been standing in his doorway for the past few minutes.

"Come inside," he said simply.

Etienne was repelled by the idea of seeking refuge there
and hesitated.

"Come inside, will you. I'll speak to them."

Resigning himself, he sought shelter in the back of the
room while the innkeeper blocked the door with his broad
shoulders.

"Come now, friends, be reasonable.... You know that
I've never tried to mislead you: *I've* always been for peace,
and if you'd listened to me you certainly wouldn't be in the
mess you're in now."

His shoulders and belly swaying, he went on at great
length, letting loose a flow of easy eloquence that was as
soothing as tepid water. And he regained all his former
success, reconquering his popularity effortlessly and naturally,
as if his comrades had never hooted him or called him
coward only a month before. Approving voices rang out:
that's right! they were with him! that was the way to talk!
And there was a storm of applause.

Standing in the rear, Etienne was sick at heart, overwhelmed with bitterness. He remembered the prophecy Rasseneur had made in the forest, when he had warned him
about the ingratitude of mobs. What idiotic brutality! What
revolting forgetfulness of all he had done! It was a blind
force constantly devouring itself. And beneath his anger at
seeing these brutes spoil things for themselves, there was a
despair at his own collapse, at the tragic end of his ambition.
What!—was it all over? He remembered that under the
beeches he had felt three thousand hearts beat in time with
his own. On that day he had held his popularity in both
hands—this people had belonged to him, and he had felt
himself their master. He had been drunk on wild dreams
then: Montsou at his feet, Paris in the distance, elected a
deputy perhaps, blasting the bourgeois with a speech, the first
speech given by a worker from the tribune of a parliament—
and now it was all over! He had awakened, miserable and
despised, and his people had just chased him away with
stones.

Rasseneur's voice rose.

"Violence had never succeeded. The world can't be remade
in a day. Those who promised you they'd change everything
overnight are either fools or knaves!"

"Hurray! Hurray!" shouted the crowd.

Who then was the guilty one?—and as he put this question
to himself Etienne's despair was complete. Was it really his
fault, this tragedy from which he himself was bleeding, the
wretchedness of some, the slaughter of others, these thin,

starving women and children? He had had this same terrible vision one evening before all these catastrophes, but even then he was being carried away by some force and swept along with his comrades. Actually, he had never led them—it was they who had led him, who had forced him to do things he would never have done without the pressure of this powerful throng pushing from behind. At every outbreak of violence he had remained stupefied by the turn of events, for he had neither foreseen nor wanted any of them. For example, could he have predicted that his faithful village flock would one day stone him? These madmen were lying when they accused him of having promised them an existence of gluttony and idleness. And beneath this self-justification, this logic with which he was trying to combat his remorse, there was the dull dread that he had shown himself unequal to the task—the constant nagging doubt of the half-educated. But he felt that his courage was gone; he was no longer at one with his comrades, he was afraid of them, of this enormous, blind, irresistible mass of people rushing onward like a natural force, sweeping everything before it, overriding rules and theories. A feeling of repugnance, due to the uneasiness of his more polished tastes and the slow growth of his whole being toward a superior class, had gradually detached him from them.

Just then Rasseneur's voice was drowned by enthusiastic shouts.

"Up with Rasseneur! He's the man for us! Hurray! Hurray!"

The innkeeper closed the door behind him and the crowd dispersed; the two men looked at each other in silence. They both shrugged their shoulders and ended by having a beer together.

This same day there was a dinner party at La Piolaine to celebrate the betrothal of Négrel and Cécile. For the past twenty-four hours the Grégoires had been having the dining room polished and the drawing room dusted. Mélanie was holding sway in the kitchen, keeping an eye on the roasts and stirring the sauces, the odor of which penetrated even up to the attic. It had been decided that Francis, the coachman, would help Honorine serve. The gardener's wife was to wash the dishes and the gardener himself would open the gate. Never had there been a gala such as this to set the large, comfortable, patriarchal house so topsy-turvy.

Things could not have gone better. Madame Hennebeau was charming to Cécile, and she smiled at Négrel when the Montsou notary gallantly proposed a toast to the happiness

of the future couple. Monsieur Hennebeau was also most
affable. His guests were struck by his good humor—there was
a rumor that he was once again in the good graces of the
directors and would soon be made an officer of the Legion of
Honor for the decisive manner in which he had squashed the
strike. Though the guests avoided mentioning recent events,
there was a definite air of triumph, and the dinner was
turning into an official victory celebration. Well, they had
been delivered at last, they could go back to eating and
sleeping in peace! A discreet allusion was made to the dead,
whose blood had so recently soaked into the mud of Le
Voreux: it had been a necessary lesson, and they were all
touched when the Grégoires added that it was now everyone's duty to go and bind up the wounds in the villages. The
Grégoires had recovered their well-meaning placidity and
were making excuses for their good miners, already envisioning them back in the mines and setting a good example of
time-honored resignation. The leaders of Montsou society, no
longer all a-tremble, agreed that the question of wages called
for some careful study. Victory became complete as they
were having the roast—Monsieur Hennebeau read a letter
from the bishop announcing the transfer of Abbé Ranvier.
All the local bourgeois were heatedly discussing the story of
this priest who had called the soldiers "assassins." While
dessert was being served, the notary resolutely announced his
position as a freethinker.

Deneulin was there with his two daughters. Amid all this
gaiety he was trying to hide his grief over his own ruin. That
very morning he had signed the papers selling his Vandame
concession to the Montsou Company. His back against the
wall, a knife at his throat, he had submitted to the demands
of the directors, finally turning over to them this long-coveted
prey in exchange for barely enough money to pay off his
creditors. At the last moment he had even accepted—and
considered it a stroke of good luck—their offer to keep him
on as a division engineer, thus resigning himself to supervise
as a salaried employee the mine into which he had sunk all
his fortune. It was the death knell of small, private enterprise, a foreshadowing of the disappearance of individual
proprietors who one by one would soon be gulped down to
feed the insatiable hunger of the monster, capital, and swept
away by the rising tide of gigantic companies. He alone was
paying the cost of the strike, and he was well aware that in
drinking to Monsieur Hennebeau's decoration they were drinking to his ruin; the only thing that even slightly consoled
him was the fine pluckiness of Lucie and Jeanne, charming in

their made-over dresses, laughing in the face of disaster, scornful of money like the attractive, emancipated women they were.

When they went into the drawing room for coffee, Monsieur Grégoire took his cousin aside and congratulated him on his courageous decision.

"What could you expect? Your one mistake was to risk putting the million francs from your Montsou denier into Vandame. You gave yourself a lot of trouble, and in spite of the fact that you worked like a dog it's all melted away—while mine, which has never left my drawer, still keeps me in decent comfort without my lifting a finger, just as it will keep the children of my grandchildren."

2

On Sunday Etienne slipped out of the village as soon as it was dark. A clear sky studded with stars was shedding a bluish light on the earth below. He headed for the canal and slowly walked along its banks toward Marchiennes. It was his favorite walk, a grassy five-mile path that ran beside the geometric waterway which stretched ahead like an endless ingot of molten silver.

He had never met anyone there, but that evening he was annoyed to see a man coming toward him. Under the pale light of the stars the two solitary walkers failed to recognize each other until they were face to face.

"Oh, it's you," murmured Etienne.

Souvarine nodded mutely. For a moment they stood still; then side by side they started off for Marchiennes. Each seemed wrapped in his own thoughts, as if miles apart from the other.

"Did you see the article in the paper about Pluchart's success in Paris?" Etienne finally asked. "After that meeting in Belleville they waited for him in the streets and gave him an ovation. . . . Oh, he's all set now, in spite of his sore throat. From now on, he can go as far as he wants."

The engineman shrugged his shoulders. He had only contempt for fancy talkers—rascals who go into politics the way other people go into law, to make a fortune thanks to their fine phrases.

Etienne was now on Darwin. He had read bits and pieces

of him—vulgarized summaries in an inexpensive edition—and
from this badly digested reading he had constructed a revolutionary theory of the struggle for existence—the lean eating
the fat, the strong masses devouring the bloodless bourgeoisie. But Souvarine lost his temper at this and expatiated
on the stupidity of the socialists who accepted Darwin—that
apostle of scientific inequality whose famous theory of natural selection was useful only to aristocratic philosophers. His
friend persisted however; he wanted to discuss the matter,
and he expressed his doubts in a hypothesis: suppose the old
society was finished, the last remnants of it swept away—
well, wasn't there a danger that as the new world developed
it would slowly be corrupted by the same injustices, with
some people sickly and others robust, with the slyer and
more intelligent people gobbling everything up, and the stupid and lazy ones sinking once more into slavery? Faced with
this vision of eternal misery the engineman cried out in a
terrible voice that if justice was not possible for mankind
then mankind would have to disappear. As long as there were
rotten societies there would have to be massacres, until the
last human being was exterminated. And the two men fell
silent again.

For a long time Souvarine, head down, walked on the soft
grass, so absorbed in his thoughts that he was following along
the very edge of the water, moving with the calm certainty
of a sleepwalker on the edge of a roof. Then, without any
apparent reason, he began to tremble as if he had run into a
ghost. When he raised his head his face was deathly pale, and
he said softly to his friend:

"Did I ever tell you how she died?"

"Who?"

"My wife, back in Russia."

Etienne gestured vaguely, astonished by this tremulous
voice, this sudden need to confide, coming from a man
generally so impassive, so stoically detached from himself
as well as from others. All he knew was that the "wife" had
been a mistress and that she had been hanged in Russia.

"Our mission had failed," related Souvarine, his eyes now
staring at the white flow of the canal between the bluish
colonnades of tall trees. "We'd spent fourteen days at the
bottom of a tunnel, mining a railroad track—only it wasn't
the imperial train that blew up, it was a passenger train. . . .
Then they arrested Annouchka. She had disguised herself as a
peasant and brought us food every evening. She was also the
one who had lit the fuse, because they would have noticed a

man. . . . I attended the trial, hidden in the crowd for six long days. . . ."

His voice choked up and he started to cough violently, as if he were strangling.

"Twice I started to cry out and rush through the crowd to join her. But what good would it have done?—one man less is one militant less, and whenever her big staring eyes met mine I knew she was telling me not to."

He coughed again.

"I was there that last day on the square. . . . It was raining, and the downpour made the awkward fools lose their heads. It had taken them twenty minutes to hang the other four— the rope kept breaking and they couldn't finish off the fourth one. . . . Annouchka was standing there waiting. She didn't see me, she kept searching for me in the crowd. I got up on a stone post and she saw me. Our eyes remained locked together. She was still staring at me even after she was dead. . . . I waved my hat, and I left."

There was another silence. The white line of the canal stretched out into infinity, and the two men walked along with the same muffled tread, as though each had fallen back into his own isolation. On the horizon the pale water seemed to pierce the sky with a slender stab of light.

"It was our punishment," Souvarine went on harshly. "We were guilty of loving each other. . . . Yes, it's good that she's dead—heroes will spring from her blood, and as for me, my heart is free of cowardice. . . . Ah, there is nothing, neither parents nor wife nor friend!—nothing to make the hand hesitate when the time comes to take the lives of others or to give one's own!"

Etienne stopped, shivering in the cool night air. He did not argue, but simply said:

"We've gone a long way. Shall we turn back?"

They slowly started back to Le Voreux, and after a few steps he added:

"Have you seen the new posters?"

The Company had had some more big yellow placards pasted up that morning. The wording was more precise and more conciliatory—the Company undertook to take back the workbook of any miner who would go down again the following morning. Everything was to be forgotten, and amnesty was being extended even to the most militant.

"Yes, I've seen them," the engineman answered.

"Well, what do you think?"

"I think it's all over. . . . The herd will go down again. You're all too cowardly."

Etienne warmly defended the miners: a man alone can be brave, but a starving crowd is helpless. Step by step they had come back to Le Voreux, and before the black mass of the mine he continued to swear that *he* would never go down again, but that he forgave all those who would. Then, since it was rumored that the carpenters had not had time to repair the casing of the shaft, he asked about it. Was it true?—had the weight of the earth against the timbers that jacketed the shaft really so pushed them out of line that one of the extraction cages scraped against them for more than fifteen feet as it went by? Souvarine, taciturn once again, replied briefly. He had worked the day before, and it was true—the cage did scrape, and the operators even had to double the speed to get it past that spot. But when the bosses were told about it they all replied with the same irritated comment: what they wanted now was coal, they'd reinforce the casing later.

"Suppose it breaks!" murmured Etienne. "All hell would break loose."

His eyes fixed on the mine which was vaguely discernible in the darkness, Souvarine summed up tranquilly:

"If it breaks, the men are sure to know about it, since you're advising them to go down again."

Nine o'clock was ringing out from the Montsou bell tower, and when Etienne said that he was going to turn in, Souvarine added, without even offering his hand:

"Well, good-bye. I'm leaving."

"Leaving?"

"Yes, I've asked for my book back. I'm going somewhere else."

Upset and amazed, Etienne stared at him. What, after two hours of walking together, to mention this only now, and so matter-of-factly, when as for himself the news of this sudden parting wrung his heart! They had come to know each other, they had worked together—it's always sad to think of never meeting again.

"You're leaving? Where are you going?"

"Somewhere—I don't really know where."

"But I'll see you again?"

"No, I don't think so."

They fell silent and stood looking at each other for a moment, not finding anything else to say.

"Well, good-bye then."

"Good-bye."

While Etienne was walking up to the village Souvarine about-faced and returned to the edge of the canal, and there,

alone now, he strode on and on, his head bowed, so shrouded
in the darkness that he was only a moving shadow in the
night. From time to time he stopped and counted the bells in
the distance. When it struck midnight he left the canal and
headed for Le Voreux.

The mine was empty at that hour—the only person he met
was a foreman, his eyes heavy with sleep. The boilers were
not due to be fired up until two o'clock for the planned
resumption of work. He began by going for a jacket he
pretended to have forgotten at the bottom of some cupboard. Rolled up inside this jacket were some tools: a brace
and a bit, a very strong small saw, a hammer, and a chisel.
Then he left. But instead of going out by way of the dressing
shed, he slipped into the narrow corridor that led to the
ladder well. His jacket under his arm, without a lamp, he
carefully went down, measuring his decent by counting the
ladders. He knew that the cage caught at 1,234 feet, against
the fifth section of the lower casing. When he had counted
fifty-four ladders he groped about with one hand and felt the
bulge in the timbers. This was the place.

Then he set to work with all the skill and composure of a
good worker who has carefully thought out his task. He
began by sawing out a panel in the wall of the ladder well,
making an opening between it and the cage shaft; then by the
light of matches quickly struck up and as quickly extinguished, he was able to check on the state of the casing and
the extent of the recent repairs.

When mine shafts were sunk anywhere between Calais and
Valenciennes, extraordinary difficulties were encountered in
getting through the permanent masses of underground bodies
of water lying in immense sheets at the level of the lowest
valleys. The only way to hold back these gushing springs was
to construct casings made of timbers held together like barrel
staves, thereby isolating the shafts in the middle of the lakes,
the dark and mysterious waves of which pounded against the
walls. In sinking Le Voreux it had been necessary to construct two casings: one at the upper level, in the crumbling
sands and white clay, riddled with fissures and sponge-heavy
with water, which lay next to the chalky stratum; and another at the lower level, directly above the coal seams, in
flour-yellow sand that flowed as easily as a liquid. And it was
here that lay the Torrent, that subterranean sea which was
the terror of the mines of the Nord—a sea with its storms
and shipwrecks, an unknown, unsounded sea that rolled its
dark waves almost a thousand feet below the sunlight. Generally, the casings held up well under the enormous pressure.

The only thing they could not stand up to was the settling of nearby strata of earth shaken loose by the constant cave-ins in abandoned galleries. As the rocks fell, they would sometimes cause fissures, which would slowly extend to the timbers and eventually warp them, forcing them into the interior of the shaft; and here lay the great danger—in the threat of a cave-in and a flood, filling the mine with an avalanche of earth and a deluge from the springs.

Straddling the opening he had made, Souvarine noted a serious bulge in the fifth section of the casing. The timbers were bellying out from the framework, and some were even out of their shoulderings. There were many leaks—*pichoux,* the miners called them—spurting from the joints and piercing the tarred hemp with which they were caulked. Pressed for time, the carpenters had merely set in angle irons—and so carelessly that they had not even put in all the screws. The sands of the Torrent contained behind the casing were obviously shifting considerably.

Using his brace, Souvarine loosened the screws in the angle irons to the point where one last push would tear them out of place. It was a mad, foolhardy job, and twenty times during the course of it he almost toppled over and plunged to the nearly six hundred feet to the bottom. He had had to grip onto the oak guides between which the cages moved, and hanging over nothingness, he made his way along the cross-pieces that connected them at intervals—sliding along, sitting down, leaning back, supporting himself on a knee or an elbow with cool contempt of death. The slightest breath would have sent him tumbling, and thrice, first without even a shudder, he caught himself just in time. First he would feel about, then go to work, lighting a match only when he lost his way among the slimy timbers. After having loosened the screws, he began on the planking itself, and the danger grew even greater. He had looked for the key piece, the one that held the others, and he set to work, boring, sawing, chiseling it down so that it lost its resistance, and all this time the water escaping in thin streams through the holes and the gaps was blinding him, soaking him in a glacial downpour. Two matches went out. Then they all got soaked and it was pitch-black, a bottomless pit of darkness.

From then on he was in the grip of fury. The breath of the unknown was intoxicating him, the black horror of this rain-battered hole throwing him into a frenzy of destruction. He attacked the casing at random, striking where he could, using the brace, using the saw, obsessed with the need to disembowel it then and there, right over his head. And he went at it with ferocity, as if he were twisting his knife in the guts of some living being whom he execrated. He was finally going to kill Le Voreux, that evil beast whose ever-gaping maw had gulped down so much human flesh! His tools crunched into the wood as he stretched out, crawled along, climbed up, climbed down, still holding on by some miracle, in a continuous shuttle, like some night bird flying in and out among the beams of a belfry.

But he was annoyed with himself, and he calmed down. Couldn't all this be done in cold detachment? He patiently waited to catch his breath, then went back into the ladder well and sealed the opening by replacing the piece he had sawed out. That was enough—he did not want to arouse suspicion by making the damage so obvious they would have to make immediate repairs. The beast had its belly wound— it remained to be seen if it would still be alive that evening; and he had left his signature—the horrified world would know it had not died a natural death. He took the time to roll his tools methodically in his jacket; he climbed the ladders slowly. It never even occurred to him to change his clothes after slipping out of the mine without being seen. It was striking three. He remained standing on the road, waiting.

At the same time Etienne, unable to sleep, was startled by a slight noise in the thick darkness of the bedroom. He could make out the light breathing of the children and the snoring of Bonnemort and La Maheude; alongside him Jeanlin was breathing with a steady flutelike sound. Convinced that he must have been dreaming, he was settling back when the noise began again. It was the rustling of a mattress, the sound of somebody trying to slip quietly out of bed. Then he thought Catherine might be sick.

"Is that you? What's the matter?" he asked in a whisper.

No one answered; there was only the continued snoring of the others. For the next five minutes nothing stirred. Then there was another rustle. And this time, certain that he was not mistaken, he crossed the room, stretching his hands into the darkness and feeling for the bed on the other side. He was amazed to find the girl sitting up, holding her breath, wide awake and on the alert.

"Why didn't you answer? What are you doing?"

Finally she said:

"I'm getting up."

"At this hour?"

"Yes. I'm going back to work."

Shaken, Etienne had to sit on the edge of the bed while

Catherine told him her reasons. She could not bear to live like this, idle, aware of the reproachful glances constantly being directed at her—she would rather go down into the mine and take her chances on being beaten by Chaval, and if her mother wouldn't take her money when she brought it home, well, she was old enough to live alone and fend for herself.

"Go away now, I want to get dressed. You won't say anything, will you? You'll be nice, won't you?"

But he remained alongside her, putting his arm around her and embracing her in grief and pity. Huddled together in their nightclothes, on the edge of that bed still warm from a night's sleep, they could feel the glow of each other's bare flesh. At first she had tried to slip loose; then she had cried softly and put her arms around his neck, holding him close in a despairing embrace. And they remained that way without any other desire, wrapped in the past of their unhappy, unconsummated love. Was it then over forever?—wouldn't they dare love each other someday, now that they were free? It would only have taken a little happiness for them to brush off their shame, that uneasiness that kept them from coming together because of all sorts of ideas they themselves did not really understand.

"Go back to bed," she murmured. "I don't want to light the candle, it would wake Mama. . . . It's time, let me go."

He wasn't listening; he was clinging to her desperately, his heart overcome by an immense sadness. He was overwhelmed by a need for peace, an invincible need to be happy, and he imagined himself married, living in a neat little house, wanting nothing but for the two of them to live and die there together. Bread would be enough for him, and if there was only enough for one, it would be for her. What good was anything else? What more was there to life?

She, however, was unknotting his bare arms.

"Please let me go."

Impulsively, he whispered into her ear:

"Wait, I'm going with you."

And he himself was astonished at what he had said. He had sworn not to go down—how then had this sudden decision issued from his lips without his even having thought of it or considered it for a moment? Now he felt so calm, so completely free of all doubts, that he clung to his decision like a man who had been saved by some happy fluke, who had finally found the one way out of his torment. He refused to listen to her frightened protests when she understood that he was sacrificing himself for her and began to fear the jeers with which he would be greeted at the mine. He laughed it all off; the posters promised amnesty, and that was enough.

"I want to work. It's my own idea. . . . Let's get dressed without making any noise."

Taking a thousand precautions, they dressed in the dark. She had secretly prepared her work clothes the night before; he took a jacket and a pair of trousers out of the closet; they did not wash for fear of rattling the basin. Everybody was asleep, but they had to go through the narrow corridor where the mother slept. As they were leaving, they lucklessly stumbled against a chair. La Maheude woke up and asked in a sleep-dazed voice:

"Who's there?"

Catherine stood still, trembling, clutching Etienne's hand tightly.

"Don't worry, it's only me," said the latter. "I'm suffocating here—I'm just stepping out for some fresh air."

"All right."

And La Maheude went back to sleep. Catherine was afraid to move, but she finally went downstairs and divided a slice of bread she had set aside from a loaf given them by a lady in Montsou. Then they softly closed the door and started off.

Souvarine had remained standing near L'Avantage at the bend in the road. For the past half hour he had been watching the miners who were returning to work—obscure shadows, moving along with a heavy, herdlike tread. He counted them the way butchers count cattle entering the slaughterhouse, and he was surprised at how many there were; even his pessimism had not foreseen that there would be so many cowards. The line kept growing and growing, and he stood erect, very cold, his teeth clenched, his eyes bright.

Then he gave a start. Though he could not see the faces of the men filing by, he had just recognized one of them by the way he walked. He stepped into the road and stopped him.

"Where are you going?"

Etienne was startled, and instead of replying he merely stuttered:

"What!—Haven't you left yet?"

Then he confessed that he was going back to the mine. Yes, he had sworn not to, but this was no way to live, just standing around with your arms folded, waiting for something that might happen in a hundred years; and besides, he had personal reasons for what he was doing.

Souvarine had listened to him, trembling. He grabbed Etienne by a shoulder and pushed him back toward the village.

"Go home, do you hear! I mean it!"

But Catherine had come up and he recognized her too. Etienne was protesting, saying he would allow no one to pass judgment on his behavior. The engineman's eyes went from the girl to his friend; then he stepped back with an abrupt gesture of surrender. When a man made place in his heart for a woman he was through, he might just as well die. Perhaps he once more had a fleeting vision of his mistress being hanged in Moscow—that last attachment of his flesh severed, setting him free to dispose of his own life and that of others. He simply said:

"Then go on."

Etienne lingered uncomfortably, looking for some friendly word so as not to separate on this note.

"You're still leaving, are you?"

"Yes."

"Then let's shake hands, old friend. A good journey, and no hard feelings."

Souvarine held out an icy hand. Neither friend nor wife.

"Good-bye for good, this time."

"Yes, good-bye."

And Souvarine, motionless in the darkness, watched Etienne and Catherine enter Le Voreux.

3

The men began going down at four o'clock. Dansaert himself was sitting in the checker's office in the lamproom, writing down the name of each miner who reported for work and seeing that he was given a lamp. He was taking all comers without comment, keeping to the promise on the placards. However, when he saw Etienne and Catherine at the window, he started, turned red, and opened his mouth to refuse them; but then he contented himself by merely crowing derisively: well, well, so the great man himself had his shoulders to the mat. There must be something to the Company after all, if the terrible champion of Montsou was crawling back to it for bread! Etienne took his lamp without a word and went up toward the shaft with the haulage girl.

But it was the jeers and the curses from the men there in the landing room that Catherine really feared. It so happened that no sooner had they come in than she saw Chaval standing among some twenty miners waiting for an empty cage. He started toward her in a fury, but stopped short at the sight of Etienne and went, instead, into a mocking performance, shrugging his shoulders theatrically. Oh well, if this other fellow was ready to crawl between somebody else's soiled sheets, he couldn't care less! Good riddance! If the gentleman liked leftovers, that was his own business! But beneath this display of contempt his jealousy was flaring up again, and his eyes were blazing. None of the other men stirred; they silently kept their eyes lowered, casting only sidelong glances at the newcomers. Then, dejected and resigned, they went back to staring at the mouth of the shaft, holding their lamps and shivering under their thin jackets in the drafts that ceaselessly swept the enormous room.

At last the cage settled on its catches and they were given orders to get in. Catherine and Etienne piled into a cart already containing Pierron and two cutters. Beside them, in another cart, Chaval was loudly telling Old Mouque that the management was dead-wrong in not taking advantage of this opportunity to get rid of the low-lifes infecting the place; but the old stableman, fallen once again into the resignation of his dog's life, was no longer angry at the death of his children, and he merely replied with a conciliatory gesture.

The cage started and they sped through the darkness. No one spoke. Suddenly, when they were about two-thirds of the way down, there was a terrible scraping. Iron creaked, and the men were thrown against one another.

"For God's sake!" grumbled Etienne. "Are they trying to squash us? We'll all end up at the bottom, thanks to that rotten casing of theirs. And they say they've repaired it!"

But the cage had passed the obstacle. It was now descending under a downpour so violent that the workers listened to the sound of the tumbling water with great anxiety. Were there so many leaks in the caulking of the joints?

Pierron, who had been working for the past several days, was questioned, but he did not want to admit his fear lest it be taken as an attack against the management, and he answered:

"Oh, there's nothing to worry about! It's always like that. They probably just didn't have time to caulk the leaks."

The torrent was pelting them, and they arrived at the bottom, at the last landing, under a veritable waterspout. Not one foreman had thought to climb the ladders and check on the situation—the pump would handle it, the caulking crew would look into it the following night. They had their hands full getting work started up again in the galleries. Before

allowing the cutters to return to their stalls, the engineer had
decided that all the men would spend the first five days on
urgent maintenance work. Cave-ins were threatening everywhere, and the passageways had so seriously deteriorated
that the timbering had to be reinforced for distances of
several hundred yards at a stretch. At the bottom, therefore,
the men were being formed into ten-man crews, each with a
foreman in charge, and then set to work in the most severely
damaged areas. When everybody had come down, a count
showed that 322 miners had returned to work—half the
number of those working when the mine was in full operation.

Chaval made the last member of Catherine and Etienne's
team, and it was no coincidence, for he had first hidden
behind some other men and then shown himself when the
foreman could have no choice in the matter. This team was
sent to clear away a cave-in at the end of the north gallery,
nearly two miles away, which was blocking a road in the
Eighteen-Inch seam. They attacked the fallen rock with picks
and shovels. Etienne, Chaval, and five others did the clearing
away, while Catherine and two mine boys hauled the refuse
to the incline. Little was said, for the foreman never left
them; but even so, the haulage girl's two lovers were on the
point of exchanging blows. Though he kept muttering that he
wanted nothing more to do with the slut, the old lover
wouldn't leave her alone, sneakily barging into her until the
new lover threatened to wallop him if he didn't leave her in
peace. They glared at each other and had to be separated.

At about eight o'clock Dansaert came by to check on the
work. He seemed in a foul temper and let fly at the foreman:
nothing was right, the timbers had to be replaced as they
went along—what sloppy work! And he left, saying he
would come back with the engineer. He had been waiting for
Négrel since morning, and he could not understand why he
was late.

Another hour went by. The foreman had called a halt to
the clearing and set everybody to shoring up the roof. Even
the haulage girl and the two mine boys were no longer
carting, but were busy preparing and bringing up the timbers.
Situated at the end of the gallery, all the way at one end of
the mine, the team was in the position of an outpost cut off
from all communication with the other crews. Three or four
times strange noises, the distant sound of running, made the
men turn their heads: what could it be?—it sounded as
though the passages were emptying out, as though their
comrades were already going up, and on the run too. But the

noise faded away into the deep silence, and they went back to wedging in the timbers, dazed by the heavy hammer blows. Finally they started clearing away again, and once more the carts began to roll.

But after the first trip Catherine came back terrified, saying there was nobody at the incline.

"I called, but nobody answered. Everybody's cleared out."

They were so shocked that all ten of them tossed aside their tools and began to run. The thought of being abandoned, of being alone at the bottom of the mine, so far from the loading station, panicked them. They had kept only their lamps, and they were running along in Indian file—the men, the boys, and the haulage girl; even the foreman lost his head and kept calling out, more and more frightened by the silence and the deserted, endless galleries. What was happening? Where was everybody? What accident could have carried them all off? The very vagueness of the danger, the fact that they did not know what the menace hanging over them was, only increased their terror.

Then, as they were nearing the loading station, a torrent blocked their way. Immediately they were in water up to their knees; they could no longer run, but had to wade painfully through the flood, obsessed by the idea that a minute's delay might mean their death.

"My God, the casing's given way!" cried Etienne. "Didn't I say we'd all end up down here?"

Ever since the men had gone down, Pierron had nervously been watching the deluge in the shaft grow in intensity. While he and two other men were loading the carts, he kept raising his head, and his face was doused by the big drops, his ears buzzed with the rumble of the storm overhead. But he was especially frightened when he noticed that the thirty-foot-deep sump below him was filling up: water was already lapping over the boards and spreading over the iron flooring— a sign that the pump was no longer able to handle the leaks. He could hear it panting away, gasping with fatigue. At this point he warned Dansaert, who swore angrily and said they would have to wait for the engineer. Twice again he spoke to him, but got no response other than exasperated shrugs. So the water was rising—what could he do about it?

Mouque appeared with Bataille, whom he was leading to work; he had to hold him with both hands, for the sleepy old horse had suddenly reared, stretching his neck toward the shaft and whinnying in deadly fear.

"What's the matter, old philosopher?—what's troubling

you? . . . Oh, it's the rain. Come along, it doesn't concern
you."

But the animal was trembling all over, and Mouque had to
drag him to work by force.

At almost the same moment as Mouque and Bataille were
disappearing down the end of a gallery, there was a cracking
sound up above, followed by the prolonged noise of something falling. A piece of the casing had broken loose and was
dropping some six hundred feet, banging against the sides of
the shaft as it fell. Pierron and the other loaders were able to
get out of the way, and the oak plank only crushed an empty
cart. At the same time a sheet of water, like a torrent
spurting from a burst dike, came pouring down. Dansaert
wanted to go up and check, but even as he was talking, a
second piece came hurtling down. And faced with this imminent catastrophe, in deadly fear, he hesitated no longer; he
gave the order for everyone to get out and sent the foremen
to warn the men in the stalls.

A panic-stricken rush began. From every gallery files of
workers came running on the double and rushed the cages.
They nearly crushed each other to death in order to be
among the first taken up. Some of them had tried to use the
ladder well, but they came down shouting that the passage
was already blocked. As each cage-load rose, the other miners stood there in anguish: that one had got by, but who
knew if the next one would make it past the obstacles
blocking the shaft? The collapse up above must still be
continuing, for they could hear a series of muffled detona-
tions—timbers splitting and cracking amid the continuous
and increasing rumble of the falling water. One cage was
soon out of service, smashed out of shape and no longer able
to move between the guides, which were probably broken.
The other was scraping so badly that the cable was sure to
snap. And there were still about a hundred men to bring up,
all of them fuming impatiently, hanging on for all they were
worth, bloodied, half-drowned. Two were killed by falling
planks. A third, who had latched onto the bottom of the
cage, fell about a hundred and fifty feet and disappeared into
the sump.

Dansaert was nevertheless trying to maintain order. Armed
with a pick, he threatened to split the skull of the first man
who did not obey orders; he wanted to get them lined up in a
single file, and he kept shouting that the loaders would leave
last, only after having sent up the others. Nobody was listening to him—he had had to prevent Pierron, white with fear,
from being one of the first to escape, driving him away with

blows each time the cage left. But his own teeth were chattering—another minute and he would be swallowed up; everything up there was giving way, water was pouring down like a river in flood, and with a murderous rain of timbers. A few workers were still running out of the galleries when, mad with fear, he leaped into a cart and let Pierron jump in behind him. The cage went up.

It was at just this moment that the team including Etienne and Chaval reached the loading station. They saw the cage disappearing and ran toward it, but they had to draw back under the final collapse of the casing: the shaft was blocked, the cage would not come down again. Catherine was sobbing, Chaval nearly choking on his curses. There were about twenty of them—were those filthy bosses going to abandon them like this? Old Mouque had slowly brought Bataille back and was still holding him by the bridle, both the old man and the horse stunned by the rapid rise of the flood. The water was already up to their thighs. Mutely, his teeth clenched, Etienne picked Catherine up and held her in his arms. And all twenty of them kept looking up and shouting, all twenty of them kept idiotically and persistently staring at the shaft—that caved-in hole from which a river was spewing forth and from which no help could any longer reach them.

On top, as Dansaert was getting out of the cage, he saw Négrel running up. By a stroke of bad luck, Madame Hennebeau had detained him that morning, just as he was getting out of bed, to leaf through some catalogs of presents for the bride. It was ten o'clock.

"What's happening?" he shouted from a distance.

"The mine's wrecked," answered the chief foreman.

And he stutteringly related the catastrophe while the engineer kept shrugging his shoulders incredulously: come now, casing just doesn't give way like that, he was exaggerating, they'd have to take a look.

"Nobody's still at the bottom, is there?"

Dansaert became uneasy. No, nobody. At least he hoped not. Still, some of the men might have been delayed.

"For God's sake!" exclaimed Négrel. "Why the hell did you come up then? You don't just leave your men like that!"

He immediately gave orders for the lamps to be counted. Three hundred and twenty-two had been given out that morning, and only 255 were accounted for now; but several of the men admitted they had left theirs below, had dropped them in the panicky stampede. They tried to call the roll, but it was impossible to establish an exact count: some of the miners had already gone, others did not hear their names

called. Nobody could agree on how many men were missing.
Maybe twenty, maybe forty. The engineer was sure of only
one thing: there were men at the bottom—when you bent
over the mouth of the shaft you could hear their shouts
through the noise of the rushing water and the falling timber.

Négrel began by sending for Monsieur Hennebeau and
trying to close off the mine area. But it was already too
late—the miners who had raced off toward Village 240 as
though pursued by the sound of the splitting casing had
already spread the alarm among the families; and bands of
women, of old men, of children, were swarming down the
hill, shouting and sobbing. They had to be pushed back, and
a ring of supervisors was given orders to keep them away lest
they hinder the rescue operations. Many of the workers who
had come up from below were also standing there, dazed,
mesmerized by the fearful fascination of the terrifying hole
from which they had just barely escaped, never even thinking
to change their clothes. The women swarmed around them in
a frenzy, begging them, questioning them, asking for names.
Was so-and-so there?—and so-and-so?—and so-and-so? They
didn't know, they stammered, they shuddered, they gesticu-
lated like lunatics, as if to ward off some abominable vision
still present before their eyes. The crowd was increasing
rapidly; lamentations were rising from the roads. And up on
the slag heap, in Old Bonnemort's shelter, a man was sitting
on the ground—Souvarine, who had not gone away and who
was watching everything.

"Their names! Their names!" cried the women in tear-
choked voices.

Négrel appeared for a moment and curtly announced:

"As soon as we know the names we will make them
available. But there's still hope, everybody will be saved. . . .
I'm going down."

The crowd waited in mute anguish. True to his word, with
calm courage the engineer was preparing to go down. He had
given orders for the cage to be detached from the cable and
replaced by a hoisting bucket, and foreseeing that the water
would probably douse his lamp, he had a spare one fastened
under the bucket, where it would be protected.

Trembling foremen, their faces pale and ravaged, were
helping with the preparations.

"You'll come down with me, Dansaert," Négrel ordered
sharply.

But when he saw that they were all frightened, when he
saw the chief foreman stagger as though drunk with terror,
he contemptuously waved him aside.

"No, on second thought, you'd only get in my way.... I'd rather go alone."

He was already in the narrow bucket, which was swaying at the end of the cable, and holding his lamp in one hand and gripping the signal cord in the other, he himself gave the order to the engineman:

"Easy, now!"

The engine started the drums turning, and Négrel disappeared into the abyss, from which the shrieks of the wretches below were still rising.

The top section was solid. He could see that the upper casing was in good condition. Swinging in the middle of the shaft, he turned his light on the walls: there were so few leaks in the joints that he had no trouble with his lamp. But at about a thousand feet, when he got to the lower part of the casing, a spurt of water swamped the bucket and, as he had foreseen, his lamp went out. From there on, his only illumination came from the hanging lamp, which was preceding him into the darkness. And despite his courage he shuddered and paled when confronted with the full horror of the disaster. There were only a few pieces of planking left—the rest had torn loose, supports and all; behind, enormous cavities were opening, and through them were bowing great masses of the flour-fine yellow sands; at the same time, the waters of the Torrent, that subterranean sea with its mysterious storms and shipwrecks, were gushing forth as though from a sluice gate. He went down still deeper, lost amid the ever-widening emptiness, spun about and lashed by the waterspout from the springs, his way so badly lit by the red star of the lamp sinking beneath him that the great shifting shadows below seemed the streets and crossroads of some distant destroyed city. There was nothing human effort could accomplish there. He could only hope to try to rescue those in danger. The lower he sank, the louder came their screams. And then he had to stop, for the shaft was blocked by an obstacle: a mass of timbers—boards ripped from the guides and partitions wrenched from the ladder well—all tangled up with the supports torn from the pump. As he was looking down, heartsick, the screaming suddenly stopped. The rapidly rising water had most likely forced the poor wretches to flee into the galleries—unless it had already stopped their mouths for good.

Forced to admit defeat, Négrel signaled to be brought up. Then he signaled them to stop again. He was still baffled by this sudden accident, the cause of which he could not comprehend. He wanted to understand, and he examined the

few pieces of casing that were still in place. From a distance,
he had been surprised by some of the cuts and scrapes he had
spotted in the wood. His lamp was flickering in the downpour, and he felt about with his fingers; he could clearly
recognize the marks of sawing and drilling, the work of
demoniac destruction. It was obvious that the catastrophe
had been planned. He remained open-mouthed as the remaining timbers cracked and came hurtling down with their
supports in a final collapse that almost took him along with
it. His courage had vanished; the thought of the man who
had done this made his hair stand on end, froze him with a
religious fear of evil, as if that man, larger than life, must
still be lurking in the shadows in punishment for his heinous
crime. He called out, he pulled the signal cord furiously—and
not a moment too soon, for he had just seen that the upper
casing, about three hundred feet above him, was beginning to
move: the joints were opening, releasing their caulking and
sending forth streams of water. It was only a matter of a few
hours now; the rest of the casing would give way and the
shaft would collapse.

At the surface Monsieur Hennebeau was anxiously waiting
for Négrel.

"Well, what happened?"

But the engineer was too choked to speak. He was on the
point of fainting.

"It's just not possible. Nothing like this has ever happened
before. . . . Did you get a good look?"

Shooting him a warning glance, Négrel nodded yes. He
refused to go into details with several of the foremen listening; he drew his uncle some thirty feet away, decided it was
not far enough, moved farther off, then finally told him in a
whisper of the sabotage, the sawed and drilled planks, the
mine with its throat cut and in its final agony. The manager
paled and lowered his voice too, instinctively responding to
the need that draws a veil of silence over the monstrousness
of wild debaucheries and terrible crimes. There was no point
in seeming frightened before the ten thousand Montsou
workers—they would see about this later. And both men
went on whispering, stunned by the fact that someone had
found the courage to go down, to hang over nothingness, to
risk his life twenty times over to accomplish this diabolic
piece of work. They could not understand this lunatic courage for destruction, and they refused to believe the evidence
in the same way that people tend to doubt stories of famous
escapes—of prisoners who get away through windows a hundred feet above the ground.

When Monsieur Hennebeau rejoined the foremen his face was twitching nervously. He made a despairing gesture and gave the order to clear the mine area immediately. It was a lugubrious, funereal departure, a silent leave-taking accompanied by backward glances at the large brick buildings, empty but still upright, which nothing could now save.

The manager and the engineer, the last to leave the landing room, were greeted by the crowd's insistently repeated clamor:

"Their names! Their names! Tell us their names!"

La Maheude was now there among the women. She was remembering the noise in the night; her daughter and her boarder must have left together, they were surely down at the bottom. And after having first cried out that it served them right, that they deserved to die down there, the heartless cowards, she had come running and was now standing in the front ranks, shivering with anxiety. She no longer had any doubts; the talk all around her about the names told her enough. Yes, yes, Catherine was there, and so was Etienne; one of the men had seen them. But there was still no agreement about the others. No, not so-and-so, but so-and-so, and maybe Chaval, though one of the mine boys swore he had come up with him. La Levaque and La Pierronne had nobody in danger, but they were carrying on and wailing as loudly as the others. Zacharie had been one of the first to get out, and despite his usual devil-may-care pose, he had wept as he embraced his wife and mother; he remained beside the latter, trembling as she did, displaying an unexpected depth of tenderness for his sister, refusing to believe she was down there as long as there was no official confirmation from the bosses.

"Their names! Their names! Please tell us their names!"

Unnerved, Négrel called loudly to the supervisors:

"Make them shut up! It's enough to drive a man to his death. We don't know the names."

Two hours had already gone by. In the initial bewilderment no one had thought of the other shaft, the old Réquillart shaft. Then just as Monsieur Hennebeau was announcing a rescue attempt from that end, word went round that five workers had just escaped the flood by climbing the rotting ladders of the old, unused ladder well; when Old Mouque's name was heard there was great surprise, for nobody had thought he was down there. But the story of the five who had escaped only doubled the tears: fifteen comrades had been unable to follow them, were lost, sealed off by cave-ins, and rescue was now impossible because there was already more

than thirty feet of water in Réquillart. All the names were
known, and the air was filled with the groans of an assas-
sinated people.

"Make them shut up!" Négrel repeated furiously. "And
make them step back! That's right, a hundred yards back! It's
dangerous here. Push them back! Push them back!"

They had to struggle with the poor wretches, who were
now imagining other tragedies—they were being chased so
that other deaths could be concealed—and the foremen had
to explain that the shaft was going to gobble up the whole
mine area. This idea stunned them into silence, and they
finally let themselves be moved back step by step; but
the number of men holding them off had to be doubled, for
they kept moving up again despite themselves, as if fascinated. A thousand people were jostling each other on the
road, coming at a run from every village and even from
Montsou. And the man high on the slag heap, the blond man
with the girlish face, kept smoking cigarettes to pass the
time, never once taking his pale eyes from the mine.

Then the wait began. It was noon, and though nobody
had eaten, nobody left. Rust-colored clouds were moving
slowly across the misty, dirty-gray sky. From behind Rasseneur's hedge a big dog, exasperated by the warm scent of
the crowd, kept up a ceaseless barking. Little by little the
crowd had spread over the neighboring ground, and it was
now encircling the mine from a distance of a hundred yards.
In the center of the great empty area rose Le Voreux. Not a
living soul, not a sound—a desert; the doors and windows,
left open, showed the emptiness inside; a forgotten tawny
cat, sensing the threat underlying this solitude, leaped from a
stairway and disappeared. The boiler fires were evidently just
going out, for faint traces of smoke were still rising toward
the dark clouds from the tall brick chimney, and meanwhile
the weathercock on the headframe was creaking in the wind
with a tiny shrill cry—the single, sad voice of these huge
buildings destined to die.

At two o'clock the situation was unchanged. Monsieur
Hennebeau, Négrel, and some other engineers who had
come on the run formed a group of frock coats and black
hats in front of the crowd, and they too remained on the
spot—bone-weary, feverish, sick at their impotence in the
face of such a disaster, only occasionally exchanging a few
whispered words, as if at the bedside of a dying man. The
upper casing must be in the final process of disintegration;
they could hear the sudden crashing sound of long, rumbling
falls, followed by deep silences. The wound was still spread-

ing: the cave-in, which had begun at the bottom, was expanding toward the surface. In a fit of nervous impatience,
Négrel had decided to see for himself, and he was already
moving forward, alone in the terrifyingly empty space, when
some of the others rushed out and grabbed him by the
shoulders. What was the use?—there was nothing he could
do about it. One of the miners, an old hand, did however slip
through the cordon and race to the dressing shed, but he
calmly reappeared—he had gone for his sabots.

Three o'clock struck. Still nothing. A downpour had
soaked the crowd, but it had not retreated an inch. Rasseneur's dog had begun to bark again. And it was not until
twenty past three that the first tremor shook the ground. Le
Voreux shuddered, solid and still upright. But a second trem-
or followed immediately, and a long cry came from the
gaping mouths: the tarred screening shed had tottered twice
and then collapsed with a terrible crash. Under the enormous
pressure the structural beams were snapping and striking
against each other with such force that they gave off a
shower of sparks. From then on the earth did not stop
shaking; tremor followed tremor on the heels of subterranean
settlings, like the rumbling of an erupting volcano. In the
distance the dog was no longer barking but howling plaintive-
ly, as if to announce the tremors that he sensed were
coming, and each time the ground shook under their feet a
wail of distress escaped the women, the children, this whole
people on the watch. In less than ten minutes the slate roof
of the headframe gave way and gaping fissures split the
landing room and the engine room. Then the noises stopped,
the subsidence halted, and once again there was a deep
silence.

Le Voreux remained in this crippled state for an hour,
looking as though it had been shelled by a barbarian army.
There was no more wailing; the enlarged circle of spectators
simply watched. Under the mass of screening-shed beams
they could see the smashed tilters, the broken and twisted
hoppers. But it was in the former landing room that the
wreckage kept building up—bricks were still raining down
among the rubble of collapsed walls. The iron scaffolding
bearing the pulleys had bent and sunk halfway into the shaft;
one cage was still suspended, a loose end of cable dangling
from it; there was a complete muddle of carts, iron flooring,
and ladders. The lamproom had by some chance remained
untouched, and its rows of bright little lamps were visible on
the left. And in the rear of its shattered housing the engine
could be seen squatting solidly on its masonry base: the

copper-work gleamed, the steel limbs looked like indestructible muscles, the enormous connecting rod jutting into the air resembled the powerful knee of some giant, reclining and confident in his strength.

At the end of this hour of reprieve, Monsieur Hennebeau felt hope revive. The shifting of the ground must be over—they might be able to save the engine and what was left of the buildings. But he still would not let anyone go near the mine, thinking it best to sit tight for another half hour. The wait became unbearable, for hope redoubled anxiety and all hearts were thumping. A dark cloud had spread over the horizon and was hastening the twilight—a sinister sunset on this wreckage thrown up by the underground tempest. They had been there for seven hours without moving, without eating.

Then suddenly, just as the engineers were cautiously moving forward, a final convulsion of the earth set them to flight. Subterranean explosions were detonating—a monstrous artillery shelling the abyss. On the surface the last buildings were toppling, crashing. First a sort of whirlpool sucked down the rubble of the screening shed and the landing room. Next the boiler house cracked and disappeared. Then the square tower housing the gasping drainage pump fell over on its face like a man cut down by a cannonball. And then there was a frightening sight—they saw the engine, torn from its masonry base, its limbs outspread, struggle against death: it moved, it stretched its connecting rod, its giant knee, as though to rise, but then it died—was shattered and engulfed. Only the tall, hundred-foot chimney remained standing, swaying like a ship's mast in a hurricane. They thought it was going to break up and crumble into dust, but suddenly it sank straight down in one piece, sucked into the ground, melted like an enormous candle; not an inch of it remained above the surface, not even the top of the lightning rod. It was all over; the evil beast squatting in its cavern, gorged with human flesh, was no longer drawing its heavy panting breath. Every bit of Le Voreux had just dropped into the abyss.

The crowd fled, shrieking. Some of the women were hiding their eyes as they ran. Horror swept the men along like piles of dry leaves. They did not want to cry out, but at the sight of the immense hole that had formed they cried out despite themselves, their throats bursting, their arms waving. The fifty-foot-deep crater of this extinct volcano extended from the road to the canal, at least a hundred and thirty feet across. The entire mine yard had followed after the buildings: the gigantic trestles, the footbridges with their rails, a whole string of carts, three railroad cars—to say nothing of the timber supply, a forest of cut poles swallowed down like straws. All that could be seen at the bottom was a mash of beams, bricks, iron, plaster—a terrifying wreckage heaped up, tangled together, begrimed by the fury of the catastrophe. And the chasm was getting larger, the fissures spreading from its edges and stretching into the fields. One crack reached Rasseneur's place and split the building's facade. Would the village itself be gulped down? How far did they have to run for shelter in this terrible twilight, under this leaden sky that seemed intent, it too, on crushing the world?

But Négrel uttered a cry of pain. Monsieur Hennebeau, who had recoiled, burst into tears. The disaster was not yet over; a canal bank burst; the water gushed out in a boiling sheet and poured into one of the fissures, tumbling like a cataract into a deep valley and then vanishing. The mine was drinking in the stream; the flood would submerge the galleries for years to come. Soon the crater was filled, and a lake of muddy water covered the ground where Le Voreux had recently been—a lake like those beneath which sleep cities under a curse. A terrified silence was upon them; nothing could be heard but the fall of the water rumbling into the bowels of the earth.

At this point Souvarine rose to his feet on the shuddering slag heap. He had recognized La Maheude and Zacharie sobbing in the face of this collapse that must be weighing down so heavily on the heads of the wretches agonizing below. And he tossed away his last cigarette and set off into the black night without so much as a backward glance. In the distance his shadow shrank and melted into the darkness. He was heading over there, into the unknown. He was calmly marching toward extermination, toward any place where there was dynamite available to blow up cities and men. He will surely be there on that day when the dying bourgeoisie will hear the pavement exploding under its every footstep.

4

Monsieur Hennebeau had left for Paris on the very night following the collapse of Le Voreux; he was eager to brief the directors personally before they could hear about it from the newspapers. The next day, when he returned, he was

perfectly calm and once again the faultlessly efficient administrator. He had apparently cleared himself of all responsibility and seemed not to have gone down in the Company's
esteem—as a matter of fact, the decree appointing him an
officer of the Legion of Honor was signed twenty-four hours
later.

But though the manager survived, the Company was reel-
ing under the terrible blow—not of the few million francs it
had lost, but of the wound in its side, the constant dull fear
of the morrow in the face of the butchering of one of its
mines. It was so panicky that it again felt a need to hush
things up. What was the point of talking about this abominable deed? Even if they were to discover the criminal, why
make a martyr of him, set him up as an example of frightening heroism that would only turn other heads and beget a
whole progeny of arsonists and assassins? In any case, it
never so much as suspected the guilty party; unable to admit
that one man could have found the courage and the strength
for such a deed, it wound up attributing the job to a whole
army of accomplices, and it was precisely this thought—the
thought that its mines were henceforth surrounded by an
ever-growing threat—that obsessed it. The manager had been
given orders to organize a vast espionage network and then
to dismiss quietly, one at a time, all dangerous men suspected
of complicity in the crime. Political prudence dictated that
action be limited to this kind of purge.

There was only one immediate dismissal, that of Dansaert,
the chief foreman. Ever since the scandal at La Pierronne's
house, he had become impossible to retain. The excuse given
was his behavior in the face of danger, the cowardice of a
captain abandoning his men. His dismissal could also be
looked upon as a tactful concession to the miners, who
bitterly hated him.

In spite of all these precautions, rumors had spread among
the public, and the directors had had to send one newspaper
a clarifying letter, denying a story in which mention was
made of a powder barrel ignited by the strikers. After a
hasty examination, the government engineer had already issued his report, which concluded that the casing had spon-
taneously ruptured due to the pressure of the shifting earth,
and the Company had preferred to remain silent and accept
the blame for faulty inspection. From the third day on, the
catastrophe had helped swell the sensationalist items in the
Paris press; people talked only of the workers dying at the
bottom of the mine, and they avidly read the dispatches
published every morning. In Montsou itself the bourgeois

paled and fell silent at the mere mention of Le Voreux, even the boldest of them hesitating to whisper to each other the legend that was springing up. The entire countryside displayed great pity for the victims—expeditions to the destroyed mine were organized, and whole families flocked there to shudder at the ruins that weighed so heavily on the heads of the poor wretches buried below.

Deneulin, who had been named division engineer, took up his duties in the full flush of the disaster. His first step was to turn the canal back into its bed, for this torrent of water was increasing the damage with every passing hour. Extensive work was necessary, and he immediately set a hundred men to construct a dam. Twice the initial barriers were swept away by the force of the water. Now pumps were being installed; it was a desperate fight—a violent, step-by-step struggle to reclaim the lost land.

But the rescue of the buried miners was what really stirred their passions. Négrel was in charge of making a final effort, and there was no shortage of willing hands—all the miners came running to volunteer in a burst of fraternal feeling. They forgot the strike, they did not worry about their pay; if they got nothing, well and good, for there were comrades in danger of death, and all they wanted was the chance to risk their necks. They were all there with their tools, impatiently waiting to be told where to dig. Many of them, still sick with fear after the accident, shaken by fits of nervous trembling, soaked in cold sweat, obsessed by never-ending nightmares, nevertheless left their beds and were among those most insanely eager to tear at the earth, as if to avenge themselves. Unfortunately the problem began with the mere decision of how to go about it: what were they to do? how were they to get down? where should they begin their assault on the rocks?

Négrel was convinced that not one of the victims had survived, that all fifteen had certainly perished, either drowned or asphyxiated; but in mine disasters the rule is always to presume that the men buried at the bottom are still alive, and he made his plans accordingly. His first problem was to figure out where they could have taken refuge. The foreman and the old hands whom he consulted were all in agreement about this: in a crisis of this sort the men had surely climbed from gallery to gallery until they reached the top stalls, so they were undoubtedly trapped at the end of one of the upper passageways. This agreed with the information given by Old Mouque, whose hazy account even led them to believe that the frenzy of the flight had made the

team split up into small groups, leaving scattered fugitives
along the way at every level. But the unanimity of the
foremen ceased as soon as they got to the question of
possible courses of action. As the passageways closest to the
top were some five hundred feet down, they could not think
of sinking a shaft. That left Réquillart as the only access,
the only point from which an approach could be made. The
problem was that the old mine, also flooded, no longer
communicated with Le Voreux, and that the only reachable
points still above the water level were some truncated galleries leading off from the first loading station. Since pumping
would take years, the best solution would be to go into these
galleries and see if at any point they ran next to those
submerged passages at whose farthest ends the endangered
miners were assumed to have taken refuge. Before reaching
this logical conclusion, much discussion had been necessary in
order to rule out a host of impractical projects.

After that Négrel made the dust fly in the archives, and
when he had found the old plans of the two mines he studied
them to determine the points at which the investigation
should begin. Little by little the hunt was inflaming his
passions, and despite his ironic insouciance about men and
things, he in his turn was caught up in a fever of devotion.
They ran into their first problems when they tried to get
down into Réquillart: they had to clear the mouth of the
shaft, cut down the service tree, root out the blackthorns and
the hawthorns—and they still had to repair the ladders. Then
the groping search began. The engineer went down with ten
men and directed them to beat their metal tools against
certain parts of the vein; in complete silence, each man
pressed his ear to the coal and listened for some far-off
answering blows. But they went through all the accessible
galleries in vain, without the echo of a reply. The problem
had become more complicated: where should they cut into
the seam? toward whom should they go, since apparently
nobody was there? But still, in a frenzy of growing anxiety,
they stubbornly kept on with the search.

From the very first day La Maheude showed up at Réquillart every morning. She would seat herself on a beam in
front of the shaft and never stir until evening. Whenever one
of the men would come out, she would stand up and question
him with her eyes: nothing? No, nothing. And she would
reseat herself and go on waiting, silent, her face hard and
inscrutable. Jeanlin too, seeing that his hideout was about to
be invaded, kept circling about like some frightened beast of
prey whose lair is about to give evidence of its depredations:

he thought of the little soldier lying under the rocks, and he was afraid that his deep slumber might be disturbed. But that side of the mine was under water, and besides, the search was oriented more toward the left, in the west gallery. At first Philomène had come along too, in order to accompany Zacharie, who was a member of the search team; but she had soon wearied of freezing there for no reason, and she now stayed in the village, listlessly getting through the days, indifferent to what was going on, coughing from morning till night. In contrast, Zacharie never let up; he would have eaten his way through the earth to find his sister. He kept crying out in his sleep—he saw her dried up with hunger, heard her call out with a voice aching from the pain of shouting for help. Twice he had wanted to dig without orders, saying that this was the right place, he just knew it was. The engineer would no longer let him go down, but he would not leave the shaft from which he was being driven; tormented by the need to be active, he was not even able to sit alongside his mother and wait, but had to continuously circle around and around.

It was the third day. Négrel, having lost all hope, had decided to abandon the search that evening. At noon, when he and his men came back after lunch to make one final attempt, he was startled to see Zacharie climbing out of the mine, red-faced, gesticulating, shouting:

"She's there! She answered me! Hurry, hurry for God's sake!"

Despite the guard, he had slipped down the ladders, and he now swore that he had heard a tapping in the first passageway of the Guillaume vein.

"But we've already been to that spot twice," said Négrel incredulously. "However, we'll soon see."

La Maheude had risen, and she had to be prevented from going down. She stood waiting alongside the shaft, her eyes searching the darkness of the hole.

Down below, Négrel himself rapped out three strokes at long intervals; then, telling his men to be absolutely quiet, he pressed his ear against the coal. Not a sound. He shook his head: the poor fellow had obviously been dreaming. Furious, Zacharie himself rapped, and when once again he heard a reply his eyes glistened and his limbs trembled with joy. Then the other men tried it, one after another: they all became excited—all of them had distinctly heard the distant response. The engineer was amazed; again he pressed his ear to the coal, and this time he finally caught a sound as light as air, a scarcely discernible rhythmic beating—the well-known cadence of the miners' call, which they tap out when in danger. Coal transmits distant sounds with the clarity of crystal.

One of the foremen who was there estimated that the block of coal separating them from their comrades must be at least 150 feet thick. But it seemed as though they could almost stretch out their hands to them, and there was an outburst of joy. Négrel had no choice but to give orders for work to get underway immediately.

When Zacharie reached the surface and saw La Maheude, they fell into each other's arms.

"Don't get your hopes up," said La Pierronne cruelly. She had strolled over to Réquillart that day out of curiosity. "If Catherine isn't with them you'll only end up feeling worse."

It was true. Catherine could very well be somewhere else.

"Shut your damned mouth," raged Zacharie. "She's there, I know she is!"

La Maheude had sat down again, mute and impassive. She went back to waiting.

As soon as the story had spread through Montsou, another rush of people showed up. They could see nothing, but there they remained, and eventually the sightseers had to be kept a distance. Down below they were working day and night. Fearing lest he come up against some obstacle, the engineer had ordered the vein to be breached by three tunnels descending and converging on the spot where the miners were assumed to be imprisoned. Only one cutter at a time could hack away at the coal in the head of the narrow tunnel, and he was relieved every two hours; the coal was loaded into baskets and passed back from hand to hand along a human chain that grew as the tunnel deepened. In the beginning the work went very quickly; one day they cut through more than twenty feet.

Zacharie had arranged to be among those topnotch workers selected to do the cutting. It was a post of honor for which there was considerable rivalry, and he would lose his temper when they wanted to relieve him after his prescribed two hours. He would cheat his comrades of their turns and refuse to give up the pick. His tunnel was soon deeper than the others—he fought the coal with such savage energy that from the entranceway they could hear the roaring of his breath, as if there were some internal forge in his lungs. When he would finally come out, muddy and black, drunk with fatigue, he would collapse on the ground, and they would have to wrap him in a blanket. Then, still staggering, he would once more plunge into the tunnel and the battle would start up again—the mighty blows, the stifled moans, the overriding murderous fury of his rage. To make matters worse the coal was becoming hard, and twice he broke his pick in exasperation at no longer being able to progress as quickly as before. He was also suffering from the heat, a heat that became more intense with every foot of progress and was unbearable at the end of the narrow tunnel, where there was no room for the air to circulate. A manually operated ventilator had been set up, but it was unequal to the task; three times, unconscious, half-asphyxiated cutters had to be brought to the surface.

Négrel lived at the bottom with his workers. His meals were brought down to him, and occasionally, wrapped in a coat, he would snatch a few hours' sleep on a heap of straw. What kept up their courage was the pleading of the wretches down there, the more and more clearly heard signal for them to hurry. It was quite distinct now, ringing out with the purity of notes sounded on a glass harmonica. It guided their progress, and they moved toward this crystalline sound just as soldiers in battle move toward the thunder of the cannon. Each time a cutter was relieved, Négrel went down, tapped, and put his ear to the wall; and each time so far there had been a rapid, urgent response. He had no doubt that they were moving in the right direction, but with what mortal slowness! They would never get there in time. True, in the first two days they had hacked through forty-three feet, but on the third day they had only managed sixteen, and on the fourth day barely ten. The coal was becoming more dense—so hard that they could now penetrate only a bit more than six feet a day. On the ninth day, after superhuman efforts, they were about a hundred and six feet along, and they calculated that they still had more than sixty feet to go. The twelfth day was beginning for the trapped men—twelve times twenty-four hours without food or fire in the glacial darkness. This horrible thought brought tears to the eyes of the rescuers and stiffened their arms to the task. It did not seem possible that human beings could last much longer; the distant taps had been growing feebler since the previous day, and the rescuers were in constant terror of hearing them no more.

La Maheude was still coming regularly to sit at the mouth of the shaft. She would carry Estelle in her arms, for the child could not be left alone from morning to night, and hour after hour she followed the progress, sharing the hopes and the discouragements. Among those who stood there waiting, and even among those as far away as Montsou, there was

feverish expectation and endless discussion. Every heart in
the region was beating in time with those underground.

At lunchtime on the ninth day Zacharie failed to reply
when he was called to be relieved. He seemed possessed,
cursing as he tore away at the coal. Négrel had left for a
moment and was not there to bring him into line; the only
ones present were a foreman and three miners. Zacharie,
probably furious at the dim, flickering light that was slowing
his progress, had been foolhardy enough to open his lamp—
despite strict orders to the contrary, for firedamp had been
escaping, and enormous masses of the gas were collecting in
the narrow, unventilated tunnels. Suddenly there was a crack
of thunder, and flame flashed from the tunnel as though from
the mouth of a cannon loaded with grapeshot. From one end
of the galleries to the other everything burst into flame, the
air serving as a train of gunpowder. This torrent of flame
swept away the foreman and the three miners, rose up the
shaft, and leaped into the daylight in an eruption that spat
forth rocks and broken timbers. The onlookers fled; La
Maheude rose to her feet, clutching the terrified Estelle to
her breast.

When Négrel and the others returned, they fell into a
wild rage. They pounded their feet into the earth—that
unnatural mother who so casually slaughtered her children in
mindless spasms of cruelty. What!—they were giving their
all, going to the rescue of their comrades, and the only result
was that still more men were lost! After three long hours of
toil and danger, when they were finally able to enter the
galleries, they began the lugubrious task of bringing up the
victims. Though neither the foreman nor the three miners
were dead, they were covered with terrible wounds that gave
off the stench of burnt flesh; they had swallowed flames, their
burns went deep down into their throats, they kept shrieking,
begging to be put out of their misery. One of the three
miners was the man who during the strike had smashed the
Gaston-Marie pump with a final blow from his pick; the
other two still bore scarred hands and cut fingers from the
bricks they had hurled at the soldiers. Pale and trembling, the
crowd doffed their caps as the men were carried past.

La Maheude was standing, waiting. At last Zacharie's body
appeared. His clothes had burned off, and the body was
nothing but a black, carbonized, unrecognizable mass. There
was no head; it had been shattered in the explosion. And
when these horrible remains were borne off on a stretcher,
La Maheude followed with mechanical step, her eyelids burning but tearless. She held the sleepy Estelle in her arms and

tragically departed, her hair whipped by the wind. Back in the village Philomène was momentarily stunned, but then her eyes gushed forth like fountains and she found immediate relief. The mother was already on her way back to Réquillart; she had brought her son home, she was returning to wait for her daughter.

Three more days went by. The rescue work had been resumed under all but insuperable difficulties. Fortunately the firedamp explosion had not wrecked the approach galleries, but the air there was so scorched, so heavy and foul, that they had had to install additional ventilators. The cutters relieved one another at twenty-minute intervals. They were moving ahead—there were only some six feet separating them from their comrades. But now they were working with icy hearts, clawing away out of mere vengeance, for the sounds had stopped; the clear, rhythmic little signal was no longer ringing out. It was the twelfth day of rescue work, the fifteenth since the catastrophe, and since that morning there had been only deathly silence.

The new accident had redoubled the curiosity of Montsou; the townspeople were organizing excursions with such enthusiasm that the Grégoires decided to do as everyone else was doing. An outing was arranged, and it was agreed that the Grégoires would drive to Le Voreux in their carriage and that Lucie and Jeanne would go with Madame Hennebeau in hers. Deneulin would show them what he was doing, and then they would come back by way of Réquillart, where Négrel could tell them just how far the galleries had reached and if there was still hope. To complete the day, they would all dine together that evening.

When the Grégoires and their daughter, Cécile, arrived at the ruined mine at about three o'clock, they found Madame Hennebeau already there, dressed in a navy-blue outfit and carrying a parasol to protect herself from the pale February sun. The sky was clear, and the air had the warmth of spring in it. Monsieur Hennebeau was there with Deneulin, and she was listening absentmindedly to the latter's explanations about the work that had been necessary to dam the canal. Jeanne, who always carried a sketch pad with her, was inspired by the horror of the theme and had started to draw, while Lucie, seated beside her on the wreckage of a railway car, was uttering cries of delight and finding it all "stunning." The dam was unfinished, allowing foaming water to stream out and cascade into the enormous crater of the engulfed mine. However, the crater was emptying out; the water, drunk in by the soil, was subsiding, exposing to view the

horrible wreckage at the bottom. Under the delicate blue sky
of this beautiful day it looked like a cesspool—the ruins of
some destroyed city that had sunk into the mud.

"Is this what everybody comes running to see?" exclaimed
Monsieur Grégoire in disappointed tones.

Cécile, glowing with good health and happy to breathe
the fresh, pure air, was cheerfully jesting, but Madame Hennebeau wrinkled her nose in disgust and murmured:

"There's no denying that it's very unattractive."

The two engineers began to laugh. They tried to interest
the visitors by showing them around, explaining the working
of the pumps and the operation of the pile driver. But the
ladies were becoming uneasy. They shuddered when they
learned that the pumps would have to work for years—
perhaps six or seven—before the shaft could be reconstructed
and the water drained from the mine. No, they would rather
think of other things; these shocking sights would only give
them nightmares.

"Let's go," said Madame Hennebeau, turning toward her
carriage.

Jeanne and Lucie protested. What, so quickly! Why, the
sketch wasn't finished! They wanted to stay—their father
would bring them over to dinner in the evening. Monsieur
Hennebeau was the only one to get into his wife's carriage,
for he too had a few questions for Négrel.

"Well, then, you go ahead," said Monsieur Grégoire.
"We'll follow along later. We want to make a short visit in
the village. . . . Go ahead, go ahead, we'll be at Réquillart
as soon as you are."

He climbed in behind Madame Grégoire and Cécile, and
while the other carriage was speeding along the canal, theirs
slowly mounted the hill.

The excursion was to be rounded off by an act of charity.
Zacharie's death had filled them with pity for the tragic
Maheu family that the whole region was talking about. They
felt no sympathy for the father—that bandit, that killer of
soldiers who had had to be shot down like some wild animal—
but they were touched by the plight of the mother, that poor
woman who had just lost her son after having lost her husband, and whose daughter might at this moment be nothing
but a corpse under the ground; and there was also, in
addition to all this, talk of an invalid grandfather, of a child
who limped as a result of a cave-in, and of a little girl who
had died of hunger during the strike. So even though the
family had partially merited its misfortunes because of its
detestable wrongheadedness, the Grégoires had decided to

demonstrate the extent of their charity, their desire to forgive
and forget, by bringing their contribution in person. There
were two carefully wrapped packages under the seat of the
carriage.

An old woman pointed out the Maheu house to the
coachman—Number 16 in the second block. But when the
Grégoires had dismounted with their packages there was no
response to their knock; they even beat their fists against the
door, but there was still no reply: the house echoed dismally,
like a dwelling place emptied by mourning, cold and dark,
long since abandoned.

"There's nobody home," said Cécile, disappointed. "How
irritating! What are we going to do with all this now?"

Suddenly the door of the next house opened, and La
Levaque appeared.

"Oh, I beg your pardon, Sir! And yours, Madame! Excuse
me, Miss! . . . I suppose it's my neighbor you want. She's not
home. She's at Réquillart. . . ."

In a flood of words she told them the whole story, repeating over and over that neighbors had to help each other
and that she was taking care of Lénore and Henri so that
La Maheude could continue her vigil at Réquillart. Having
spotted the packages, she began to talk of her poor widowed
daughter and to recount her own wretchedness, her eyes
shining with covetousness. Then she hesitatingly murmured:

"I have the key. If Monsieur and Madame really want to
go in . . . The grandfather is there."

The Grégoires looked at her in amazement. What!—the
grandfather was there? But nobody had answered their
knock. Could he be asleep? And when La Levaque had
finally opened the door, what they saw froze them on the
threshold.

Bonnemort was there, alone, his eyes wide and staring,
nailed to a chair in front of the fireless chimney. The room
around him looked larger without the cuckoo clock and the
varnished pine furniture that had formerly cheered it up; the
only things left against the raw green walls were the portraits
of the Emperor and the Empress, their pink lips smiling
down in official benevolence. The old man did not stir, nor
did his eyes so much as blink at the sudden light from the
open door; he was like an imbecile, and he appeared not to
have even noticed all the people coming in. At his feet was
his plate of cinders—as if he were a cat and a place had been
provided for him to mess in.

"Pay no attention to him if he doesn't behave properly,"
said La Levaque obligingly. "Something seems to have

snapped inside his head. He hasn't said a word for the last two weeks."

Just then Old Bonnemort was shaken by a horrible hawking sound rising from his very entrails, and he spat a thick black blob into the plate. The cinders were soaked with this muddy mixture of coal—all the coal from the mine was coming up from his throat. But he had immediately resumed his immobility, and he no longer moved except at long intervals to spit.

Uneasy, sick with disgust, the Grégoires nevertheless tried to say a few friendly and encouraging words.

"Well, my good man," said the father. "Have you caught a cold?"

The old man kept his eyes fixed on the wall and never turned his head. A heavy silence fell once again.

"Somebody should make you a nice cup of tea," added the mother.

He maintained his mute rigidity.

"You know, Papa," murmured Cécile, "someone did tell us he was crippled, but then we forgot about it. . . ."

She stopped in deep embarrassment. After having set out a pot of stew and two bottles of wine on the table, she had begun to undo the second package and was drawing from it an enormous pair of shoes. It was the present for the grandfather, and holding one shoe in each hand, she stood there staring in utter confusion at the swollen feet of the poor man who would never walk again.

"Well, old fellow, they come a little late, don't they?" resumed the father to introduce a cheery note. "Never mind, they'll come in handy somehow."

Bonnemort neither heard nor replied, and his terrifying face remained as cold and hard as stone.

Cécile furtively set the shoes against the wall, but though she tried to be careful, the nails clattered against the floor and the enormous shoes remained an embarrassing presence in the room.

"No use expecting any thanks from him," exclaimed La Levaque, who had looked at the shoes with a glance of deepest envy. "You might just as well give a duck a pair of spectacles, if you don't mind my saying so."

And she talked on, hoping to draw the Grégoires to her own house, where she was sure she could touch their hearts. Finally she thought of an excuse; she began to tell them how wonderful Henri and Lénore were—so sweet, so darling, and so intelligent that they answered questions like little angels! They'd surely be able to tell the lady and the gentleman whatever they wanted to know.

"Won't you come for a moment, sweetheart?" asked the father, pleased to be able to leave.

"Yes, I'll be along in a minute," Cécile answered.

She remained alone with Bonnemort. What kept her there, trembling and fascinated, was that she thought she recognized this old man: where had she seen that square, livid face tattooed with coal? And suddenly she remembered—she saw herself surrounded by a screaming mob, she felt the cold hands tightening around her neck. Yes, this was the man, she recognized him. She stared at the hands resting on his knees, the hands of a crouching worker whose entire strength is in his wrists, hands that were still strong despite his age. Little by little Bonnemort seemed to be rousing himself; he became aware of her, and in his imbccilic way he seemed to be examining her, too. A fiery flush rose to his cheeks, a nervous twitch pulled at his mouth, from which a thin stream of black saliva was dribbling. They remained staring at each other in fascination—she blossoming, buxom, and fresh from long hours of idleness and the well-fed comfort of her race, he swollen with dropsy, as pathetically ugly as some broken-down beast of toil, ruined by the destruction, from father to son, of a hundred years' backbreaking labor and hunger.

Ten minutes later, surprised at Cécile's continuing absence, the Grégoires returned to the Maheu house and uttered a terrible cry. Their daughter, her face blue, was lying on the ground, strangled. The fingers around her neck had left the red imprint of a giant's clutch. Bonnemort, tottering on his lifeless legs, had fallen alongside her and was unable to get up. His fingers were still crooked into claws, and his wide, staring eyes were imbecilically fixed on the Grégoires. He had smashed his plate when he fell, and the cinders had scattered, splattering the entire room with muddy black spittle; the enormous pair of shoes were still aligned against the wall, safe and sound.

It was never possible to reconstruct exactly what had happened. Why had Cécile drawn near him? How had Bonnemort, a man unable to move from his chair, been able to get at her neck? Once he had got a grip on her, it was obvious that he must have clung relentlessly, squeezing, stifling her cries, falling to the ground with her, holding on till her last gasp. Not a sound, not a moan, had penetrated the thin partition between the neighboring houses. The only explanation was that it had been a sudden fit of madness, an inexplicable impulse to murder aroused by the girl's white

neck. So savage an act seemed incredible on the part of this
old cripple who had always lived like a good man, always
been like an obedient animal, turning his back on new ideas.
What unconscious bitterness could have slowly festered within him and risen from his entrails to his brain? The horror of
the deed made them conclude that he could not have known
what he was doing, that it was the crime of an idiot.

Meanwhile the Grégoires were on their knees, sobbing,
strangling with grief. Their adored daughter, that so-long-
desired daughter who had been showered with all their
wealth, whom they went on tiptoe to watch over while she
slept, whom they had thought never well-enough fed, never
plump enough! It was the collapse of their entire existence—
why go on living now that they would have to live without
her?

La Levaque was screaming wildly:

"My God, what's the old bastard done? Who could have
imagined such a thing? . . . And La Maheude won't be
coming back till evening! Do you think I ought to run and
get her?"

Crushed, neither the mother nor the father replied.

"Don't you think that would be best? . . . I'm going."

But before she left, she spotted the shoes again. The whole
village was in a stew, a crowd was already forming outside.
Somebody was sure to steal them—and besides, there were
no more Maheu men left to wear them. She quietly carried
them off. They would be just about right for Bouteloup.

At Réquillart the Hennebeaus, accompanied by Négrel,
waited a long time for the Grégoires. The engineer had
come up from the mine and was explaining things to them:
they were hoping to reach the trapped miners by that evening, but in all likelihood they would find nothing but corpses
to bring up, for there had been no break in the deathlike
silence. La Maheude, pale as a ghost, was sitting on a beam
behind the engineer and listening when La Levaque came
running up to tell her about the fine piece of work the old
man had just done. She merely shrugged with impatience and
irritation. But she returned home with her.

Madame Hennebeau all but fainted. How terrible! Poor
Cécile—she had been so gay that day, so alive only an hour
earlier! Monsieur Hennebeau had to take his wife into Old
Mouque's shack for a minute. He loosened her clothes with
clumsy hands and was troubled by the scent of musk that
rose from her open bodice. Her face streaked with tears, she
embraced Négrel, who was horrified by this death that put a
sudden end to his wedding plans; her husband watched them

console each other and experienced a sense of relief. This tragedy settled things nicely; he would rather put up with his nephew than risk having him replaced by his coachman.

5

At the bottom of the shaft the marooned wretches were screaming with terror. The water was now waist-high. The noise of the torrent stunned them, and the last falling pieces of the casing made them think the final crack of doom was sounding, but what finally drove them mad with fear was the whinnying of the horses locked up in the stable—the terrible, unforgettable death cry of an animal being slaughtered.

Mouque had let Bataille loose. The old horse was standing there trembling, his dilated eyes staring at the ever-mounting water. The loading station was rapidly filling up, and by the reddish glow of the three lamps still burning under the vault they could see the greenish flood rising. Then suddenly, feeling the icy water soak his hide, Bataille started off in a furious gallop, plunged into one of the haulage galleries, and disappeared.

The men followed the animal in a wild flight.

"There's no damn use hanging around here," shouted Mouque. "We'd better try Réquillart."

Now they were swept along by the hope that they could get out by way of the neighboring shaft if they could only reach it before the passage was blocked. All twenty of them were pushing and shoving, one behind another, holding their lamps up high so the water would not snuff them out. Luckily the gallery was on a slight incline, and they sloshed along, fighting against the flood for some two hundred yards without the water gaining on them. Forgotten superstitions reawakened in their terrified hearts; they invoked the earth, for it was the earth that was avenging itself, making the blood flow from the vein because one of its arteries had been severed. One old man was stammering forgotten prayers and turning his thumbs out to appease the evil spirits of the mine.

But at the first crossroad an argument broke out. The stableman wanted to go to the left, some of the others swore they could take a shortcut by going to the right. A whole minute was lost.

"Go ahead, croak if you want to—I don't give a damn!"
Chaval shouted brutally. "I'm going this way."

He took the turning on the right and two of the men
followed him. The others continued to race behind Old
Mouque, who had grown up at the bottom of Réquillart. Yet
he himself hesitated, did not know where to turn. They became confused, and even the old-timers could no longer
recognize the maze of tunnels that seemed to have tangled
into a twisted skein before their very eyes. At every fork in the
tunnel uncertainty made them stop dead, yet some decision
had to be made.

Etienne was running last, held back by Catherine, who was
paralyzed by exhaustion and fear. Left to himself, he would
have gone to the right with Chaval, for he believed that the
latter had chosen the best route, but he had let him go, even
at the risk of never getting out again himself. In any case, the
group kept splintering; some of the other men had set off on
their own, and there were now only seven behind Old
Mouque.

"Put your arms around my neck and I'll carry you,"
Etienne said to the girl on seeing her falter.

"No, let me be," she murmured. "I can't go another step.
I'd rather die now and have it over with."

They were some fifty yards behind the others, and he was
about to pick her up in spite of her resistance when the
tunnel was suddenly blocked: an enormous mass of rock had
given way and was now separating them from the others.
The flood was already lapping against the rocks, and there
were cave-ins on all sides. They had to double back. Eventually they completely lost their sense of direction. It was the
end; they would have to give up any idea of getting out by
way of Réquillart. The only hope left was to make for the
upper stalls, from where they might be rescued if the waters
went down.

Finally Etienne recognized the Guillaume vein.

"Good!" he said. "Now I know where we are. Damn it, we
were on the right road, too! Well, to hell with that! . . .
Listen, let's go straight ahead—we'll climb up the chimney."

The water was beating againt their chests and they could
only inch along. As long as they still had some light they
would not give up hope, and in order to save on oil they put
out one of the lamps; later they would empty its fuel into the
one still burning. They had just reached the chimney when a
noise behind them made them turn. Had the others, also
finding their way blocked, returned? They could hear a roaring sound of breathing in the distance, and they could not

understand this storm that was churning up the foam as it drew nearer. They screamed when they saw a huge, whitish mass emerge from the darkness and fight its way toward them through the narrow timbers crushing against its sides.

It was Bataille. After leaving the loading station he had galloped wildly through the dark galleries. He seemed to know his way about in this underground city, where he had been living for eleven years, and his eyes could pierce the eternal night in which he had spent his life. He galloped, he galloped, bending his head, lifting his feet, racing through these narrow tunnels that were filled by his great body. Road succeeded road, crossroad after crossroad spread out before him, and he never hesitated. Where was he going?—over there, perhaps, toward the vision of his youth, to the mill on the banks of the Scarpe where he had been born, to the confused memory of the sun burning in the sky like some enormous lamp. He wanted to live, his animal memory was awakening, the desire to breathe once more the air of the plains urged him on and on in search of the hole, the way out into the warm air, into the light. And a spirit of revolt swept away his former resignation—after having blinded him, the mine was now trying to kill him. The pursuing flood was lapping at his thighs, stinging his rump. The farther he plunged ahead, the more narrow the galleries became, and their roofs got lower and their walls bulged. But still he galloped on, scraping his hide, leaving bits of flesh hanging from the timbers. The mine seemed to be closing in on him from every side, trying to trap him, to smother him.

As he came into sight, Etienne and Catherine could see that he was being strangled between the rocks. He had stumbled and broken both forelegs. In a final burst of energy he dragged himself along for a few more yards; but his flanks would no longer pass through, and he was ensnared, garroted by the earth. His bleeding head was craned forward, his large troubled eyes still searched for some crevice. The water was rapidly rising over him and he began to whinny, to emit the same long, horrible death cry with which the other horses had previously died in the stable. The final agony of this old animal—broken, immobilized, struggling in these depths so far from daylight—was terrible to behold. His cry of distress never ceased; even when the flood covered his mane it issued only the more hoarsely from his raised and gaping mouth. There was a final gurgle, the muffled sound of a barrel being filled. Then a heavy silence fell.

"Oh, my God, take me away!" sobbed Catherine. "Oh, my

God! I'm afraid, I don't want to die! . . . Take me away!
Take me away!"

She had seen death. The collapsed shaft, the flooded mine—
none of it had breathed such terror into her face as the
clamor of Bataille's final death cry. She could still hear
it—her ears were ringing with it, every inch of her flesh
trembling from it.

"Take me away! Take me away!"

Etienne had caught her up and was carrying her. It was
not a moment too soon—they were soaked to the shoulders
even as they scrambled up the chimney. He had to help her,
for she no longer had the strength to grapple with the timbers.
Three times he thought she was slipping from his grasp, falling
into the bottomless sea whose rising tide was roaring beneath
them. They were able to catch their breath for a few minutes
when they reached the first roadway and found it still dry,
but the water reappeared and they had to hoist themselves
higher up. Hour after hour they continued to climb, the flood
chasing them from roadway to roadway, always forcing them
to continue their upward scramble. At the sixth roadway a
respite filled them with feverish hope—they thought the
water level had stopped rising. But then there was an even
stronger upsurge and they had to clamber up to the seventh,
and then the eighth. There was only one more, and when
they got there they watched anxiously as the water inched
upward. If it didn't stop, would they have to die like that old
horse, crushed against the roof, their lungs filled with water?

They could hear the thunderous sound of cave-ins at every
moment. The entire mine was shaken, its narrow guts bursting with the immense flood that was gorging it. Forced
back into the ends of the galleries, the air accumulated,
became compressed, and exploded with great violence among
the splintered rocks and the churned-up soil. It was the
terrifying din of internal cataclysms—like a part of the
prehistoric struggle when floods were turning the earth upside
down, burying the mountains under the plains.

And Catherine, shaken and dazed by this continuing collapse, joined her hands together and kept stammering the
same words over and over again.

"I don't want to die . . . I don't want to die. . . ."

To reassure her, Etienne swore that the water was no
longer rising. They had been on the run for six hours now—
help was sure to be sent down. He said "six hours," but he
did not really know, for they had lost any exact sense of time.
Actually, a whole day had already gone by while they were
climbing up through the Guillaume vein.

Soaked to the skin and shivering, they settled down. She undressed without embarrassment and wrung out her clothes; then she put her trousers and jacket back on so they could finish drying on her. Since she was barefoot and he had his sabots, he forced her to take them. All they could do now was wait, so they lowered the lamp wick until there was only a feeble glow. But cramps churned their stomachs and they realized they were dying of hunger—until then they had hardly been conscious of being alive. When the catastrophe had occurred, they had not yet eaten, and now their sandwiches were waterlogged, turning into a soup. She had to lose her temper before he would accept his share. As soon as she had eaten, she fell into an exhausted sleep on the cold ground. Tormented by sleeplessness, he watched over her, his head in his hands, his eyes staring.

How many hours went by this way? He could not have said. All he knew was that down the hole of the chimney in front of him he had seen the water reappear, the black, moving flood, the beast whose back was continually swelling toward them. At first it was no more than a thin line, a supple, lengthening snake; then it widened into a wriggling, crawling spine; and before long it reached them and lapped at the sleeping girl's feet. Though he was worried, he hesitated to wake her. Wasn't it cruel to rouse her from this repose, from this oblivious ignorance that was perhaps cradling her in a dream of fresh air and life under the sun? Besides, where could they escape to? Wracking his brain, he remembered that the inclined plane was in this part of the vein and that it connected with the one used by the loading station above. It was a way out. He let her go on sleeping as long as possible, watching the rising water, waiting for it to drive them on. Finally he lifted her gently, and she shuddered violently.

"Oh, my God, it's true! . . . My God, it's beginning all over again!"

Remembering everything, she cried out at finding death so near again.

"No, be calm," he murmured. "We can get through, I swear we can."

To reach the inclined plane they had to walk doubled over, once more soaked to the shoulders. Then the climb—a more dangerous one this time—began again, now through a completely timbered passageway over a hundred yards long. At first they attempted to pull the cable and fix one of the cars at the bottom, for if the other one came down while they were climbing it would crush them. But it would not

budge; something was blocking the mechanism. They had to
risk it, not daring to use this cable that kept getting in their
way, breaking their nails against the smooth timbering. He
went behind, supporting her with his head whenever her
bleeding hands made her start to slide. Suddenly they
bumped into a splintered beam that barred the way. The
earth had poured down—a cave-in made it impossible for
them to go higher. Luckily there was a door at that point,
and they came out into a passageway.

They were thunderstruck at seeing a lamp glowing before
them. A man shouted out furiously:

"A few more idiots no smarter than I am!"

They recognized Chaval, who was blocked by the cave-in
that had filled the inclined plane; the two men who had
started off with him had been left by the wayside, their skulls
split open. He himself had been wounded in the elbow, but
had had the courage to crawl back on his knees to take their
lamps and search their clothes to steal their sandwiches. Just
as he was making off, a final cave-in behind him had sealed
the gallery.

He immediately swore to himself that he would not share
his supplies with these people who were crawling out of the
ground. He would kill them first! Then he recognized them
and his anger subsided; he began to laugh, a nasty, gloating
laugh.

"Oh, it's you, Catherine! You've had your nose put out of
joint and you want to come back to your man, do you? Fine,
fine, we'll give it a whirl together."

He pretended not to see Etienne. Stunned by this encounter, the latter had protectively put his arm around the
haulage girl, who was clinging to him. But there was no way
out of the situation, and so, just as though they had left each
other as good friends only an hour earlier, he merely asked
Chaval:

"Did you have a look back there? Can't we get out
through the stalls?"

Chaval was still snickering.

"Oh sure, through the stalls! They've collapsed too. We're
between two walls, in a real mousetrap. . . . But you can go
back along the plane—if you're a good diver, that is."

It was true; the water was rising, they could hear it
lapping. Their retreat was already cut off. Chaval was right—
it was a mousetrap, a section of gallery blocked at both ends
by massive cave-ins. There was no way out; the three of
them were immured.

"Staying, are you?" added Chaval mockingly. "Well, I

guess there's not much else you can do, and if you don't bother me, I won't even say a word to you. There's still room here for two men. . . . We'll soon see which of us will croak first—unless help comes, which seems unlikely."

Etienne continued:

"If we tapped against the walls, maybe they'd hear us."

"I'm sick and tired of tapping. . . . Here, take this stone and try it yourself!"

Etienne picked up the piece of sandstone, which Chaval had already worn down, went as far back along the vein as he could, and beat out the miners' call, the prolonged drumming with which men in danger signal their presence. Then he placed his ear against the wall to listen. Twenty times over he stubbornly began again. There was no answering sound.

During this time, Chaval pretended to be calmly setting his possessions in order. First he placed his three lamps against the wall: only one was burning; the others would be used later. Then he set out his two remaining sandwiches on a piece of timber. That was the buffet—if he took care, he could easily last two days on that. He turned around and said:

"You know, half of it's for you, Catherine, when you get really hungry."

The girl remained silent. To find herself between these two men was the final misery.

And so their terrible life together began. Seated on the ground a few feet from each other, neither Chaval nor Etienne so much as opened his mouth. In response to a comment by the former, the latter put out his lamp, an unnecessary luxury of light; then they both fell silent again. Uneasy at the way her former lover kept looking at her, Catherine had lain down near Etienne. The hours dragged by; they could hear the tiny murmur of the ever-mounting water and, from time to time the violent shocks and distant explosions that announced the final collapse of the mine. When the lamp was empty and they had to open another to light it, fear of firedamp made them hesitate for a moment, but they would rather have been blown up then and there than try to endure in the dark, and nothing did explode; there was no firedamp. They stretched out again, and once more the hours began to pass.

Startled by a noise, Etienne and Catherine looked up. Chaval had decided to eat: he had cut a sandwich in two and was chewing it slowly so as not to be tempted to swallow it all at once. They watched him, tortured by hunger.

"You're sure you don't want any?" he said to the haulage
girl in his provocative way. "You're wrong, you know."

She had lowered her eyes, fearing she might give way, her
stomach torn by such a cramp that her eyelids were swollen
with tears. But she knew what he wanted; that very morning
he had breathed down her neck, for seeing her with the other
man had aroused in him one of his former furies of desire.
The looks with which he was trying to attract her had a
flame that she well knew—the flame of his attacks of jealousy, when he would pummel her with his fists and accuse
her of abominations with her mother's boarder. And she did
not want this; she was terrified lest in going back to him she
would set these two men against each other here in this
narrow cave where they were breathing their last. My God!—
couldn't they meet their fate as good friends?

Etienne would rather have starved to death than beg
Chaval for a mouthful of bread. The silence grew heavier
and they seemed to be living through an eternity as the slow,
monotonous minutes dragged hopelessly by, one after the
other. They had been imprisoned together for a day. The
second lamp was growing dim and they lit the third.

Chaval began his other sandwich and growled:

"Come on, don't be a fool!"

Catherine shuddered. Etienne had turned aside to avoid
influencing her. Then, as she did not move, he said in a low
voice:

"Go ahead, child."

Then the tears she was choking back began to flow. She
wept for a long time, unable to find the strength to rise, no
longer knowing if she was hungry or not, her entire body
aching with pain. Etienne had gotten up and was pacing back
and forth, vainly beating out the miners' call, furious at being
forced to spend the tail end of his life crammed up against a
rival whom he detested. There was not even room for them
to be able to croak far enough away from each other! As
soon as he had gone ten steps he had to turn back and bump
into that man! And she, the poor girl, they were fighting over
her even in the bowels of the earth! She would belong to the
survivor—if he went first, that man would steal her from him
again. There was no end to it, hour followed hour, the
revolting promiscuity grew worse as the air was fouled by
their breaths and by the filth of their bodily functions carried
out in one another's presence. Twice he rushed at the rocks
as though to force them open with his fists.

Another day was ending, and Chaval, seated beside
Catherine, was sharing his last half-sandwich with her. She

was chewing each mouthful painfully, and he was making her pay for every bite with a caress, stubbornly determined in his jealousy not to die without having possessed her once more, right before the other's eyes. Exhausted, she was about to let him have his way, but when he tried to take her she pleaded:

"Oh, let me alone, you're breaking my bones!"

Etienne, trembling, had put his face to the timbers so as not to see. He turned around and leaped toward them wildly.

"Let her go, damn it!"

"What business is it of yours?" said Chaval. "She's my woman—she belongs to me, doesn't she?"

And out of bravado he grabbed her again and held her tight, crushing his red moustache against her mouth while he said:

"Stop bothering us, will you? Why don't you take a walk and get lost!"

But Etienne, his lips white, shouted:

"Let her go or I'll strangle you!"

Understanding from the sound of Etienne's voice that he was about to bring things to a head, Chaval sprang up at once. Death was being too slow about it for them—one or the other had to go right now. The old struggle was beginning all over again, here in the earth where they would soon be sleeping side by side forever; and they had so little room that they could not swing their fists without skinning them.

"Watch it!" roared Chaval. "This time I'm going to eat you alive!"

At this Etienne went mad. His eyes clouded over with a red mist, his throat was congested by a rush of blood. A need to kill came over him, an irresistible physical need, like the violent fit of coughing that follows on the irritation of a bleeding mucous membrane. It rose in him, burst beyond his control under the pressure of his inherited taint. He had grasped at a slab of shale in the wall and was tearing at it, ripping loose a large, heavy piece. He raised it in both hands, his strength increased tenfold, and he brought it down on Chaval's head.

The latter had not had time to jump back. He toppled forward, his face smashed, his skull split. His brain had splattered against the roof of the gallery, and a purple jet was spouting from the wound like the steady jet of a spring. The smoky star of the lamp was reflected in the pool of blood which immediately formed. The shadow of the black form filled the sealed-off cave; the body on the ground looked like the black hump of a pile of slack.

And Etienne bent down and stared at him, his eyes wide.

So he had really done it, he had killed. In a dazed way he remembered all his struggles, his futile fight against the poison that slept in his muscles, the alcohol slowly accumulated and passed down by his ancestors. Though he was drunk with nothing more than hunger, the distant drunkenness of his forebears had sufficed. His hair stood on end in horror of this murder, but despite the repugnance born of his education, joy was making his heart beat faster—the animal joy of an appetite finally satisfied. And then he felt proud, the pride of the stronger. A vision of the little soldier had appeared before him, his throat slit by a knife, killed by a child. Now he too had killed.

But Catherine, bolt upright, cried out:

"My God, he's dead!"

"Are you sorry?" Etienne asked savagely.

She was gasping, babbling. Then she tottered and threw herself into his arms.

"Oh, kill me too!—let's both of us die!"

She grasped him by the shoulders and clung to him, and he clung to her too, and they hoped they would die. But death was in no hurry, and they unwound their arms. Then, while she covered her eyes, he dragged the poor wretch away and threw him down the inclined plane to get him out of the narrow area in which they had to go on living. Life would have been impossible with that corpse at their feet. They were terrified when they heard it sink and send up a geyser of foam. What, had the water already filled the hole? Then they saw it; it had overflowed into the gallery.

And then there began a new struggle. They had lit the last lamp, and its dying light showed them the flood rising steadily, stubbornly, unceasingly. First the water reached only to their ankles, then it lapped at their knees. By taking refuge at the top of the sloping gallery they gained a few hours' reprieve, but the flood overtook them and came up to their waists. Standing at bay, their backs pressed against the rock, they watched it keep rising and rising. When it reached their mouths it would all be over. The lamp, which they had hung up, was casting a yellow glow over the rapid swell of the tiny waves; it paled, and they could see only a semicircle of light that kept decreasing, as if devoured by the darkness that seemed to spread with the flood; and suddenly the darkness enveloped them—the lamp had gone out with a splutter of its last drop of oil. It was complete, absolute night—the dark night of the earth in which they would sleep without ever again opening their eyes on the light of the sun.

"God damn it!" Etienne swore dully.

Catherine had taken shelter against him, as if she had suddenly felt the shadows grab for her. In a low voice she repeated the miners' saying:

"Death blows out the lamp."

Nevertheless their instinct fought against this threat, and they were animated by a feverish desire to live. Using the lamp hook, he began to claw wildly at the shale while she helped him with her fingernails. They managed to make a sort of elevated platform, and when they had both hoisted themselves up on it they sat with their legs dangling and their backs bent, for the vault above forced them to keep their heads down. Now the water was only chilling their heels, but they soon felt the cold at their ankles, their calves, their knees, as it advanced with invincible relentlessness. The platform was not level, and it became so wet and slippery that they had to hold on tight to keep from sliding off. It was the end—how long could they wait, imprisoned here on this niche where they dared not move, exhausted, starving, with neither bread nor light? And most of all they suffered from the darkness, which kept them from seeing the approach of death. A heavy silence reigned; the water-swollen mine was still. Now they could only sense the sea beneath them, its silent tide swelling up from the depths of the galleries.

Hour after black hour went by, and they were not even able to keep count of them, for their notion of time had grown more and more confused. Their torments, which should have made the minutes drag, sped them by. They thought they had been imprisoned only two days and a night, but actually the third day was already drawing to a close. All hope of rescue had vanished; nobody knew they were there, nobody could possibly get down there, and even if the flood spared them, hunger would finish them off. They had thought of rapping out the signal one last time, but the stone had been left behind, under the water. Besides, who would hear them?

Resigned, Catherine had rested her aching head against the vein; suddenly she sat up with a start.

"Listen!" she said.

At first Etienne thought she was referring to the faint noise of the steadily rising water. Wanting to calm her, he lied.

"That's me you hear. I'm moving my legs."

"No, no, not that. . . . Over there, listen!"

And she pressed her ear against the coal. He understood and did the same. For a few moments they held their breaths. Then, very far away, very feeble, they heard three widely spaced raps. But they still could not believe it—their ears were buzzing, or maybe the coal was cracking in the seam. And they had nothing with which to rap out a reply.

Etienne had an idea.

"You've got the sabots. Take them off and tap with the heels."

She tapped, beating out the miners' call; then they listened and once again they heard the three raps in the distance. They began all over again dozens of times, and each time the raps replied. They wept, they embraced each other at the risk of losing their balance. Their comrades were finally there, they were coming. As though their rescuers had only to poke a finger through the rock to free them, a surge of love and joy swept away the torments of the wait, their rage at the useless calls for help, so long unanswered.

"Isn't it lucky that I leaned my head back!" she cried gaily.

"What sharp ears you have," he replied. "I didn't hear a thing."

From then on they took turns, one of them always listening and ready to reply to the faintest signal. Soon they could hear the sound of the picks: they were beginning to work their way toward them, they would open a gallery. Not a sound escaped them. But their joy was short-lived. Laugh as they might to hide their fears from each other, it was no use; little by little despair reclaimed them. At first they had gone in for long, detailed explanations: they were obviously coming from Réquillart, the gallery being opened went down through the seam, maybe they were even opening more than one—they could hear three men at work. Then they began to speak less and less, and eventually, as they got to estimating the enormous mass that separated them from their comrades, they stopped speaking at all. They continued their reflections in silence, calculating the days and days it would take a worker to cut through such a block. Nobody would ever get to them in time, they would be dead ten times over. And as their anguish deepened, they hardly dared exchange a word; they automatically replied to the signals with a drumming of the sabots, but hope was gone and they were only responding out of a mechanical need to let the others know they were still alive.

One day went by, then two days. They had been at the bottom for six days. The water had stopped at their knees, neither rising nor subsiding, and their legs seemed to be dissolving in the icy bath. They were able to draw them up for an hour or so, but then the position would become so uncomfortable that they would be gripped by terrible cramps and have to let their feet dangle again. They had to keep propelling themselves back on the slippery rock every ten minutes. The sharp edges of the coal cut into their backs, and they had continuing and intense pain in their necks from having to keep them bent so as not to crack their heads. And it became more and more stifling as the air, driven back by the water, grew denser in the cloche-like area in which they were confined. Their muffled voices seemed to come from far off. Their ears began to ring, they would hear the pealing of a wild tocsin, the stampede of a herd under an interminable hailstorm.

At first Catherine suffered horribly from hunger. She would raise her poor clenched hands to her throat, draw deep rasping breaths, groan heartbreakingly for hours on end, as if pincers were tearing at her stomach. Etienne, strangled by the same torments, was feverishly feeling around in the dark when his fingers touched a half-rotten piece of timber alongside him. Shredding it into bits with his fingernails, he gave a handful to the haulage girl, who gulped it down greedily. For two days they lived on this worm-eaten wood; they devoured it completely, then, desperate at having finished it, scraped themselves raw trying to claw out other pieces that were still too solid and whose fibers resisted. Their torment increased, and they raged at not being able to chew the fabric of their clothes. His leather belt afforded some relief. He tore out pieces of it with his teeth, and she chewed them to a mash and forced herself to swallow them. It occupied their jaws, gave them the illusion of eating. Then, when the belt was gone, they returned to the cloth, sucking on it hour after hour.

But soon these violent fits calmed, and hunger became no more than a deep-seated dull pain, the slow, progressive ebbing of their strength. They would probably have died if they had not had as much water as they wanted. They would simply lean forward and drink from the hollows of their hands, and they did so time and time again, scorched by such a burning thirst that not even all this water could quench it.

On the seventh day, as Catherine was bending over to drink, her hand bumped into something floating in front of her.

"Look here. . . . What's this?"

Etienne felt around in the darkness.

"I don't know—it feels like the cover of a ventilation door."

She drank, but as she was dipping her hand in for a second

mouthful the "thing" bumped against it again. She uttered a
terrible cry.

"Oh my God! It's him!"

"Who?"

"Him—you know who. . . . I felt his moustache."

It was Chaval's body, which the flood had floated to the
top of the inclined plane and was now pushing toward them.
Etienne stretched out his hand and immediately felt the
moustache and the smashed nose; a shudder of repugnance
and fear went through him. Gripped by a terrible nausea,
Catherine had spat out the water still in her mouth. She was
sure that she had drunk blood, that all the deep water in
front of her was now the blood of that man.

"Wait," stammered Etienne, "I'll shove it away."

He kicked out at the corpse and it floated off. But soon
they could once more feel it bumping against their legs.

"God damn it, get out of here!"

And after the third attempt Etienne had to give up. Some
current kept bringing it back. Chaval didn't want to leave, he
wanted to be with them, against them. He was a gruesome
companion, adding his pestiferous stench to the already foul
air. For one whole day they drank nothing, struggled, preferred to die, and it was only on the next day that suffering
made them relent; though they had to push the body away
each time they drank, they drank nevertheless. It had hardly
been worthwhile splitting his skull if in his stubborn jealousy
he was again to come between them. Even dead he would be
there to the very end, to keep them from coming together.

Another day, and another. Every time the water stirred,
Etienne would feel a light tap from the man he had killed—
just the nudge of a neighbor reminding you of his presence.
And each time it happened Etienne shuddered. He kept
envisioning him, swollen, green, his red moustache on his
smashed face. Then he would forget what had happened—he
had not killed him, Chaval was swimming over and was
going to bite him. Catherine was now being shaken by
violent fits of weeping, endless, interminable, after which she
would fall into a state of numb prostration. Eventually she
became irresistibly sleepy. He would wake her, she would
mumble a few words, then she would immediately fall asleep
again, without even having opened her eyes. Fearing lest she
drown, he had put his arm around her waist. It was now he
who would reply to their comrades. The sounds of the picks
were drawing nearer, he could hear them behind his back.
But his strength was also diminishing, and he had no heart
left for tapping. The men knew they were there—why ex-

haust himself further? He no longer cared if they came or not. The endless waiting had so stupefied him that for hours on end he would forget what it was he was waiting for.

One bit of relief gave them some comfort. The water was subsiding, and Chaval's body drifted away. It was nine days since the rescue work had been started, and now, the first time they were able to take a few steps up and down the gallery, a violent explosion threw them to the ground. They groped for each other, then remained in each other's arms, wild with fear, understanding nothing, thinking the catastrophe was beginning all over again. There was no sound; the noise of the picks had stopped.

As they were sitting side by side in a corner of the gallery, Catherine suddenly gave a little laugh.

"It must be nice outside. . . . Come, let's go out."

At first Etienne fought against this madness, but then even his sounder mind was touched by the contagion and he lost his sense of what was real. All their senses were beginning to play tricks on them, especially those of Catherine, who was restless with fever and tormented by a need for words and gestures. The buzzing in her ears had become the murmur of running water, the songs of birds; she could smell the strong perfume of crushed grass, and she could clearly see big yellow spots floating before her eyes, spots so large she thought she was in the open, near the canal, in the wheat fields on a bright sunny day.

"Oh, how hot it is! . . . Take me, why don't you? Let's always stay together, yes, always and always!"

He held her tight, and she snuggled up against him for a long time, all the while continuing her happy, girlish babble.

"How silly we were to wait so long! I would have been willing right away, but you didn't understand, you sulked. . . . And then, do you remember that night at our house when we couldn't sleep, and we lay there without looking at each other, just listening to each other's breathing and wanting to be together?"

Her gaiety was infectious, and he joked at the memory of their mute tenderness.

"You slapped me once—oh yes, you did!—on both cheeks!"

"It was because I loved you," she murmured. "You see, I wouldn't let myself think about you, I told myself it was all over—but still, deep in my heart I knew that some day we'd be together. . . . All we needed was the opportunity, a little bit of luck, didn't we?"

An icy shudder ran through him, and he wanted to shake off this dream; but then he repeated slowly:

"Nothing is ever over. It only takes a little bit of happiness to start things going again."

"Then you'll keep me this time? This time it's for good?"

She fell back in a near-faint. She was so weak that her low voice was fading away completely. Terrified, he held her against his heart.

"Are you in pain?"

She sat up in surprise.

"No, not at all. . . . Why?"

But the question had roused her from her dream. She stared wildly into the shadows, twisted her hands, and burst into another fit of sobbing.

"Oh my God, my God, how dark it is!"

Gone were the wheat fields, the scent of grass, the song of larks, the great golden sun; there was only the ruined and flooded mine, the stinking darkness, the mournful dripping of this cave in which they had been agonizing for so many days. Her confused sense now increased the horror of it; she was back in the grip of the superstitions of her childhood, and she saw the Black Man, the dead old miner who came back to the mine to wring the necks of bad girls.

"Listen, did you hear that?"

"No, I don't hear a thing."

"Yes, it's the Black Man. . . . You know. . . . Look! There he is. . . . The earth has emptied all its veins of blood to avenge itself because we cut one of its arteries . . . and he's there, look, you can see him! . . . He's blacker than the darkness. . . . Oh, I'm afraid, I'm afraid!"

Shivering, she fell silent. Then, in a very low voice, she continued:

"No, it's still the other one."

"What other one?"

"The one who's with us, the one who's dead."

The vision of Chaval kept haunting her, and she would speak of him wildly, telling of their miserable life together, of the only time he had been nice to her—that time at Jean-Bart—and of all the other days of insults and beatings, when he would all but kill her with kisses after having battered her with blows.

"I tell you he's coming, he's going to keep us from loving each other even now! . . . He's jealous again. . . . Oh, make him go away, keep me, keep me—all of me!"

She had flung herself at him wildly, found his lips and passionately pressed her own to them. The shadows lightened, she saw the sun again, she laughed once more a tranquil lover's laugh. Trembling at the feel of her against his flesh, at the half-naked body under the shredded jacket and trousers, he clutched her to him in a reawakening of his virility. And this was their wedding night at last, here at the bottom of this tomb, on this bed of mud. They felt the terrible need not to die until they had known happiness—the obstinate need to live and to create life one last time. They loved each other in despair of all else, in death itself.

Afterward there was nothing. Etienne was seated on the earth, still in the same corner, and he had Catherine's motionless body stretched across his knees. Hour after hour went by. For a long time he thought she was asleep; then he touched her and she was very cold, she was dead. Nevertheless he did not move lest he awaken her. The thought that he had been the first to have her as a woman and that she might be pregnant roused all his tenderness. Other ideas—the desire to go off with her, the joy of their life together later—kept recurring, but so vaguely that they seemed scarcely to brush against his face, like the breath of sleep itself. He was growing feebler, and he had only strength enough for a tiny gesture, a slow movement of his hand to assure himself that she was really there, like a sleeping child, in her icy stiffness. Everything was fading away, the darkness itself had vanished, he was nowhere, beyond space, beyond time. True, something was rapping alongside his head—blows that were becoming louder as they drew nearer—but at first he had been too lazy to get up and reply, too weighted down by an immense fatigue, and now he no longer knew what it was; he just kept dreaming that she was walking before him and that he was hearing the faint clip-clop of her sabots. Two days passed, and she had not moved; he kept running his hand over her mechanically, reassured by her tranquillity.

Etienne felt a shock. Voices were calling out, rocks rolling to his feet. When he saw a lamp he wept. His blinking eyes followed the light; he could not get his fill of it, he was in ecstasy before this reddish point that barely dispelled the darkness. But his comrades were carrying him off, and he let them insert spoonfuls of bouillon between his clenched teeth. It was only when they got to the Réquillart gallery that he recognized someone—the engineer Négrel, who was standing in front of him; and these two men who despised each other, the rebellious worker and the skeptical boss, threw their arms around each other's necks and sobbed mightily in a tremendous outpouring of all the humanity within them. It was an expression of great sadness, of the wretchedness of generations, of the depths of grief into which life can sink.

At the surface La Maheude, prostrate beside Catherine's dead body, was uttering cry after cry, long, unending lamentations. Several bodies had already been brought up and aligned on the ground; Chaval, who they assumed had been crushed by a cave-in, and a mine boy and two cutters who were also in the same state—their skulls empty, their bodies swollen with water. Some of the women in the crowd went out of their minds, ripping their skirts and clawing their faces. When they finally brought Etienne up, after having gotten him accustomed to the lamps and given him a little to eat, he looked cadaverous, and his hair had turned completely white; people drew back and shuddered at the sight of this old man. La Maheude stopped shrieking and looked at him stupidly, her eyes wide and staring.

6

It was four o'clock in the morning. The cool April night was beginning to warm at the approach of day, and the stars were fading in the clear sky as dawn purpled the east. There was a faint stir passing over the black, sleeping countryside, the vague rustle that precedes awakening.

Etienne was striding rapidly along the road to Vandame. He had just spent six weeks in a hospital bed in Montsou. Though he was still pale and extremely thin, he had felt strong enough to leave, and he was leaving. The Company, still fearing for its mines and proceeding with its successive waves of dismissals, had informed him that it could not keep him on. It had, however, offered him help in the form of a hundred francs, along with the paternal advice to give up mining work because his strength would no longer be equal to it. But he had refused the hundred francs. He had already received a reply from Pluchart—a letter calling him to Paris and including the money for the trip. It was his old dream come true. After leaving the hospital the previous day, he had spent the night at the Bon Joyeux, widow Désir's place, and he had got up very early; there was only one thing he still wanted to do before taking the eight o'clock train from Marchiennes—say good-bye to his comrades.

The road was turning pink in the light of the dawn, and

Etienne stopped for a moment. It was good to breathe the pure air of this early spring. It would be a beautiful day. Slowly the light spread, and the life of the earth was rising with the sun. Then he set off again, sharply rapping the ground with his dogwood stick, watching the distant plain emerge from the mists of the night. He had seen nobody; La Maheude had come to the hospital once, and had then probably been unable to return. But he knew that all of Village 240 was now going down at Jean-Bart and that she too had gone back to work there.

Little by little the deserted roads were filling with people; pale, silent miners were constantly passing him. The Company was said to be taking advantage of its victory. When the hunger-vanquished men had returned to the mines after two and a half months on strike, they had had to accept the system of separate payment for timbering—that disguised wage cut now rendered more hateful than ever for being stained with the blood spilled by their comrades. An hour of labor was being stolen from them, and they were being forced to go back on their pledge not to submit; the necessity of breaking their word left the taste of gall in their throats. Work was beginning again everywhere—at Mirou, Madeleine, Crèvecoeur, La Victoire—and everywhere in the morning haze, all along the shadowy roads, there was a trampling herd, lines of men trodding past with hanging heads, like cattle being led to the slaughterhouse. They were shivering under their thin cloth garments, shuffling along with crossed arms, swaying hips, and backs humped by the *briquets* lodged between their shirts and their jackets. And in this mass return, in these black, silent shadows that never laughed or raised their eyes, one could sense the teeth clenched in anger, the hearts swollen with hate, the resignation due solely to the demands of the belly.

The closer Etienne got to the mine the more of them he could see. Almost all of them were walking separately, and those who came in groups were following each other in a single file, already exhausted, weary of the others and of themselves. He saw one man, very old, whose eyes were glowing like hot coals under his pale forehead. Another man, a young one, was breathing heavily, like the breath of a pent-up storm. Many were carrying their sabots in their hands, and the soft sound of their heavy wool stockings on the ground could hardly be heard. It was an endless flow, a crushing defeat, a forced march of a beaten army moving along with hanging heads and sullenly burning with its need to take up the battle again and be revenged.

Jean-Bart was emerging from the shadows when Etienne arrived; the lanterns hung on the trestles were still glowing in the growing dawn. A steam exhaust was rising over the dark buildings like a white plume faintly tinged with carmine. He went up the stairs of the screening shed and made his way to the landing station.

The descent was beginning and the men were coming up from the dressing shed. For a moment he remained immobile amid the confusion of sound and movement. The iron flooring was shaking under the rumble of the carts, the drums were turning and unwinding their cables, while all around were bellowing megaphones, ringing bells, hammers pounding into the signal block; and once again he was face to face with the monster swallowing down its ration of human flesh—the cages rising and plunging, endlessly gulping down full loads of men with the insatiable hunger of a voracious giant. Ever since his accident he had felt a nervous horror of the mine. The plunging cages tore at his guts. He was unable to bear it, he had to turn away.

But in all the vast, still-dark room, uncertainly lit by the dying lanterns, he could not see one familiar face. The barefoot miners who were waiting, lamps in hand, stared at him with wide, nervous eyes, then looked down and turned away in embarrassment. In all probability they knew him and bore him no ill will; on the contrary, they seemed to fear him, and were blushing at the idea that he might be reproaching them for their cowardice. This attitude made him feel as if his heart would burst; he forgot that these were the wretches who had stoned him, and he began again to dream of transforming them into heroes, of leading the people, that natural force that feeds upon itself.

A cage was loaded with men, the batch disappeared, and as some others came up he finally saw one of his lieutenants in the strike, a fellow who had sworn to die rather than give in.

"You too!" he murmured, heartsick.

The man paled and his lips trembled; then, with a gesture of excuse:

"What do you expect? I've got a wife."

He recognized everybody in the new group that was now surging up from the dressing shed.

"You too! You too! You too!"

And they all shuddered, they all stammered out in throttled voices:

"I've got a mother . . . I've got children . . . We have to eat . . ."

The cage had not yet reappeared and they awaited it gloomily, in such anguished awareness of their defeat that they avoided looking at one another and stubbornly kept their eyes fixed on the shaft.

"What about La Maheude?" asked Etienne.

There was no reply. One of them indicated by a sign that she would be coming. Others raised their arms, trembling with pity: ah, the poor woman! what misery! The silence remained unbroken, and when Etienne held out his hand to say good-bye they all shook it firmly, putting into this silent handclasp their rage at having submitted, their feverish hopes for revenge. The cage was there, they got in, they sank down, swallowed by the chasm.

Pierron had appeared, his foreman's open lamp attached to his leather cap. Since the previous week he had been in charge of a crew at the loading station, and the men moved aside, for his honors had gone to his head. Though unhappy to see Etienne, he nevertheless went over to him; he was greatly relieved when the young man told him of his departure. They chatted. His wife was now in charge of Le Progrès, thanks to the good offices of all these gentlemen who were so kindly disposed toward her. But he broke off to lash out at Old Mouque, accusing him of not having sent up the stable litter at the prescribed time. The old man listened, his shoulders bowed. Then, fuming at this reprimand, before going down he too shook Etienne's hand the same way the others had—a long clasp, hot with suppressed rage, a-quiver with future rebellions. And this old hand trembling in his, this old man who forgave him the deaths of his children, so moved Etienne that he watched him disappear without saying a word.

"Isn't La Maheude coming this morning?" he asked Pierron after a moment.

At first the latter pretended not to have understood, because even talking about bad luck is contagious. Then, as he left under the pretext of having some order to give, he finally said:

"La Maheude, did you say? . . . Here she comes now."

True enough, La Maheude was coming up from the dressing shed, lamp in hand, wearing trousers and a jacket, with a cap pulled tightly over her head. It was a charitable exception on the part of the Company, which had been moved by the fate of this poor woman who had been so cruelly stricken, to permit her to go down again at the age of forty; and since it did not seem a good idea to send her back to hauling, she was given the job of operating a small ventilator that had just been installed in the north gallery, in those infernal regions under Tartaret, where there was no ventilation. For ten hours at a stretch, her back breaking, her flesh roasting in temperatures of over a hundred degrees, she turned her wheel at the end of the fiery tunnel. She earned thirty sous.

When Etienne saw her—pitiful in her man's clothing, her breasts and belly more swollen than ever, as if from the humidity of the stalls—he stammered in astonishment, unable to find the words with which to explain that he was leaving and had wanted to say good-bye to her.

She looked at him without listening, and she finally said:

"You're surprised to see me here, Etienne? . . . It's true that I threatened to strangle the first member of my family to go down again, and yet here I am—I should strangle myself, shouldn't I? . . . Oh, I'd have done it a long time. ago if it weren't for the old man and the children at home!"

And she went on in her low, weary voice. She was not excusing herself, she was simply relating the facts—that they had almost died of hunger, and that she had finally made up her mind to it so they wouldn't have to leave the village.

"How's the old man?" Etienne asked.

"Just as gentle and clean as ever. . . . But his brain's cracked. . . . You know that they let him off for that business? There was some talk of putting him in the madhouse, but I wouldn't hear of it—they'd have done him in with a little something in his soup. . . . Still, what he did has done us a lot of harm, because now he'll never get his pension—one of the gentlemen told me it would be immoral to let him have one."

"Is Jeanlin working?"

"Yes, the gentlemen found him a job on top. He makes twenty sous. . . . Oh, I'm not complaining, the bosses have behaved pretty well to me—as they themselves have pointed out. . . . The boy's twenty sous and my thirty sous make fifty sous in all. We'd have enough to eat on if there weren't six of us. Estelle shovels it in now, and the worst of it is that we'll have to wait four or five years before Lénore and Henri are old enough to go down."

Etienne was unable to restrain a gesture of grief.

"Them too!"

La Maheude's pale cheeks had flushed and her eyes had begun to blaze. But her shoulders sagged, as though under the crushing weight of destiny.

"What do you expect? They'll go just like the others. . . . The others all lost their lives down there, now it's their turn."

She stopped; they were in the way of some trammers

pushing their carts. Dawn was streaking through the large dusty windows and washing out the lanterns with a grayish light; every three minutes the engine started rumbling, the cables unrolled, the cages went on swallowing men.

"Let's go, you loafers, hurry!" shouted Pierron. "Load up, or we'll never get done today."

He was staring at La Maheude, but she did not budge. She had already let three cages go down; now, as if suddenly awakening and remembering Etienne's first words, she said:

"So you're leaving?"

"Yes, this morning."

"You're right to go. It's better to be elsewhere, if you can get away.... And I'm glad to have seen you because at least this way you'll know I don't bear you any grudge. Oh, there was a time after all those deaths when I could have killed you, but after a while you get to thinking and you begin to realize that it's really nobody's fault after all.... No, no, you're not to blame, everybody's to blame."

Now she was talking quite calmly about her dead—her husband, Zacharie, Catherine—and her eyes filled with tears only when she spoke of Alzire. She had regained her old reasonableness and was able to judge things quite clearly. In the long run, to have killed so many poor people would bring misfortune on the bourgeois. They would surely be punished for it someday, because everybody has to pay the piper. The poor wouldn't even have to take a hand in it—the whole business would blow up all by itself, and the soldiers would fire on the bosses just as they had fired on the workers. There had been a change in her centuries-old resignation, in the hereditary discipline which was once again making her bow under—she was sure that injustice could not continue much longer and that even if there was no more God, another would spring up in his place to avenge the wretched of the earth.

She was speaking softly, looking about her suspiciously. Pierron was approaching, so she raised her voice and said:

"Well, if you're leaving you'd better stop at the house to pick up your things. . . . There are still two shirts, three handkerchiefs, and an old pair of trousers."

With a wave of his hand Etienne refused these few items that had escaped the secondhand dealers.

"No, it's not worth bothering about. The children can use them. . . . I'll get some things in Paris."

Two more cages had gone down, and Pierron made up his mind to address La Maheude directly.

"How about it, over there? We're waiting for you! Isn't it about time to wind up your little chat?"

But she turned her back on him. Who was he to act so eager, the turncoat! The descent was none of his business. His crew at the loading station already hated his guts. And she stubbornly remained standing there, lamp in hand, chilled by the drafts despite the mildness of the season.

Neither she nor Etienne could think of another thing to say. They stood looking at each other, their hearts so full that they longed for some word to exchange.

Finally, just to say something, she remarked:

"La Levaque is pregnant. Levaque is still in prison, so Bouteloup is taking his place in the meantime."

"Ah yes, there's always Bouteloup."

"And listen, did I tell you?—Philomène's gone."

"Gone?"

"Yes, she left with a miner from the Pas-de-Calais. I was afraid she'd leave the two brats with me, but she didn't, she took them with her. . . . How do you like that?—a woman who's always spitting blood and looking as if every minute will be her last!"

She mused for a moment, then went on slowly:

"The things they've said about me! . . . You remember how they used to say we were sleeping together. My God! After Maheu died, I suppose that might very well have happened if I'd been a bit younger—but now I'm glad it never did, because we'd have been sorry."

"Yes, we'd have been sorry," Etienne repeated simply.

That was the last thing they said. A cage was waiting for her and she was being angrily summoned, threatened with a fine. This decided her, and she shook his hand. Deeply stirred, he kept looking at her, so ravaged and worn, with her ashen face, her graying hair straggling out from under her blue miner's cap, her all-too-fecund body rendered shapeless by the cloth trousers and jacket. And in this final handshake he felt again what he had felt in the long mute clasp of his comrades—a promise to meet again on the day when they would take up the struggle once more. He understood perfectly; the calm faith that sustained her shone out from the depths of her eyes. Good-bye for now—next time it will be the real thing.

"Did you ever see such a damn loafer!" Pierron shouted.

Shoved and jostled, La Maheude piled into a cart along with four others. The cord was pulled to hammer out the meat signal, the cage started and dropped into the darkness, and then there was nothing but the speeding cable.

Etienne left the mine. Below, in the screening shed, he saw a creature sitting with its legs spread out on a thick bed of coal. It was Jeanlin, who had been hired to "clean" big lumps of coal. He was holding a large block of coal between his legs and was hammering off the fragments of shale; he was so enveloped in the soot formed by the fine coal dust that Etienne would never have recognized him if the boy had not lifted his monkey's snout and shown his protruding ears and tiny greenish eyes. He gave a mocking laugh, cleaved the block with a final blow, and disappeared into the rising cloud of black dust.

Once outside, Etienne followed the road for a time, lost in thought. All kinds of ideas were buzzing in his head. But then he became aware of the fresh air and the open sky, and he breathed deeply. The sun was rising gloriously on the horizon, and the whole countryside was joyously awakening. From east to west the immense plain was flooded with gold. The living warmth was rising, spreading, in a surge of youth pulsating with the rustling sounds of the earth, the song of the birds, the murmur of the streams and the woods. It was good to be alive; the old world wanted to experience still another spring.

And filled with this hope Etienne walked more slowly, his eyes turning from left to right, drinking in the gaiety of the new season. He thought of himself and he felt strong, matured by his hard experience in the depths of the mine. His education was complete; he was setting out armed, a fully aware soldier of the revolution who had declared war on society after seeing it and condemning it for what it was. His joy at the idea of rejoining Pluchart, of becoming, like him, a leader to whom the masses listened, inspired him to think of speeches and to polish their phrases carefully. He mulled over ways to broaden his program, for the bourgeois refinement that had raised him above his own class only increased his hatred of the bourgeoisie. He felt a need to cover these workers, whose stench of poverty now troubled him, with glory—to show them that they alone were great, they alone pure, that they were the sole source of the nobility and strength in which humanity could retemper itself. He could already see himself on the speakers' platform, sharing the people's triumph—if only the people didn't devour him.

High above him, a lark's song drew his attention to the sky. The last of the night mist had formed into small red clouds that were now melting into the limpid blue, and they seemed vaguely like the faces of Souvarine and Rasseneur. Yes, there could be no doubt about it—everything went to pieces when each man scrambled for personal power. For example, that famous International, which should have brought about a rebirth of the world, was crumbling into impotence after having seen its formidable army divided and splintered by internal quarrels. Could Darwin be right? Was the world merely a battlefield, with the strong devouring the weak for the sake of the beauty and perpetuation of the species? The question continued to trouble him, though he had supposedly, with scientific smugness, settled it. But his doubts were dispelled by a most engaging idea—he would elaborate on his old theory in his first public speech. If one class had to be devoured by another, wouldn't it be the people, still fresh and strong, who would devour the pleasure-weary middle classes? New blood would make the new society. And in this expectation of a barbarian invasion that would regenerate the old exhausted nations he found once more his absolute faith in a coming revolution—the real one, the one made by the workers—the flames of which would color the dying century with the same purple fire that was now bleeding across the sky.

He kept walking, dreaming, striking at the pebbles in the road with his dogwood stick, and whenever he looked up he recognized some familiar spot. For example, at the Fourche-aux-Boeufs he remembered that that was where he had taken over leadership of the crowd on the morning they had wrecked the mines. Today that backbreaking, deadly, ill-paid labor was beginning all over again. Over there, from more than two thousand feet below the surface, he thought he could hear the sound of heavy, regular, continuous blows: it was the men he had just seen going down, his black comrades hammering away in silent rage. True, they had been defeated, they had left the field littered with their savings and their dead, but Paris would have cause to remember the rifle shots at Le Voreux, for the blood of the Empire itself would flow from this incurable wound; and though the industrial crisis was drawing to a close, though the factories were opening one after another, nevertheless a state of war had been declared, and peace was no longer possible. The miners had stood up and been counted; they had taken the measure of their strength and had shaken the workers of all France by their cry for justice. Their defeat had thus reassured no one; the bourgeois of Montsou, haunted in victory by a dull dread of what the strikes might bring in their wake, kept looking over their shoulders to see if this terrible silence did not somehow conceal their inevitable end. They realized that the revolution would be reborn again and again—perhaps the very next day there would be a general strike, a coalition of workers backed up by emergency funds that would supply them with bread while they held out for months. Even this time the old crumbling society had been jarred; they had heard it cracking under their feet, and they could sense that other jolts were on the way, and still others, and that it would go on until the old edifice would totter and collapse, sink and be sucked into the chasm, just like Le Voreux.

Etienne turned left and took the Joiselle road. He remembered how he had kept the mob from rushing Gaston-Marie. In the sparkling sunshine he could see the distant headframes of several mines—Mirou on the right, Madeleine and Crève-coeur side by side. Everywhere there was the rumble of work; the picks he had thought he could hear hammering away in the bowels of the earth now seemed to be sounding out from one end of the plain to the other. One blow, and another, and still more, from under the fields, the roads, the villages smiling in the sunshine: all the obscure labor of that underground prison, so deep down under the enormous mass of rock that you had to know it was there before you could make out its great painful sigh. And now it seemed to him that perhaps violence did not speed anything up after all. Those cut cables, torn-up rails, smashed lamps—such useless effort! What an accomplishment for three thousand destruction-bent people racing wildly across the countryside! He was vaguely becoming aware that legal action might one day prove more terrible. Now that he had let off the steam of his bitterness, his reason was maturing. Yes, La Maheude's solid good sense had enabled her to understand—next time they would do it right: they would organize calmly, learn to know one another, band together in unions whenever the law allowed; then one day, when they felt themselves shoulder to shoulder, when they knew themselves to be millions of workers against a few thousand idlers, they would seize power and become the masters. Ah, how truth and justice would then spring awake! The glutted and crouching god, the monstrous idol hidden in the depths of his tabernacle in that distant unknown place where he fed on the flesh of the poor who had never seen him, would die instantly.

But Etienne was leaving the Vandame road and coming out on the highway. To the right he could see Montsou stretching down the hill and disappearing. Ahead of him were the ruins of Le Voreux, the accursed hole which was still being drained by three pumps day and night. On the horizon, he saw the other mines—La Victoire, Saint-Thomas, Feutry-Cantel—and to the north were the tall towers of the blast furnaces and the coke ovens, smoking in the clear morning air. If he didn't want to miss the eight o'clock train he would have to hurry—there were still almost four miles to go.

And beneath his feet the heavy, stubborn hammering of the picks was still going on. His comrades were all there—he could hear them follow his every stride. Wasn't that La Maheude under the beet field, her back breaking, her harsh breathing rising in time with the rumble of the ventilator? To the left, to the right, farther along, he thought he could recognize the others, under the wheat fields, the hedges, the young trees. Now the April sun was high in the sky, blazing gloriously, warming the teeming earth. Life was springing from her nourishing flank, buds were bursting into green leaves, fields were trembling under the push of the grass. On all sides seeds were swelling and stretching, thrusting through the plain in search of warmth and light. There was a whispering rush of overflowing sap, the sound of seeds spread in a great kiss. Again, again, more and more distinctly, as if they too were rising to the surface, the comrades were continuing to hammer. Under the flaming rays of the sun, in this morning of youth, it was with this sound that the countryside was heavy. Men were springing up—a black, avenging army was slowly germinating in the furrows, sprouting for the harvests of the coming century. And soon this germination would sunder the earth.

Afterword

Each literary generation fashions its own blinkers and then insists that they allow unimpeded vision. My generation grew up with a mild scorn for the writers of naturalistic fiction who flourished in the late nineteenth and early twentieth centuries. Some of them we took to be estimable and others talented: we did not mean to be unfair. Many naturalists had a strong feeling for social justice, and if irrelevant to their stature as writers, this seemed to their credit as men. Zola's great cry during the Dreyfus Affair could still rouse us to admiration. His great cry could stir even those of us who had reached the peak of sophistication where Flaubert was judged superior to Balzac, Stendhal to Flaubert, and all three, it need hardly be said, to Zola—for Zola was tendentious, Zola was rhetorical, Zola was coarse, Zola knew little about the new psychology. With such wisdom, we entered the world.

Everyone had of course read Zola earlier, in those years of adolescence when all that matters in our encounter with a novel is eagerly to soak up its experience. Then *Germinal* had stirred us to the bone. But later we learned that literary judgment must not be defiled by political ideas, and Zola, that damp and clumsy bear of a novelist, became an object of condescension.

It was wrong, hopelessly wrong—like those literary fashions of our own moment which two or three decades from now will also seem all wrong. Reading *Germinal* again, and reading it with that emotional readiness which middle age can sometimes grant, I have been overwhelmed by its magnitude of structure, its fertility of imagination, its reenactment of a central experience in modern life.

Still, it should be admitted that if we have been unjust to
Zola these last few decades, some of the blame must fall on
his own shoulders. He talked too much, he pontificated too
much about Literature and Science, he advertised himself
too much. We are accustomed in America to bemoaning the
redskin dumbness that overcomes so many of our writers
when confronted with a need to theorize about their craft,
and behind this complaint of ours there is often a naïve
assumption that European writers have commonly possessed
the range of culture we associate with, say, a Thomas Mann.
It is not true, of course. What had Dickens or Balzac to say
about the art of the novel? As for Zola, there can hardly
have been a modern writer so repeatedly confused about the
work he was doing. Consider the mechanical scientism to
which he clung with the credulousness of a peasant in a
cathedral; the ill-conceived effort to show forces of heredity
determining the lives of his characters (so that a reader of
Germinal unaware of the other volumes in the Rougon-
Macquart series can only with difficulty understand why
Etienne Lantier should suddenly, without preparation or con-
sequence, be called "a final degenerate offshoot of a wretched
race"); the willful absurdity of such declarations as "the same
determinism should regulate paving-stones and human brains";
the turgid mimicry with which Zola transposed the physiological theories of Dr. Claude Bernard into his *Le Roman expérimental*. About this side of Zola—the journalist preening himself as scientist-philosopher—Angus Wilson has remarked:

> ... he must present his artistic method as though it were
> a solid intellectual scheme, lend that air of culture and
> education—of which in reality he knew himself to be
> deficient—to present as a logical theory what was in
> fact the form in which his individual genius expressed
> itself.

Yet we ought not to be too hasty in dismissing Zola's
intellectual claims. If his physiological determinism now
seems crude, his sense of the crushing weight which the world
can lower upon men remains only too faithful to modern
experience, perhaps to all experience. If his theories about
the naturalistic novel now seem mainly of historical interest,
this does not mean that the naturalistic novel itself can
simply be brushed aside. What remains vital in the naturalistic novel as Zola wrote it in France and Dreiser in America
is not the theoretic gropings toward an assured causality;
what remains vital is the massed detail of the fictional worlds

they establish, the patience—itself a form of artistic scruple—
with which they record the suffering of their time.

In looking back upon the philosophical improvisations of
those late nineteenth century writers who were driven by
conscience to surrender their Christian faith and then to
improvise versions of rigid mechanism and spiritualized secu-
larism, we like to suppose that their "ideas," once so earnest-
ly studied by literary scholars, were little more than impedi-
ments they had to put aside, dead weight on the tissue of
their work. You ignore Dreiser's pronouncements about
"chemisms"; you agree with Huysman's remark about Zola:
"Thank God he has not carried out in his novels the theories
of his articles, which extol the infusion of positivism in art."
There is of course something to be said for this view of the
matter, but less than we commonly suppose, for the announced ideas behind a novel, even those thrust forward by
the author as direct statement, ought not to be confused with
the actual play of his intelligence. We may judge these
announced ideas as tiresome or inert or a mere reflex of
fashion; we may be irritated by their occasional appearance,
like a mound of fossil, along the path of the narrative; yet in
the novel itself the writer can be engaged in a play of
intelligence far more supple than his formal claims lead us to
suppose. A reductive determinism is what Zola flaunts, as
when he places Taine's not very brilliant remark, "Vice and
virtue are products like sugar and vitriol," on the title page of
Thérèse Raquin; but a reductive determinism is by no
means what controls *Germinal* and *L'Assommoir.* When we
say that a work of literature "takes on a life of its own," we
mean in part that the process of composition has brought
textural surprises, perhaps fundamental shifts in perspective,
which could not have been foreseen by studying the author's
original intention.

Even among ideas we regard as mistaken, sharp discrimi-
nations must be made when trying to judge their literary
consequences. A writer infatuated with one or another kind
of psychic charlatanism is hard to take seriously. A writer
drawn to the brutalities of fascism rouses a hostility that no
creed of esthetic detachment can keep from spilling over into
our feelings about his work. But when writers like Zola and
Hardy and Dreiser were attracted to the thought of Darwin
and Huxley, or to popular versions of their thought, they
were struggling with serious and urgent problems. They may
have succumbed too easily to the "advanced ideas" of the
moment—precisely the kind that date most quickly. Still,
they were grappling with questions that gave them no rest,

just as a half-century later Sartre and Camus would be
grappling with the questions raised by existentialism, a school
of philosophy that may not last much longer than determinis-
tic scientism but which has nevertheless helped to liberate
valuable creative powers. As Harry Levin[1] has said in
partial defense of Zola:

> Surely no comparable man of letters, with the exception
> of Poe, had tried so hard to grasp the scientific imagina-
> tion. His contemporary, Jules Verne, led the way for
> writers of science fiction to tinker with imaginary gad-
> gets. Science for them has been an Aladdin's lamp, a
> magical fulfillment, an easy trick. . . . For Zola it was
> much tougher than that; it was behavior under pressure;
> and the literary experimenter was both the witness of the
> behavior and the gauge of the pressure.

Insofar as a writer's ideas enter his literary work, they
matter less for their rightness or wrongness than for their
seriousness. And at least with some writers, it is their seriousness which determines whether the ideas will release or block
the flow of creative energies. Zola shared with many late
nineteenth and early twentieth century writers what I have
elsewhere called a "lust for metaphysics." Christianity might
be rejected, Christianity might be remembered, but its force
remained. Among those who abandoned it there was still a
hunger for doctrine, a need for the assuagements of system.
They wished to settle, or continuously to worry, the problem
of their relation to the cosmos. To us this may seem a
curious need, since we are more likely to be troubled by our
relation to ourselves; but in the last half of the nineteenth
century the "lust for metaphysics" was experienced by people
whose moral and intellectual seriousness cannot be questioned.

One large tendency in nineteenth-century literature, cours-
ing through but not confined to romanticism, is an impulse
to spiritualize the world, to distribute the godhead among
numberless grains of matter, so that in a new if less tidy way,
purpose can be restored to the cosmos and the sequence of
creation and re-creation be made to replace the promise of
immortality. Toward the end of the nineteenth century men

[1]From Professor Levin's scholarly study of French nineteenth-century
fiction, *The Gates of Horn,* I have borrowed several citations, and wish
here to record my debt.

like Zola could no longer accept transcendental or pantheist derivatives from Christianity, yet they wanted some principle of order by means of which to locate themselves in the universe; whereupon they proceeded to shift the mystery of the creation onto the lawfulness of the determined. What then frightened reflective people was something that we, in our benumbed age, seem to accept rather easily: the thought of a world without intrinsic plan or point.

The transfer from *telos* to causality, insofar as it preserved a premise of meaning, enabled writers like Zola and Dreiser to make their lives into a heroic discipline—heroic because radically at variance with the ideas they expounded. It was almost as if they were reenacting in secular charade the paradox of Calvinism: that a belief in the utter worthlessness of man, living in a world blinded by God's grace, could yet drive the faithful to zeal and virtue.

Zola went still further than those writers who transferred the dynamic of faith into a fixity of law. Like Balzac before him, he yielded to the brilliant impiety of transforming himself into a kind of god, a god of tireless fecundity creating his universe over and over again. The nineteenth-century novelist—Dickens or Balzac, Hardy or Zola—enacts in his own career the vitalism about which the thought of his age drives him to a growing skepticism. Zola's three or four great novels are anything but inert or foredoomed. He may start with notions of inevitability, but the current of his narrative boils with energy and novelty. *Germinal* ends with the gloom of defeat, but not a gloom predestined. There is simply too much appetite for experience in Zola, too much sympathy and solidarity with the struggles by which men try to declare themselves, too much hope for the generations always on the horizon and always promising to undo the wrongs of the past, for *Germinal* to become a mere reflex of a system of causality. Somehow—we have every reason to believe—Zola's gropings into the philosophy of determinism freed him to become a writer of energy, rebellion, and creation.

II

Germinal releases one of the central myths of the modern era: the story of how the dumb acquire speech. All those at the bottom of history, for centuries objects of manipulation

and control, begin to transform themselves into active sub-
jects, determined to create their own history.

Now we cannot say that this myth has gained universal
acceptance in our culture, nor that those of us who register
its moral claims can do so with the unquestioning credence
and mounting awe we suppose characteristic of men in ancient cultures. Still, we might remember that insofar as we
know Greek myth through Greek drama, we know it mediated by individual artists, and with the passage of time,
mediated in directions increasingly skeptical. The myth in
Germinal—if we agree, however hesitantly, to call it a myth—
is one that may have some parallels in earlier cultures, but it
takes its formative energies from the French Revolution. It is
the myth of the people and more particularly, of the proletariat. They who had merely suffered and at times erupted
into blind rebellion; they who had been prey to but not part
of society; they who had found no voice in the cultures of the
past—they now emerge from the sleep of history and begin
the task of a collective self-formation. This, of course, is a
schematized version of historical reality, or at least a perspective on historical reality—which may indeed be the dis-
tinctiveness of whatever modern myths we have. Where traditional myths appear to us as transhistorical, a frieze of
symbolic representation, our own take their very substance
from the materials of history, magnifying and rendering
heroic the actions of men in time. Some idea of this kind
may have led Thomas Mann to write that "in Zola's epic,"
made up as it is of events taken from everyday life, "the
characters themselves are raised up to a plane above that of
everyday life."

The myth of *Germinal* as I have been sketching it is close
to the Marxist view of the dynamics of capitalism, but to
yield ourselves to Zola's story is not necessarily to accept the
Marxist system. Zola himself does not accept it. At crucial
points he remains a skeptic, as we may imagine Euripides to
have been, about the myth that forms the soul of his action.
His skepticism is not really about the recuperative powers of
the miners, for it is his instinctive way of looking at things
that he should see the generations crowding one another,
pushing for life space, thrusting their clamor onto the world.
His skepticism runs deeper. Zola sees the possibility that in
the very emergence of solidarity—that great and terrible
word for which so many have gone smiling to their death!—
there would be formed, by a ghastly dialectic of history, new
rulers and oppressors: the Rasseneurs, the Plucharts, and

even the Lantiers of tomorrow, raised to the status of leaders
and bureaucrats, who would impose their will on the proletariat. Zola does not insist that this must happen, for he is a
novelist, not a political theoretician. What he does is to show
in the experience of the Montsou workers the germ of such a
possibility. As it celebrates the greatest event of modern
history, the myth of emergence contains within itself the
negation of that greatness.

(Is it not this note of prescience, this intuition all too
painfully confirmed by recent history, which explains why
Georg Lukacs—the east European Marxist critic who always
starts with heterodox insights and ends with orthodox dog-
mas—should attack Zola's work as mechanistic and passive,
lacking in revolutionary dynamism? We have here a confron-
tation between a writer's honesty and an ideologue's tenden-
tiousness, between Zola's myth of a collective entry into
consciousness and Lukacs' pseudomyth of "socialist realism."
The true myth is a story arising from the depths of common
experience; the pseudomyth, a manipulation of that story in
behalf of the false collective declaring itself the "vanguard of
the proletariat.")

At the center of the novel is the mine. Dramatic embodiment of exploitation, the mine nevertheless makes possible
the discipline through which to overcome exploitation. But
for the moment, man's nature still bows to his history, personal need to the workings of the market. The mine has a
"natural" awesomeness, with its crevices and alleys, depths
and darkness: its symbolic power arises organically, spon-
taneously, and not as a willed imposition of the writer. And
then, in a stroke that does bear the mark of will, Zola creates
an astonishing parallel to the miners. The mine-horses share
the misery of the men, but without the potential for motivated rebellion; the mine-horses represent, as a gruesome
foreshadowing and with an expressionist grossness that de-
feats critical scruples, what the men may yet accept or sink
to.

The mine is voracious and unappeasable, a physical emblem of the impersonality of commodity production. It
"seemed evil-looking, a hungry beast crouched and ready to
devour the world." It "kept devouring men . . . always
ravenous, its giant bowels capable of digesting an entire
nation." But this suggestion of a force bursting out of the
control of its creators gains its strength not merely from the
intrinsic properties of the mine. Here Zola does come close to
the Marxist notion that men must beware of fetichizing their

predicaments; they must recognize that not in mines or factories lie the sources of their misery but in the historically determined relations between contending classes. And here surely historical associations come into play, associations which even the least literate reader is likely to have with mining—a major industry of early industrialism, notorious for its high rate of exhaustion and accident. As always in *Germinal,* the mythic and symbolic are of the very substance of the historical. And thereby Zola can fill out his myth with the evidence of circumstantiality. The more he piles up descriptions of the mine's tunnels, shafts, timbering, airlessness, and dampness, the more are we prepared to see it as the setting for the apocalypse with which the book reaches its climax.

In a fine piece some years ago William Troy remarked that the great scene in which Etienne and Catherine are trapped in the mine

> ... brings us back to an atmosphere and a meaning at
> least as old as the story of Orpheus and Eurydice. For
> what is the mine itself but a reintegration of the Hades-
> Hell symbol? The immediate and particular social situa-
> tion is contained within the larger pattern of a universal
> recrudescence . . . Etienne emerges from his journey
> underground to *la vita nuova* of his own and of social
> experience. ("The Symbolism of Zola," *Partisan Review,*
> December 1937.)

The Orpheus-Eurydice motif is there, Etienne experiences a recrudescence, though of a somewhat ambiguous kind, and the mine is surely the symbolic center of the book. Yet we should be clear as to how Zola achieves these effects. Zola controls his narrative with one overriding end in mind, and that is to show not the way men are swallowed by their work (surely not new) nor how a hero can emerge healed from the depths (also not new) but the gradual formation of a collective consciousness. When Maheu, that superbly drawn worker, begins to speak to the manager, "the words were coming of themselves, and at moments he listened to himself in surprise, as though some stranger within him were speaking." The stranger is his long-buried self, and this transfigura-tion of Maheu is at least as morally significant as that of the individual protagonist gaining access to self-knowledge in the earlier nineteenth century novel.

Etienne reads, Maheu speaks, La Maheude cries out: ev-erything is changed. Gathering their strength and for a time delirious with fantasies of freedom, almost childlike in the pleasures of their assertiveness, the workers become what Marx called a class for themselves. And then, with his uncanny gift for achieving mass effects through individual strokes, Zola begins to individualize his characters. He does this not to approximate that fragmentized psychology we associate with nineteenth-century fiction but toward the end of preparing the characters for their new roles: Etienne in the pride and exposure of leadership, Maheu in the conquest of manhood, La Maheude as the voice of ancient grievance, and even the children, led by the devilish Jeanlin, who in their debauchery release the spontaneous zest that the overdisciplined life of the miners has suppressed.

The strike becomes the central action, and thereby the myth of emergence takes on the sharp edge of conflict. The workers are shown in their rise to a noble solidarity and their fall to a brutal mob—better yet, in the ways the two, under intolerable stress, become all but indistinguishable. ("Do not flatter the working class nor blacken it," Zola told himself in notes for *L'Assommoir*.) And nothing is more brilliant than Zola's intuition—it speaks for his powers of insinuating himself beneath the skin of the miners—that after the horrible riot with which Part Five closes, he sees the men continuing their strike, digging in with a mute fatalism, "a great somber peacefulness," which rests far less on expectations of victory than on a common yielding to the pathos of standing and starving together. Defeat comes, and demoralization too, but only after Zola has charted with a precise objectivity the rhythms of struggle, rhythms as intrinsically absorbing for the novelist (and at least as difficult to apprehend) as those of the individual psyche in turmoil.

Again, it should be stressed that the myth Zola employs is not the vulgar-Marxist notion of an inevitable victory or of a victory-in-defeat ending with noble resolves for the future. True, he shows as no other European novelist before him, the emergence of a new historical force, and he reveals the conflict that must follow; but its outcome remains uncertain, shadowy, ambiguous. The more serious versions of Marxism speak of historical choice: freedom or barbarism. It is a choice allowing for and perhaps forming the substance of tragedy. *Germinal* shares that view.

III

A work of modern literature may employ a myth and perhaps even create one, as I think *Germinal* does, but it cannot satisfy its audience with a composed recapitulation of a known, archetypal story. With theme it must offer richness of variation, often of a radical kind, so as slyly to bring into question the theme itself. The hieratic does not seem a mode easily accessible to modern literature. We want, perversely, our myths to have a stamp of the individual, our eternal stories to bear a quiver of nervous temporality.

The picture Zola draws of Montsou as a whole, and of Montsou as a microcosm of industrial society, depends for its effectiveness mainly on the authority with which he depicts the position of the miners. Just as the novel is a genre that gains its most solid effects through accumulation and development of narrative, so the action of Zola's book depends on his command of an arc of modern history. If he can persuade us that he sees this experience with coherence and depth, then we will not be excessively troubled by whatever intellectual disagreements we may have with him or by our judgment that in particular sections of the novel he fails through heavy exaggeration and lapses of taste. Two lines out of tune in a sonnet can spoil our pleasure, since a short lyric depends for its success on verbal unity; but in a novel whole episodes can be out of tune without necessarily spoiling our pleasure, since an extended prose fiction depends mainly on such large-scale effects as narrative thrust and character development.

Again we reach an interpenetration of commanding myth and historical material—what I take to be Zola's great achievement in *Germinal*. A stranger arrives, slightly removed from the workers because of his superior intellect, yet required to enter their lives and ready to share their troubles. So far, the pattern of the story is not very different from that of much fiction composed earlier in the nineteenth century. But then comes a radical shift: the stranger, now on the way to being a leader, remains at the center of the book, but his desires and reflections do not constitute its central matter. What engages us primarily is the collective experience of the miners, the myth of their emergence. In Part Five of *Germi-*

nal, both the most original and the most exciting portion of the novel, this entry into consciousness is shown in its two-sidedness, and with a complexity of tone that unites passionate involvement and dispassionate removal. In his notes for the book Zola understood that he must remain faithful to his story as archetype:

> To get a broad effect I must have my two sides as clearly contrasted as possible and carried to the very extreme of intensity. So that I must start with all the woes and fatalities which weigh down the miners. Facts, not emotional pleas. The miner must be shown crushed, starving, a victim of ignorance, suffering with his children in a hell on earth—but not persecuted, for the bosses are not deliberately vindictive—*he is simply overwhelmed by the social situation as it exists.* On the contrary I must make the bosses humane so long as their direct interests are not threatened; no point in foolish tub-thumping. The worker is the victim of the facts of existence—capital, competition, industrial crises.

For this perception to be transformed into a dramatic action, Zola relies mainly on the narrative increment that follows from his myth of the speechless and the symbolic suggestiveness of the mine. In saying this I don't mean to imply that everything which occurs in the novel is necessary or appropriate. The narrative is frequently flawed by cheap and lurid effects. Zola, as someone has remarked, had an overwhelming imagination but only an uncertain—and sometimes a corrupted—taste. That the riot of the miners should be a terrifying event seems entirely right; that it should end with the ghastly *frisson* invented by Zola is a sign of his weakness for sensationalism. Zola tries hard to present his middle-class characters, the Hennebeaus and Grégoires, with some objectivity and even sympathy, but he usually fails. Not, I think, for the reason William Troy gives: ". . . the inherent unsuitability of naturalism, a system of causality based on quasi-scientific principles, to the practise of literature." I doubt that local failures in a novel are ever to be traced so directly to philosophical conceptions. Zola fails because in this novel he is not interested in such people at all. They are there because his overall scheme demands it, because he feels an obligation to "fill out the picture." Sensing as much, we read these inferior portions with a certain tolerance, assuaged by the likelihood that further great scenes

with the miners lie ahead. The mediocre intervals come to
serve as "rests" helping Zola create or regather suspense. M.
Hennebeau, the mine manager, is a partial exception, if only
because he is a figure of power and power is always fascinat-
ing for Zola. Still, the subplot of Hennebeau's personal
unhappiness and his envy of what he takes to be the miners'
unsoiled virility is obviously weak—just how weak one can
see by comparing it to D. H. Lawrence's treatment of similar
material. And again, the immersion of Etienne and Catherine
in the mine, once the strike has been lost, is both a scene of
considerable power and a scene marred by Zola's lack of
discipline when he has the body of Chaval, the girl's former
lover, float horribly up to them in the darkness. Zola does not
know when to stop.

To notice such flaws can be damaging, and to write as if
Germinal were no more than the sum of local incidents could
be a strategy for dismissing the book entirely. But this seems
a poor way of dealing with a novel. Germinal, like many
works of fiction, depends upon effects that are larger, more
gross, and less open to isolated inspection than picking out
scenes of weakness would suggest; it depends upon the large-
muscled rhythms of the narrative as a whole. We are dealing
here with a writer of genius who, in both the quality of his
imagination and the occasional wantonness of his prose, can
sometimes be described as decadent. One remembers T. S.
Eliot's remark that Dickens was "a decadent genius," a
remark accurate enough if the noun is stressed at least as
much as the modifier. The decadence of Zola, which has
points of similarity to that of Dickens, comes through in the
excesses of local episodes, the vulgarities of particular par-
agraphs, the flushed rhetoric with which Zola seeks to "reinforce" material that has already been presented with more
than enough dramatic vitality. The genius comes through in
the mythic-historical sweep of the narrative as a whole. And
at least this once, Zola himself knew exactly what he was
doing:

> Everyone in the world [he wrote] analyzes in detail
> nowadays, I must react against this through the solid
> reaction of masses, of chapters, through the logic, the
> thrust of the chapters, succeeding each other like super-
> imposed blocks; by the breath of passion, animating all,
> flowing from one end to another of the work.

If what I have been saying has validity, it follows that
there will also be frequent episodes of brilliance—else how

could the novelist achieve his large rhythms of narration? And there are, of course, such episodes. Two kinds may be distinguished: those persuading us of Zola's authority as imaginative historian (substantiating detail) and those persuading us of his psychological penetration into a given moment of the action (illuminating detail).

The first kind is to be found mainly in his treatment of the miners at the peak of crisis. Etienne reading a Belgian socialist weekly, hastily and poorly absorbing its contents, seeking to make up for years of waste as he is "gripped by the uneducated man's methodless passion for study" and then overcome by "the dull dread that he had shown himself unequal to the task"—all this bears the thick circumstantiality of the actual. Zola knew the kind of men who were drawn to socialist politics: not merely learned bourgeois intellectuals like Marx and Kautsky, but self-educated workers like Bebel, straining with ambition and stumbling into knowledge. This command of his material is shown even more subtly in the portrayal of the inner relationships among his three radicals: Rasseneur, the most cautious and experienced, clearly on the way to becoming a classical Social Democrat; Souvarine, also a classical figure, though of the anarchist-terrorist kind who declares the need "to destroy everything . . . no more nations, no more governments, no more property, no more God or religion" and then to return to "the primitive and formless community"[2], and Etienne, the sincere unformed worker, open to a wide range of possibilities but determined—his aspiring intellectuality prods his ambition—to make a place for himself on the stage of history.

The second and more striking kind of detail shows Zola's imagination at work somewhat more freely, releasing incidents which do not depend directly on the overall design of the novel. On the simplest level there is the pathos of the mine girl Mouquette, hopelessly generous with all she has (her body to the men, her affection to almost anyone, her bared bottom to the strikebreakers), who offers Etienne a dozen cold potatoes to still the hunger of the Maheu household. It is a trifle, but from such trifles affecting novels are

---

[2]The reader of *Germinal* may be tempted to see Souvarine as a remarkable anticipation of certain contemporary figures, and indeed he does talk as if he belonged to an esoteric New Left faction. But it should be remembered that by the late nineteenth century the anarchist-terrorist, often in popular stereotype, had become a familiar presence in European culture. Zola was here drawing upon a fund of common material, and what is notable about Souvarine is not the conception behind him but the detachment, even the ironic coolness, with which he is presented.

made. On a level hard to apprehend in strictly rational terms, there is Etienne finding himself a place to hide, after the riot, in one of the hated mines. (A little bitterly, one remembers Fabrice's chestnut tree, emblem of innocence, in *The Charterhouse of Parma*.) But the greatest of such imaginative strokes concerns the strange old Bonnemort, introduced at the outset as a ghost of a man embodying the exhaustion of the workers' lives. He has nothing to say, he is barely alive, until at the strike meeting, amid the predictably rousing speeches

> . . . everybody was surprised to see old Bonnemort standing on the tree trunk and trying to make himself heard. . . . No doubt he was giving way to one of those sudden fits of babbling that would sometimes stir up the past so violently that old memories would rise from his depths and flow from his lips for hours. It had become very quiet, and everybody listened to the old man, so ghostly pale in the moonlight; as he was talking about things that had no obvious connection with the discussion, long stories that nobody could understand, their astonishment increased. He spoke of his youth, told of his two uncles who had been crushed to death at Le Voreux, then went on to the pneumonia that had carried off his wife. Through it all, however, he never lost hold of his one idea: things had never been right and they never would be right.

Without rhetorical strain, this passage summons the losses of the past, the whole unreckoned waste that forms our history. The mode is grotesque, but for readers with a measure of historical imagination, Zola achieves something far beyond the limits of what that descriptive usually suggests.

IV

Zola is not a fine writer. His style aspires toward a rich and heavy impasto rather than toward a lucid line-drawing, and often it is marred by excess. In *Germinal* the writing is nevertheless effective at two points: first, the passages describing the mine with that wary respect for the power of the actual a novelist must have, and second, the episodes in

which he evokes the surge of conflict and the passions of
enraged men. In these episodes the prose can be extremely
effective, combining mass and speed—as long as Zola stays
with his central purpose, which is to depict the sensations of
men who have thrown off the discipline of society but not yet
discovered the discipline of self. Nor need we succumb to any
version of "the imitative fallacy"—that in its internal quali-
ties a style must reflect the matter it is trying to convey—in
order to recognize at least some correspondences as proper
to the relation between style and subject. One does not write
about the collapse of a mine in the style of James analyzing
an exquisite heroine.

Zola achieves the effect of speed, but not the light or
nervous speed of a Stephen Crane or an Isaac Babel. Especially in Part Five of the novel, his style is that of a rumbling
and heavy speed—a leaden speed. The writing is rarely
nimble or graceful; the sentences are weighted with qualifiers
and prepositional phrases, as well as with accumulating
clauses which repeat and magnify the matter of their prede-
cessors. Admittedly, this prose is highly rhetorical: it employs
organic metaphors of anger, release, and cataclysm
("Nature," says Zola, "is associated with our griefs"), and it
depends heavily on Zola's hoarse and rasping voice. For what
he is trying to do seems decidedly risky, even from the
vantage-point of eighty-five years later: he is giving dramatic
embodiment to a collective as it disintegrates into a mob, and
since he must keep his attention mainly on the group, which
has of course no individuality of consciousness or will, he
finds himself forced to speak in his own voice. That, in the
actuality of composition, is the paradox the novelist must
face when he tries to dramatize the conduct of a group. His
effort to create an action of extreme objectivity, a plot of
collective behavior, leads the novelist to a style of extreme
subjectivity in which he finds himself driven to "impersonate"
the group. At its worst, this kind of writing can seem willed—
an effort to do for the action through rhetoric what film
makers try to do for their stories through music. At its best,
the writing has a coarse strength and even splendor—what
might be called the poetry of naturalism.

Still, it would be foolish to claim for Zola that his prose
can yield the kind of sentence-by-sentence pleasure that can
be had from the prose of a writer like James or Flaubert.
Zola is often careless as a stylist, sometimes wanton, occasionally cheap. His trouble, however, is not that his prose
lacks nicety of phrasing or epigrammatic neatness; it is that
he does not content himself with a utilitarian plainness but

must reach out for the ornamental and exalted, seeking
through rhetorical fancy-work to establish his credentials as a
literary man. Like other half-educated novelists and journal-
ists of the late nineteenth century, Zola was painfully suscep-
tible to those charms of the "literary" that he claimed to
dismiss.

His style, like almost everything else in *Germinal,* is interesting mainly when considered in the large. One then encounters a phenomenon I do not pretend to understand, and
which seems to be an essential mystery of literature. For long
portions of the novel Zola yields himself entirely to the
passions of the miners, and his prose becomes strongly, even
exorbitantly, passionate. We are swept along, as we are
meant to be, by the surge of men in revolt; we are with
them, the starving and the hunted, and the language heaves
and breaks, sweeping across us with torrents of rhetoric. But
let us not be frightened by that word "rhetoric": it bears the
strength, not only the weakness, of Zola's novel. Here is a
passage in which Zola describes (he is always strong in
parallel effects, grotesque doublings) the behavior of the
miners' children during the strike:

> The scamps had become the terror of the countryside,
> which they had invaded, little by little, like a savage
> horde. At first they had been satisfied with the yard at
> Le Voreux, where they rolled around in the piles of
> coal, becoming black as Negroes, and played hide-and-
> seek through the stacks of timber among which they
> wandered as though in a virgin forest. Then they had
> taken over the slag heap, where they would slide on
> their behinds down the bare parts, still hot with interior
> fires, and dart among the brambles of the older parts—
> hidden all day and as busy as mischievous mice with
> their quiet little games. Enlarging their territory still
> further, they fought among the piles of bricks until
> blood flowed; raced through the fields, eating all sorts of
> juicy herbs without bothering about bread; searched the
> banks of the canal for mudfish, which they swallowed
> raw; and roamed ever further afield, traveling as far as
> the forest of Vandame, where they would stuff them-
> selves with strawberries in the spring and hazelnuts and
> huckleberries in the summer. Soon the whole immense
> plain belonged to them.

Rhetoric, yes; but a rhetoric which accompanies and sus-
tains a remarkably strong evocation. The passion Zola pours

out finds its match, its justification, in the incidents he imagines. Yet, as we read into the depths of the book, we grow aware that there is another Zola, one who draws back a little, seeing the whole tragedy as part of an eternal rhythm of struggle and decision. This Zola, as if writing from some timeless perch, is finally dispassionate, withdrawn from his own commitments, and capable of a measure of irony toward the whole human enterprise. Zola the partisan and Zola the artist: for those who like their "commitment" straight, in the duped formulas of "socialist realism" such ambivalence is detestable. But I take it to be a sign of Zola's achievement. If there has ever been a novel concerning which one might forgive a writer his unmodulated passions it is *Germinal;* yet precisely here Zola's "scientism" proves to be an unexpected advantage, enabling him to achieve an esthetic distance that gives the book its ultimate austerity.

There is still another doubleness of response in *Germinal.* Hardly a Zola critic has failed to note the frequency with which images of fecundity occur in the book—repeated scenes in which, along and beyond the margin of his central narrative, Zola displays the unplanned and purposeless creativity of existence. Henry James, in his essay on Zola, remarks:

> To make his characters swarm, and to make the great central thing they swarm about "as large as life," portentously, heroically big, that was the task he set himself very nearly from the first, that was the secret he triumphantly mastered.

Now this "swarming," for many nineteenth-century novelists, can be a source not merely of narrative energy but also of a mindless and pseudoreligious sentimentalism. Everyone has encountered it as a special kind of fictional cant: the generations come, the generations go, etc. Asserted without irony, such declamations often constitute a kind of psychic swindle, convenient enough for novelists who fear the depressing logic of their own work or who need some unearned lilt in their final pages. That Zola does approach this kind of sentimentalism seems beyond doubt, but again and again he draws back into a baffled stoicism, evading the trap his romantic heritage has set for him. "A black avenging army" is "germinating in the furrows"; "soon this germination would sunder the earth." But even as such sentiments fill Zola's final pages there is no simple assurance—indeed, no assurance of any kind. Despite the sense of a swarming procreation which keeps the race alive, Zola ends on a note of anguish; he does not propose an easy harmony between the replenishments of nature and the desires of men. Etienne, clumsily balancing his idealism and his ambition, goes out into the world. To one reader at least, he enters neither upon personal triumph nor the "final conflict" promised by the dialectic of history, but upon a journey into those treacherous regions of the unknown where sooner or later all men find themselves.

—Irving Howe

SELECTED BIBLIOGRAPHY

Works by Emile Zola

Early Novels
   La Confession de Claude (Claude's Confession), 1865
   Le Voeu d'une morte (A Dead Woman's Wish), 1866
   Les Mystères de Marseille (The Mysteries of Marseilles), 1867
   Thérèse Raquin, 1867
   Madeleine Férat, 1868
Les Rougon-Macquart
   La Fortune des Rougon (The Fortune of the Rougons), 1871
   La Curée (The Kill), 1872
   Le Ventre de Paris (Savage Paris), 1873
   La Conquête de Plassans (A Priest in the House), 1874
   La Faute de l'abbé Mouret (The Sinful Priest), 1875
   Son Excellence Eugène Rougon (His Excellency Eugène Rougon), 1876
   L'Assommoir, 1877
   Une Page d'amour (A Love Affair), 1878
   Nana, 1880
   Pot-Bouille (Restless House), 1882
   Au Bonheur des Dames (Ladies' Delight), 1883
   La Joie de vivre (Zest for Life), 1884
   Germinal, 1885   (Signet Classic 0451-519752)
   L'Oeuvre (The Masterpiece), 1886
   La Terre (Earth), 1887
   Le Rêve (The Dream), 1888
   La Bête humaine (The Beast in Man), 1890
   L'Argent (Money), 1891
   La Débâcle (The Downfall), 1892
   Le Docteur Pascal (Doctor Pascal), 1893
Les Trois Villes (The Three Cities)
   Lourdes, 1894
   Rome, 1896
   Paris, 1898
Les Quatre Évangiles (The Four Gospels)
   Fécondité (Fruitfulness), 1899
   Travail (Work), 1901
   Vérité (Truth), 1903
Short Stories and Plays
   Contes à Ninon (Stories for Ninon), 1864
   Nouveaux Contes à Ninon (More Stories for Ninon), 1874
   Théâtre (Thérèse Requin, Les Heritiers Rabourdin, Le Bouton de Rose), 1878

Le Capitaine Burle (Captain Burle), 1882
Naïs Micoulin, 1884

Critical and Polemical Works

Mes haines (My Hatreds), 1866
Le Roman expérimental (The Experimental Novel), 1880
Les Romanciers naturalistes (The Naturalist Novelists), 1881
Documents littéraires (Literary Documents), 1881
Le Naturalisme au théâtre (Naturalism in the Theater), 1881
Nos auteurs dramatiques (Our Playwrights), 1881
Une Campagne (A Campaign), 1882
Nouvelle Campagne (New Campaign), 1897
La Vérité en marche (Truth on the March), 1901

Biography and Criticism

Bédé, Jean-Albert. *Emile Zola*. Columbia Essays on Modern Writers, 69. New York and London: Columbia Univ. Press, 1974.

Grant, Elliott M. *Emile Zola*. Twayne's World Authors Series, 10. New York: Twayne, 1966.

———. *Zola's 'Germinal': A Critical and Historical Study*. Leicester, England: Leicester Univ. Press, 1970.

Hemmings, F. W. J. *Emile Zola*. Rev. ed. Oxford: Clarendon Press, 1966.

———. *The Life and Times of Emile Zola*. New York: Scribner's, 1977.

Howe, Irving. "Zola: The Poetry of Naturalism." In his *The Critical Point: On Literature and Culture*. New York: Horizon Press, 1973, pp. 59-76.

James, Henry. "Émile Zola, 1902." In his *Notes on Novelists; with Some Other Notes*. London: Dent & Sons; New York: Scribner's, 1914, pp. 20-50.

Josephson, Matthew. *Zola and His Time*. New York: Book League of America, 1928.

King, Graham. *Garden of Zola: Emile Zola and His Novels for English Readers*. New York: Barnes and Noble, 1978.

Levin, Harry. "Zola." In his *The Gates of Horn: A Study of Five French Realists*. New York: Oxford Univ. Press, 1963, pp. 305-71.

Lukács, Georg. "The Zola Centenary." In his *Studies in European Realism*. London: Hillway, 1950, pp. 85-96.

Pritchett, V. S. "Zola." In his *Books in General*. London: Chatto & Windus, 1953, pp. 110-22.

Schor, Naomi, ed. *Zola*. Yale French Studies, 42 (1969).

Turnell, Martin. "Zola." In his *The Art of French Fiction*. New York: New Directions, 1959, pp. 91-194.

Walker, Philip D. *Emile Zola*. New York: Humanities Press, 1968.

Wilson, Angus. *Emile Zola: An Introductory Study of His Novels*. Rev. ed. London: Secker & Warburg, 1965.